King's Folly

JILL WILLIAMSON

BETHANYHOUSE
a division of Baker Publishing Group
Minneapolis, Minnesota

© 2016 by Jill Williamson

Published by Bethany House Publishers
11400 Hampshire Avenue South
Bloomington, Minnesota 55438
www.bethanyhouse.com

Bethany House Publishers is a division of
Baker Publishing Group, Grand Rapids, Michigan

Printed in the United States of America

ISBN: 978-0-7642-1424-0

Library of Congress Control Number: 2015956729

This is a work of fiction. Names, characters, incidents, and dialogues are products of the author's imagination and are not to be construed as real. Any resemblance to actual events or persons, living or dead, is entirely coincidental.

Cover design by LOOK Design Studio

Author is represented by MacGregor Literary, Inc.

16 17 18 19 20 21 22   7 6 5 4 3 2 1

King's Folly

THE KINSMAN CHRONICLES

King's Folly
Darkness Reigns: Part One
The Heir War: Part Two
The End of All Things: Part Three

KEY PLAYERS

ARMANIA

House Hadar

Echad [EE-kad]-**Rosâr Hadar**, king of Armania

+ **Schwyl**, Echad's onesent
+ **Captain Lebbe Alpress**, captain of the King's Guard
+ **Filkin Yohthehreth**, prophet to Rosâr Echad

Avenelle/Mother Rosârah, mother of Echad

Brelenah-Rosârah, Echad's first wife, Wilek and Inolah's mother

+ **Sir Rayim Veralla**, captain of the Queen's Guard
+ **Hawley**, Brelenah's onesent

Wilek [WILL-ek]-**Sâr Hadar**, son of Echad and Brelenah

+ **Sir Kalenek Veroth**, Wilek's High Shield
  ◦ **Novan**, Kalenek's backman
+ **Agmado Harton**, Wilek's backman

+ **Dendrick**, Wilek's onesent
+ **Lebetta**, Wilek's concubine

Laviel-Rosârah, Echad's second wife, Janek's mother

Janek-Sâr Hadar, son of Echad and Laviel

+ **Sir Jayron**, Janek's High Shield
+ **Oli** [OH-lee] **Agoros**, Duke of Canden, Janek's backman
+ **Timmons**, Janek's onesent
+ **Mattenelle**, Janek's concubine
+ **Pia** [PEE-ah], Janek's concubine

Thallah-Rosârah, Echad's third wife, Trevn's mother

Trevn-Sâr Hadar, son of Echad and Thallah

+ **Sir Cadoc Wyser**, Trevn's High Shield
+ **Hinckdan Faluk**, Earl of Dacre, Trevn's backman
+ **Beal**, Trevn's onesent

5

Valena-Rosârah, Echad's fourth wife

+ **Hrettah-Sârah Hadar**, daughter of Echad and Valena

+ **Rashah-Sârah Hadar**, daughter of
. Echad and Valena

Ojeda-Rosârah, Echad's fifth wife

Others in Everton

Father Tomek, high priest of Arman, tutor to Trevn

Eudora Agoros, Oli's sister

Pontiff Barthel Rogedoth, head of the Rôb Church

Admiral Hanray Vendal, admiral of the king's fleet

Captain Aldair Livina, captain of the *Half Moon* and the *Arzah*

The Omatta Clan

Rand, leader of the Omatta

Meelo, Rand's son

Teaka, Rand's mother

SARIKAR

House Pitney

King Jorger Pitney, king of Sarikar, the God's King

Princess Nabelle Barta, Jorger's daughter, widowed mother to Zeroah

Zeroah Barta, Nabelle's daughter, betrothed to Wilek Hadar

+ **Mielle Allard**, Kalenek's ward, honor maiden to Lady Zeroah

Prince Loran Pitney, King Jorger's second-born son and heir

Princess Saria Pitney, Prince Loran's daughter

RUREKAU

House Orsona

Nazer Orsona, emperor of Rurekau

Inolah [IN-oh-la]**-Sârah Orsona-Hadar**, Nazer's wife, daughter of Echad and Brelenah

+ **Ree**, Inolah's nurse

Prince Ulrik Orsona, son to Nazer and Inolah, heir to the throne of Rurekau

Prince Ferro Orsona, son to Nazer and Inolah

Princess Vallah Orsona, daughter to Nazer and Inolah

MAGONIA

Ruling Clan

Mreegan, Magonian Chieftess
+ **Kateen**, First of Mreegan's Five Maidens
+ **Astaa**, Second of Mreegan's Five Maidens
+ **Roya**, Third of Mreegan's Five Maidens
+ **Eedee**, Fourth of Mreegan's Five Maidens
+ **Rone**, number One of Mreegan's Five Men
+ **Nuel**, number Two of Mreegan's Five Men
+ **Vald**, number Three of Mreegan's Five Men
+ **Morten**, number Four of Mreegan's Five Men
+ **Torol/Thirsty**, number Five of Mreegan's Five Men
+ **Magon**, a great shadir, bonded to Mreegan and Charlon

Also in Magonia

Charlon, a kidnapped woman
Onika [ON-ik-ah], a blind girl
+ **Rustian**, Onika's dune cat

Grayson, a boy with a gray rash
Jhorn, a prisoner
Burk, a thief

TENMA

Priestess Jazlyn, the Sixth Great Lady of Tenma
+ **Qoatch** [KO-ach], Jazlyn's eunuch slav, a seer

+ **Gozan**, a great shadir, bonded to Jazlyn

THE GODS OF THE FIVE REALMS

Arman, the father god
Athos, god of justice and law
Avenis/Avennia, god/goddess of beauty
Barthos, god of the earth/soil
Cethra/Cetheria, god/goddess of protection
Dendron, god of nature
Gâzar, ruler of the Lowerworld, bringer of death
Iamos, god/goddess of healing
Lâhat, god of fire

Magon, goddess of magic
Mikreh, god of fate and fortune
Nivanreh, god of travel
Rurek, god of war
Sarik, god of wisdom
Tenma, the mother god
Thalassa, virgin goddess of the sea
Yobat/Yobatha, god/goddess of pleasure and celebration
Zitheos, god of animals

The Five Realms

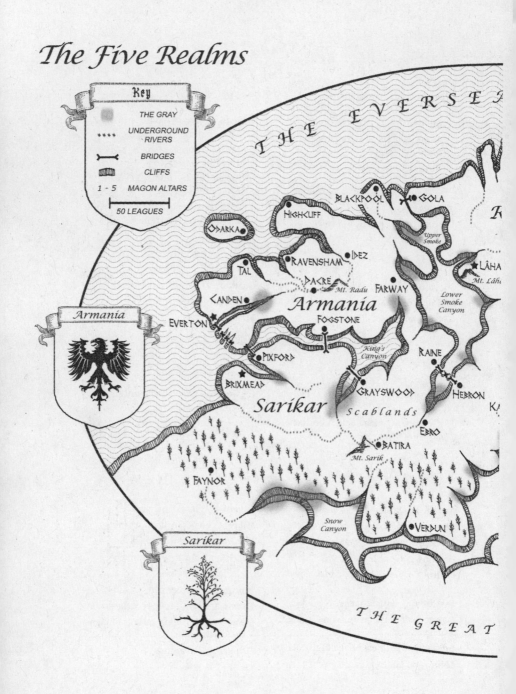

Key

THE GRAY
UNDERGROUND RIVERS
BRIDGES
CLIFFS
1 - 5   MAGON ALTARS
50 LEAGUES

THE EVERSE[A]

BLACKPOOL • GOLA

HIGHCLIFF

ODARKA

Upper Smoke

RAVENSHAM • IDEZ

TAL

DACRE   Mt. Radu   FARWAY

LÂHA

Mt. Lâha

CANDEN

Armania

FOGSTONE

Lower Smoke Canyon

EVERTON

King's Canyon

RAINE

PIXFORD

BRIXMEAD

Sarikar

GRAYSWOOD

HEBRON

Scablands

EBRO

BATIRA

Mt. Sarik

FAYNOR

Snow Canyon

VERDUN

THE GREAT

Armania

Sarikar

The king did evil in the eyes of Arman. He erected altars to Barthos, consulted black spirits, and sacrificed his sons in the fire, following the detestable ways of the priests of Rôb.

—Prophetess Onika, House Hadar 871

PART ONE

DARKNESS REIGNS

PROLOGUE

Aldair Livina sat at the table in the great cabin of his privately owned ship, the *Half Moon*, looking over his most recent chart of the Eversea. After an eleven-night voyage north-northwest from the Port of Everton, he had discovered a new island. He had named the isle *Bakurah* in honor of the first ripe fruit of the season. Aldair hoped that this island would be the first of many.

Father Tomek believed that the Five Woes had come upon them at last. Aldair wasn't convinced that the world was ending, but he appreciated the challenge set before him. And the pay.

The *Half Moon* was a lateen-rigged ship built for exploring. Smaller, lighter, and faster than the merchant tubs that frequented the Eversea, or the king's galley ships, it took only fifteen men to sail her and no oarsmen. It had taken three days to circle the new island, which Aldair believed to be slightly smaller than Odarka. Strangely, the water on its northern side was a great deal warmer and bluer than the aqua waters of the Eversea. Aldair succumbed to boldness and scratched the word *Northsea* on the chart above the newly discovered isle.

After rounding the isle, the *Half Moon* had started the long journey home for supplies. Any moment now they would reach the Everton Harbor. Since dusk grew nearer, Aldair had given the order to sail between the cliffs and the reefs. It wasn't the safest route, but his men had taken the journey countless times. And if they didn't reach the harbor before dark, they'd have to anchor out for one more night. Everyone was eager to get home. Tonight Aldair would sleep in his own bed in his own house. He would give his crew five days' leave before returning with haste to Bakurah with a second ship to explore the isle while Aldair sailed the *Half Moon* farther into the unknown.

The ship suddenly quivered as if the anchor chain were running out of the hawser pipe. Aldair straightened and stilled, feeling the movement. Bottles of wine rattled on the sideboard. His inkwell shook its way across the table. That hadn't felt like a reef. And there were no shallows here that they could be up against, yet the trembling continued as if the vessel were dragging over soft ground.

It had to be another earthquake. Ground shakers were common in the Five Realms, ever more so in the past year. Dozens of ships had been lost, capsized by massive waves. Surely this minor tremble was nothing to worry over.

Yet shouts rose outside his cabin. Aldair left his chart and went to the door, opened it, and ran smack into the ship's boy.

"Captain!" Ottee said. "Your presence is requested on deck, sir."

Aldair pulled the door closed and followed the boy. Thunder cracked overhead, though the graying dusk sky was clear. A glance over the rail revealed very little surf. The water was instead marred by endless rings, similar to those produced when one jarred the side of a washtub.

Thunder rolled again, though not from the sky. From land—and this time it did not stop. Aldair spotted movement at the rock wall of the cape. Silt and rocks raining down. Boulders. The surf churned white and foamy against the cliffs. That landslide would push a wall of water toward them in a matter of minutes.

"Landslide!" Aldair yelled, jogging onto the main deck. They'd dropped sail to slow into port, and there was no time to raise them and get up enough speed to turn.

Ottee yelled, "Captain on deck!"

"I have the deck," Aldair said to Carlus Breck, the first mate. "Hard a port."

Breck yelled the order down the hatch to the helmsman, who was manning the whipstaff in steerage.

"Drop the port anchor," Aldair added. "We've got to turn now."

Breck echoed the order to two sailors and added, "Go, go!"

The men scurried across the deck toward the bow as Aldair watched the water. If they didn't turn, the wave might roll them. The dropped anchor line would hopefully swing them around in time.

"It's going down!" Breck yelled, staring at the cape.

Chunks of rock the size of houses fell and plunged into the sea, creating a swell that rippled out toward them. Aldair waited, tense, for the anchor to dig into the sea bed. He didn't have his charts handy to know how deep—

There! The ship trembled as the anchor struck bottom. A tug and the bow swung around just in time to meet the water, which rolled monstrously large toward them. Some of the sailors cheered. One stumbled at the sudden movement.

"Hang on!" The order ripped from Aldair's mouth. He grabbed the port rail and hunched down to protect himself as the mountain of water raised them up. He could hear the strain on the timber as the anchor line held taught.

Ottee yelped and slid toward him. Aldair reached out and grabbed the boy, helping him get a grip on the rail while watching the movement of ship and water. Mikreh's teeth! They were going to clear it!

He hadn't realized he'd been smiling until the sound of timber splintering off the port bow made him frown. No, no!

The ship lurched, twisted roughly, then jerked as the anchor line snapped. They hadn't let out enough line! Without the anchor's support, the wall of water pushed the ship backward. The incline was so steep that the men tumbled about, grabbing for anything to hold on to.

"Gods help us!" Aldair yelled moments before the ship jolted from the stern.

They'd hit something. The reef, he guessed, despair welling within him. The wave surged past, yet they remained in place, jerking back and forth, the reef chewing up the hull.

"Check the bilge!" he yelled, starting for the stairs. "And the forward and stern bulkheads!" He needed to see for himself what he already sensed. Was there time to fother the leaks? The nearest beachhead was a good hour south, likely longer with the dinghy towing them. Could they make it?

Halfway down the steep steps, his boots met water. Nortin, who worked the pumps, looked up at him. "It's up to my knees, Captain"—which Aldair could plainly see—"but it's past my waist at the bow."

Wolf waded through the water from the aft, eyes bright with fear. "She's breaking apart at the stern, Captain."

"Abandon ship!" Aldair yelled, turning back up the stairs. "Launch the dinghy!"

The men scrambled to the main deck and set to work. The cliff continued to crumble, sending more waves that caused the ship to thrash against the reef. The fate of the *Half Moon* was out of Aldair's hands now, sitting helpless on the reef, grinding apart bit by bit.

The freeboard was nearly under at the bow. They needed to get off before they were all in the water and the waves threw them between the ship and the reef. Most of his men couldn't swim.

It spoke well for his crew that they were able to launch the dinghy in a sea that had quickly become loppy. One by one they boarded the dinghy. Aldair was last to leave his doomed vessel for the smaller one.

"Get us away from the ship," he told the oarsmen, "then take us into port."

The men rowed hard. Gradually, stroke by stroke, they put open water between themselves and the wreckage. A leak sprouted through a hole knocked in the dinghy's side when the men had launched, so those who weren't rowing set to bailing with hands and hats. The rough sound of the *Half Moon* grating against the reef faded with each pull of the oars that carried them toward home.

By now the sky had blackened. Night was upon them. The surging waves came in bunches, pushing the dinghy south, toward the harbor. They would indeed make it to land before the night bells tolled, but home? For Aldair?

There was no longer any evidence of the *Half Moon* on the empty sea. No sign of the rocky peninsula. Cape Waldemar was gone. Completely. The entire cliff, which once had housed two score of upscale homes and over fifteen hundred people, had gone into the deep. Maybe Father Tomek was right about the Five Woes.

Aldair's family. His home. His boat. All gone.

WILEK

A procession of fifty men made their way through the cool desert night from the royal retreat in Canden toward The Gray. Fifty-one men, technically, though the king did not count the wailing convict riding in the cage since the man would soon be dead.

Despite the glow of the full moon, twenty guards carried lit torches. For once they entered the thick fog of The Gray, the moonlight would be snuffed out.

Prince Wilek Hadar rode on his father's right, a few paces back from the carriage, as was customary. The only one allowed to ride ahead of King Echad—or Rosâr Echad, as he preferred to be called—was Pontiff Rogedoth, the high priest of the Rôb faith. Only on the night of an offering was this permitted.

The first hint of warm mist tickled Wilek's nose and he flinched. His heart pounded in his chest, warning him to rein his horse around and flee this cursed place.

He could not do such a thing if he wanted to remain in the king's favor, and he believed his father was close to naming him Heir. Therefore, he must remain strong.

It was childish, really, for a man of four and twenty years to fear this place. Yet as drops of moisture beaded over Wilek's sleeves and the torchlight fizzled in the damp air, he found it difficult to breathe. He fought to draw in the humid air without calling attention to himself. As far as he knew, only his grandmother and Kal were aware of his phobia.

The moonlight suddenly vanished, bathing the desert in darkness but for the dwindling torches. Wilek clutched Foxaro's reins, his chest tight.

They had fully entered The Gray, the dominion of Barthos, god of the soil.

Several of the horses nickered and lashed their tails. The prisoner's keening grew louder. Foxaro lifted his head, ears stiff, eyes wide and white. He shuffled his feet and tried to turn back.

"Whoa, boy. It's all right." Wilek held the horse firm and tried to calm down. His fear was making things worse. He breathed deeply and slowly, trying to steady his heartbeat. He leaned forward and petted Foxaro's neck, which, after a few strokes, steadied his own shaking hands.

"We'll get through this, Fox," he whispered. "We always do." He scratched Foxaro's withers. The horse nickered, the sudden darkness forgotten.

It was easier to be brave when someone needed you to.

Wilek glanced back at the cart carrying tonight's caged offering. Inside the iron bars sat a middle-aged man. The convict. Had killed another in a tavern brawl. Wilek had failed to negotiate a lighter sentence. The man would die tonight, just as the others had.

Just as Chadek had. Small hands holding tight—

"Halt!" a voice cried up ahead.

Wilek shook off the memory of his brother Chadek as the procession slowed to a stop. He glanced at Kal, who met his gaze with a somber expression. Kalenek Veroth, Wilek's shield, sat his horse like a demigod, his warrior hair twists loose around his scarred face. Like all King's Guards, he wore a deep blue tabard over his blacks. But rather than King Echad's red Barthos insignia, he bore Wilek's five gods emblazoned in white on his breast. Kal also wore the gold belt of a shield. He hated these offerings almost as much as Wilek, but for another reason entirely.

Ahead, shadowed men holding torches dismounted and moved forward on foot. They slid their torches into brackets on the shrine and dim light flashed off the bronze. Once all were in place, the men returned to their horses, the shrine now fully visible.

It had been built on the edge of a cliff that overlooked a deep canyon. Ten paces from the shrine, a half-circle of melon-sized rocks separated the holy ground from that of the desert wilderness.

The shrine itself was like any other in Armania: a five-sided bronze platform with five pillars that held up a pointed roof. In the center of the clearing between the altar and rock barrier stood a bronze pole of the god the shrine represented. This shrine honored Barthos, and it was Barthos's likeness that stared down at Wilek now. The god of soil had a man's body and a canine's head with long pointed ears, a shaggy mane, and three eyes. Wilek looked up into those eyes and shuddered.

Inside the shrine, a chest-high box had been built over a trapdoor. That door opened to a chute that carried the offering down a steep slope into the sulfurous canyon of Barthos's realm. The sight of the box brought a memory of small eyes peering over the top, small hands gripping the ledge, the Pontiff prying those hands loose so his brother would fall.

Movement shook Wilek away from the haunting past. Pontiff Rogedoth and Wilek's father exited the carriage and walked forward. The king, hugely overweight, was in his late sixties, ill, and rarely walked anymore, preferring his rollchair. Rogedoth was a decade younger, though his hardened expression made him look as old as the king. The men stepped over the rock barrier and approached the pole. They knelt before it and muttered a prayer. When they finished, four guards were called forth to help the king stand. Then he and the Pontiff walked around the pole five times before ascending the shrine. In the center of the platform, they turned and looked out at the men.

"Bring the offering," Father yelled, his voice as large as his ego.

Two guards went to the back of the cart and set about removing the convict from the cage. This was no simple task, as the "offerings" nearly always fought back.

"No!" The convict backed into the corner of his cage, as far from the guards as possible. Torchlight glistened in eyes wild with fear.

The guards called forth two more, who jabbed pikes between the iron bars at the man's back until he had no choice but to move toward the opening.

The first guards caught his arms and pulled him from the cage, dragged him toward the shrine. The others followed.

"No! Please!" The man dug his bare feet into the chalky gray dirt. "Don't put me in there. I'll serve you. I'll do anything!"

Wilek closed his eyes and reminded himself that Athos, god of justice, had answered his prayers that Father would only sacrifice criminals deserving of death. This man was guilty. Still, Wilek wanted to be far away from this place, in his bed, tangled in Lebetta's comforting arms.

"Assume the formation," the king yelled.

Wilek looked up. The guards had the convict inside the barrier now, on his knees before the Barthos pole. Wilek nudged Foxaro toward the line of rocks. Father demanded his son occupy the very center of the arc. This was considered the best position one could have short of the honor bestowed on the Pontiff and king in conducting the ceremony. One more small sign Wilek hoped meant he'd be declared Heir.

King Echad didn't believe in the right of first blood. He would choose his Heir when he was ready and not a moment sooner. With two sons of age and a third nearly so, the longer he tarried in making a decision, the more divided the realm of Armania became. Hopefully Father would declare Wilek his Heir soon and end the matter.

Kal rode up on Wilek's right. Agmado Harton, Wilek's new backman, appeared on his left and, thankfully, remained silent. The muscular nineteen-year-old had only been serving Wilek these past two weeks since Wilek's previous backman had moved to Grayswood to marry. This was Harton's first time attending the offering, and Wilek had warned the chatty young backman to be silent until it was over.

The other King's Guards moved their horses until, side by side, they formed a wide arc along the rock barrier.

"Prepare the offering," the king yelled.

The pikemen prodded the convict in the back, and he cried out as the sharp weapons forced him to his feet. He began walking around the pole with the guards, five times as was customary before approaching the shrine.

As the convict walked, the Pontiff spoke. "We, the children of man, sit in the shadow of Barthos's glory. Our sins bind us in misery and we deserve his wrath. Barthos shakes the foundations of the earth again and again to warn us of his displeasure. He casts the shadow of death over his children to remind us to revere him."

Wilek held in his contempt. No god forced the king to make these offerings. They were fueled by superstition. Something Wilek was powerless to fight.

"Barthos alone can lift this shadow," Rogedoth continued. "Only he can still the ground, can save us from our afflictions, can deliver us from the grave. We thank Barthos for his kindness. We proclaim his wonders to all who have ears."

Rosâr Echad looked down to the guards. "Bring forth the offering."

The guards and the convict had finished circling the pole and approached the platform. When they reached the steps, the convict shied back. Another jab of a pike sent him scrambling up the steps until he stood between Father and the Pontiff.

The convict fell to his knees and clutched the hem of Father's velvet robes. "Rosâr, have mercy! I beg you. Don't send me to Barthos." He fell forward and hugged the king's ankles.

Father lost his balance and grabbed hold of one of the bronze pillars to keep from falling. "Get him off me!" he yelled.

The guards pried away the convict. It took some doing, but they finally managed to drive the man to the other side of the platform and into the chute box. The convict gingerly touched the shards of broken glass that had been set along the top edge of the chute box a few years back.

No place to hold on anymore. Wilek pushed away the unwelcome thought and tried to think again about Lebetta.

"You have been convicted of wrongdoing and sentenced to die," Father said. "Tonight you will atone for yourself and all Armania."

"Not The Gray. Please! Anywhere but The Gray. I beg you, Holy Rosâr, have mercy!"

Rogedoth lifted his gaze to the Barthos pole. "Here is our exchange, Barthos! Here is our substitute. Here is our atonement. This man will go to death so that we might earn your favor and proceed to peace and long life." The Pontiff yanked down the lever that opened the trapdoor. The convict dropped, yelped, reached for the jagged top of the chute box.

He did not hold on long.

As he slid down the chute, his scream stabbed through Wilek, who swallowed and eased Foxaro back a step. The man's cries and pleas continued as he slid toward the bottom of the canyon, but the clarity of his words was drowned by the growing distance.

Now they waited.

Gâzar, god of the Lowerworld, take him swiftly.

Time passed and the men grew restless. They ignored the convict's distant imploring and began to talk and joke with one another.

"Is it over?" Harton whispered.

"No," Wilek said. "We must wait for Barthos to accept the offering."

"What if he doesn't?" Harton asked.

"He always does." Wilek had witnessed over two hundred sacrifices.

"Gods," Harton said. "They don't do anything like this in Highcliff."

"Welcome to the court of Rosâr Echad," Kal said, his tone tinged in disgust that only Wilek would recognize from having known him so long.

Something rattled in the distance.

"Is that a snake?" Hart asked, eyes wide.

"Silence!" Rogedoth yelled, then lowered his voice. "He comes."

The men fell mute. The only sounds were the nickers and slapping tails of the horses, the steady hiss of the mist against the torches' flames, the convict's distant pleas, and the rattling.

The rattling rose in pitch until it became the familiar, maniacal screeching cackle that frequented Wilek's nightmares. The sound intensified. Foxaro's ears twitched.

The screeching stopped.

A breath of silence.

A shriek pierced the night, horrible and lingering: the cry of a man being eaten alive.

Wilek gritted his teeth and scratched Foxaro's withers, pretending he was back in Everton outside the stables, getting ready for a ride to the beach. Foxaro loved to run on the wet sand where the air was cool.

"Your Highness." Kal nudged his arm. "It's over."

Wilek jumped, exhaled a shaky breath, sickened by the eerie silence. He glanced at Harton. His backman clutched the pommel of his saddle, face pale, eyes haunted and staring past the shrine.

King Echad might force his son to attend the monthly offerings, but once they were over, Wilek was always the first to leave.

"Let's go." Wilek backed up Foxaro from the stone barrier until he had room to turn. The King's Guards urged their mounts to part, and Wilek kicked his heels into Foxaro's flanks. The animal took off through the throng of blue, red, and black uniforms, as eager as Wilek to leave.

As Foxaro carried him away, the mist dampened his face, and soon his hair clung to his cheeks. He did not slow until Foxaro carried him out of The Gray and into the moonlight.

He found the road and waited for Kal and Harton to catch up. He did not wait long. Hooves pounded the dry desert. Kal appeared and reined his horse in front of Wilek's.

"Are you well?" Kal asked.

"Same as always," Wilek said.

They let their horses walk along the road toward the lights of Canden. In the distant blackness, rivers of orange fire snaked down the foothills of Mount Radu. The last earthquake had destroyed two dozen homes in the mountain village outside of Dacre. Hearths had caught fire, and then, due to the dryness of the area, the hills had too.

Harton shot out of The Gray and circled Kal and Wilek's horses, coming alongside Wilek's left. "That was harrowing. You do that every month?"

"So long as the earthquakes continue," Wilek said. "My father fears that Barthos is angry he stopped human sacrifices at the end of the Centenary War."

"Did the king really kill his own sons?" Hart asked. "Because that's what I've heard, and I—"

"*Harton*," Kal snapped.

The young man leaned forward in his saddle to see around Wilek to Kal. "What?"

"I don't mind questions, Kal," Wilek said. "It's good to question. It's something I intend to do more of if I ever become king." Something his father should do more of. He accepted every word his corrupt advisors uttered—never bothered to confirm a single fact for himself.

"You mean *when* you become king," Harton said.

"No, Hart, I mean *if*. Don't mistake me. The chance I'll someday rule is greater than ever before. But my father remains an impulsive, superstitious man, and I often fail to please him. To answer your question, yes. Years ago the king did indeed sacrifice three of his sons to win Barthos's favor. We were at war then, and the Pontiff convinced my father that only the most precious offerings would appease the god of the very soil we were fighting over. Father rose to the occasion and encouraged many of his most trusted men to do the same. Fifty were fed to Barthos that day." Wilek paused to let that sink in. "These earthquakes have my father worried. If they should continue . . . who knows? He may decide to make another *precious* offering to his favorite god."

"His?" Harton asked. "You don't serve Barthos?"

"I have chosen my five," Wilek said. "Barthos is not one of them." He would never worship the god who took his brother.

MiELLE

The carriage jerked forward, making Mielle's stomach flutter. She watched the dilapidated buildings of the Sink as they rolled past, the worn faces of the people going about their lives.

For decades the war had devastated their realm. It had orphaned Mielle and her sisters, and later taken her eldest sister's and nephew's lives. Now the Woes were doing the same. Too many children were orphaned each time an earthquake shook the Lowerworld. Too many were left homeless when their homes turned to rubble. The only person Mielle knew of who cared was the king's first wife, Queen Brelenah. She'd overheard Prince Wilek speak often of his mother's worries to Kal. If Mielle could earn a position with Lady Zeroah, once the young woman married Prince Wilek, Mielle might get a chance to speak with his mother about other ways to help the orphans in the Sink.

It was her only hope.

There was far too much riding on this interview. If she were not chosen for the position, what then? A position with the launderer or tanner or tailors would never pay enough, let alone get her any nearer to Queen Brelenah. She clasped her hands and tried to squeeze out her jitters.

The carriage jolted and the road became smooth. Mielle grasped the window's ledge, keenly aware that the bump they'd just experienced had been where the dirt road of the Sink became the cobblestone of Procession Way.

They were getting closer.

She glanced at Kal, the man who had practically raised her. She loved seeing him in his uniform. Unlike most soldiers, Kal wore his hair coils loose around his face, probably to further hide his scars. His eyes were closed as they always were when he was worrying. Poor man. He worked hard to provide for Mielle and her sister Amala. Getting this position would lift a great burden from Kal's shoulders and likely open doors for Amala to find a place in the future. No more daydreaming. Mielle must focus.

"Kal," she said, "why isn't Lady Zeroah called princess like her mother?"

Kal opened his eyes and glanced at Mielle. "In Sarikar, only children of the king and of the heir apparent are titled prince or princess. So Princess Nabelle is a princess because she is the daughter of King Jorger. But as she is not his heir, her daughter is not a princess."

"But once Lady Zeroah marries Prince Wilek, she'll become a princess, right?"

"Yes, she'll be Zeroah, Princess of Armania."

And someday, perhaps, Queen of Armania.

Kal looked her over, his scars keeping his smile flat. "Wouldn't Livy like to see you looking so fine?"

Mielle's heart pinched at the mention of her older sister. "Do I look like her?"

Kal's eyes flickered as they studied her face. "A little. You have her nose."

A big nose.

"But her hair was naturally curly, like Amala's. You look more like your mother."

Mielle couldn't remember her mother to know whether or not that was a good thing. She leaned forward so she could see the houses outside. They had turned off Procession Way and were passing down High Street, the richest part of the city outside the palace walls. "Why doesn't Princess Nabelle live at Castle Everton with the other royals?"

"Don't know. My guess is she doesn't appreciate the corruption at court."

The word *corruption* made Mielle shiver. "Nurse Darlow said court can be dangerous, and I should be careful who I trust."

"She's right. Trust no one. Not even your mistress or her mother, should you be accepted to the position. Just because one is quiet does not mean one is not scheming."

"Why do so many want to go to court, then?"

"Because there's wealth and power to be had when one is near royalty. There are also men looking to catch wives." Kal waggled his eyebrows.

Mielle did not find such a comment funny. "I don't want wealth or power."

Well, maybe a little, to help the orphans. "And if I wanted a husband, I would catch my own."

Kal laughed. "I don't doubt that. Simply show Princess Nabelle that you're obedient and hardworking and you'll do fine."

He made it sound so easy, but obedience never came easily to Mielle. "What if the princess doesn't like me?"

"She doesn't want to like you. She wants to know you'll be a help to her daughter." The carriage slowed to a stop. "We're here."

The driver came around and opened the door. Kal climbed out first, then helped Mielle down. Kal offered his arm, and Mielle grabbed it the way he'd taught her. It felt strange. Like they were playing a game. She suddenly felt like an impostor. She was no lady! She climbed cliffs and swam in the Eversea and—

"Relax," Kal told her. "You're leaving finger marks on my arm."

Mielle doubted that, but she softened her grip and took a deep breath to calm her nerves. Before her waited Fairsight Manor, fashioned of clean yellow firebricks with stripes of brown airbricks on each of three levels. Its exterior was grander than Castle Everton's—newer, anyway. The castle, gray and in constant repair from crumbling bricks, had been built centuries ago.

Kal led Mielle up a short but wide staircase of brown brick to a set of black iron doors where a man dressed in green and brown was waiting.

"Good day to you, Sir Kalenek," the man said, eyes averted from Kal's face.

Kal nodded. "Hoyt."

"Please come inside," Hoyt said.

Mielle hated how people never really looked at Kal. They were embarrassed by his scars. He never let on that he noticed, but she knew it bothered him.

She clung to Kal's arm as they entered a cool, narrow hallway with a high ceiling. The floors were stone lined with fragrant rushes. The walls were stone painted gold and covered in framed paintings. Everything was so colorful and splendid. If this was frugal Sarikarian decor, Mielle could not imagine what Castle Everton must look like inside.

Despite herself, she couldn't keep from being thrilled. But she wouldn't lose herself. She must not forget Margeet and her little brothers or Jespa, Lareno, and baby Hooj—all homeless after the last quake.

Mielle peeked into every open doorway they passed. There was a dining hall that sat over two dozen people, a chamber with a carpeted staircase that split in two directions to reach the second floor, and a Temple Arman with a bronze shrine of the sunbird Nesher.

Up ahead, Hoyt stopped outside an open set of iron doors. "Please wait in the drawing room."

Mielle walked inside and stopped, taking it all in. The stone walls had been painted lavender and crisscrossed with fine white lines. Elaborate candelabras hung from a pale pink ceiling, though the candles weren't lit—two wide windows on the far wall let in plenty of sunlight. Fancy chairs upholstered in gold satin had been arranged around a white brick hearth.

"It's so lovely," Mielle whispered.

Kal sat on one of the satin chairs, propping an elbow on the dark wood arm.

Wood. She glanced around the room again. All the furniture had legs and arms of wood. A table against the wall was made entirely of it. The realm of Sarikar was famous for its trees, which were rare in Armania. Selling even a single piece of wooden furniture here could enable Mielle to rent an apartment in the Sink for two years.

"How do you feel?" Kal asked. "Remember everything I told you?"

"Yes, Kal. Stop worrying." But in all honesty, she wasn't sure.

The door opened and Hoyt returned. "Her Royal Highness will see you now, miss."

Mielle exchanged her nervous look for Kal's encouraging one and followed Hoyt. They passed into a huge room covered in murals. As their steps over the stone floor echoed off the high ceiling, the beauty distracted Mielle from her apprehension. "What room is this?"

"The ballroom, miss," Hoyt said. "The princess hosted a ball here three weeks ago on her thirty-first ageday."

A ball. Mielle stared at a mural of a man kissing a woman's hand, enthralled by the expressions on their faces. Her foot caught on the edge of a carpet, and she just kept herself from falling. Hoyt, it seemed, had not noticed. Mielle gathered her skirt and hurried after him.

At the end of the ballroom, Hoyt knocked twice on another iron door and pushed it open. "Miss Mielle Allard, Your Highness," he said, stepping aside.

Mielle entered and flushed, searching the room for the princess, uncertain where to look. The room was vast, painted gold as well, though the floor was carpeted in a huge turquoise rug. A simple throne of pale wood sat at the far end of the room under a canopy of cloth of gold. A woman sat there. Mielle took two steps, then remembered to curtsy.

Tuhsh! She was messing up already!

"Come forward," the woman said.

Two rows of vacant chairs upholstered in turquoise satin formed an aisle to the throne. Mielle walked carefully, trying to be graceful. She stopped two paces from where the princess sat and curtsied again.

Mielle had never seen a woman as beautiful as Princess Nabelle. She couldn't be thirty-one years of age! She sat her throne with perfect posture in robes of gold and green. She had the blackest skin and hair, which fell in waves over her shoulders and down past her elbows. Her eyebrows were two thin arcs over eyes the color of apricots that nearly glowed in her dark face. She wore a simple gold circlet on her head and no other jewelry save a ring on each hand.

"You are ward to Sir Kalenek Veroth?" the princess asked.

Mielle fought to keep her voice even. "Yes, Your Highness."

"Your mother was Lady Olah?"

"Yes, Your Highness." If Mielle only had to repeat, *"Yes, Your Highness,"* the entire interview, she might actually obtain the position.

"Lady Olah was one of my honor maidens before I married. Did you know that?"

Mielle's breath caught. "No, Your Highness." She knew very little about her mother.

"Who has educated you these past years?"

"First my sister Livy. Now my nurse, Darlow. Kal has taught me much as well."

"Your sister Liviana died in the Centenary War, is that correct?"

"Yes, Your Highness."

"Many would criticize my hiring you as honor maiden to my daughter. Can you guess why?"

Mielle knew all too well. Kal and Darlow had talked of little else these past few days. "Because I'm orphaned and my family has had bad fortune. People will say I'm poor, unconnected, and cursed by Mikreh's hands. They'll say a girl like me would not be a blessing to Lady Zeroah's retinue. They'll also fault me for being . . . tall."

"Very perceptive. How do you think I should respond to such concerns?"

Mielle had also practiced the answer to this question. "You could tell them that Miss Mielle Allard came from a highborn family. Her parents gave their lives for their realm. Miss Mielle cannot make up for the grievous loss of her beloved parents, sister, and nephew. But she makes consistent sacrifices to the gods, devotedly serving Cetheria, who she feels made her tall and strong so she can see danger coming from afar and thwart it." Her heart pounded, but she held eye contact with the princess, hoping her answer would satisfy.

"Cetheria is the only Armanian goddess worth serving," the princess said. "And what is your position on the Heir War?"

"That Prince Wilek should someday rule Armania."

"*Sâr* Wilek is his official title, and you will use it."

Curse her careless tongue! Mielle curtsied. "Yes, Your Highness."

"Well, you are plain enough and well-mannered," the princess said. "Clearly well fed. Sâr Wilek swears my daughter could do no better in regard to your character. You may as well meet her. Flara, take Miss Mielle to Lady Zeroah's chambers."

Flara? Confused, Mielle turned and saw the woman who answered to Flara standing beside Hoyt. She must have come in after Mielle.

"You brought your belongings, I assume?" Princess Nabelle asked.

"No, Your Highness." Wouldn't that have been presumptuous?

"Hoyt, inform Sir Kalenek that he may go. Ask him to send Miss Mielle's things."

"Right away, Your Highness." Hoyt left.

Go? She was sending Kal away? But what if Lady Zeroah didn't like her? Mielle opened her mouth to speak.

"This way, miss." Flara crossed the back of the receiving room and held open a second iron door.

Mielle hesitated only a moment, then curtsied once more to the princess and followed Flara, assuring herself that this was a good thing. If the princess sent Kal away, Mielle must have gotten the position, even without having met Lady Zeroah.

Flara looked to be in her late twenties and wore a simple green dress and brown sandals. She led Mielle through a series of short hallways until they came to the foot of the grand staircase. Up they went, and Mielle marveled at the softness of the red carpet underfoot.

"When you're waiting on her ladyship, simply knock twice, open the door, and enter," Flara said. "You don't have to wait for permission."

"But what if she's dressing?" Mielle asked.

"Only females are permitted to enter Lady Zeroah's chambers," Flara said. "Servants have been dressing her since she was a babe. She's not shy."

What must it be like to have someone dress you?

At the top of the stairs, Flara led Mielle down yet another hallway. The walls were gold here as well, lined with rushes that made the corridor smell sweet. Flara stopped in front of a single black iron door, knocked twice, and entered.

Inside, warmth embraced Mielle. Tapestries had curtained off a triangular section of what seemed to be a much larger room. A fireplace in the far corner filled the area with heat. Two large picture windows fed sunlight into the chamber. A slight girl about Mielle's age sat embroidering on a longchair before the window closest to the hearth. She wore a pink satin dress with a black belt and a two-tiered skirt that reached her calves. Black beads lined the hem of each skirt. Her hair had been braided into dozens of tiny braids that were wrapped in a coil atop her head. Intent on her sewing, she did not look their way when the door opened and closed.

"Pardon, Lady Zeroah." Flara bobbed a quick curtsy.

The girl looked up. Her face was slender with delicate features: a small nose, small eyes, small lips—the opposite of Mielle in every way. She had her mother's skin tone, but eyes set a little too far apart and a pointed chin made her not nearly as pretty. Her eyelashes, though, seemed longer than any Mielle had ever seen. Nor had she ever seen anyone with so much hair.

Lady Zeroah's eyes quickly switched from Flara to Mielle. "Yes?"

"This is Miss Mielle Allard, lady. The princess bid I bring her to you."

"You're the one Sâr Wilek recommended to my mother." The girl's voice was soft and airy.

"I am." Mielle curtsied.

"No, you must not curtsy to me. Not yet, anyway." Lady Zeroah set down her embroidery and stood. "It is nice to meet you, Miss Mielle. May I call you Mielle?"

"Yes."

Lady Zeroah smiled. "Then you must call me Zeroah, though not in front of my mother. You may go, Flara."

"Yes, lady." Flara quickly slipped from the room, closing the door behind her.

"Won't you sit?" Zeroah motioned to the end of the longchair.

"Thank you," Mielle said, relieved by the girl's friendliness.

When they were both settled, Zeroah eyed Mielle. "I have some questions for you. It's important that you be completely truthful."

"As you wish." Though Zeroah's tone made Mielle nervous.

"What is your favorite color?"

That was all? "Red."

"Mine too, though my mother forbids me to wear it. She says it's too brash. Do you have any siblings?"

These simple questions made Mielle relax. "A little sister named Amala. She's twelve."

"I have a brother who is eleven. He lives with my uncle in Pixford. So you and I are both the oldest."

Mielle wanted to correct her, to say that she wasn't the oldest, but the middle child. But she didn't think it the time to mention Livy. She was dead, anyway. So Mielle supposed she *was* oldest now.

"Do you like to ride?" Zeroah asked.

"Oh, yes! I mean, I think I will. I've never ridden but have always wanted to. I like animals very much. Kal used to have a cat named Hinney."

"I adore cats. My mother is allergic, so I cannot have one. Plus she fears the little beast might scratch my face. What is your favorite way to spend an afternoon?"

"Swimming in the Eversea." Which seemed a very pleasant idea at the moment; this room was sweltering!

"I cannot swim," Zeroah said. "Perhaps once I'm married I shall be permitted to learn. Mother thinks it too dangerous. Do you like embroidery?"

Mielle wrinkled her nose. "Not very."

"You will have to learn. It is Mother's favorite task for me, so it will be for you as well. Do you want to be my honor maiden? Or are you here because your guardian is forcing you?"

"I must have some profession." One Mielle hoped would give her the means to help her less fortunate friends. "Many girls my age aren't so lucky."

"What is your age?"

"Sixteen."

"I am fifteen. We are both adults now. Strange, isn't it? I do not feel like an adult. Not really."

They stared at each other for a long stretch of silence. Should Mielle say something? What was Zeroah thinking? It would help to know what was expected of her. "What are my responsibilities as an honor maiden?"

"Most importantly I need someone who will speak honestly with me and will guard my inmost secrets with her very life. Even from my mother."

Keep a secret from the princess? Was that allowed?

"Do you refuse?" Zeroah asked.

"I'm only wondering whether or not you are testing me."

"Well, of course I am."

"Yes, but testing me how? Do you want to see whether I'll speak honestly to you? Do you want to know if I'm capable of discretion in keeping your secrets from your mother? Or did your mother ask you to find out whether I would be willing to keep secrets from her?"

"The second one. Some things I wish my mother not to know."

"Then I would do that for you, lady," Mielle said. "After all, I'm *your* honor maiden, not your mother's. My duty is to you." At least that's how Mielle saw it.

Zeroah smiled. "I am glad to hear it, but how can I know you speak the truth? Perhaps my mother told you to say that."

Gracious. Why would anyone's mother be so deceitful? "I could tell you a secret of my own?"

"Oh, I should like to know a secret! No one tells me anything worth knowing."

"Very well. My secret is this: I'm trying very hard to act the part of a proper lady today. But the truth is, I'm a hopeless chatterbag who daily embarrasses her guardian with my wild ways. Though now that I'm here, I promise to behave."

Lady Zeroah laughed. "I shall keep your secret, Mielle. And you may talk as much as you like with me."

"You're very kind." Mielle liked Lady Zeroah already.

"You are so clever to have puzzled out all the possibilities of what my question might have meant. I was being honest, but many women at court are not. I am ever so glad I shall have your sharp mind to help me analyze potential motives." Zeroah grabbed Mielle's hand. "Now I shall tell you a secret, but you mustn't tell anyone, upon pain of death."

"I swear to secrecy, lady."

"I am afraid of Sâr Wilek. I can hardly speak when we are together. It is so humiliating."

"But he's kind, isn't he? He seems so, and Kal believes he is. Why does he frighten you?"

"Because . . . he holds my happiness in his hands. I confess I do not trust him with it."

"Why not? I should think that most girls would be thrilled to marry a prince."

"I so desperately want him to like me—to someday love me. But . . . have you met Rosâr Echad?"

Mielle shook her head.

"He has five wives, dozens of concubines, and claims whatever girls please him, whether they are servants, honor maidens, or other men's wives. He has an irritable temper and always has his way. What if the son becomes the father? I have seen Rosârah Brelenah's unhappiness. Rosârah Thallah is equally dejected. How could I ever be happy living like that?"

Mielle didn't know.

"Mother said I have no right to happiness. That my life will belong to my husband. But something in me thinks a husband's life should belong to his wife as well. They should love each other. He should not have other wives. That is how things are done in Sarikar."

"Sounds nice," Mielle said.

"There is more," Zeroah said. "Sâr Wilek has a concubine. The Honored Lady Lebetta. She was given to him on his ageday almost ten years ago. She is dazzlingly beautiful. I see how he looks at her. He loves her, Mielle. Ten years, they have been together. How will I ever compare?"

Mielle shook her head at the tragedy of it all. She hadn't considered that a rich daughter of a princess might have trials.

"Forgive me," Zeroah said. "I have dumped all my burdens into your lap. I have never had a friend before and am so glad you will be living with me for now and forever. Will you miss your sister terribly?"

Forever? "I will miss her, but she can be difficult at times." Would Mielle never go home again?

"Perhaps when she has grown a little older, she can be an honor maiden too."

"Oh, she would like that," Mielle said. "It's her greatest joy to wear fancy dresses. Why is it so hot in here?"

"I chill easily. Mother does not want me to fall ill."

"Oh. Is that your real hair?"

Zeroah laughed. "Yes, though it is not all attached to my head anymore. Whenever my hair has been cut over the years, the braids have been saved for embellishments. Does it looks silly?"

"Not at all. You look like a princess."

"That is the idea."

"Do you spend much time at Castle Everton?"

"Very little. Mother says we may go only when the sâr invites me. He has only done that twice since I have been in Armania these three months. He is very busy, working for his father."

Mielle frowned. How could Zeroah earn the prince's favor if she never saw him?

"What is wrong? What are you thinking? Tell me, Mielle. You must!"

"Why would the prince invite you to Castle Everton if he thinks you don't like him? If I liked a man, I'd do all I could to be near him. He would have no doubts about my affection."

Zeroah's eyes bulged. "But that is not proper."

"Why must a lady sit around and wonder whether or not a man admires her? If he will not say so, why can't I? Then I'll know. And if he doesn't admire me, I won't have wasted days pining over the question."

"That will not do with Sâr Wilek. We will be married whether we like each other or not."

"Which is why you must let him know that you like him."

"But I cannot!"

"He's to be your husband. You must!"

Lady Zeroah pressed her hands against her cheeks. "Let us talk of something else." She stood and tugged Mielle toward the door. "Come, I will show you the manor."

"Are you angry about what I said?"

"Of course not. I told you I wanted an honest friend. You are a gift from Arman, Mielle. I cherish you. But I cannot be forward with the sâr. I will have to find another way."

Mielle took hold of Zeroah's arm. "Then I shall help you."

CHARLON

After months of freedom. A prisoner. Again.

Huddled in the corner of the wagon, Charlon ached to get free. There were others here. Prisoners. Boys taken from the slums of Bar-Vorak earlier this evening. Just like she'd been taken. Grabbed . . . Dirty hands on her arms. Throwing her roughly into the wagon. No one had touched her in four months. Until now.

Charlon trembled. Tried not to think of it. She was safe. For now. In her corner. Perhaps the men would not hurt them. She wondered again where they were going. All night the wagon had been driving. Hours and hours in the darkness. None could guess where it was headed.

Dawn broke. Charlon gauged the situation. There were five captives in the wagon. Four male children and herself, who was neither male nor a child. Despite how she looked. Two men sat at the driver's seat. Three more rode on horseback. One on either side of the wagon, one behind. Armed with shard clubs and whips. They had short, cropped hair. Brightly colored turbans and kasahs: the thin blankets Magonians tied around themselves for clothing. Charlon wore one too. It had been her disguise. She hoped it would continue to save her from evil men. Evil Magonians.

But why take children? To sell as slaves? Charlon knew too well how lucrative the slave market was. Especially with the young and innocent.

She peeked over the side of the wagon. Studied the landscape. Sandy ground sprinkled with cacti and shrubs. Everywhere the same. She had no idea where they were. Where they might be going.

"Got to pee," one of the boys whispered to another.

"So go," said an older one, motioning to the side of the wagon.

The first boy crept toward the bed wall. Eyes fixed on the man riding along-side. The man seemed to ignore him. The boy stood and fumbled with the folds of his kasah.

A whip snapped through the air. The boy collapsed, an anguished cry soft on his lips. A thin line of blood split his cheek.

The older boy scowled at him. "Hey!"

"Stay in the wagon," the man said, voice calm.

Charlon sank lower in her corner. Staring at the whip in the man's thick hand. Heart pounding within. Warning her to get away. Away before she was hurt. *Go*, her heart said. *Go now!*

But she remained. Going would bring pain. How could this have happened? Six years she'd lived a nightmare. After her brother had sold her. To that scorpion.

Yet she'd escaped. And for four months . . . She'd been doing fine for four months.

The gods were punishing her. For leaving. Leaving her master. The thought brought anger. Hot and bold. Not even a slave should suffer such cruelty. Gods be hanged! Charlon would serve only goddesses. Goddesses from now on. Males brought nothing but pain. Pain and betrayal.

Gods included.

"Please." The boy who had been whipped rose to his knees, bouncing and grabbing himself. "I got to pee."

"Pee, then," the calm man said. "But don't stand or get near the side."

The boy opened his mouth. No words came forth. He glanced at his friend, then back to the man. "But I'll make a mess."

"Where you're going, no one will care," Calm said.

Charlon's chest tightened. Such words made her want to leap. Leap from the wagon and run. *Run*, her heart said. *Run now!*

"Just hold it and stop making trouble," the older boy said.

But the younger boy had more to say. "But how much farther 'til—"

"No talking!" yelled one of the drivers, his voice thirsty and rough. "Stop encouraging them, Vald."

Vald spat on the ground but said nothing.

Silence. From then on. Silence until the sun was hot in the sky. Imagined fears kept Charlon company. Goaded her. Haunted memories touched her. Again and again she forced them away. They always returned. Always.

The wagon neared a hill. Slowed as it ground through drifting sand to the top of the ridge. On the other side, a valley. Prickly green bushes, huge cacti, tangles of whitethorn and cat claw. Growing thick from crags of sand and rock. Beyond lay a camp. Several white tents. One red.

The wagon descended into the valley. The red tent sat on a perfectly round hill. A tart on an overturned bowl. The white tents ran side by side in two long lines. Maybe a dozen on each side. A narrow, dusty path between them.

The wagon slowed to a stop in the middle of the camp. Vald rode away. Charlon's heart still pounded within. She stared at the red tent, drawn by the color of blood.

Would she bleed? Would these men make it so?

The red tent on its hill reigned at one end of the path. The white tents blocked Charlon's view of the other end of camp. All but the top of a bronze pole stretching into the air. Twice as high as any tent. Charlon squinted, trying to see which deity crowned the pole. Too far to tell. Until a cloud moved. The sun reflected off two red stones in the face. Gleaming eyes.

Magon.

Charlon's breath caught. The altars! This must be one of the five. She had learned of Magon's altars as a child. Each had a different rune carved into the base. One of five runes Magon had taught her first followers. Each altar required a different sacrifice.

Her heart trilled in fear. They would be sacrificed. Five boys. Killed on Magon's altar.

No. Four boys. One woman in disguise.

Run! her heart screamed. But she gazed at the pole. Prayed to the goddess. Prayed hard. *Have mercy, great goddess. I give my life in service. Don't let me bleed. Please, magnificent one. I beg you. Don't let them touch me. Don't let them—*

"She's ready." The calm one, Vald, had returned.

The driver cracked the reins. The wagon jerked forward. Turned in a circle. Rolled away from the camp. They were leaving! Magon had answered her prayer.

But they did not go far. The wagon stopped in the middle of the shallow valley.

"Out," Vald said, waving his shard club. "Time to run."

The boys stood, slowly. Some had been sleeping. The one nearest Charlon left a wet mark on the worn wood. The backside of his kasah was dark from moisture.

Charlon pushed to her feet. Followed the boys to the wagon's edge. Eyes watching the men. Must keep away. She jumped down to hot sand. Feet burning. She kicked aside granules to reach the cooler layer beneath the surface. The boys did the same. None had sandals.

"I'm hungry," a small boy said.

"I'm thirsty," said another.

"Why'd you bring us here?" asked the oldest.

"For the hunt," Vald said.

The boy who'd wet himself asked, "What we hunting?"

Vald chuckled. "*You* aren't hunting, lad. You're the game. The Chieftess and her maids are hunting you. So I suggest you move quick and find a place to hide."

"Come on. Let's go!" And the oldest took off.

The other boys scattered. Charlon ran too. The man's words settled in her mind.

They were being hunted.

Wagon wheels creaked. Charlon glanced back. The wagon heading back to camp. With it the men on horseback. But other horses were coming. She quickly counted six riders. Females. Approaching fast. Pikes in hand.

Goddess, no!

Charlon faced forward. Sprinted after the boys. Most had stopped. Crouched behind bushes or cacti. None hidden well. Charlon wanted to live. Needed to disappear.

Feet smarted from hot sand, sharp rocks, prickly plants. She ignored the pain. Ran faster. Must crest the hill. Then she could hide. Sprinted up the slope. Arms pumping. Legs spinning.

Behind her a boy screamed. Agony ringing out. Farther away another boy yelled. Closer, a third. The piercing cry echoed off the rocks.

Charlon pushed harder.

More screams came. Clomping hooves grew nearer. The sounds urged her legs to move faster . . . faster . . . faster.

Pain exploded in her belly. Charlon collapsed. Slid down the incline on the hot sand.

Don't, don't!

Her gaze drifted to her waist. The tip of a wooden spear protruded from her stomach.

Don't.

A keening moan sighed from her lips. Her body pulsed with heat. She pushed to her knees. Focused. The retreating rear of a horse. Galloping back into the fray. The rider must think her dead.

She was not. Not dead yet.

Reaching behind, fingers grazed wood. Gripped the shaft. Pulled the spear backward. Pain swelled within. Dizziness swept over her. She held her breath. Kept pulling, pulling. The spear slid free. Fire inside. Hot and draining. She gasped. Dropped the pike. It clattered against rocky sand.

Fingers trembling, she untied the shoulder of her kasah. Folded it into a long strip. Wrapped it around her waist. Once. Twice. Tied it as best she could. Her breasts were exposed now. No matter. Nothing mattered now but survival.

She stood. Her vision blackened. She paused to let it pass. Once her eyesight cleared, she stepped toward a tangle of brown branches. Three steps and she collapsed. On hands and knees. Crawling the rest of the way. Burrowing through thorny prongs. Scratching her skin. No matter. Must hide. The hunters would return.

No strength left. She fell into tingling darkness.

"How'd he get in there?" A man's voice. Low and rough. Thirsty.

"Must have crawled in after he got hit," another man said. Calm. Vald.

Then a more distant voice. Tight. Nervous. "Here's the spear that got him! Must have hurt to pull this out."

"Tough little pinch root," Thirsty said. "Times like this I want to flee to Rurekau."

Footsteps approached. "Don't let the Chieftess hear you say that," Nerves said.

"Am I saying it to her face?" Thirsty asked. "No. I'm saying it to the backside of a dead boy, who's about to become a burnt offering. Now shut up and bring the hatchet. I'll have to cut him out."

The voices pulled Charlon toward the pain. She groaned, wanting to keep away.

"Holy goddess, the kid's still alive," Thirsty said.

"What should we do?" Nerves asked.

"Slit his throat," Vald said. "Put him out of his misery."

"Don't!" Charlon gasped in a deep breath. A sound like a braying pig.

"Easy now," Thirsty said. "You've made a bed in a patch of sticky snare. We're trying to cut you out."

"Don't kill me," Charlon rasped.

"Can't have only four sacrifices, can we?" Thirsty said.

"No sacrifice," Charlon said. "Don't want to die."

"Neither do I," Thirsty said. "And if I come back without you, I'll be number five."

"Can't you reach him yet?" Nerves asked. "Pull his legs."

"I'm trying, but—"

Galloping hooves approached. The hacking stopped.

"Why aren't you done?" a woman asked.

"This one dug his way into sticky snare," Thirsty said. "We're cutting him out."

Charlon turned her head. Squinted through the branches. The woman sat on a white horse. Wore animal pelts and skins. Dozens of furry tails hung around her waist. Formed a short skirt. Dangling above her knees. She dismounted in a single leap. Approached Charlon's hiding place.

"Don't . . ." Charlon's voice was but a whisper.

The woman crouched. Peered into the snare. Their eyes met briefly. Tan face painted with red and black streaks. Hair pulled back. Dyed with bright red paint. Paint smeared along her skin at the edge of her hairline.

Her eyes lit with fire. Turned to burn another. "You let us hunt a *woman*?"

Behind Charlon the men grunted.

"Looks like a boy to me," Thirsty said.

"You've seen many boys with breasts?" Even her voice burned now.

Branches cracked as the men moved. *Don't touch. Please don't.*

"Little breasts," Vald said.

Nerves snickered.

"Cut her out of there, but do *not* kill her," the woman said. "Mreegan will want to speak with her." The woman strode back to her horse. Mounted. Galloped away.

Charlon would not die. Not this moment, anyway.

"Speak with her about what?" Nerves asked.

The hacking resumed. "Either way, Roya will make trouble," Thirsty said.

Charlon fell into darkness. When she next opened her eyes, she was being carried.

By a man.

Touched!

Don't!

She screamed. Struggled. Pain pulsed through her. Blurred her vision. "Let go!" The smell of sweat and blood. Her stomach twisted. She pushed her elbow into the man's gut.

Drop me. Please, let go!

His hold tightened. "Not going to hurt you." The voice belonged to Thirsty. "Can't speak for the Chieftess, though. She's a hard one to figure."

Chieftess? Charlon gripped his arms. Dug fingernails into flesh. "Put me down."

"Hurt me if you must, woman, but I'm trying to help."

Men never helped. "I must walk."

"You can't," Thirsty said. "You're dying. The only way you're going to live is if the Chieftess heals you. And I'm not saying she will."

The Chieftess wanted to speak to her.

Muscles relaxed. Mind stayed sharp. Thirsty's man smell gnawed. Twisted. She needed to run. Run far away.

Thirsty carried her into the camp. Up the hill to the red tent. He stopped before two men. Men standing on either side of a door.

"I've brought the woman," he said.

The door flap shifted. Thirsty carried her into darkness. She smelled blood and something earthy. Starchy. Strained to see. Woven straw mats on the floor. A pile of furs. Gnarled whitethorn branches. Lashed together. A throne. A woman sat there. A pale newt on her shoulder.

Chieftess Mreegan of Magonia.

A bare-chested man stood to one side. Waved a huge palm branch over the Chieftess. On the other side, a woman. Standing regal, like a statue.

Thirsty dropped to his knees before the throne. Kept his hold on Charlon. Bowed his head. Did not speak. Charlon studied his closed eyes. Lashes thick against dark skin. She willed him to put her down. He did not.

"She's near death," the Chieftess said.

Thirsty opened his eyes. "I fear she has little time left."

The Chieftess's cold gray eyes focused on Charlon's. Probing. The newt watched her as well, its eyes red. "Who stuck her?"

"The Fourth," Thirsty said.

"Then my Fourth shall take her place. Prepare her for sacrifice."

41

The woman beside the throne left.

"Why did you dress like a boy?" the Chieftess asked Charlon. "Why have you cut short your hair?"

"Boys draw less attention," Charlon whispered. "Less than girls."

Gray eyes probed deeper. Chilling. "You've been hurt. Before."

She knew. Could see the pain within. Charlon could hide only by closing her eyes.

A clap of hands. "Bring her to my bed."

Thirsty stood. Grunted.

Charlon's eyes flashed open. "Don't!" She tried to struggle. Too weak.

Thirsty held her captive. "You're safe now," he said. But men lied. Always.

A few steps and he knelt again. Laid Charlon on the pile of furs. Leaned back. She was free! She pushed to hands and knees. Crawled over the furs. No way out.

She turned. They were watching. Thirsty. The Chieftess. The man with the palm. Her arms wobbled. Darkness flashed. She fought to stay awake. Failed. Fell.

Hands grabbed her. Stretched her out. She heard her own whisper. "Don't."

"Remove the kasah," the Chieftess said.

Rough fingers fumbled with the knot at Charlon's waist. She opened her eyes. It was Thirsty. He would hurt her. She reached out to stop him. But her hand barely rose off the furs. Her strength was fading. She was dying. Finally. Eyes closed forever.

What would happen? Would she see her mother? In the Lowerworld? Would Gâzar let her in? She'd never served him well. Never pledged her life to any god. Until Magon.

Thirsty pulled the kasah from Charlon. The wad of fabric slid under her back. Unwound from her body. Suddenly she was naked but for blood. Blood everywhere. Cold air from the man's palm leaf tingled her skin. Everyone was staring. She closed her eyes. To hide. They could not see within. They could not take everything.

A hand touched her side. Her eyes sprang open. A groan of pathetic protest. The Chieftess was kneeling beside her now. Eyes closed. Murmuring. Foreign words.

Slowly, word by word, her voice grew. Louder. Until her words rang with authority. Power. *"Magon âthâh. Tihyéna shel yâd. Âtsar dâm. Râphâ zōt chêts. Pârar môwth."*

Charlon grew cold. The pain increased. The Chieftess removed her hand. Examined Charlon's wound. With the kasah's pressure it had oozed blood. Now blood poured forth. Ran down her side. Bubbled. Boiled.

Charlon shivered violently. What had the Chieftess done?

Breath wafted from her lips. A white cloud from within. Frost formed dust-like layers on the tent walls. Breath misted from the mouths of the Chieftess, Thirsty, and the palm man. Their hair turned white. The newt stiffened, as did the furs beneath Charlon. Blood stopped flowing from her side. Frozen by bitter cold.

Charlon blinked. Her eyelashes stuck together. She could not open her eyes. Could not see. Panic lit her heart. But it beat slower. She'd thought she was dying before. This time, it was real.

Then she was gone from the tent. Standing in a field of grass. Grass greener than any she'd seen before. It stood as high as her waist. Rippled in the wind. Swayed like a blanket on a clothesline. In the distance a person walked toward her. Too far away to tell if it was a man or woman. Charlon blinked. The person appeared half the distance closer. Another blink. Nearly there. It was a woman. Blink. A young woman. Blink.

It was Chieftess Mreegan.

She stopped in front of Charlon. Looking down. Eyes probing within. Hands reaching toward her. Wanting to touch. To touch without harm. Charlon reached as well. Their hands met, fingers sliding over palms, gripping. Painless.

Charlon was touching another person. And she wasn't afraid.

"I know who you are," Mreegan said. "You cannot hide your true self from me. Do not fear. You will not die today. You will serve me like Mreegan does."

"But you're Mreegan," Charlon said.

"No. I am Magon, goddess of magic."

Charlon gasped and opened her eyes. She was in the tent again. Warm now. The walls were no longer frosty. She blinked. No ice melted from her lashes. No cloud came from her lips. She glanced at her side. Crusty blood smeared her brown skin. Smooth skin. Completely healed. As if she'd never been wounded.

The Chieftess draped a soft white fur over Charlon's bare body.

Charlon instantly felt safer. "You're Magon?"

The woman raised an eyebrow. "She showed herself to you, did she? Magon is my shadir. She gives me her likeness. No one remembers what I really look like. Least of all me." The Chieftess stood. Walked away from the bed of furs. "Five, get her some clothing. My Fifth, some food."

Thirsty and the statue woman—who must have returned at some point—scurried from the tent.

"You showed yourself to this child?" Mreegan said.

Charlon did not understand. Who was she talking to?

"I don't believe it," Mreegan said, turning and gazing into nothingness. "She cannot be that old." Mreegan strode back to the bed of furs and looked down on Charlon. "How old are you?"

"Nineteen," Charlon said, still confused.

"Have you altered your age with magic? I wouldn't have guessed you more than twelve." The newt crawled down Mreegan's arm and she cradled it against her stomach.

"I know no magic. I've always been small," she said, then added, "lady."

Mreegan smirked and stroked her newt. "I am no *lady*. You will address me as Chieftess. What's your name?"

"Charlon."

"How did you come to live on the streets of Bar-Vorak, Charlon? Your accent confuses me."

"I was born in Rurekau, Chieftess. In Larsa. When I was thirteen, my brother . . . I became a slave. To a brothel in Lâhaten. Months ago I escaped my master's home. Fled to Magonia. I'd heard women were treated better. Better in this realm, but . . ." Charlon trailed off. She didn't want to insult Magonia's ruler.

"But there's trouble for a poor woman everywhere," Mreegan said. "I was once like you. Even though we are exalted in the mother realms, some men still find a way to hurt women here. I'm sorry you've suffered in my realm."

Tears flooded Charlon's eyes. Mreegan blurred before her.

"You have a new home now. Welcome to our tribe, Charlon," Mreegan said. "Magon led you to us. She tells me you will help us in the future. After today's sacrifice I will have only four maidens. You will be my Fifth. Part of my inner circle."

Too many thoughts. All at once. Magon led Charlon here? The woman who'd thrown the spear, sacrificed? Charlon to become the Fifth Holy Maiden of the Magonian Chieftess? "I'm not a maid," Charlon blurted out, cheeks burning. "My master, the brothel—"

Mreegan lifted her hand. "You've been healed. Made whole. What once was is no more. You are again a maid."

A ludicrous statement. Underneath the white fur, Charlon ran her fingers over her healed side. "But how?"

Mreegan offered a glowing smile. "Nothing is impossible with Magon. I'm glad you have come to us, my Fifth. I look forward to the revelation of Magon's plan for you. Rest now. Seeing the goddess takes great strength."

Mreegan reached toward Charlon. Charlon flinched. But the Chieftess merely waved her hand past Charlon's eyes and whispered. There was no choice. Charlon's eyes fell closed and she slept.

Trevn

In the 760th year of House Hadar's reign, the disciples of Lady Omari Gasta split off from Armania in what later became known as the Great Parting. King Nathek Hadar had outlawed magic, but to Magon's disciples, magic was the next step in the development of humankind. Patriarchy had become archaic. Gender did not give value, nor was magic evil in and of itself. They formed the nation of Magonia in the east and built shrines and temples to the goddesses they worshiped.

The people of Magonia quickly became divided. There was little food and many disagreements over politics and the treatment of men— especially male mantics. A series of murders sparked a civil war, which ended with the nation of Magonia dividing in two. Those with a more aggressive view on mantics seceded to northern lands with Lady Omari and founded the nation of Tenma, setting their minds on becoming the most powerful nation in the Five Realms. And so the mother tribes have been rebelling against House Hadar to this day.

—from *A History of the Five Realms* by Pontiff
Vremmel Gerke, House Hadar 806

W hat are your thoughts, Sâr Trevn?" Father Tomek turned his bulging eyes on Trevn. The high priest was mostly bald with a fringe of white hair stretching from ear to ear around a dark brown, wrinkled scalp. Despite his old age, his posture was straight and his shoulders broad from years of sword training as a lesser prince. "Can you expound on this passage?"

Trevn stared at the old scroll before him. In all honesty, reading about the mother tribes made him think of the Yobat/Yobatha debate, which brought to mind temple prostitutes, which reminded him of his brother Janek's threats to send one to his bedchamber when he least expected it.

But he would not say *that* to Father Tomek.

Trevn focused on the words etched into the clay. "Mantics, mainly female ones, felt oppressed by the Armanian king, so they seceded from Armania." Trevn couldn't blame them. Armanian kings—or rosârs, as Father liked to be called—had the tendency to oppress, especially their children. "Yet some of the mantics took their newfound independence too far, and today men are oppressed in the mother realms."

"Good," Father Tomek said. "The mother realms warred with us for over one hundred years. Wasn't their freedom enough?"

"The west has superior resources," Trevn said. "Most of Tenma and Magonia stands desolate, so the mother realms built cities on the eastern seaboard. For decades their only food came from the Eversea, which was why they wanted our land."

"Was that all? They merely wanted our land to grow food?"

"Not exactly. Tenma was also hungry for power and wealth. They wanted wood for ships. They wanted to rule everything."

"Yet your father gained us peace. How and at what cost?"

"The Ten Year Truce ended the fighting and enabled free trade at neutral ports. But those border cities quickly divided and began imposing taxes on anything that crossed the borders. So while the treaty enabled trade, a tax war has made trade terribly expensive."

"Good. There was another repercussion from the treaty, one that—"

"Illegal entry laws," Trevn said, thinking of the protestors he'd talked with yesterday.

Father Tomek sighed, and Trevn realized he'd interrupted. "I was referring to the gods, Sâr Trevn. Think on it. Tomorrow we'll discuss it further."

Trevn straightened in his chair, eager to leave. "I'm dismissed?"

"Have you finished transcribing your five pages?"

"Almost." He had only five pages to go.

"Transcribing the holy book is the most important part of a priest's training. Why is that?"

Because the holy book was full of holes? Trevn fought back a grin. "Because the act of writing increases the chance the writing will be remembered." This Trevn had found true with the maps he'd drawn.

"I shall read until you're finished," Father Tomek said, walking to his desk.

Trevn bit back a sigh. There was no task more arduous than transcribing. It made his back ache, his hand cramp, and his eyes squint until a headache was induced. But stalling would not get it done faster, and if he tarried too long, he'd miss his ride into the city.

Trevn fetched his vellum pages and the original holy pages from the cabinet Father Tomek kept under lock and key when he was not in the classroom. He returned to the table, spread out his work, and began to write.

Trevn barged into Hinck's chambers and dropped his scrolls and hipsack on the floor inside the door. His friend and backman had been in Highcliff for three weeks, celebrating his majority ageday. Hinck had returned to Castle Everton late last night and, from the size of the lump on the bed, was still sleeping.

Trevn approached and gave the lump a shake. "Hinck! Get up, we're going out."

Hinck moaned and pulled the covers over his head.

Trevn set his foot on the side of the bed and heaved himself up. He stepped awkwardly over the feather mattress to Hinck's side. Jumped once. "Now!" Twice. "If you don't hurry . . ." Three times. ". . . we'll miss the carriage."

"Woes!" Hinck's voice came muffled from under the blankets. "Not the rooftops. I just got back."

Trevn jumped again. "Absolutely the rooftops." Another jump. "What better place to spend such a glorious day?" Trevn leapt off the bed and landed on the wooden floor with a thud. "I haven't been able to go since you've been gone. Now get up."

The lump shifted. "Trev, I'm tired. Take Beal with you."

"Beal has gained my mother's permission to avoid the roofs. Keep complaining and I'll have Father find me a new backman."

Hinck threw off the blankets and sighed, staring at the ceiling. "Aren't you even going to ask about my ageday?"

Trevn made it a point never to ask personal questions. People would always tell a prince more than he wanted to know if he was patient enough.

"Move. Now." Trevn found Hinck's clothing from the previous day in a heap on the floor. It smelled clean enough, so he pitched it at Hinck's face. "We'll have to run." He walked to the door to retrieve his hipsack. He threaded the strap over his head and arm and settled the sack on his right side. The leather maps he tucked under his arm.

When he looked back, Hinck was sitting on the edge of the bed in only his trousers, turning his tunic right side out.

Hinck had a round face, small eyes, and a huge smile that bared teeth and gums—though he wasn't smiling now. He had darker skin than Trevn and soft muscles that showed a halfhearted commitment to swordplay. His shoulder-length black hair was thick and trapped in the single braid of a non-soldier. A week past fifteen, he also had a feather of hair on his upper lip.

Hinck pulled on his tunic, which made broken strands of hair frizz out around his face. He stuffed his foot into one boot and scanned the floor for the other. "You'll drop the maps if you carry them that way."

"One time, I dropped them," Trevn said. "And only because I upset that bird's nest."

"And who had to fetch them for you? Me. I almost died trying to climb up the side of Mama's Shelter with all those maps." Hinck bent down and reached under his bed. "It's worth my time to do it right."

He took the maps, squatted, and unrolled each on top of another, spreading them out on the floor in a stack. Once they were flat, he re-rolled them together in one thick cylinder. He slid them inside a map tube, pushed in the stopper, and put the strap over his head. "Lead the way, Your Impatientness."

Trevn darted into the hallway and sprinted to the servants' stairs. Down, down he went around the curling stairs. He surprised a maid, who screamed and dropped a pile of fabric.

"Sorry!" Trevn called back.

Seconds later Hinck called out a "Sorry!" of his own.

Trevn grinned. Hinck was slower than a snail in stormmer.

He reached the ground floor and slowed to make the left turn. Past the laundry, the buttery, the store, and into the vast kitchen where the aroma of baked bread filled the air. He poured on the speed, dodging servants.

A crash sounded behind him. Hara, the cook's voice. "Oh, that boy!"

Trevn chuckled and veered toward the corner exit where Hawley, Queen Brelenah's onesent, presided over three male servants and a dozen wicker baskets filled with bread.

They'd made it!

Hawley glanced at Trevn as he ran past, his face hardened against any hint of approval.

Trevn knew better. Hawley liked him. The man took food to the Sink daily, at the command of his queen. It had been too long since he'd given Trevn a ride.

Outside, the sun burned down, making him wish he'd changed into lighter clothing. The carriage was there, waiting. Trevn ran to the front and climbed aboard.

The driver stood, hands raised in protest. "Wait just a minute, lad. What do you think you're . . ." He cleared his throat and bowed. "My pardon, Your Highness."

Trevn ignored him, stepped onto the driver's seat—leaving a dusty boot-print—then hoisted himself to the roof. He slid onto his stomach, grabbed the front trim of the carriage, and swung around so he lay looking out over the driver's seat.

The driver was staring. New driver. Trevn had never seen him before. Their eyes met, and the man looked away. He made to sit down just as Hinck arrived. The driver offered Hinck a hand up, but Hinck's hands were filled with pastries.

"Want one?" he asked the driver.

"Thank you, no, lord. I've eaten," the driver said.

Hinck shoved a pastry in his mouth and accepted the driver's assistance. He lumbered up to the roof and sat beside Trevn. "Must you knock down so many servants, Your Discourteousness?"

"It's a gift," Trevn said. "You're just upset because I beat you. Again."

"I'm never racing. But by the time the person you knock down looks up, I arrive. *I* get the dirty looks. *I* get the curses. They all think *I* ran them down."

"Then run faster next time." He watched Hinck take a bite of pastry. "Aren't you going to offer me any?"

"Noh, Yer Bosshinessh." Hinck swallowed and said clearly, "These are mine. If you want some, next time slow down and steal your own."

"Isn't it a privilege to steal for your prince?"

Hinck took a huge bite and moaned. "So good." He licked his fingers and squinted.

Hinck was incapable of winking, yet he continued to try. His failure made Trevn wink all the more.

"The bread has been loaded, sir," a man said from below.

"Are we all ready, then?" Hawley called out.

That was Trevn's cue. He reached over the side of the carriage to give the answering knock, but—

"Yes, Mister Hawley, we are ready," a girl said.

Who was *that*? Trevn hung his head over the side and peeked into the carriage. Across from Hawley sat his brother Wilek's intended, Lady Zeroah, with a girl who looked very familiar. A striking girl with ginger skin, very big eyes, and a pink dress. Where had he seen her before?

She glanced up, saw him, and gasped.

Trevn winked and straightened himself back on the roof. Hinck lay on his stomach now, still eating.

"Everyone *else* ready?" Hawley called out from below.

Trevn rapped his fist three times on the side of the carriage and clutched the trim.

"Off we go, driver," Hawley said.

The carriage started to roll.

Hinck shoved the last of his pastry into his mouth and grabbed hold, cheeks bulging. "Whooss in thrrr?"

"Lady Zeroah and her maid." Though that other girl had not been dressed like a maid. She'd been wearing pink, and Princess Nabelle was stringent about her servants wearing the green and brown of her homeland.

The carriage rolled around the side of the castle toward the front gates where a crowd of protestors stood, shaking their fists. Trevn had spent some time with them while Hinck had been away. Some were Athosian priests, warning of apocalypse. But the majority were acolytes of Dendron or waterbearers, who wanted the king to investigate some illegal evenroot harvesting they claimed was killing plant and animal life and poisoning underground rivers and cisterns. And Trevn's father—the most unpopular Armanian king in a century—ignored them.

Trevn pushed to his knees and waved at his newest friends.

"Long live Sâr Trevn!" someone shouted.

"I'll try my best!" he yelled back.

The crowd cheered as the carriage passed through the gate. Not one person threw a stone or rotten piece of fruit.

Trevn laughed and waved, enjoying their attention. Back in Sarikar, where he'd spent much of his childhood, few had appreciated his spirit. Here in Armania, though, things were different.

"What was *that* all about?" Hinck asked.

Trevn lay back down as they rolled past the crossroads of High Street. "I can get away with anything here in Armania. The people love me!"

"Because they don't know you very well."

"Then they'll love me even more once they get to know me." It was a nice change from the stuffiness and judgmental glares in Sarikar.

The carriage drove down Procession Street, deep into the heart of Everton. Hawley would spend about two hours in the Sink, distributing bread to the poor, apparently assisted by Lady Zeroah and her pink-clad friend. That gave Trevn a few hours to explore before he needed to catch his ride home.

The carriage reached the Blackwater Canal and turned into the Sink, where it slowed and rattled over the narrow dirt road. Despite the horrible stench and the sight of so many poor, Trevn loved the Sink. The tiny adobe buildings were crammed so close together and had such flat clay roofs that Trevn could run and leap from one to another.

As they approached the bend where the carriage would nearly touch the roof of the Lazy Man's Inn, Trevn pushed up to a crouch.

"Get ready," he told Hinck.

Hinck sighed. "I'm ready."

In one, two, three! Trevn leapt off the carriage. His feet skidded a little on the fine layer of soot the inn's chimney left on the rooftop. He caught his balance and took off on his road in the sky. Over the next two inns, down to the roof of the chandler's shop, up over the public bathhouse, up higher onto Mama's Shelter, then a big jump down to the roof of the leatherworks, which reeked of urine.

He paused and looked over the ledge. Below, an alleyway separated the leatherworks' roof from that of the currier's. Trevn glanced back. Hinck was moving slowly, as usual. But at least he'd been willing to come. Trevn's first backman had asked to be reassigned after one week in Trevn's service. And Beal, his onesent, refused the roofs before ever trying.

Hinck caught up, panting. "Are we stopping?"

"Not quite," Trevn said. "I want to study the harbor."

Hinck groaned and plodded back along the roof. "I'll take the long way, thanks."

"Meet you there." Trevn walked back to the far side of the leatherworks roof to get a running start. He crouched down and grinned.

He was a squirrel. And squirrels could nearly fly.

He shot off, sprinting as fast as he could. At the edge of the roof, he leapt. His arms circled and his legs churned as he ran through the air. He landed a bit off kilter and slid onto his knees and right hand, catching himself on the edge of the currier's roof. He looked down to the alley below, met the gaze of a boy looking up.

The boy waved. Trevn waved back, then pushed to his feet and continued on.

Over the tenement housing and around the Temple of Rurek, which was far too tall to climb in a hurry. Another group of tenements and he arrived on the red-and-brown striped roof of Thalassa's Temple. From here he could look out to the Eversea, examine the shoreline, and watch the ships. He sat down to wait for Hinck, annoyed that he'd let him carry the maps. He withdrew the grow lens from his hipsack, eager to put his time to good use studying the coastline.

Everton had been built on the cliffs overlooking the sea. The nearest beach-front was a league south of the city. His father had a manor house there—Seacrest, it was called—but Trevn never visited now that his elder brother Janek had all but claimed it as his own.

Trevn quickly found the place where Cape Waldemar had been. He moved the grow lens from his eyes and squinted. Moved the grow lens back and looked again. He studied the shape of the cliffs, mentally comparing them to the maps he'd drawn. Five Woes! The cape was truly gone. He'd definitely be making some changes to his maps today.

Extraordinary, the power of nature. And a little terrifying.

Trevn peered out to the horizon. The harbor was filled with ships, coming and going from the Port of Everton. Trevn saw eight merchant cogs, three merchant stoneclads from Rurekau, one angle-rigged barge bearing a Sarikarian flag, several dozen fishing finships—some single-masted, some double—and a myriad of houseboats, sailing skiffs, and even a few reamskiffs. Not one wandered far from shore.

In the past hundred years many a ship had gone looking for new land, only to return with negative reports. Trevn felt they hadn't gone far enough. There was more out there, beyond the bowl, he just knew it. And if the Athosian priests were correct and the Five Woes were upon them, they needed to find land soon.

Footsteps approached, but Trevn kept his gaze on the sea. "You have my maps."

Fabric rustled, and the wooden tube thumped against the roof and rolled to stop by Trevn's leg. "Your precious maps . . ." A gasp for breath. "Your Mag-nanimousness."

"Big word," Trevn said. "You're smarter than you look."

Hinck shrugged and fell down beside Trevn, still fighting for breath.

Trevn dug into the map tube. He found the map of the harbor and unrolled it on the rooftop. He anchored the corners with stones from his hipsack so the wind couldn't whip it away.

"What's all that smoke?" Hinck asked.

Trevn looked up, annoyed to be pulled away from his map now that it was finally in front of him. "Where?"

Hinck pointed east, to a distant gray cloud that filled the sky.

Trevn went back to his map. "That's Mount Radu. It caught fire in yesterday's quake. Didn't you see it on your way back?"

"It was night, and I was sleeping."

Trevn found the bit of coastline he'd been studying. He looked up at the land through his grow lens, then back at the map. "It really did collapse. Not just part of it. The entire thing."

"What did?"

"Cape Waldemar. It's gone. As are the houses that were built on it."

"Five Woes," Hinck said, staring blankly at the missing cape.

"Captain Livina resided there," Trevn said. "He was at sea when it happened, but his children, his mother, his entire household, perished."

"Wasn't he admiral of the king's fleet? The one your father forced into early retirement?"

"The very one," Trevn said, sorry for the man. "I'd like to get closer, but I'd have to ask Father."

Hinck snorted. "Gods forbid you speak to the man."

"It's wisest not to, as you well know."

"How can a whole cape be gone?"

"Fell into the Eversea during the big earthquake two weeks back." Trevn handed Hinck the grow lens. "I think the cracks have something to do with where they strike."

Hinck held the grow lens to his eye and shuddered, then set his palm over his heart in the sign of The Hand and kissed his fingers, as if such an action might actually protect him. "I hate earthquakes."

"I hate that people die because of them, but they have a glorious majesty. Not even my father can stand against such power."

"Careful. If the rosâr hears you saying such things, he'll sacrifice you to Barthos."

"On the contrary, my pessimistic backman. The Hideous Rosâr, may he die a thousand deaths, would agree, though he'd give credit to Barthos. And if my father ever tried to sacrifice me, I'd run away."

Hinck handed back the lens. "You're fast, but not that fast."

"Even better, I'd steal a great ship and sail past the bowl until I found new land, which I'd name Trevonia."

"You want to be rosâr?"

"Not here. Never here. And never *rosâr*." As if being king wasn't good enough, Father had titled himself rosâr back before Trevn had been born, along with declaring the titles of rosârah, sâr, and sârah for the queens, princes, and princesses respectively. Father's pretension had been to set his dynasty apart from others, but the words were nothing more than ancient Armanian translations for king, queen, prince, and princess. And no matter how many people Father had sent to the pole for misspeaking, many continued to use the more common titles. "But I'd be king of Trevonia. I'd make it my mission to explore every corner of the world and map it all."

Hinck rolled his eyes. "I think that's already been done."

"How wrong you are. See how Cape Waldemar is no more? I will now create the first map to show it. The world is always changing, Hinck."

"I shall strive to remember that, O Enlightened One."

Trevn ignored Hinck's snark. He removed a wedge of charcoal from his hipsack and set about sketching a new shoreline without the cape.

"Since you refuse to ask about my ageday," Hinck said, "I'm just going to tell you."

Finally.

"I did not receive the gift of a concubine. So you were wrong."

"I'm afraid that sometimes happens," Trevn said, "though it's rare."

"Father said I might be seventh in line for the throne, but that doesn't mean I get to live like a prince. So you owe me one gold piece."

"Have my backman fetch it for you," Trevn said.

Not even a smirk from Hinck. "Father *did* invite a temple prostitute to our home, though."

Trevn glanced at Hinck. "Which temple?"

"Mikreh. The Duke of Highcliff would never do anything the rosâr wouldn't."

"Of course not."

"Mother was furious."

Trevn erased a mistake with the side of his pinky finger. "I can imagine." The woman was from Sarikar like Princess Nabelle and her stately daughter Zeroah. Dancing prostitutes were never appropriate. Was the girl in pink from Sarikar too? Why had she seemed so familiar?

He finished sketching the new coastline and sat back to look over his work.

"Anyway," Hinck said, "I spent the whole hour of first sleep with her."

"*What?*" Trevn glared at his friend. "Have you forgotten our pact so soon?" He lifted his fist to show the R-shaped scar etched into the side of his pinky and palm.

"But you should have seen her, Trev. She was amazing. And I wanted to . . . you know, to be a man."

Trevn rolled his eyes. "You need a woman to become a man?"

"Will nothing I do ever impress you?"

Trevn peered through his grow lens to check the shape of the coast against what he'd drawn. He seemed to have captured it perfectly. "If your goal in life is to impress me, I suggest you find a new goal."

Hinck sighed.

"Do not sigh as if I've disappointed *you*," Trevn said. "Renegades stand against the establishment that confines us—that forces us to conform to *their* ideals. Manhood at fifteen is their decree, Hinck. It's steeped in superstition. It means nothing. One might be a man at twelve. Another at seventeen. Each man lives his own life."

"Then let me live mine. You telling me to do the opposite of the establishment is you confining me to *your* ideals. I was curious. That was part of our pact too, in case *you've* forgotten."

"I've forgotten nothing. Curiosity is good and natural. But not when you follow their traditions, not when you support the very thing we're trying to— Do you feel that?"

The roof began to sway. A rumble hummed from below. On the streets, people screamed, and unseen objects rattled and clinked. Out to sea, waves crashed against the cliffs, swelling higher than Trevn had ever seen. He grinned, in awe of the majesty of it all. He had never been outside for a—

"Earthquake!" Hinck yelled.

WILEK

The floor trembled.

Wilek stopped in the foyer and set his hand against a fluted pillar. Muted screams echoed throughout the stone walls of Castle Everton. Overhead, chandeliers rocked on rattling chains. Two paces from where he stood, a candle slapped against the stone floor. Across the room, another fell. Then another and another.

Please let raining candles be the worst of this quake. Wilek had once thought the castle unmovable, but over two dozen earthquakes this past year—and three in two weeks!—had proven him false. How much more could the old stone walls take?

Kal grabbed his arm. "We must go outside, Your Highness."

Before Wilek could decide whether or not to concede to his shield's wishes, the shaking stopped.

Kal's grip on Wilek's arm remained tight, dark eyes met his. "Are you well?"

"Fine. That was a short one." Wilek took a deep breath and tugged his arm free. He kicked a candle out of his way and watched the white wax roll across the foyer until it bounced off a pillar. "That was the third in two weeks. People will panic."

"And the Athosian priests will take full advantage of the paranoia," Kal said.

Those priests had caused trouble enough. Father would have to do something about them. Perhaps Wilek should check on the king . . . suggest a plan. The more useful he made himself—especially in times of crisis—the better his chances of being declared Heir.

Wilek turned back to Kal to get his shield's opinion on the matter and saw Harton running toward them. The lad's belt and sword were tucked under one arm and his tabard had bunched up over his hands as he tied the laces of his britches.

"Three quakes in a fortnight!" Harton seemed giddy at the prospect. He let his tabard fall into place and pulled his sword belt round his trim waist. "Dendron is terrible fierce about something. Guess he didn't like the rosâr's sacrifice to bad-breath Barthos."

"Your place, Harton!" Kal snapped. "And why are you late? Again?"

Now fully dressed, Harton turned a repentant gaze on Kal, then quickly bowed his head to Wilek. "Forgive me, Your Highness. I . . . slept in. I only mentioned Dendron . . . I mean . . . I didn't mean to insult Barthos."

Agmado Harton "slept in" at least four times a week, a shortcoming Wilek had temporarily overlooked due to the boy's amiable disposition. When three people spent almost every hour of every day in the same company, it was much more pleasant if those people got along.

Wilek gripped the young backman's shoulder. "Listen well, Harton. I do not begrudge each man his choice in which gods he kneels to. But should my father hear such slander against Barthos from your lips, he'll have you flogged."

Harton's throat bobbed. "Yes, Your Highness. I shall guard my tongue from now on."

"See that you do." Though Wilek doubted such a thing was possible for this magpie.

The high-pitched flutter of women's voices rose from the back of the castle. Mother.

Wilek strode across the foyer toward the inner courtyard. Kal and Harton kept pace on either side.

Over three hundred years ago, Castle Everton had been built in the shape of a letter *A*, to honor Arman, the creator god. King Echad had recently started renovations on the northern end with the intent of remodeling the castle into a *B* for Barthos. The foyer, which filled the entire crossbar of the A, separated the castle entrance from the inner courtyard in the A's center: his mother's favorite place to hold a court of her own apart from the king.

"They started early today," Kal said.

"Mother feels any time between breaking her fast and second sleep is a good time for court." Being surrounded by her followers—and her throng of tiny dogs—gave Wilek's mother joy and purpose. Arman knew how little attention the king gave his first wife.

A pillar in the foyer had collapsed. A group of courtiers stood around the wreckage. At the back of the foyer, two Queen's Guards were holding open the main doors to the courtyard. Courtiers filed inside, holding one another and exclaiming over the ordeal they'd just survived.

"Harton," Wilek said, "send these people back through the garden to the northern wing until we can get someone to inspect that pillar. Guard!" Wilek waved one of the Queen's Guards over. Like the King's Guard, their uniforms were blue tabards over blacks but for Queen Brelenah's green branch insignia on their chests instead of Father's red Barthos heads. "Find Lady Lebetta and see that she is safe," he told the guard. "Bring word to me at once."

Harton and the guard ran off.

The crowd parted somewhat at Wilek's approach; those who saw him bowed. Many were too overcome to notice their surroundings. The second guardsman at the doors gave Wilek a quick bow of the head as he and Kal stepped outside.

Wilek scanned the courtyard and saw no immediate damage. He fought his way through the chaos that only three score of courtiers, their servants, a squadron of guards, and a dozen of his mother's tiny dogs could create after a natural phenomenon. The animals yipped and bit at his ankles as he walked toward the open colonnade. Women were scattered, sitting or lying on blankets on the pebbled ground. Perhaps some had fainted. None were his mother.

The moment Wilek made eye contact with Princess Nabelle of Sarikar, she pushed through the bodies toward him. The mother of his betrothed was a flawless woman—in appearance, anyway. Today her typically regal expression had been replaced with fear.

"Sâr Wilek, may you live forever." The words came quickly as she sank into a low curtsy.

"You are well, I hope, Princess?" he asked.

"Yes, but I fear for my daughter."

Wilek frowned. "Lady Zeroah was injured?"

"Wilek!" His mother lunged past Princess Nabelle and threw her arm around his neck. The other arm held one of her dogs, which sniffed Wilek's tunic. "Oh, my son. Thank Arman! How relieved I am to see you well. I detest those horrible quakes."

He gave her a gentle squeeze. "Are you well, Mother?"

"All but my nerves." She pulled back and set her hand to her heart. "I declare one day those quakes will stop my heart forev—" Her gaze latched on to Princess Nabelle. "Oh, Lady Zeroah!" She gripped Wilek's arm, and the dog she was holding yipped. "Oh, Wilek, your betrothed!"

"Time to be a hero," a crackly voice said from behind him.

"Gran." Wilek stepped back to allow his grandmother into their circle. The Mother Rosârah was a tall, lean old woman whom Father tried to ignore but Wilek's mother refused to let be forgotten.

Wilek glanced into the colonnade and behind the wicker chair his mother used as a throne. No sign of Lady Zeroah. "She is not here?"

"They went to the Sink," Princess Nabelle said. "Zeroah and her new honor maiden."

Wilek glanced at Kal, but his shield's scarred face showed no emotion.

"Such a sweet girl," Mother said, leaning on Wilek for support. "Hawley was taking food to the poor, and Miss Mielle suggested that she and Lady Zeroah go along. Arman only knows what madness this quake might have stirred in the city. Lady Zeroah's guards might have been overpowered. The almshouse might have collapsed!"

Wilek wrapped his arm around his mother's waist and helped her back to her throne. He righted a footstool beside it as she settled her dog on her lap. "Princess Nabelle, won't you sit?"

"Thank you, but I would rather stand." She wrung a handkerchief between her fingers.

Gran plodded up and sat on the chair beside Mother's throne. "Well, I'd rather sit."

"It was only a tremor," Wilek told them. "Lady Zeroah's guards are well trained. I'm certain she is fine. But to ease your minds, I will go at once."

Princess Nabelle curtsied again. "Thank you, noble sâr. You are most kind."

"He'll make an excellent king," Gran said. "I'll have the minstrel write a song about this."

"Find her and bring her back to us, my son. Make haste!" Mother reached for Princess Nabelle's hand, and the princess graciously moved to the queen's side.

Wilek kissed his mother's cheek, then he and Kal left the courtyard and started for the west wing, the quickest route to the stables. Kal sent a boy to run ahead and tell Master Crossett to saddle their horses, then followed silently on Wilek's right.

"I am certain they are well," Wilek said. "It was a little quake."

Kal merely nodded.

Harton ran up behind them. "Some guards have set up a barrier to keep people out of the foyer."

"Well done," Wilek said.

The castle seemed deserted and devoid of any other damage save more candles fallen from wall sconces. The men exited through the western doors and found a crowd of servants huddled on the terrace.

"The quake is over," Wilek told them. "Return to your posts at once."

The servants meandered toward the castle, shooting Wilek furtive glances as if he were mad to suggest they go back inside. At the foot of the terrace steps, three horses stood saddled and waiting. Wilek slowed as he approached his mount. The black horse before him was not his stallion.

"Where is Foxaro?" he asked Master Crossett.

The marshal ran his fingertips along the bridge of the stallion's nose. "Sorry to say, Your Highness, but Prince Janek took Foxaro to Seacrest. I hope Gibolt will serve you well. He's an excellent horse."

Wilek's chest tightened. Janek! That arrogant, bothersome . . . He had no time for such games. He mounted Gibolt and set off. Kal and Harton quickly caught up. They rode three abreast, heading for the front gate.

Not even an earthquake could drive away the crowd of protestors. They caught sight of Wilek and pressed against the iron bars, their cries increasing in volume and fury, no doubt fueled by the superstitions of the Athosian priests. The guards saw Wilek coming and pushed back the crowd so that the gates could be opened.

"Let the prophet speak!" someone yelled from the crowd.

The protestors fell silent and backed away from a stooped, scrap of a man with slits for eyes and skin like a raisin.

"Everton staggers!" The man's voice was raspy yet full of authority. "Armania is falling; the king's words and deeds oppose Athos, defying his glory. He parades his sins, does not hide it. Five Woes to him! He has brought disaster upon himself and all of Armania. Justice will come from the hand of Athos. Stop, Prince of Armania, and answer for the crimes of your father!"

Those slit-like eyes focused on Wilek, who looked away. Crazy Athosians. Wilek should stop and answer. He wanted the people to know he cared—that he was not his father. But would they even listen? And what could he say about the earthquakes? He was powerless to stop them. Besides, Lady Zeroah was waiting—could be hurt.

Wilek urged the stallion into a canter. The protestors got out of the way, but their indignant cries filled Wilek with guilt. Once Lady Zeroah was safely returned to Castle Everton, he would try to speak with them. A prince should not ignore his people, whether he had answers or not.

Wilek, Kal, and Harton rode down Procession Street until it came to an end at the cliffs where the waterwheels lifted seawater up into the Blackwater Canal. The stench of sewage and rot overpowered the fresh sea smell as they neared the poorest part of Everton. Here they turned left onto the Sink Road, which followed the canal inland along Echo Crack.

Dust clouded his view as if a contingent of King's Guard soldiers had just passed through. The poor visibility and debris in the street forced the horses to slow. Merchant booths had collapsed, wheels had broken off carts and wagons. Several awnings had been ripped from their braces and hung limply down the sides of buildings. They passed by two buildings that had collapsed into a pile of rubble that spilled out into the street. Every so often someone ran up and begged help. At Wilek's nod, Kal threw each a coin.

"That prophet could be right," Harton said. "My nurse used to say the father realms would someday fall and Magonians would rule all."

A bolt of fire ran through Wilek's veins. "Senseless! Athosian prophets are nothing but play actors. They rewrite ancient prophecies and terrorize the people with doomsday claims. Look to the original texts and you'll find a very different message."

No one spoke for the space of ten paces. Wilek should not have snapped.

"I thought you were from Highcliff, Hart," Kal finally said.

"Indeed," Harton said. "But my nurse was Magonian. When I see a disaster like this—like Cape Waldemar—it reminds me of the bedtime stories she used to tell."

Delightful bedtime adventures for a child. "I have no intention of letting Magonians take over my reign," Wilek said.

If he ever got to reign.

Ahead, the adobe brick almshouse came into view, looking sturdy and undamaged. Thank Mikreh! If Lady Zeroah had perished, the king would have seen it as a sign against Wilek as Heir.

Regret washed over Wilek at his selfishness. He hated how the Heir War plagued his every thought, but Janek was deceitful and would use any means to win the title of Heir for himself. Wilek must take care.

The almshouse had been built at Mother's command to help the destitute. Rosârah Brelenah herself came once a week to feed her people. It pleased Wilek to learn that his mother and Lady Zeroah shared this interest. Perhaps, once he and Lady Zeroah were married, his mother would occupy much of his wife's time so that Lebetta would not fear being replaced.

Lady Zeroah's guards let them inside. From the realm of Sarikar, they wore green-and-brown striped tabards with the crest of the evergold tree bright over their breasts. Sarikar did not invite each royal to choose their own insignia. Everyone wore the crest of their king.

Wilek stopped to let his eyes adjust to the darkness and the mess. Shelves had tipped over and lost their contents to the dirt floor, which was covered in muddy patches from spilled soup. A lone table remained standing. Behind it stood a woman in a pink dress who jumped when she saw them enter.

"Kal!" It was Miss Mielle. She ran to Kal and embraced him. For the first time, Wilek realized the girl was nearly as tall as her guardian.

"Where is Lady Zeroah?" Wilek asked one of the guards.

"Out back, serving soup," he said.

Excellent. "Harton, with me." Wilek started for the back door, but Mielle released Kal and stepped in Wilek's way.

She curtsied to him, wobbling slightly. "Good midday, Your Highness. Thank you for helping me to a position with Lady Zeroah. I'm most grateful. We are already dear friends."

Wilek smiled, always amused by how Mielle managed to mix up the order of protocols and never seem the wiser. "You are most welcome, Miss Mielle."

Kal, as always, corrected her. "You must wait to speak to the sâr until he first speaks to you, Mielle."

"But he spoke, didn't he?" She looked innocently flummoxed. "I thought he had."

"To the guard, yes," Kal said. "But not to you."

"Oh." The word was weighted with such forlornness that Wilek could not leave it be.

"Forgiven and forgotten, Kal," Wilek said. "Walk with me, Harton. I must determine whether or not Lady Zeroah is ready to depart."

Harton followed Wilek toward the back door. "That's a big girl," he said. "Put a sword in her hand and I'd think twice about crossing her."

"Don't let Kal hear you say that," Wilek said, despite the truth of Harton's words.

They exited through the back door and into a muddy clearing where Lady Zeroah stood dishing up bowls of soup, a Sarikarian guard on each side. Lady Zeroah Barta was a pretty girl. Short and slender with thick black hair that today she wore in a combination of braids, beads, and loose curls. It was all tied back under a cowl to keep it from the cauldron flames and from slipping into someone's bowl. Her skin was the color of dark chocolate, a tinge lighter than her mother's, since her father had been Armanian. She had her mother's golden eyes. She wore a dress in two shades of blue, the hem of which was now muddy. Her body had very little shape to it . . . yet. Her mother's stunning figure gave Wilek hope of that someday changing.

The line of dust-covered people before her table sent a twinge of guilt to Wilek's heart. Why had he never come here? No wonder the people hated him. Perhaps he should help.

He walked to her side and picked up an empty bowl, held it out. She did not see him, too busy talking to the small girl she was handing the bowl to.

Next in line was a boy of maybe nine. His tired eyes locked onto Wilek and flashed wide. "It's the sâr! The Dutiful! The First Arm!" The boy sank into a squat.

The outcry quickly caught on as others in line bowed to their prince. Lady Zeroah turned her head. Golden eyes latched onto his. She gasped and sank into a deep curtsy.

"I am grateful to see you well, lady," Wilek said. "From the damage I have seen on my ride here, the earthquake must have been a great deal stronger than it felt inside the castle. Our mothers and I were concerned for your welfare."

Her eyes shifted to meet his, wide and wary like a frightened mouse. "Your Highness." She looked at the ground and mumbled, "Good midday."

Bother. Wilek grew weary of these meetings. He could plainly see she was terrified of him. Trying to father his heir on this girl would likely be an awkward chore. He wondered if telling this to Lebetta would ease her anger at his coming nuptials. Likely not.

Lady Zeroah straightened, reached for the bowl he was holding. She took it, careful not to touch him. "I thank you." She ladled soup into the bowl, but her shaking hand spilled soup over the side and onto her finger. She closed her eyes and winced. Had it burned her? Or was she merely embarrassed?

The boy was on his feet now and grabbed the bowl. "I thank you, lady."

"Let me clean the side," she said, reaching for a rag.

"No need. That's what the gods gave me a tongue for." The boy grinned and staggered off, slurping at the bowl.

Wilek withdrew his handkerchief and handed it to Lady Zeroah.

"Thank you, Your Highness." She carefully took the proffered linen and dabbed the moisture from her hand, keeping her eyes downcast. Her chest heaved, as if she were short of breath.

Gods help him. How was he to stomach being married to this jittery butterfly? One wrong word and she would fly away. If only he could marry Lebetta instead.

"Your Highness," Lady Zeroah blurted suddenly. "Would you honor me with a walk?" A deep breath. "In the queen's garden when we return to Castle Everton?"

Well, this was new. Every moment they spent together seemed to cause the poor girl agony. Did she relish an increase of torture?

Still, he saw no way out of it and gave a polite lie. "I would be delighted, Lady Zeroah."

"Helping!" A woman in a black cloak ran toward them, waving her arms. "Helping me! Is hurt. My daughter!"

Wilek was struck by her strange accent and bronzed skin. Could she be from the mother realms? It was difficult to tell sometimes. All this talk of prophecy was making him jumpy.

"Where is your daughter?" Lady Zeroah asked.

The woman pointed down the street to an alley. "Is in tiny street. First house. Is inside. Trapped. My daughter."

"There is nothing but adobe houses down that alley," Wilek said. If an adobe house had collapsed, the girl was likely dead. Adobe bricks were mercilessly heavy.

"But you will go with her, yes?" Zeroah asked, turning her golden stare on him.

"Absolutely," he said, wishing he would have jumped to it without having to be told. He was far too used to having everything done for him. But here was his chance to help his people. "Harton, fetch Kal. We will assist this woman."

Harton darted inside the building and returned a moment later with Kal. The three men followed the strange woman to an alley that was cluttered with dust and fallen bricks. Midway down, he could barely see that the back side of a tenement had collapsed. The woman stepped deftly through the rubble. Kal followed, hand on the hilt of his sword. Wilek doubted very much this old woman had planned an ambush, but he appreciated his shield's caution.

The woman stopped at what once had been the corner of the tenement.

The back wall was gone, now a pile of broken adobe and dust that bared the inside of each home on the three levels of the building. The woman pointed to a bare foot sticking out from a section of fallen wall. A foot with reddish-brown skin. This must be a Magonian family. Or Tennish. Illegal immigrants in Everton. Why?

"Harton, help me lift," Kal said. "Your Highness, try to grab the girl."

Kal and Harton gripped the end of the broken wall and lifted, both grunting with the effort. Wilek reached for the bare ankle, which was now a fully bare leg. Was this girl naked?

Clumps of straw and mud from the roof's insulation covered the rest of her body. Wilek brushed aside the debris until he found—not a girl, but—a young woman underneath. She was clothed, after all, wearing the red sheath of a temple prostitute. Wilek lifted her in his arms and carried her back down the alley. She groaned when he laid her on the packed dirt, then looked at him. Her eyes were gray, like polished rounds of a dirty diamond. She must be from the mother realms.

"*Te segees*," the girl said.

"*Te des emjar*," Wilek replied in rusty Tennish. He had learned the language as a child but had not spoken a word of it since the war ended and the truce kept Armania's borders closed to the mother realms.

Those gray eyes widened at his comment, and she spoke quickly to her mother, too soft and fast for Wilek to understand.

"They're from Magonia," Kal said.

"How can you tell?" Wilek asked. "I guessed Tenma."

"The accent. And the red dress is in honor of Magon's red lakes."

"I have never seen eyes like those," Wilek said.

"She's a mantic," Kal said. "Evenroot turns the eyes gray."

A mantic. A chill ran up Wilek's arms at the idea of magic, illegal in the father realms. He had never, in fact, seen magic done.

Kal had grown up in Raine and fought in Magonia during the war. His Tennish was much stronger than Wilek's. "Ask them why they are here," Wilek said. "How they got here."

Kal asked the woman, then translated. "She says they always lived here."

"Tell her who I am and that I will have them arrested if they lie to me again."

Wilek caught some of Kal's next words. *This is your sâr, the First Arm of Armania.* Then Kal's fluency lost him.

66

The mother gasped and fell to her knees. "My prince! To me. Be forgiving." She rubbed her hands on the ground and scrubbed her face, leaving smudges of dirt and adobe dust on her skin. Then she prattled on to Kal.

"She says, 'The Chieftess of Magonia is coming to rule Armania,'" Kal said. "'For centuries the prophets have spoken of this time. Any day now, the old world will fall to ruin.' They came here through Ebro, then Grayswood, and Pixford. Her daughter was trained at the Temple of Magon, which helped them cross the border and earn rides with merchants." Kal grunted. "Says her daughter knows many ways to please a man."

Of that Wilek had no doubt. Her other words disturbed him. Every realm had their own translations of the Root Prophecy, but this sounded like the Magonian Chieftess might be plotting something. "My father rules Armania," Wilek said.

The woman wiped dirt over her daughter's face. "Forgive us, most noble prince. From the earth we come. From Barthos. We honor god of Armanian king. You must be taking to be wife. My Fina. Girl is beautiful, yes?"

"Yes," Harton mumbled from behind them.

"Pleasing you, my daughter. Making wonderful wife. For a prince. Being Father to the Deliverer. You may be."

"I have no need of a wife." Especially one who spun magic.

"Saved her life, my prince," the woman said. "Insult Magon, you do. To refuse. If not wife, add to your harem, no? My daughter?"

Wilek had no harem. He looked back to the girl, Fina, and her eyes of glass. His brother Janek would have already thrown the girl up over his horse and ridden away, but Wilek had trouble enough balancing two women in his life. Plus his father would never allow a Magonian woman in the castle, no matter how beautiful or exotic she appeared.

"Kal, give them some coin and see that everyone vacates this building. It is dangerous and must be knocked down." Wilek retreated down the alley.

Bootsteps slapped the packed dirt behind him and Harton slowed on his left. "You're just going to leave her?"

Wilek glanced back. Kal was walking toward them, so he waited for his shield to catch up. "Upon our return to the castle, send some men to arrest them. They are in our realm illegally, and we must learn more of this Magonian plot to usurp the throne."

"I live to serve," Kal said.

"You're going to *arrest* her?" Harton said.

"Never underestimate the power of a woman, Harton," Wilek said. "Especially one of our enemy. Lady Zeroah awaits."

Another full hour passed before all the soup had been dispersed and Lady Zeroah declared the task complete. Wilek felt glad for having helped. Shortly thereafter Hawley and the women were loaded into the carriage. The Sarikarian guards led the way on horseback. The carriage followed. Wilek, Kal, and Harton brought up the rear.

That was when Wilek saw them.

His youngest brother, Prince Trevn, and Hinckdan Faluk, the young Earl of Dacre, were riding atop Lady Zeroah's carriage. The boys were facing forward, paying no attention to them.

"Do you see them?" Wilek said to Kal.

"Rosârah Thallah won't be happy," Kal said.

"Why not?" Harton asked. "The rosâr gave permission, didn't he? That's what I heard."

"He did," Wilek said, "but Rosârah Thallah will have looked for her son after the earthquake. I fear this was bad timing for Trevn's adventure. No woman keeps a tighter bridle on her son than the third queen."

"So he's in trouble," Harton said.

"Indeed," Wilek said. "But trouble is nothing new for Trevn. He will survive."

"Wilek, finally!" Hrettah yelled.

Wilek dismounted in front of the castle and handed his reins to a boy. His twelve-year-old half sister, Princess Hrettah, ran down the front steps of the castle and gave a quick curtsy as his rank required. Rashah, age five, followed. She curtsied as well, then flung her arms around Wilek's waist.

He patted Rashah's back. "Is everyone well?" he asked. "Your mother? The rosâr?"

"Trevn is gone," Rashah said, eyes wide. "His mamma was crying."

Wilek winced. "Trevn is fine, Rashah. He is there." Wilek pointed to Trevn and Hinck, who were sliding off the back of the carriage roof.

"Trevn!" Rashah yelled, running toward the carriage. Trevn caught her up and threw her upside down over his shoulder. She shrieked giggles and kicked her bare legs until her dress fell to her waist.

68

Wilek's onesent, Dendrick, approached. "The rosâr wants to speak to you right away, Your Highness."

Wilek nodded, happy for an excuse to cancel his garden walk with Lady Zeroah. He needed to speak with his father about the Magonians. "A moment, Dendrick. I must speak with Lady Zeroah."

"Very good, sir."

Wilek walked to the carriage to wait for his betrothed. Her guards opened the door and handed Lady Zeroah to him. She quickly stepped back and curtsied. He offered his arm again, and she took it.

Miss Mielle climbed from the carriage next. "Who were those boys on the roof?"

"Sâr Trevn and the Earl of Dacre." Wilek led Zeroah toward the castle entrance. Kal and Miss Mielle followed. "My half brother enjoys adventures he cannot find inside the castle walls."

"Sâr Trevn did much of the same in Sarikar," Lady Zeroah said. "Or so I heard from my cousin."

Unsurprising. Wilek's youngest brother had spent his childhood in the realm of Sarikar, a gesture of peace between the two nations. But now that Trevn's ageday approached, their father had called him home.

"I must cancel our walk in the garden," Wilek told Lady Zeroah. "My father has summoned me."

She seemed to deflate a little, and he felt her arm tremble. "I understand, Your Highness. Likely many people need aid after such an earthquake."

"Indeed." But hopefully not many more Magonians.

They entered the castle foyer and Lady Zeroah spoke again, looking at the floor. "Might I join you tonight for dinner in the great hall?"

Woes! Never before had Lady Zeroah asked anything of him. Had Princess Nabelle put her up to this? Wilek had not realized until now, but he hoped his marriage would change little of his life. This girl seemed suddenly determined otherwise. But he must keep her happy. "Certainly," he said, forcing a smile. "I shall see you then." He released her arm, bowed. She countered with a curtsy. Then he turned on his heel and strode for the vestibule that led to the west wing, eager to escape.

Mielle

Prince Wilek walked away, posture like a flagpole, Kal and the other King's Guard right behind him. Zeroah watched them go, a look of forlorn hopelessness on her face.

This would never do.

Mielle hurried to her lady's side. "What happened?"

"He canceled our walk," Zeroah said in a small voice, staring at the floor. "His father summoned him."

Mielle had no argument for that. "Well, perhaps he will see us at dinner, and you can try again." Zeroah had managed to convince her mother to move into her apartment in Castle Everton under the pretense of accepting Rosârah Brelenah's long-standing invitation to the Court of the Queen. This also afforded Zeroah many a chance to see Sâr Wilek and get to know him better.

Zeroah looked up, wincing. "I asked if we might join him for dinner."

"Oh, well done!" Mielle said. In the two weeks she'd been working for Zeroah, Mielle had been encouraging the girl to be brave.

Zeroah bit her bottom lip. "I vex him; I can tell. What can I do?"

"You must relax. All this worry is upsetting you. Let us be proactive. Might we return to Queen Brelenah's court?"

"I overheard that she has retired for the day. But . . ." Zeroah lit up. "Perhaps we might risk the court of the king?"

"I thought you hated going there."

"I do. But the rosâr is not there. This very minute Sâr Wilek goes to a meeting with his father. I suspect court will be far less intimidating with the rosâr and his advisors away. Do you agree?"

"Yes! Let us go at once." A thrill kindled in Mielle's stomach. She was going to the court of the king!

The Presence Chamber of Rosâr Echad was on the first floor of Castle Everton, at the very top of the A-shaped building. A quick walk through the cactus garden in the courtyard brought them to the entrance.

A crowd had assembled outside the chamber. Many were servants of those within. Others were merchants, tradesmen, priests, and entertainers, all gleaming in their finest ensembles, all hoping for a chance to meet the king. Only nobles could enter the Presence Chamber without invitation. Zeroah's guards parted the crowd, bringing murmurs to Mielle's ears.

"It's Lady Zeroah!"

"The sâr's betrothed."

"Who is that with her?"

"Where is the princess?"

Four King's Guards stood before a set of intricate bronze doors, pikes in hand. The ruby Barthos insignia on their chests looked villainous compared to the gold thread of the Sarikarian tree. Mielle suddenly wished she were Sarikarian instead.

The guards opened the doors, and Mielle and Zeroah entered, arm in arm. Inside, Mielle's courage shattered. The room was packed! Sunlight streamed in through the small windows lining the back wall, making the gold draperies and lavish clothing of those inside gleam like jewels. Although servants stood along the walls, fanning massive palms, the air was stale and warm with the unpleasant odor of too many bodies crammed together.

"Lady Zeroah, what a pleasure!" A plump woman with graying hair swept up before them. She wore a brown-and-white gown with so many ruffles she resembled a feather duster. At least a dozen ropes of red and orange beads had been twisted around her throat and completely hid her neck from view.

"Lady Durvah, good midday," Zeroah said. "May I introduce Miss Mielle Allard, my friend and companion."

"How do you fare, Miss Mielle?" Lady Durvah asked, tugging on a strand of beads.

"I am well, thank you," Mielle said.

"How is your mother, the princess?" Lady Durvah asked Zeroah.

As Zeroah answered, Mielle took in the room. The chamber was much smaller than the Throne Room but had the same blue silk-covered walls. Golden drapes ran along the molding and bunched in each corner, falling in waves to the floor. They met in the center back wall and fell in a cascade behind a bronze throne cushioned in blue silk, which, as Zeroah had predicted, was blessedly empty.

A young woman stepped up to Mielle. "Good midday, ladies." Silky voice, unfairly beautiful face. She was small and curvaceous, dressed in a bloodred gown with white and black ribbons holding gathers in place. Her hair hung in a cascade of gold and brown ringlets under a chaplet of beaded red flowers. "Lady Durvah, is that your husband speaking with Keshelle Malton?"

"Is it?" The plump woman turned, her ropes of beads clacking. Her expression darkened. "Avron, come here at once!" She shuffled away, shaking her finger in the air.

The young stranger chuckled. "Poor woman. Elderman Avron Jervaid is generally unpleasant in every way. Lady Durvah has borne her husband's infidelities with such composure, but his flagrant behavior so distresses her she cannot help but overreact. Perhaps a leash might be the answer to her problems."

Mielle and Zeroah glanced at one another.

"Lady Zeroah, won't you introduce me to your acquaintance?" the young woman asked.

"Yes, of course," Zeroah said. "This is Miss Mielle Allard. Mielle, this is Lady Eudora Agoros. Her mother is Sârah Jemesha, the rosâr's sister."

Mielle curtsied. "I am pleased to know you."

Lady Eudora threaded her arm with Zeroah's and led her toward the nearest corner. "You have come to court before with your mother, but now that you are here alone, you must allow me to give you my own private tour. Your friend may join us."

Zeroah glanced over her shoulder and shot Mielle a worried expression. Mielle hurried after them. Lady Eudora stopped in the corner and turned to face the full room, golden draperies at her back. Mielle positioned herself on Zeroah's opposite side.

"There is no place better to pass the time than in the court of Rosâr Echad, may he live forever." Eudora paused and looked pointedly at them both. "Courtiers from all corners of the father realms come to show patronage to the rosâr, no matter the cost. Many young men come to court in hopes of making their fortune—too often by marriage to a wealthy young heiress. But they must take care. The wrong woman could be their downfall." Lady Eudora nodded to a handsome young man in a green-and-black tunic, who was standing in a group of men. "Jarmyn Koll was expelled from court after he got Lady Madara Vohan with child, and she only fourteen at the time. He is only present today because the king is not. And beyond the men, those three women? Each of their husbands sits on the Wisean Council. In the turquoise and lavender is Elessia Hearn, wife of Sherriff Irlond Hearn. Aarella Trumboke is wearing white and red. She is married to Governor Estin Trumboke. And in the sage green is the Duchess of Highcliff, Zura Faluk, married to the duke. Their son, Hinckdan, is a close friend of Sâr Trevn's and an earl himself."

"The Earl of Dacre?" Zeroah asked.

Eudora raised one perfect eyebrow. "Indeed."

"He was the one riding atop our carriage with Sâr Trevn," Zeroah told Mielle.

Eudora sighed. "Yes, Sâr Trevn is very wild. It is expected, his mother being who she is."

Mielle wanted to ask what Eudora meant by that, but Zeroah spoke first.

"The earl is in line for the throne as well, is he not?" Zeroah asked. "Seventh, I believe."

"Why, Lady Zeroah!" Eudora frowned. "Surely you of all people know that Armania is locked in an Heir War?"

"Well, yes," Zeroah said, cheeks darkening. "I know full well that Armania does not practice inheritance by birth order. I only thought—"

"Not by birth order *alone*," Eudora corrected. "One must be related to the rosâr by blood to become Heir. Therefore it is entirely possible that Hinckdan Faluk could be granted the title. But since he has never even spoken to the rosâr, it is unlikely."

"Oh," Zeroah said. "I see."

"And you do not want the earl as Heir. Surely you desire Sâr Wilek on the throne, hmm?" She smiled, so focused on Zeroah that Zeroah looked away.

"Of course," Zeroah said. "Since that is his wish."

Eudora pursed her lips. "My, you are so very agreeable. Sâr Wilek will adore you. Look there." Eudora jutted her chin toward an exotic-looking man. His head was shaved bald, and he had some kind of tattoo running down the sides of his neck. "Sir Garn. He is the emissary from Rurekau who brought Sir Jayron here. Sir Jayron is Sâr Janek's new shield, a gift from the Rurekan emperor. Rurekans do not grow warrior's braids. Sir Garn came on a great ship that still sits in Everton's harbor. He had an affair with Carressa Reman, honor maiden to Rosârah Laviel, then discarded her in favor of Lady Jadel, the young third wife of the former Admiral Livina. Sir Garn and Lady Jadel carried on for several months until the lady suddenly died. It was whispered that she was poisoned, either by her husband the admiral or by Carressa, though the physician declared the cause of death was ague."

"How dreadful!" Zeroah said.

"The admiral fell into such a consumption that the rosâr demanded his early retirement. Five weeks later the admiral also lost his family, his home, and his ship in the collapse of Cape Waldemar. The king promoted Hanray Vendal to admiral. Oh, look! There is Lilou Caridod." Eudora's eyes followed a curvaceous woman, whose hair was done up in a fat bun of yarn braids. She was standing with a second woman and a young man. "*She* is the rosâr's newest mistress. An actress friend of Rosârah Ojeda's. You do know that the fifth queen was an actress?"

Zeroah nodded. Mielle did as well. The Sink had been buzzing with the news of the king's marriage to a commoner.

"The rosâr took up with Lilou the moment Rosârah Ojeda's stomach began to bulge. He appointed her to a post in Rosârah Ojeda's bedchamber! The fifth queen hates her, calls her a 'lecherous girl.' And she is ever so obnoxious, but we all must like her. The rosâr declared that whoever was Lilou's enemy was his as well." Eudora rolled her eyes. "Do be ever so sweet to Lilou's face, at least, or you may find yourself standing before the Rosâr's Bench. Oh, and the Honored Lady Zenobia, first of the rosâr's harem. She is the one speaking with Lilou."

Lady Zenobia wore a two-piece beige dress and a ruby in her nose that was as big as a pea, both marks of a royal concubine. Despite her age, no lines marked her skin and her hair was as black as ink.

"No concubine is permitted at court," Eudora said. "Except Lady Zenobia. And no one knows why the king made the exception. Some say it is because she has bewitched him with mantics. It is also said that is why Rosârah Ojeda has been so very ill during her pregnancy."

Zeroah gasped and met Mielle's eyes. Oh, this Eudora was full of herself and her ability to captivate with gossip. It would take Mielle all afternoon to calm Zeroah down after this.

"The young man standing with the women," Eudora said. "Do you know him?"

"I confess I do not," Zeroah said.

"He is Kamran DanSâr, Lady Zenobia's youngest at six and twenty," Eudora said. "Lady Zenobia has borne the king four sons and a handful of daughters." Eudora raised one eyebrow. "Can you guess how many children the king has fathered?"

"I cannot," Zeroah said.

"Do try," Eudora said. "Miss Mielle, take a guess."

"A dozen?"

Eudora cackled. "So naïve, you girls. The answer is thirty-eight. That he has claimed, anyway. How many children are you prepared to give your future husband, Lady Zeroah?"

Zeroah's eyes bulged.

Mielle's gaze caught on Rosârah Thallah, the king's third wife, who was standing in the corner opposite them with a group of women, all of them short and very round. "What do you know of Rosârah Thallah?" Mielle asked, hoping to rescue her lady from Eudora's rudeness.

"She was a trade marriage from Rurekau. Is aunt to the current emperor. It is a wonder Sâr Trevn was even born. The rosâr found her so ugly, he cast her out upon arrival! She fought back by writing to her brother, and only by pressure from the Rurekan emperor did Rosâr Echad do his duty to father a child on her. Poor dear. I do believe she cried daily for the first three years of her marriage until she became pregnant. Never comes to court when the rosâr is present. She is nearly mad, they say."

The doors opened then and a young man in a foreign uniform entered. His head was shaved bald, and he had the trimmed shadow of a beard sculpted around his jaw and the tip of his chin. No, that was black ink. A tattoo?

Eudora sucked in a sharp breath. "My pardon, ladies. Sir Jayron has come and I must speak with him. Enjoy your midday." She sauntered across the room toward the young soldier.

"And I thought *I* was a chatterbox," Mielle said.

"Now you know better," Zeroah said. "Let us depart before we are accosted by another who wishes to gossip for my benefit. I am exhausted after having spoken to two souls."

They withdrew from the chamber in a hurry, hands clasped between them. Zeroah led Mielle back through the courtyard and into the foyer. They passed under an archway into the vestibule that led to the east wing. Much of Castle Everton was old and ugly compared to Fairsight Manor. The corridors were chilly and dark, no matter the time of day, with walls of thick stone, chipped in places, and too few torches to light the way.

"Lady Eudora had much to say," Zeroah said. "I am still reeling."

"That Sir Jayron is devilishly handsome," Mielle said. "He and Lady Eudora would make a beautiful pair."

"I heard my mother tell Flara that many men love Eudora," Zeroah said. "She applied to be my honor maiden, but Mother felt her a poor influence. She also said, 'Lady Eudora is no maiden.' I suppose that is what another might have told us of her." Zeroah's eyes popped.

Mielle clasped Zeroah's arm and they laughed at the scandalous nature of such a comment. The girls reached the end of the vestibule and turned into the east hallway, almost running into a woman coming around the corner from the opposite direction. A peppery, woodsy smell engulfed them. Had this woman bathed in hyssop?

"Oh, excuse me," Mielle said, for she had been in the lead and going the fastest.

"Why, hello, *children*," the woman said. "It has been a while since I saw such young people in this part of the castle."

This woman was stunning—more so than even Lady Eudora or Princess Nabelle. She wore a plain turquoise top and skirt. No ruffles. No lace. Just smooth fabric hugging her curvy form and revealing lots of dark flesh: a flat stomach, slender arms, the side of one long leg. A ruby stone glittered on the side of the woman's nose. This was a royal concubine.

Relief flashed through Mielle at the realization that she would never be beautiful enough to be a concubine.

Zeroah and the woman were glaring at each other. Mielle filled the awkward silence with words. "Enjoy the midday," she said, pulling Zeroah away.

"Afraid of me, are you?" the woman asked.

Mielle glanced back. She did not like the concubine's superior tone or the way Zeroah looked ready to attack. "We don't want to keep you from your important business."

"I *do* have important business," the woman said. "A wedding to plan."

"Congratulations," Mielle said.

Zeroah spoke for the first time. "And whom are you marrying, mistress?"

"You should well know I am marrying Sâr Wilek. Likely before he marries you."

Such words! This must be Prince Wilek's concubine, the one Zeroah so feared. "You're lying," Mielle said. "Sâr Wilek would never marry you."

The concubine's eyes flashed. "Silence, you stupid girl."

Far from stupid. Mielle smiled. "He's already told you that, hasn't he?"

"You know nothing," the concubine spat.

"We must retire to my mother's apartment for first sleep," Zeroah said, tugging Mielle away.

"Yes, run along, *children*," the woman called after them. "Sâr Wilek will be waiting for me. We always spend first sleep together."

"Not for much longer!" Mielle yelled.

"Do not bait her." Zeroah squeezed Mielle's arm as they rounded the corner. There were tears in her eyes. Not until they were safely within Princess Nabelle's apartment did Zeroah let her emotions overtake her.

"Evil woman. I hate her!" She threw herself onto a longchair and wept.

The door opened and Princess Nabelle entered. "What is wrong?"

Mielle held her tongue, hoping Zeroah would explain.

Princess Nabelle strode to Mielle's side and took hold of her elbow. "What has happened? Answer me."

"A woman spoke rudely to us," Mielle said, uncertain how much Zeroah wanted her mother to know. "She implied that she and Sâr Wilek are to be married soon."

"It was *her*." Zeroah sat up, wiped her eyes. "She said she was going to marry him before I did."

"Lady Lebetta?" the princess asked.

Zeroah sniffled. "She said I was a child."

"Well, you are certainly behaving like one."

"But, Mother! She was horrible!"

Princess Nabelle grabbed Zeroah's arm and shook her. "Stop whining! When my father betrothed you to Sâr Wilek, my life changed forever. I had to move here. I had to infiltrate Rosâr Echad's court. And I have spent the past ten years fighting with immoral men in hopes that you will have a better future. That our realm will fare better for all our toils. You will do your part."

"But how can I . . . ?" Zeroah broke off in a sob.

"I will hear no more, Zeroah. We have been over this. The palace is filled with conniving women. If you do not grow a spine, once you are rosârah, women like Lady Lebetta will destroy you. You must learn to play the game. This . . . ." She gestured to Zeroah's tear-streaked face. "This is how you lose."

Wilek

Father's royal apartment originally had been on the fifth floor, but first his laziness, and later his ailments, prohibited the man from climbing to such heights multiple times a day. Therefore the royal apartment had been moved to the ground floor of the castle's west wing.

The King's Guards outside the Throne Room saw Wilek coming and opened the doors. The hall was vast, walled in blue silk and bronze panels that were decorated with faces of the gods. Wilek crossed the worn white marble floor that scores of commoners had trod upon over the centuries. The throne itself—or shrine, as Wilek was prone to think of it—was made of bronze, with four legs that ran up the side of the chair in pillars to support a pointed canopy roof. Five bronze busts perched on top—Gâzar, ruler of the Lowerworld; Lâhat, god of fire; Mikreh, god of fate; and Yobatha, goddess of pleasure—each on one corner. Barthos, god of soil, stood upon the pinnacle. These were his father's five chosen gods.

King Echad Hadar sat wedged onto his throne, surrounded by his Wisean Council of advisors and a cacophony of chatter. The king had once been a muscular man. But sometime around Wilek's twentieth ageday, his father had gained an abnormal amount of weight. His stomach ballooned, his chin multiplied, his muscles turned to flab, and his eyes sank into doughy cheeks.

To hide his girth he wore velvet robes and heavy capes in Armanian shades of blue and brown. He had a short, pointed beard that had been dyed black to hide the gray, and eyebrows penciled darker with kohl. Under a massive crown, hundreds of black warrior's braids threaded with jeweled beads hung to his elbows. They were none of them attached to his head. His illness had caused his hair to fall out. Wilek shuddered to think about what had become of the fighting man—or men—whose hair made up his father's wig.

Pontiff Rogedoth stood on the king's right, as always, in the position Wilek would occupy if and when his father declared him Heir. Wilek and the Pontiff did not get along. The man was far too controlling and often acted as if he were king. He believed priests, being so close to the gods, were superior to others. For some reason, Father put up with his nonsense.

The herald blew Wilek's call on the trumpet, one short note and four long ones. "His Royal Highness, Wilek-Sâr Hadar, the First Arm, the Dutiful."

The bustle around the king ceased. Wilek bowed low to his father, who waved him forward.

"We must increase the offerings to Barthos, my son," Father sputtered, eyes wide and eager. "His anger is plain. How many in the prison are sentenced to die?"

Wilek struggled daily to temper his father's impulsiveness. "I am glad to see you well, Father," he said. "How fares the castle?"

"Havoc!" said Canbek Faluk, Earl of Ravensham. Hinckdan's uncle was a greasy bachelor obsessed with sand cats. He owned several as pets and was currently wearing a cape of tan and black fur, buttoned at the throat with a fang as long as Wilek's hand. "Two dozen servants were injured in my home and one was killed when a chunk of stone fell from the ceiling not three paces from where I was taking my morning repast."

"Rosârah Laviel twisted her ankle," Avron Jervaid said, entering the room after Wilek. "She was descending the stairs when it hit." Jervaid was an ugly man with pitted skin and an onion-like nose. He was the wealthiest merchant in Everton and owned a fleet of thirty-eight ships, though his fear of water kept him from sailing himself.

"I am of a mind to move to my yacht," Canbek said.

"Are you daft?" Jervaid glared at Canbek. "Have you so soon forgotten how Captain Livina's *Half Moon* went down? Boats are no safe haven from the earthquakes. I have lost four ships myself from their malevolence."

"What about the city?" Wilek asked, seeking facts over panic. "Two buildings collapsed in the Sink, that I know of, and a third tenement structure will have to be knocked down before it falls on anyone. My men report at least twenty dead and some fifty injured. Has Captain Alpress given a King's Guard report?"

"He is busy at present in the castle foyer," Father said. "Those pillars are load-bearing. They must be repaired at once, or the crossbar will fall."

"The hub on the larger waterwheel broke," Jervaid said. "And a boy fell off the south end of the Cobweb Bridge. He'd been walking the rail on a dare."

"Forget the city," Canbek said. "I require a new apartment. And the Sun Chamber is still a shambles from the quake two weeks ago. The rosâr has had to meet his mistresses in his bedchambers."

"Those women have no business in my private rooms," Father said. "Tell the master builder and his crew that if the repairs on the Sun Chamber are not complete by the next full moon, they'll all be fed to Barthos!"

"But, Father, if the builders are sacrificed, who will repair the castle?"

"I'll hire builders from Sarikar! Think, boy. There is more than one way to shine a coin."

"What of the sacrifices, Your Highness?" Pontiff Rogedoth asked, pulling Wilek's attention away from the throne. He spoke slowly, calmly, always looking into the eyes of his subject. "Barthos could again shake the ground at any moment, maybe even destroy the castle. We must act quickly."

"I agree, worthy rosâr," Jervaid said. "Barthos is a fierce god, one we must not provoke."

Father grunted and turned his beady eyes on Wilek. "Son? What say *you*?"

Wilek would not encourage his father to murder more people to mollify his superstitions. "I do not know the number of prisoners sentenced to death."

"Find out," Father said. "Nothing matters more than appeasing Barthos."

"Indeed, sire, you are very wise," Rogedoth said, and the other men nodded, whether they truly believed it or not.

Beaming bootlickers . . . Wilek found another matter far more pressing. "Did you know Magonia means to take over our realm?"

Rogedoth turned his amber gaze on Wilek. "They've threatened for years. It is nothing new."

"I just arrested a Magonian woman and her daughter who were living in the Sink," Wilek said. "They moved here, illegally, because they believe the prophecy is at hand, that their Deliverer is coming to destroy us."

"A superstitious people, Magonians," Father said, as if the Magonian belief in prophecy was somehow worse than the five garments of clothing Father wore each day, or the five-stemmed candelabra that hung about the castle, or the fact that Mother had named Wilek "*Willek*" but the rosâr changed the spelling to five letters. Most people in the mother realms believed his name was pronounced Wile-ek.

Clearly Magonians were the superstitious ones.

"Regardless, Father, we cannot allow them to break the treaty, can we?" Wilek asked.

"Absolutely not," the king said. "Any illegal foreigners found in Armania are to be arrested and sentenced to sacrifice. Those you arrested today will go to Barthos next full moon along with three others. I'm raising the sacrifice from one to five from now on."

"A clever idea, sire," Rogedoth said. "That should please Barthos."

A pang of regret kept Wilek silent. The Magonian women he met that morning would be killed because of his report. He hesitated now to broach the topic of the Athosian priest at the gate for fear his father would sentence him to death as well.

"It's good to sacrifice more convicts," Jervaid said. "But we don't want Magonian scum crossing our borders either. We should send word to Raine and have them increase the guards at the Cross Canyon Bridges."

"Actually," Wilek said, "the women I met this morning came from Ebro to Pixford."

Rogedoth scoffed, nose pinched in disgust. "You'd think those prudish Sarikarians would recognize debauched women passing through their realm and arrest them."

"On the contrary," Canbek said. "Sarikarian men have such temperate wives, they probably bring the Magonian wenches across the border in packs."

Several of the men laughed, including the king.

Wilek did not. "Do not forget, Lord Ravensham, that my betrothed is from Sarikar."

"Indeed, Your Highness." Canbek nudged him. "Fortunate, then, that your concubine is not."

The men laughed harder.

"You misunderstand my meaning," Wilek said, though he doubted anyone could hear him over their guffaws. "Princess Nabelle is also from Sarikar and is usually one of your number. It is callous to—"

"Yes, yes," Father said. "It was a joke, son! You're too intense. You must learn to laugh."

Wilek gritted his teeth and forced a small smile. He feared his inability to revel with this group was perhaps the one thing keeping Father from naming him Heir. Janek never struggled with revels. "We should increase security on the Sarikarian border as well."

"Indeed," Rogedoth said. "But this is King Jorger's blunder. If Magonians are crossing his borders, he must be made to take action against it."

"Dictate a letter to King Jorger warning him of the Magonian trespassers," Father snapped at Schwyl, his onesent.

The discussion droned on. The first sleep bells tolled, yet long after them the men continued to plague the king with trivial matters: squabbles over marital dowries, merchant disputes, a series of stolen ships, a scandal involving a young lord and some missing jewels, a shortage of grain and produce at market, and a plea from a farmman claiming a mantic destroyed his crop with a spell. The Wisean Council should have ruled on these matters already, on their own, but these men lived for the power Rosâr Echad's presence provided. And Rosâr Echad lived to be needed.

Wilek had better things to do than join in the bootlicking. There was much to be done in the city. In the present, however, he wanted to escape to his chambers where he would find Lebetta, warm and waiting.

When his father finally dismissed them, Wilek went to his chambers with Kal and found Lebetta standing inside the door in her black robes. Kal swept through until he was satisfied all was safe, then left them alone.

Lebetta gazed at him, her eyes dark and sultry, and threw off her robes, revealing a sheer black gown. "You're late."

Wilek's eyes absorbed every curve. "You know how the rosâr can be." He circled her waist with his arms and pulled her close. He wasn't an overly tall man, but Lebetta's soft flesh pressed against him made him feel like a demigod. He nuzzled her neck and feasted on her spicy smell, her velvety skin.

Lady Zeroah's face flashed before his mind, unbidden. Lebetta was a woman where Zeroah was a skinny child. He pushed thoughts of Lady Zeroah away and gave himself over to the soft warmth of the one woman who knew him better than anyone.

Movement jostled Wilek awake. Lebetta was sitting on the edge of the bed, watching him.

"How late is it?" he asked.

"Nearly evening. You sent a guardsman to check on me after the quake today. Can I expect more of that, now that your bride-to-be is living in Everton?"

She was angry. She was always angry of late. "I cannot be so many places at once. The guardsman assured me you were safe."

"But you went to *her*. I don't like her. Or her little honor maiden. If I can't marry you, then I should have a say in whom you marry. Why don't I have a say?"

It was impossible to follow her. "You spoke with Lady Zeroah? When?"

"Why shouldn't I? The way we came upon each other in the hallway, it would have been rude not to."

"Etta, I cannot have you causing trouble with my betrothed."

"That child caused the trouble, not me. She shouldn't get to marry you, Lek. I've known you longer."

"Not true. I met Lady Zeroah just after she was born. Five years later on my majority ageday, I received you both as gifts, you as my concubine, Lady Zeroah as my future bride."

"But I came home with you that day, and I've been here ever since."

His nerves began to smolder. He could not have this conversation again. "You question my devotion?" He reached for her hand, but she stood and stepped away from the bed.

"Any woman would question the devotion of a man who marries another."

He wanted to scream. "I'm not just any man, Etta. I'm a prince of Armania. It's my duty to serve my realm and produce a legitimate and noble heir."

"Noble . . . what a filthy word. You'll marry her, then. And she'll take my place in your bed."

"Yes, I'll marry her. But she will have her own chambers just as you have. Just as I have. Very little will change. I'll see her only at dinners and formal gatherings."

"But you'll lie with her."

"It's my duty!"

"Grave duty indeed."

He took a deep breath, hoping to calm himself. "How can I appease you, Etta? Tell me how to mend your anger and I shall do it."

"Marry me."

Woes! This was getting old. "You know full well it is against the king's law for a man to marry a concubine. If I become king someday, perhaps I can change that law. For now, the subject of marriage is closed." *And please never speak of it again.*

"I thought you loved me."

He climbed out of bed and pulled her into his arms. "I do." He tipped up her chin and kissed her softly.

She turned her face and pushed away from him, but he grabbed her and kissed her again. For a moment she relaxed against him, but again she broke away, this time looking into his eyes.

"If you truly love me, then I would ask something else."

He paused, dreading what she might want now. "Go ahead and ask."

"Make me one of Lady Zeroah's bedchamber women. The positions will be filled long before you marry. It's the highest honor in the realm for a woman to serve the rosârah."

Wilek didn't know how to answer. He might never become rosâr in the first place. "Why would you want to?"

"Because it's an honor. And it's a way to be a bigger part of your life. As one of her ladies, I'll hear all the important things, attend all the important events. You must get me a position, Wilek! I want to be where she is—where you'll be."

"You would have to serve her well, Etta. Treat her with respect. Be obedient to her every command. I would not think it easy."

"I'll have to do that anyway. At least as one of her servants I'll get paid."

He could not see this ending well. "I will make the suggestion."

"Not a suggestion, Wilek. A *recommendation*. And to Princess Nabelle. There's a difference and you know it."

"I will think on it." He could just imagine how the princess would react to such a recommendation.

Lebetta released him and stepped back. "You're not going to do it, are you? It's because you hate me. I'm nothing to you but a body to warm your bed."

He rubbed his temples. "I don't wish to fight, Etta."

"I'm merely trying to provide for my own happiness since you will not. Your brother's concubines are paid, did you know that? Prince Janek offers jewels and fancy titles, sometimes eats with them at *their* table."

Bringing up his brother was the deepest of insults. "I must dress for dinner, Etta. We are through discussing this. You may go."

"I'm not going anywhere," she spat.

Wilek strode to the door and opened it, held it wide, staring at Etta as he spoke. "Kal, Lady Lebetta requires an escort from my chamber."

"It would be my honor." Kal walked inside, but before he reached Lebetta, she screamed and stormed out.

Wilek stood still, heart pounding hot with anger. He watched until she turned the corner at the end of the hallway, then pushed the door closed.

"Are you well, Your Highness?" Kal asked.

Well enough. "Send a boy to fetch Dendrick. I must dress for dinner."

TREVN

A few days after Trevn had moved back to Armania, he had asked the heralds to stop announcing him with his trumpet song, a custom he found pompous and unnecessary. The heralds had all agreed, so long as Trevn arrived before the king. So Trevn made a habit of showing up early whenever possible to spare himself the pomp every time he entered a public room.

Trevn nodded at the herald as he and Hinck passed into the great hall for dinner. The narrow room stretched out long before them. Five tables spanned the dais, and another fifty covered the floor. Father cared more for superstition than symmetry.

On the dais, the center table belonged to the king. Since he had not yet arrived, his fifth, newest bride, Rosârah Ojeda, sat alone, near bursting with her first child. The other four tables were designated for the other four queens and their children, though now that Wilek and Janek were of age, their tables belonged to them and their mothers were merely guests. In another two months the same would happen with Trevn's table, though he might forget to invite his mother to dine.

The princes and princesses were permitted to invite nobles to dine at their tables. Concubines and the king's stray children were not allowed on the dais and had tables assigned on the floor.

Trevn and Hinck approached the dais by way of the center aisle. All five queens were now present, as were the princesses Hrettah and Rashah and their nurse. No sign of Wilek or Jan—

"Little brother, there you are!" Speak of the demon himself, Prince Janek popped up from one of the floor tables, his face beaming, one arm outstretched in greeting, the other holding a potted plant.

Janek knew how handsome he was, how strong, and how his very presence made women swoon and men eager to pledge lives of service to his cause, no matter how perverse. What bothered Trevn most was how quickly Janek could go from furious one second to a gleaming smile the next. He was the best actor in the Five Realms.

Janek had been sitting at the Agoros table, which belonged to the family of Sârah Jemesha, Father's sister. At a quick glance, it was full of all Janek's dearest acquaintances: the type of people who blindly followed idols. The kind of people Trevn loathed. Not a potential Renegade among them.

A funny sound came from Hinck's throat, a cross between an indecipherable word and a whimper. Not surprisingly, he was gazing longingly at cousin Eudora.

Janek put his arm around Trevn's shoulder, smelling of wine, women's perfume, and the soil from his plant. "I've been meaning to introduce you to Lady Kyree of Fogstone." He twisted Trevn around to see a girl who had been standing behind him.

Lady Kyree was about Trevn's age. She was a nervous, silly girl who talked faster than her brain could manage. As the daughter of Baron Faxon, Trevn had met her often enough over the years.

Trevn nodded politely. "How do you fare, Lady Kyree?"

"Magnificently, Your Highness," she said. "And Lord Dacre. What a day! Good evening to you both."

Hinck jerked his attention to Lady Kyree. "Evening." His eyes bounced right back to Eudora, who, as always, pretended to have no idea that Hinckdan Faluk, Earl of Dacre, existed.

Janek drew Trevn a step closer to Kyree. "Lady Kyree is staying with the Agoros family for a few weeks. Cousin Eudora has been gracious enough to share her with our little group."

Eudora shot Janek a glare. The young women around her giggled.

"Indeed, that's quite right," Kyree said. "My mother sent me for a visit. Sâr Trevn, did you know Lady Eudora and I were second cousins?"

"I did." Didn't everyone?

"Oh, well, I suppose you would. How foolish of me. You're a sâr of Armania! I suppose it's a sâr's duty to know all about his subjects."

"A duty my brother takes *very* seriously," Janek said. "I'm sure he knows you've reached your majority, Lady Kyree. You had a celebration, did you not?"

"I did! Of course, you were both invited. Though I know Fogstone is a desperately long journey for sârs to attend a simple ageday party. We had a suckling pig and fifteen eels, in honor of my age—isn't that fun? And dancing too! Never before had I danced so much that my feet—"

"My brother was no doubt buried in his studies," Janek said. "He's to join the priesthood, you know."

Lady Kyree frowned. It could be difficult to follow Janek's quick-changing subjects. "The priesthood is a noble profession," she said, finally, and, for Kyree, quite succinctly.

"Do not despair, lady," Janek said. "Priests are permitted to take concubines."

Kyree touched her face. "Oh, yes. I suppose that's true. I had, um, heard that, I mean. We have but one temple in our barony. It's staffed by an elderly widower."

Trevn saw where Janek was taking this. He needed to leave before he and Lady Kyree were thoroughly embarrassed. He twisted out from under Janek's arm and stepped away. "My mother is expecting us, Janek. Enjoy your dinner, Lady Kyree."

"Thank you, I shall. I could smell it in the hallway, and I told Eudora that it was going to be delicious. Didn't I, Eudora? I do think I smelled eel and perhaps—"

"Trevn," Janek said, "ask your mother if your new concubine might move in to your chambers tonight. Honored Lady Kyree, what say you?"

Her eyes flashed wide. "Oh . . . well . . ." Her bottom lip trembled. "The rosâr. He would have to speak with my father . . . I'm not at all certain he would allow me to become a, um . . . however respected such a position is, I . . . I don't think he would approve."

"But might he consider it?" Janek asked.

"That's enough, Janek," Trevn said.

"Enough stalling, yes," Janek said. "Come, lady, don't be rude. What is your answer?"

Seated at the table beside Eudora, Fonu Edekk spoke up. "If Sâr Trevn won't have you, maybe Hinckdan will."

The sound of his name jerked Hinck from his Eudora-induced reverie. "Don't answer them, lady," Hinck said. "They're playing games."

Kyree's brow crumpled. "I don't understand. Eudora?"

Eudora and her friends burst into laughter.

Kyree bobbed a quick curtsy. "I beg your highnesses excuse me." She turned and ran from the great hall.

Janek shrugged at Trevn. "I don't think she likes you."

Trevn funneled his anger into words. "You mock me for being young, but I ask you, who is more juvenile: The man who pours himself into knowledge? Or the man with no interests beyond humiliating his peers and misusing women?"

Low hums from Janek's friends.

"A cutting rebuke, little brother," Janek said. "I'd take offense if you weren't a virgin."

Fonu snorted.

One of the concubines tittered.

Always with Janek, it went back to sex. "Forgive me," Trevn said, "but it's not my goal to bed every girl in the Five Realms."

"It's my fault," Janek said. "I should have never allowed Father to send him away. The Sarikarians have ruined him. Not only is he devoutly chaste, he thinks himself better than everyone else."

Typical that Janek would now blame an entire realm for his losing an argument. "You're a slave to gratification," Trevn said. "History teaches us that living for pleasure alone is a good way to bring ruin on oneself. Take heed from the catastrophes of those who have come before you, and pick up a scroll." Trevn pushed past Janek and strode to the dais.

"He always ends with a scroll," Janek said behind him. "Does he think me illiterate?"

"Aren't you?" Fonu asked, and laughter rang out.

Trevn jogged up the steps past his father's table, far enough away now that he could no longer hear Janek and his friends.

"You shouldn't fight with him," Hinck said.

"Janek might be able to best me with a sword, but a debate is an intellectual battle. Even at six years my senior, his brain is no match for mine."

They walked behind Wilek's table where Grandmother and Queen Brelenah sat together, Brelenah with two tiny dogs on her lap and three more grazing the table.

"One doesn't need much of a brain to act like a ruffian," Hinck said. "He's a dangerous enemy."

"He's an imbecile."

"So are you to overlook his power, Your Stubbornness."

A fair point. Trevn sighed. Why did everyone think they could tell him how to live?

They reached his mother's table. Trevn sat down on her right. Hinck on Trevn's right.

Everything about Queen Thallah was swollen. She had a bulbous nose; fish eyes; massive breasts that hung to a plump midsection; and short, stumpy legs like a pair of pillar candles. She also had the biggest hands he had ever seen on a female, hands that had slapped him senseless more than a few times.

"I saw you speaking to Sâr Janek and his friends." Mother leaned her cheek toward Trevn.

He kissed her quickly. "Good evening, Mother."

"What did he say?"

"Nothing much."

"Truthful lips endure forever, Trevn. I'm still angry with you for abandoning me this midday."

"I am clever, Mother, but not even I can predict earthquakes."

She banged a massive paw on the table, shaking the goblets of wine and bowls of food. "To rude words, deaf ears, Trevn. I've spoken with the rosâr. Since you continually risk your life traipsing all over the city unattended, he agrees that you should have a shield."

Sands no. Trevn gritted his teeth. "Completely unnecessary. The Armanians love me. Besides, a shield could not keep up." Nor could anyone wishing to do him harm.

"Captain Veralla assigned Sir Cadoc Wyser to the position," Mother said. "The captain says he is the best available."

"Mother, I—"

A trumpet cut him off. The king's tune. Trevn stood with the rest of those in the great hall and watched their rosâr enter.

Father had gotten old in Trevn's absence and had given up swordplay. That and several illnesses over the years had turned muscle to flab. Add five layers of clothing, including an embroidered tabard and a thick velvet cape, and the man waddled down the aisle like a duck, even with five attendants carrying the hem of that insanely long cape.

Every eye watched until Father sat in his throne at the high table. With a wave of his hand, he permitted his subjects to sit and continue eating.

"It's not only your reckless excursions that have caught my concern,"

Mother said. "Prince Janek humiliates you every chance he gets. And you allow it. Part of Sir Cadoc's job is to keep you from speaking to Prince Janek or any of his patron friends. You've fallen victim to their pranks for the last time. No woman will trick herself onto you again."

Trevn's anger balled up in his throat and he fought to keep it there. "That was well over a year ago."

"A foolish son brings grief to his mother. The subject is closed. Sir Cadoc starts his shielding duties first thing tomorrow." She leaned in front of him. "Hinckdan, how is your mother?"

"Very well, Your Highness, thank you," Hinck said, reaching for the wine.

Trevn sat back and tuned out the conversation. Months away from his majority ageday, finally gaining a true measure of freedom, and now he was to have a shadow.

Movement at Wilek's table caught his attention. Wilek had still not arrived, but two young women curtsied to Queen Brelenah and took the seats on her left. Lady Zeroah and the girl from the carriage this midday. The mystery girl had changed from the pink dress into a light blue one. She was big, but not like his mother. She must be close to six feet tall. Her arms were as thick as Trevn's, though he visited the practice field less than Hinck.

Perhaps Lady Zeroah had been saddled with a shield of her own.

The thought made him smile, but this woman was too young and wore no sword. She reached for a bread roll and knocked over her goblet. Wine bled into the tablecloth. She ripped the roll in two and pressed both sides into the liquid. Grabbed another roll and did the same. Lady Zeroah and Queen Brelenah were oblivious to the chaos, locked in conversation with one another.

A servant passed by the table, saw the mess, and stopped to help. The girl pulled a handkerchief from her sleeve, but Lady Zeroah had finally noticed the situation and a quiet word sent the girl's hands to her lap to stay. She watched in silence as a second servant arrived and helped the first mop up the mess. A new goblet was set before the girl and filled to the brim. The servants departed.

The girl glanced at Lady Zeroah, who was again talking to Wilek's mother. Her hand came up from her lap. Tentative, long fingers curled around the stem of her goblet. She picked it up, glanced to her left, then to her right. Wide brown eyes met Trevn's and grew even wider.

He winked.

She turned her head so fast that wine sloshed over the rim of her goblet and down her arm.

Trevn chuckled.

"What are you laughing about?" Mother asked. "For Cetheria's sake, eat something. You're far too skinny. One morsel helps in the next." She grabbed a lamb's leg, dunked it in a tureen of gravy, and dropped it on his trencher.

Trevn's cheeks stung. He wanted to leave, to get up and stride from the room, to show his mother he would no longer tolerate public humiliation. Instead he picked up the leg of lamb and poured his fury into eating.

WILEK

Wilek stopped on the threshold of the great hall, Kal beside him. "Why not skip dinner tonight?" Kal asked.

"Because Lady Zeroah asked to meet me. It's rude to desert her twice in one day. I must keep her happy if I am to put my best foot forward for Heir." He made eye contact with the herald at the door. "Announce me."

"Yes, Your Highness." The herald picked up his trumpet and blew Wilek's call, then announced, "His Royal Highness, Wilek-Sâr Hadar, the First Arm, the Dutiful."

Every person but the king went to their feet—even Janek—and bowed as he walked past. Lady Zeroah stood beside his mother at his table, watching him—actually looking at him. How odd. Lebetta's usual seat at the royal concubine table was unsurprisingly empty.

Wilek stopped before the king's table and bowed deeply to his father, who waved him on with barely a glance as he sucked on a leg of lamb.

Wilek jogged up the steps. Kal took his place on the wall. A servant pulled out Wilek's chair, which had a sleeping dog on it. Mother scooped the creature into her arms, and Wilek sat between Mother and Lady Zeroah.

The women, and everyone else in the great hall, reclaimed their seats.

Mother snuggled the puppy to her cheek. "Where have you been, my son?"

"Forgive my lateness," Wilek said. "I was detained."

"Young people are too busy these days," Gran said.

"Is anything wrong?" Lady Zeroah asked, looking directly into his eyes.

Her golden stare raised goose bumps on his arms and made him smile. "Nothing at all."

She glanced away, took a shaky breath, then looked back. Smiled again. Curious.

"The lamb is dry tonight," Gran said. "Take it with gravy."

Wilek filled his trencher. One of the dogs on the table sniffed and licked his food. He pushed it away. He hadn't come here to eat. He must talk with his betrothed so his father would see he was the best choice for Heir. "How was your first sleep, Lady Zeroah?"

She glanced at Mielle. "It was good."

Good. "And you, Miss Mielle? Did you enjoy your first sleep?"

"I didn't sleep, Your Highness. I was far too upset."

"I hope it was nothing too dire," he said.

"You must not," Zeroah whispered to Miss Mielle, then added something Wilek couldn't hear.

Mielle met his gaze, then looked down. "Nothing important, Your Highness."

Something was going on between these two, but Wilek was too tired of female drama to try to puzzle it out. He searched for something else to say, but the remainder of his day had held nothing that would interest a lady. "Is the wine good?"

"Very."

Gods, he needed to do better than this. "Did you enjoy your time at the Sink?"

"Yes, thank you."

Three words must be Lady Zeroah's limit for dinner conversation. He sat back in his chair, bored already. Lady Zeroah and Miss Mielle whispered again. On his left his mother and grandmother were whispering too. He was surrounded by women with secrets.

"Too much food," Gran yelled suddenly, making him jump. She pushed her trencher toward the dogs on the table.

"I am full as well," Mother said on a sigh. "Let us retire, Avenelle." She elbowed Wilek and murmured, "Enjoy your conversation. I insist."

Gran leaned around his mother. "Yes, boy. Do the job right."

Wilek stifled a groan. One secret revealed, at least. "Good evening, Gran, Mother."

Mother gathered up two of her dogs. "Lady Zeroah, Miss Mielle, thank you for the lovely company. I hope to soon see you at the court of the queen."

"I hope so as well, Your Highness," Lady Zeroah said. "Good evening. To you as well, Your Highness," she added to Gran.

How was this fair? Nine words to his mother, six for Gran. Each received at least double his three. Wilek watched the two queens depart the great hall, arm in arm, heads bowed in conversation, leading, between the two of them, a dozen honor maidens and five dogs.

Whispered words pulled Wilek's gaze to the girls. They really were girls, giggling and telling secrets. But maybe all women were, regardless of age.

Lady Zeroah smiled at him, then took a sip of wine.

Why so much smiling today? Had the girl taken too much wine?

"Sâr Wilek," she said, "there are so many poor in Armania,"—she paused, her voice unsteady—"in Everton, especially. My heart breaks for the men who want to support their families but cannot. Is there no way to provide more jobs for your people?"

It was the longest sentence he had ever heard from her lips. A sentence with some substance too. "There are plenty of jobs in Everton for a man willing to work."

Her eyes lit with something like anger. "You believe your people lazy?"

What? Her tone was almost defiant. Miss Mielle glared at him over Lady Zeroah's shoulder. "I didn't say that, but many a man has turned down a good job in hopes of something less taxing. I have seen it happen."

Lady Zeroah looked down her nose at her trencher. "It is easy for you and me to judge a man for wanting a less taxing job when neither of us has ever done hard labor in our lives."

Oh ho! "Lady Zeroah, are you picking a fight with me?"

She met his gaze and held it, a tremor of pulse at her throat. "I, um, only seek to understand your coldness, Your Highness."

He grinned at her naiveté. "Not cold, lady, merely cynical. Years of listening to men make pleas to my father have hardened me. It would be much simpler if no one ever lied. But men lie. And cheat. And are lazy."

"Miss Mielle knows many men who are eager for jobs, is that not so?" Lady Zeroah asked her honor maiden.

"Indeed," Miss Mielle said. "Women too, and orphaned children."

"Are you so hardened that you cannot tell good people from the bad?" Lady Zeroah asked.

This conversation had the makings of an ambush. Wilek had a feeling Miss Mielle was behind much of it. "There are plenty of good people in our realm, but we were talking of those seeking jobs. With all due respect, lady, there are jobs enough for everyone in Everton if they are willing to seek one out and do the work. Just today I assigned work to four men who came looking."

"Oh," Lady Zeroah said softly. "Forgive me, Your Highness. I am but a child speaking on matters I know little about."

Did she even realize how true a statement that was? "Don't apologize. Your compassion and your willingness to speak frankly . . . Both are qualities I greatly admire."

Lady Zeroah beamed then, a smile almost as wide as one produced by his brother's backman Hinckdan. It remained only briefly, before she wrestled it away, but for a moment she had been radiant. Miss Mielle nudged her, and she turned her golden eyes his way once more. "Thank you, Your Highness. You are very kind."

"You are most welcome, lady," Wilek said. They talked all through dinner, and Wilek rather enjoyed the attention. Miss Mielle nudged Lady Zeroah a few more times and whispered here and there, but Lady Zeroah seemed truly interested in how he spent his days, which was something Lebetta had never cared about. From now on he would put more effort into getting to know Zeroah. After all, she would be his wife—possibly his queen—and the mother of his children. It would be best if they could get along. Nor would it hurt for Father to see them together often, to remind him that Wilek would soon marry—while Janek had long ago ruined his own betrothal.

So when Lady Zeroah stood to depart, Wilek asked her to attend a private dinner the following night. She accepted and made her exit from the great hall with Miss Mielle.

Now he simply needed a chaperone to keep Miss Mielle from interfering. He also must keep Lebetta from finding out.

By the time Wilek left the great hall and started back to his chambers, the sky was black and thick with stars. Weeks had passed since the offering at The Gray, and the moon was now a mere sliver. Knowing that the next sacrifice was far off gave him a measure of peace.

He and Kal entered his chambers. They appeared empty.

Kal walked into Wilek's closet, then checked the privy. "All is well," he said. "I'll be outside until the night bells. Harton will relieve me."

"Send for Lady Lebetta," Wilek said. She must still be angry with him to not be waiting here.

Kal bowed his head. "Yes, Your Highness. And a boy to tend the fire?"

"No, it's fine. Thank you, Kal."

Kal left, and Wilek sat on the longchair before his cast-iron fireplace. He stared through the damper door at the red-hot coals smoldering in the firebox. That was his heart at present. Likely Lebetta's as well. His marriage to Lady Zeroah would change everything. But what could he do? His father and Janek would have him order Lebetta not to speak on the subject of his marriage again at the threat of being banished and replaced.

The problem was, Wilek had never treated Lebetta like a concubine. She was so much more than that. She was his best friend, his confidante. He loved her.

A knock on the door and Kal entered with a boy. Both looked somewhat anxious.

"Give your message," Kal told the boy.

"Lady Lebetta is not in her chambers, Your Highness," the boy said. "Her maid said she'd gone out."

"Out? Where?"

"Maid didn't know. But Master Beal saw her with Sâr Janek."

Cold rage slid down Wilek's spine. "The Honored Lady Lebetta with Janek? Where did Master Beal see them?"

"He said he . . ." The boy took a short breath. "He saw 'em enter Sâr Janek's chambers."

But Wilek had seen Janek at dinner. How long had he remained? "Thank you. You may go."

The boy turned away.

"Wait. Find Dendrick and tell him the Honored Lady is to be brought to me as soon as possible."

"Yessir."

Wilek trailed the boy to the door and slammed it behind him. "First my horse, now my concubine. I am sick of his games!"

"He's always enjoyed needling you," Kal said. "I'm sure Lady Lebetta wouldn't . . . She's been loyal to you all these years."

"There is no such thing as loyalty. Everyone wants something from me. A favor. An audience with the king. And Janek is the worst. He seeks to goad me into a duel. If I am dead, there is no one to compete for Heir."

"Now you're being paranoid," Kal said. "Janek is not your equal with a sword. You must trust people."

"I trust you, Kal. And Dendrick. That is all I can afford." He paced to the fireplace and back to his bed. "This cannot go unpunished. What shall I do, Kal? Advise me."

"I could drug him while he sleeps, make him a eunuch."

Wilek's lips parted. "You would do that?"

"If you wished it."

Years prior to becoming Wilek's shield, Kal had been training to be an assassin. Wilek sometimes forgot just how dark the man's past had been. Before he did something he might forever regret, Wilek forced himself to say, "What else do you advise?"

"Appeal to your father. Ask him to invoke justness."

"I don't want one of Janek's concubines. Father will think me petty to complain of this. Perhaps I am."

"No," Kal said. "If you allow this, Janek will only take more. You'll soon be married. You cannot risk Lady Zeroah to his scheming, or any of her maidens."

Wilek looked at Kal then. "This was why you hesitated to place Miss Mielle with Lady Zeroah. Fear of Janek."

"Not only Janek. You must know how quickly the young honor maidens at court are deflowered," Kal said, "whether it be by a courtier, Prince Janek, or the rosâr himself. Lady Zeroah and Mielle are safe enough for now, but . . ." The scars pinching Kal's face made his expression even more dire.

Wilek had been a fool. He paid little attention to the liaisons at court. Perhaps that should change. While Wilek did all the work of Heir, Janek had been manipulating the people who whispered to the king. Wilek was suddenly unsure any of the Wisean Council supported his claim as Heir. "Whom do we have at court?"

"I cannot say for certain. Kamran DanSâr attends. He supports you over Janek."

"Father cares little for the opinion of one of his strays. We need someone of importance there, to be my eyes. I will set Dendrick upon it." Wilek walked out onto his balcony and gripped the railing.

Kal followed him. "What are you going to do about Lady Lebetta?"

"That depends on what she has done. Will you stay?"

"If that's your preference."

"Lebetta is prone to moments of hysterics. Your presence might help keep her temper in check."

"I shall do my best to look foreboding."

With his scars, it required no effort. One glimpse at Kal and children ran the other way.

They came inside and sat by the fire. Time writhed along. The longer Lebetta took, the colder Wilek's rage became. How dare she enter his brother's chambers? She belonged to him.

The familiar *knock, knock-knock* made Wilek stand. The door opened, and Lebetta slipped inside, Dendrick behind her, looking cautious.

Lebetta offered Wilek a sheepish smile, which faded when she caught sight of Kal. "I wasn't feeling well, so I went to the healer. Must have lost track of the hour. Found Dendrick waiting outside my chambers. Did you need something?"

She dared lie? "When did Sâr Janek take up the healing arts?"

Her eyelashes fluttered. She opened her mouth, but no words came forth.

"You were seen with my brother, entering his chambers."

She snapped out of her daze and shrugged off his question as insignificant. "You were angry. I thought you'd like some distance."

Wilek flinched as if she had struck him. "At this point, it matters not whether you shared his bed. But I would still like to know."

Her eyes widened with remorse and fear. "Lek, please. It meant nothing. I am yours."

Wilek gritted his teeth, stunned by her audacity. His arm flew out to the side, pointing in the direction of Janek's chambers. "Until you were also his!"

"It wasn't like that. You have to believe me."

Wilek replied with a rude snort. "I *have* to? My reports say you walked into his chambers voluntarily."

"Yes, but there are things you don't know, things I can't explain."

"Try."

A tear ran down her cheek. "It's for your safety. To protect you." She knelt at his feet. "Please, Lek. All I have done is because I love you."

"Did he threaten you?"

"No."

"Me? He threatened me?"

She shook her head.

"Then explain yourself!"

"I can't."

Wilek stepped back from her, pulling free from her touch. "Why, Etta? I demand you tell me what . . ." His voice broke. She would not meet his eyes. She would tell him nothing. He drew a calming breath, but it didn't ease the anger, the hurt. "You go too far in so many ways. I've overlooked much that my father would have punished."

"Lek, please."

"You are dismissed forever from my service." He exhaled a shaky breath. "I banish you from Castle Everton and the city. You'll be compensated so you may start a life elsewhere. Be gone by tomorrow evening."

He expected her to throw herself at his feet again, beg forgiveness, confess all that had really happened, all she was hiding. Instead her expression hardened. Her eyes glittered.

"You can't banish me."

Wilek fought against the anger choking him and kept his voice steady. "Kal, escort Lady Lebetta to her chambers. Inform the guards she is to remain there until transport can be made to her new home."

"You can't do this!" She scrambled to her feet and tried to slap him, but he caught hold of her wrist, then caught the other when she raised it against him as well. Kal pushed between them and grabbed her waist.

"No!" She thrashed against Kal, but he easily dragged her toward the door. Dendrick opened it, and two guards in the hall ran toward them. "He'll kill you! Janek will be Heir. Is that what you want?"

"What do you mean?" Wilek asked. "Who will kill me? Janek?"

"Let me stay! Please, don't cast me out."

"Explain yourself and I will consider it."

"I can't!"

"You leave me no choice." Wilek waved at Kal to continue. The guards stepped forward and assisted the shield in removing Lebetta from the room.

"I hate you!" she screamed as the three men hauled her away. "You're weak! Gullible! If you ever rule this realm, you'll be killed the moment that crown touches your brow."

Her words stabbed, and he turned away, unable to look upon her. The door shut, silencing most of the struggle. Weary, Wilek sank onto the edge of his bed, breath clogged in his chest. She had always been able to wound him with words.

"Do you wish to be alone, Your Highness?" Dendrick asked. Wilek's onesent stood just inside the door.

"Was I wrong, Dendrick?" He had been. He knew it.

"Your father would have her executed."

"No." Wilek's heart seized at the very idea. "I don't wish that." He would let her fret for a few days, then call her back.

"I only meant that you have gone easier on her than he would have," Dendrick said.

"But why would she . . . ?" He understood none of this. "What did she mean? Could there be a plot against me?"

"There is always a plot, Your Highness. I'll investigate at once. It might be nothing. She loves you, I am certain," Dendrick said, "but loving a concubine is like holding a lit candle without a holder. At some point you will get burned."

"My father will demand I replace her." Father had never understood why Wilek had only one concubine. To have none at all . . .

"Was your decision final, Your Highness?" Dendrick asked.

"I know not." No. It felt like his chest had caved in.

Why had this happened?

"Why not wait a few days?" Dendrick said. "Tell no one about the banishment. I could chase down the guards, keep Lady Lebetta confined to her chambers. That way, if you change your mind, no one will know it ever happened."

"You're wise, Dendrick," Wilek said. "I will heed your advice."

"You honor me, Your Highness."

"No, Dendrick, *you* honor me."

Wilek barely slept that night. Early the next morning, he set off for Janek's chambers, Kal and Harton chasing after him.

"What are you going to do?" Harton asked.

"Get some answers."

Sir Jayron, Janek's Rurekan shield, was standing outside the door to Janek's chambers. Despite his shaved, henna-covered chin and head that lacked even one warrior's tail, he wore a King's Guard uniform. As Janek's shield, his tabard bore Janek's insignia of a black great ship. He bowed his head ever so slightly. "Sâr Wilek."

"I must speak with my brother," Wilek said.

"He's not up yet," Sir Jayron said.

"Then I will wake him."

Sir Jayron scowled at Wilek. "If you'll wait a moment, I'll tell him you're here." He slipped into the room.

Wilek counted to ten, then went inside. Kal and Harton followed.

Sir Jayron was standing beside the bed, shaking Janek's shoulder. "Your Highness?"

Janek wasn't alone. Wilek's heart flipped, thinking Lebetta might have come here. But no. There were two women. Janek's concubines.

Janek groaned and pushed onto one elbow. "What time is it?"

"Time to get up and answer for your crimes," Wilek said.

Sir Jayron strode toward Wilek. "I told you to wait in the hall."

"You didn't actually," Wilek said.

Kal lunged past Wilek to meet Sir Jayron, toe-to-toe. Wilek slipped around them. Sir Jayron made a grab for Wilek's arm, but Kal pushed him back. He fell onto Janek's bed. One of the women screamed.

"Enough!" Janek yelled, eyes red with sleep. "Guards, outside."

"But, Your Highness," Sir Jayron said, "I cannot protect you if I'm not here."

"My brother is no threat to me."

"Don't be so certain," Wilek said.

Janek climbed out of bed and pulled on a robe. "Wait in the hall, all of you."

Wilek nodded to Kal and Harton. The two shields, Harton, and both concubines left.

"Is this about your horse?" Janek asked once they were alone.

"This is about Lebetta."

"Who?"

"My concubine."

"Oh, is *that* her name?"

"Don't. I want to know what you did."

Janek grinned. "In detail?"

Wilek punched him. His brother flew back against the wall, knocking into the tapestry that covered the window. He grabbed it to keep from falling, but it ripped and he slammed to the floor, the tapestry heaped in his lap.

Janek flexed his jaw and rubbed it with his palm. "What was *that* for?"

"Because of you I had to . . ." He caught himself. "I threatened to banish her."

Janek's eyes widened. "You wouldn't banish Lady Lebetta. She's been here forever."

"You threatened her somehow. Threatened me."

"Is that what she said?"

"Tell me what's going on."

Janek reached for Wilek. "Help me up."

Wilek paced to the other side of the bed and folded his arms.

Janek pushed to his feet and straightened his robe. "I was only trying to help. Face it, brother. She has too much power over you. I mean, look at you! A lowly concubine has brought you to my chambers, throwing punches. Are you going to arrest me? What would our father say to that, I wonder?"

"Let's ask him."

"You cannot take your brother's concubine, Janek," their father said.

"Or my horse," Wilek added, feeling childish the moment he had said it.

They had been unable to see the king so early, so they returned to the Throne Room a half hour before the Rosâr's Bench to make their case. Father had dismissed all his bootlickers to see his sons, who now stood side by side before the throne.

"Wilek, your devotion to that woman is unnatural," Father said. "Stop being content with so little. Build a harem, spread your attentions to many. Choose five women by the end of the week. I want a list of their names."

Wilek didn't want a harem. "But, Father. I'm to marry in a few months. Can this wait until after the wedding?"

"Absolutely not. Better to have your harem in place before your wife makes her home here. And, Janek, as a sâr of Armania, you can take most anything you want, but you cannot take from me or your brothers without permission. If you do so again, you will face the pole. Is that clear?"

"Yes, Father." Janek bowed deeply to Wilek. "My most humble apologies if I offended you, brother."

Wilek said nothing.

The muted sound of the trumpet announced the hour of the Rosâr's Bench.

"My cue to leave," Janek said, prancing toward the back door. "Enjoy your time with the people, brother."

Wilek glared after him.

Father raised one kohl eyebrow at Wilek. "Choose new women, my son, and be happy." Then, to the herald. "Let them in."

The doors were opened, and the council filed in. Then the guards let in the patrons, who lined up along the wall to wait their turn to petition the king.

Wilek half listened to each request, his thoughts still on Lebetta. Should he forgive her right away? No. She had betrayed him. He must not forgive so easily. To appease his father, he would choose a harem. Such an act would frighten Lebetta. Perhaps enough to tell him the truth.

CHARLON

You must focus!" Mreegan yelled. "Ask the shadir to give power to your runes."

Charlon looked up from her mat, where she knelt. She had drunk ahvenrood juice. Could see into the Veil. Could see the shadir. They moved about in blurs of color. Unseen by the men in the tent. Every so often one stopped, stared at her.

They were formless, yet constantly moving. Boiling masses of colored smoke. Once, she thought she saw three eyes staring at her from a green cloud, but they blinked away.

"The shadir ignore me." And the ahvenrood poison was killing her. She could feel it within, destroying.

"Shadir answer sincere acolytes," Mreegan said. "Tell them the purpose for the power you seek, which is to serve me and the realm of Magonia."

Serve Mreegan? Was that Charlon's purpose?

Mreegan's newt scurried over the furs to Charlon's altar mat. Its tongue darted out, tasted the leather. Charlon's runes, she'd drawn them perfectly on the mat. In her own blood. But she was weak. So weak.

Mreegan loomed over her. "You feel nothing?"

"Tired. And thirsty." Poison eating her bones. Formless shadir gloating.

"Not the slightest surge of cold?"

Charlon glanced up. "Like when you healed me?"

Mreegan stalked away, red cloak billowing behind. Her newt darted after her. "That was the power Magon gave me to heal your wounds. You must find a shadir that responds to you. Go again to the altar. Only when you find your shadir can I continue your training. Find it soon, or the poison will kill you."

A threat? "You won't heal me?"

Mreegan crouched to pick up her newt. "To what purpose? I cannot keep a maiden unable to join with a shadir."

Charlon stood, legs trembling. Hobbled out of the red tent. Chastised. Forlorn. From the hilltop she glanced across camp to the altar and the gleaming ruby eyes on Magon's idol.

Why *did* she want this? Not to obey Mreegan's wishes. Yes, Charlon had been safe here. Eighteen painless days. Plenty of food. As the Fifth Maiden, no man could touch her. Mreegan promised freedom. Charlon knew better. Service as a maiden was another form of slavery. Honorable, true. But Mreegan could not be trusted. If Charlon could not join with a shadir, Mreegan would let her die.

Father had beat her. Brother had sold her. Men had forced her. Years of pain. Bondage.

No more.

Magon had saved her once. Charlon would pray to Magon again. Only at Magon's altar would she find answers. The shadir. The black spirit that might power her spells.

Slow steps down the hill to keep from falling. At the bottom she edged down the dirt path. White tents on both sides. People staring. Judging. Knowing she would die next. Knowing deep down she mistrusted Mreegan.

Refusing to yield fully to Mreegan? Did that keep the shadir at bay? Did the black spirits sense she would eventually rebel?

To join with a shadir, one must be true. But Charlon had lied. She didn't want to serve Mreegan. Charlon wanted freedom. Value. Power. Stature.

She wanted to be Chieftess.

Mreegan ruled cruelly. Killed the boys. Killed the maiden who'd speared Charlon. Killed to drive fear. So that none would stand against her. But Mreegan had no power that Magon did not give.

Magon.

The goddess of magic could give Charlon power. Charlon would have to bow, though. But Magon had saved her life. For that, Charlon was grateful. If she must serve someone, only a goddess was worthy.

She reached the altar. Sank onto brittle knees. The poison worked quickly. She must hurry.

She fell prostrate. Gripped handfuls of sand, rubbed it on her face, and screamed the only name that could save her. "Magon! I will serve only you. I am your servant. Heal me of this poison, and teach me the ways of the mantic. Give me power over runes, over soil and plants and animals, over human flesh and hair and bone, over humors of body, earth, and sea." She lowered her voice. "If you find me worthy, make me Chieftess someday. I want to rule—not by strength alone, but with compassion. I want to be Mother to your people. Be my master, Magon. Only to you will I bow."

The ground chilled. Sand grew stiff with cold. Charlon lifted her head, looked up the Magon pole. Her breath clouded white before her. Hid the idol in fog. A figure in red stepped out of the cloud. Stood before Charlon. Clear and bright with eyes of fire.

Magon, the goddess of magic.

"Rise, daughter. I have found you worthy." Though Magon's lips moved, the voice came from inside Charlon's head.

Charlon stood. Legs now strong. Standing, yet still so small before a goddess.

"I shall be your power," Magon said, "but you must tell no one, especially not Mreegan. Tell her you found your shadir. That she is called *Eemahlah*, which means mother. For as your mother is gone, I shall be a mother to you, so that you, in time, can be Mother to my people."

"Thank you, goddess," Charlon said, her voice but a whisper.

"Remain loyal to Mreegan until her time ends. Then, and only if I deem you worthy, will I set you up as Chieftess."

"I will do as you—"

In a blink, Magon vanished. Charlon was back on her face in the sand. Lying before the altar. Warmth flooded her body. She had been healed! But deep within, an icy pool waited, ready to be drawn from, ready to provide power.

She was a mantic. And her shadir was a goddess.

"Thank you," she rasped, throat tight with tears. "Thank you."

Charlon returned to the red tent a mantic. But Mreegan wanted proof. *"Show me,"* she'd said. Sent Charlon to gather cuttings and humors. Prepare a spell.

Very well.

Charlon asked Thirsty, who Mreegan called Five and everyone else called Torol. He had been kind. Was kind still. Let her pluck a hair from his short mane. Smiled and wished her luck. Expected her to fail. Thought her too new to cast a mold of another human.

Charlon forgave him.

She returned to the red tent. Set up her mat and bowl and knife and the hair Torol had given. Knelt down. Took a swallow of ahvenrood juice. Let it absorb within. When she could see the Veil, she sliced her fingertip with the knife. Blood dripped into the bowl.

Patience. Let it pool.

When she had enough, she drew runes in blood on the smooth leather mat. Concentrated on Magon, the runes, the intended result.

Before she had worked in fear, hoping a shadir would take pity. Now she worked in confidence, knowing Magon would lend the power she needed.

The cold place in her belly pulsed. Grew. Magon was ready.

When Charlon finished the last rune, she fell across her mat and spoke her request. "*Eemahlah âthâh. Tsamad ani. Ten shel cheber tokef.*"

She sat up and tugged out one of her hairs. "*Bara* Charlon . . ." She dropped her hair into the bowl. Picked up Thirsty's hair. ". . . *tselem ba* Torol." She dropped his hair into the bowl. She lifted the bowl above her head. Repeated her request. "*Ten shel cheber tokef. Bara* Charlon *tselem ba* Torol."

Magon chuckled inside Charlon's head. Charlon could not see her but knew she was near. Icy cold spread slowly. Out from the deep of her stomach, through her veins. She set down the bowl and bowed over the runes. The cold engulfed her, pimpling her skin and frosting her eyelashes. She did not blink, for fear her lashes would stick. She wanted to watch the effects of her first spell. Wanted to see Mreegan's reaction.

Charlon's dainty, feminine hands swelled. Skin darkened to a reddish brown. Black hairs sprouted on the backs of her fingers and up her arms. Shoulders, chest, and waist widened. The fabric of her tunic tore down her back. Her skirt's waistband cut into her sides. The stench of man sweat covered her. Limbs and spine lengthened. No pain in the growth. Just a good stretch.

When warmth embraced her again, she looked to Mreegan's throne.

Three had stopped fanning his palm branch. He stared, eyes wide, lips curled. Impressed. "Truly you are blessed by the goddess to have mastered such a spell so quickly," he said.

"My shadir is powerful," Charlon replied, though her voice was male and gruff. Torol's voice. "Magon has blessed me greatly." This half-truth should please Mreegan and pacify Three, but Charlon meant it as praise to her goddess, whom she could already feel within, healing her of the ahvenrood poison.

Mreegan stared, expression bland. She stroked the sleeping newt on her lap. "Leave us," she said to Three.

He swallowed and set down his palm. Glanced once more at Charlon as he left.

When they were alone, Mreegan spoke. "You were arrogant to cast a mold as your first spell. Your shadir could have punished you for asking too much too fast."

Magon would never hurt Charlon. "How long does it last?" So strange, to have a man's voice!

"With only one hair each, only a few hours. For the magic to last longer, the offering must be greater. A small lock of hair will give you a full day. A finger or toe can get you several weeks. If you wish your subject no harm, a steady offering of blood will also work."

"What if my subject is dead?"

Mreegan raised one eyebrow. "Dead molds are difficult. You must appeal to your shadir, offer something of value in trade, and change your runes and spell, of course. You need much more practice before attempting something so ambitious."

Charlon bowed to her. Not to Mreegan, really. She bowed before Magon, spoke words to the goddess. "Thank you. I would never have learned without your excellent teaching."

"What name did your shadir give?" Mreegan asked.

"Eemahlah," Charlon said.

"The mother." Mreegan pursed her lips in thought, waved her hand. "Dismissed."

Charlon gathered her tools and left the red tent, still looking like Thirsty. Outside, a cluster of men and women stood on the hill, staring.

Someone whistled sharply. Two men pushed Torol out of the crowd. He stood alone, facing her. Facing himself. Cheeks flushed crimson.

"You look good in foxtails, Torol," Nuel yelled. The crowd chuckled.

Charlon was still wearing her dress. The bodice had torn up the back, and the skirt had ridden up high and tight across her—his waist.

Torol fell to his knees, rubbed his hands in the dirt, and wiped it on his face. "The goddess has blessed you. Forgive my doubt."

"I already have." Charlon walked past, chin held high, careful to touch no one.

Everyone stared. She had shown strength. She had impressed them.

Still, so embarrassing to wear a man's skin and walk in it. She liked the strength and size of his body. But her own smallness no longer mattered. With Magon's help, she would never be weak again.

Mielle

The King's Guards led Lady Zeroah and Mielle to the private dining room on the second floor of Castle Everton. It was a spacious room with walls paneled in royal-blue silk piped with stripes of gold. A large iron fireplace divided the end wall. The floor was polished stone with a huge silk rug featuring Nesher the sunbird covering much of it.

A long stone table in the center of the room was set for four, two on each side, with bronze bowls clustered in the center. A candelabra hung overhead, filled with dozens of thin taper candles. The light reflected off the bronze dishes, making everything gleam.

Zeroah's guards remained outside, while a bowl boy seated them on the fireplace side of the table. The chairs were wickerwork and cushioned in blue-and-gold brocade. Mielle eyed the empty chair across the table. Prince Trevn would sit there. She tried to recall if he looked anything like Wilek. She had barely seen him the first time and had been too embarrassed to take much notice the second.

Since her first day in Zeroah's service, Mielle had done all she could to ease Zeroah's jitters around Prince Wilek. Tonight it was Mielle's turn to be nervous. Prince Trevn had winked at her. Twice. She had told no one, of course. Surely he had meant nothing by it. Flara had said that Prince Trevn was known as the Explorer Prince. That he was full of mischief and climbed the castle walls like a squirrel. Having seen him atop their carriage, Mielle did not doubt it.

The bowl boy returned. "May I present Wilek-Sâr, the First Arm of Armania."

Lady Zeroah pushed back her chair and stood. Mielle hurriedly copied her.

She felt massive in a bright orange-and-green silk dress beside petite Zeroah in her elegant gold gown.

Wilek entered, resplendent in a blue tunic with gold accents. Mielle complimented herself on how well the gold dress she had chosen for Zeroah matched his ensemble.

Zeroah curtsied deeply to Wilek, and, again, Mielle copied her. She caught sight of Kal out in the hallway. No sign of Prince Trevn.

Mielle's heart sank, figuring he had decided not to come, but then she heard the sound of distant footsteps, pounding nearer, running. Wilek and Zeroah turned to the doorway, all three of them ensnared by the commotion.

A gangly boy bounded into the room and slowed to a dramatic stop, cheeks flushed maroon. He panted and grinned, lifted one hand in a casual wave. "Hello," he said, his voice low and pleasant.

"Lady Zeroah and Miss Mielle, I present my brother Trevn," Wilek said.

Prince Trevn Hadar was a hand taller than his brother and all arms and legs. Both princes had dark brown skin, brown eyes, and black hair, but that was where the similarities ended. Wilek's hair had been cornrowed into five warrior's braids that were bound at the nape of his neck. His features were narrow, his eyes and mouth small. He stood with stately posture, his tunic and trousers crisp and smooth.

Trevn's hair was shorter, perhaps chin-length. It was tied back high on his head and poofed out like a rabbit's tail. He had a long neck that seemed longer with such short hair. His face was round, as were his nose, cheeks, and eyes. Even his ears were round, and they stuck out a bit too far on the sides of his head. He wore a dark blue tunic with gold buttons and black trousers. His clothes were wrinkled. The top two buttons on his tunic weren't fastened. In fact, the top button was missing altogether, a loose thread the only sign it had ever existed.

"Pleased to see you again, Sâr Trevn," Zeroah said.

"Indeed, lady," he said. "Strange that we lived so long in each other's realms."

"But no longer," Zeroah said. "We both call Everton home now."

He nodded and glanced at Mielle.

A jab to her side made her jump. Caught staring! Zeroah shot her a wide-eyed glare and bobbed her knees a little.

The curtsy! Mielle's cheeks flamed. She curtsied to Prince Trevn, trying not to dip as low as she had for Wilek. She wobbled. Oh, tuhsh. What must he think of her?

She could speak now, since both had spoken. Right? "Pleased to meet you, Sâr Trevn." She added another curtsy, hoping it made up for the lateness of her first.

Trevn chuckled, and she glanced at Zeroah. Had she done something wrong?

"Shall we sit?" Wilek suggested, and as they took their seats, she watched Trevn looking around.

"I've never eaten in here. In fact, I didn't even know this room existed before tonight."

"But don't they call you the Explorer Prince?" Mielle asked. "I'd have thought you would've inspected every room of the castle by now."

He smirked, which made his ears stick out more. "Dining rooms are only interesting when they're full."

"Full of people or full of food?"

"Yes."

Mielle laughed. "So, if you hadn't been invited here tonight, you might have come anyway, drawn by the sound of people's voices and the smells of food?"

"That's doubtful. I prefer my chambers at night."

"Really? Why? I would think you—"

"*Miss Mielle.*"

Zeroah's scolding tone turned Mielle's head. "Yes, lady?"

"You must not badger the sâr with questions," Zeroah said softly.

Mielle blinked, confused. Hadn't that been the plan? Both princes were watching her now. "Forgive me, Your Highnesses, if I did something improper," she said. "I've never been to a private dinner before."

Trevn laughed deeply and slouched in his chair, tipped it back on two legs, and held the table with his thumb and two fingers. "Think nothing of it, Miss Mielle. It's nice to talk to someone who isn't all rules and perfect manners. In fact . . ." His chair fell forward and clumped against the floor. "I hereby abolish all rules for this evening. We shall each say whatever we want without fear of giving offense."

"Trevn is a revolutionary," Wilek told Zeroah. "Someday he will write new laws."

"Really?" Trevn asked. "Me?"

"You'd rather Janek do the job?"

"Only if you want advice on debauchery."

Wilek cleared his throat. "Well, if Lady Zeroah does not mind, we can neglect protocol tonight."

Mielle thrilled at the idea of omitting the rules for one evening. "Could we?" she asked Zeroah.

Trevn wrinkled his brow. "Please say yes, lady. We cannot all be perfect like our mothers."

Zeroah fought a smile and inclined her head to Trevn. "As you wish, Sâr Trevn."

"Good." He slapped his hand on the table. "That's settled."

Wilek complimented Zeroah on her dress, so Mielle seized the moment to continue her conversation with Prince Trevn. "So? What do you do when you're not exploring?"

Trevn folded his arms. "For myself, I draw maps. For the realm, I study. As the third son of a king, I'm to be a priest."

The boy who jumped off a moving carriage? A priest? Mielle did not believe it. "Which gods do you worship?"

"Oh, none of them."

She tried not to laugh. "What kind of priest will you be if you worship no god?"

"Well, I have to choose my five when I reach my majority. Until then I could worship this bowl if I wanted to." He nudged one of the bronze bowls in the center of the table.

He was joking again, but his words puzzled her. "But you study the gods."

"Oh, yes. The gods *and* the faiths. See, in Sarikar, as Lady Zeroah well knows, they exalt Arman above all other gods. But here in Armania, we follow Rôb, which is to worship five gods of one's choosing."

"That's ironic, isn't it?" Mielle asked. "With our realm being named after Arman."

Trevn shrugged. "My parents named me, and I'm not all that fond of them either."

It took great effort not to laugh at that. "What does a priest do?"

"In Armania it's all about learning the pecking order of the gods, which can change by the minute. One day Dendron might be more powerful than Thalassa. But another day, Thalassa might rule over all. Priests must have a thorough understanding of the gods so they can advise the king whom to serve each day. If a priest chooses a god that's overpowered by another, the king is angry with the priest for his poor advice. Too many errors from a priest of Rôb, you could face the pole or worse."

"So much responsibility!" Mielle said. "How can anyone know the minds of gods?"

"It takes a certain intelligence to become a priest."

A snort from Wilek.

Trevn glanced at him. "I mean, since there is so much to learn."

This brought laughter from Wilek. "The church chose you for your unparalleled mind, is that it, brother?"

Trevn smiled into his lap, but if he was embarrassed, he quickly recovered. "Of course, no one can truly know the mind of any deity. They're unknowable and can never be completely understood."

"Except by those with a *certain intelligence*," Wilek said.

"I just meant that by careful study, priests can advise others. Stop laughing. We can."

Thankfully the food arrived then, distracting the princes from their disagreement. First came a serving of stuffed button mushrooms and honey-glazed turnips. Then a carrot-and-caraway soup that was very strong. The main dish was baked fish with white-wine sauce and gingered green beans.

Mielle ate everything that was set before her and fought the urge to lick her fingers. It all tasted divine.

She asked Trevn questions throughout the meal and learned much about him—he talked more than she did! She hoped Zeroah was asking Prince Wilek as many things.

The final course was a chewy, sweet cobbler with a crunchy topping that Trevn called date nucato. There was also a platter of brittle nut fondants shaped like little flowers and trees. Mielle savored every bite.

"What do you enjoy, Miss Mielle?" Trevn asked suddenly.

Here was a chance she hadn't seen coming. "There is little to enjoy with so many suffering. Did you know there are thousands of orphaned children in Everton?"

"I do, actually." Trevn slapped the table. "That's where I've seen you before. With the protestors outside the castle gate."

Mielle blushed. "It was before I took the position with Lady Zeroah. I don't recall ever seeing you there."

He grinned. "A hemp cloak is disguise enough for that crowd. They are so frenzied by their cause, they pay no attention to who is listening."

"Why do you go?"

He shrugged one shoulder. "I'm new here. Best way to learn what is going on is to hear what people complain about."

"Well, I'm complaining about the orphans. We must do something for them. They are starving. The almshouse cannot possibly feed them all."

"Then we'll do something," Prince Trevn said.

"What?"

"I know not. You must give me more than a breath to think on it."

"I will give you until tomorrow."

His eyebrows lifted high. "You are quite demanding, Miss Mielle. I will make a demand of my own. Tell me what else you like to do besides championing orphaned children."

"Very well. Before I took a position as Zeroah's honor maiden, I spent much of my time on the beach near Echo Crack. There's a place where you can climb down. Someone has tied a rope to a post at the top."

"You like to climb?"

"Very much. Fear thrills me."

"Does it?" He looked at her strangely, blinked. "Um . . . and what did you do at the beach? Swim?"

"Sometimes. My friends and I held dances there. Do you like dancing?"

He wrinkled his nose. "I know not."

"How can one not know such a thing?"

"I'm too young to attend balls. But I've been taught to dance in grueling practices with serving women three times my age. Mother does what she can to ensure I won't embarrass her on my ageday celebration."

Mielle giggled. "I'd like to see you dancing with those serving women."

"Are all women this cruel?" Trevn asked Wilek, but Wilek wasn't listening. He had turned in his chair as Dendrick, Prince Wilek's onesent, entered the room.

The man stopped at the end of the table and bowed to Prince Wilek. "Forgive the intrusion, Your Highness, there is an urgent matter."

Wilek nodded at Lady Zeroah. "Excuse me." He got up and followed his onesent from the room.

"I hope nothing is wrong," Zeroah said quietly.

"It's likely our father," Trevn said. "He summons Wilek all the time. Urgent this. Urgent that. I'm so thankful I'm not being considered for Heir."

A man's cry from outside the room made Mielle jump. That had been Prince Wilek's voice.

Trevn sprang from his chair and ran to the door, holding it open with his hand. "Where's Wilek?"

"We should stand," Zeroah whispered to Mielle. So they did.

Dendrick returned, slipping past Trevn at the door. He stopped inside and bowed. "I beg your pardons, Sâr Trevn, Lady Zeroah, Miss Mielle. An emergency has arisen. Sâr Wilek will be unable to return. Please accept his apologies. He requests you permanently accompany him to dinner from now on in the great hall."

"It will be an honor," Zeroah said, lips curving in a small smile.

Trevn was not so easily appeased. "What's happened? Speak, man!"

"Forgive me, Your Highness," Dendrick said. "You'll have to ask Sâr Wilek."

"Trevn!" A large woman in turquoise robes burst into the dining room and gripped Trevn in a hug. "Thank Mikreh you're all right." She released him and gasped in several short breaths. "When I heard," she panted, "I feared death was in the pot."

Trevn grabbed the woman's arms. "Mother, what are you talking about?".

"The Honored Lady Lebetta is dead! Murdered, they say. I feared someone had poisoned you all." She scowled at his clothing. "What *are* you wearing? You're dressed like a windmill. I insist you let Beal choose your clothing from now on."

Dead? Mielle pressed her hand over her heart. Lady Zeroah simply stared out the door, eyes glazed.

"Lady Lebetta was not with us tonight, Mother," Trevn said. "Wilek and I were dining with Lady Zeroah and her honor maiden Miss—"

"Dendrick! What news?" Trevn's mother rushed up to the onesent, who immediately quitted the room. Queen Thallah gave chase. "You will tell me at once!"

Zeroah swayed.

"Lady!" Mielle put her arms around Zeroah's waist. "Will you look at me?"

Zeroah's eyes flickered around the room and finally stopped on Mielle.

"Do you hear me?" Mielle asked her. "Can you speak?"

"I . . ." Her eyelids fluttered.

"Lady Zeroah isn't feeling well," Mielle said to Trevn. "We should retire at once. Will you fetch her guards?"

"Certainly." Trevn rushed out of the room. Seconds later Doth and Ephec ran inside.

Doth swept Zeroah into his arms. "Hold open the door," he told Ephec, who was already on his way out of the room.

Mielle followed them out and curtsied to Trevn in the hallway. "Thank you for dinner, Sâr Trevn," she said. "Please thank Sâr Wilek." Then she added, "And give him our prayers."

"Certainly, Miss Mielle," Trevn said. "Good evening to you both."

"Yes, good evening." Mielle rushed after the guards and Lady Zeroah, hoping there were no murderers about.

WILEK

Wilek ran. Mind a haze, body numb. Down the stairs, walls blurring around him. Through the foyer and out into the courtyard. Up ahead, a crowd in the queen's garden. Beneath the statue of Mikreh. Wilek pushed men aside until he reached the marble slab that held the god of fate and fortune. He stepped into a puddle of blood.

Lebetta lay on her left side, lower arm stretched above her head, the other bent at the elbow and falling over her waist, fingers touching the stone ground.

A groan came from his lips. He dropped to his knees and reached for her, but men swooped in, took hold of his arms, held him back.

"Take care, Your Highness," someone said. "We don't know what killed her. Must take precautions."

"Hang precautions!" He strained against them, wanting to take her in his arms. "Release me at once!"

"Your Highness, please. 'Til we know for certain what killed her, touching her is dangerous."

"I don't care." He only wanted to hold her.

"Wil." Kal's voice. Kal's scarred face before his. Kal's hand on his shoulder. Wilek blinked, eyes blurred with moisture.

"We'll restrain him if we must, Kalenek. The rosâr ordered an investigation, and I won't have any trouble. Not even from a sâr. Now, if he'd like to help . . ."

"We must find who did this, Wil," Kal said. "She deserves that, don't you think?"

She did. Someone had taken her life, and that person must pay. Wilek nodded, gave up his fight against the men. They moved away. He sat back on his heels, throat tightening, gaze locked on her lifeless body.

Kal squatted on his right, comfortably silent.

Footsteps crunched over the gravel behind him and stopped on the marble slab. Trevn, looking down on the scene. "Gods."

Gods, indeed. Why take Lebetta's life? She loyally followed her five gods. She didn't deserve death.

"Do they know what happened?" Trevn asked.

"Not yet," Kal said.

"I'm sorry, brother." Trevn stepped closer to where she lay. "Did she write something?"

"A rune, we think," said one of the guards.

Rune? The word pulled Wilek's attention to Trevn, who was circling Lebetta's body, studying the ground. Wilek pushed to his knees and peered over her side, looking where her fingers touched the marble slab. He could barely see swipes of blood on the pale stone.

"Move the light closer," Trevn said, as if reading Wilek's mind.

A guard passed his candlestick to another, who set it on the ground. The light cast eerie shadows over Lebetta's body and the statue of Mikreh.

Wilek could see shape in the writing now. "A rune?" The weakness of his voice shocked him, so he spoke again, this time with as much authority as he could muster. "Who can read runes?"

No one answered.

He tried again. "Who is capable of reading runes, even if they are not in present company?"

"Perhaps a priest," someone said.

"Runes are Magonian witchcraft," Trevn said. "No Rôb priest could read them."

Wilek thought of the Magonian women from the last earthquake. "Harton?" He spun around and located his backman in the crowd. "Copy this rune and take it to the women in the dungeon. See if they can translate."

"Yes, Your Highness." Harton left the scene.

"Boy," Wilek said to a young servant. "Fetch Pontiff Rogedoth. Tell him to come immediately." Surely the Pontiff would know the runes of his enemy.

"Yes, Your Highness." The boy sprinted away.

For the first time, Wilek looked at the faces around him. Besides Uhley the physician, most were guards or servants. His mentor and friend, Rayim

Veralla, captain of the Queen's Guard. Lebbe Alpress, captain of the King's Guard. For some reason Zeteo Agoros, Wilek's uncle by marriage, standing with Mahat Wallington, a local merchant.

Wilek breathed deeply. "Captain Alpress, close off the courtyard. I don't want people gawking at her. No one but the physician need be here."

Alpress barked orders at the servants and his guards. The crowd scattered. Servants went inside. Guards took position around the garden. Wilek glanced up at the inside walls of the castle, looking for lit rooms or faces that might be looking down.

He saw nothing.

Grief threatened to choke him, but he wrestled it back. "How did she die?" he asked Uhley.

"Loss of blood, from first glance," the physician said. "But I see no wounds. It's most strange."

Wilek needed to know more. "What happened? Who found her?"

"We did," Zeteo Agoros said. He and Mahat Wallington had not left at Captain Alpress's orders. "Mahat and I had cut through the garden after leaving a private party in Rosârah Laviel's apartments."

"Did you see anything?" Wilek asked.

"Just her, lying there," Master Wallington said. "Saw no one else."

Silence stretched out, and Wilek's heart seized with the gory reality before him. He heard himself make a strange noise, almost a growl.

"Perhaps you shouldn't be here, Your Highness," Rayim said. "Can I take you somewhere?"

"There is nowhere else I want to be right now. Uhley, how long until you complete your investigation?"

"Half an hour or so. Then I'd like to move her to the deadhouse to examine her further, determine the exact cause of death."

Deadhouse. Cause of death. Dead. Gone forever. Had his actions somehow caused this? He had been trying to make a point. He never really wanted her gone.

That thought sent him on another trail of confusion. "Lady Lebetta was confined to her chambers. Rayim, find out who let her leave her rooms and why. Gather anyone who saw her tonight, see what they know."

"Yes, Your Highness." Rayim departed.

Giving orders helped distance himself from his emotions. "Dendrick, notify her parents. Invite them to the castle to gather her belongings. They should start preparations for last rites and . . . shipping."

With that one word, he lost himself again. Gods! His Lebetta, dead. And she believed he had banished her because of Janek.

Thoughts of Janek made him want to cast blame. Might his brother have killed her? He could think of no reason why. Janek was a trickster, not a sadist. Then who would take her life? She had no enemies that he knew of, though she had upset Lady Zeroah and Miss Mielle the other day. Surely neither of them . . . A ridiculous line of thinking. Besides, those ladies had been with him when she died.

Harton returned with a wax tablet and stylus. He crouched beside Lebetta and squinted at the rune.

"She couldn't have been out here long," Kal said. "The courtyard is busy this time of evening."

Yes, that was true. "How could someone have killed her so quickly?"

"Perhaps she was killed elsewhere and brought here to be found," Harton suggested.

"Then why no blood trail?" Trevn asked, rounding the body again. "If she was moved here, bleeding as she was, we would see blood coming from one of the entrances."

"Found none," Captain Alpress said. "Whatever happened, she fell here."

"With your permission, Your Highness, I'd like to roll her to her back," the physician said.

Wilek nodded. "Permission granted."

"Don't smudge the rune," Harton said. "I'd like a better look in daylight."

Uhley positioned himself above Lebetta's head and took her left hand in his gloved one. "Would someone wearing gloves grab that arm?" He pointed to the hand Lebetta had drawn with.

Kal took hold of Lebetta's right wrist. He and Uhley rolled her until she lay on her back, arms at her side.

She looked peaceful, lying there, though the blood that coated the left half of her body belied that peace. Wilek could see no blemish or bruise on her face or head. His gaze caught on the tiny mole at the corner of her right eye. He'd kissed it hundreds of times. Memories flooded him, squeezed his chest.

"Drice," Uhley said, backing up from her body. "See the holes by her left ear? Just under the lobe? She bled out there and through her ear. I suspect the majority of the drice took the simple route in through the ear."

Wilek looked to her ear. The dried blood did seem thickest there. "Drice are from the east, right?" he asked.

122

"Tenma, mostly," Kal said.

"Someone must have brought them here," Uhley said. "But they don't kill without being provoked."

"Perhaps whoever set them on her starved them first," Trevn suggested.

"They're a tool of mantics," Kal said. "Saw them used in the war."

Mantics.

Lebetta devoured by drice? "They are still alive?" Wilek stared at her body, wondering if the beasts were gnawing at her viscera and might break through her skin at any moment.

"Likely so," Uhley said. "She should be burned at once or they'll roam free . . . eventually."

Wilek turned away, horrified. He could not allow drice to roam the castle. But burning Lebetta would not allow her body to be preserved for the journey to Shamayim. He would have to petition Gâzar to receive her ashes and rebuild her body. He swallowed his grief. "See to it, then. I will inform her parents."

Uhley ordered a litter brought, and Lebetta's body was moved to it by reluctant guards wearing gloves.

Just as the men carried the litter away, Pontiff Rogedoth arrived in his night robes, scowling. "Why have you summoned me at this hour?"

Wilek had wanted to go to the pyre house to be with Lebetta every moment until her body turned to ash, but the Pontiff must not be ignored.

Barthel Rogedoth was a proud man with small features and tight skin over a bony skull. He wore his receding gray hair in a single fat plait that ran down his back to his knees. His priest's lock was so long, it darkened to black in the middle of his back.

Wilek explained about Lebetta and the rune.

Rogedoth's scowl deepened. "This is absurd. Who cares what happened to a concubine?"

Wilek steeled himself. "I do. Can you translate the rune?"

"Of course not," Rogedoth spat. "You will need a mantic to tell you its meaning, and there are none in Armania. At least none who would help you."

Wilek breathed through his nose to calm himself. Rogedoth's bluntness had always grated on his nerves. "Every man has a price."

"With the rosâr sacrificing illegal immigrants to Barthos, no price is high enough to come forward."

"A pardon is."

"For a concubine?" Rogedoth shook his head. "I am going home, Sâr Wilek. Do not summon me again."

"I will summon whomever I like, Pontiff," Wilek snapped. "You are not above the throne."

"Perhaps not. But you do not sit on the throne."

The man strode away, forcing Wilek to bite back his anger. Now was not the time to take on Rogedoth.

"Arrogant shrine-kisser," Trevn mumbled.

"This from the priest-in-training?" Wilek asked.

Trevn shrugged. "Honesty is a virtue."

Wilek glanced down to the bloody writing on the marble slab. "There must be someone in the city who can read mantic runes."

"By the time you unearth them, you could have walked to Magonia and back ten times," Harton said.

Father would never permit Wilek to enter Magonia. "We must keep looking, Hart. I have to know what this rune means. Captain Alpress, if you need me, I'll be at the deadhouse."

Lebetta's parents were waiting at the deadhouse with Dendrick when Wilek, Kal, Harton, and Trevn arrived. Nikk Obert was a short, tidy man with more hair in his eyebrows than on his head. His wife stood a full head taller than him and was three times as wide. Wilek had only met them twice before. Should he embrace Senja? Shake Nikk's hand? He simply stood there, stupidly, his boots and knees stained in their daughter's blood.

"I am so sorry," he finally managed to say.

"I am to blame, Your Highness," Senja said, wringing her skirt in her hands. "If only she had heeded my warning."

"Have you discovered any new information?" Nikk asked Wilek.

"Unfortunately no," Wilek said. "Madame Obert, what warning did you give your daughter?"

"Lebetta had been worshiping black spirits. I disapproved. Told her to stop. She accused me of being old-fashioned, said the spirits gave freedom and power."

Wilek's thoughts spun. Worshiping black spirits was against the law in Armania. It angered the gods and priests both. Wilek could not imagine Lebetta getting involved with something so dark. "Where did she worship them? With whom?"

"She never said. I assumed it was here at the palace with you."

"I have never worshiped black spirits." The very idea was insulting. "Harton!" He waved his backman over. When Harton reached him, Wilek took the wax tablet and showed it to the Oberts. "Do you recognize this? Lady Lebetta drew it."

"Where would she learn to draw runes?" her father asked.

"From the black spirits." Senja's voice cracked. She made the sign of The Hand. "Gods forgive her, but only black spirits know the runes."

"And the mantics who worship them," Harton added.

Senja moaned, eyes filled with tears.

"Thank you, Harton." Wilek shoved the wax tablet into Harton's hands and shooed him back to Kal.

"Please, Your Highness." Nikk took his wife's hand. "Find out who did this to our daughter."

"I shall," Wilek said. "You can count on it."

An awkward moment of silence fell over them.

"Lebetta left few of her valuables in our home," Senja said. "Might I have permission to search her chambers for anything I could add to her grave offering?"

"Yes, of course. I'll add to it as well. She won't go into the next world empty-handed."

"We will send her by sea," Senja said. "Start the procession at our home and wind our way outside the city limits to the quay. We must give her every chance to reach Shamayim."

It was the best they could do. Had she been his wife, Wilek would have chosen the same, though then the procession would have begun at the castle.

"It might not matter," Nikk said. "If she'd been worshiping black spirits, no amount of wealth or distance travelled will appease Athos when she stands before his bench."

This comment set Senja wailing again. Worshiping black spirits. How could that be Wilek's Lebetta? What had she been involved in and why?

Less than an hour later, Zithel Lau, a medial priest, performed a last rites ceremony with as many votive offerings as Wilek and Senja had time to gather.

The night bells tolled just as Uhley lit Lebetta's pyre. Kal stood on Wilek's right, Trevn on his left. Harton and Dendrick were around somewhere. But as Wilek stared into the flames that consumed her, he felt ultimately alone. Senja's keening nearly undid him.

Watching Lebetta's body burn, something in him died. She had taken part of his heart with her to the Lowerworld.

He would never forget her.

Her ashes were swept into an urn that would be sent out to sea in a shipping ceremony. This way Lebetta could sail to Shamayim and have her body restored in the afterlife.

Uhley handed the urn to Wilek, who instantly passed it to Lebetta's parents. He promised to visit them when he had answers and stumbled back to the castle. Dendrick and Kal followed silently, allowing him his grief.

A short while later, he fell into his bed. His cold bed. Lebetta would never come to him again. He would never hold her in his arms. Never kiss her soft lips or hear her throaty laugh. There was no life without her. No joy. There was only an unimaginable hollowness that made him ache all over.

Images from the night haunted him. Her pale, lifeless body. His boots standing in a puddle of blood. The flames of the pyre destroying her beauty forever.

Tears blinded him even from the darkness of his chambers. His chest and throat burned from the magnitude of his despair and the added remorse that he had banished her.

He should not have done it.

He should not have.

CHARLON

The low moan of a horn woke Charlon. She sat up. "What is that?"

"One has blown the lure," Roya, the Third Maiden, said. "The Chieftess is calling."

Charlon threw off her furs. Scrambled to her feet. Stepped over the wriggling form of Eedee, who was slowly waking.

She dashed out of the tent into the cool night. Clouds hid the moon and the hour. Tents around her rustled. Those within rose to the lure's call.

Since Charlon had first met Mreegan, they had traveled all of Magonia. This was Altar Five. In the shadow of Mount Magon. Something important would happen here.

Tonight.

The cold place within told her so.

Charlon had been learning. From the other maidens. From Mreegan. And from the goddess Magon. Mreegan had once started as a Fifth Maiden too. Someday Charlon would succeed her. Become Chieftess. She was growing stronger each day.

The magic came easily now. Charlon had entered a world of wonder. Learned to be a mantic. Faster than any other in decades, Mreegan told her. A lie. Magon confirmed that it had been faster than any mantic ever, including Mreegan herself.

Charlon's skill surpassed even the Chieftess.

Someday she *would* rule.

Tonight, however, Charlon must remain the humble Fifth Maiden.

Her run slowed as she reached the hill and started up. Light flickered inside the red tent. As she neared, voices could be heard.

Along with the Five Maidens and several dozen acolytes, the Chieftess kept her Five Men, titled One through Five. One and Two stood guard outside the red tent, shard clubs in hand. Charlon stopped before Rone, the strapping man who was also called One. He had danced with Charlon during her induction ceremony. It was custom, the first should welcome the last. She had let him touch her hands. It had not been easy, despite his beauty.

He had never spoken to her. The maidens said he was seventy years old. That Mreegan kept him young because he was her favorite. He wore nothing but a kasah around his waist and the lure around his neck, which was made from a massive cheyvah horn. Cheyvah, a real beast, Charlon had learned. Not a myth.

"I heard my Chieftess call," Charlon said. "Has she need of me?"

Rone jerked his head at Two, also known as Nuel, the man on the other side of the door. Two pulled the tent flap aside and went in.

Charlon's heart thudded at the mystery of what was to come. She glanced at the lure, caught herself staring at Rone's muscular chest, and looked away.

Nuel returned and nodded to Charlon. "Remain silent and watch."

Charlon pulled aside the deerskin flap and entered. Chieftess Mreegan lay facedown, naked, in the center of her tent. Two men knelt on either side, drawing on her back. Four—also called Morten—used a mixture of ahvenrood and kohl. Five—Torol—used ahvenrood and blood. Kateen and Astaa, the First and Second Maidens, stood at Mreegan's head, overseeing. Kateen held Mreegan's newt on her shoulder. The creature looked down on his mistress, his tongue flicking in and out.

Torol glanced up at Charlon, smiled, then continued his work. He was also beautiful—all the men were. Torol had short hair that grew in coils, full lips, and light brown eyes.

The image on the Chieftess's back took shape. They had drawn a square with four lines coming out from the top and one from the side. "The Hand mythos?"

Everyone glared at Charlon. Torol passed a bloodied finger across his lips, a hint to be silent, then went back to work. Lines were drawn on the bottom of the hand as well.

Charlon recognized it now. Inhaled a sharp breath. It was the symbol the Five Men wore. Tattooed on the backs of their necks. A box with ten lines coming off it, like a square sun.

The men set aside their bowls. The women helped the Chieftess stand. Mreegan turned slowly to face Charlon as her men set about dressing her. They draped her body in furs and skins, added a huge white fur cape, and placed circlets of brass and turquoise on her head. Torol picked up a comb and began brushing her hair.

"The Kabar hands are sacred," the Chieftess told her. She reached out and took hold of Charlon's hand, drew it forward, and held it palm up between them. She set her own hand on top, palms together. "Stretch out your thumb."

Charlon obeyed, and Mreegan wrapped her thumb around the side of Charlon's hand. Charlon did the same.

"The earth is our home, but ahvenrood gives us power over it," Mreegan said. "Humans, animals, demons, and beasts—all bow before those who wield the ahvenrood, who join hands with shadir, who become like gods." Mreegan pulled Charlon's hand against her. "Hasten to the altar, daughter. The time draws near."

Charlon bowed and backed out of the tent. The flap fell shut, and she turned, ran. Down the hill. Back to her tent. She now understood. The image on the Magonian flag. On the men's necks. The Kabaran hands. The symbol of mantics.

Inside, Roya and Eedee stood before two large bowls. One filled with kohl paste. The other with red ochre. They painted hair and faces. Covered their bodies in hand-printed versions of the Kabaran symbol.

"Mark yourself as much as you can," Roya told Charlon. "I'll help you with the other side."

Because the Chieftess had shown her, Charlon understood. She slid up to the bowl. One hand in red, the other in black. She pressed a black print over the soft flesh of her thigh. She glanced at the others, noting where they put their prints, and copied them. Arms, legs, thighs . . . scrubbed red ochre into her hair.

But she could not make the reverse side of the Kabaran hands on her own.

When she was done, Roya came to Charlon and reached out.

Charlon stepped back. "Don't."

Roya met her gaze. "I won't hurt you."

Charlon knew but did not like it. Not when people touched her. She gritted her teeth. Nodded.

Roya set to work. She quickly turned Charlon's single prints into Kabaran hands. The powdery pastes dried quickly. Kateen and Astaa returned and painted their bodies as well. When all were ready, the Five Maidens each took a sip of ahvenrood juice and ran to the altar at the end of camp. The area was packed with acolytes who were dancing to the beat of tribal drums. Only Chieftess Mreegan and her men were missing.

The Five Maidens climbed onto the flat stone altar, and as Charlon's eyes opened up to the Veil, she began to dance. Charlon loved how dancing made her feel. No man could touch her. She was free. She was safe. And with Magon as her shadir, she was powerful.

The lure blew again. The dancing stopped. All heads turned. Looked up the path. Here came the Five Men. Bringing the Chieftess. Rone walked in front. Two through Five carried the throne on poles that ran under the chair. Mreegan sat regal, splendid, her newt on one shoulder with its tail curled around her neck. The men wore skirts of grass and bone. Bare chests marked with bloody prints of Kabaran hands. And in the Veil, the shadir swirled around them, colors murky and dark.

The maidens fell to their knees, rubbed dirt on their faces to show their reverence. Charlon copied them, as did the acolytes on the ground.

From her throne, Mreegan lifted one hand. "Stop."

The men stopped walking.

"Show me your faces."

Movement rippled through the crowd as each man, woman, and child lifted their dirt-covered faces and fixed their gaze on their Chieftess.

Mreegan extended her arm and snapped her fingers. Rone turned to face the throne and issued a soft command. Five men from the crowd moved quickly, bending their bodies into three steps before Mreegan's throne. Two bent at the waist and locked their arms around each other's torsos. Two more fell to their hands and knees, curling their heads between their arms. The last threw himself prostrate on the ground.

Mreegan slid off the throne, carefully placing her feet on the first two backs. She stood and lifted her chin, waited until she was certain everyone was watching, then stepped to the next row of men, to the last, and finally to the ground. She approached the altar and climbed into the middle of the circle of kneeling maidens.

She spun around, whipping her white fur cloak out behind her, and yelled, "Behold, I say to you, that in those days the root of Arman will be destroyed and usher in the end of all things. There will be mourning and great weeping heard throughout the land. Brother will turn against brother, and their swords will dash each other to pieces. And Armania, the glory of realms, the beauty of the goddess's eye, will no longer be the head of all things."

She paused. Charlon could hear only her own breath. The crowd was silent, as if the Chieftess's words had frozen time. There was more to the prophecy. The people awaited it.

"I will bring peace between Mother and Father," Mreegan yelled, "and the two will be reconciled. From the line of Arman and Magon will come a Deliverer who will be ruler over all. He will crush the foreheads of our enemies, the skulls of all who come against us."

The crowd cheered. Several cried out, "Deliverer!"

"Our Deliverer will not be conceived until Mother and Father are reconciled," Mreegan said. "The signs are upon us. The Father will come soon, and our Deliverer will swell within the Mother's womb."

More cheering.

A white cloud drifted up to Charlon's chin. She heard Magon's voice within. *Ready yourself, Mother. Your time has come.*

Mreegan held up her hand to silence the crowd. "Magon has chosen who will birth the Deliverer. Prophecy states the least will overpower the greatest, and so will she, as the least, become the greatest. Arise, Fifth Maiden!"

The crowd gasped. Charlon's breath caught. The Chieftess had chosen her. Just as Magon had said. She stood and walked to the front of the circle, faced Mreegan. Both were clouded in white from the shadir in the Veil. Was Magon still here?

"Enter the circle and kneel before me," the Chieftess said.

Charlon stepped between Kateen and Astaa, knelt on cold stone she could not see beneath the white fog.

"You have pledged yourself to me, have you not?"

"I have, Chieftess." But only in service to Magon.

"Do you accept this calling to birth the Deliverer?"

"I do." Though she knew not what it meant.

"In this you will soon become Mother."

Just as Magon had promised!

Mreegan drew a small knife from her belt and sliced the end of her middle finger. She pressed it against Charlon's forehead. Charlon stiffened at the contact. The newt ran down Mreegan's arm and perched on Charlon's shoulder. Charlon did not mind its touch.

"I bless this maiden in her task to fulfill prophecy," Mreegan yelled. "I send her out to make peace with the Father, to reconcile with him, to conceive, and to birth the Deliverer through which Magonia will become the head of all things."

The people burst into a cheer. A chill ran up Charlon's spine. She smiled, though she still did not understand. How would she fulfill this role?

When the cheering subsided, Mreegan said, "We must leave Magonia. We will not return. Rise, my children, and celebrate the coming of a new dynasty."

The people shot up like birds into the air. Music began, an eerie sound of pipes and harp over a steady, thumping drum. The maidens resumed their altar dance. The shadir continued to swoop and swarm. Occasionally Charlon saw eyes, always in threes, but never a fully formed creature. No sign of Magon.

"You will need to change your appearance," Mreegan said. "Men in the father realms are vain about women. Only the most beautiful and voluptuous will capture their notice."

Charlon bowed her head, shamed by her smallness. "I am your servant."

"Do not disappoint me, Mother," Mreegan said, taking back her newt.

"I won't," Charlon said. She mustn't.

WILEK

Wilek stepped into the courtyard. The night was warm. He walked the winding path through the queen's garden, tiny rocks crunching underfoot. Around the bend of the five ironwood trees he saw her. Lebetta. She smiled and ran toward him.

Three steps and she stumbled, clutched her stomach, moaned.

Wilek reached her just as she collapsed into his arms. "Etta, what's wrong?"

Her body convulsed, slipped. He adjusted his grip and nearly dropped her. Her stomach was covered in blood. It ran down her sides and legs, and seeped into the loose gravel underfoot.

No longer gravel. Sinksand.

"I've got you," Wilek said as the sand crawled up their legs. He reached for the drooping branch of an ironwood tree, but a sound from the grove stilled his hand. A rattle, like stones in a leather pouch.

Not Barthos. Anything but that.

Up to his waist now, Wilek searched for another way out. The rattling quickly built to a high-pitched, raving cackle.

He struggled to wade away, but Lebetta slipped again. He pulled her close just as a shadow crossed her face.

Wilek looked up.

Barthos loomed overhead, three eyes glittering, teeth a jagged row of fangs that dripped rancid saliva. The god of soil opened its maw, roared, and bit down—

Wilek gasped awake, sat up in bed, heart pounding inside his chest.

133

A dream. A heinous, violent, torturous dream.

He set his face in his hands and breathed deeply through his nose to try to calm himself. His chest ached. How could she truly be gone? In his half-dazed state, tears came easily. Father would be annoyed. He blinked away his weakness despite the fact that no one was here to witness it.

Why did he care what Father thought? Ten years was a long time to love someone. He *should* grieve. Should wear black today. To honor Lebetta.

A one-syllable laugh burst from his mouth. Wearing blacks for a concubine would infuriate Father.

So what?

He shoved fear of his father aside and climbed out of bed. He *would* wear black today. He owed her that much.

He reached for the bell cord and stopped. The windows were dark. No need to wake Dendrick. He lit a candlestick in the fireplace and carried it through his dressing room and into his wardrobe. The room was nearly as large as his bedchamber, with walls covered in racks and hooks and shelves and cabinets. He had no idea where anything was, except his weapons in the armory alcove off the wardrobe's front end. A quick study showed boot and sandal shelves on the far wall and what appeared to be clothing folded on the shelves in between.

He lit three wall sconces to see better and set about looking for anything black, pulling out the items one by one. The first was a cloak, the second a robe. He tossed both to the floor and kept looking. By the time he found a pair of black trousers halfway down the first wall, the pile of clothing on the floor was ankle deep. The next few items were trousers as well. Dendrick was a meticulous man. Tunics on the other side, perhaps?

Sure enough, tunics, tabards, and cloaks filled the shelves on the opposite wall. But he couldn't find anything solid black. How could that be? The closest was a black tunic that buttoned to the neck and had gold cord stitched around the cuffs, collar, and shoulders.

It was his best option, but the gold cord bothered him, so he fetched a dagger from his armory and began slicing it off. By the time he had managed to dress himself, the dawn bells had rung and pale light filtered in through his bedchamber windows.

Wilek opened his chamber door, eager to be seen and set rumors ablaze, to show everyone his pain. Kal and two women stood outside. They broke off their conversation and all three stared.

Kal bowed curtly. "Good dawning, Your Highness."

The women curtsied. Ruzana and Duette, two of the five he appointed to his harem to appease his father. They wore the traditional two-piece gowns of concubines and each had a ruby nose ring. Their dress reminded him of Lebetta and the ache returned.

"I'm going to the great hall," he said, passing between Kal and the women.

Kal followed alongside. "Those women spent the night in the corridor," he said in a low voice. "They were here before I took the shift from Harton."

Wilek sighed and turned around. "Ladies, I must explain. In my chambers is a bell to summon Dendrick. If I need anything, I ring him and he assists me."

"But what if you need us?" Ruzana asked.

"Any of us," Duette added.

"I'll ask Dendrick to fetch you for me," Wilek said.

"As you wish, Your Highness." Ruzana stepped closer, curtsied again. "Please know that we can help in many ways. Fan you or give you massages. All of us are accomplished singers and musicians. We can also dance and recite poetry."

As could every concubine in the palace. "Your list of accomplishments are great, indeed. If I have need of you, I'll send Dendrick." He spun around and walked away.

Kal followed in silence until they reached the grand staircase. "Interesting tunic. I've never seen threads come out of seams like that. Shall I ask Dendrick to prepare some fresh mourning clothes for tomorrow?"

"If you think that necessary," Wilek said.

"I honestly do, Your Highness."

The king was not in the great hall for the morning repast. The royal family rarely was. So Wilek ate alone, garnering all the sympathy he could. Every wide-eyed glance that landed on him lifted his mood. *For you, Etta.* The people would talk. Rumor would spread. He could hear it now.

The First Arm mourns his concubine!

Surely not!

I saw him myself, dressed all in black.

For a concubine?

Can you believe it?

It's unheard of.

He really did love her.

He had. He still did.

Servants brought him trays of food and he ate slowly, eyes focused on the table Lebetta would have been sitting at.

Halfway through his meal, Dendrick approached and bowed low.

"Do you need something?" Wilek asked.

"Good dawning, Your Highness. I'm sorry I missed dressing you this morning. You should have awakened me."

"I managed on my own."

"Yes, I see that, sir." Dendrick's throat bobbed. "A summons has arrived from your father. I'm afraid he wishes to discuss your attire."

Word traveled fast. Wilek fought back a smile. "The king awake so early?"

"The prophet Yohthehreth, I believe, saw you and went to the rosâr. Might I, um, groom your jacket before the meeting? Perhaps tidy your hair?"

Wilek had not thought to groom his hair. "Thank you, Dendrick. You always strive to help me look my best. But I am making a point this morning. It is the only way my father will hear me."

"Of course, Your Highness."

"I'll make sure he knows you opposed my decision."

"Thank you, Your Highness."

Kal and Dendrick waited outside the king's bedchamber. Wilek entered and found his father sitting in his rollchair, eating breakfast at a table before his fireplace. The room smelled strongly of the vapor bath Father's attendants were preparing and the scented garlands prescribed for the king's ailments.

"Good dawning, Father." Wilek gave a low bow, much deeper than custom required.

"What's this nonsense you're wearing?" Father snapped as he bit into a hard-cooked egg, which crumbled bits of dried yolk into his pointed beard.

Wilek looked down at himself and feigned surprise. "You dislike it?"

"It looks as if you took it off a dead man in the Sink."

"I confess, I found it myself in the middle of the night. It is difficult to see with only a candle. Dendrick begged me to change, but I wanted to look as shabby as I feel."

"You know full well that mourning is for family."

"Lebetta was family to me. She was my wife in every way but the law."

The king growled. "Wives are for bearing children. She did none of that, did she? In ten years, not one pregnancy."

"I *will* mourn her, Father."

"You will not! The mere suggestion is preposterous."

The fact that she had mattered to Wilek should have been reason enough, but the king was not a compassionate man. "I loved her. I want to honor her memory. I must."

Father glared at him, face oily and tense. "Fine," he barked. "Take the day to wear your blacks. Tomorrow this ends."

One day would not be enough. "I want the full five months for Lebetta."

The king's nostrils flared as he glared at Wilek. "Five *days*."

"Five weeks."

"Fifteen days."

Wilek set his chin. Lebetta deserved the full five months and nothing less. But if he pushed, he might find himself spending the night in the dungeon. Then who would see his blacks? Fifteen days was long enough for word to spread and people to know how he felt. "Fifteen days. Thank you, Father."

"Now get out of my sight. And have Dendrick find you something more suitable. I won't have my son looking like a commoner, even if he does look like a fool."

"Yes, Father."

Wilek strode from the aromatic bedchamber with as much pomp as the king entering the great hall. Kal and Dendrick were standing right where he left them.

"Well?" Kal asked.

"He gave me fifteen days."

Kal nodded his approval. "Well done."

Wilek had wanted more. "She deserves the full five months."

"Finding her killer will honor her more," Kal said. "Come with me to question the Magonian women."

"Forgive me, Your Highness," Dendrick said. "Might we change you first? You will look more foreboding in your official blacks."

"I would have put them on if I could have found them, Dendrick." But Wilek had made his point with the king. He saw no reason to refuse. "Lead on."

Dendrick's tense expression faded some. "Also, Your Highness, you had planned to invite Lady Zeroah to dine with you in the great hall from now on. Last night after you departed, I took the liberty of passing on that invitation. She accepted."

The last thing Wilek wanted at the moment was to spend time with a child so utterly opposite of Lebetta in every way, but he supposed he must.

"I hope I did not overstep," Dendrick said.

"Not at all," Wilek said. "Your doing so likely mended my rude departure. Thank you for thinking of it." Dinner was hours away. He could worry about Lady Zeroah then. "Now, find me my blacks, Dendrick. I have a murderer to catch."

TREVN

After breaking his fast, Trevn left his chambers with his wax tablet and rune sketch. Cadoc, his new shield, was waiting outside. The man was shorter and younger than most guards, but his muscular arms and near dozen braids bound in a warrior's tail were warning enough. And while Trevn loathed having a shield, he did like the way his hunting horn insignia looked on Cadoc's tabard. It was the first time anyone had worn the mark. Trevn himself was not allowed to wear it until his ageday.

"Your Highness," Cadoc said in his slow, measured voice. "How are you this morning?"

"Slightly bitter to see you as always." Trevn started down the hall to the main staircase, trying to decide whether or not he wanted to make Cadoc run today. So far he had been unable to lose the man.

"Trevn!"

He turned. Hinck was sprinting toward them. Trevn had only seen his backman move this fast when he was trying to keep up on the roofs.

Hinck reached him and dragged him by the arm several paces away from Cadoc. He stuffed a scrap of parchment into Trevn's hand. No, it was paper. In Armania, correspondence on such a medium was as rare as the trees it came from.

"From Miss Mielle." Hinck raised his eyebrows.

"For me?"

"She certainly wouldn't write to me, now would she?"

139

Thinking of Miss Mielle made Trevn's mouth go dry. Why would she write? Demanding his solution to the orphans' plight, no doubt. "Did you read it?"

Hinck bowed low, sweeping his arm dramatically to the side. "I am but a humble backman."

He had read it. "What does it say?"

Hinck straightened. "Read it yourself, fool. It is one sentence long."

Trevn glanced at Cadoc, who was watching them, then unfolded the paper and read.

Sâr Trevn,

Would you be so kind as to meet me in the queen's garden in the quarter hour before first sleep?

With reverence and gratitude,

Mielle Allard

She wanted to meet. Why? He had never before received a note from a girl—a woman. Miss Mielle was of age. "How did you get this?"

"A maid from Fairsight Manor handed it to me when I was leaving the practice field this morning. I told her correspondence should go through Beal, but she said this was unofficial and asked me to pass it to you."

Unofficial. "What does *that* mean?"

Hinck shrugged. "Who cares? A pretty woman wants to meet you in the garden. Go and thank Mikreh."

"You think her pretty?"

"More of a lioness, like Cetheria in human form. Give her a sword and I'd kneel for fear she'd cut off my head."

"It would be your arm," Trevn said, "she's quite clumsy. You think I should go?"

"Why wouldn't you?"

"Forgotten my disaster with Shessy Wallington already?"

"Miss Mielle isn't Shessy, Trev. But if you don't trust her, don't go."

Trevn nodded and shoved the paper underneath the lid of his wax tablet. "What are you going to do?" Hinck asked.

"I guess we'll both find out later. Father Tomek will be waiting." He walked toward the stairwell, feeling somehow more alive. Cadoc shadowed him, which somewhat dampened the thrill of having a pretty woman ask to meet him.

She was pretty, he decided. Not only for the reasons Hinck said. Trevn had enjoyed talking to her. She was smarter than any girl he knew. Liked to climb. Hated rules and injustice. And when she smiled, it somehow pinned him to his chair.

What could she want from him? The mere thought that she might be looking to take advantage of his position made him queasy. He actually slowed a little to catch his breath.

Surely she wasn't like Shessy.

He wavered back and forth all the way to the classroom. Father Tomek had yet to arrive. Trevn sat at his desk and pulled out Miss Mielle's note. Read it again, wondering.

Father Tomek strolled into the room and up to his desk. "Good morning, Sâr Trevn."

Trevn shoved the note under his tablet and traded it for one of the rune sketches he had copied late last night.

"Father, did you hear what happened to the Honored Lady Lebetta?"

"Who?"

"Wilek's concubine. They found her in the courtyard last night, eaten by drice." He carried his drawing to his tutor's desk. "She drew this in her own blood. Do you know what it means?"

"Gracious me, what a terrible thing." Father Tomek took the drawing and frowned as he studied it. "Mantic runes?"

"We think so, but Wilek cannot find anyone to translate them."

"Yes, well, that's unsurprising. I might be able to help, but I'll need to consult some old scrolls. May I borrow this?"

"You may keep it. I have another copy."

"How wise. You'd make an excellent scribe if you didn't have to be a priest."

"Won't I make an excellent priest too?"

Tomek twisted his lips. "That remains to be seen. Now take your seat. Today's discussion is on the Mythos of The Hand, which is . . . ?"

"The basis for most religions in the Five Realms." Trevn grabbed a sheet of velum from the cabinet where he'd left it to dry yesterday and returned to his desk.

"Why is the hand a sacred symbol?"

"Because the hand of Arman created the world, so the hand is revered. Plus, a hand has five fingers, which is why many believe the number five is providential."

"Very good. Which is the oldest religion in the Five Realms?"

"Armanite," Trevn said. "Most believe that Arman created the world and rules as father over it. Armanites believe Arman is the only god."

THE MYTHOS OF THE HAND

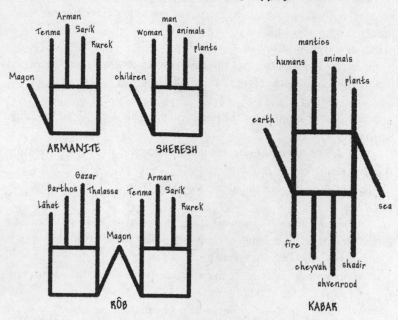

"How does that differ from the Rôb and Sheresh faiths?"

"Rôb believes in multiple gods. Most followers choose five to follow devotedly. Sheresh believes that man is above all—that even the gods serve man."

"How is Kabar different from Rôb?"

"Kabarans worship black spirits, often in conjunction with evenroot powder. They believe mantics are demigods set apart to rule lesser men."

"Which religion does not believe Arman is father and creator?"

"Kabarans do not believe in Arman at all. The Sheresh believe he was a mantic."

"What do you think of that belief? Arman as a mantic?"

Trevn shrugged one shoulder. "Why would a god need black spirits for power?"

"Indeed." Tomek walked to the shelves on the far wall. Trevn spied the corner of the note sticking out and admired one curve of the loopy handwriting. He pulled it out and read it again.

"Which religion is supreme in each of the Five Realms, generally speaking?" Father Tomek asked. "My sâr, are you listening?"

"Huh?" Trevn's eyes jerked up, and he shoved the note onto his lap, his face hot. Father Tomek watched him from across the room, clay tablet in hand. Which religion where, he had asked. "Um . . . Armania is Rôb, the realm of Sarikar is Armanite, the Sheresh dominate Rurekau, and Magonia and Tenma follow Kabar, though they have different methods of worship."

Father Tomek carried the tablet to his desk. "So far you have studied the Root Prophecies for Sheresh and Kabar. Each faith has its own version of the Root Prophecy. I'd like you to compare them. This tablet includes the prophecy for Rôb. Listen carefully as I read."

Father Tomek began, and Trevn glanced to the note in his lap, reading it again. If something was wrong with her family, she would have asked Kal or Lady Zeroah for help. Her servant had told Hinck it was unofficial. Maybe she just wanted to see Trevn again, to ask about the orphans. He wanted her to want to see him again.

His stomach tingled at the thought of meeting her. He would have to go alone—lose Cadoc somehow. The castle roof would be best. Lots of privacy. But she had already suggested the queen's garden.

"Sâr Trevn?"

Good thing the note hadn't gone to Beal. His onesent would have shown it to Mother. Beal was too old and stuffy for Trevn's tastes. Trevn used Hinck for the work of backman *and* onesent, especially when he wanted to hide something from his mother.

A hand on his shoulder. "Your Highness."

Trevn jumped and stuffed the note between his knees. "Yes?"

Father Tomek was standing over him, one hand on his shoulder, the other holding the clay tablet. "How late did you stay up last night?"

Trevn swallowed. Father Tomek thought him tired from what had happened to Lady Lebetta. Perhaps he could work this to his advantage. "I went to the deadhouse with Wilek. Uhley had to burn Lady Lebetta's body because of the drice. But I was asleep before the dawn prayer bells."

"Have you copied your pages?"

Trevn winced. "Not yet. I slept late."

"If I let you skip lessons this day, will you promise to give me your full attention tomorrow?"

Trevn straightened. "Yes!"

The old man smiled. "Copy your pages and you may go."

Trevn scrambled out of his chair to the cabinet that held the holy scrolls. He gathered his things and brought them back to his desk. He had to concentrate to keep his hand from shaking as he transcribed. He hoped Father Tomek wouldn't make him redo them.

When he finished, he returned the holy scrolls to the cabinet and laid out his five pages of vellum on the shelf above to dry overnight.

"All done?" Father Tomek asked.

"I am."

"Go, then. Get some rest. But tomorrow morning I expect your full attention."

Back at his quarters Trevn again assured a concerned Cadoc that all was fine. "I'm just tired. Stayed up too late. Father Tomek is letting me sleep it off. After that, I think I'll work on my maps. You'll wait out here. Inform Beal I'll take my midday meal in my chambers."

"Yes, Your Highness."

Trevn shut the door and grinned. This would be the ideal way to spend his time until he could meet Mielle.

He quickly spread his Armania maps on the floor of his chambers, studying the coastlines and cracks. He subscribed to Pollon's teachings on the cracks. Pollon had taught that if the earth had split once before, it would again. Cape Waldemar had extended off the northern side of the Echo Crack, and Trevn was certain the cape's demise was partly related to its location.

Beal arrived at midday with a tray of food. His onesent was a middle-aged man, thin, with sunken cheeks and ashen skin. His voice wheezed, likely from overuse of the evergold smoking pipe he kept in his pocket at all times. He set the tray on Trevn's table. "Your meal, sir."

Trevn didn't bother to look up. "Return to help me dress for dinner. I'll remain in my chambers until then."

"So long indoors?" Beal rasped. "Are you ill?"

"Tired. Did no one tell you I was up until dawn with my brother Wilek? His concubine was murdered."

"I heard that much, Your Highness, but was unaware you were present."

"I accompanied my brother to the deadhouse. Now leave me, and don't concern yourself or my mother. A few hours' sleep will be just the thing."

"Of course, Your Highness."

The moment the door closed, Trevn approached the candle clock on his wall. He pushed the time pin into the wax at half an hour before first sleep. That would give him plenty of time to reach the queen's garden.

He went back to his maps until the clatter of the pin told him it was time to go.

Trevn tied the strings of his sandals together and hung them around his neck. Then he slipped out to his balcony and scrambled up the stone carvings of vines that ran up the wall. They were cool under his hands and feet since his window was in shadow until long after midday. When he reached the roof, he moved quickly over the hot stone that the sun had baked all morning, hoisted himself over the crenellation, and jogged to the roof garden. There he took a bench and put on his sandals. A shame that Miss Mielle hadn't suggested this garden. Easier to get to and much more private.

Trevn hurried to the servants' stairs, which was the quickest route to the ground floor. He circled down and only upset three maids.

He realized then that word might reach his mother that he had been on the servants' stairs again. She would know he had tricked Cadoc, lied to Beal, and taken advantage of Father Tomek's generosity.

It could not be helped. If she found out, he would deal with it, but he wasn't going back now. He would be careful of the time, returning before the evening prayer bells tolled and Beal came to dress him for dinner.

Trevn slipped outside onto the courtyard's wide gravel lawn of white marble. It ran around the perimeter, surrounding an open colonnade of red granite on one end and the vast cactus garden on the other.

It was eerie to be here after last night. Lady Lebetta had been murdered on the far end of the garden. Did Miss Mielle know this? The courtyard and colonnade seemed deserted. Queen Brelenah had temporarily moved her court indoors to honor her son's loss.

The gravel crunched underfoot as Trevn followed the maze of pebble paths that wound through clusters of cacti, prickly trees, tiny flowers, shrubs, and palms. He turned down a path that curved under a grove of trees and found Mielle waiting on a bench by the summer flory, which had not yet bloomed. She saw him coming and stood. She was wearing a red-and-yellow dress that bared her ankles and the brown sandals she wore. Her feet were dusty. As was her skirt.

"Did you walk here?" he asked, pointing.

She glanced down. "Oh, no. I went in there," she said, pointing at a grove of ironwood—five trees that had been gifts to the garden from Queen Brelenah's brother, King Jorger of Sarikar. "I wanted to see how high I could climb."

"You climbed an ironwood tree?" They were quite prickly.

"Two of them. First I went up that one with the low branch. But it's thin at the top, and I couldn't get very high. So I climbed the one in back. Oh, I forgot." She curtsied.

Trevn fought back a smile. He didn't want to let down his guard until he knew she could be trusted, but her mere presence winded him more than his run had. He swallowed, suddenly nervous, though he couldn't imagine why. "Why have you asked me here, Miss Mielle? Is something wrong?"

She sighed. "Nothing is *wrong*. Do you really want to know?"

He had asked, hadn't he? "Of course. I will help, if I can," he added, knowing better than to give a promise he could not keep.

"I need information." She smiled, all innocence and charm.

He should have guessed. Miss Mielle was like every other female, looking to further her position at court, a place Trevn was still too young to even attend. He took a steadying breath to keep from yelling. "I am sorry to disappoint, Miss Mielle, but I cannot be bought or bribed or seduced in any way."

Her brow pinched. "Seduced?"

"You want something from the king, or you simply want to get close to me to gain power or influence at court. Well, it won't happen."

She gasped. "I want nothing of the sort! I thought you were kind. I wouldn't have come to you otherwise."

Her reaction puzzled him. She wanted information from him, yet she was acting like he had wronged her. "I do not understand. What information do you seek?" He steeled himself against the coming request, confused, yet hopeful that she might yet redeem herself.

"Anything about your brother Sâr Wilek."

She was after Wilek? This was somehow worse than using him to get a favor from the king. "Why not ask Lady Zeroah to gain favor with him?"

"I don't want a favor! I simply wish to help Lady Zeroah. She wants nothing more in life than to please her future husband, but he is so distant. We had

146

high hopes for dinner last night, but now the lady is melancholy. I can barely get a word from her."

His anger fell away. She wanted to help Wilek and Lady Zeroah.

Miss Mielle went on. "With this horror over his concubine's death, my lady is at a loss for how she can ever bring him comfort, and I cannot stand to see her so distressed. You were so kind at dinner, I hoped you might help. Forgive me for wasting your time." She moved to walk past him, but he stepped in her way.

"I'd be happy to help," Trevn said, suddenly eager to please this woman he had been so certain wanted to use him. "But I . . . I know little about . . . such things."

Miss Mielle offered up that wide and glowing smile. "I'm not asking for tips on romance, Your Highness."

A small relief. "What, then? I know nothing of grief either."

"He is your brother."

"Half brother. I spent the last ten years in Sarikar. I barely know him."

"But Lady Zeroah said you and he are friends. Understanding his interests and dreams will help her know him better."

"He has never once told me his dreams," Trevn said.

"Must you make everything so difficult?" Miss Mielle set her hands on her hips. "What's his favorite color?"

Trevn shrugged. "Men don't talk of favorite colors."

"Well, does he like to dance?"

"I know not. I told you I am not permitted to attend balls until I reach my majority."

"Does he like music? What's his favorite instrument?"

Trevn knew that much. "He owns a lyre. I heard him playing it once in this very garden. He plays poorly, though."

Miss Mielle's eyes lit up. "Indeed! That is precisely the kind of information I needed." She darted forward and pressed her lips against his cheek.

His cheek.

His stomach leapt. Trevn wanted to leap too, but he kept his expression passive, as if the kiss held very little interest for him.

Her dark brown eyes searched his. "Anything else?"

Trevn tried to look like he didn't desperately want another kiss, but quick words betrayed him. "He once remarked that pear crispels are delicious."

For that, he received a kiss on his other cheek.

Trevn liked this game. Perhaps he could negotiate longer kisses for larger secrets. He would need to strategically plan a way to seek out the answers. For now, he threw out another useless fact. "He prefers boots to sandals."

"Thank you," Miss Mielle told him. This time she kissed him on the lips. She was exactly the same height as he was. Her face was so close that her eyes blurred into one. He could still feel the burn of her lips on his.

"He hates his mother's little dogs," Trevn whispered, and this time he took his own kiss.

A man cleared his throat. Trevn and Miss Mielle sprang apart.

Rayim Veralla, captain of the Queen's Guard, bowed, as was proper. "Your mother is looking for you, Your Highness. She is most concerned for your well-being."

Sands! How did she even know he was gone? "I . . ." He swallowed. "Um . . . wanted a walk in the garden." He had never before felt such heat in his face.

"I see that. I'm to escort you to your mother's apartment immediately."

The words sent fire up Trevn's spine. He didn't want to leave Miss Mielle, but no excuse to stay presented itself in his overwhelmed brain. So he bowed to her. "Miss Mielle, please forgive my mother's rude interruption. I wish you a good midday."

She curtsied deeply. "Thank you for your assistance, Sâr Trevn."

Trevn studied her flawless skin, the curve of her throat, full lips, straight nose, bright eyes, thick braids of hair, the—

"Shall we, Your Highness?" Captain Veralla said.

"Yes, of course." Dazed, Trevn followed the captain but kept his focus on Miss Mielle until he walked into a rosebush and thorns stabbed his legs. "Ahh!"

Captain Veralla spun around, hand on the hilt of his sword. Then smirked. "Best to face forward when walking, my sâr."

"Good idea." But Trevn risked one last glance back to Miss Mielle. She was giggling. Yes, very funny. Yet he smiled despite his embarrassment.

Captain Veralla held open the garden doors for Trevn. He met the man's gaze as he passed through. "Are you going to tell her?" Trevn asked.

"Tell who what, Your Highness?"

"Tell my mother what I . . . what you saw."

The captain continued to the grand staircase. Trevn walked alongside him. "I'll tell her I found you in the queen's garden. Should she ask whether or not you were alone, I won't lie. But I doubt she'll ask me. You, however, should be prepared to answer for yourself. She's very protective of you."

Trevn's heart was still racing from that last kiss. "She will be angry if she learns about Miss Mielle."

They started up the stairs. "No mother likes to see her child grow up. Your majority has nearly arrived, but when your mother looks at you, she will always see the face of her babe."

Trevn grimaced. "You know a lot about mothers."

"That's because I have one. And seven brothers before me. And five children of my own, including a girl who reached her majority this year. You, however, are your mother's only son. She will guard you fiercely as long as she can."

Trevn sighed. If his mother would have another son, perhaps that boy could be the priest and Trevn could be an explorer. But the king had cast her aside. Her only lover now was a bottle of wine.

"May I make a suggestion, Your Highness?"

"I suppose."

"Next time, take Cadoc with you to meet your Miss Mielle. He will give you privacy and keep your secret. Your mother might have employed him, but you are his master. Once you are of age, he will answer to none but you and the rosâr."

Really? Trevn hadn't thought of Cadoc as an asset. "An excellent suggestion, Captain Veralla. Thank you."

"Just you stay away from my daughter, though."

Trevn had never even met Captain Veralla's daughter, and by the look in the man's eye, he never wanted to. "I will do so."

Queen Thallah's apartment was decorated in the Rurekan style. Everything was gold or yellow. The walls were covered in weapons that had supposedly belonged to her ancestors. There were three swords and a pike mounted in the sitting room alone.

In a corner of the room cowered Cadoc and Hinck, and Queen Thallah paced angrily before them like a fat sand cat, turning only as Trevn cleared his throat.

"Trevn!" Mother ran to him, embraced him in one of her smothering hugs. "It's worry that kills, son of mine. Father Tomek gave you the afternoon off, but you hadn't checked in with me. When Cadoc said he lost you, I nearly went to your father. Thank Mikreh that Captain Veralla begged a chance to seek you out. How humiliating would it have been to claim you missing to the rosâr with you here all along? Well? What have you to say for yourself? Where were you?"

"Walking in the queen's garden."

She leveled a glare at Captain Veralla. "That is where you found him?"

"Yes, Your Highness. As always, he left a trail of unhappy servants in his wake. I had only to follow the destruction to the garden, and there he was."

Her angry eyes flashed back to Trevn. "Doing what in the garden?"

He could not mention Miss Mielle. To do so would bring her to his mother's attention, and she would devise some way to keep them apart. "Studying the scene of the crime. Lady Lebetta was murdered last night, and her killer has yet to be—"

"Oh, Trevn!" His mother fell onto her sofa. "You don't know what I suffer for your sake. The women here give me no respect. They all plot to use you against me."

She had moved on to theatrics. The worst was over. "Mother, no one will use me against you."

"You won't mean to betray me, no, but youth and parchment take any impression. You run headlong into adventures without first considering the consequences." She rolled to her feet and waddled to him, clutching his hands in her massive ones. "You are my joy. I simply worry about the future. I simply worry too much." She hugged him close.

"As you said, Mother, it's worry that kills." He pulled away. "Trust me to take care of you."

"I know you will." She gazed at him so long he turned away, looked at the door. "Yes, go get dressed for dinner," she said, patting his arm. "I will see you there."

Trevn, Hinck, and Cadoc walked in silence to Trevn's chambers. When they arrived, Trevn waved them all inside and closed the door.

"How did this happen?" he asked.

"It's my fault," Hinck said. "I came to meet you after your lessons, but Father Tomek said he let you go early. So I came here to see what you had decided to do about . . . you know. But you were already gone. And when I came out, Cadoc, well, he . . ."

"I could tell from the look on his face he hadn't seen you. I entered your chambers, confirmed you had left, and informed your mother of the situation."

Trevn looked from Cadoc to Hinck, mustering up his most disappointed frown. Captain Veralla was correct. They were his to command, and he needed them on his side. "I apologize, Cadoc. I'm not used to having a shield. But *I* am your master, not my mother. From now on, I will ask your help when I want to meet someone privately without my mother's knowledge."

"I appreciate that, Your Highness," Cadoc said.

Hinck's grin claimed his entire face. "So you met her? And there'll be a next time?"

Trevn fell into his chair by the fireplace and smirked. "I hope so." He would meet her tomorrow, if he could make his list by then. The more information he could gather about Wilek, the longer Miss Mielle's lips would be on his.

WILEK

Unfortunately every avenue of investigation failed to yield results. The Magonian women in the dungeon claimed to be illiterate and swore they weren't mantics. The guards he had posted at Lebetta's door affirmed that she had not left, yet a chambermaid had seen her walk past the laundry in the basement. Those were his only clues besides the mysterious rune. How had Lebetta gotten out of her room? Could she scale the walls like Trevn, or were the guards lying? And what had she been doing in the basement? The lack of logical answers left Wilek cross and irritable.

He arrived late to dinner so that all would see him enter. The herald played his tune, and he moved slowly up the aisle, proudly bearing his official blacks, which Dendrick had found within moments of entering Wilek's wardrobe. Father was not here. Ill, so his attendants claimed. Wilek knew better. He was hiding.

The people stared and murmured. Wilek relished every shocked expression. Until his eyes met Lady Zeroah's. Again, he had forgotten she would be here. He winced inwardly, knowing that his scene might cause her pain.

His mother and Gran merely stared, silent, perhaps for the first time in their lives. It would not last long. A servant pulled out his chair and he sat. Kal took his post on the wall.

"Good evening, ladies," Wilek said. "I trust you all enjoyed first sleep?"

"*Wilek*," his mother breathed.

Wilek drained half his goblet of wine, hoping it might dull his frazzled nerves. Lady Zeroah glanced about the great hall, from the king's table to the floor, to Trevn's table. "You are the only one wearing blacks, Your Highness," she said softly.

He steeled himself. "I mourn the Honored Lady Lebetta."

"I see." Her chin trembled and she pushed back her chair. "I *am* sorry for your loss. I shall leave you in peace until the five months have . . ." She stopped and set her hand on the edge of the table as if to steady herself. "Will you be wearing black to the wedding?"

Mikreh's teeth. "I shall mourn Lady Lebetta only fifteen days," he said. "I mean no offense."

She took this in, nodded. "Then we will return after that time." She stood, pulled her skirt out from the legs of her chair. "Mielle, let us depart."

"You are leaving?" Wilek asked.

"I am afraid we must." Lady Zeroah curtsied. "Enjoy the rest of your meal, Your Highness. May you find peace in your time of grieving." She walked past him, down the steps, Miss Mielle at her side.

"She handled that well," Mother said.

"I've always liked her," Gran said. "Quiet, but those eyes are so intelligent. She'll make a fine queen."

"I'm glad you both approve," Wilek said.

Mother frowned at him. "How terribly rude of you to wear blacks to sit with your betrothed. You risk your marriage and position as Heir with such behavior."

"I must mourn her, Mother."

"You're a good boy," Gran said. "This quail is divine, Brelenah. I think Hara discovered a new spice."

"It *is* good," Mother said. "Tastes like cumin, only sweeter. Cinnamon, perhaps?"

Gran had a way of saving Wilek from lectures. She could maneuver a conversation better than anyone, leading his mother into a debate over the cook's culinary surprises. *Had* he done the right thing? Just because Lebetta was gone and he was suffering did not change the fact that he must marry Lady Zeroah in two months' time. He would need to make peace with her, and soon.

He remained in the great hall long after Mother and Gran had gone. With only fourteen more days to wear his blacks, he might as well make the most of it.

A chorus of laughter pulled Wilek's attention to the Agoros table. Janek was there now, holding court. Over half of those at the table were watching Wilek. Janek said something softly, and they all laughed again.

Wilek sighed.

"Wilek?" He turned and saw Trevn pull out the chair on his right. "May I?"

"Please," Wilek said.

Trevn sat and ate a berry off Lady Zeroah's abandoned trencher. "Was Lady Zeroah feeling ill?"

"I don't think she appreciated the color of my tunic."

Trevn glanced at Wilek's clothes. "Oh, right."

"Nor does the king. Nor does my mother. Nor does Janek, who mocks me to his friends. Does it bother you, brother?"

"Not at all. Mourn if you must. It's your right." He grinned. "I rather like the fit it gave our father."

That others knew that Wilek had annoyed the king made him smile. "I confess, that was part of the reason I did it."

"What's your favorite color?" Trevn asked.

Wilek frowned, thought it over. "Uh . . . I suppose I prefer blue. Why?"

"Just wondering. What's your favorite pastime?"

"Well, I enjoy music, both playing it and listening to it."

"How about food? What's your favorite?"

Of all the bizarre . . . "Trevn, why do you ask these things?"

He shrugged. "Because I want to know you better."

Oh, well, no harm in that. "All right. I like fish, and Hara's rose pudding is divine."

"Rose pudding, fish. Got it. Um . . . whom do you most admire?"

"Rayim Veralla. Kal. Gran. My mother." When Trevn didn't respond with another question, Wilek asked, "Is that all? Have I satisfied your curiosity?"

"Almost." Trevn furrowed his brows, like he wasn't sure what he wanted to say next. "What weather do you like?"

"Cloudy, so it's not so hot."

"Moon or stars?"

"I abhor the moon. It reminds me of . . ." Wilek stopped. He'd never told anyone but Kal and Gran how much he hated the offerings in The Gray. Trevn, he supposed, might understand. "It reminds me of the night Chadek was killed."

Trevn's eyes swelled at those words, then he smiled. The boy found humor in Chadek's death? "That's great. To know, I mean. It's terrible that it happened. Human sacrifice is an archaic practice."

"And you to be a priest?"

"Wasn't *my* idea."

Wilek chuckled, but it felt wrong to laugh while wearing black, and it quickly died. "I do not worship the Rôb Five like Father, his council, and the priests. I substitute Arman for Barthos." It was on Wilek's insignia.

"Because of the sacrifices?"

"Partly. Arman demands sacrifice of life service, while Barthos demands sacrifice of life blood. Service gives more value to a man's life than a one-time outpouring of his blood. Arman values life over death, and so do I." He caught sight of Dendrick walking toward them. "Anything else, Trevn? Dendrick is coming, and it looks as if he has something on his mind."

"No, that's good. Thanks, brother." Trevn slapped Wilek's shoulder and dashed away, sprinting through the great hall as if it were on fire.

How very odd.

As Dendrick ascended the stairs to the dais, he glanced back at the blur that was Trevn. "Your Highness, a messenger has just arrived. Your father requests your presence in the Throne Room."

Wilek stood and followed his onesent along the dais to the exit on the far end.

"Nice blacks, brother," Janek yelled from the Agoros table.

Janek's minions snickered. Wilek ignored them but caught the gazes of the Honored Ladies Pia and Mattenelle. For the first time ever, his brother's concubines looked on him with something like respect.

A handful of advisors were already in the Throne Room with the king when Wilek arrived. Among them were Pontiff Rogedoth, Canbek, Jervaid, and Princess Nabelle. A sharp stench drew Wilek's attention to a man in clothing so filthy he could have been pulled from the Blackwater Canal.

"Wilek!" Father yelled. "Finally. Read the message again for my son."

The filthy man cleared his throat and read from a scroll. "'Rosâr of Armania, hear our cry. The city of Farway is no more. On the fifth day of the second week of the third month of spring, an earthquake swallowed our fair city into the depths of the Lowerworld, killing thousands, including my father, mother, and three sisters. We are a deserted people without home, food, or even water. Please send assistance at once to Farmman Geffray's claim.' Signed, 'Estin Dobry, Earl of Farway, which is no more.'"

Wilek leaned against the wall, stunned. Into the Lowerworld? He couldn't fathom such a thing. "Underground, you mean?"

"It's the Five Woes come at last," Canbek said. "I warned you. I've been saying it for—"

"Oh, shut up with your woes," Jervaid said. "I tell you the whole thing is impossible: woes and earthquakes that swallow cities."

"We all saw what happened to Cape Waldemar," Rogedoth said. "Barthos is angry still."

"Arman is angry," Princess Nabelle said, glaring at the Pontiff.

"An entire city, though?" Jervaid said. "I don't believe it."

Wilek did not like the idea that the Five Woes were upon them; still . . .

"Why would the boy lie?" he asked.

"To pilfer money from the rosâr's coffers," Jervaid said. "Probably killed his father for the earldom."

"That's ridiculous," Wilek said. If anyone was pilfering, it was Jervaid. "Estin is fourteen. He needs our support." He looked to the messenger. "Why is he staying on a farm?"

"His father's advisors were farmmen, the lot of them," the messenger said. "With the city gone, that's where the food is."

"I say we send someone to confirm this claim," Jervaid said. "We cannot take the word of this lout."

"Wilek will go," Father said, looking to him.

The command shocked him senseless. "To Farway?"

"Take fifty men including yourself, no more, no less. If Farway is truly gone, the people must have angered Barthos. Set up a shrine and make sacrifices. One for every five survivors. There is a Gray at the northernmost tip of the King's Canyon."

"You are very wise, sire, to think of such things," Rogedoth said.

No, he was insane. The both of them were. Wilek would never sacrifice anyone to Barthos.

"Why must you send Sâr Wilek?" Princess Nabelle asked.

"I trust no one else," Father said. "Janek will accompany me to Canden next moon."

Wilek had a feeling his father only wanted to get rid of the embarrassment of Wilek's blacks. It would take ten days to reach Farway. The rest of Wilek's mourning period would be seen by no more than his forty-nine men and any commoners they saw along the way. But he wavered only a moment. Anyone else would obey Father's command to sacrifice survivors. Plus, being so close to the border between Armania and Magonia, perhaps he could find a mantic to translate Lebetta's rune.

"I will leave the day after tomorrow," Wilek told the messenger.

"Excellent," Father said. "Go now and prepare."

Trevn

Trevn sat on the bench inside the rotunda of the roof garden, bouncing one knee, worried. Miss Mielle was late. He didn't like how it made him feel powerless and at her mercy. He jumped up and jogged down the steps, around the curved path to where Cadoc stood guard.

His shield looked up. "Patience, young sâr. She comes now." He nodded across the roof.

Indeed a woman was coming toward them, alone. Trevn ran back to the rotunda, to his spot on the bench. Moments later he heard the *slap* of approaching sandals on the stone path.

Then Miss Mielle came into sight. She had changed her hair. It was done up in dozens of minibraids, part of them twisted into a knot, the rest hanging down her back. She wore a green dress with gold ribbon lines down the seams that made her look even taller.

Trevn popped to his feet. What was it about this woman that made it difficult to even breathe? "Hello, Miss Mielle."

She climbed the three steps to the platform and curtsied but did not meet his gaze. Her forehead was wrinkled, and her eyes glinted with distrust as she looked around the rotunda, up to the ceiling, behind him. Something was wrong.

"My, this is . . . remote," she said. "No one should ever find us up here."

That was the idea. He tried a smile.

"Because you can't risk being seen with me again." This she said to the floor.

He stared at her, afraid to speak or move. He had seen his mother behave like this and feared Miss Mielle was working her way toward an outburst.

She walked past him, sat on the bench, still avoiding his eyes and still looking very angry. "I assume you have some information to share or you wouldn't have summoned me."

His chest burned. Something had changed. He feared speaking would only make it worse. He walked slowly toward her and sat down, careful to leave a large space between them.

"Well? Let's hear it," she said. "Lady Zeroah needs all the help she can get."

Trevn wanted to know what was wrong but was hesitant to upset her further. "I remembered that he collects knives. She might give him one, as a present."

This information softened her demeanor. "That's helpful. Anything else?"

"His favorite color is blue. His favorite pastime is music—playing the lyre and listening to it."

"You already told me that."

"No I haven't." He'd told her that Wilek played the lyre but not that music was his favorite pastime.

"Yes you have. Because I told my lady, and she interviewed a player to learn about the instrument."

"Well, I have more. He prefers any kind of fish. Favorite dessert is rose pudding. He most admires Captain Veralla, Sir Kalenek, his mother, and Grandmother. He likes cloudy weather because it is cooler. And he hates the moon. Want to know why?"

She shrugged and looked away, as if disappointed in his efforts.

He had imagined this information would earn him a long and thankful kiss. Now he simply wanted to lighten her mood. He also hoped Wilek wouldn't find out he had told anyone. "Please use this information with care, Miss Mielle. If he learns I told you . . ."

Her eyes rolled up as if he were a silly child. "I shall be most discreet, Your Highness."

Trevn bit the inside of his cheek, trying to decide if he should tell her or not. He really did want to help Wilek and Zeroah find happiness together. "It's the sacrifices."

She looked at him for the first time since entering the rotunda. "Which sacrifices?"

"The full moon sacrifices at The Gray. Once a month my father goes to Canden to sacrifice a convict to Barthos. It reminds Wilek of when our father sacrificed some of our brothers."

Miss Mielle's lips parted. "The king killed his own sons?"

"You didn't know? It was before I was born. Wilek was nine. Father dropped them into The Gray as sacrifices. Got his advisors and nobles and soldiers to sacrifice their children too. There were fifty Armanian males offered to Barthos that day. Newborns to grown men. All for favor to win the war."

Miss Mielle stood up, hands balled into fists. "Fifty?" she yelled.

Trevn flinched. "That is why Wilek hates the full moon."

She twirled away from Trevn and paced to the wall, her green skirt fluttering out behind her, briefly revealing part of her leg. "Of all the horrible, monstrous . . ."

"Miss Mielle, forgive me for asking, but is something bothering you? You seem upset."

She spun around and stalked toward him. "Do I?"

He shrank back as she neared. "Did I do something?"

She plopped down beside him and folded her arms.

He wanted to reach out and touch her but didn't dare. "Miss Mielle?"

"Yes?"

"You don't have to kiss me if you don't want to. I'm happy to help Lady Zeroah any way I can. I want her and my brother to find happiness. You as well."

She sighed, deflated a little. "Sâr Trevn, I am but a servant to my lady. My happiness matters not, now or ever, it seems."

"Oh." So what was she saying?

"I was introduced to your mother today."

"Ah." Mystery solved. That explained everything.

"Since your father was feeling ill, Lady Zeroah and I visited the king's court. This time, however, his advisors were there—and your mother, who I understand only comes when the king is gone." Her eyes were glossy with tears, which she somehow managed to keep from leaking out. "We should never have gone. Your mother approached us, greeted Lady Zeroah. Talked of you and how clever you are. I told Rosârah Thallah that you and I had dined with Sâr Wilek and Lady Zeroah. I said you were charming and kind. Do you want to know what she said?"

No. He really didn't.

"She pointed out two young ladies who were at court. Said she was searching for your wife and wondered which of the ladies I found more handsome. I told her I could not choose, that both were lovely. Then she asked my age. When I told her, she said that I was, unfortunately, too old to be one of your concubines. Apparently she seeks some of those for you as well."

He swallowed. "My majority ageday is approaching."

"Oh, I'm well aware. Your mother could talk of little else. She mentioned the scandal of Sâr Wilek's mourning his concubine and advised Lady Zeroah to consider marriage to you instead, since you both match in fives. She thinks you stand a better chance of being declared Heir. And then she told Lady Zeroah that Sâr Wilek chose a harem of five women."

Trevn choked on a sharp breath and coughed. "He did?"

"Indeed. There was much discussion as to which woman he'll sleep with first. Some of the men are placing bets."

Trevn could only imagine. It was one of the reasons he hated court. But why was any of this his fault? "Why do you care so much about Wilek's harem, anyway? It's not like you wanted to be in it."

Her chin trembled. "I don't want to be in anyone's harem! Your mother said that to hurt Lady Zeroah in hopes that she might marry you and help your position to be declared Heir." She stood and crossed the platform, arms folded.

"I have never wished to be Heir."

"Are all nobles so awful? I always believed court would be the epitome of romance and refinement. Imagine my horror when I was informed that I am thirty-six days too old to be your concubine and, in the next hour, was propositioned by *three* greasy old men, who are each at least twenty years my senior. When I slapped the boldest of them, *your mother* scolded me for it. Apparently she thinks young maidens have no value in this world beyond who they can bed. But pity on me that the boy I *did* like is out of my reach, even in the basest sense. One month too old to be your concubine, which of course your mother assumed I was eager to be."

Silence descended. Trevn hoped the worst had passed, but then Miss Mielle spun around and yelled again.

"I can't believe you think I want to be in a harem!"

"I never said that." Trevn stood but kept his distance. "I just wondered why Wilek's harem bothered you. I should have known my mother was causing trouble. She excels at that."

"Don't pretend to care about my feelings. You don't care that Sâr Wilek's

new harem has broken my lady's heart. You don't care how horribly men behave at court. Why should you? You're going to turn out just like them. And
I don't want to have anything to do with you!" She grabbed her skirts up in
one hand and fled.

Trevn watched her go, clueless how to stop her or if he should even try.

WILEK

Wilek's contingent to Farway had assembled in front of Castle Everton. A commotion outside the gate captured his attention. A carriage had arrived—Princess Nabelle's, if he was not mistaken. The guards managed to push back the protestors and open the gates so the carriage could enter. It stopped at the bottom of the castle's front steps. Wilek went down to greet it, wondering whom he might find inside.

The coachman beat him to the door and helped Lady Zeroah step to the ground. Wilek had thought she wasn't going to visit until his fifteen days of mourning had passed. And here he was, still wearing his blacks. He caught sight of Miss Mielle inside the carriage; the girl didn't appear to be getting out.

Wilek glanced behind him to Kal. "Go around and greet Miss Mielle. Harton, with me." He approached Lady Zeroah, who curtsied. Wilek greeted her warmly. "Lady Zeroah, what a splendid surprise."

She met his greeting with nervous eyes. "I heard you were departing on a journey that would keep you from us for too long, and I could not stay away."

A choppy line of words, no doubt rehearsed, but coming from her he knew it had taken effort. "You honor me, lady."

Her lips twitched into a small smile. "I try." She reached through the open door of the carriage and withdrew something from the seat inside—a long, narrow whitewood box, stained with coiling black burns. She handed it to him. "I brought you a gift."

Intrigued, he took it from her and opened it. Inside, a long bronze dagger gleamed on a bed of green velvet. A dirk, actually, two hands long and crafted like a broadsword, sharp on both edges and the point. The hilt was made of glossy brown wood, as dark as his skin. Instead of a pommel, a bronze sunbird capped the end, its wings wrapped partially around the wooden grip. In the place of a crossguard, a clawed foot reached out on either side to protect the hand.

"Do you like it?" she asked softly.

He could barely breathe he was so taken with the weapon. "It's glorious, thank you."

"It was my grandfather's," she said. "King Jorger wished me to give it to you for a wedding gift, but I thought you might like to have it early."

Wilek glanced into her golden eyes. "I like it very much, lady. I collect daggers."

Her relieved smile softened her posture. "I am so pleased. I pray you won't have need of it on your journey."

Oh, but Wilek would not bring this with him, as much as he would have enjoyed studying it on the long ride. It was much too valuable to take to a disaster area where desperate people might steal it. "Worry not, lady. My men will keep me from harm."

"I will pray for your safe return at every toll of the bells." She swayed—had she lost her balance?—leaned forward, up on her toes, and kissed his cheek, bringing with her the fresh smell of rosemary. "Farewell, my sâr," she whispered. Before he could answer, she spun around and clambered into the carriage.

Stunned, Wilek stared at the open door but could see only her voluminous skirt as she sat back against the seat. He set the dagger in its box and handed it to Harton. He moved her skirt inside and closed the carriage door, then clutched the window opening and peeked inside.

"Farewell, lady, and thank you again for the gift."

Zeroah nodded from the shadows, her shy self again.

"Good-bye, Kal!" Miss Mielle hung out the opposite window, waving at Kal. She pulled herself inside and turned her attention on Wilek.

"Good midday, ladies." Wilek stepped back from the carriage and signaled the driver.

The carriage pulled away. Miss Mielle leaned across Lady Zeroah and waved out the window. "Good midday, Sâr Wilek!"

Zeroah peeked out as well and offered a tiny wave.

Wilek waved back, oddly content. "Well, what do you make of that, Kal?"

Kal came to stand beside him. "I missed the entire exchange."

Harton stepped between them, dagger box under his arm. "Lady Zeroah gave our sâr a knife and a kiss on the cheek."

"Lady Zeroah?" Kal said. "I don't believe it. The kiss, I mean."

"Perhaps Mikreh will smile on my marriage after all," Wilek said. "Do you think it possible?"

"Indeed I do, Your Highness," Kal said.

"Give that box to Dendrick, Hart," Wilek said. "See that he puts it in my armory. I want it kept safe until I return."

"Yes, Your Highness," Harton said, starting up the front steps.

Wilek felt joyful for the first time in days. "Are we ready to depart?" he asked Kal.

"Another half hour should have all the men gathered and ready," Kal said.

"Good," Wilek said. "Just long enough to bid Mother and Gran farewell."

Alone, Wilek could ride a well-trained horse to Farway in five days. With fifty men, the 140-league journey would take closer to ten.

On the fourth midday the Sandacre Valley came into view. A little over a year had passed since Wilek had last traveled this way, and the changes in the land startled him. What should have been golden wheat fields were nothing but dead stalks. The distant hills of Mount Radu were burned black. The closer they came to the city of Dacre, the worse the fires were. Smoke hung bitter on the air. It tickled the nose and made the throat sore until everyone sounded ill.

That night, Wilek sent a messenger ahead to announce his arrival in Dacre. He would rest there one night and speak with the governor about the fires. He stood outside his tent and watched the rivers of fire, orange and bright in the darkness, snaking down the slopes of Mount Radu. A peachy smoke cloud hung over the mountain, lit by the flames. The black silhouettes of buildings blocked some of his view of the fire, as if they were barring the way from destruction.

They reached Dacre just after the morning bells the next day. The majority of Wilek's party went around the city to set up camp on the east side. Wilek would meet them there tomorrow evening. He kept ten men with him in the city, including Kal, Harton, and Dendrick.

Dacre itself had remained unscathed from the fires. Though the mountain still smoldered, the wind had shifted in the night, and the smoke was lighter than it had been. They headed straight for The Crooked House, the most reputable inn in Dacre and the place Wilek always stayed when he passed through. He looked forward to sleeping on the soft feather bed in the upper suite.

This early, the inn was fairly empty. Dendrick set off to notify the governor of their arrival. Wilek sent Kal to look for mantics who might translate the rune, which left Harton to guard his suite door while he bathed and rested.

The familiarity of the suite set him at ease. The door to the private bedchamber, the worn desk with the wobbly chair and a rough gray robe folded over it, the roundstone fireplace with a steaming iron bathtub waiting before it—everything just where it was supposed to be.

Wilek relaxed in the warm water, wondering over the condition of Farway, if young Lord Estin's message was true, and if it was, what that would mean for Armania in the form of displaced people, lost resources, and the myriad of end-times prophecies that would rage. Many would think it the Five Woes, come at last. Could it be? Wilek allowed himself to consider it. Surely not.

His thoughts drifted to Lebetta and the rune and how he might be able to find a translation. He tried to relax, but his mind refused, so he finished his bath and put on the gray robe. He may as well eat something and dress to meet the governor.

Wilek opened the door and stepped into the hallway, empty but for Harton and a woman. His backman was holding a maid up against the wall with his body, his mouth pressed to hers. The girl whimpered, turned her head, squirmed, got her hand free, and tried to push Harton back, but he grabbed her wrist and pinned it against the wall, murmuring softly in a language Wilek did not understand.

"Harton. Is this how you guard my door?"

Harton fell back from the woman, who instantly fled down the hall and stairs. "Your Highness, good midday. The maid came to ask if you were hungry."

"And you didn't see fit to inquire of me?"

"I was just about to."

"Yes, it looked like it. If I give you a task, can you manage it without stumbling over some woman on the way and forgetting?"

"Of course, Your Highness."

"I would, indeed, like some food. Send Dendrick to me as well."

"Yes, Your Highness." Harton strode down the hall, leather armor creaking.

Wilek watched him, eyes narrowed. It occurred to him how little he knew his backman. The fact that Harton had been caught shirking his duties while forcing himself on a woman who had a message to deliver to Wilek, that he showed no remorse whatsoever . . . Wilek would have to consult Kal. He hated to think of finding yet another backman—people would believe the position cursed!—but he needed a man he could trust. He was no longer certain he could trust Agmado Harton.

Wilek met with Governor Albak in a room Dendrick and the innkeeper's staff had prepared on the ground floor. The governor of Dacre had a face like a cabbage, all wrinkles and folds. He spoke in a harsh whisper, but that might have been due to the smoke.

"Always pleased to speak with you, Highness." Though his narrowed eyes and guarded expression belied his words. "How can I be of service to the throne?"

"By telling me how you fare. Are the fires a threat to the city? Have you many casualties?"

The governor relaxed a bit. "Fire never reached the city. Wind blew it north. Over three dozen homes in the hill villages were lost. One old hermit burned with his house. No other casualties to report, though the entire population is afflicted by the smoke. We all might sound as if we're on our death boats, but the physicians assure me it will clear when the fires do."

"That's excellent news," Wilek said. "Have you seen any mantics around Dacre?"

"Mantics? Never seen any of them, though we had some Magonians pass by the outskirts of the city. Sent my sheriff after them, but he found no trail."

Uneasiness crept upon Wilek. "Which way were they headed?"

"West, toward Canden," the governor said.

Wilek and Kal exchanged glances. The Magonians could be headed to Everton.

"If they have mantics in their group, they could hide their trail," Kal said.

"Suppose that's true," the governor said.

"Thank you, Governor Albak," Wilek said. "I'll leave five men behind. Four to track the Magonians and one to work with you. He'll make a list of your needs, and when we stop on our way back, I'll take your concerns to Everton and the rosâr."

The governor bowed. "Much appreciated, Your Highness."

"See that no need is neglected," Wilek said. "The people are my top concern."

The next morning, just after the dawn bells, Wilek and his remaining men met up with the other forty and renewed their journey. Over the next few days, they passed an endless trail of bruised and battered refugees headed toward Dacre. Most were caked in dirt or mud. Some smelled of sewage, some limped, some wore arm slings, some carried packs or cauldrons, some pulled carts, some had mules or camels laden with belongings.

All were looking for a new home.

When Wilek passed camps along the road, he sent Dendrick or Kal to question the people. The reports were eerily similar:

"The ground fell out from under me."

"The whole field caved in."

"Everything sank to the Lowerworld."

"The floor collapsed."

"The ground gave way."

"It was like a trapdoor opened up beneath me."

"The Five Woes for sure. The gods are done with us."

They came across a weeping man, caked in mud. "Couldn't find my family," he said. "Dug as long as I could, but the mud took everything."

"What do you mean, mud?" Wilek asked.

"The ground fell clean away in places," the man said, "but most of the city drowned in a bog of sinksand. Swallowed even the temple."

Swallowed the temple.

They continued on. Wilek had never fully doubted young Lord Estin's word, but at the same time, he hadn't fully believed it either. But to hear the panic and sorrow in these people's voices . . . to see their shocked expressions . . . to witness their tears of loss. Something dire had happened in Farway. Whatever it was, it chilled Wilek's soul.

Midmorning on the tenth day they came to the fork that led to Farmman Geffray's land, and Wilek sent the majority of his group on with Dendrick to announce his arrival. He, Kal, and Harton rode ahead to see what was left of the city.

In the past the temple spire was the first thing anyone saw when nearing Farway, but Wilek saw no sign of a city on the horizon at all. He thought they should have come to the city gatehouse by now. In Armania every city gate was the same: two round stone towers on either side of a pointed arch with a statue of Rosâr Echad standing beside the right tower and a set of guards manning an open iron gate. All they saw was barrenness until they came to a post jammed into the middle of the road. A leather sign nailed to it was burned with the following text:

Go no farther.
What once was Farway is no more.

Wilek dismounted and stepped slowly past the sign. A dozen paces ahead the road fell away, like the cliff edge of a canyon. Leagues ahead and to both sides, a gaping chasm had opened up where the city of Farway had once stood. Craggy walls of sediment stretched down some ten levels deep to a muddy bog. The occasional bubble of dirty water grew and popped, like a cauldron at slow boil. Wilek saw no sign of the temple spire or the city gates. Muddy lumps might have been stone walls, pillars, or roofs, but there was no way to tell.

"Holy gods," Harton muttered.

Kal grabbed Wilek's arm just above the elbow. "Keep back from the edge, Your Highness, in case the ground is soft."

Wilek took a step back. "If I wasn't seeing it with my own eyes . . . How could this be? Where did it all go?"

"Underground?" Harton suggested.

Clearly. "But where did the underground go?" Wilek asked.

"Into the ream?" Kal said of the subterranean freshwater rivers.

"Which could be why the wells are dry." Standing here raised an army of gooseflesh on Wilek's arms. He had seen enough. They mounted and headed for Farmman Geffray's land.

As they backtracked, Wilek noticed other things. Cracks in the ground, fractured cisterns that were dried up, and huge puddles flooded with muddy water.

"The Lowerworld has been doing a lot of rearranging lately," Harton said.

"So it seems," Wilek said, wishing he knew why.

They arrived at Geffray's farm. If Wilek hadn't known a disaster had taken place, he might have thought this the location of a festival or tournament by the number of people, though most were dressed in rags. Tents were everywhere, ranging from fine quality to bedsheets tacked against overturned wagons. Beyond the farm in a distant field, Wilek could see the sweep of regulation blue army tents that his men had raised. He was glad they had thought to stay out of the people's way.

At the farmhouse a guard immediately escorted them inside. They were led to a room where Dendrick was sitting at a table covered in scrolls with young Lord Estin and a middle-aged man.

Dendrick stood and announced Wilek. "His Royal Highness, Wilek-Sâr Hadar, the First Arm, the Dutiful."

"Lord Estin," Wilek said.

"Your Highness, thank you for coming," Lord Estin said.

He and the stranger stood and bowed, both eyeing Kal's scars warily. Estin was near Trevn's age, with the bony shoulders and stretched limbs of a boy growing too quickly into a man. Dark circles rimmed bloodshot eyes.

"This is Elderman Raeden." The boy gestured to his associate. "We are the last of the official government of Farway. The others were lost when the city . . . fell. Won't you sit and join us?"

Wilek and Kal sat across the table from the other three.

"How many casualties?" Wilek asked.

"Impossible to know for certain," Estin said. "Elderman Raeden has compiled several lists. One naming bodies that have been claimed, another for those who were seen, um, drowning. Do you have the total casualties, Elderman?"

Elderman Raeden reached across the table and riffled through some scrolls. He found what he was looking for and unrolled it. "At last count that list totals nine hundred and forty-three souls."

Wilek's heart sank. "That many?"

"I'm afraid so, Your Highness. We also started a list of those reported missing. That total is . . ." Raeden picked up another scroll and read from it. "Three thousand two hundred and seventeen, but we suspect it's truly much greater."

Greater than four thousand, lost. "What was the population of Farway?" Wilek asked.

"Last census was after the war," Raeden said. "At that time the population of Farway was eight thousand two hundred forty-two. It's grown some since, not a lot, mind, but . . ."

"Do you have a list of survivors?" Wilek asked.

"No," Raeden said. "We do have a list of over four hundred orphans."

Wilek pulled out a chair across the table from Estin and sat, shocked by the magnitude of what had happened here. "You must have some guess at the total living and dead."

Estin nodded. "My guess is that sixty to seventy percent of our population perished in the, uh . . . Gods!" Estin rubbed his eyes. "I still don't know what to call it."

"They're called fall-ins where I'm from," Harton said. "Small ones are fairly common."

"And you're from?" Estin asked.

"Rurekau, originally."

"What?" Wilek said, straightening in his chair. "Kal said you were from Highcliff."

"Trained in Highcliff, Your Highness," Harton said. "Not born there."

Wilek met Kal's gaze and could tell from the set of the man's jaw that he hadn't known that either.

"A fall-in, then," Lord Estin said. "A fall-in pulled our fair city into the Lower-world."

"What are you dealing with now?" Wilek asked. "What are your plans?"

"This morning we were focused on recovering survivors, but I think we've given up hope of finding any more," Estin said. "So now we'll focus on getting the survivors medical attention and temporary shelter. Once everyone has somewhere to go, we'll try to place orphans into families."

"Children are vulnerable," Raeden said. "A guard patrol stumbled onto a slaver headed for Raine with a caravan of a dozen children. We arrested him, but who knows what else is hidden in the chaos."

"We need to dig new cisterns," Estin said. "We're quickly running out of water."

"And we'll have to appoint a new sheriff to sort out the hundreds of fights over animals and equipment that people helped themselves to or mistakenly claimed as their own," Raeden said.

"After that, we'll think about relocating and rebuilding," Estin said. "But I don't know where we could rebuild or if we should. I had hoped the rosâr would advise me." Estin met Wilek's gaze, looking every bit his young age.

"I will advise you in his absence," Wilek said. "That is why I've come."

Lord Estin sighed. "I'm incredibly thankful. As the youngest son, I wasn't groomed to rule."

"You seem to be handling it well," Wilek said.

"Elderman Raeden has done most of it," Lord Estin said.

"I hope you can see that is not the case," Raeden said. "This young man has saved hundreds of lives with his quick thinking. Mikreh blessed us all when he spared him."

"Where were you when it happened?" Wilek asked the boy.

"Walking across the practice field. I don't remember falling. But I woke up with my face in a pool of mud, still gripping my waster. I don't know the man who pulled me out, but we did our best to help others. There was little we could do. We watched a house sink under the mud with people trapped inside, screaming. It was terrible to watch and be helpless. Elderman Raeden was outside the city."

"I was evicting tenants from some nearby farmland," Raeden said. "Ironic, isn't it? Today there are seven families in that house, including the one I evicted. I was inside when the shaker came—just a gentle one. I bid the family good-day and headed back to the city. There I found a mob of people congregated outside the city gates. Over their heads I could see the temple spire tip sideways. I pushed to the front and found men with shovels and picks, breaking up fallen walls and hauling the bricks, branches, furniture—anything they could find—trying to make bridges so people could crawl out, but the mud kept sucking everything down."

Wilek had no words. He could not even imagine what these men had lived through.

After a long moment of silence, Estin stood. "You must be hungry. Let me show you the dining hall."

Wilek followed Estin to a room in the back of the farmhouse. It must have once been the front sitting room, as it had a fireplace and tapestries on the walls. Three long tables had been crammed inside and were packed with people. The walls were also lined with people, some sitting, some standing, all holding a bowl or chunk of bread.

"I'm terribly embarrassed, Your Highness," Estin said. "I assure you there is plenty to eat. I'll have a maid bring a tray to the study. You and your officers are welcome to eat there. Elderman Raeden and I can clear the table and—"

"Do not think of it," Wilek said. "We brought food enough with us. We will eat at our camp."

Estin bowed. "Thank you, Your Highness. You're a good man."

Such a compliment from one so young made Wilek smile. "As are you, Lord Estin."

Wilek made plans to meet Estin and Raeden first thing in the morning to start on the recovery efforts, and then he, Kal, Harton, and Dendrick left the farmhouse.

The makeshift camps of refugees ran one into another across the entire field, creating a web of guy ropes and clotheslines between tents and wagons that would be easier for Wilek to go around. Tired from days in the saddle, he chose to walk Foxaro. His men followed suit with their mounts. They took their time, regarding the people along the edge of the encampment.

Sorrow creased every face. Not one child was giggling or running about. These people had suffered a harrowing ordeal.

And Father wanted him to make sacrifices to Barthos. Such a thing was unthinkable.

"Agmado Harton!" a woman yelled.

A pretty young woman stood holding a child's hand a few steps from a crowded campfire. She walked toward them, glaring all the while at Harton, and nudged the child toward him. "Here's the result of taking your pleasure, you foul dallier."

Before Harton could respond, two men stood up from the campfire, and Kal whisked Wilek away. "Best leave Harton to them, Your Highness. That's no place for you. Dendrick, take care of the horses."

Wilek and Kal walked on toward their camp. "That child looked at least eight years old," Wilek said, glancing back. "Harton would only have been eleven."

"I'm beginning to think Harton has a habit of bending the truth," Kal said.

Wilek sighed at that. "You think him older?"

"Don't know what to think," Kal said.

At Wilek's tent Kal assigned several guards to the door and went back for Harton. Wilek ate his evening repast alone and pondered the grievous things he had seen and heard. He was still eating when Kal returned with Harton. The backman had a bloody nose and his tabard had been ripped down the front.

Wilek wasted no time with his accusations. "You are older than you claimed, Harton, and a Rurekan citizen."

This seemed to throw Harton off guard. "Uh . . . yes, sir. I wanted into the King's Guard, but you have to be under twenty to join the ranks, unless there's a war. No one asked about my citizenship."

Wilek gestured to Harton's ripped tabard. "What happened back there?"

"Kalenek cannot hold a sword," Harton said, sneering at the shield. "There is something wrong with his—"

Kal cuffed Harton's ear. "He's talking about you, boy."

"Are her allegations true?" Wilek asked.

Harton shrugged. "I passed through these parts years ago and paid her well. Don't whores take precautions not to get with child?"

The servant girl in Dacre came to mind. Wilek wanted none of this. He had never been concerned with what his men did in their spare time, but if it reflected poorly on him . . . "Regardless," he said, "the child is yours?"

"She can have him," Harton said. "What would I do with a child?"

Wilek released a slow breath. "I don't think she fears you will take the boy away. I think she hopes you will assist her in raising him."

"I can't raise a child. I told her the same."

"If you don't want children, you should take more care where you plow fields," Kal said.

"No, sir," Harton said, angrily now. "Women who bed men for coin should know how to take care of such . . . matters. It's not my problem."

"Typical Rurekan morals," Kal mumbled.

Harton glared at Kal. "You dare speak of morals?"

"Enough!" Wilek set his jaw, furious that he had hired a Rurekan as his backman. "In light of the suffering this community has endured and this woman's public display and how it may reflect on House Hadar's reputation, you will give her money to provide for the child. Do so in public so that witnesses will see it happen."

"But I brought no coin," Harton said. "Didn't think I'd need it."

"I will loan you a gold," Wilek said.

Harton's mouth gaped. "But that's two week's wages!"

"Fair point," Wilek said. "I will loan you two. This is not a game, Harton. I will not allow your behavior to taint my retinue. Do you understand me?"

Harton lowered his head. "Yes, Your Highness."

"Dismissed," Wilek said.

Harton stormed out of the tent.

Wilek fell back in his chair. "What say you, Kal?"

"About Harton or Farway?"

"Yes."

Kal took a deep breath. "Harton has become increasingly worrisome. He is late most mornings because he is not alone. He moves through women quickly. And there have been some altercations between some of the serving women in Castle Everton."

"He has hurt them?"

"No, the serving women fight with each other over him. He's as virile as Prince Janek."

Wonderful. "I have no time for this."

"Don't worry yourself with Harton," Kal said. "I'll handle him. What about Farway? What do you think of Lord Estin?"

"Remarkable, for one so young," Wilek said. "Remarkable regardless of age. He is more organized than Dendrick. I only hope I can offer him something he has yet to accomplish."

"One so young simply wants the assurance he is doing the right thing," Kal said. "Hold his hand for a week and you will have a devoted man for life."

"A better man I could not buy."

"He might make a good backman," Kal said.

Wilek chuckled. "Farway needs him more than I do." He sat silently for a moment, lost in thought until an idea presented itself. "Will you do something for me, Kal?"

"If I can."

Wilek withdrew a roll of leather from his pocket and held it out. "Take the rune sketch into Magonia and find a translation." He was asking a lot. Kal would not only be temporarily abandoning his role as Wilek's shield, he would be illegally entering Magonia and returning to the place that had scarred him during the war. "You hesitate. Think no more on it. I should not have asked."

"You are my sâr," Kal said. "You can ask anything you want of me. You can demand it."

"I would never demand something like this, not of you. It would almost relieve me if you said no. If something happened to you while chasing after a mystery that might not be solvable . . . I would not forgive myself."

"Every mystery has an answer," Kal said. "We must learn who is plotting against you. I will go, but I require coin and a backman. *Not* Harton."

Wilek grinned. "Name the man and he is yours."

"Novan Heln," Kal said. "He is young enough to pass as a backman and light-skinned enough to not stand out in Magonia."

"A wise choice," Wilek said, wondering if Novan might make a good backman if it came to that. "What Harton said about you not being able to hold a sword. What did he mean?"

Kal sighed heavily, looking at his boots. "They were beating him badly when I arrived. I drew my blade and scared them off. All but one. He and I crossed swords. I nicked him, and he ran. Then I lost my grip. Only the women and Harton were still there, but . . . it was embarrassing, Your Highness."

"It happens," Wilek said. "At least you had already chased off the men. Might have lost you otherwise."

"That thought crossed my mind as well," Kal said.

"Leave in the morning," Wilek said. "I want you back as soon as possible."

Kal nodded and left to make the necessary preparations. Wilek sat alone in his tent with his thoughts, surrounded by death. He was tired of death. A sâr should be strong, should lead with courage and purpose. His father lived in fear, and Wilek wanted to be different—had to be. For too long he had been complacent, unsure. In coming to Farway he had saved these survivors from the horror of human sacrifice. He had made a difference here.

Too bad the people could not choose the Heir.

Something grew within him. Like a father protecting his child, Wilek must protect his people from the evil that continued to rise against them. Whether that be from Janek, an assassin, their own king, or the wrath of an immortal god.

Whether or not he ever became Heir or king, he would not let evil win.

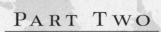

PART TWO

THE
HEIR WAR

TREVN

In those days the root of Arman will be destroyed and usher in the end
of all things. There will be mourning and weeping throughout the land.
Brother will turn against brother, and their swords will dash each other to
pieces. There will be earthquakes, floods, mountain fires, sinksand, and
rocks that fall from the sky. And Armania, glory of the Five Realms, beauty
of the gods' eyes, will no longer be the head of all things.

Out of Magon will come one who prospers by deceit. He will crush
the heads of those who stand against him. Therefore the gods will raise
up for you many prophets. Their words will save the obedient and deliver
peace throughout the realms.

—Rôb prophecy from the prophet Greela, House Hadar 468

T his prophecy is partly responsible for the duration of the Centenary
War," Father Tomek said. "Can you tell me why?"

Easily. "My forefathers were afraid that compromise with the mother realms
might bring about the fall of Armania," Trevn said.

"Correct. Now read me the Kabaran prophecy and look for differences."
Trevn read from the second tablet.

Behold, I say to you, though the root of Arman will be destroyed, peace
shall come between mother and father, and the two will be reconciled.
And you, Magonia, though you are small among the five clans, from you
will come a deliverer who will rule over all. He will crush the skulls of his

enemies, turn their citadels to dust, and Magonia will become the ruler of nations.

—Kabaran prophecy from the prophet Theria, Magonia 4

"What do you notice?" Father Tomek asked.

Trevn pushed the tablets together and studied them. "They both talk of peace but in different ways. Rôb says a deceiver will come but prophets will bring peace. The Kabaran prophecy talks of a deliverer. Perhaps the same deceiver referenced in the Rôb prophecy?"

"Perhaps. Both are called the Root Prophecy. Why are they different?"

"They were spoken by different prophets," Trevn said, which made him think of Filkin Yohthehreth. "Why are no new prophecies recorded by my father's prophets?"

"They record them, but none have come to pass. There hasn't been a true prophet born in Armania in over 120 years."

A bold statement. "So, my father's prophets are pretenders? Rogedoth's as well?"

"It's not a popular view, but it's mine. That's partly why I'll never sit on the Wisean Council."

"You should." Father's advisors were imbeciles.

"I'm not good at telling a man what he wants to hear. Have you finished your pages?"

"Yes. I finished early today. I have plans and didn't want to have to hurry."

"I praise you for your forethought," Father Tomek said. "You are dismissed."

Trevn left the classroom. Cadoc was waiting in the hallway, looking a bit pale.

"Are we still doing this, Your Highness?"

"Of course." Trevn grinned and sprinted away. "Try to keep up!"

Trevn and Cadoc lay side by side on the roof of the carriage. Cadoc kept shifting, which made his scabbard scrape against the wood.

"Hold still," Trevn said. "You'll give us away."

"Let it be known that I dislike this plan. I suspect Miss Mielle will too."

"That shows how little you know Miss Mielle," Trevn said.

The soft voices of Lady Zeroah and Miss Mielle drifted up to his ears. Trevn listened to them climb into the carriage. The doors clicked shut. He had already asked Hawley not to signal him today. The man climbed up beside the driver, winked at Trevn, and they were off.

A thrill flamed within Trevn's chest. Today he would know whether or not Mielle Allard was a Renegade.

Trevn kept his head down until they passed the protestors at the gatehouse. Then he wasted no time. "I'm going in."

Cadoc nodded and braced himself: one hand over the far edge of the carriage, the other held out to Trevn.

Trevn took hold and slipped over the side. He fell fast, legs flailing a bit before finding the open window. "Lower me!" he yelled, which Cadoc did, little by little.

The women screamed, which made Trevn grin. They were hitting his legs too, as if he were some kind of villain. Once his backside rested on the window ledge, he let go of Cadoc's hand and slid inside, landing in a crouch on the floor of the carriage.

The screaming ceased.

Lady Zeroah and Miss Mielle were sitting across from one another against the far wall of the carriage, watching him, wide-eyed.

"Good midday, ladies," Trevn said, quite pleased to have frightened them.

"Sâr Trevn." Lady Zeroah inclined her head.

Miss Mielle slid down the bench and slapped his shoulder repeatedly. "You reckless madperson!"

Trevn slipped to his knees and grabbed her hands. "Miss Mielle, I promise you I have no intention of marrying or taking concubines or building a harem. Rest assured, my mother will continue to behave poorly and try to run my life, but I will make my own decisions. I realize friendship with me is a risk. I hope it is a risk you will consider taking." He gazed up into her deep brown eyes and pinched his brows into the penitent expression that had always worked on his mother.

Miss Mielle said nothing. Merely stared. The carriage rattled around them, horses' hooves clomping, tack jangling.

Then finally: "Kal says I should avoid you."

Did he? Kalenek Veroth's caution was to be applauded. "And you have! Just look what I had to do to get a word with you. Will you forgive me for my part in upsetting you?"

She glanced to Lady Zeroah and back, stiff posture wilting. "I forgive you, Your Highness."

Trevn grinned and slid up to sit beside her. "Will you come with me? To the roofs?"

Her eyes doubled in size. "I mustn't abandon Lady Zeroah. Besides, who would chaperone us?"

"Cadoc is with me. And Lady Zeroah has Hawley and the kitchen maids, isn't that right, lady?"

"Indeed, Your Highness," Lady Zeroah said. "Do go, if you like, Mielle. But be careful."

Trevn pulled Miss Mielle to the window. "I will bring her to the almshouse in two hours, lady."

Miss Mielle gripped the sides of the window, looked out and up. "How will we get up there?"

"Turn your back to the window and lean out. I will lift you, and Cadoc will pull you up."

At this moment most women would have refused. Not Miss Mielle. She spun right around and nearly crawled out herself.

Sands, he liked her.

Unfortunately, when Hawley saw what was happening, he slowed the carriage to a crawl, which greatly minimized the risk and Trevn's thrill. Once Miss Mielle lay on the roof between Trevn and Cadoc, the carriage resumed its regular speed.

"We are approaching the drop to the Sink," Trevn said. "It will become quite bumpy."

"Is that where we jump?" Miss Mielle asked.

"After the turn where the cobblestone ends."

"Don't be afraid, Miss Mielle," Cadoc said.

"Oh, I'm not afraid," she said, eyes wide and eager.

The carriage jolted as it hit the dirt road of the Sink and rattled over the pothole-filled road. Trevn pushed to his knees, eyeing the distance to the bakery. Miss Mielle mimicked his actions.

"See that long brown roof?" Trevn pointed ahead. "The road narrows there. The carriage will slow to avoid hitting the buildings. That's where we jump."

Trevn went first. The moment his feet made contact with the roof, he spun around to watch Miss Mielle, who was already hurtling toward him, her hindrance of a skirt clutched in one fist at her hip. He skipped aside to catch her, but she landed fine, skidding a bit on the soot. Cadoc landed hard, weapons jangling. He stumbled but quickly caught his balance.

Seeing them both safe, Trevn turned and ran. Over the inns, down the sloped roof of the chandler's shop, up to the bathhouse, then to Mama's Shelter, and down to the leatherworks. He bypassed the leap over the alley and went Hinck's way, which was longer but safer. Roof to roof he ran until finally climbing onto the red-and-brown striped roof of Thalassa's Temple, where he sat in the center.

Miss Mielle sank to her knees beside him, studying the view. Several tendrils of hair had escaped the knot of braids on her head and framed her face. "It's wonderful up here."

Trevn pointed. "That used to be Cape Waldemar. The earthquake pulled it under the sea." He fished his grow lens from his hipsack and passed it to Miss Mielle.

She squinted through the lens and sighed. "I lived there as a child. When my parents died, Kal and Livy moved in to take care of us."

"I'm sorry," he said, wondering what had happened later that forced them to live in the Sink.

Miss Mielle shook off her sorrow with a flip of her hair. "I want to go there and get a closer look. Not today, but soon."

So did Trevn. And now he had reason besides his own curiosity. "Next week perhaps? The rest of this week will be consumed with my ageday ball." He paused. "Would you come?"

"To a sâr's ball?" She shook her head. "That wouldn't be proper."

"It would if I invited Lady Zeroah."

She gave him that slow smile that twisted his insides into a knot. "I will convey your invitation to Lady Zeroah. I'm sure she will accept."

Trevn released a careful breath, not wanting her to know how much she intimidated him. "And will you dance with me there?"

She flushed, but her eyes lit with joy. "I won't refuse, though won't it upset your mother?"

Oh, it would. Trevn was counting on it.

Trevn had barely taken his seat in the great hall for dinner when his mother attacked. "You were seen walking with a woman in the Sink. Who was she?"

Just like that, his happiness over a perfect day with Miss Mielle vanished. "If your spies were unable to identify her, perhaps you should employ better ones."

"Proud talk brings a rod of discipline. I know who she was." Mother glanced pointedly to Wilek's table where Miss Mielle and Lady Zeroah were sitting with Queen Brelenah and Grandmother. "Really, Trevn. After what happened with Shessy Wallington, how can you be so careless?"

Trevn picked at a wedge of cheese. "Do you know how rare it is to find a girl willing to run the roofs?" He doubted there was another in all of Armania who would.

"A sâr should not run the roofs at all. Now, about your ball, I invited two groups of young ladies and requested they dress appropriately. Potential brides will be dressed in Hadar blue. Potential concubines in pink."

Of all the . . . "Father Tomek says a priest should avoid concubines." Nor would a Renegade take one, curious or not.

"Concubines are the fashion for sârs," his mother said. "I won't have people mocking you for not following the trend. Your reputation is everything."

Trevn agreed. But the core of a Renegade's reputation was to oppose everything fashionable and conventional.

"The night of your ball you will choose your favorite for a wife. I will choose as well, and hopefully Mikreh will bless us with agreement. I care less about your choices of concubines. Pick ten. That should please your father."

"Ten!" Trevn barely knew what to do with one woman. "Not even Janek has ten concubines."

"Which is why you should have more. Listen to your mother. Now, remember, not everyone is able to attend."

Trevn rested his elbows on the table and fisted his hands together over his mouth.

"For a wife, do seriously consider Princess Saria."

"Saria is like a sister to me." A pesky sister.

"And you must also think of your cousin Mihah for a concubine. She will be better trained than most. No realm instructs women in the art of lovemaking like Rurekau. It still shocks me that the rosâr has cast me aside."

Trevn dropped his head into his hands. His day had gone from blissful to nightmarish in too short a time. His only comfort was imagining the look on his mother's face when he chose Miss Mielle for the first dance at his ball.

KALEΠEK

Five days' ride southeast from what had once been Farway brought Kal and Novan Heln within sight of the border. The southern crack of the great Smoke Canyon stretched out before them like a gaping wound. Before it, the city of Raine. The Rôb temple spire pierced the skyline. Beyond, the Cross Canyon Bridges looked like nothing more than a few gray hairs coiling over the golden chasm.

Not since the war had Kal come this far east. The gleam of the yeetta's obsidian knife flashed in his memory. He touched his gloved hand to his face and pushed the nightmare down.

The second largest city in Armania, Raine stretched several leagues across at its widest point. It stank of rot and sewage without a nearby sea and waterwheel to flush clean its canals. The tolls and taxes on the bridge brought in a tremendous amount of wealth for Lord Edekk—and crime, since he kept most of the money in his own coffers.

Kal stopped to buy them each a change of clothing so they could travel out of uniform. He took a room at the Cracked Cistern, a sandstone inn owned by a man who dealt in impossible situations. The tavern on the ground floor was packed. Kal preferred to have his back against the wall, which afforded him the best view of potential threats, but the only empty table was in the center. He claimed one of the four chairs. Novan sat across from him.

A bowl boy approached their table. "Hungry or thirsty?"

"Both," Kal said. "And I'd like to see Eenar."

The boy frowned. "Two coppers for stew, four for mutton, one for ale. Pay first."

Kal withdrew a ten-penny from his coin purse and handed it to the boy. "Two muttons, two ales. Eenar?"

"I'll see if he's in." The boy scurried away.

Kal scanned the room, uncomfortable with his back to so many. Most of the patrons were in groups of two. A man in a Magonian kasah with a knife on his belt sat alone. A shriek of laugher pulled Kal's glance to behind Novan. A woman in a group of six was cackling, head thrown back in utter delight. Her companions laughed as well, though it seemed more at her expense.

Movement in the doorway captured Kal's attention: a man in torterus-shell armor with a jagged scar across his cheek that made Kal's scars tingle. Eenar.

Kal stood. "Wait here," he told Novan and made his way around the tables. Eenar stepped into an alcove that held a shrine to Mikreh. Kal followed him.

"Didn't expect to see you again," Eenar said.

Kal hadn't intended to return. "I need a pastone into Magonia. Or a mantic. Whichever is easier."

"You won't find a mantic this side of the border. The hazak monitor them."

"The mantic needn't be practicing. I seek a rune translation."

"I couldn't find such a person without asking my Magonian contacts."

Kal was afraid of that. "I'd rather not call attention to myself. A pastone, then."

"It'll cost you a gold."

Kal withdrew the coin from his purse and handed it to Eenar. "Anything going on in Magonia I should know about?"

"I hear the Chieftess and her court are in the father realms."

The news rocked Kal. Had the party seen near Dacre included the Magonian Chieftess? Headed to Everton to fulfill her dubious prophecy? "She passed through Raine?"

Eenar shook his head. "Went around the Ebro Tip. King Jorger should take more care with his eastern border."

Kal would have to send word to Wilek. "Any idea why she'd break the treaty?"

"I put nothing past a Magonian female. They—"

"Sir Kalenek!" Novan's voice.

Kal stepped from the alcove in time to see a man in a red uniform grab Novan by the front of his tunic.

Kal dodged around the tables and wedged himself between Novan and his attacker, who was half a head taller than Kal. "Is there a problem?"

The man's eyes flitted over Kal's scarred face. "He was asking about runes."

"Why is that your business?" Kal asked.

"I am hazak. We guard the border from mantics."

"Do you sense magic in me or my companion?" Kal asked.

The man hesitated.

"We're not mantics. Look." Kal held up his hand, baring his shield ring. "We're on the rosâr's business. We seek a mantic murderer."

"There are no mantics in Raine," the man said. "We see to that." He stomped away.

The bowl boy arrived then, holding a tray. He transferred two plates of mutton and two mugs of ale to the tabletop.

Kal glanced across the room to the alcove. Eenar had gone. He fell back into his chair and pulled his mutton close. "I do the questioning, Novan. You do what I say. That clear?"

"Yes, sir." Novan sat down and started eating without question. Kal liked that about him. Harton talked far too much for his liking.

They ate in silence. Just as Kal swallowed the last of his ale, the bowl boy returned and set a small stone on the table. It was engraved with the insignia of Magonia on the top. Kal nodded at the boy and picked up the stone, flipped it in his palm, and verified the insignia of King Echad on the back.

He pocketed it. "We leave at dawn."

Crossing the bridge at night was prohibited, so Kal and Novan rose with the dawn bells. They dressed in plainclothes, which included head scarves to keep off the sun, and then it was down to the stables to rent camels for the journey into the desert. The stableman taught them the commands to make the camels sit, stand, walk, run, and stop. Kal's was a creamy-white female, Novan's a golden male. They mounted and set off for the bridge.

"They're so high, sir." Novan clutched the saddle horn with both hands. "Why can't we take the horses?"

"I don't like the height either," Kal said. "But camels are more practical in the desert and don't need as much water. Plus our fine horses would stand out. I aim to blend in."

Even this early the line at the border was considerable. As they waited, Kal studied the zigzagging bridges with trepidation. Fifteen stone arches connected a series of buttes and mesas across the narrowest section of the canyon, which was still a two-league distance. A camel could walk two leagues in less than two hours, but combine that distance with the awkward staircases, paralyzing height, and two-way traffic, and it would take half the day to cross.

The gatekeeper noted their pastone without comment and waved them under the entry arch. The Smoke Canyon gaped below, a half league deep, its floor a wilderness of rock crags, hoodoos, and cracks. Jagged rock walls displayed layers of sediment in a rainbow of earth tones. River holes gaped like pores across the rock face and spilled water in stripes down the wall.

The first bridge ended on a butte. The guard at the bridge house inspected their pastone and sent them on. A set of long, shallow stone steps twisted down the butte to the start of the next bridge. Kal and Novan came to a standstill behind two men wrestling a team of oxen and a cart down the steps.

Kal sighed, seeing no way around.

"I'll try to help them." Novan gave the command for his camel to sit.

Helping had not occurred to Kal, which shamed him. In his years of royal service, he'd grown used to having the right of way.

The men readily accepted Novan's assistance. The boy took hold of the back of the cart, and the three of them got the animals moving. At the start of the next bridge, the men insisted that Novan and Kal go around.

Bridge after bridge, they made their way across the canyon. Novan's camel had a tendency to run, and the boy was constantly trying to slow him down. Halfway across the eighth segment, they passed under a stone arch topped with a statue of the goddess Magon.

Kal shivered. They had entered Magonia.

Novan reached the ninth bridge house ahead of Kal, who arrived in time to catch the Magonian guard trying to charge Novan to enter.

One look at Kal's sword and scarred face and the man changed his mind.

"I bet the oxen men won't be so fortunate," Novan said as they rode on.

Yes, well, sometimes being horribly disfigured came in handy.

As they neared the other side, the small sections of stairs on the buttes and mesas began to go up, and Novan fell behind. He eventually had to get off his camel and bribe it with carrots to make the climb. By the final bridge, Kal had also gotten down to walk. They managed to drag the camels to the other side, where they could see the city of Hebron stretched out before them. It didn't look all that different from Raine, except for the abundance of red-tile roofs and the gold-clad spire of the Temple of Magon that gleamed like a star in the setting sun.

"It's beautiful," Novan said.

Kal merely grunted and led his camel toward the bridge house and solid ground. The guard there took one look at Kal's pastone and waved them through. They mounted their camels and rode into the city of Hebron.

"Where do we look first, sir?" Novan asked.

"In Lifton," Kal said.

"That's another week's journey. Why not look here?"

"Hebron devours ignorant foreigners," Kal said. "It's dangerous enough to ask questions in daylight; it's suicidal to ask them at night. If we keep moving, we look like men on a mission, and men on a mission aren't helpless."

After one stop at the public well to water the camels and fill their jugs, they rode quickly for the city gates. Not until they were outside did Kal slow his pace.

"Will our water last until Lifton?" Novan asked.

"No, but we can get more. Cisterns are usually dry out here so we'll watch for stepwells."

"What are those?"

"Doorways to the underground rivers of the ream."

"Won't people be living in them too?"

"Stepwells get a lot of traffic, so people don't tend to linger. If we can't find one, we'll milk ground cones. They grow above the reamways. Their roots are long and deep and transport water to the surface."

"Like a fountain?"

"More like tears. You can fill a jug halfway overnight."

They rode until dark. Kal found a grove of sticky snare that would hide them from the road. The moment Novan dismounted, he collapsed.

"Have you been drinking your water?" Kal asked.

"I'm trying to save it," Novan said.

What were they training the young soldiers these days? "That's a mistake. You need to take small sips every so often. Eating will make you thirstier, so try to wait till we stop. Here are some ground cones. I'll show you how to milk them."

Kal crouched beside the plant with a clay bowl and handkerchief. He cut off the blossom on top, and the stalk instantly began oozing liquid. He sheathed his knife and pushed the stalk over the bowl. It began to drip: *pat, pat, pat.* "That'll take a while. Help me make camp."

They set up a lean-to by hanging one end of a fold of linen on a sticky snare bush and anchoring the other end with rocks. They placed their leather bedrolls inside to keep their bodies off the still-hot sand. Kal took first watch. Novan fell instantly asleep.

Kal woke screaming.

Novan loomed over him, sword drawn. "Sir? What's wrong?"

Kal sucked in a long breath. "Only a dream." It happened all too often. Yeetta warriors carving his face with shards of obsidian. Kal could barely speak of such things without folding in on himself. There was too much buried there.

"Must have been intense." Novan sheathed his sword and kicked the air, growled, and punched his thigh. "I can't feel a thing. That blasted camel was using my leg for a pillow."

Novan's camel lay with its chin on the bedroll. It blinked bulbous brown eyes at Kal.

They packed up camp, which inspired Novan's camel to rise and help. Novan had to continually push the animal aside and finally tied the beast to a nearby cactus. After that the work was quickly done, despite the camel's mournful howling.

Three days later they came to their first stepwell. It was marked by a waist-high wall made of stone, which was the same color as the sand and would have been nearly impossible to see if not for the red wavy lines carved into the side. A set of long, shallow steps descended underground like those of the Cross Canyon Bridge. Novan's camel trotted up to the wall and extended his head over the top.

"Are you thirsty already?" Novan commanded the camel to sit. The moment he dismounted, the camel lurched back to its feet and ran toward the stairs, nearly knocking over Kal.

"Haht, you dumb camel. Haht!" Novan yelled as he chased the animal down the stairs.

"He's fine," Kal yelled after him. "He can't go far."

A great splash rose from below.

Unless he swam the river. Next time they'd have to remove the saddlebags before getting too close to water.

Kal had the opposite problem and had to fight to get his camel down the stairs. They emerged onto a stone slab in an underground cavern and found

Novan's camel knee-deep in the river, kicking up water and making a spectacle of himself. The river spanned about six paces. A group of men stood on a sandbank on the other side, wet from the waist down—muimacs, Kal guessed, by their mismatched clothing.

Kal quickly counted nine men. Four were laughing at the camel. Two were staring at Novan, who was staring back; all eyes narrowed as they regarded each other. A seventh man lay on the ground, dead by the look of his vacant stare. The last two men crouched over him, one pulling off his boots, the other checking his pockets.

"Think they killed him?" Novan whispered.

"Not likely. Muimacs don't kill unless provoked. They're scavengers."

"If they didn't kill him, what did?"

"Oh, any number of things. Or people. Or he could have died of thirst." Though not likely in a stepwell. "He could have been living on that sandbank."

Two more of the muimacs turned back to the task at hand, and between the four of them, they quickly stripped the man to nothing.

"Why take his clothing?" Novan asked.

"The muimacs take everything from the dead. As long as we live, they won't bother us. Help me fill the jugs."

Soon they were riding again. Kal glanced back several times, and he finally noted with relief the dark shapes of the muimacs moving off to the south. *Good.* He'd never liked the idea of being followed by men waiting for him to die.

Wilek

A day shy of two weeks since their arrival at Farmman Geffray's claim, Wilek and his contingent headed back toward Everton, leaving young Lord Estin with a council of trustworthy advisors and a plan to rebuild his barony. As they traveled, Wilek pondered the distant cliffs, still awed that Farway had perished so suddenly. It had never occurred to him that the tunnels and caverns of the ream could collapse. Knowing that any moment the ground might fall, he anxiously watched it . . . the hooves of the horses around him . . . the wagon wheels. He missed having Kal to talk with. Harton had not been his chatty self ever since Wilek had ordered him to pay the woman in Farway.

By the time they reached Dacre, Wilek was eager for the feather bed in his suite. He bathed, ate his fill of hearty stew, and slept the day away, while the majority of his men took a well-earned evening off.

That night Wilek dreamed he was floating. Invisible. He sailed out of his room, past the sleeping guards outside his door, and drifted along the hallway to the stairs. Down he went, gliding on his stomach as if swimming through the air, though his arms hung limply beneath him. Downstairs, dozens of men were carousing in the tavern. Several couples danced before the fireplace to a lutist's song. Harton was one of their number.

The door blew open on a gust of wind, inspiring shrieks and laughter. Before the bowl boy could cross the crowded room to close it, Wilek floated outside.

He sailed through the dark streets of Dacre until he reached a horse harnessed to a cart full of hay. He made a bed for himself in the hay, yawning heavily. The cart rolled forward. As the gentle movement lulled him to sleep, he heard a woman speak.

"*Magon âthâh. Ten lo tardemah.*"

"Wilek."

The voice drew Wilek from the arms of sleep. He opened his eyes to darkness. He was lying on a bed of furs. Moonlight spilled through a hole in the ceiling and painted a diagonal white stripe across a dirt floor. He was in a tent?

Movement in the darkness. A woman dressed in a white gown.

"Who are you?" His voice came out hoarse; he coughed and wished for water.

"Don't you know me, Lek?"

His skin prickled at that voice. She stepped into the beam of moonlight, and her face and posture twisted his heart. "Lebetta?" It couldn't be. He sat up, pushed to his feet, reeled as a wave of dizziness washed over him. "You're not real."

She approached slowly. Her every step, every motion, grabbed him in a sense of familiarity. "I assure you, Lek, I'm flesh and blood."

She sounded like Lebetta. The spicy smell of hyssop smelled like Lebetta. She even had the tiny mole at the corner of her eye. "How . . . ?" His voice broke. Oh, how he missed her. "I saw you dead."

"My mortal life has ended. But Gâzar sent me back. Back to you. For one night. You earned his favor."

"Gâzar? Why?" Wilek paid him no more tribute than any other.

"Does it matter? Would you turn away this gift?" She stepped into his arms and kissed him, trembling.

His mind fogged, and he drew back. "You fuddle my thoughts."

"It's my immortality. Don't be afraid." She kissed him again and whispered, "I love you."

He melted into her, succumbing to the desire she stirred within him. Gâzar had sent her back. He accepted the generous gift, pulled her close.

"No. Don't!" She pulled away, cursed, and muttered foreign words he didn't understand.

Lethargy fell over him like the heat of a summer day. His eyes drooped, and suddenly he was in bed again, the woman who claimed to be Lebetta standing over him, her eyes bright gray.

"Who are you?" he whispered as he drifted to sleep.

When next he woke, it was still dark. He felt confused, heavy. His head pounded as if he had consumed an amphora of wine. He had dreamed. Gâzar had sent Lebetta back to him.

He blinked, examining his surroundings, dismayed to find himself still in a tent. The moon had shifted away from the hole, leaving the glowing orange remains of a campfire the only light. His right hand tingled, as if he had slept on it. He tried to move it, but it was stuck. Somewhere close, a woman was chanting.

"Lebetta?" A foolish thing to say. It had left his mouth before he could think.

"Shh," a woman said. "Go back to sleep."

The voice wasn't Lebetta's. It was unfamiliar, not as husky, and had a faint accent. He blinked rapidly, his focus clearing some. The mystery gray-eyed woman sat beside him, holding his hand. No, she had tied his hand to hers with a thin hemp cord.

"What are you doing?" Wilek tugged his hand, and hers came with it.

"The time has come. Mother must make peace with Father."

She was Magonian. Eyes of a mantic. Slowly his mind began to clear. He pulled his hand again. "Stop this at once. Guards!" No one came. "I command you to—"

She whispered and his voice went mute. He tried again. Nothing. He attempted to sit, but his body wouldn't move either. Gods, what was happening?

The woman continued chanting. The language was familiar. An ancient Armanian dialect. He did his best to understand.

"*Shelno yâdyim rakas.*" Our hands bound.

"*Mopheth rakas am.*" A symbol . . . bound people?

"*Rakas nephesh.*" Bound souls?

Bound? What was she doing? He tried to move, speak, but her spell had left him mute and frozen. He shivered. Breath hissed from his lips. Why was it so cold?

"*Magon âthâh.*" Magon, come.

"*Tsamad shelno yâdim.*" Bind our hands.

"*Qadosh Magon, lâqach hay âz nêzer êmer, pôal . . .*" Holy Magon, take the separate . . . um . . . he searched for the word. Separate deeds? Desires? Will?

"*Dabaq netsach. Bara am ekhad.*" Join forever. Make into one.

Ice pooled in his chest. *Oh, gods. Stop it. Stop now!*

She did. She slipped the cord free without untying the knot. Warmth filled Wilek's body, though not entirely. Coldness lingered inside. She held the cord above him, untangling it. A stone amulet hung from one end. Smooth and green, it looked like jade with a rune carved into the surface of both sides. Two *V*s, facing each other, crossing, with a dot in the center of the diamond they formed.

She put the cord over her head and tucked the amulet into the neckline of her kasah. Bloodred slashes wrapped her hand from where the cord had been. Wilek lifted his own hand, surprised when it obeyed. Indeed, his hand was also covered in red lines. Burns. And the rune had seared its mark in the center of his palm.

The bizarreness of such a ritual cowed him. Charlon was merely glad it was over. Surely such a bond would make things easier.

The thoughts stunned him. He knew her. Knew her name—could feel her. He opened his mouth and found he could speak. "What magic is this?"

"We're soul-bound, you and I." She stood and walked toward the dying fire. "Armanians call it married."

Shock rattled through him. He sat up, looked around. They were alone in the tent. "I didn't agree to marry you."

"In Magonia a woman claims her mate. Binds her soul to his. I mastered you."

"I'm not Magonian."

"That matters not. First you gave me your body. Then you gave me your soul."

A small cry escaped Wilek. "We did nothing but kiss."

"My enchantments have clouded your memory."

He could tell she was lying. But how could he know that? He tried to make sense of it. "You looked like Lebetta. How did you know so much about her? About us?"

"I petitioned Magon. Reached beyond the Veil."

Beyond. "You're a mantic." Mantics communed with the black spirits—with the dead. That this woman had bothered Lebetta in the afterworld filled him with fury. "Did you kill her?"

"Of course not."

"Then what do you want? Is this because of a prophecy?"

She smiled. "My soul-bound reads me well."

"I am not your soul-bound. I am betrothed to another." Lady Zeroah. He had already insulted her by publicly mourning his concubine. How could he possibly explain this?

"Fidelity isn't necessary, Lek, only—"

"*Don't*. Don't ever call me that."

Her gray eyes bulged, horrified. He could feel her emotions. Regret. Fear. She looked down, pursed her lips, fought her guilt. Of what?

She looked at him with a gaze that chilled. "You will give me a child. Then I'll—"

"Guards!" Wilek made to stand, but Charlon lifted her hand and whispered, forcing him back against the furs, again immobile. He whimpered. *Holy gods, what was this?* "Guards!" he screamed as loud as he could.

"They're not here. When in Dacre, the Prince of Armania always stays at The Crooked House. The innkeeper showed me your room. I waited under the bed. Once you slept, I cast a spell to carry you away."

Invisible? Wilek recalled his dream.

"You should rest." She walked to him, leaned down, reached for him.

"Don't," he said, and again felt her horror. Tears welled in her eyes.

She touched the side of his neck. A twinge. He flinched. His throat felt thick. Vision clouded. Eyes fell closed. But his mind remained shocked by all that had taken place.

He had always believed his father would be the one to kill him. Apparently not.

TREVN

Beal dressed Trevn for his ageday ball in a ruffly blue-and-gold tunic Mother had commissioned. The only thing Trevn liked about it was that it bore his insignia of the hunting horn, which symbolized high and noble pursuits. Both Father and Mother hated it, as it had nothing to do with any of the gods.

Beal started on Trevn's hair. Once Trevn took his priestly vows, he would start wearing his hair in a single priest's lock. Tonight Beal was braiding it into fifteen cornrows.

Hinck and Cadoc stood watching the scene, no doubt with great amusement. Trevn did not find his situation at all humorous.

"It is an ensemble befitting a prince," Beal wheezed.

Trevn glared at the ruffles in the mirror. "Does Mother think I'm female? Why does she do this to me?"

"Torture is what mothers do best." Hinck gestured to his own sleek maroon-and-black ensemble. "Will this do? Or should I find something with frills?"

"You can shut up."

Hinck blinked, one eye more closed than the other, but nowhere close to a successful wink. "Can but won't. So tonight we hunt you a wife?"

Trevn heaved a deep sigh. "That and ten concubines."

"*Ten?* So unfair. How old is Miss Mielle, anyway?"

"Sixteen. One month too old to match in fives."

"Well, *that's* a shame," Hinck said.

Trevn wanted none of this, especially the ruffles. "We should have waited for Wilek to return." Beal tugged too hard and Trevn winced. "He was going to help convince Father to have my ageday at sea. What's the point of being a sâr if you cannot have what you want?"

"So you can give me what I want," Hinck said, his smile larger than normal. "I'll take your ten concubines, Your Generousness."

Cadoc snorted. "Well, that would be generous."

"Oh, no," Trevn said. "If I have to suffer, so do you."

When they finally approached the great hall, Mother's onesent Arkil was standing outside the doors, waiting. "The rosâr has already arrived," he whispered.

"Good," Trevn said. The shorter this event, the better. "May as well announce me."

The guards opened the doors and revealed a great hall transformed. Most of the tables had been removed to create space for dancing. The room was a wash of blue and pink dresses but for a few matronly types dressed in dark colors. Men stood in clusters by the outer walls where tables laden with food ran lengthwise. Everyone was standing, except the king, who sat on his throne, which had been moved from the Throne Room to the dais for this special day. Trevn's mother stood on Father's left. An empty chair to the right of the throne awaited Trevn. To the far right Janek stood behind the cup table, which held six golden cups: five small tumblers and a large goblet.

Five Woes of misery; Wilek should be cupbearer. The herald blew Trevn's call on the trumpet, which twisted Trevn's stomach. The song ended and the herald announced in a loud voice, "His Royal Highness, Trevn-Sâr Hadar, the Third Arm of Armania."

All faces turned his way. The crowd bowed like a slow, rolling wave as Trevn walked past. He reached the dais much sooner than expected, climbed the steps, and knelt.

His mother sang a song, which wasn't half bad, after which Pontiff Rogedoth must have read an entire chapter from the Book of Rôb, because Trevn's knees went numb while he waited. Then came the part everyone knew by heart. The cupping.

"To become a man," Father said in a booming voice, "a boy requires faith in the gods, who give us life."

Janek lifted the first tumbler and poured the contents—wine—into the goblet.

"To become a man," Father said, "a boy requires health, without which he will die."

Janek poured the second cup.

"To become a man, a boy requires wisdom, without which he will become a fool."

In went the third splash of wine.

"To become a man, a boy requires love, without which he will have no heir."

Janek dumped the cup of love.

"To become a man, a boy requires prosperity. If he honors the gods, is blessed with good health, wisdom, and heirs, he will indeed find it."

Janek poured the final cup, then lifted the goblet in both hands.

"Cupbearer, bring forth the cup," Father said.

Janek carried the cup around the table and handed it to Trevn. The gold felt cool in his sweaty grip; the dark liquid trembled.

"Drink, boy, from the cup of manhood," Father said.

Trevn drank very slowly, breaking tradition. Lore said the faster one drank, the longer he would live. A foolish superstition that Trevn intended to prove false by living a hundred years. Behind him, whispers rose from the assembly, and he caught his mother's glare. He finished and handed the cup to Janek, who carried it back to the cup table.

Father stood and set his hand on Trevn's head. "I dub thee, Trevn-Sâr Hadar, the Curious. You are now a man."

Curious? That was his title? Fitting, he supposed. As per the ceremony, Trevn repeated, "I am now a man."

The crowd burst into cheers. It might be an archaic ritual to provide nobility with yet another reason to celebrate, but Trevn's throat tightened and it took effort to maintain an indifferent expression.

He then claimed the seat beside his father and received his showering, in which the guests paraded past with gifts. He received pendants, brooches, rings, buckles, daggers, swords, capes, tunics, boots, jewelry for his future wives and concubines, several dozen amphoras of wine, mirrors, three slaves—two female, one male—four horses, ornate rugs, a handful of perfumes and ointments, lampstands, cups and bowls, incense holders, crowns, tapestries, and paintings.

His mother gave him a set of wedding cuffs.

His father gave him his own signet ring and a seat on the Wisean Council, which Trevn intended to avoid as long as possible.

Janek gave him a stallion, a potted tree, and said in his ear, "Borrow Pia and Mattenelle anytime you like."

Miss Mielle gave him a shard of roof tile on a cord. "From yesterday," she whispered, fingering a similar tile at her neck that ran beneath the bodice of her gown. "I kept the other half."

Lady Zeroah gave him a wooden map tube and fifty sheets of map paper.

Father Tomek gave him a prayer stone that was said to have belonged to the prophet Zyon Ottee.

Then it was time to dance.

The band began a traditional somaro. Trevn led his mother to the center of the hall. She wore a hideous purple-and-green gown that made her look like a bunch of grapes. She was a great deal shorter than he was, and he had to release her for the twirls, as her girth did not easily fit under his arm. She looked happy, though. She wouldn't for long.

Tradition stated that Trevn would dance the first half of the first song with his mother, then pass her off to the king and choose his own partner. Mother had nagged him all morning about the only three acceptable choices for his first dance.

But he had already chosen.

When the strings and flutes stopped playing and only the percussion remained, Trevn led his mother to the king, who was standing at the foot of the dais stairs. He handed her off, pretended not to see her mouth the name *Brisa Hadar*, then turned to face the crowd.

In the circle of pink and blue dresses, Miss Mielle was easy to spot. She was wearing green, standing beside Lady Zeroah, who wore silver.

A deep breath and Trevn crossed the room. The percussion continued, seeming in time with his steps and rattling nerves. He stopped before Miss Mielle and bowed. She curtsied. He extended his hand.

People started to whisper.

Her hand slid into his and he pulled her to the center of the room. The flutes and strings burst into song, and they danced. Trevn kept his eyes on Miss Mielle's, not wanting to see his mother or father or anyone else.

"You're nervous," she said.

Was it that obvious? "So are you."

"Everyone is staring. How do you ever get used to it?"

"I ignore them. You look very pretty tonight."

"As do your ruffles." She smirked.

Sands, he liked her more and more each day.

The song ended before he was ready to let go. He returned Miss Mielle to Lady Zeroah's side and suddenly felt awkward, standing in the center of the circle alone.

"Sâr Trevn."

His mother was walking toward him, dragging his second cousins Brisa and Trista by the arms. A fake smile contrasted the twin daggers of her eyes. She released the cousins and grabbed his chin—digging in her fingernails as she kissed his forehead. "Greet your cousins."

Let the drudgery begin. Trevn bowed to the girls. "Good evening, cousins."

"Are you going to marry us both?" Trista, at ten, wrinkled her nose as if marrying anyone was disgusting.

"No, Lady Trista, I—"

"The sâr is merely looking tonight," Mother said. "But he does plan to marry one woman. For now."

Trevn shrank a little and sent a pleading look to Hinck, who was smirking over by the food table.

"I'm going to marry my father," Trista said.

"Forgive my sister, Your Highness," Brisa said with a small curtsy. The elder of the Duke of Odarka's daughters was but four months Trevn's junior and more intense than his mother. "Trista is but a child. She has an unfortunate habit of speaking her mind."

"So have I," Trevn said to Trista, then leaned down and whispered in the little girl's ear. "I prefer a wife closer to my age, but let's allow your sister to think I'm picking you, just for fun."

Trista brightened at this.

"Would you dance with me, Lady Trista?" he asked in his full voice.

Trista curtsied. "Yes, I will, Sâr Trevn."

He offered his arm and she nearly tackled him, giggling all the while. He led her to the middle of the room, then told the band, "A rengia, please." Rengias were the fastest type of dance, and Trevn felt his young partner up to the task.

The band set upon the lively tune. Trevn and Trista stomped, twirled, and laughed. Thankfully some other couples joined in the dancing, including Hinck, the bootlicker, who was dancing with Brisa. These two girls were Father Tomek's granddaughters, though only Trista seemed to have been blessed with the man's easygoing nature.

When the song ended, Trevn caught sight of Shemme, Cook Hara's daughter, wearing pink. She was the skinniest girl he had ever seen—an oddity when she stood beside her overweight mother. Trevn had knocked her over plenty of times on his runs through the castle. He owed her. She would be his next dance.

He approached and said, "Good evening, Miss Shemme."

Her eyes bulged and she backed up a step, knocking into a girl in blue. "I'm sorry," she told the girl, falling into a bony curtsy at the same time. "Good evening, Your Highness."

"Will you dance?" he asked.

"It's my duty to obey, Your Highness."

He frowned. "But do you want to?"

"May Athos deal with me, be it ever so severely, but I have pledged my heart to another. To become your concubine would dishonor him."

Trevn's cheeks burned. Curse his mother's ridiculous invitations. "I ask but for one dance, Miss Shemme. If you would rather not, I understand."

"No, please. My mother would be so happy if I danced with you."

"Very well." Perhaps next time Trevn ran through the kitchen, he would knock down Cook Hara.

The current song was a nevett, a rather upbeat tune that required little touching. This was good, as Shemme had no coordination and managed to kick him twice *and* step on his heel.

Hinck joined them with a girl Trevn had never seen before—a much more graceful dancer than Shemme. When the song ended, Trevn thanked Shemme and started toward Hinck, but his mother grabbed his arm and yanked him aside.

"Poorly done, Trevn. I'm so desperately embarrassed."

"What? What did I do?" Besides totally defy her.

"You made a mockery of yourself, dancing the first with an honor maiden. Then you slighted Lady Brisa twice by dancing with her little sister, then with a kitchen maid."

"I didn't mean to slight anyone. You said Trista was one of your top choices." She raised both eyebrows.

"I'm not going to marry either of them." So what did it matter if he had a little fun?

"Why wouldn't you marry them?" Mother hissed. "They're Hadars! Embarrass me again, and I'll see you chained in your room till you marry and give me a grandson."

Of all the ridiculous . . . "I'm a man now, Mother. You no longer decide for me."

"Care to wager a bet?"

Her time to control him had come to an end. "Let's ask Father right now."

She squeezed his arm, held him there. "Gods and kings cannot be everywhere, so mothers were created to protect their children from disaster. That's all I'm trying to do, Trevn."

He gritted his teeth, but accepted her words as a temporary peace offering. "Fine. Who would you like me to dance with next?"

Having gotten his goodwill, she smiled. "Lady Brisa, if she'll have you. Jeanon Yohthehreth is the next highest in rank. Then Nolli Jervaid—she's Wisean Jervaid's second-eldest girl. Very pretty. Then Windelle Veralla."

"Rayim Veralla's daughter?" The man who had caught him kissing Miss Mielle?

"She is the lowest of those I would approve as your wife. Her parents are nobly born, and the captain is highly decorated and respected. Dance with every girl in blue before dancing with those in pink. Understand? You should also ask Lady Zeroah to dance before any of the potential concubines. You would do well to steal her from your brother."

Trevn scowled. "That will never happen, Mother." Before she could reply, he approached Brisa. They managed to dance a stiff corroet and have a stiffer conversation. He then worked his way down his mother's list. Jeanon Yohthehreth was clumsy and pimpled and wouldn't meet his eyes. Nolli Jervaid was nearly as short as little Trista—he stepped on her feet three times. Since he promised Captain Veralla—who was on guard over by the door—never to look on his daughter, he tried to dance with Miss Windelle while keeping his gaze elsewhere.

He tried several times to find Miss Mielle in the room, and while he saw Lady Zeroah and Princess Nabelle conversing with his devious mother, Miss Mielle seemed to have vanished.

MIELLE

Mielle sat on a chair wedged between the food table and the corner of the great hall. One moment she'd been dancing with Trevn, the next she was being harangued by Princess Nabelle and banished to this chair. For a while her defiant nature had her standing on the wicker seat so she could see over the wall of bodies blocking her view. But watching Trevn dance with girl after girl only made her feel sorry for herself, and she sat down to sulk.

She knew what Kal would say. And now that Princess Nabelle was aware of Trevn's favor, she would forbid her to see him as well.

It wasn't fair.

"Why does my brother's favorite hide in the corner by the pickled beets?" Prince Janek stood three steps away. He looked like a warrior on extended leave: strong but quickly going soft. He was a beautiful man with a defined brow, sleepy eyes, full lips, and a shadow of a beard. His only blemish was a small scar on the tip of his nose.

Mielle popped to her feet and curtsied. "I'm not hiding, Sâr Janek," she said. "Princess Nabelle asked me to wait here."

"You upstaged her precious girl. Mothers are such controlling creatures, are they not?"

That gave Mielle pause. "I don't remember my mother."

"She was a noblewoman. You should be wearing blue, I would say."

"I'm the wrong age," Mielle said. "Sixteen."

"A shame, that. And you Trevn's favorite." Janek tapped his finger against his scarred nose, then gasped, flashing her a dazzling smile. "Why, Miss Mielle. I am twenty-one. We match in fives, you and I."

"Oh." What an awkward thing to say. She stepped back until her legs struck the chair she'd been sitting on.

Janek stepped closer. "Trevn cannot legally have you, but I can. And I share everything with my brothers." He whispered, "I gifted Trevn my concubines tonight."

The mere thought made Mielle's eyes water. "Excuse me, my sâr, I must look for Lady Zeroah." She stepped around him, but he cut off her path.

"Miss Mielle, this is Mikreh's doing. The god of fate knows it is the only way you and Trevn can be together." He grabbed her arms and pulled her to him. "Let us go to my father at once. Surely he will agree when he hears Trevn's plight."

"No!" Mielle stomped on his foot and, when he let go, dashed back to her chair.

He caught her waist with his arm and pulled her against him. "My, my," he whispered in her hair. "How unladylike to lose one's temper."

"Let go!" She elbowed his stomach and tried to pull his arm off her waist.

"Sâr Janek!" Princess Nabelle's voice. "Unhand Miss Mielle at once."

Princess Nabelle stood like a goddess, glaring regally at them both. Just behind her Lady Zeroah looked on in horror.

Sâr Janek released Mielle, and she ran to Zeroah. They clasped hands. Tears were already leaking from Mielle's eyes as Zeroah pulled her toward the exit.

Princess Nabelle joined them a moment later and called for a carriage.

"We have stayed at the castle long enough," she declared.

As they waited, the princess demanded Mielle repeat Sâr Janek's every word. Once Mielle had done so, the princess decreed that they would stay away from Castle Everton until Sâr Wilek returned.

Mielle did not cry fully until she was alone in her bed at Fairsight Manor that night. Life for an honor maiden simply wasn't fair.

KALEПEK

Near sunrise on the fifth day, the first red lake came into view. The sun peeked over the horizon and shot an arrow of white light across the glossy surface. Having lived near the Eversea so long, for Kal it wasn't the vastness of the lake that captured his awe but the stillness and rich color.

"That's a sight," Novan said.

"It's poisonous," Kal said, not wanting the boy to get too enchanted. "Even to the touch."

"What makes it so?"

"Evenroot. Magonia's chief export. They've overharvested to the point of spoiling all four great lakes and many of the rivers in this part of the ream."

"So, anyone who drinks the water must become a mantic or die?"

"There were still plenty of safe reamways here six years ago," Kal said.

Novan seemed to consider this. "How much farther to Lifton?"

"A few hours. There's a stepwell near here. We'll stop for water before entering the city." Better to have no business in Lifton but to find a mantic and depart.

It was midday when they reached the stepwell. This close to Lifton, Kal had expected it to be overrun with people, but it was deserted. A black charcoal slash on the stone wall said why.

"Contaminated," Kal said, shaken. He didn't like seeing a freshwater source go bad. "We must press on to Lifton and pray there's clean water to be—"

A scream from below straightened Kal's spine. He met Novan's gaze.

"I know you took it!" a man yelled in Tennish. "I saw that witch with it."

"Who? Onika?" a child replied. "She's not too smart. Probably dropped it somewhere. We should look aboveground."

"Get me that sack, boy, or you're dead!"

Novan whispered, "Can you understand what they're saying?"

Kal drew his finger across his lips and pulled his sword.

A boy scampered up the steps like a nimble squirrel. He was slight, maybe as old as twelve. He caught sight of Kal and slowed, eyes wider than a camel's as they flicked over Kal's scars. One glance at Novan and he chose his protector.

"Help me!" the boy cried, running toward Novan. "He's going to kill me!"

Kal reached out and snagged the boy's arm. His skin was dark for a Magonian and was covered in blotchy gray patches like a rash of dried mortar. Kal let go immediately, not wanting to catch whatever ailed the boy. "Is he your master?" Kal asked in Tennish. "Your employer?"

The boy hid behind Kal. "He's nothing to me. Says I stole his sack, but I didn't! You're Rurekan, yeah?" he said in the Kinsman tongue. "I can help you. I know the four cities better than the mapmakers. I'm good with animals too. Don't let him kill me!"

The boy's pursuer emerged at the top of the steps. The man had short hair, reddish skin, and wore the insignia of a Magonian yeetta warrior, which was a shard club across the Kabar hands. The yeettas had invaded Armania at the end of the Centenary War and slayed thousands of innocents. Women. Children.

Livy and their infant son.

Butchered in their beds.

One blink. Two. Kal felt himself slipping back in time to that night. It was all happening again.

He gauged his enemy. A shard club swung from the man's belt. The polished length of hardwood was lined with obsidian shards, spaced apart like the jagged teeth of a fang cat. Effective in a melee, but one-on-one it didn't stand a chance against a sword.

"This ain't your business, stranger," the man said in Tennish.

Filthy yeetta liars. Kal charged.

The man dodged Kal, pulled his club, and swung for Kal's legs, then darted back, lunged, and swung again. Typical. This was how the yeetta fought. They had to keep their distance because one well-aimed cut of the sword could splinter their weapon. But they were quick, and while Kal's sword had the power to destroy wood, the obsidian shards could decapitate a fang cat with one powerful blow.

Kal made to parry the next swing, but the club reversed as the man twisted and tried to hamstring Kal. Slashed his clothing but didn't cut him.

The man thrust out, spun into a side cut. Kal parried reflexively, perfectly, forgetting he wasn't fighting another sword. Had he turned his parry and met the club with the cutting edge of his blade, he would have destroyed it.

The yeetta slid back. Kal pressed forward. Yeetta scum had murdered Livy, murdered their son, cut Kal's face. They all deserved to die.

A tingle ran up his sword arm.

No! He must end this now. Quickly. Before it happened again.

He went after the man with all the hatred in his heart, pressing forward, taking hard cuts. He drove his opponent toward the half wall until the man's backswing struck stone. The man faltered, and Kal's quick downward cut across the neck ended the fight. The man collapsed, dead.

Kal's sword fell from his numb grip. He looked down on the yeetta. The blood. Horror pooled within him. Deep breaths failed to calm as he slowly returned to the present.

Again it had happened. He had stepped into a nightmare and killed without thinking. Numb, he scrubbed sand over his blade to clean away the blood—left-handed, since his right hand hung useless. When he finally looked around, the camels stood staring, but Novan and the boy were gone.

He ran down the stepwell stairs, sword in his left hand, hoping he wouldn't need to use it.

Beneath the ground the air instantly cooled. The river gurgled past. He saw no sign of life, but footprints on the soft silt veered a sharp left along the bottom edge of the stairs. Kal followed them back to the stone wall of the cavern. Up ahead, Novan stood before a waist-high cave, fabric sack in hand.

"He gone?" Kal asked, flexing his right hand as feeling started to return.

Novan gestured to the cave. "Someone's in there with him." He handed the sack to Kal. "Looks like turnips."

Kal sheathed his sword and took the sack, glanced inside. Not turnips. It was filled with small evenroot tubers.

Something tickled his shins. Was he bleeding? He glanced down and froze. A full-sized dune cat threaded itself between his legs, purring like a kitten; its weight and pressure caused him to stumble back a step.

"Hello there, cat," he said, reaching down to pet it. The dune cat arched its spine into Kal's hand and twisted through his legs again. Kal smiled, intrigued by the animal.

"That's mine!" The boy shot out of the cave and grabbed hold of the sack. Kal held tight until Novan pulled the boy away.

"You speak two languages?" Kal asked.

The boy struggled against Novan. "My mother is Magonian, my father Rurekan. Now give it back! My family will starve."

Kal lifted the sack. "You plan to eat these, do you?"

A nod. "Mother sent us to scavenge, but that yeetta tried to steal it."

"That yeetta is dead," Kal said. "Show me your hands."

The boy's eyes flew wide. He tucked his hands behind him. "Don't prune my hands. I'm not a thief!"

"I'm not going to cut you." The feeling in Kal's right hand had returned, so he grabbed the boy's wrist and jerked his hand close. He saw none of the red pustules that normally came from touching evenroot, but his fingernails were rimmed in dirt. He'd been digging. "You're a liar is what you are." He threw down the boy's hand. "You can't eat evenroot."

"You know what that is? Oh, you're right. I'll tell you the truth."

"I doubt that," Novan mumbled.

"If I don't return with that bag, my sister will be killed. She's just a wee thing. Three years old. But the blackard tied her up until I harvest a sack of root. He's too big to climb into the cracks and reach the good stuff."

"I don't believe this," Novan said.

"You offered yourself as a guide if I helped you," Kal said. "You'll guide us now. First to clean water. Then to the man you sell root to."

The boy's eyes lit up. "I can take you anywhere, for a price."

"The price has been paid with that yeetta's life," Kal said. "And I seek no destination. I need to find a mantic."

The boy gasped. "A mantic? To translate a rune?"

Kal frowned. "How do you know that?"

"Onika! It's him!" The boy jerked away and scampered into the cave.

Novan crouched outside the tunnel. "His mouth never stops. Reminds me of my little brother. Probably talks in his sleep too."

Kal squatted beside Novan. Deep inside the cave, the boy had stopped beside a woman. Hisses and indiscernible words floated out to Novan and Kal.

Footsteps brushed the stairs. They both stood and drew their swords.

"Sands alive!" Novan sheathed his blade and ran toward his camel, which was halfway down the steps and coming fast.

"Don't let him near the water!" Kal yelled. "The poison will kill him."

"Haht!" Novan grabbed for the camel's reins, but the beast barreled past, knocking Novan onto his rear. That camel did what it wanted to do, and it seemed to want a swim.

But it stopped suddenly on the riverbank, put its head down near the water, moaned, and drank nothing.

Novan took hold of its reins and pulled back. "Let's go find a carrot, yeah?"

The camel bellowed, clearly unhappy to be denied his swim and drink, but allowed Novan to lead him back up the stairs.

"Most animals can sense the poison." The boy ran out from behind Kal and chased after Novan. "Can I feed him?"

"The rescuer needs to be rescued," a woman said.

The voice sent a chill up Kal's arms. He turned around. Beside the cave stood a young woman. She had white skin, hair like wheat, and eyes like diamonds. Was she a spirit? A mantic who had binged on evenroot? Surely not. Such a person would have died.

The woman looked at him—or through him—as if she didn't see him at all. He marveled at the gem-like quality of her eyes and studied the rest of her. She wore the traditional kasah of the mother realms, this one blue and yellow. The baggy way she had tied it around herself did nothing to hide her curves. A surge of attraction ran through Kal and he looked away, surprised at himself.

"You saved the boy?" she asked.

The mesmeric sound of her voice made him shiver. "My name is Kalenek Veroth. Who are you?" *Better question, what are you?*

"Onika." She smiled, shy and young, still looking through his soul. "It's nice to finally meet you, rescuer. Now, we must hurry. The Lowerworld grows weak with thirst. Soon it will level the mountains and swallow the land."

Every word gripped his nerves. Was this magic? "Are you a mantic?"

Onika laughed, a deep, enchanting sound, and her smile and joy were so pure, Kal knew he would keep her safe even at the cost of his life. Nothing mattered but that this woman live.

"I'm a prophet. My foreknowledge comes from Arman alone. I need no ahvenrood to see what he shows me. If we hurry, we can reach the lake before sohar and hire a barge."

"And where are we going?" Kal asked.

"To Kaptar, to the man who will translate your rune. Then to the sea." She put her fingers in her mouth and whistled sharply. "Rustian!" The dune cat bounded out of the cave and to her side. Onika set her hand on the animal's head, and together they set off for the stairs.

She was blind.

Kal had seen mules trained to guide the blind—once seen a dog—but never a cat. In fact he had never seen a domesticated dune cat of any kind.

He followed them up the steps, admiring how she and the cat moved in sync, oddly thankful she couldn't see his scarred face. "How do you know I seek a rune translation?"

"Arman showed me." She said this without a shift in her stride or a twitch of her head. No point, Kal supposed, if she couldn't see.

The boy ran down the stairs to walk beside Kal. "I'm called Grayson. What happened to your face? My parents gave me up, afraid of my rash. I don't blame them, though. I bet people are afraid of you too. I sure was. We've been waiting for you all year. Onika thought you'd come by now. Expected you last spring."

"Grayson," Onika said.

"We're going with them, aren't we?" he asked. "I thought you were sure."

"We'll talk of this later," she said.

So many questions flooded Kal's mind. He would really rather talk of them now.

They reached the surface. Novan stood feeding his camel a carrot. He saw Onika and stared, lips parted, brow furrowed. A narrowed glance to Grayson. "This your baby sister?"

"Onika is my friend." Grayson took Onika's hand and led her around the wall, then stopped and bent over the yeetta's body.

"Is she a ghost?" Novan whispered to Kal.

"Says she's a prophet. Says we're to take her on a barge across the red lakes to Kaptar where we'll find a man who'll translate the runes."

"That's quite a journey isn't it?"

"A few days depending on the wind."

"You believe her?"

"I don't know," he said. All he knew was that feeling of needing to keep her safe. "But if she knows a mantic . . ." He walked toward them. Grayson, who was now crouched beside the yeetta, pulled his hands from the man's pockets and popped to his feet.

"How can we be sure your man is in Kaptar?" Kal asked.

"Oh, he'll be there," Grayson said. "Can't be anywhere else 'cause he's in prison with Dun."

"Our friend Dunmore was captured by Tennish mantics," Onika said. "Jhorn freed him. They made it back to Magonia but were taken prisoner in Kaptar. They're to be shipped back to Tenma for sentencing next week. Unless we help."

"We're trying to slip in and out of this realm quietly," Novan said. "We can't walk into a Magonian prison."

At Novan's logic, Kal's resolve to follow her, even die for her, snapped like an ironwood branch.

"I know you'll help us because I've seen it," Onika said.

Her voice brought back the lenitive feelings. Kal needed to take care around this woman. He waved Novan over to the camels to discuss the situation.

"She claims she's a prophet, so we're supposed to believe whatever she says?" Novan asked.

"She knew about the rune," Kal said. "This mission was dangerous from the start. But this woman could take us to one who could give us the answers we seek with no trouble."

"Breaking into a prison is more trouble than facing a mantic," Novan said. "Plus a blind woman and a boy won't be much help in a fight."

That much was true.

"We already know the boys tells lies," Novan said. "They could lead us anywhere. Could be they mean to rob us. Besides, if they sell evenroot regularly, they should know a mantic nearby. I think it's a trick."

Why hadn't Kal thought of that? "Smart thinking, Novan. We'll continue on to Lifton. Surely we'll find a mantic there." Yet disappointment weighed down Kal's shoulders as he approached Onika. He hadn't so much as looked at another woman since Livy died six years ago. That Onika had captured his attention seemed important somehow. Though from the way Novan was watching her, it could be like that for every man. Perhaps she was a witch. Had put a spell on them both.

"I thank you, Miss Onika," Kal said, "for your offer to help us find your mantic friend, but we've decided to try our luck in Lifton."

Onika frowned, glassy eyes narrowed. "Do be careful, Kalenek Veroth. A yeetta warrior was killed today, and many will be looking for his murderer. Grayson said you killed him. Once I tell the sheriff, word will spread, and they'll hunt you down with magic."

Such a threat from a young woman surprised Kal. "Blackmail is a risky way to deal with armed men, Miss Onika," he said. "I could kill you both now and end my trouble."

"But you won't," Onika said, focused on the air between them. "You're both far too honorable."

Novan snorted. "Wish we could say as much for you."

"I do regret this course of action," Onika said, "but my offer has not changed. Once the men are free, Jhorn will translate the rune."

Kal weighed his options. It could very well be that Onika was bluffing. Yet it mattered not. It was dangerous enough to travel in Magonia, even with the pastone. It would not do to have people looking for him. "Novan, there's rope in my saddlebag. We'll have to tie them up."

"Not me!" Grayson sprinted away.

Onika merely stared at Kal with those fathomless eyes. "Your realm is in danger. You must take word to your prince if your people hope to survive the coming destruction."

"Soothsayers have been predicting the fall of Armania for centuries," Kal said.

"You're a broken man, Kalenek Veroth. The past haunts you, benumbs your sword hand, but there is one who can set you free, who can help you find sleep again."

If she had stabbed him he would have been less shocked. "Who do you work for? Captain Alpress?"

"Liviana trusted in Arman. So did you once."

"Enough!" Kal grabbed her arms and squeezed, shaking her. "What did Arman ever give Livy? A torturous death by depraved yeetta witch slaves, that's what."

"Sir?" Novan set his hand on Kal's shoulder.

Onika's glassy eyes stared at his throat, her brow furrowed, her lips a trembling frown.

Kal released her, took two steps back. His hands had left red marks on her pale arms. How could she know such things? Livy's name . . . his hand . . . ?

She looked through him then, fierce and terrible. "Wail, for the day of destruction is near!" Her spellbinding voice seemed to come from inside Kal's head. "Arman is about to destroy the earth and make it a vast wasteland. He will devastate the surface of the land and scatter the people. The foundations of the earth will be violently shaken, broken up, collapsed. Mountains will tremble like a tent in a storm, fall and not rise again.

"The earth will be void, swallowed into the sea, the land washed away and withered. Throughout the land the story will be the same—only a remnant will endure, like stray grapes left on a vine after harvest. The remnant will set sail and begin anew. In northern lands they will give glory to Arman. In the lands beyond the sea they will praise his name."

A silence followed that was greater than any Kal had heard in his life, as if even the insects, birds, and wind had all paused to regard this woman.

Novan made the sign of The Hand.

Prophet indeed. A chill snaked up his arms. "When would you like to leave?"

Grayson led them back the way they'd come. Onika refused to ride. Humming an eerie melody, she walked beside Grayson, and the dune cat leaned against her left leg. Kal and Novan rode behind the odd threesome. The red lake came into view again, but this time they headed toward it, keeping to the outskirts of the city. Soon the walls of Lifton rose up on their right. Shadows of clouds muted the heat of the sun and reflected off the scarlet surface of the water.

"What a sight," Novan said.

"What is it, Master Heln?" Onika called back.

"I was remarking on the beauty of the red lake," Novan said.

"Aside," Onika said, and the dune cat leaned hard against her leg, pushing Onika's steps to the right, giving the camels room to come abreast. She glanced up toward Novan, almost on target. "Will you describe what you see?"

"I can try," Novan said. "Do you understand colors?"

"I went blind when I was seven," Onika said. "I remember colors."

"The water is scarlet except where the sun touches it," Novan said. "There it's golden, almost orange. Fluffy white clouds have passed in front of the sun, which is low on the horizon and completely opposite the town clustered on the shore. Walls the color of the sand surround buildings of the same, all but the roofs, which are red-clay tile that match the water. The lake is so massive, I can't see the distant shore. Only the gleaming sun hiding behind the clouds."

Onika smiled. "I can see it."

"That's not all, Miss Onika. It seems as if the town and the sun are shouting good midday across the expanse, but it might be the distance is too great for them to hear one another."

Onika chuckled, but it ended in a forlorn sigh. "They can hear each other well enough, Master Heln. The sun warns the town that today might be peaceful, but disaster is coming. After the sun sets a third time, the red lakes will rise up against the land and wash it with poison that will bleed into the reamways below. Many will die. We should fill our jugs before boarding the barge."

Her words made Kal's mouth run dry. "Does it matter which barge we take across?"

"Bargeman Wymer is expecting us," Onika said. "He'll take no other passengers."

"How can he be expecting us?" Novan asked.

"I spoke to him yesterday," Onika said. "We were going to sell the ahvenrood tubers to the yeetta soldier to raise funds for the barge and to bribe the Kaptar prison guards."

A ridiculous plan for a blind woman. "I see that worked well," Kal said.

"It was a mistake to try to rush the prophecy," Onika said. "I should have trusted Arman. He brought you to me, as promised."

Had he? Kal wasn't so sure.

They followed the city wall until it stretched out into the lake like a jetty. Grayson led them along the shore, far enough away from the water to keep their feet dry.

They came to a fenced stone house that had been built on the edge of the lake. Behind it, a barge bobbed on the water's surface.

A red-skinned man opened the gate for them. "Made good time, I see." He was white-haired with a row of crooked teeth. "How long till the shaker comes, Miss Onika?"

"Hello, Wymer," Onika said. "Two full days will pass before the ground will tremble with the morning sun."

Wymer nodded once. "If we're quick, we'll make it."

"You believe her?" Kal asked.

"I always believe her," the old man said.

"Wymer," Onika said, "this is Kalenek Veroth and his backman, Novan Heln."

"How do, Misters? Fancy a float across the Upper Sister, do ya? Bring your beasts back."

Kal and Novan led the camels after Wymer to the dock. Gulls soared overhead. The wind was cool and fresh. Kal glanced over the edge of the dock to where the reddish water rushed up the sandy bank, spread thin, and sizzled as the foam sank into the sand. The grasses around the lake were yellow and shriveled. Kal didn't relish the idea of riding over poisoned waves.

The barge was twenty paces long with rails along both sides. It had a small wooden barn in the center and rows of wooden crates on either end. Kal was glad to see water and other provisions already stocked. They loaded both camels into the barn, Kal's beast groaning and straining the entire time while Novan's pranced on as though he rode a barge every day. Both were shackled to keep them still while on the water.

"We ready to go?" Kal asked once the job was finished.

"Soon as my watermen show," Wymer said. "Takes four to push this load."

Kal left Novan and Grayson in the barn and found Onika sitting with her dune cat on a wooden crate at the bow of the barge. Kal sat down away from her, in the far left corner, pondering her prophecy and trying not to think about her strange beauty.

A few minutes later, four men boarded. They wore long-sleeved tunics and gloves to protect themselves from any splash from the poison water. Wymer came out of the barn and greeted them. The men picked up longpoles from the floor along the rails, and Wymer untied the barge from the dock. At the captain's word, the men pushed off. Once they were floating lazily away from the dock, two of the men went around to the other side. All four spaced themselves out like wheels on a cart, put their longpoles over the rail, and began pushing.

"Is it this shallow all across?" Kal asked as Wymer joined him at the front.

"Nope. They'll switch to sweeps when it gets deep."

They slowly picked up speed, and the city of Lifton came into view around the jetty wall. Hundreds of piers and docks branched out over the surface of the lake. Boats, barges, and reamskiffs sat tied to them, waiting for someone to take them on a voyage. Most of the boats were wood—Magonia had several huge forests in the south, which provided a sizable logging industry. But this close to Rurekau and Tenma, many of the boats were poured stone, which came from a special white sand only found around volcanoes. It produced a substance much lighter than concrete or bricks and was used for wagons, boats, and Rurekau's famous stoneclad warships.

Kal was thankful they had bypassed Lifton. It was a better city than Hebron, but trouble dwelled in cities. Kal was glad to have avoided it.

Novan exited the barn and joined Kal, leaning on the side rail and gazing out at the water. "I can't get over how big it is," he said. "It's like the Eversea without the waves."

"It has some." Kal looked over the side at the waves that curled and broke against the side of the barge. "They're just not as big."

"It smells like rain instead of salt water."

"I do like the smell," Kal said. "Pity we can't swim in it."

The farther they drifted, the smaller Lifton became. By sunset there was nothing to see but water and sky in every direction.

That night, the watermen took shifts to sleep so that two could continue rowing. Novan volunteered to take a shift.

"Many thanks, Master Heln," Wymer said, "but my passengers should rest and enjoy the journey."

Kal liked Novan, but sometimes the boy was a little too good. Novan left Wymer and approached where Onika sat, her dune cat curled in a ball at her feet.

"So, what's the cat's name?" Novan asked.

She jumped a little, glassy eyes staring into nothing. "Rustian."

"How did you train a dune cat?"

She lifted her chin and turned her face in Novan's general direction. "I didn't. He's always been with me."

"Someone must have trained him," Novan said. "Sand cats are wild. I had a friend who got attacked by one once. Stepped on a den of kits."

"Any mother would attack someone who stepped on her babies."

"I suppose. Does it bother you to speak Kinsman?"

"It is Jhorn's language and therefore my first choice. We rarely speak Tennish."

"Oh." A pause. "Can I pet him?"

"You'll have to ask him. I'm not his master."

Novan squatted at Onika's feet and reached out. "Mind if I pet you, Rustian?"

He must have succeeded, because Kal could hear the great cat purring all the way across the bow. Onika and Novan laughed, and the scene looked to Kal like the makings of a happily forever. Jealousy twisted his stomach into a stone, which only made him angry. He was a fool to waste soft thoughts on the prophet woman. He rolled over and desperately sought sleep.

Kal woke with a jolt, still smelling the reek of blood from battle, dagger in hand, uncertain where he was. The rhythmic *glub* of sweeps in water brought him back. The barge. He was in Magonia. At least he hadn't screamed when he woke.

"Is your sleep troubled often?"

At Onika's voice, Kal started and sat up, which made his head spin. It was pitch black. He sheathed his dagger. "How do the watermen know where they're going?"

"The Kaptar watchtower is lit," she said. "They simply follow the light."

Kal scanned the darkness until he saw what she meant. A small yellow flame burned in the distance, no bigger than a spark from where they sailed. "How did you know it was there?"

"Grayson told me."

Silence stretched between them, and Kal had the sudden urge to please this woman, to earn her favor. "Miss Onika, I'm sorry I grabbed you earlier."

"You're a broken man, Kalenek Veroth. Until you heal you'll continue to risk hurting others. Arman warns you by weakening the source of your violence, but you press on to do the will of hatred. You must submit to him in order to be free."

Kal had no response to that.

"You should speak with Jhorn about the war," Onika said. "Many soldiers survived with physical wounds that healed, but they never knew to heal the wounds inside. Jhorn learned to do both."

Kal's heart pinched. Any other time he would have ended this conversation, but the darkness hid his fear of the subject. "How can anyone heal a wound inside?"

"I know not. You'll have to ask Jhorn."

"And will I learn?" He felt bad the moment he put her to the test, as if she were a possession to perform on demand.

"Someday. But not for a very long time."

Kal squeezed his right hand into a fist, testing the feeling there. "We'll see."

İпоlaн

Empress Inolah stood with the maidservant in the dark passage. The only light came from the woman's candle and a thin slot on the wall to her left.

"See the latch, Empress?" the maidservant asked, resting her fingers on a wooden knob that protruded from the skeleton of the wall. "Pull down to open the door. Pull up to close it again." Her fingers moved to the slot. "Always look before entering."

Inolah peered through the slot. The room was vast and bright. A dark shape jerked across the windows. Up, down, up, down.

Ferro, jumping on the bed.

Inolah's heart leapt. "I see Ferro." She placed her hand on her pregnant belly, remembering when she had carried her second son. Eight years had gone too quickly. She hoped that this next child would always know freedom.

The maidservant pulled down on the latch. Something in the wall clicked, and a door popped open. "You must hurry."

"I shall." Inolah slipped into the room. "Ferro."

"Mama!" Ferro leapt off the bed and ran to her. She swept him up and sat on the edge of the bed, nuzzling her cheek against his. He was a sturdy boy with big brown eyes and a shaved head. A new henna tracing—a crown of interlocking squares—had smeared just above his left ear. She smiled and kissed the smear.

"Mother."

Her eyes lifted at the sound of Ulrik's voice. Her eldest son stood beside a large desk, one hand gripping the back of the chair. Ulrik was sixteen. He had a new tracing as well. A cheyvah tail circled his shaved head and ended with the thick black spike tip ringing one eye. Her breath caught to see it. Every day he looked more like his father, the emperor.

"It's not safe," Ulrik said. "If Father finds you here . . ."

"I don't want to sleep in this room," Ferro whined. "I want my old room."

"I know, dearest." Inolah wanted to promise that he could go back soon, but her husband, the emperor of Rurekau itself, had grown far too unpredictable. She had no idea what he might do if he found out she had defied him in speaking to her boys.

She set Ferro down beside her. "Go back to jumping, Ferro. Mama needs to talk to Ulrik."

Ferro leapt to the bed without need for convincing.

Inolah hurried to Ulrik's side. "There is little time," she said softly so that Ferro wouldn't hear.

"He will find us, Mother," Ulrik said. "And kill us."

"It is your constitutional right to leave. He has broken too many laws."

Ulrik sank onto the chair, his expression troubled. "He would never forgive me. I would lose my place as his heir."

"If you remain here, you will die. Ferro and Vallah too." Or the boys might become just like him, and Vallah nothing but a pawn in his quest to dominate the Five Realms.

Ulrik nodded. "When will we leave?"

"Tonight. I will come just after night bells."

"Dinner with Father. That's the last time we'll see him?" Ulrik asked.

"I'm afraid so," Inolah said. "Do not tell Ferro. He won't be able to keep a secret."

That made Ulrik smile. "You can count on me, Mother. I shall take care of things."

"I love you, Ulrik. Until tonight." She kissed him on the cheek, caught Ferro for one more squeeze and kiss, then slipped back into the passage.

Inolah laid Vallah's folded dresses on top of the packed food to hide the provisions. That was the last of it. Two hours more until night bells rang. She wished she and her children were already in Jeruka, boarding the ship to Everton.

The door to her room burst open. Her husband, Emperor Nazer, stormed inside. He was bare chested as always, his muscles covered in henna tracings and gold chains. The tracing on his head dripped down over both eyes, making them dark and daunting.

Inolah stood and curtsied deeply. "Your Eminence."

He slapped her so hard she stumbled, just managing to catch herself on the bed. He grabbed her braids in his fist and tugged. "You saw the boys? How?"

Had the maidservant told? "You have no right to keep them from me."

"I have every right. You have poisoned them against me for the last time. Bring her."

A guard entered the room, holding Vallah in his arms.

"Mama!" The six-year-old reached for Inolah, arms outstretched.

Inolah stood, heart heaving in her chest. "Nazer, she's your child."

"A female. Good only for a marriage trade. And I've made one. She leaves in the morning. Blame yourself."

The shock produced instant tears. "You wouldn't. She is too young."

"Ferro said he saw you today. Tell me how you did this and I will reconsider the trade."

And just like that, he won. "There is a passageway in the walls. I entered through Mikreh's shrine." She kept secret the doorways into her room and the library. Perhaps they could still escape.

"Find the door in Prince Ulrik's room and seal it," Nazer commanded the guards. "Move him and Prince Ferro to my chambers for the time being. Two guards remain in this room at all times—with eyes on the empress. She will remain here. Receive no visitors. No messages." He lowered his voice and glared down on Inolah. "Try to see my sons again without permission and your nurse dies."

"You go too far," Inolah rasped. "Against the Rurekan constitution, against the treaties with Armania and the mother realms."

"I no longer need treaties." He drew his fingers hard down her cheek and gripped her throat. "Why must you continually defy me?" He squeezed. "Don't think I won't kill you . . . once you deliver my son." He palmed her belly with his other hand.

Inolah struggled to breathe. "My father would wage war against you."

"The fool would never know."

"Mother would miss my letters." Nazer squeezed harder. Dizziness wrapped Inolah in a flash of darkness.

"Letters can be forged. No one will miss you." Nazer shoved her to the floor and stepped over her as he left the room, taking Vallah with him.

Inolah curled into a ball on the scratchy rug and listened to Vallah's screams fade away. She remained until she had cried out all her tears. The emptiness left only anger and determination in its place. Arman would not look lightly on such evil. Inolah must find a way to escape with her children before Nazer ruined them all.

TREVN

Trevn was late. He ran through the castle with Cadoc and Hinck close behind. Mielle had requested he meet her in the market square before their visit to Cape Waldemar. Apparently she had errands. He continually forgot she was employed.

Trevn darted around the corner to the grand staircase and collided with a woman. Knocked her to the floor. Something small skidded past his foot and clacked against the wall. "Sorry!" he yelled, scrambling to his knees. Hinck descended on the victim, so Trevn found the object she had dropped and picked it up. A stone, etched with runes. His heart panged. The same runes the Honored Lady Lebetta had drawn before dying.

"Let go of me, you oaf!" a woman yelled. Eudora. One of Trevn's first cousins.

"Forgive me, lady." Hinck stepped back but kept his lovesick gaze on Eudora. The weak-kneed feather heart, anyway.

Eudora smoothed her skirt and curtsied shortly to Trevn, all the while scowling. "You really should slow down, Your Highness."

"Apologies, cousin." Trevn held up the stone. "I believe this is yours. What is it?"

She snatched it back. "Just a luck charm to ward off evil. Please excuse me." She curtsied again and stalked away.

A luck charm? Trevn supposed that Lady Lebetta might have drawn such a mark as she lay dying. Halfway down the hall, Eudora looked back and then increased her speed. He heard his mother in his head: *The guilty man runs.*

223

"She's hiding something," Trevn said. "Follow her, Hinck. See where she goes."

Trevn and Mielle left Cadoc at the carriage with the driver and walked to the edge of Cape Street, which was now on a bluff overlooking the Eversea. They stood side by side and studied the damage. On their left, the remnants of a stone foundation stuck out of the ground. On the right, the circular imprint of what had once been a basement cistern. Below, nothing but waves crashing against rocky cliffs. No sign of any rubble.

"It's really gone," Mielle said. "It's strange to think of my old house at the bottom of the sea." She took hold of Trevn's hand, making his whole arm tingle. "Perhaps the fish are enjoying my old bedroom."

"What might they see inside?"

"A mural of the First Story covered the wall opposite the bed. I used to lie under the covers and imagine I was there when Arman became Nesher and created the land. There was an image of Nesher perched on Tenma's arm. She was gazing at the sunbird with an intense expression. I always wondered if she was sad that her husband was going away. The next pane showed the sunbird flying above the sea. In another he'd spread his wings and was gliding over the water. Then one where he'd landed. Cactus and flowers were sprouting from his wings. The whole story was there. How Rurek and Sarik grew from the land. The people tree. It was beautiful." She tugged his hand. "Let's go down there."

"We can't. A boat that close to the cliffs would be dashed against the rocks."

"Not exactly there. Down to the beach. Where my rope is."

Trevn agreed, happy for any excuse to spend more time with Mielle.

They were headed back to the carriage, arm in arm, when a woman screamed. "My boy! Someone help me, please! He took my boy!"

Trevn scanned the area until he caught sight of the woman, standing on the edge of the street beside a wool merchant, pointing up the coast. In the distance a man dodged through the crowd, a small child thrown over one shoulder.

"Ask the driver to call the watch," Trevn told Mielle. "Cadoc, with me!" He sprinted after the man. Passed by shops, taverns, and into the bedlam of noise and people that was the market, then out into a dank alley where all was dim. The tall buildings with their overhanging roofs blocked out the light of day and enhanced the senses. Trevn's boots slapped over muddy ground and rotten food. Where the market had smelled pleasant, the alley stank like a pig's trough. He had entered the seedy underbelly of Everton's Sink. Hives of criminals hiding from the arm of the king. His father would send all these people to Barthos without a second thought.

Trevn rounded a sharp corner and slipped in a puddle of mud, going down hard. Five Woes, how disgusting.

He pushed himself up and looked after his quarry. The alleyway ended in nothing but blue sky. He approached the end and stopped at a cliff overlooking the Echo Crack. Trevn peered over the ledge and caught sight of the kidnapper. He was walking a narrow path that led to a river hole in the cliff wall.

"Your Highness, wait." Cadoc stopped beside him, looked over the edge himself. "He could have a band of outlaws in there."

True.

"There is another way," Mielle said.

Trevn spun around, livid that she had followed. "You were meant to remain with the carriage." He winced inwardly at the authoritative sound of his own voice.

Mielle raised her eyebrows. "Was I? I grew up here, don't forget. I know this place better than you both put together."

"Is there another way into that cave?" Cadoc asked, pointing at the river hole.

"We must not abandon the child," Trevn said. He wanted to make peace but was still angry Mielle had ignored his command. "Lead on, Miss Mielle."

His formality earned him a glare, but she guided them back to Sink Road, where Trevn found Captain Veralla and informed him of the situation.

"Ho, up! Squad!" Veralla yelled at the King's Guard who'd been searching for witnesses. "Fall in behind me." He nodded to Mielle. "Lead the way, miss."

Mielle took off at a run. Veralla shot Trevn an amused smile, and together they traversed a different series of alleys and backstreets to the mouth of a cave that was crowded with squatters.

Captain Veralla grabbed Mielle's arm, then Trevn's. "Here you'll both wait with Cadoc until we return. I'll leave three more guards with you."

"But we want to come!" Mielle said.

"Out of the question," Veralla told her. He turned his authoritative gaze on Trevn. "I trust you'll handle this?"

Trevn nodded. He too wanted to accompany the soldiers, but he couldn't risk putting Mielle in danger. If he went in, she would follow.

"I don't need handling," Mielle grumbled. "I know my way around my own city."

Trevn chose not to reply.

A few seconds later, Mielle grabbed Trevn's hand. "Do you have any coin?" My, she certainly blew east and west. "Some," Trevn said.

"Let's go buy some food." She glanced around at the squatters. "Please, Trevn?" The way she said his name turned him to custard.

Trevn nodded, and their party of six trekked back to the market. He purchased six baskets and enough food to fill them, which they took back to the squatters at the cave.

Trevn had never served the poor before. He talked to them often enough, but today Mielle's somber reverence for these people tied his tongue in knots. Besides, he was covered in so much filth he likely looked like her waitman, so he followed in her wake until Veralla and his men returned, towing between them ten adult men and three women.

"Take them to the dungeon," Veralla told his second. "Then send another squad back here."

"What about the missing boy?" Trevn asked the captain.

"Better come take a look," Veralla said. "You as well, Miss Mielle."

They followed Captain Veralla deep into the cave, which turned out to be a tunnel. The smell of pitch was heavy from torches in braziers along the wall. They suddenly entered a vast cavern where they found themselves high above the ground, looking down on a scene that stole Trevn's breath.

It was some sort of factory. Lit torches mounted on crude lampstands stood throughout the open area, which was covered with individual millstones and bronze urns filled with a white mixture.

Children were everywhere. Over a hundred of them. Skin and bones with eyes overly large in their dirty faces. Some sat in pairs, spinning millstones. Some stood over urns, pounding poles into the white stuff, breaking it down. Into what? Some kind of flour?

"What is this place?" Mielle asked Veralla.

"Evenroot milling. Some harvesting too, it looks like." He motioned to a series of small tunnels in the inner wall of the cavern.

"Evenroot in Armania?" Mielle said. "I didn't think it grew here."

"It grows everywhere," Trevn said, examining the urns again now that he knew what he was looking at. "It's illegal to harvest here."

"I'm going down." Mielle spun and took hold of the sides of a ladder that ran

226

along the wall to the ground. Trevn thought to stop her, but he wanted to explore this place too. He waited until she was far enough down that he could follow.

"Go with them, Cadoc," Veralla said.

"Yes, sir."

Trevn glanced back to Veralla and decided to get a jump on Mielle. "Send some of the guards for food—and lots of it."

"An excellent idea, Your Highness," Veralla said.

Trevn climbed down. His boots slipped a few times on the smooth rungs. At the bottom he followed Mielle, who had already begun gathering the children into a huddle.

"You will not work here another day," she told them. "You're all going home."

"Got no home," a boy said.

"Then we will find you one, won't we, Sâr Trevn?"

Gasps rose, and over a hundred sets of eyes locked onto his. He saw them examine his muddy clothing with doubt, but it wasn't long before each and every face realized his garments were not made of rags, just filthy.

"It's him!" a girl said.

"The sâr rescued us!" yelled another.

"Hooray for the sâr!" a boy said.

"Hooray!" the children sang, and rushed him like a mob.

It shamed Trevn that his first thought was fear. Tiny hands and bony arms grabbed his legs, arms, and waist, hugging, shaking his hand, clapping him on the back. "Not I," Trevn tried to say. "Captain Veralla and his men arrested your captors."

No one cared. They continued to thank him until the soldiers returned with several dozen women carrying baskets of food. The women and Mielle bade the children sit in circles, and as they passed out lunch, Trevn began to explore the cavern. He crouched over an urn of white powder and examined it. It looked no different from flour. The temptation to taste the substance seized him, and he quickly moved on.

He next approached the wall. Most of the tunnels were too small for him to enter. Past the end of the evenroot tunnels, Trevn reached a natural river hole that was only two hands' breath shorter than he was tall. No water trickled from it, though the sides showed various stains from different water levels that had once flowed through here.

Footsteps sounded behind him, and he glanced back just as Mielle stepped past him up into the river hole.

"After you," he told her, smirking as he climbed inside.

"It's dark in here," she called back. "I can't see the end."

"It's part of the ream; it might not have an end."

She screamed.

"What's wrong?" He stepped toward her.

Mielle had crouched down. "I think it's dead." From over her shoulder he could see a puddle of pale light illuminating a creamy-colored lizard.

Mielle gasped, pointing behind Trevn's head. "There's another one!"

The front half of a lizard hung limply from a hole in the wall. It too looked dead. The reamway walls were covered in holes, most the size of Trevn's fist. Water dripped from many, drying on the rock before it reached the bottom. Wasn't the water supposed to flow freely in the ream? They weren't in a drought, that he knew of.

"These are baby cheyvah," Mielle declared.

Nonsense. Trevn grinned. "Cheyvah are myth. And they're massive."

She gestured at the wall. "Clearly not!"

"I will take one back to Father Tomek. Perhaps he could find a sketch in the archives."

"What killed them? Did they drown when the tide came in?"

"The tide doesn't come this high." Trevn didn't see any abrasions on the first creature. Its legs and tail were curled inward, stiff. It had webbed feet and gills. Not a lizard at all. "These have gills. They must live in the ream."

"*In* the water? We drink lizard water?"

"*Newt* water." Trevn shrugged. "I never drank a newt, but probably their excrement."

She punched his arm. "That's disgusting."

"Hey!" He grabbed her hand and pushed it behind her back. She punched his shoulder with her other hand, so he grabbed that one too. She ducked under his arm and untangled herself, scampered toward the mouth of the river hole, turned back, and raised her eyebrows.

"Giving up so easily?" she asked.

He sank to his backside and leaned against the curved wall, stretching out his legs. If she wanted to, she would come back. He hoped. It would be a good experiment anyway.

She did come back. Slowly. Staring at him all the while. He swallowed, nervous from the look in her eyes.

"What?" he asked.

She sat on his lap and kissed him. Her lips were cold, but her breath was warm.

She pulled back. "Princess Nabelle forbade me to see you."

"Why?" he asked, shocked. "She cannot do that."

"As my employer she can. It would upset Kal if I lost my position. I need it to help provide for my sister and hopefully find her a place someday. If the princess is angry with me, she could keep my sister from a good position."

This was no good. "I could speak with her and—"

"That would only make her angrier."

"Then I'll help your sister find a position. She could serve my mother." At Mielle's horrified expression, he added, "Or my grandmother."

"That would be better, I think," Mielle said.

"You could serve Grandmother too, if you want."

"Thank you, but I adore Lady Zeroah. She needs me. Once she and Sâr Wilek marry, I'll no longer work for Princess Nabelle."

"So we bide our time in secret?" Trevn asked, liking the sound of that.

Mielle nodded. "If you don't mind. Will you help with the orphans? You see the problem is bigger than even I imagined, don't you?"

"I see now. I won't abandon them."

That made her smile. "We will help them together," she said, eyes glinting in the low light. "No matter what anyone says. I would give up my position with Lady Zeroah for this, Trevn. It's more important than anything."

He understood. This was her cause. She would fight even the king to get her way. "You're a Renegade." Trevn fisted his hand and twisted it to show Mielle his mark. "See this *R*?" He traced it with his finger. "Hinck and I marked ourselves Renegades when my father ordered us back to Everton. We were happy living in Sarikar. We liked their ways. So Hinck and I, we made two vows. First, not to let this realm change us, and second, to change this realm for the better."

"I'm a Renegade because I care for orphans?" Mielle asked.

"Not only that. You're honest and brave. You would never pass by a wrong without speaking out or helping. You do what you believe is right, no matter who stands in your way."

Mielle set her forehead against his. "Have you a knife? I want to be a Renegade."

✦　✦　✦

That evening Trevn returned to the castle, stiff with dried mud, Cadoc at his side. They entered the foyer and found his mother and a half-dozen King's Guards waiting.

His first thought was for Wilek. "What has happened?"

"Seize him," Mother yelled.

Trevn held up his hands, confused. "I'm not going anywhere."

"You most certainly are. To the rosâr." Mother glared at the guards. "Well? Obey me!"

The guards stepped toward him. Cadoc moved between them and drew his sword.

"There is no need to touch me," Trevn said, frustrated yet determined to finally end this ridiculousness. "Do not forget, I outrank my mother now, though she seems happy to ignore that fact. It is time we both speak to my father about this issue of dominance. We shall see what the rosâr has to say on the matter."

"Indeed we will." Mother pointed through the vestibule that led into the west wing. "After you, my son."

Trevn walked as slowly as he could to his father's apartment. The dead newt hung in a bundled handkerchief Mielle had tied to his belt. His feet were damp inside his boots and stuck awkwardly to the leather. He was shocked his mother hadn't insisted he change. She likely planned to use his filthy appearance against him.

When they arrived outside Father's office, the guards said the king was in conference.

"Apparently he's busy, Mother," Trevn said.

"We will wait." She took a seat by the fireplace.

The only other chair was beside hers, so Trevn stood in front of the door, Cadoc at his side. That way they could enter before—

The door opened. King Jorger of Sarikar stood holding it with one hand, still looking inside at Father, who sat on his throne. "I suggest you deal with it, and soon."

"She was a *concubine*," Father said. "We later discovered she'd been meddling with black spirits. If Mikreh cursed her, he had good reason."

"Your foolishness will bring down House Hadar someday, Echad, mark my words. I only hope my loved ones are in Sarikar when it happens."

"Now, see here, Jorger—"

The Sarikarian king turned his back and walked away. Two of his Royal Guards followed him. "That man tires me," he mumbled. "I shall rest before dinner." He came face-to-face with Trevn and stopped, looked him up and down. "Been wrestling pigs, have you, Sâr Trevn?"

"Chasing criminals in the Sink, actually," Trevn said with a bow.

The king grunted. "Yes, well, your father is a madman, but you already know that." He charged past, cloak dragging heavily. His guards jogged to keep up.

Trevn entered Father's office wondering why crotchety old Jorger had traveled to Armania. His mother already knelt before the throne, head bowed, waiting to be spoken to. She must have sneaked past when Trevn had been talking to King Jorger. Father was ranting to Janek, who stood on his right in Wilek's place. A potted flower occupied the bench seat on Father's left, so Trevn claimed the chair on the side wall. The only other person in the room was Schwyl, Father's onesent, who leaned against the wall opposite Trevn with a ledger and quill in hand.

"Barthos curse his lands and wither his trees!" Father sputtered, face flushed.

"Why come all this way to rant about a dead concubine?" Janek asked.

"He dared accuse me of carelessness," Father said. "Princess Nabelle and her daughter have always been safe here. I heard no hint of them being unhappy. I thought they were staying in the castle. Why was I not informed when they returned to Fairsight Manor? Find out who knew she left and send them to the pole."

"Princess Nabelle keeps her own servants," Trevn said. "Ours might not have realized she was gone. Sending some poor waitman to the pole won't change that."

"What are you doing here?" Father asked, frowning at Trevn's attire.

"My mother tried to have me arrested." Trevn gestured to his mother, who was still kneeling before the king.

Father glared down on his third wife. "Woman! I've told you to stop meddling in Trevn's affairs."

"He was with Miss Mielle Allard," Mother said.

Father's gaze turned to Trevn. "Why are you covered in dirt?"

"I was in the city when a man abducted a boy. Cadoc and I chased them into the Sink, where we discovered an evenroot workhouse with over a hundred and fifty captive children," Trevn said, hoping this news would distract his father.

"An evenroot workhouse?" Father's eyes blazed. "In my city?"

"Indeed, Father. I would like to build a sleephouse for the orphan captives and any others who have been made homeless by the earth—"

"He is changing the subject," Mother said. "Miss Mielle Allard does not match him in fives."

"Janek, do all your friends match you in fives?" Trevn held his breath, unsure whether or not his brother would support him.

"That would be impossible," Janek said. "Not even the Wisean Council matches in fives or even tens, right, Father?"

"That's true," Father said. "Thallah, if Trevn hasn't married the girl or declared her his concubine, I don't care what he does with her. Stop wasting my time."

"But he hasn't chosen a bride yet," Mother said, "or even one concubine."

"Why no concubines, son?" Father asked. "I expected your list days ago."

Trevn scrambled for an excuse. "Mother invited too many to my ageday. I cannot decide."

Mother's dagger glare speared Trevn. "He who takes crooked paths will be found out!"

"I think I can help, Father," Janek said. "I'll take Miss Mielle as a concubine. She matches my fives. That way Trevn could borrow her from time to time without angering Athos." He winked at Trevn. "Or his mother."

Trevn shot to his feet. "You will not!"

"Who?" Father asked. "Who is this woman you both want?"

"She is Lady Zeroah's honor maiden," Mother said.

"Out of the question!" Father roared. "I have enough trouble with King Jorger as it is. I'll not do a thing to further upset the man."

Trevn relaxed. Thank Arman for that.

"Now, all of you, get out!" Father yelled. "It's time for my massage. And, Trevn, get me that list. I don't care how long it is. I'll do what I can."

"Thank you, Father." Trevn bowed and strode from the room. As soon as the door shut behind him, he ran, not wanting Janek or his mother to catch up and cause more trouble. Cadoc, who had waited outside, gave chase.

They returned to Trevn's chambers, where he found Hinck sitting at the table, gnawing on a chicken leg. "Cadoc, will you wait outside?" Trevn removed the bundle holding the dead newt and handed it to his shield. "And have someone deliver this to Father Tomek."

Cadoc took the bundle and left Trevn alone with Hinck.

Trevn pulled off his boots. "What news of my cousin?"

Hinck wiped his mouth with his sleeve. "Why, hello, Hinck. How was your day, Hinck? Terrible, you say? Oh, I'm so very sorry to hear that."

Sands, no more drama, please. "Just tell me." Trevn entered his wardrobe and peeled off his dirty clothes.

"Your demand is my duty, Your Exasperatingness!" Hinck yelled after him. "Lady Eudora went to her apartment. I waited outside for *over an hour* before she came out. It was terribly boring and cold. And I was starving."

"Which I see you've remedied, poor wee babe." Trevn found a white tunic and put it on.

Hinck next spoke over a full mouth. "She then went down to the underbuilding of the east wing and passed through the dungeon."

Trevn found a worn pair of trousers he knew to be comfortable and pulled them on. "You followed her?"

"Yes. Until she went through a door that, when I reached it, was locked."

Trevn came back into the main room, lacing his britches. When he finished, he sat across from Hinck at the table and helped himself to a piece of chicken. "Locked from inside?"

Hinck shrugged. "It had a keyhole. I didn't see whether she used a key or if someone let her in." Hinck tossed his chicken bone on the table and leaned back in his chair. "How was the Cape?"

"An adventure. But my mother and Janek seek to ruin my fun." Trevn explained what had happened in the Sink and since he had returned.

"Evenroot milling. Sands," Hinck said. "But Miss Mielle should be safe from Janek at Fairsight Manor, at least."

Trevn sighed. "But far from me."

"She wants the Renegade mark. She'll be one of us forever. Seems promising, though I can't imagine a woman would really cut herself."

"Mielle would." And hopefully not her whole hand.

"Oh, it's Mielle now without the *Miss*, is it? What else went on in the Sink?"

Nothing Trevn would ever tell Hinck. "I dislike how Janek is getting cozy with Father in Wilek's absence. I bet he knows where Cousin Eudora went in the bowels of the castle. I want you to start spending time with him and his friends."

"Janek? Why?"

"That rune Eudora carried is no coincidence. She is part of his retinue. This will be safer than you following her everywhere."

"There you go again, changing my life with a few casual words. Do you even know your brother? He'll never call me friend."

Likely true. "So make it about Eudora. Everyone knows you love her." He sighed. "This is important, Hinck. A woman has been murdered. There must be a link somewhere to the symbol. I cannot go. You can."

"You mean to use me. As always."

"Why shouldn't I? We're royalty. Our mere existence marks us as pawns in a game that never ends until we sail away on our death boats. I may have stumbled upon a sphere of influence that could harm Wilek. I must confirm or deny it."

"Eudora will laugh at me. Remember what she did when the Rurekans were here and my mother tried to make us dance?"

"Of course they will all mock you ruthlessly. They mock everyone. But this is the only way."

"I don't know . . ."

"Hinck, if something should happen to Wilek, Father will certainly make Janek his Heir. . . . Can you imagine Janek as rosâr?"

Hinck grimaced. "It's a night terror I have every so often."

"So you see why you must do this."

A heavy sigh. "They'll ask why I'm not serving you."

"Tell them I'm busy with my lessons."

"All the time? Even *you* don't read that much." He pursed his lips. "I could tell them you're with Miss Mielle?"

That brought a grin to Trevn's face. "An excellent notion. Janek will be thrilled."

Hinck

Hinck awoke early and rode toward Seacrest. He took his time, enjoying the cool morning air and imagining the worst the day ahead might hold.

Hinck was an earl but never got to act like one. He had spent the last ten years with Trevn in Sarikar, complacent in the sâr's shadow. Whenever they had visited Everton, Hinck had suffered scores of humiliating practical jokes from Janek and his friends—some with violent consequences.

Trevn knew this, of course. It still shocked Hinck that Trevn felt sending him to face them alone a justifiable request. But he must stop pitying himself. He had known what it meant to be Trevn's backman upon accepting the position. And Lady Eudora *had* been carrying a stone with the same rune the Honored Lady Lebetta had drawn in her dying moments.

Hinck arrived at Seacrest and handed the boy his horse with as much indifference as he could muster in hopes of imitating the behavior of Janek's friends. That included barging in the front door, and the racket he made sent five servants scrambling into a line to greet him. Their behavior so surprised him that he almost apologized for his rudeness.

Timmons, Janek's onesent, stood center front. "Your lordship. How can I be of service?"

Hinck forced himself to answer with confidence. "I've come to visit Sâr Janek."

"I see, sir. I didn't realize you and Sâr Janek were friends."

Hinck flushed, annoyed that a servant would question him, but not surprised that Janek had trained his man to be particular. "Sâr Trevn gave me the day off. My father has encouraged me to make new acquaintances, so I figured . . ." Hinck's bravado dwindled. "Will he see me, do you think?"

Timmons shrugged. "Sâr Janek's moods change more than the tides, your lordship. I shall announce you, and I daresay his answer won't be long in coming." Timmons left Hinck in the foyer. The other servants scattered.

Hinck should have written first, but that would have given Janek opportunity to decline. Showing up unannounced was a gamble, though. He forced himself to keep from pacing, worrying what was to come and hoping Janek might refuse him so he could go home.

Timmons returned. "Your lordship, the sâr would like to speak with you."

"Excellent." Though inside, Hinck cringed. He knew Janek wouldn't pass up an opportunity to ridicule Hinckdan Faluk in front of his peers.

Hinck followed Timmons through the house. The walls were masoned sea stones with a row of shells nested along the top, around the windows, and on the door frames. Furniture had been crafted from driftwood and cushioned with blue-and-gold damask. Everything was vaguely familiar. Hinck had been to Seacrest a few times as a child, long before Janek had claimed this place for himself.

The courtyard seemed smaller than Hinck remembered. It was much greener too. Someone had put in a garden. Paths of white gravel separated sections of plants and trees. In the center a blue canvas canopy covered a graveled area. On the far end Janek sat on a driftwood throne, holding a potted plant on his knee. His concubines shared a blanket by his feet. Eudora's brother—Oli, Duke of Canden—reclined on a longchair, tossing a leather ball up and down. Fonu perched on a stool between Oli and Janek, a goblet in his hand that was likely filled with wine. Hinck also recognized Sir Jayron, Janek's Rurekan shield, standing beside the throne, his arms folded. Lady Eudora sat beside Shessy Wallington on a longchair, their heads tipped toward one another as they whispered and giggled. Heat flooded Hinck at the sight of Eudora, and while no one had yet seen him, he quickly looked away.

"Your Royal Highness," Timmons said. "May I present the Earl of Dacre."

All faces turned to Hinck, who gave Janek a deep bow.

"Dacre Dan," Janek said, looking Hinck over like one might a potential tunic. "You bring a message from my puppy brother?"

"I have no message, Your Highness," Hinck said, softly.

Janek's brows sank, reminding Hinck of Pontiff Rogedoth for some reason. "Then why are you here? You want something?"

"I ask no favor but your company." He tried to hold a confident posture and firm voice.

"Shouldn't you be chasing Trevn all over the realm? Isn't that what back-men do, Oli?"

The duke, expressionless, tossed and caught his ball.

"Sâr Trevn has dismissed me for the day," Hinck said.

Another frown from Janek. "Dismissed his servant? Why?"

"*Janek*," Oli said. "He's no more a servant than I am."

"Well, fetch me a drink then, Oli, and show him how the job is done."

Oli threw the ball at Janek. It thwacked off his chest, released a small burst of feathers and dust, and rolled over the gravel, stopping in the middle of the open area.

"You almost hit my sandvine!" Janek yelled, frowning at the white sliver of a bud in the pot. "Timmons, take this inside where it will be safe from my careless guests."

"Yes, Your Highness."

Everyone watched in silence as Timmons retrieved the potted plant and carried it into the house.

"Why are you here?" Janek asked Hinck.

"He's come for Eudora," Sir Jayron said, his gaze cold.

As if on cue, everyone looked at Eudora. Fonu snorted. Oli dipped his head to hide a smirk. Yet Eudora watched Hinck, her eyes sparkling.

Janek raised his eyebrows. "Have you?"

Hinck kept his gaze on Janek, though he could sense Eudora awaiting his answer along with everyone else. He had rehearsed this reply on the ride over, knowing someone might make the accusation. He hoped he wouldn't botch it. "Lady Eudora's presence always thrills my soul, Your Highness, but I didn't come here to pursue her."

Someone—Fonu, Hinck thought—oohed.

"Why did Trevn dismiss you?" Janek asked.

"He had lessons this morning and plans all afternoon," Hinck said.

"Dallying with that honor maiden of Lady Zeroah's, I bet," Fonu said.

This made the ladies giggle.

Hinck pounced on that theory. "I suspect that's his plan exactly."

"An encouraging turn of events." Janek scooted to the edge of his throne and clasped his hands. "So the young earl, dismissed by his lascivious young master, seeks the favor of my company. Well, why not? Perhaps you can help me reach that fickle brother of mine before he goes the way of Wilek."

"I wonder if Sâr Wilek has captured the killer of his concubine yet," Oli said.

"Didn't I tell you?" Fonu said. "It was I who killed her. An accident, of course. Do not waste tears for her. She died in ecstasy."

"Do shut up, Fonu," Eudora said. "This is nothing to joke about. I always liked Lady Lebetta."

"You would," Fonu said. "She probably taught you all your tricks."

"Tricks you'll never experience," Eudora said.

"Temple prostitutes have better tricks than you," Fonu said.

"Only a man who cannot win a woman frequents the temple harems," Eudora said.

"Plenty of real women favor me," Fonu said, "it's your type that—"

"Friends!" Janek's voice cut through the ribbing. "I'll not have you deviants corrupting the young earl with your bawdy talk."

A moment of silence passed as everyone exchanged glances, likely trying to decide whether or not Janek was being serious. That's what Hinck wanted to know. He decided to brag a little and, hopefully, prove he was one of them.

"I'm fifteen," Hinck said. "On my ageday my father bought me an hour with a temple prostitute. So nothing you say will shock me."

This made everyone burst into laughter. Hinck's cheeks burned, bewildered by their reaction.

"So we can say what we want," Fonu said, grinning at Janek.

"Not *everything*," Janek said. "Like you, Fonu, Hinckdan hasn't yet learned Lady Eudora's tricks."

Shessy Wallington gasped. Eudora shot Janek a glare that could smelt ore.

Fonu snorted. "What good is a lady when he's had a temple prostitute?"

"Enough," Eudora said, standing. "You're all worse than children." Shessy stood with her, and the two swept into the house without another word.

Hinck watched them go, sorry that Janek and Fonu's teasing had fallen on Eudora. But he would be less nervous with her gone, so perhaps it was a blessing.

"Come, Hinckdan," Janek said, standing. "Let me show you my garden."

Janek strolled down a gravel path, so Hinck chased after him, eager to obey for some strange reason.

"Much is in bloom now," Janek said. "There's the cat's claw. The coral leaf is fantastic. Roses, always going strong. I like them in mass. Gives me some color. A little prickly leaf and some bitterbrush. I put in this pea stone path. I love the sound it makes when you walk on it and the pale contrast against all the green."

"It's wonderful," Hinck said, slightly bewildered, as though he'd stepped into a different world where Janek was almost normal.

"The pond is fed from the sea," Janek said. "I've got an underground duct on both sides. Moving water gives a restful feeling, and I wanted to create a sense of peace when people enter the garden. How did you feel when you first came in?"

Scared out of his mind. But Hinck said, "Peaceful."

Janek nodded. "Then it's working. Good. I hear the gods in my garden, Hinckdan. Dendron and Barthos share energy and wisdom when I touch soil, leaves, or blossoms. All this beauty is my offering. Dendron and Barthos both fell in love with Magon, started a war over her. But they don't need her. Together nature and soil give life. There's magic in that, Hinck. Power."

And maybe a little insanity?

They returned to the courtyard, where Oli, Sir Jayron, and Fonu were laughing about something. Janek took his throne, and Hinck stood awkwardly beside it.

"The ladies have given you their seat, Dacre Dan," Janek said, gesturing to the longchair. "Relax in the company of greatness."

"I'd throw my ball at you again, Janek," Oli said, "but I'd have to get up, and you're not worth the exercise."

"Hinckdan," Janek said. "Fetch His Grace's ball. I abuse him greatly, and pelting me with a scrap of leather is his only release."

Hinck collected the ball. Oli held out his hand to catch, but Hinck pitched it at Janek instead. The ball smacked the sâr on the left shoulder, leaving a dusty mark before falling to his lap.

Everyone stared, mouths gaping as they waited to see how Janek would respond.

A smirk. "Oh, I do like the sparks in you," Janek said to Hinck. "Trevn must bore you to madness with all his maps and history lessons."

"Sometimes," Hinck said, which was completely true.

"But I cannot let you strike me without consequence. You aren't the Duke of Canden, you know."

"You're going to punish me?" Hinck asked, feeling slightly faint.

"I'm going to test your worth."

"Janek, let it go," Oli said.

"This is an opportunity to mold a future soldier."

"He's not a soldier. Nor am I, as there's no war at present."

"There's always a war!" Janek snapped. "We are in battle every day, fighting for our place in this world. Young Hinckdan must as well. He issued a challenge with his toss of the ball. I shall meet it. Should he pass my test, I shall claim him as loyal. Should he fail, I'll have him flogged on the pole and shipped back to Trevn in a death boat."

"He's joking," Oli said to Hinck. "He won't really kill you."

Hinck wasn't so certain. He ground his teeth to keep his chin from trembling.

"Must you play with everyone?" Oli asked Janek. "He's too young to stand up to your challenges."

The duke might have been trying to help, but his insults were almost as bad as Janek's threats. "I'm not afraid of a challenge," Hinck said.

"See, Oli? He's not afraid. Besides, this challenge doesn't require brawn. Hinckdan Faluk, Earl of Dacre, I challenge you to tell me what bodymark hides under Lady Eudora's clothing."

The blood drained from Hinck's face.

"Why does he get this challenge and you sent me to fight in the diamond?" Fonu asked.

"We all saw how the earl glowed in Lady Eudora's presence," Janek said. "I must know if he is capable of taking what he wants. If he cannot charm that drick, he is useless to me."

Oli swung his legs off the longchair and stood. "You call my sister a drick?"

"I test you all," Janek said. "And you remain here only because you continue to pass my tests."

Hinck's mind galloped with the reality of this challenge. "How long do I have?"

"Five weeks," Janek said. "And if any of you breathes a word of this to Lady Eudora, you'll all face the pole."

Oli rolled his eyes. Fonu and Sir Jayron glared at Hinck, who pondered the challenges before him. Two tasks from two sârs. To fail Janek's challenge would inevitably mean failing Trevn's. Eudora's runestone had started this, so getting closer to her might at least help him find answers for Trevn, even when he failed Janek's challenge, which, of course, he would.

"Very well," Hinck said. "I accept."

Janek leaned back and smiled the smile of a man who enjoyed playing with people's lives. "Good. Now sit and relax, Dacre Dan. You're safe. For now."

Hinck perched on the edge of the longchair, but he didn't relax or feel the least bit safe.

Charlon

Five days' travel from Dacre across the King's Gorge to catch up with the Chieftess in Sarikar. This land had trees. Bizarre yet beautiful. Mreegan's camp hid in a canyon. Charlon dismounted and handed her horse to Vald, number Three. Ordered Torol to take Prince Wilek to her tent. It felt good, ordering the men. But she had failed. Could not lie with the prince. Could barely touch him.

Now she must confess.

Reluctantly she approached the red tent. No hillock in this canyon. The men had erected the Chieftess's tent on a cliff. Charlon climbed rocky switchbacks. Felt the prince within. The soul-binding allowed him to see what no man should. He knew her heart. Her desires. Her fears.

She could sense him as well. His frustration and anger choked her. His wrists burned from the ropes holding him. He cursed his stupidity. He must escape. He could not.

Magon help her. She pushed his thoughts down. Tried to ignore him. Approached the tent.

Rone stood guard outside. Opened the tent flap. "Welcome back, Mother." Kindness and respect for the Mother, fueled by fear.

No time for pleasantries. She entered. Knelt before the throne where Mreegan sat.

The Chieftess lit up with a smile, stroked the pale newt on her lap. "You have him?"

"Yes," Charlon said. "All went as planned." *Almost.*

Mreegan cocked her head. "You pity him."

The words pinched Charlon's heart. "He is sad."

"Good. If he is beaten, he won't cause trouble."

Charlon's quest was trouble enough. "His emotions cut deeply."

"You must rule him," Mreegan said.

Charlon bowed her head. "Yes, Chieftess." If only it were that easy.

Mreegan slipped off her throne. Squatted in front of Charlon. Set her hand on Charlon's abdomen.

Charlon stiffened. The cold place inside flared. *Get away!* Charlon's heart said. But she fought to remain still.

Mreegan muttered. Searching. The newt crawled down to Mreegan's wrist, its tongue tasting Charlon's tunic. "There is no child in you." Mreegan stood and returned to her throne.

Of course there was no child! Charlon had barely been able to touch the man. Why had Magon put this before her? It was a mistake. She could not. Heaviness pressed down.

"What is the problem?" Mreegan asked.

Hide the truth. "He hates me. His sadness saddens me. His fear frightens me. His anger angers me. I cannot control it."

"That's what it means to be soul-bound," Mreegan said. "Make the magic work in your favor. Force his emotions to mirror yours. You must be his master, not the other way around. We remain in this canyon until you conceive. Dismissed."

Despair! "Yes, Chieftess." She left. So heavy. So burdened. How could she succeed? What had been done to her . . . she must do. Do to another. She could not! Not do it. Not—

She must! She was new. Reborn by Magon. No longer a victim. And this was a man. The enemy. How many had he abused? In the name of pleasure? How many? She would do to him what he deserved. She must!

It was the only way. To become Mother.

In her tent, the prince. Alone. Hands bound behind to the center pole. Head hanging low. Sorrow swelled off him. Like heat from a fire. Charlon staggered under its power.

Focus. Time to work the magic. Bleeding him would pain her. She had taken hairs the first time. Hair would work again. "We must cut your hair," she said in Kinsman. So strange to speak her childhood language again. "Only women are permitted long hair."

The prince glanced up, eyes bloodshot. "A warrior's braids are a matter of honor in Armania. Cut them, and you make me a laughingstock."

Tears welled. She forced them back. "I need part of your body. To cast my spell. You'll miss your hair less. Than a finger."

An arrow of hatred stabbed within. "I'll die before I let you touch me again."

"Give me a son. And you can die anytime you like."

He sputtered, confused, frustrated. "What kind of a person are you? To take Lebetta's face and voice and smell." Great anguish stretched between them. "Do you even care how you played with . . ." Voice trailed off in a tremble. He panted through his nose. "Why am I trying to reason with a witch?"

Charlon couldn't bear his grief. She must get away. At least find help. She yanked the door flap aside. "Torol!" she cried in Tennish. He stood outside. Obedient, always. "We must cut this man's hair. Apply the rune. Call the First and Third. And someone to hold him."

"Yes, Mother."

Torol returned with Kateen, Roya, and two lesser men, both carrying shard clubs. The women prepared the tattoo ink. The men held the prince. Torol came at his braids with an obsidian knife. Prince Wilek turned his head, and Torol's blade sliced his cheek. The prince growled. Thrashed his legs. Trying to kick someone. He pulled against the center pole. Screamed. Twisted his shoulders from side to side. The tent bobbed and shook. His fury pooled in Charlon's gut. So much anger. She fought back a scream.

The men grabbed him. Forced him down. Held his head. His arms. Torol sawed his braids until they were severed. Handed them to Charlon.

The prince saw them. Anger melted to despair, defeat. Bloodshot eyes met hers. "Bind my hands. Cut my hair. Use magic to force me to your will. But I'll *never* be Magonian. I'm a sâr of Armania." Rage grew within. "I don't recognize our marriage. Nor will anyone in Armania. You waste effort on a plot that will fail."

"Once I carry your child, the Armanian king will accept our marriage," Charlon said.

The prince laughed. Ironic joy swelled through Charlon. "You don't know my father. He'd sacrifice any child of our making to Barthos, just to protect his throne."

She sensed his honesty. "Not his own grandson."

"Are all Magonians so ignorant of history? My father killed three of his sons before my very eyes. I was nine. He is a ruthless man who cares only for his superstitions. You cannot blackmail him. You cannot trick him. He is the master of all evil games."

Charlon had no words. Failure would become her doom. She carried the prince's warrior locks to her altar mat. Cut some hairs. Sprinkled them into a bowl. Drank ahvenrood juice.

A quick spell ended the prince's obstinance. The men carried his limp body to Charlon's bed of furs and laid him on his stomach. Torol held the prince's head. Roya knelt at his side, bowl of ink in one hand, needle in the other. She dipped it and pressed it against the prince's neck. A groan. A twitch. Torol held him steady. The pain irritated Charlon as well. She gritted her teeth. Focused on the shadir who were curling and smoking in the Veil. Magon stood beside them, proud, confident.

Roya worked slowly. Meticulously inked the slav rune. When she finished, Charlon cast a spell of obedience. Now he would be compelled. To obey the command of any mantic. Her task would be simpler now.

The trance did not stop his thoughts. His mind was active. Dreams of fear and pain. Longing for his dead woman. *His thoughts nauseate me,* Charlon told Magon. *I hate being soul-bound. No man belongs within. Nor do I want to see what lies in his soul.*

If you want to succeed, you must do this for me, Magon said. *Then you may someday take Mreegan's place.*

So Charlon wore an expression of indifference. Pretended to be brave. But it was a lie. It was all a lie.

KALEПEK

Kaptar had been built in a valley. Concrete walls surrounded the end of the Upper Sister to keep the poisonous lake water at bay. In the city itself, the wall contained a dam to divert waters in case of flooding. The water was currently so deep the watermen were still using sweeps. This put the barge high enough that Kal could see over the dam to the red-tile roofs in the city.

The Kaptar pier floated on the surface and was tied to the dam with ropes so it could rise and fall with the water level. A stone staircase ran up the side of the dam. The bottom steps were green with algae and descended below the water level. Some three dozen watercrafts were tied to the pier. The steps were crowded with people hauling cargo.

How were they going to get the camels up those steps?

Grayson, eating a roll, approached Kal. "You hungry, Sir Kalenek? There's cheese rolls in the barn. I ate five already. Onika says it's because I'm growing. Says I'm taller than ever."

"How would Onika know how tall you are?" Kal asked.

"She puts her hand on my head."

Kal regarded the pale woman. Novan was yet again sitting with her on the wooden crates at the bow. "Time to load up the camels, Novan," Kal yelled. A deep roll of thunder resounded, pulling Kal's eyes up to a clear sky. The thunder did not cease but amplified. On shore, someone screamed. Kal ran back to the bow. A dust cloud rose up on the other side of the wall.

"What's happening?" Novan asked.

246

"Earthquake!" Wymer yelled, running toward them from the stern. "Help us paddle her back from the pier."

Kal and Novan each grabbed a sweep and set to work. The pier bobbed, slamming the tied watercrafts against itself and each other as the waves convulsed. Kal paddled with all his strength, watching the dust cloud billow higher and higher. People scrambled over the wall and down the stairs. Some crawled into boats or reamskiffs and pushed out into the lake.

The thundering stopped as suddenly as it had begun. Cheers went up from the boats. Kal stopped rowing and noted fewer roofs showing over the wall than before.

"Did a lot of damage," Kal said, unnerved that this had happened exactly when Onika had prophesied.

"How can you tell?" Novan asked.

"Look at the rooftops," Kal said. "Not nearly as many buildings still standing."

A *pop* tore his attention to the dam. Stone grinded against stone. The wall cracked down the center and slowly gave way, crashing back into the city and ripping the pier like a piece of muslin. Water surged through the opening ahead of them.

"Sweeps!" Wymer yelled. "Pull hard!"

Kal dragged his sweep through the water, lifted it, and dragged it again. He paddled as fast and hard as he could, glancing back in horror just as the dam walls fell.

"Keep at it, men!" Wymer yelled. "Pull! Pull!"

Kal pulled until his arms burned, but they were no longer moving backward. Around them reamskiffs and boats slid past. The strength of seven men wasn't enough to keep their barge out of the current.

"Hold on!" Wymer yelled. "We're going through!"

Kal yanked the sweep inside and wrapped his arms around the rail. Oddly enough the barge wasn't moving terribly fast. It glided into the crack the fallen walls had made, tipped, held for a moment as the port side scraped against the broken wall, then sailed over the hump and down into what must have once been a street.

The water carried the barge in a rush past the remains of buildings. Debris floated alongside: produce, wood scraps, patches of grass roof, and the occasional body. The barge twisted, struck a stone building, then jerked back the other way. It spun slowly in a circle until it faced the opposite direction and the bow hit the same building again. The watermen used longpoles to try to keep them straight.

The farther they floated, the more cluttered the water became. Furniture, market stalls, entire roofs drifted down the makeshift river. Kal could no longer tell where the road might have been. The barge struck a floating roof like a peal of thunder. Water and bits of grass rained down.

"Inside the barn!" Wymer yelled. "We must keep dry."

They hunkered down in a mass of bodies between the two rows of stalls. One of the camels was braying. Onika and Grayson hugged each other. Novan had his arms around them both.

The barge bobbed wildly over the waves and jerked whenever it made contact with something solid. Kal wished he could see where they were going.

A sudden collision threw them all on their faces. A second jolt came when something rammed them from behind. Water gushed underneath the prow doors. Wymer yelled and climbed up on the half wall of a stall to keep clear of the water. Novan picked up Onika and sat her beside Wymer.

But the water immediately receded.

"Bit afraid to open the doors," Wymer said.

"Then leave them closed!" Grayson yelled.

"We have to know what's going on out there," Novan said. "What if more waves—"

The bow dropped, leaving them hanging at a steep angle. Grayson yelped and grabbed one of the poles that held up the roof. Someone's pack slid across the floor. Kal caught it with his foot.

No one moved for several seconds. "I'm going to look." Kal tucked the pack into a stall and walked carefully down the steep incline to the bow. He spread his feet wide before the doors, then pushed one open. It swung slowly at first, then flipped around the outside corner of the barn, slammed, and swung partway back.

They were floating a good three paces above the water line.

How could that be?

A quick glance and it all made sense. "We're on top of a building!" Kal yelled. "We need to get off or we'll be stuck when the water recedes."

Wymer joined him at the door. "Now that's a fix. Men, get your poles and head out back. See if we can find something to push off of. Sir Kalenek, we could use the help of you and your man."

"Novan, with me," Kal said.

They followed Wymer out the aft doors and found sweeps. The end of the barge had stopped against the outer city wall.

"On my mark," Wymer said. "And when we fall, you best hold on. Now!"

Everyone pushed. Something scraped beneath them, a sound like pulling a nail as big as a man. The barge shifted in tiny jerks. Kal imagined a roof of red tiles with the hull snagging each row.

The barge began to slide, rumbling like an avalanche as it ground over the rooftop. Kal tucked the sweep under his arm and grabbed the rail with both hands.

The barge fell. Kal's stomach flipped. All sound stopped.

The bow hit first, nearly jerking Kal's arms from his body. Seconds later the stern plunged into the debris-clogged water. The splash was tremendous, but their forward motion left the greater part of it in their wake. Water spots on Kal's left sleeve gave him pause. No water seemed to have touched his skin.

The barge rocked and banged. Kal clutched the rail until Wymer walked past and opened the doors to the barn. They had survived.

"Everyone alive in here?" Wymer asked.

"We're fine!" Grayson called.

Wymer looked up past Kal's shoulder, his eyes wide. Kal turned and saw a woman sitting on a rooftop and holding a little girl in her lap.

Novan lifted a hand and waved.

The little girl waved back.

A soft whistle. "Rustian?" Onika whistled again. "Has anyone seen the cat?"

No one had.

"We're going to have to stay on the barge till the water fades," Wymer said.

"Can we steer ourselves to some kind of clearing?" Kal asked, wanting to wait out the flood over open ground.

"No place like that in this city," Wymer said.

"How far to the prison?" Onika asked.

"Can't imagine anyone in the prison survived," Wymer said. "But we might as well sail that way. Could take days for this water to drain."

The men set to driving the barge through the cluttered water. Kal and Novan stood at the bow and used their sweeps to push debris out of the way. As they scraped past a building, Grayson called out.

"Rustian! On the rooftop!" The boy ran toward the rail. "I'll get him for you, Onika."

"Don't be a fool!" Kal snapped. "Come away from there."

But it was too late. Grayson had already climbed over the rail and up the side of the building. They managed to stop the barge and reverse their direction, but the boy was out of reach. Kal watched helplessly as Grayson held on with one hand and stretched his other toward the cat.

"Come on, Rustian." The boy's fingers brushed the cat's leg. Rustian pushed against Grayson's hand, purring. The roof tiles shifted. The boy adjusted his grip.

All that movement was too much. The tiles began to slip, one at a time. The cat hissed and leapt over Grayson's head, landing with a thud on the floor of the barge. The boy let out a small yelp and fell. Kal bent over the rail and reached for him, just grazing the boy's leg before he plunged beneath the water.

Kal went to his knees and squeezed between the railing, leaning out over the water. The moment Grayson's head bobbed above the surface, Kal grabbed him and pulled. The boy weighed next to nothing, and Kal easily dragged him aboard.

"You fool!" Kal gave him a good shake. "You think the cat couldn't take care of itself? It got up there, didn't it?"

Grayson coughed and sputtered, gasping in breaths. "I'm fine. I'm not hurt."

"But the poison," one of the watermen said.

Indeed. Kal's hand and arm already itched fiercely. He peeled off his glove and found red pimples had dotted his skin. A thrill of panic rose in his chest. Surely so little water wouldn't kill him. But the boy . . . He'd die in agony.

Novan offered Grayson his hand to help him stand.

Kal waved him back. "Don't touch him. The sores ooze contagion."

"Red water doesn't hurt me," Grayson said.

"It's poison," Kal said. Yet the boy's skin remained blotchy gray, while Kal's arm had completely broken out in pustules.

"I have some salve that'll help with the pain," Wymer said. "Come inside and I'll make you comfortable."

Everything happened too quickly for comfort. Kal collapsed onto a bedroll. A fever came upon him. It was difficult to breathe. His arm burned as if covered in flames. He couldn't bend his elbow. He fell in and out of sleep, tossing and turning, restless.

Shadir swarmed him, whispering in his ear to follow them to Gâzar's court where Livy was waiting. Kal knew the creatures were lying. Livy had followed Arman. She would never step foot in Gâzar's court. Still, he wanted desperately to go. To see if he might find her.

He overheard people talking but understood nothing. A guard. A prison. A pit.

Kal drifted between that strange reality and his familiar nightmares of the war, which were worse than ever. And this time they did not end, because he did not wake.

TREVN

After a tiring morning on the practice field, Trevn walked back to the castle with Cadoc. Swordplay had never been a favorite pastime, but lately it had served as a release for Trevn's pent-up frustration over not being allowed to visit Mielle. Today, however, despite his fatigue, he still felt unsettled, restless.

"I'm going to climb," he told Cadoc. "Care to accompany me?"

Cadoc's displeasure was evident as he looked up the side of the castle. The shield was no faintheart—had followed Trevn places Hinck had never been willing to go—but he had not yet forced himself up the walls after Trevn. Perhaps this was his line in the sand. "You'll go straight to your chambers?"

Trevn gave the man a curt nod. "I will. I promise."

"Then I will meet you there, Your Highness."

"Very well." Trevn pulled off his boots and sword belt and handed them to Cadoc.

Cadoc tucked the things under one arm. "Please don't fall."

"Never on your watch," Trevn said, grinning. "If I decide to fall, it will be when Beal is under me. I'd prefer a new onesent, anyway." He grabbed hold of the vine stonework that trimmed the castle walls and hoisted himself up and to the left, leaving his shield on the ground outside the eastern entrance of the castle.

Trevn scaled the wall steadily, moving diagonally from balcony to balcony. When his arms tired, he took short breaks by sitting on balcony ledges.

Before he had met Mielle, his days had passed in a haphazard state of busyness, drawing maps and exploring the castle or the city. Now nothing compared to being in her presence, and he hadn't seen her in over a week. Why would Princess Nabelle disapprove of his friendship with Mielle?

He pondered this as he approached the underside of a balcony on the fourth floor. The soft hum of men's voices slowed his ascent. He didn't wish to be seen, especially not eavesdropping.

He backtracked a little so his head remained below the balcony, where he could pass underneath. The sound of his own name stopped all movement.

"How can you be sure?" A man's voice, deep and grating. Trevn recognized it immediately as belonging to Filkin Yohthehreth, his father's favorite prophet.

"I know what I heard." This from a voice that Trevn could not place. One of Yohthehreth's disciples, perhaps?

"But if Father Tomek is an Armanite, he must be teaching the sâr the same," Yohthehreth said.

"The rosâr says his uncle is no devout follower of any one god, but His Majesty has always been blind where his relations are concerned."

"Indeed," Yohthehreth said.

"We should investigate the matter ourselves. If he is teaching the sâr lies . . . Should the boy ever become rosâr—"

"Sâr Trevn will never sit on the throne of Armania," Yohthehreth snapped. "If all goes to plan, Sâr Janek will be king for a very long time. After that, Rosâr Janek's heir."

Trevn's heart pulsed in his ears so loud that he was certain the men could hear it. He pulled himself as high as he dared, peering between the stone rails. He caught sight of the men but was too close to see more than the folds of two robes against the stone floor of the balcony: one white, the other cobalt. Yohthehreth was the prophet in white, but who was the Rôb priest?

"Find out for certain what god Father Tomek serves," Yohthehreth said. "Then we'll know how to proceed."

"It will be done, lord."

The robes fluttered. Trevn saw the soles of the men's sandals as they walked away. The priest wore a silver cuff around his ankle. It was adorned with the shapes of the Rôb Five chiseled out of turquoise.

Trevn continued his climb, reeling with all he'd overheard.

"Find out for certain what god Father Tomek serves."

"Sâr Trevn will never sit on the throne of Armania."

"If all goes to plan, Sâr Janek will be king for a very long time."

With all the questions these words raised within Trevn, the biggest was why Wilek had not been mentioned. Fear for his brother's welfare made Trevn's arms tremble. He needed to speak to Father Tomek right away.

By the time he climbed around the corner of the castle, Cadoc was waiting on his balcony. Normally Trevn would slow down to punish Cadoc's impatience. Today he crossed the wall like a spider evading a stomping sandal. He reached his balcony and tumbled over the rail.

Cadoc helped him stand. "Would you like a drink, Your Highness?"

Trevn gasped in air and pushed past Cadoc. "I must go immediately to Father Tomek." He ran into the hallway, bare feet slapping the stone floor.

Cadoc's boots thumped behind him. "Your Highness, wait!"

Trevn ran all the way to Father Tomek's chambers and let himself in without knocking. His tutor was sitting at his table, which was covered in piles of scrolls.

"Sâr Trevn." Father Tomek stood and bowed. "Is something wrong?"

"You're in danger, Father."

Cadoc lumbered into the room, closed the door behind him, and stood wheezing and clutching his knees.

"Sit down, both of you." Father Tomek gestured to a longchair before his balcony.

Trevn had no patience for formalities. "I overheard Filkin Yohthehreth and a priest speaking about you. About us."

Father Tomek took Trevn by the arm and led him to the longchair. They sat together, side by side. "Start from the beginning and tell me everything."

Trevn related the tale with as much detail as he could. "What does it mean?"

Father Tomek glanced at Cadoc, his expression pinched as if trying to surmise the man's soul with a mere glance.

"Cadoc is trustworthy," Trevn said. "I'd stake my life on it."

"Then he has my trust as well," Father Tomek said. "I am what they say, though I've never hidden that from you."

"What's so bad about worshiping Arman?"

"Nothing whatsoever. But you were raised in Sarikar, where Arman is everything. In Armania, priests of Rôb refuse to give any one god absolute authority for fear that god will become a tyrant. The Armanite faith is considered archaic and dangerous."

"If they're so certain Janek will rule, why do they care what I learn?"

"Because someday they'll die, leaving behind a younger generation of priests to lead the king. You very well might rise to be a high priest or even Pontiff."

They feared Trevn might influence the king to worship Arman alone. "But what of Wilek? They never spoke of him, as if he didn't exist."

"That bothers me greatly. Could be the Farway claim was a trick to lure Sâr Wilek out of the city, where he would be vulnerable. Heir wars can be ugly things."

Trevn's stomach clenched at the very idea of someone trying to kill Wilek. "What shall we do?"

"Pray for his safe return. Trust Arman to protect him. I will go to Captain Veralla and ask his advice as well."

Good idea. Veralla and Wilek were close. "Thank you, Father. Please be careful."

"My god will keep me safe."

Trevn hoped so.

"I discovered the identity of your dead newt." Father Tomek stood and walked to his desk. He picked up a scroll and unrolled it. Trevn came to stand beside him. There was a sketch of the long, pale newt. Beneath it, the tiniest writing.

"What language is that?"

"Ancient Armanian. It says that the letaha lives on evenroot. Isn't that fascinating? What kills us, feeds this creature."

Strange more than fascinating. "So how did it die?"

"My guess is starvation. Especially if someone was harvesting all its food."

A mantic, perhaps. One who had something to do with Lady Lebetta's death, Eudora's runestone, or both. "Did you learn anything about the runes Lady Lebetta drew when she died?" Trevn asked.

The old man shook his head. "Nothing yet, but I shall keep looking. You are welcome to join me in the archives. Two sets of eyes are better than one."

"I will think on it," Trevn said, hesitant to spend hours of free time with his tutor, who would likely turn the search into extra lessons.

Halfway back to his chambers, Trevn and Cadoc came upon Hinck in the hallway.

"Come with me," Trevn said. "I've something to tell you."

"Don't you want to know how I fared with Lady Eudora today?" Hinck asked.

"I'm sure you'll tell me."

"She wasn't there. That's what. How can I succeed in Janek's challenge when I never see Lady Eudora? I'll face the pole for certain."

"We have bigger things to worry about at present than your courting my cousin."

"Oh, I'm sorry, Your Carelessness. Never you mind my unscarred back. Do tell. What catastrophe has befallen the youngest sâr of Armania this day?"

The pinched look on Hinck's face made Trevn feel bad, but now was not the time to baby him. "In private, Hinck," was all he said.

Once they were in Trevn's chambers with the door secured—and Cadoc had made sure no one hung underneath his balcony—Trevn told Hinck all that had happened.

"Go to your father," Hinck said.

That would help no one. "I must get a better look at the local priests, see if one of them wears an anklet of the Rôb Five."

"Oh yes. Walking around the castle and inspecting every priest's ankle won't draw any extra attention to your actions."

"Maybe I should visit court."

This comment brought a heavy silence.

"I am of age now," Trevn said.

"You've been of age for several weeks. People will wonder why you go now. They will think you seek to bolster your own position for Heir."

"Let them," Trevn said. "I want to see who panders to my father. I want to hear the gossip firsthand."

"It will only sicken you," Hinck said.

No doubt it would. "I do not go for my own enjoyment," Trevn said. "I go to be Wilek's eyes and ears."

"May I make a suggestion?" Cadoc asked.

"Please," Trevn said.

"You might also visit Rosârah Brelenah's court. See who spends time with her."

"Excellent notion, Cadoc. I shall attend both." How tedious the morrow would be. He turned his attention to Hinck. "You'll keep watch for anything strange in Janek's crowd?"

"Beyond the everyday oddities, you mean? Because today Prince Janek made us all weed his sandberry patch."

"You know what I mean, Hinck. You, Cadoc, and Tomek are the only people I trust in this castle. I need your help."

"Like I have anything better to do," Hinck said. "*I'm* not a sâr."

The next morning a single knock preceded Hinck's arrival. Cadoc let him in and shut the door behind him. Trevn waved away the garment Beal was holding. "Too lacy. What else is there? Something a knighten would wear. Plain but at the same time . . . I don't know, strong."

"I will look again, Your Highness," Beal rasped, retreating into Trevn's wardrobe.

"What are you doing?" Hinck asked, coming to stand beside him.

Trevn took a bite of fig bread. "Readying for court," he said between chews. "I need people to like me. Especially Queen Brelenah."

"You're a prince. People will like you for that alone. And if you're worried about Brelenah, take her a puppy."

Trevn swallowed. "I'm not taking her a puppy."

"At least they'll welcome you. How am I supposed to proceed with Lady Eudora? She despises me."

Beal returned and held up a dark blue tabard with silver embroidery.

"Perfect," Trevn said. "Find whatever things match it."

"Of course, sir." Again Beal entered the wardrobe.

Hinck raised one eyebrow. "Lady Eudora? You were about to save my hide?"

Trevn raised two eyebrows back and grabbed another fig roll from the tray. "How is this my problem?"

Hinck glanced at the wardrobe and whispered, "Because you sent me to Janek and he gave me an impossible task, and if I fail him, I fail you and get my back shredded. If you want me to find answers about the rune, I need your help winning Lady Eudora. Or at least knowing how to talk to her. She won't even look at me."

"What makes you think I can help?" Trevn asked.

"You're doing fine with Miss Mielle."

Trevn scoffed. "That's different. Miss Mielle is madly in love with me."

Cadoc laughed, and both Trevn and Hinck turned toward the door where he was standing.

"Something funny?" Trevn asked.

"Only if I may speak freely."

"You may always speak freely, Cadoc," Trevn said.

"You both amuse me in your quests for female affection," Cadoc said. "It is not as difficult as you make it."

Hinck leaned closer. "Share your secrets, then, Cadoc."

Trevn continued eating, pretending he didn't desperately want to hear Cadoc's answer, but he stopped chewing so he could hear clearly.

"Treat her well," Cadoc said. "Speak to her interests, let her talk while you listen, look for ways to compliment her without sounding like a charmer."

Hinck's expression grew eager. "Give an example."

"Sâr Trevn once told Miss Mielle she was honest and cared for people. She seemed to like that, didn't she?" Cadoc asked.

Trevn scowled. "How did you know that?" They'd been in a river hole when he'd said that.

"It's my job to hear," Cadoc said.

Trevn disagreed, but now was not the time to reprimand his nosy shield. "Well, I meant it, what I told her."

"My point exactly," Cadoc said. "Make your words genuine. Otherwise just ask questions to get her talking. The man who listens wins the woman."

"Ask questions." Hinck stared out the balcony window. "But what if she's not there?"

"If she's not there today," Trevn said, "we'll find out where she is and send you to her."

Hinck slumped in his chair. "Very well."

Beal exited the wardrobe carrying a cushion that held a gold circlet with various buckles and baubles piled in the center.

"All right, Beal," Trevn said. "Help me dress. I have a host of nobles to impress."

"The king requested you enter and remain silent until he calls for you," the herald said.

"Very well." Trevn had come to observe, not cause disorder. He left Cadoc outside with the other guards and servants and stepped into the Presence Chamber. There he met a wall of bodies and heat. Incense burned in braziers, but rather than mask the body odor, the combination created a stench that rivaled that of the Sink. The chamber was packed with courtiers, all with their backs to him, all silent. Loud voices in the front of the room led Trevn to believe he'd entered upon a fierce argument.

"How long have you betrayed me and our son by embracing this human as a husband?" a man yelled.

"What betrayal?" a woman replied. "Have you not made sport of your affections for human females? What you made acceptable for yourself, you have made acceptable for me."

"Fool woman! You disrespect your son when you disrespect me."

"We have no son between us," the woman said. "Lâhat was begotten of Barth."

A gasp from the crowd and a cry of rage from the man. "Treacherous villains, die, all three!"

Ah, a play was being acted out. The theater was Father's latest craze. This must be *Magon's Betrayal*, when Dendron learned that his wife had taken up with a human man.

Trevn walked the perimeter of the room until the throne came into sight. Before it, four actors were dressed in bright robes. A short man in green with a thin priest's lock was pretending to strangle a tall man in brown: Dendron attacking Barth. Behind them a woman in red cowered with a young man in robes of red, brown, and orange. They would be Magon and her son Lâhat. Trevn glanced at the priest's feet, but his costume billowed on the floor, hiding his ankles from view.

The play went on. Barth begged Magon's help, and she used her magic to turn him into Barthos, god of the soil. Trevn wondered why his father so hated magic when it had, supposedly, created the god he so revered.

Dendron and Barthos began their war, yelling out their circumstances for all to hear.

"I, Dendron, send vines to bind you and stop your breath."

Barthos clutched his throat as if vines were actually choking him. "I shake the earth and break the vines that bind me," he croaked.

Dendron staggered about in the pretend earthquake. "The rain pours down with such vastness that you are drowned."

This went on and on. In the real story, their war lasted a thousand years. For the sake of entertainment, the actors jumped quickly to the end. Dendron realized he could not destroy Barthos, so he cursed him instead, taking away his human form and turning him into the mythical cheyvah dragon. Then he turned his wrath on Magon, cursing all humans who called on her for power. Not only would they be feared and hated, their magic would require poison, the use of which would bring death and fierce cold.

Dendron's final curse came down upon Lâhat. Dendron made him god of fire, which could only burn with the aid of Dendron's wind. Lâhat would have no power that was not ordained by Dendron. Never would Magon's ice be able to come near Lâhat's fire, or the two would destroy one another. So Dendron forever separated Magon from her son.

"Curtain!" someone in the crowd shouted.

The audience applauded.

"Well done," the king yelled, clapping wildly. "Actors, come forward! And my son as well. Herald? The trump for my youngest son."

From across the room the trumpet played Trevn's tune. The crowd murmured and shifted, looking around to see where Trevn might be standing.

Trevn walked toward his father's throne and bowed deeply.

The king's sweaty face lighted in a smile. "Ah, yes. Excellent. Come stand beside me, my son."

Trevn obeyed, and when he reached his father's throne, he saw the four actors standing in a row before the king. The men bowed. The woman curtsied. Trevn recognized the king's stray son Kamran DanSâr in Lâhat's robes, and it was Zithel Lau, the medial priest of Rôb, who had played Dendron. The last two were a Rurekan soldier and a woman he had never seen before.

"Sâr Trevn, what did you think of the play?" Father asked.

"Very well acted," Trevn said, though he had little interest in theater.

"Indeed," Father said, all of his attention bestowed on the female who had played Magon. "Your skills are to be praised."

"Yobatha is delighted with your offering." This was said to the performers by Filkin Yohthehreth, Father's head prophet, who, as always, was dressed in white robes.

Trevn stiffened to see the man who was so offended by Father Tomek's Armanite faith. Their eyes met. Yohthehreth bowed.

"Good morning, prophet," Trevn said as politely as he could manage.

"Is the goddess Yobatha among your chosen five, Sâr Trevn?" the prophet asked. "You have selected, haven't you?"

Trevn had been so obsessed with Mielle, he had yet to pick his five now that he had come of age. Normally he would have been happy to admit that fact, but he would not earn the trust of these men today by being himself.

"I have, prophet," Trevn lied, mind spinning with what to say. "But I must test each to see if we fit well before I pledge my faith."

"A wise decision," Yohthehreth said. "Will you tell us your five?"

Meddlesome prophet. Trevn fought to keep his expression indifferent as he spun out another flowery excuse. "I am a young man. My desires and concerns are not as important as my father's or even yours, prophet. My choices couldn't possibly interest this court."

"Do tell, my son," Father said, "for your choices greatly interest me."

"Very well." Woes, he would have to choose. Which gods would a typical, newly-of-age prince find appealing? He thought of Janek, and the answers came easily. "First and foremost, I worship Yobatha, for I seek nothing more each day than pleasure and joy for myself."

The crowd chuckled.

"Second, I revere Avenis, who is the only one capable of sending beautiful women my way." Someone guffawed at this. A man. Trevn went on, "Mikreh, of course, for he holds my fate in his very hands. And lastly I've chosen Rurek and his bride, Cetheria. As the youngest son of a king, I cannot be too careful with my life. Only Rurek, god of war, and his protector queen are equipped to keep me safe from harm." Trevn looked pointedly at Yohthehreth then. *Your move, prophet.*

Yohthehreth smirked. "Sensible choices for one so young, Sâr Trevn. There is safety in an abundance of counselors. If you will listen well to the advice of your five and accept their instruction, you will prosper in all you do."

Rubbish and nonsense, Trevn wanted to say.

"A fortuitous prophecy," the king said. "Schwyl, mark that down in my chronicles."

"Yes, Your Highness," Schwyl said.

It was customary to give the sign of The Hand when a prophet spoke over one's life, so Trevn placed his hand over his heart, then pressed his fingertips against his lips. He said nothing.

Father reached out to Schwyl. "Help me up. I must retire for a spell."

Already Father was leaving? Trevn did his best to assist Schwyl in prying his father from the throne. Once the man was on his feet, Schwyl smoothed out his robes and helped the king into his rollchair.

"Enjoy your time at court, Trevn," Father said. "Perhaps you will meet some young women here to add to your list, yes?"

"Perhaps," Trevn said.

Father nodded once, as if the matter was settled. "With me, Miss Caridod." The actress who had played Magon took hold of the two poles behind the king's rollchair and pushed him away. One shoulder of her costume robe had slipped off her shoulder, giving Trevn a glimpse of bare skin decorated in a black tattoo that looked eerily like the rune Lady Lebetta had drawn in blood.

Trevn stepped after them, but someone caught him by the arm. He jerked free and wheeled around.

The man bowed. It was Hinck's uncle, Canbek Faluk, the Earl of Ravensham. The same man who had accosted Mielle upon her last visit here. His hair glistened from whatever oils he had used to slick it back into a tail. The gutted face of a white sand cat stared hollowly at Trevn from the man's shoulder.

"Who was that woman, Lord Ravensham?" Trevn asked, watching her push the rollchair out the back door of the chamber, which led to the king's drawing room.

"Lilou Caridod is the rosâr's newest mistress," Canbek said. "Sâr Trevn, may I introduce Sir Garn, the ambassador from Rurekau, here on the emperor's behalf to negotiate several matters with your father."

The Rurekan who had played the part of Barthos bowed. The man looked fortyish and well built. He was bald as a vulture with abstract henna tracings down both sides of his neck. All members of the Igote—the Imperial Guard of the Emperor—shaved their heads. So, not just an emissary, then, but a trained killer. Interesting.

Trevn inclined his head. "How is your volcano, Sir Garn?"

"Mount Lâhat is smoking, as always, Your Highness."

"Sâr Trevn shares your passion for ships, Sir Garn," Canbek said.

"How fortuitous," Garn said. "Perhaps you might join me in my plea toward your father that Armania import sand."

Trevn had to stretch logic to find the man's connection from ships to importing sand. "Why would we need sand? For bricks?"

"For arenas. Immensely popular in Rurekau for tournaments and challenges. All of our executions and sacrifices to the gods take place in arenas. Emperor Nazer knows that the gods love to be entertained."

A rather vulgar idea.

A man and a young woman stepped up on Trevn's right, standing patiently until he acknowledged them. "And you are?"

"My pardon, Your Highness," the man said. "I am Keson Orrey, one of the rosâr's minstrels. This is my daughter Fairelle. May she sing for you?"

Trevn slid back a step. "Oh, I don't think—"

"Go ahead, girl," Keson said. "Sing 'The Great Parting.'"

Fairelle closed her eyes a moment, then opened them slowly, keeping them half-lidded. She sang low and monotone. "*Deep in the reign of noble House Hadar, the Mother tribes fled to the east afar. . . .*"

This. This was why Trevn preferred to keep to himself. While Fairelle sang, Trevn studied her. She was slender. Dressed in green and gold layers. Her hair was pulled back in cornrows that ended at the crown of her head and fell back into dozens of tiny braids. The look made her forehead seem huge. Time crept along in agony as she sang all six verses of the ancient song. Finally she closed her eyes and bowed her head. Finished at last.

Trevn faked a wide smile. "Very nice."

"Sâr Trevn." A large woman waved her handkerchief at him and pushed between Sir Garn and the bard, completely ignoring proper etiquette. "My daughter would so love a position in your mother's household. Does the rosârah need any honor maidens?"

"I know not, Lady . . ." He did not know her name. Not that it mattered. She went on to ask the same of the other queens and even Lady Zeroah's household, as if Trevn would know such things.

Trevn's time in the Presence Chamber was nothing but nonsense from that moment forward. A nonstop current of people swirled around him, asking favors or flirting. Somehow he had lost their respect, as all ignored the command of not speaking to a sâr until acknowledged by him. No wonder his brothers stayed away. As the nobility of Armania continued to accost him, he edged slowly toward the exit and finally managed to open the doors.

"Cadoc!" he yelled, and his shield emerged from the shadows. "Sands, that was a spectacle!" Trevn said. "How can my father stand it?" As they walked away, he went on to tell Cadoc all that had happened inside.

"You were too nice to them," Cadoc said. "Your father has trained the people to know that if they dare speak to him without asking first, they face the pole. You must set boundaries or the people will take advantage. Did you learn anything useful inside?"

"Perhaps." Trevn thought of the tattoo under Lilou Caridod's shoulder blade. "Though I know not what."

MIELLE

Mielle loathed court. Lady Zeroah had been brave to ask her grand-father, King Jorger, to intervene with Princess Nabelle. Lady Ze-roah felt that in Prince Wilek's absence, it was imperative that she been seen in Castle Everton each day to remind everyone that Sâr Wilek would soon return, that they would be married, and that, hopefully, he would be declared Heir.

Though King Jorger hated just about everyone in Armania, he heartily agreed with his granddaughter's wisdom.

Princess Nabelle raised the point of the murdered concubine, Prince Janek's appalling behavior to Mielle, and Mielle's *"ongoing flirtations with Sâr Trevn"*—which Mielle felt was a terribly unfair way to put the matter. The king still sided with Zeroah. Her mother was displeased but congratulated Zeroah on using her head for once.

So Mielle sat on a cushion behind the thrones of Queen Brelenah and the Mother Rosârah in the colonnade, watching Lady Zeroah dance with some courtier. Nothing pleased Queen Brelenah more than watching couples dance—besides her dogs, of course. The day was proceeding as slowly as the one before until the herald's trumpet broke the monotony with a familiar tune on his trumpet.

"His Royal Highness, Trevn-Sâr Hadar, the Third Arm, the Curious."

Mielle's heart raced. She rose to her knees on the pillow. The dancing had ceased. It *was* Trevn! How dashingly regal he looked as he approached the thrones. Much better than when he had been covered in mud from the Sink.

"Forgive the interruption, Your Majesty," Trevn said, stopping before the throne. "I hoped I might join you today."

The sound of his voice made Mielle's stomach ache to speak with him. She traced the scarred line of the *R* she'd scratched into the side of her hand and wondered when he might see it.

"You're most welcome here, Sâr Trevn," Queen Brelenah said. "Do you dance?"

"I'm capable of dancing," Trevn said.

The crowd chuckled.

"He danced very well at his ageday ball," his grandmother said.

"Oh, yes! I heard that," Brelenah said. "Would you dance for me, Sâr Trevn?"

"Alone?" Trevn asked, eyes bulging slightly.

Another round of laughter from the crowd.

"Gracious, no. I don't approve of solo dancing except from jesters."

"And you cannot ask him to tumble about in that silk damask," his grandmother said.

More laughter.

Lady Zeroah, who now stood beside the throne, whispered in the queen's ear.

"Is that so?" the queen asked. "Sâr Trevn, Lady Zeroah tells me you danced your first public somaro with her honor maiden."

Zeroah! Heat rushed over Mielle.

Trevn grinned: wide and perfect. "That's correct. Miss Mielle is a close friend."

Close friend.

"Wonderful! Miss Mielle!" The queen glanced around her feet, as if Mielle might be curled against her legs like one of her pups. "Where are you, girl?" Two of her dogs pushed to their feet and yipped.

"Here, Your Majesty." Mielle stood, slightly dazed that Trevn had again publicly acknowledged their friendship. He watched her with a half smile as she made her way forward.

"Come dance with Sâr Trevn," the queen demanded. "I want to see what all the talk was about. My apologies for not attending your ball, Sâr Trevn. Without Wilek here, I just didn't feel up to a party. The Mother Rosârah told me everything, though. Let's see, they were playing a somaro, yes?"

"Yes, Your Majesty, the 'Ages of Man,'" Trevn said.

"Pipers? Play on."

Mielle stepped past the throne and the song began. Trevn took her hand, and it was like going back in time to his ball.

"This ensemble suits you better than your ageday one, Sâr Trevn," Mielle said.

"I chose it myself," Trevn said. "I didn't expect to find you here."

"Lady Zeroah appealed to King Jorger, who gave her permission to attend Rosârah Brelenah's court until Sâr Wilek's return. Though Princess Nabelle has still forbidden me to see you."

Trevn glanced at the princess, who was standing on Lady Zeroah's other side. "She does look cross."

"She won't speak out against the queen's wishes," Mielle said. "Maybe later in private."

"So this could be our last dance until Wilek returns?"

"Doubtful. If Rosârah Brelenah likes us, do not be surprised if you and I dance until the midday bells toll."

"You cannot know how overjoyed I am to find you here. I visited my father's court this morning for the first time, and I am still recovering."

Mielle laughed. "That, I understand completely."

"How fare the orphans?"

"Better. Without homes, they are still in danger. The almshouse cannot feed everyone. There is likely no easy solution."

"I have several ideas. First, a sleephouse. I've drawn plans for such a building based on military barracks. That way we can house many in a single room. Second, evaluations. If we can find a skill or an affinity for a particular trade, a child might be assigned as an apprentice. And perhaps my father would give tax allowances to those who take on orphan wards."

"Oh, Trevn!" Mielle's eyes widened at her public use of his given name. She glanced to the throne and lowered her voice. "You are brilliant."

"It won't happen overnight," he said. "I'm not entirely certain where to begin. My father did not respond when I first broached the topic."

"It's a start, though. And I'm certain you—"

The song ended and they were forced to stop talking. The queen applauded, upsetting one of the dogs on her lap. It jumped to the ground and stretched.

"A fine pair of dancers," Queen Brelenah said. "You must go again. Pipers—"

"Perhaps the sâr would like to dance with some of the other young ladies," Princess Nabelle suggested.

Rage swelled up from Mielle's stomach. Of course the princess would intervene and try to crush Mielle's joy. She kept her head down, hoping no one would see the anger in her eyes.

The suggestion seemed to completely puzzle Queen Brelenah. "Well, I am uncertain."

"Perhaps it's Princess Nabelle who wants a turn with my grandson," Trevn's grandmother said.

The crowd chuckled.

Queen Brelenah frowned. "No, I am quite put out by the suggestion, Princess. I so like them together. Miss Mielle is too tall for the other men. Sâr Trevn, what say you? Would you dance again with Miss Mielle? Or would you rather choose a new partner?"

"I prefer Miss Mielle to any other partner, Your Highness, excluding yourself and my grandmother."

The queen waved her handkerchief. "Such a charmer, you are. I don't dance myself. Avenelle? Will you dance with your grandson?"

"Pish," the Mother Rosârah said. "I can see by the gleam in his eye he wants to dance with the honor maiden. Play on, pipers, and let the youngsters dance."

And dance they did. Until the midday bells rang and beyond.

Hinck

Hinck had not seen Lady Eudora at Seacrest since that first day. He suspected she'd had enough of the unpredictable environment. Deep down he wondered if it was his fault. Was she staying away because of him? If so, how would he ever manage to complete Janek's challenge?

But when he stepped into the garden that morning, there sat Lady Eudora on a longchair with one of her honor maidens. Hinck stared a moment before giving Janek the proper greeting. The sâr sat his wicker throne, holding his potted plant. At least it looked like the same one.

"You see Lady Eudora has returned to us, Dacre Dan?" Janek said. "We shall endeavor to treat her well today. Thankfully Fonu is absent. He tends to steer the conversation to bawdy topics."

"I shall do my part to honor the lady," Hinck said, dipping his head toward Lady Eudora.

She rolled her eyes and looked away, fanning herself with a red-stemmed ruffle leaf. An awkward silence ensued but for the rush of distant waves.

Gods, she truly hated him.

"Did you miss the fact that my mother, the rosârah, is here today, along with the Pontiff?" Janek asked.

Hinck's eyes cast about until he located Rosârah Laviel and Pontiff Rogedoth sitting on side-by-side wicker chairs. Five Woes! He bowed to the Pontiff. "Your Eminence." Then another bow to the queen. "Your Highness."

Rosârah Laviel stood, looking bored, and curtsied to her son. "The heat tires me, Janek. I will retire." She started toward the house, brushing past Hinck as if he were completely invisible, leaving behind a cloud of hyssop. The woman was a goddess, dark and perfect despite being twice Hinck's age. Her shiny black hair parted in the middle and had been combed flat and straight as a horse's mane, down to her narrow waist.

"I shall join you, Laviel," the Pontiff said in his slow voice. The balding man scowled at Hinck as he passed by, or perhaps it was simply his ridged brow that made him look angry.

No one spoke as the pair made their way toward the house. Hinck turned to watch, taking note of the way their gaits dovetailed, Laviel's hair and Rogedoth's priest's lock swaying together like pendulums.

"Finally," Janek said when the door shut. "You are Mikreh's blessing, Dacre Dan. I thought they would never leave."

Janek's greeting gave Hinck some comfort over the fear that the pair had left because of his arrival. "Do they visit often?"

"Once or twice a week. Mother holds no court of her own, nor will she attend any in the castle. When she gets lonely, she comes to hound me for legitimate grandchildren."

Hinck snorted. "Rosârah Thallah does the same to Trevn."

"Does she? Will my little brother obey his mother?"

"Have a child? Trevn?" Hinck chuckled and shook his head. "Trevn prides himself on disobedience, especially to his mother."

"Mikreh's teeth, he and I do have something in common," Janek said.

"I grow bored," Eudora said. "Perhaps I shall join your mother indoors."

"Do not go, lady," Janek said. "I will see you properly entertained. Oli. Fight Hinck."

Fight?

"I'd rather not," Oli said. "Why don't we recite a play?"

"Oh, yes," Eudora said. "A play would be diverting."

"I want to see blood," Janek said. "Come now, Dacre Dan. Be a good sport and let Oli bloody you up a little."

Was he insane?

"But Oli will kill him!" Eudora said.

Well, Hinck couldn't let *that* slide. "I know how to fight, lady."

Eudora met Hinck's gaze. "He'll still kill you. Oli doesn't know his own strength."

"I do so," Oli said. "There's none stronger my age."

"Prove it," Janek said.

"I'm six years Hinck's senior," Oli said.

"So? He's a man now," Janek said. "And he says he can fight. Stop talking back and obey me at once."

Oli sighed and got up. "Very well."

"Oh, Oli. Go easy on him," Eudora said. "Please?"

Hinck watched Eudora carefully. Was she worried for him? He considered winking at her, but what if Trevn was right and he couldn't wink?

Oli walked to the middle of the graveled courtyard. Hinck joined him, feeling very small. Oli stood a full head taller than him with arms as thick as Hinck's thighs. Oli raised his fists, so Hinck pulled his up to his face—probably too high.

How had he gotten himself into this?

Oli took a swing. Hinck dodged it. Oli punched again. Hinck ducked right into Oli's cross. He staggered under the force, head ringing.

"Don't let him get away with that, Hinck!" Janek screamed. "Get him!"

Hinck did the only thing that had ever worked on Trevn. He faked a swing to Oli's face and punched him in the stomach.

Oli grunted. Hinck's knuckles stung.

Janek whooped. "That's better!"

"I *was* going to go easy on you," Oli said through gritted teeth.

"Don't bother," Hinck said, confidence soaring now.

But Oli punched Hinck so fast he couldn't react. Gut, ear, jaw, ribs, and square in the nose. Something crunched, and Hinck collapsed on his back in the gravel, clutching his face.

"Oh!" Eudora cried out.

Hinck couldn't believe how quickly Oli had moved—or how badly his nose hurt.

"Oli, you dog," Janek said. "Couldn't you have played with him a little? You're a terrible entertainer."

"Because I'm not an entertainer," Oli said. "I don't play with my victims. I destroy them and move on to the next. Care to step into the ring, *Your Highness*?"

A gust of lavender rolled over Hinck. He opened his eyes. Eudora was kneeling at his side, studying his face. "Oli, you beast, you broke his nose!"

Broken? Panic shot through Hinck, but he couldn't take his eyes off Eudora: her pinched brow, frowning lips.

"Let me have a look." Oli crouched on Hinck's other side. "Gods, I did. Sorry about that. I can try to push it back. Shall I, Hinck?"

Push it back?

"Yes, do, Oli. He was on the cusp of being handsome."

Wait, what?

"Only if you want me to, Hinck," Oli said.

He nodded dumbly, lost in Eudora's half praise.

"Janek, ask Timmons to bring a cut of raw meat," Oli said.

"Ask him yourself," Janek said.

Eudora squeezed Hinck's hands. "Be strong, Lord Dacre."

"This will hurt." Oli took hold of Hinck's nose and jerked it to the side.

Hinck's nose crunched in a spike of agony. He screamed, but overall the pain lessened.

Eudora glanced over his face. "Better."

"There will be a bump," Oli said, sitting back.

Eudora smiled, her eyes focused on his. "A battle scar."

"That was no battle," Janek yelled from somewhere. "Oli pummeled him!"

Oli stood and looked across the yard. "Did you send Timmons for a steak?"

"It's not my job to play fetch," Janek said.

"Shall I go, lady?" Eudora's honor maiden asked.

"Yes, Kless. And I with you. I'll bring you some water, Lord Dacre. We'll be right back."

Footsteps crunched over gravel. Hinck thought about sitting up, but someone came into view above, potted plant hugged in one arm, smirking down. Janek. His ridged brow made him look so much like Pontiff Rogedoth that Hinck wondered how hard Oli had struck his head.

"You're welcome," Janek said.

"For what?" Hinck rasped.

"Fonu and I have a bet going. He thinks you don't stand a chance with Lady Eudora. Thanks to me, you now have her attention. That's all the help I'll give you, so make the most of it." He walked toward the house.

Hinck pushed himself to sitting. He and Oli were alone now, Oli sitting on the side of his longchair, hands clasped. Hinck wanted to stand, but his head throbbed to the point of dizzying him.

Eudora returned in a rush of footsteps and knelt beside him, pressed a stone cup to his lips. "Here. Drink."

He sucked down the cool water, praying he wouldn't choke or sputter in her presence. How could a beaten man look dignified before such a lady?

"Oli, help him up." Eudora stepped away and Hinck was shuffled to Eudora's longchair. Then Oli retreated into the house the way Janek had gone.

Eudora sat beside Hinck, a bowl in her lap that held a slab of raw meat, the water cup in her hand. Kless stood at her side, holding another bowl. Hinck couldn't see what was inside it.

Eudora picked up the meat with her fingertips. She wrinkled her nose and lifted the bloody mass toward him. He shut his eyes just as the cold meat slapped over his face, covering his eyes, nose, and mouth. He reached up to adjust it, and she swatted his hand aside.

"I know it's distasteful, but it will help. I've seen my father do it."

"Can't breathe," he managed to mumble.

"Oh! I'm sorry."

The cold meat slid up on his face until his mouth was free. He gasped in a breath, the tang of blood bitter on his lips. "Thank you."

"Kless, set that by my feet and fetch some fresh rags."

"Yes, lady." Footsteps crunched away.

Then they were alone. Hinck's mind raced as quickly as his heart. He should talk to her, ask her questions before he lost his chance. "So, um . . . your father taught you this?"

"You aren't the first to be needlessly wounded in this company. Oli has been Sâr Janek's backman since they were boys." She lowered her voice. "Oli could easily best the sâr now, but it wasn't always that way. Sâr Janek used to dominate, especially with fists."

"But not now?"

"Once he discovered women, he lost interest in fighting. He's getting soft. And fat. But don't tell him I said so."

He heard a smile in her voice and steered the subject away from Janek. "You don't approve of fighting?"

"Bloodsports are barbarous. But Sâr Janek always gets his way. Oli's the only person who can talk him out of things."

"You seem to hold your own."

"Propriety is a woman's friend in public, but when I am alone with him . . ."

Hinck fell silent as he imagined all she implied. Finally he managed another question. "What interests you, Lady Eudora?"

"I like playacting. I like wearing pretty dresses that make men stare. I like dancing. Do you dance, Lord Dacre?"

"Yes, though I have little opportunity in Sâr Trevn's service. I danced more than he did at his ageday ball. His mother forbid him to dance a second with Miss Mielle Allard."

"She is so plain. What does he see in her?"

"Adventure. She ran the roofs with him."

"That explains it." She laughed softly. "I well understand the pressure to marry. Father has lost me to Lord Ravensham in many a game of dice, though Mother says I'll not be given so freely to anyone."

The tone of her voice burned Hinck's cheeks. "Uh . . . so you must, uh, choose between Sâr Janek or my uncle Canbek?"

"Oh, no. There are many others. Prince Ulrik of Rurekau, but I won't live in a realm that abuses women. Lord Rystan, of course."

"But he's thirteen."

"He won't be thirteen forever. There are several princes of Sarikar I could marry, though I wish a prudish husband as little as an abusive one. There is you."

His heart nearly stopped. "Me?"

"You *are* in the royal line, which makes you my parents' fourth choice after Sâr Janek, Sâr Trevn, and Prince Ulrik."

Gods, Trevn too? "They want you to wed royalty."

"My parents want me to be a rosârah, so I understand Sâr Trevn's reluctance to obey his mother's demands. Haven't your parents tried to marry you off? As an only child, I'd think your mother would be adamant about it."

"She is, but my father wishes me to marry for love. They were an arranged marriage. My father had once loved another."

"A tragic and common tale."

The raw meat smell was turning his stomach. "It doesn't matter. I belong to Sâr Trevn, and he gives me little time to meet anyone. I'll likely die a bachelor, having fallen from a rooftop while trying to rescue one of the sâr's precious maps."

Eudora giggled and removed the steak from Hinck's face, thank the gods. "That's enough of that." She dropped the meat in the first bowl and lifted the second into her lap. It was full of water. Kless had returned and was standing behind Eudora. She handed her lady a rag. "Now let me wash off that blood and we'll see what's left of you."

Hinck did not complain.

When he finally passed through the house on his way out, he thought it deserted until he heard the low murmur of a man's voice coming from the altar room. Four guards exited, leading a woman and sobbing little girl away, both with hands bound. The woman wore a plain brown dress, but the gold silk gown the girl wore rivaled that of any queen. *How very odd.* Voices were still talking in the altar room, so Hinck slowed and peeked inside.

A couple knelt before the altar, holding hands, foreheads pressed together with heads bowed in prayer. Queen Laviel and Pontiff Rogedoth.

The murmured prayer stopped. The queen looked up into Rogedoth's eyes and beamed, kissed his cheek. He pulled her into a tight embrace.

What in the Five Realms?

Hinck found Trevn hunched over the table in his chambers, scribbling on some map.

"I've returned from yet another day of abuse for your benefit, Your Stupendousness."

"Are you calling me stupid?" Trevn asked without looking up.

"Aren't you even going to look at me?" Hinck asked.

"Do you wish me to?"

"Very much."

Trevn sighed. He set down his charcoal and regarded Hinck. His eyes flashed wide. "Did you spend your day in the practice pens as a pell?"

"At Seacrest, per your command."

"You're purple. Shall I ring Beal to fetch the physician?"

"No, thank you. I'm fine."

Trevn shrugged and went back to his map.

Unbelievable. Trevn would never ask, so Hinck had to tell him. "Janek made me fight Oli. Said he did it to make Eudora sympathetic to me. Apparently Fonu bet him I'd fail the challenge, so now Janek wants me to succeed."

"Five Woes, they're a bunch of barbarians."

Janek was, at least. "It worked, though. Eudora was livid with Oli for harming my '*potentially handsome face.*'"

"*Potentially* handsome? Her compliments are as backward as mine."

"Yes, I noticed."

"That's good, though. Did you get to speak with her?"

"Lots. She played nursemaid on me, so I asked as many questions as I could."

"About the stone?"

"Not yet. But we had a nice chat about parents and controlling sârs who try to ruin our lives."

"That *is* encouraging."

"I also saw Pontiff Rogedoth and Queen Laviel praying in the altar room. They have two prisoners. A woman and a little girl, both bound. The girl looked wealthy. The woman her nurse, perhaps. Rogedoth and Laviel were very . . . intimate with each other."

That made Trevn look up. "Intimate how?"

"Holding hands. She kissed his cheek and he hugged her."

"Your mind lives in the Blackwater Canal. You think they're having an affair, don't you?"

"I think they have been for years." Hinck paused, working up the courage to share the theory he had invented on the ride home. "I think Rogedoth is Sâr Janek's father."

Trevn burst out laughing. "What gave you *that* idea?"

"The eyebrows. Next time you see Janek and Rogedoth together, look closely and see if I'm not right."

"I think you're crazy, but I'm intrigued by the idea of Rogedoth and Queen Laviel working together. That would explain a lot."

Hinck took it as a compliment. "Who is the little girl, do you think? Some kind of sacrifice for Barthos?"

"Gods, I hope not," Trevn said. "Try to find out."

As if Hinck didn't have enough to find out. "How did court go?"

"I hated it—my father's court, I mean." Trevn shared all that had happened, ending with Lilou Caridod's tattoo. "Someone should question her."

"Don't look to me, Your Ignoramus."

"Excuse me?"

"Lilou Caridod. Do you truly know nothing? Your father decreed that no one is to speak ill of her. She is his favorite. You must wait for him to cast her off before you question that one."

"Why?"

"How should I know why kings do what they do?" Hinck racked his memory for something about Lilou to give his prince. "Some say she's a witch."

"Because of the tattoo?"

Hinck shrugged.

"Ask Janek about her."

Hinck groaned. "I feel as though I need a break from Janek's company."

"No, Hinck. You are so close. I can feel it. You must persevere."

Q·OATCH

Qoatch, eunuch slav to Priestess Jazlyn, Sixth Great Lady of Tenma, stood alone outside the doors of the Throne Room, close enough to hear if the priestess were to summon him, yet far enough away that he couldn't overhear the private discussion. His Great Lady had been called before High Queen Tahmina, and he desperately wanted to know why.

Her shadir had gone with her, of course. There were several slights drifting along the corridor that he could ask to spy, but shadir—especially slights—were never to be trusted.

The doors opened, and Jazlyn strode out and down the hallway. Her shadir, Gozan, lumbered alongside. A great shadir, in his natural form, Gozan stood twice Jazlyn's height. He had the face of a rat, a man's chest and arms, and legs like a standing fang cat. His skin was black as coal and covered with coarse hairs. Thick arms and beefy shoulders curled forward from muscles too big for such slender legs to support.

Qoatch trailed behind them, silent as always. Shadir were grotesque. It was a mercy from the Great Goddess that so few people were able to see them. Qoatch only had the ability because Jazlyn had put a spell on him so that he could carry messages to the creatures on her behalf.

"Pack my things," Jazlyn told Qoatch without looking back. "Enough for a trip to and from Lâhaten and for at least a week in that loathsome city."

"Yes, Great Lady." *To Rurekau? Why?*

She said nothing more until they reached her chambers and the door was securely closed. "Lâhaten! Two months, I will be gone." She began pacing. "She wants me to confront Emperor Nazer about the Rurekans abducting our women and girls. She knows I detest traveling outside Tenma. Why does she torture me? Gozan, do you know her motives?"

"Her shadir told me nothing, Great Lady," Gozan said.

Jazlyn growled and turned her glare on Qoatch. "Answer."

Only when Jazlyn demanded Qoatch answer was he permitted to speak. "Perhaps she trusts only you to accomplish the task?"

Jazlyn sighed and changed the angle of her pacing. "Yes, yes, I know. I'm her hands and feet. But is it my fault the other Great Ladies are incompetent? Answer me that, eunuch."

No lady was more persuasive than Jazlyn. "You'll be High Queen someday, Great Lady. These struggles will result in a crown."

"I have a crown." She stopped before a full-length mirror and adjusted the gold-and-pearl diadem on her head that marked her a Great Lady of Tenma. Another sigh. "Answer, Qoatch."

"Yes, but not *the* crown, Great Lady," he said, hoping his words would comfort her.

"The seer speaks wisdom," Gozan said. "Someday you shall be High Queen; then you can send the Great Ladies wherever you like. Order *them* to cross the desert to Rurekau."

Qoatch kept his gaze averted from the shadir. He never felt comfortable when the creature agreed with him.

Jazlyn nodded, the words sinking in. "But Tahmina will likely live another hundred years. Even if she died, Sixth is far too low to inherit the throne."

"A fatal sickness could come upon the others," Gozan said. "If they die, their shadir will be freed and will not stand against us. The seer knows how to do this."

A prime example of how dangerous the shadir truly were. They knew too much. About everything. Qoatch tried to keep his expression plain. Jazlyn rarely deigned to look upon her eunuch, but she did now. Qoatch's heart raced to see those fathomless gray eyes meet his.

"Could you really make them sick?" When he didn't reply, she added, "Answer me."

What to say? "That would be treason, Great Lady."

"I wasn't asking you to do it," she snapped. "Only wondering if you had the skill. I need to know what you're capable of in case I need to use you against the Rurekan emperor. Answer me truthfully, eunuch slav, are you a capable assassin?"

Gozan's rattish gaze bored into him, daring him to lie. "I suppose, Great Lady. All eunuchs are trained in the herbal arts." This was a stretch of the truth. Qoatch had been trained better than most.

Yet his answer seemed to satisfy. Jazlyn turned back to the mirror, lifted her chin, and adjusted her crown. "Good to know."

When Jazlyn—and her shadir—left to dine with the High Queen and the other Great Ladies, Qoatch set about packing her things for the coming journey.

Duvlid arrived, carrying a tray of newly mixed lotions, which he set on Jazlyn's dressing table. "I've brought new beauty creams for the Great Lady."

To all but a select few, the man was a castle servant, but Duvlid never visited without dual motives. Thankfully Qoatch did not see any shadir in the Veil who might eavesdrop. "You bring a message?" he asked.

Duvlid stepped close and whispered, "The time has come, seer. Tomorrow night."

The words made Qoatch feel as though he were standing on the point of the temple spire, one moment away from falling to his death. The organza dress he was holding crinkled in his fierce grip, but he realized that with this journey, the great goddess Magon had given him a way to escape fate. "It cannot be tomorrow night," he said. "Priestess Jazlyn leaves for Rurekau at dawn to negotiate the human trade situation with Emperor Nazer. You'll have to wait."

"The Kushaw have waited long enough," Duvlid snapped. "Do it on the road. When you return, the women will be cast down."

Qoatch could never attempt such a feat with Gozan watching. Only by urging his lady to fast could he keep the shadir away.

"You know what happens if you fail," Duvlid said, then left the room.

For a long moment Qoatch stared into nothing, shocked that this day had finally come. He rallied himself to the cause. The Kushaw had been working for years to free Tennish men—men who were worthy of equal rights with women. Qoatch had been trained to do his part in destroying tyranny in Tenma. He had but one task. But, Great Goddess, he could not do this!

He could not kill the woman who had saved his life.

TREVN

I will send a prophet before that great and dreadful day comes. And those who listen, who turn their hearts to me, they will be spared when I strike the land with total destruction.

—*The Holy Book of Arman*, chapter 12

Trevn set down his quill and leaned back in his chair, staring at the last line of the Book of Arman. It seemed absurd that the recent earthquakes could be related to this prophecy, that, with all of time to choose from, Arman might bring destruction during Trevn's lifetime.

He shook off the dismal thought and let the joy of having finished this arduous task sink in. After two years of hard work, he had completed his transcription of the holy text. Now he could be ordained as a neophytic priest. Not that he wanted to be a priest. Still, a swell of pride warmed his chest. He had done a tremendous amount of work. Such a feat might please even his father.

Another thought to shake away. Father wouldn't care, nor would his mother, who only wanted him to marry and have sons and upstage his brothers. Father Tomek, however . . . He would rejoice at Trevn's accomplishment.

Trevn left his room and found Cadoc leaning against the wall in the hallway outside. "We're going to see Father Tomek," Trevn said. "I have news that cannot wait."

✦ ✦ ✦

Father Tomek, being royalty, lived on the fifth floor in the crossbar. As a young prince he had once resided in the very chambers that now belonged to Trevn. Now an aging lesser prince and mere priest, he had been relocated many times over the years. Not that the man gave a whit about such things.

Trevn entered without knocking. A single candle burned on a wall sconce above the bed, casting enough light that he could see the shape of a body under the covers.

Sleeping? This early? He slowed his footsteps and whispered, "Father Tomek?"

"Praise to the God," a weak voice replied. "Close the door, Sâr Trevn, and come."

"Cadoc is with me. Shall he wait in the hallway?"

"No, no. Bring him."

Cadoc entered and closed the door. It was then that Trevn noticed the smell. A bitter, almost sour stench permeated the room. The smell of sickness.

Pinpricks traveled up Trevn's arms as he approached the bed. "Father, are you ill?"

The old man moaned. "All is lost. I found it this afternoon, there on my desk."

The desk was empty but for a charred stack of parchment. Trevn reached for the first page.

"Don't touch it!" Father Tomek cried. "Cadoc, stop him! It's poisoned."

Trevn pulled back his hand, bewildered. Before he could ask, Cadoc plowed into him like a soldier on the practice field. The impact knocked Trevn the equivalent of four steps. His right shoulder slammed against the wall. A ceramic vase slipped off its shelf and shattered on the floor.

"For sand's sake!" Trevn yelled. "I didn't touch it!"

Cadoc released Trevn, stepped back. "Sorry, Your Highness."

"It's covered in poison," Father Tomek said. "Burned by magic to destroy it and whoever touches the pages."

Trevn's mouth went dry. "You touched it?"

"I won't survive the night."

"Nonsense!" Trevn cried. "I'll call for the physician at once."

"You'll call no one," Father Tomek said. "They must believe they've succeeded or they might come after you. Now tell me, how much of the Holy Book have you transcribed?"

"First tell me who 'they' are," Trevn said. "Filkin Yohthehreth?"

"Don't play games with me, boy. I have little time. Answer my question."

The intensity of his voice brought tears to Trevn's eyes. "All of it. I finished only just."

"You finished transcribing a book that sits there on my desk? How?"

That was the Holy Book? "I've, uh, been taking original pages to my chambers each night. I wanted to work faster." He swallowed his guilt. "To surprise you." And to keep his mind off the fact that he could see little of Mielle these days.

Father Tomek cackled. It was a wheezing sound, rather than his regular laugh. "You delightfully disobedient boy. I should punish you greatly for such an act, but the God used your ambition for good. Wonderful irony, isn't it? You have the original last pages?"

"The last chapter, yes, in my room. Shall I fetch it?"

"No! You must hide everything. The original chapter *and* your copy. Take care. They'll come looking to see what you've been transcribing. Cadoc, he will need extra protection."

"I'll see to it, Father," Cadoc said.

"I don't understand," Trevn said. "Why destroy your book?"

"You've been transcribing the Holy Book of Arman, not Rôb."

"I know. Father, if you're dying, let me try to get help."

"There's nothing any physician can do for me, my boy. Do nothing but hide the book for now. It must survive! After my shipping, visit my son Barek and tell him all that you know. He will help you." Tomek began to cough. Blood misted from his lips.

Trevn searched frantically on the bedside table for a handkerchief. Cadoc handed his own to Trevn, who nodded his thanks and dabbed the blood from his mentor's lips and chin.

"One more thing," Father Tomek said. "The rune marking you gave me."

"Yes?" Trevn asked, eager.

"The Lahavôtesh was a sect of Chokmah Rôb that started in Sarikar. The rune was its insignia."

"Eudora said it is a symbol to ward off evil."

"I suppose it could mean that to some nowadays. People are very superstitious in Armania. There are so many false gods, it's hard to keep track of them all. I left the research on Lahavôtesh in our classroom, under the tablets of the Five Woes. Read them for yourself." The old man gasped in a breath. "Would you recite to me?" Another breath. "From the book?"

Trevn knew only common sayings and children's stories from memory. All that came to mind was the creation story from the wall mural of Miss Mielle's childhood home. "In those days, Arman lived in the heavens with his bride Tenma and their two sons, Sarik and Rurek."

In the midst of Trevn's story, Father Tomek began coughing up blood again. Trevn swallowed his tears and took care of his mentor. By the time he finished the story, Father Tomek had stopped breathing. Eyes were closed. Lips curved in a slight smile.

Father Tomek was dead.

Someone had poisoned him.

Someone who hated Arman. Who? Which god opposed Arman?

"Forgive me, Father," Trevn said, both to Father Tomek and to Arman, the father god Tomek had served so relentlessly. "I won't rest until I avenge you." He clutched his mentor's sleeve and wept.

News of Father Tomek's death reached Trevn before morning prayer bells the next day. He was relieved not to have to report to his classroom and feign ignorance. He dressed in his blacks and went about his day, aching inside, but keenly aware of everything and everyone.

Someone had killed Father Tomek and destroyed the Holy Book of Arman. That person might come for him next.

Let them. Last night Trevn had hidden the book in a secret room in his mother's apartment. No one would find it, not even if they tumbled the place.

The book was safe.

Father Tomek had been well loved. Piles of flowers quickly became a nuisance at the castle gates. Trevn was summoned to the Throne Room to help plan Father Tomek's memorial. He sat silently among his father's council members, trying not to openly glare at Yohthehreth, whom he knew was guilty of something, or Janek, whom Yohthehreth wanted as Heir over Wilek.

"His body might be contagious," Yohthehreth said.

"Perhaps he should be burned," Janek said.

"He was a prince of Armania," Trevn said, disgusted with the cowardice around him. "He must have a sâr's last rites and shipping."

"Agreed," Father said. "The physician knows how to handle contagion."

Contagion. His dear mentor's body lay on a slab in the pyre house, alone.

At that moment, a soldier arrived, breathless—one of Wilek's men. He handed a missive to Schwyl, who read it, then handed it to Father. The eyes of every man in the room fixed on the king, waiting as he read.

Father let out a cry.

"What is it, Father?" Janek snatched the message and read it. "Wilek is missing. His contingent was attacked east of Dacre. They believe it was the Omatta."

The room erupted into turmoil, everyone talking at once. The king moaned. Trevn clamped his eyes shut, praying that this news was false, tempted to grab Yohthehreth and shake him, demand answers.

"They'll want a ransom, I suspect?" Avron Jervaid asked.

Canbek grabbed Jervaid's arm. "One must not negotiate with outlaws."

"This is the sâr!" Hinck's father said. "We must bring him safely home."

"All is not lost," Jervaid said. "We have Sâr Janek, and Sâr Trevn after him."

Surely Wilek wasn't dead. "If they'd wanted to kill him, he'd be dead!" Trevn said, thinking of Father Tomek. The room fell silent, and he realized he'd shouted. He tried again, this time in a more reasonable tone. "If they've taken him alive, they want something. We must wait for their demands."

"Well said, my son," Father said. "I'll order Wilek's men to find the Omatta and bring him home. If they fail, they can all feed Barthos next full moon."

The men clucked their agreement and began arguing whether or not to send a second army to search for Wilek.

Trevn sat dazed. His logic had calmed his father and the council, but he felt as though his world had ended. All at once he had lost the two men who mattered most to him. It was too much to bear.

KALENEK

When Kal finally woke, he had no strength. Each breath felt as if his lungs had shriveled to prunes. Wymer brought him a cup of water, which he gulped eagerly.

"You're a strong man, Sir Kalenek," Wymer said. "Many have died from less of the water's touch."

"Where are we?" Kal's voice came out a soft whisper.

"Outside the Kaptar prison," Wymer said. "Couldn't reach the lake. Too many felled buildings. Met a guard on a raft who said Miss Onika's man had been put in the solitary pit. Master Heln figures since we are stuck here, we might as well give in to Miss Onika. She won't let up, so Master Heln means to let her see the man's body."

Novan seemed to have taken charge. Good. "How many days since I touched the water?"

"Three."

Three days? "And Grayson?"

"Healthy as a camel and bouncing off the walls. Not a hint of what you went through, though he's grown a bit."

Grown?

Kal fell asleep, wondering what Wymer could have meant. When next he woke, he was able to sit and eat some dried fish. Wymer helped him stand, and Kal found his legs as strong as ever. Only his right arm, blistered and swollen, was still weak.

Novan rushed toward him. "The way everyone was talking, I was afraid you'd die, sir. I'm glad you didn't."

"As am I. What's this you've planned for tomorrow?"

"To enter the prison and search for Miss Onika's man. Will you be well enough to lead us?"

"I'll be fine." *Hopefully.*

Novan nodded. "I promised to bring Grayson as well."

This instantly sat wrong with Kal. "Whatever for? The errand will be much faster without that mischief-maker."

Novan leaned close and whispered. "It's for Miss Onika, sir. If we come back without her man, she'll never believe we did our best. Better to bring Grayson along as her eyes."

Kal humphed. Novan was too smart for his own good.

Kal went back to bed, but he'd slept enough. He stood, wanting to sit outside in the fresh air. Low voices pulled his gaze across the barn. Onika was standing with Novan in one of the stalls. Rustian was perched on a nearby fence post, watching them with lazy eyes. Onika patted the brown camel's nose. The moment she stopped, the creature nudged her hand, eager for more attention. Novan said something Kal couldn't hear, and Onika laughed.

Jealousy twisted Kal's stomach into a stone. He berated himself for such childish emotions and found comfort in the fact that come morning, they'd find Jhorn's body and have reason to leave the prophetess behind forever.

When Kal woke the next day, he caught a young stranger going through Onika's pack.

"Hey! Get away from there!" he yelled.

The stranger jumped to his feet and spun around. "It's me, Sir Kalenek. Grayson."

It was. Yet it wasn't. The boy had grown a full hand taller, his voice was decidedly lower, his face had thinned, and his hair now hung in his eyes.

"What happened to you?" Kal asked.

Though he looked near of age, his bottom lip trembled as if he might cry. "The water," was all he said.

"The water made you grow?"

"The root did." Onika's voice, coming from where she rested on her bedroll. The moment Kal looked her way, Grayson ran out of the barn. Onika was sitting up, a blanket clutched to her chest. "It's not his fault, and I won't have anyone bully him about it."

"Didn't mean to bully him," Kal said. "I just want to understand."

"It's Jhorn's place, not mine. Don't ask Grayson about it again. Please."

All Kal could think to say was, "Yes, ma'am."

The prison was a low stone building with a single watchtower that sprouted up from the center. The receding flood had painted the walls with varied stripes of wetness. Kal, Novan, and Grayson climbed off the barge, which was now partially sunk in the muck. The ground swarmed with insects, and off it rose a rotten stench that turned Kal's stomach.

The threesome slogged toward the prison's front entrance. Kal opened the door, and water gushed over his boots. *No!* He kicked off the moisture, afraid he'd put himself in bed for another three days, but all was well. The leather had kept the poison water from his skin.

Inside, Novan lit a torch in the darkness. The prison was small, and they quickly found the mess hall. Tables were scattered against the entrance, having been moved by the floodwaters. Novan passed the torch to Grayson, and he and Kal moved the tables aside to make a path. Soon they were standing in the middle of the room on a stone floor that was crawling with black bugs.

"We're looking for a trapdoor?" Kal asked.

"The guard said there are six," Grayson said in his new wobbling voice. "But he didn't know which Jhorn was in."

They found one. Dirty leather stuck out from all four sides of the stone lid. Kal crouched and tugged on it. "To block the light. Blasted yeettas love torture."

"Perhaps it kept out the water," Novan said.

Kal grunted, doubtful that a scrap of leather could have held back the weight of a flood.

The lid was kept in place by two pegs inserted through iron loops. Kal pounded them out with the butt of his dagger, then prised up the lid with the blade. Cool air wafted from below. Remarkably, there was no water inside. Nor were there any prisoners.

"Shock me," Kal said. "Could be Onika's man *is* alive."

This enthused Grayson, who scampered off and soon yelled, "Found another one!"

"Sir, that boy is the strangest thing I've ever seen," Novan whispered.

Kal thought so too. "His body has aged, but his behavior hasn't."

By the time they caught up, Grayson had already kicked out the pegs. Kal shoved his dagger into the crack and lifted the stone.

The pit was filled with water. Kal drew back just as a body bobbed into the opening.

Grayson screamed.

Instantly Kal thought of the war, of the bodies that had been tortured and eventually drowned. He looked away and fought off the memory.

"We'll have to turn the body," Novan said, "so Grayson can identify it."

"It's not Jhorn." Grayson ran off, searching for the next pit and taking the torch with him.

"How can you tell by looking at his back?" Novan hollered after him.

"He's got feet!" was Grayson's cryptic reply.

Novan rubbed his face. "Four more pits and it'll be over, sir."

"Let's get it done," Kal said, eager to leave this place and these people.

The third pit was completely dry and empty.

The fourth was filled with water but no body.

The fifth looked dry. Kal leaned down to peer inside, and a clump of dirt hit him in the face. An arm hooked his waist and a fist punched, though there was no strength behind it.

"Get him off!" Kal yelled.

Novan grabbed Kal and his attacker, pulling them away from the hole and each other.

It was an adolescent, grinning from ear to ear. "No warden? So I'm free to go?"

"Don't you leave me here, Burk!" a man yelled from the pit.

"Jhorn!" Grayson held the torch down to the dark opening.

The prisoner yanked free from Novan and sprinted toward the exit.

"Shall I chase after him?" Novan asked.

"Let him go," Kal said, wiping the dirt from his face. "Help me with our rune reader."

Between the two of them, they managed to hoist Jhorn out of the pit. The man was short and light, like a child or perhaps a dwarf. He seemed quite hairy, but perhaps that was simply the filth of prison life.

"Is that you, Grayson?" the man asked.

"Yes, sir." Grayson dropped the torch and fell to his knees to hug the man. "I fell in the lake water."

"Oh, my boy. For how long?"

"Not long. Sir Kalenek pulled me out."

Kal retrieved the torch, which illuminated Jhorn.

Well, ship me to Shamayim . . .

He had no legs.

Kal stared, knowing he was being rude, yet struggling to understand what he was looking at. Jhorn's legs ended just above the knee. Each pantleg had been sewn closed over the stump.

It was too late to stop Kal's mind from circling back to the war, to the melees where he had trod upon severed limbs. *This* was the man Onika claimed had learned to heal his battle wounds?

"To answer your question," Jhorn said, looking from Novan to Kal, who were both still staring, "I lost my legs in the war."

"Ah," was all the answer Kal could manage.

"That must have hurt, sir," Novan said.

"I thought I'd died," Jhorn said. "When I woke and found myself with no legs, I wished I had. But that was the past."

The man had neatly ended discussion on the matter, so Kal said the next thing that came to mind. "You're Armanian."

Jhorn smirked. "So are you."

"Some of the pits were flooded and some were dry," Grayson said. "I prayed you were in a dry pit and you were!"

"Not totally," Jhorn said. "We had a steady leak. Had to work to keep the water draining into the privy hole. What happened, anyway?"

"An earthquake broke the dam," Kal said. "The lake flooded the entire city."

Jhorn nodded. "Onika was right. We have little time."

Novan and Kal exchanged dark glances.

"Let's get out in fresh air, shall we?" Novan said.

Grayson jumped to his feet. "What about Dun?"

"In his cell?" Jhorn asked.

Grayson's eyes widened. "Guard said everyone in the cells drowned."

A heavy moment of silence passed.

"I could carry you backsack, Master Jhorn," Novan said. "Then you could take a look in the cells."

"I'd appreciate that very much," Jhorn said. "Grayson, you wait here."

"But I want to come!"

"You'll do as you're told," Jhorn said in a tone that settled the matter.

Grayson hung his head. "Yes, sir."

Kal had no desire to see more dead. "We'll meet you at the barge."

Novan crouched in front of Jhorn and lifted the legless man to his back. Kal gave Novan the torch. They left together, parting ways in the hall. Light streamed in the open front door, so Kal and Grayson had no difficulty finding their way out. They had barely stepped onto the barge when Onika rushed toward them, fingers gripping the tail of her dune cat.

Grayson hugged her around the waist as if he were still a much shorter boy. "Jhorn's alive!" He went on to tell the full story of the search, adding far more detail about the dead body than Onika likely cared to hear. "But Dun wasn't there. Novan carried Jhorn to look for him in the prison cells."

Onika nodded, tears in her crystalline eyes. "He is in the arms of the God now."

"Don't say that!" Grayson yelled, pushing away from her. "That's not true!"

Novan stepped up onto the barge and helped Jhorn sit on a wooden crate at the bow.

"I'm afraid it is, boy," Jhorn said. The legless man wiped tears from his eyes. Those caught in his bushy beard glittered in the sunlight.

"No!" Grayson yelled. "You're wrong!" He ducked into the open barn door, footsteps quickly fading.

"I'm so pleased to hear your voice, Jhorn," Onika said.

"Thank you for coming," Jhorn said. "Are you well? These men hurt you?"

"We're all fine," Onika said. "They're good men."

Jhorn glanced at Kal and nodded. "See to the boy, Onika?"

"Rustian." Onika reached out her hand. "To Grayson." The cat threaded around her legs and stopped with its head under her hand. Together they moved into the barn.

"That never ceases to amaze me," Kal said.

"And just who are you?" Jhorn asked.

"Sir Kalenek Veroth, shield to the First Arm of Armania."

"If you're his shield, what are you doing here?"

"Sâr Wilek sent me on a mission to get a rune translated. Miss Onika said if I helped free you, you'd be able to help me."

"I'm no mantic, but I'll take a look."

"I'd appreciate that," Kal said, relieved that he might have finally reached the end of his mission. He withdrew the rolled leather from his pocket and handed it to Jhorn.

"Hmm . . . It's not one of the five mantic runes. Where'd you find it?"

"Drawn in blood beside a dying concubine."

"Ominous. Whose concubine?"

"Does it matter?"

"With concubines, it always matters."

Kal supposed that was true. "Sâr Wilek's concubine."

"Prince Wilek's old enough to have a concubine, is he?"

"He's been old enough for ten years."

"I suppose it has been that long. Wasn't sure he'd make it to manhood, the way his father made sacrifices. Does he still?"

"Rosâr Echad visits The Gray each full moon," Kal said. "But he hasn't again sacrificed his own blood."

Jhorn grunted and narrowed his eyes at the scrap of leather. "Like I said, I'm no mantic. The only symbol I recognize is this one here, though it's no rune. Surprised you didn't see it." Jhorn traced his finger down one line, over a shorter line that crossed it, and along the five short lines in an arc above. "This is your mark, isn't it?"

Kal's arms pimpled. It was the mark of a Knife, a royal assassin. "What makes you think that?"

Jhorn shrugged. "Onika said an assassin would save us."

But Onika had called him rescuer. "All this time she thought I was an assassin?"

"Aren't you?"

"Years ago. I gave up knifing when I married." Kal studied the symbol of the knife within the rune mark. If Lady Lebetta had been killed by a Knife, only one person could have given the order: King Echad. "You have my thanks, Jhorn. But I still need a translation for the runes before I can return to Armania."

"There's no time," Jhorn said. "You must return now and take us with you."

Oh no. Kal had had enough company to last a lifetime. "Why would we do that?"

"A true prophet is born to serve the king. I've protected her for years, waiting, but she must go to Sâr Wilek at once. For counsel, mind you, not as a bride or concubine. Grayson goes as her onesent, I as her shield."

Kal looked to Novan and had to fight to hold in his shock. He couldn't imagine a legless man being anyone's shield. And Grayson, a onesent? It was laughable.

"You doubt her still?" Jhorn asked. "Surely you've heard her prophesy?

During the Great War, priests of Rôb murdered every last true prophet. Since then the king has had only false prophets, and the realm has suffered for it. The Five Woes are upon us. Onika is not certain how long we have. A month, maybe? Two at most. It'll happen before summer ends. We must warn Sâr Wilek to evacuate Everton or the realm of Armania will end forever."

Onika had a gift. Kal had seen her power. But the Five Woes of myth? That he could not grasp. "If I agreed—and I'm not saying I do—why Sâr Wilek and not the rosâr?"

"King Echad has been compromised for decades," Jhorn said. "Salvation for Armania will come through The Heir who convinces the king, as Onika has prophesied. Unless you think her a charlatan."

She wasn't that, but Kal didn't like feeling cornered.

"There's more you need to know," Jhorn said. "Grayson is gifted. He doesn't fully understand it yet, nor do I, but he must be protected."

"Gifted how?" Kal asked. "He grows fast?"

"Evenroot doesn't affect him the way it does you and me," Jhorn said. "Legend says a root child is conceived by a woman who takes evenroot during her pregnancy. The magic is in his blood, and the child is born with powers. I think that's why his skin is the way it is."

A mantic that required no root?

"He ages faster than most, and if he takes evenroot or gets into the poison lakes, his aging accelerates for a time," Jhorn said. "If he fell into the lake, my guess is he'll grow another few inches before the effect wears off."

"How old is he really?" Kal asked.

"Just over eight," Jhorn said.

"Eight!" No wonder he talked so much and could never sit still.

"If the mother took root when carrying a child, wouldn't she die?" Novan asked.

"She did die," Jhorn said.

"Who was she?" Kal asked.

"A woman named Darlis Nafni."

Nafni was Queen Laviel's maiden name. "Related to the second queen?" Kal asked.

"Sisters," Jhorn said. "Darlis died in childbirth, leaving Laviel with her child."

"How did you end up with him?" Kal asked. "And how do you know all this?"

"I found him by accident in Canden," Jhorn said, "while I was recovering from the loss of my legs. I had been one of Laviel's personal guards before the war, so I noticed the boy's nurse and recognized his skin when I saw it again. I knew Laviel would try to use the child to put her son on the throne, so I stole him away and came to Magonia."

"You kidnapped the queen's nephew?" Novan asked.

"I did what I had to," Jhorn said.

"Then Everton is the last place the boy should go," Kal said. "With his skin and the way he prattles on, he won't escape Rosârah Laviel's notice for long."

"I don't plan to keep him in Everton for long," Jhorn said. "I simply want him to stay with Onika until her prophecy has been fulfilled."

"Keep him with Onika . . . why?" Kal asked.

"Arman won't let his prophet die young," Jhorn said. "Onika has seen herself years into the future."

"You want the boy to live," Novan said. "You believe her prophecy about the destruction of the land."

"If Grayson stays with Onika, he will survive the Five Woes," Jhorn said. "Will you help us? Every moment we tarry, more will die. We must get Onika to Sâr Wilek."

Or at least her message. It looked like Kal would be spending a lot more time with these people. He met Novan's gaze. "Could you find your way back alone?"

Novan's expression sobered. "I think so, sir."

"One can travel much faster than all of us together," Kal told Novan. "I'll write a coded message to Sâr Wilek and advise him to question you as a witness to what we've discussed here. Return to Hebron. Gather your horse in Raine, and ride for Everton at top speed. Tell Sâr Wilek what happened here in Kaptar. Tell him Onika's prophecy about the destruction of the Five Realms. Say nothing of Grayson for now, but give my recommendation that Everton prepare for a seaward evacuation. Let nothing stop you."

WILEK

Wilek trudged alongside the man called Torol, shivering with each step. It mattered not that the sun hung high in the sky or that sweat trickled down his back. He had been cold since meeting Charlon. Her magic had changed him. He could hear her, back in her tent, casting some spell and talking to her demons. The farther he went from her side, the more he thought of her.

They had taken his clothes and forced him to wear a kasah as a skirt, leaving his chest bare. All the Magonian men dressed this way. He felt ridiculous and all the more naked without his hair.

Torol led him toward a cistern, around which several men were pounding sticks into bronze pots. Wilek eyed a rocky ledge, wondering if he would survive a jump off the side. He drifted toward it.

His own body fought him. Every limb, every muscle repelled from the cliff. The disorientation caused him to stumble. His ankle twisted and he fell. He caught himself on hands and knees, wincing at his stinging palms.

Torol offered him a hand. "The compulsion takes some getting used to. It will force you to obey, and it won't let you run away or harm yourself, so don't bother trying."

Compulsion. How many spells had they placed on him after shearing his hair? He stayed close to Torol, wanting to avoid the unwelcome tug the compulsion inflicted.

They reached the cistern. The men who weren't pounding poles into pots were sitting in pairs at small millstones, working as teams to spin. A half-dozen

293

poles were stacked by the cistern's edge with a pile of gloves. Torol picked up a pole and set of gloves and handed them to Wilek. "Find an urn and mash root. When you're finished, take it to the men at the wheels."

Wilek pulled on the gloves. "Is it flour?"

"Ahvenrood. Get busy before one of the maidens catches you standing around."

Wilek found an urn filled with chunks of starchy root and mirrored the other men by pounding the end of his stick into them, though he did so warily, not wanting to touch the stuff of magic. Slowly the chunks broke apart and turned to mash. As Wilek worked, he plotted the many ways he might kill Charlon. If she were dead, would he be free of the soul-binding?

The mere thought of her death made his eyes sting with sorrow. Madness! Between the soul-binding spell and the compulsion, he doubted his body would let him harm her. He needed to think. To do something that—

"Another load, Father."

Behind Wilek a man dropped the handpoles of a pull cart filled with small evenroot tubers.

"Yeah, I'm talking to you," the man said. "Get over here and unload this."

The invisible hook of the compulsion yanked Wilek forward until his body slammed against the cart, knocking the wind from him. He held tight to the cart's side to keep from crumpling.

A gray-eyed woman stood on the other side of the cart, the Third Maiden, he thought. Roya. "You'll obey the Chieftess's men, Father."

"Yes," Wilek said, without wanting to.

"That's better." She reached across the cart, smirked.

He didn't understand. Did she want him to take hold of her hand?

The other men watched eagerly. Torol frowned and gave a slight shake of the head. What did he mean? Obey her or refuse?

"Well, Father?" Roya asked.

Touching her as lightly as possible, Wilek took hold of her hand.

"Fool," she spat, and slapped him hard across the face.

His cheek burned. Wrong choice, apparently.

"Never touch a maiden without being ordered," Roya said.

He looked to his feet, hating her, hating them all.

She walked around the cart, pointed at the ground. "Kneel before me."

Before he could decide, his knees hit the ground and his spine bowed low until his forehead touched the dirt.

"Lazy fool!" Roya yelled. "Get up and empty this cart."

Wilek sprang to his feet and grabbed an armful of the dirty tubers.

"Here," Torol called, waving Wilek to a large rock where a kneeling man was slicing the tubers into chunks.

Wilek carried the tubers to the rock and dumped them in the small pile beside the man, then marched back to the wagon to fetch another load. His body moved of its own accord.

Roya laughed, as did several of the men who were watching. Anger pooled within Wilek. Was this how his slaves felt? Fear and shame and having no control over their own choices?

When the cart was empty he slowed, until Roya ordered him to return to his pot of root and finish it. He grabbed up his pole and pounded so fast his hand blurred.

"Better." Roya walked away.

Wilek felt her hold on him release. He loosened his grip on the pole and flexed sore fingers, glad it was over.

"It'll get easier," Four said.

"Why do they call me Father?" Wilek asked.

"Maiden Five, the one called Mother, she will give birth to the Deliverer. You are her One."

"One what?"

"Mate. Servant. Slav. Whatever she asks of you. The Chieftess keeps Five Men to do her bidding. Mother has only one. You."

Wonderful. "Will the, um, Mother claim other men?"

Four shrugged and picked up Wilek's urn. "Perhaps. We've never had a Mother before." He carried the urn to a pair of millers and traded it for an empty one, which he filled with chunks of tubers and brought back to Wilek. "It's best if you don't fight."

Four's hair had been cropped short, like Wilek's. He had a sun-like rune inked on the back of his neck. Wilek scratched his neck, sick over his next question. "Do I have a mark here? Like yours?"

Four nodded. "The rune holds the spell that compels you."

"Is it permanent?"

"Never heard of a man who had it removed. Though I've never heard of a man who left the Chieftess's service either."

Never left? "Then how do new ones arrive?"

"When one of the men is killed."

Killed. Not dies. But killed, as if by intention.

For the first time Wilek was thankful for his father. The man was cruel, possibly insane, but in upholding laws prohibiting magic, he had shielded the Armanian people from such atrocities.

"Stop talking and get this root milled!" Roya yelled as she strode between them. "I need water hauled for my bath."

"If we all spit on her at once, she could have her bath now," Wilek mumbled.

Four's eyes widened and he spoke no more to Wilek.

Perhaps Wilek should guard his tongue more carefully. At least Roya hadn't heard him. She continued to bark orders, and whenever she commanded him, the runes on his neck itched fiercely. He rubbed them, but only obedience brought relief.

Never in his life had he imagined such misery existed. Even with the protection of gloves, Wilek's hands were blistered from using the pole. The men worked nonstop until all the tubers had been cut, pounded, and milled, their starchy mixture spread on wire screens to dry. When they finished, they hauled buckets of water to each of the maiden's tents for bathing.

"What now?" Wilek asked Three after the baths had been delivered.

"Now we eat," Three said.

Thank the gods. Wilek left his gloves behind and followed the men to a tent in the center of camp. The smell of something fried drifted from inside. Three and Four ducked inside, but Wilek's legs carried him on.

He looked back. "I cannot stop walking."

"You're being summoned," Three said from the tent's doorway. "Be polite. When in doubt, say nothing."

Wilek faced forward, wondering where his legs would take him. Charlon's tent, likely, but he passed by hers and climbed the hill to the red tent.

The Chieftess.

A man armed with a shard club held open the flap, and the first thing Wilek noticed on entering was that Charlon was here. And that he felt safer with her close by. She stood on the other side of a throne. Their eyes met, and she glanced down. Shame welled inside him—her shame. What did she regret?

He tore his gaze from Charlon and inspected his surroundings. It was colder here than in Charlon's tent. The Chieftess sat upon a fancy throne of woven whitethorn branches. A man stood on one side, fanning her with a fat palm branch—the woman was hot?

The Chieftess herself was solemn, though attractive like any Magonian woman with her reddish-gray skin and gray eyes. She didn't look all that impressive for a ruler. Nor did her tent. A mismatch of fur pelts, leather scraps, and straw mats covered the floor. The Chieftess wore versions of the same. Why hadn't this nomadic woman conquered Armania long ago? A compulsion on the king would have done the trick.

"Prince Wilek Hadar, welcome," the Chieftess said in the Kinsman tongue. "Won't you kneel?"

He paused, waiting for his knees to bend automatically. When they didn't, he said, "I prefer to stand."

The Chieftess chuckled. "Men are always hard to break," she said to Charlon. "Royal men are the worst. *Brak*."

His knees slammed onto the straw mat, the weave biting his skin. A white lizard slithered up to him. Its blue tongue shot out and tasted his thigh.

"You don't yet believe," the Chieftess said, "but Magonia will soon rule the Five Realms."

All five? Wilek scoffed. "Impossible."

"*Hâcâh*," the Chieftess said.

And Wilek could no longer speak. His hands slid off the mat on their own, rubbed the dirt, then spread the dust on his own face. He recalled the Magonian mother doing this after the earthquake and seethed inside. He owed no honor to this witch.

The lizard scampered toward the throne, climbed the Chieftess's leg, and settled on her lap. She stroked its back. "Our rule has been prophesied for centuries. Even your priests know this. You are fortunate to have been chosen. The Father will be remembered in our new history"

Wilek wanted to rail at her, to tell her she was a fool and demand she release him from these insulting spells. But as he couldn't speak, he could only listen. He tried to raise his head so he could at least glare at the hateful woman, but he couldn't even do that. His breath puffed out in a frosty cloud, its size the only evidence of his anger.

"Seems he would rather be elsewhere," the Chieftess said. "Take him to your tent, Mother. I won't receive him again until you carry his child."

His child, the mad witches. The moment the Chieftess released his body and voice from her hold, Wilek stood and said, "I won't be an accessory in your war against the Five Realms."

"Go before I silence you forever," the Chieftess commanded.

Suddenly Wilek was moving out the door and down the cliffside. His legs didn't stop until he was inside Charlon's tent. Beside the waiting tub of bath-water, he found a folded kasah, which he used to wipe the dirt off his face.

Charlon entered the tent. "You're hungry. Come and let us eat."

Wilek *was* hungry. Desperately so. Thirsty too. And itchy. He scratched the insides of his forearms where a rash had grown. Reluctantly he followed Char-lon to the mats surrounding the fire in the center of the tent. A feast awaited, set out in bowls. He wondered which of the men had done this.

Charlon knelt on the mats. Wilek sat across from her, on the other side of the fire. He tore into the food like a starved animal, wolfing down bites, stopping only to itch. It was the first food he had eaten all day. Some kind of roasted bird and chunks of cactus. Bland, but hot.

"You've been poisoned," Charlon said, pointing to his arms. "The starch from the ahvenrood sometimes gets on your skin. I could heal you, but I won't."

Wilek should be afraid, yet Charlon had no fear for his life, so why should he? "Why not?"

She smiled, and though she was smaller than Lady Zeroah, he could see that she was older. "That bit won't kill. And it will be good, for you to see the Veil."

Mythical nonsense.

She sensed his doubt. "The Veil is where we see the spirits. Spirits that al-lowed me to speak with your woman. Want to know? How she died?"

Wilek choked on the half-chewed meat in his mouth. He fell into a coughing fit, grabbed a jug of water, and washed it away. He regained his composure and peered at the witch through half-lidded eyes, wary. "If you mean to ma-nipulate me with your lies, don't bother."

"The binding spell grieves you," Charlon said. "I feel your emotions. Just as you feel mine. I only wish to ease your sorrow."

"To ease your own."

"Perhaps. Would you rather—?"

"Just tell me."

"You are sure?" she asked. "You might not like it."

Wilek wasn't sure at all. He knew better than to mess with black spirits. But whatever she had to say could be no worse than knowing nothing. "Who killed her?" he asked.

"Drice. In her perfume bottle."

"Who put them there? She must have had some idea."

"She did. Wouldn't tell me. To protect you."

"How does that protect me?"

"The one who left the drice. He was a mantic. Lebetta feared my shadir would tell his. That he would learn she betrayed him. And he would follow through on his threat to kill you."

"How did she leave her room that night? Where did she go?"

"She didn't say how she left. But she went to speak with Prince Janek. To ask to be his mistress."

"What?" Being a mistress would be a demotion from concubine. "What did he tell her?"

"She was killed before she could see him."

Why Janek? "Did she love Janek?"

"No. But she needed to stay. In the castle. To protect you. Prince Janek was the only way."

"Then why did she go to him before?"

"To punish you. So you would know. What it felt like to share the one you loved."

The words struck like a blow to the chest. "So I'm to blame for everything? If I hadn't banished her she would still be alive." And if he'd agreed to marry her, she would never have gone to Janek in the first place.

"Being cast from your favor brought death sooner. But Lebetta had refused to help those who sought to do you harm. Her murderer would have lost patience. At some point. Taken her life anyway."

"Who? Who wanted to do me harm? And how? Why not simply kill me and be done with it?"

"She didn't say."

Silence stretched between them. Wilek scratched his arms and realized he believed every word Charlon had spoken. He felt a fool yet could think of no reason for her to invent such a tale. He felt her sincerity. Her honesty. Now that the words were in his mind, they seemed true. Lebetta had been asked to betray him. She had refused. And her refusal had ended her life.

"Can you speak to her again? Can I speak to her?"

"That would counteract my goal."

Because she wanted him to give her a child. Could he negotiate? Agree if she let him speak to Lebetta? Was it worth it?

Of course not! How could he even consider it?

Wilek ate his fill, then lay down on his mat in the corner. Exhausted from a day of hard labor, sleep came quickly.

A dream of Lebetta being sacrificed to Barthos woke him in the middle of the night. He felt ill. Feverish. The rash on his arms burned, and even though he couldn't see it in the dark, he could feel several raw bumps.

You're going to die, a voice taunted in his head.

That one lies, a lower voice said. *Ask my help and I will free you.*

"Who's there?" Wilek asked, heart racing.

In a flash of light, a plume of yellow smoke cackled and passed over where he lay.

A purple fog followed it, curling and smoking in wreaths above his chest. Three dark eyes peeked out from the cloud and blinked at him. *You want to be free, don't you?*

He lies! the yellow one shrieked, flashing past again. *You don't need his help. Kill the woman and you'll be free.*

Kill Charon?

Her words came back to him then. Was this the Veil?

Terror fell like a net. "Go away!" Wilek yelled. "You have no power over me!"

The purple one vanished, but the yellow continued to circle his torso. It passed over him, disappeared into the ground on one side, came up on his other side, and passed over him again.

Charlon woke and whispered words in a language he didn't understand. The yellow spirit vanished, as did the fierce itching on his arms. They felt smooth again. He began to slip back toward sleep.

Before losing himself to the night, a single and clear thought came to him. Charlon had made a mistake in casting a soul-binding spell. Roya had abused him that afternoon at the cistern. The compulsion spell could force him to do anything. Yet Charlon, who wanted his child, had not forced him to sleep with her. Their soul-bound connection made her merciful toward him.

He must find a way to exploit that mercy and escape.

TREVN

What is the Lahavôtesh? Some would say it is freedom. A sect of the Rôb faith founded by Prince Mergest III, the Lahavôtesh serves as a popular outlet for Sarikarians who find the rules and pious lifestyle of the Armanite faith oppressive. Followers meet in each other's homes, often in secret, as King Ormarr opposes all that deviates from the Book of Arman. The king has recently disinherited his eldest son and deposed him as heir, claiming the Lahavôtesh is a cult that is causing dissention for the realm of Sarikar. Prince Mergest and his followers disagree. They defend their sect as being superior to Armanite, insisting that the Lahavôtesh focuses on peace, love, and forgiveness compared to Armanite's punitive legalism.

—Father Lamis, high priest of Armanite, House Pitney 507

My study of the Lahavôtesh sect has brought forth a revelation. I have spent the last six years learning ancient Armanian, and my recent fluency has led me to a translation. The word *tesh* means "followers." *La* is an article meaning "the." And *havôt* means "powerful shadir." This group is not a sect of the Rôb faith but one of Kabar, the faith of the mother realms. Followers beware.

—Father Lamis, high priest of Armanite, House Pitney 513

This was the research Father Tomek had left for Trevn in his old classroom. He found the scrolls underneath the clay tablets that spoke of the Five Woes, just as Father Tomek said he would.

Growing up in Sarikar, Trevn had heard the stories about how Prince Jorger had been made Heir after his older brother's disinheritance. Trevn's tutors had always been Armanian and had only taught him House Pitney's political history. Trevn had never known the reason behind Prince Mergest's fall until this very moment.

Could it be coincidence that the Kabaran sect used as its insignia the very rune combination Lady Lebetta had drawn in blood as she lay dying? Trevn thought not. Which would mean the Lahavôtesh were active in Armania. Were Cousin Eudora or Lilou Caridod part of this sect?

Trevn still was not sure, nor was he certain how to find out.

"My pardon, Your Highness," Cadoc said.

Trevn glanced up. His shield was standing in the doorway. "Yes?"

"Your father has summoned you."

"Again?" Trevn wanted to scream. In Wilek's absence, Janek had become Father's number one, which made Trevn number two, which meant more meetings than ever before. This was the third time in the same day! "Very well. First I must visit my mother's apartment."

Once the documents Father Tomek had left for Trevn were safely stored away in the secret room in his mother's apartment, Trevn set out to meet his father.

He arrived at the royal apartment and found his mother, the king, and Princess Nabelle waiting in Father's office. Dread seized him like a cloud of steam.

"Sit, Trevn," Father said. "We must discuss an important matter."

Trevn sat.

"It is tradition for Armanian and Sarikarian royalty to intermarry," Father said. "Keeps our interests mutual. With Wilek gone, everyone is a bit concerned. Right, Princess?"

"Indeed," Princess Nabelle said. "The people of Sarikar have been anticipating my daughter's wedding to Sâr Wilek for a decade. Even more so after what happened with Sâr Janek and Princess Nolia."

Trevn didn't like where this conversation was headed or the smile on his mother's face. "Lady Zeroah greatly admires my brother Wilek," he said carefully. "They will make a fine match."

"Wilek might be dead," Father said.

The man may as well have punched Trevn in the gut. "He is not dead, Father."

The king raised his hand. "Hear me out. He might be. If so, we are left with no pending marriage treaties with Sarikar. King Jorger informed me that should Lady Zeroah be cast aside, he will cease free trade between our realms and demand payment in full on all our debts. We have plenty of debts to Sarikar we cannot pay, my son. If we cannot pay, King Jorger can declare war."

War. The word shocked Trevn. "He wouldn't do that."

"Oh, he would love an excuse to cut off our sinful, Rôbish heads," Father said, practically scowling at Princess Nabelle. "Now, I think our army would stand a fair chance against him, but I'd rather it didn't come to that. You see where this is going, don't you?"

He certainly did. "You want me to marry Lady Zeroah." The words came out whispered and strange, like someone else had said them.

"I love the idea," Mother said.

Father glared at her, then said to Trevn, "Janek offered, but they don't match in fives. You and Lady Zeroah are the same age. I see Mikreh's favor in that."

"No," Trevn said.

Father glared at him. "You think I give you a choice?"

"I won't take my brother's bride," Trevn said.

"Fools die from lack of judgment," Mother snapped. "Sâr Wilek is likely dead!"

"You don't know that," Trevn snapped back. He took a deep breath and tried to be reasonable. "It's only been a couple months since he left. Assuming the worst is irrational. Lady Zeroah turns sixteen in, what, eight months? If Wilek is still missing then, I will marry her to keep peace between our realms. But I see no reason to panic until we know for certain."

The room fell silent but for Mother's sudden weeping.

"I suppose we can wait until then," Father said. "Princess Nabelle, what say you?"

"It is a fair compromise," Princess Nabelle said. "I doubt my father would object to waiting eight more months, as long as we sign an agreement."

"Fine. I'll have the papers drawn up," Father said, ready to move on to the next thing. "Trevn, you will come here and sign them with Lady Zeroah. Tomorrow, an hour before midday. Is that convenient, Princess?"

She nodded.

"Tomorrow, then, Trevn," Father said. "Dismissed."

✦ ✦ ✦

Trevn returned to his chambers in a daze, Cadoc at his side. When they arrived, they found Hinck outside the door, arguing with a priest in blue robes. It was Zithel Lau, the medial priest of Rôb who had playacted as Dendron in *Magon's Betrayal*.

"What's this?" Trevn asked.

"He said he had permission to search your room," Hinck said.

"I've been sent to retrieve your apprentice copy of the Holy Book, Your Highness," Lau said.

The words instantly set Trevn on edge. "Sent by whom?"

"Pontiff Rogedoth."

"Leave," Trevn said. "If the Pontiff wants to speak to me, he may set up an appointment in the usual manner. I am a Prince of Armania. I will not be treated like a commoner."

"The Pontiff won't be pleased," Lau said. "The church is the highest authority in the realm. Above even the rosâr."

"Is that a fact?" Trevn asked. "Let us go to my father now so you can give him this news."

The priest paled.

"No? If you are unwilling to speak to the rosâr, this conversation is over. If I catch you near my chambers again, I will have you sent to the pole. Is that clear?"

"Yes, Your Highness." As Lau scurried away, Trevn caught sight of a silver ankle cuff on his leg.

"Lau!" he called out.

The man turned back, bowed. "Yes, Your Highness?"

"Your ankle cuff. Do all medial priests wear one?"

Lau looked down at his foot, lifting his robes until the cuff showed. "No, Your Highness. This was a gift from the Pontiff when I took my vows. He gives each of his acolytes something unique."

Trevn faked a smile. "How thoughtful."

Lau nodded, bowed, then fled.

Trevn watched him go, seething. He had to do something, quickly. "Hinck, summon two guards to watch my door." He started for the grand stairs. "Cadoc, with me."

"Where are you going?" Hinck called after him.

"To see Pontiff Rogedoth."

✦　✦　✦

The Pontiff did not reside in the castle but in the Priest House attached to Temple Everton. The temple had been built between the castle and High Street. It was white marble and had five towers, each with five-tiered roofs. Diamond-paned windows with blue glass glittered in the light of the setting sun. Not quite as old as the castle, the temple had been built some two hundred years ago when King Halak II had converted to the Rôb faith.

Trevn and Cadoc tied their horses at the door of the Priest's House, on the back side of the temple. Trevn had never been inside the Priest's House before, and its extravagance surprised him. He thought priests lived humbly. The Pontiff certainly didn't. Marble floors, silk rugs and tapestries, golden lampstands, wooden furniture—not even the king owned this much wood. Trevn supposed privilege came with power.

The Pontiff's onesent led them to the receiving room to wait. Trevn found the room similar to the king's Presence Chamber. It even had a throne.

Trevn felt every bit a Renegade in confronting the Pontiff, but if what Lau said was true, the Pontiff felt himself above the king. Why, then, would he answer the demands of the youngest sâr? What if the man refused him?

"Sâr Trevn." The deep voice made Trevn jump. Pontiff Rogedoth entered from a door on the side wall, his onesent in tow. "I am pleased you came by. There is a matter I wish to discuss with you."

Was there? "I hope it explains why you sent a priest to search my chambers."

"It does." The Pontiff sat on his throne and did not offer Trevn a seat. In fact there were no other chairs in this room. "Have you chosen a new tutor?"

"I have not. As you can see," he said, motioning to his black attire, "I am still mourning."

"That is commendable, Your Highness. If you need suggestions for a new tutor, I would be happy to provide a list."

"Thank you," Trevn said, "but why were you searching my chambers?"

"Concerns have arisen as to the curriculum Father Tomek taught you."

"Why not ask me? Is not a civil conversation simpler than trespassing?"

The Pontiff didn't answer right away. Trevn noted the man's extremely pronounced brow, which reminded him of Hinck's speculation regarding the Pontiff and Queen Laviel. Could Hinck be right that the man was Janek's father?

"I will grant you a civil conversation," the Pontiff said. "It was common knowledge that Father Tomek was a follower of Arman. No one would begrudge him his right to choose which five to follow. The father god is mighty, indeed. What you might not know is that Father Tomek was a devout Armanite.

He served no god but Arman. He also had in his possession a copy of the Armanite text. That document is pure heresy and has been outlawed by the Rôb church for centuries."

Trevn struggled to keep his expression passive. That Pontiff Rogedoth might have had something to do with Father Tomek's death made his hands tremble. "I fail to see what Father Tomek's possessions have to do with me," Trevn said.

"Simply to confirm he did not lead you astray."

Madness! "I assure you, had he done so, I would have told my father immediately." Lying came so easily. Did the Pontiff have the same ability?

"Most gratifying to hear, Your Highness. Bring the manuscript you transcribed as part of your apprenticeship for my inspection. It could be that Father Tomek misled you to transcribe his illegal tome."

"I think I would have noticed," Trevn said, realizing he was a terrible priest, for it hadn't occurred to him to wonder why he had been transcribing the Armanite book over the Rôb.

"Most certainly. But only the text will set my mind at ease."

My mind, the man had said, as if he were the master of this investigation. Of killing Father Tomek. Five Woes, a murdering priest.

"No matter to me," Trevn said, scrambling for a way to stall. "I have made little progress, though."

"It has been two years, Your Highness. How far along are you?"

"Oh, maybe half." Trevn hoped that sounded convincing. He shrugged. "I will have my pages sent to you, if you like."

Rogedoth's smile looked more like a snarl. "Your cooperation is most appreciated."

Trevn left Rogedoth's luxurious quarters with a mission in mind. Back at the castle he asked Beal to fetch a copy of the Rôb text and take it to his old bedchamber in his mother's apartment. Then he returned to his chambers, where he found two guards stationed outside the door. Inside, Hinck was pacing before the hearth, brown furrowed in despair.

"What happened?" Hinck asked.

Trevn relayed Rogedoth's demand.

"You think Rogedoth was involved in Father Tomek's murder?" Hinck asked.

"Seems likely. I cannot give him my book, so I will transcribe a new copy."

"So quickly?"

"I only need to do half. You will help me stall by spreading rumors about me and Miss Mielle and secret outings. I'll write to her and explain. Will you take her my message right away?"

"Of course."

Trevn scratched out a plea to Mielle and sent Hinck to deliver it. Then he gathered all the map tubes he could, emptied them, and gave them to Cadoc to carry. Trevn grabbed a stack of parchment, and they set off for his mother's apartment.

When they arrived, Beal was waiting with the Book of Rôb.

Trevn took the tome from him. "Is my mother here?"

"She is still at dinner, Your Highness," Beal wheezed.

"Dinner." Trevn hadn't realized it was so late. This was good, though. "Thank you, Beal. You are dismissed for the evening."

"Yes, Your Highness."

Beal bowed and departed. Trevn led Cadoc into his mother's bedchamber, closed the door, and went into the privy, where a secret door led to a short passageway.

"How did you find this place?" Cadoc asked.

"I followed my mother here as a boy," Trevn said, stepping into the dark space. "Back then she still cared about advancing her own causes at court. Now she only cares about advancing me. Hand me that candlestick."

Cadoc lifted the candlestick from the privy wall and passed it to Trevn.

Trevn held it aloft, squinting. He stepped to the second secret door and pushed it in. The room wasn't much bigger than the privy. It was triangular in shape, a space left behind by the architecture of the rooms beyond. Cobwebs and dust coated walls of unfinished stone. It was furnished with a small stone desk and stool, brackets on the wall to hold candlesticks, and a basket hanging from the ceiling that held a dead plant. The map tube holding his Book of Arman still hung from a nail on the wall. The two scrolls Father Tomek had left concerning the Lahavôtesh lay on the desktop.

Trevn set the candlestick on the desk. "Once Mother stopped coming here, I claimed the space as a fort. There are two peekholes. One looks into the sitting room, the other into her bedchamber. She would rage at her servants, looking for me. Never knew I was right there, watching." Laughing. "This will be a safe place to hide while I transcribe."

"While everyone thinks you are out with Miss Mielle," Cadoc said.

Yes. "Was I wrong to ask it of her?"

"I think she'll be eager to help."

Trevn hoped so. "Hang the map tubes there." He pointed at the dead plant. Cadoc reached up for the basket.

Trevn wiped a swath of dust off the desk with his sleeve and set the parchment and Book of Rôb down in the clean space. He began transcribing right away. It did not banish his sorrow over losing Father Tomek, his fear for Wilek, his dread at possibly being forced to marry Lady Zeroah, or his worry that he might have lost Mielle forever. Still, it was a relief, truly, to have something to distract from the madness.

The next midday, Trevn was summoned to his father's office to sign the betrothal agreement. He and Lady Zeroah sat before the king's desk. Father and King Jorger had already signed, as had Trevn's mother and Princess Nabelle.

Trevn read the agreement twice, carefully looking for any loophole that might force the wedding sooner. It seemed written to his specifications. "What did Miss Mielle say about this?" he whispered to Lady Zeroah.

"She does not know," Lady Zeroah said. "Please, do not tell her. Sâr Wilek will return. There is no need to upset anyone."

A nice thought. Trevn glanced around the room. Two footmen stood by the door. Five of his father's guards were posted outside. Word would likely get out. It always did. He hoped Wilek would return soon.

Trevn nodded to Lady Zeroah and signed his name.

KALENEK

Wymer and his men opted to go their own way, so Kal led Grayson, Onika, and Rustian out of the city, with Jhorn atop the female camel. Horses would speed their journey back to Everton, but the only horses Kal had seen still living in Kaptar were carrying yeetta guards, who didn't look willing to share.

They passed out of the city, and Kal scanned the horizon. "Is there higher ground nearby?" He didn't want to camp in the valley in case another flood came in the night.

"There are hills to the southwest," Jhorn said. "About six leagues."

So Kal veered southwest. They traveled all day under the scalding sun, digging up desert ground cones when they found them and sucking on the roots. They gathered bits of wood—mostly tumbleweeds of sticky snare and the occasional cat's claw branch. It was nearly sunset by the time they reached the foothills.

Grayson, Onika, and Rustian had fallen behind, so Kal halted the camel. As they waited, Jhorn shared about his time in the war. He had fought in the Scablands Invasion, just south of Raine. It had been one of the bloodiest battles in the Centenary War. Jhorn told the story in detail, sharing how he fell in battle after a yeetta shard club severed his right leg and half his left.

"How about you?" he asked Kal. "Where were you stationed?"

Kal merely shook his head. Hearing Jhorn's nightmare had been bad enough. He didn't want to relive his own.

"Talking about it helps," Jhorn said. "You wouldn't think so, but it does."

"I've never seen skin like Onika's," Kal said, deliberately changing the subject. "Are there more like her in Magonia?"

Jhorn watched Kal for a long moment. "Never seen any," he said, finally. "Five years back I found the cat scratching at my door. It wouldn't come in. Wouldn't eat. Kept scratching and mewing until I followed it to a river hole in a nearby stepwell. There sat Onika, thirteen years old, blind and spouting prophecies. You have children, Sir Kalenek?"

Kal hated that question. He should say yes and be done with it. Instead he said, "Of a kind."

Jhorn looked down from the camel. "What *kind* of children, then?"

Now he had to explain. "When I married, my wife had two younger sisters she cared for who became part of our household. When she died, they became my wards."

"That's good of you," Jhorn said.

It had been. Until he had lost their fortune to Captain Alpress's blackmail. "They are good girls." Which made Kal wonder if Mielle had kept away from Sâr Trevn. Somehow he doubted it.

The others had nearly caught up. In the distance beyond them, Kal caught sight of movement. He withdrew his grow lens and peered through. "Someone follows us. Looks like the young man who shared your pit." Kal handed the lens up to Jhorn.

Jhorn took a look and sighed. "Burk is a thief and a bully. If he reaches us, we will need to take care."

They climbed the hill to the summit. They had no tents, but Kal built a fire from the wood scraps, and everyone gathered around for warmth. Everyone but Kal, who continued to watch the young thief's approach.

Jhorn borrowed Kal's knife and began to whittle the fat end of a cat's claw branch. Grayson teased Rustian with a bit of rope. Onika stared into the flames. Could she see the brightness? Her face was pink, having been burned by walking all day under the sun. Tomorrow Kal would give her his head scarf to protect her skin.

"The one comes who will seek to end my calling," she said suddenly, her eyes shifting. "He will not deter me for long."

It had been days since Kal had heard Onika prophesy. The power of her voice squeezed his heart. He followed her gaze to the approaching boy, who was but fifty paces out and moving closer.

"Should I send him away, Onika?" Kal asked. "I won't allow anyone to harm you."

"Trials come to us all, Kalenek Veroth, as you well know." She stood and crept away from the campfire. Three steps and she stumbled on a clump of sagebrush.

Grayson popped up and took her arm. "I'll help you to your bedroll, Onika."

The sound of approaching footsteps pulled Kal's attention to the newcomer.

"Jhorn! I hoped I'd find you," the boy said in Kinsman as he stopped before the fire. He was gaunt and greasy with shrewd eyes. His hair was dyed rusty orange and twisted into short locks like a rat's tail cactus. He looked at Kal, up and down, as if gauging an opponent. "You were at the prison."

Jhorn dropped his whittling to his lap and regarded the young man. "Burk, this is Sir Kalenek Veroth. We have him to thank for our freedom."

The boy bowed low, his arm sweeping across bony hips. "I thank you, noble knighten. If not for you, we might have died in that pit."

"We want no trouble." Kal set his hand on the hilt of his sword. "What do *you* want?"

Burk lifted both hands, his expression all eyes. "Only to travel with you. I can catch wattlelop and squirrels with my sling. Plus I trained for a time with the Rurekan army, so if you give me a sword, I—"

"Rurekau your home?" Kal asked.

"I was born there, but I don't call anyplace home."

Kal didn't want the thief here. He was a fugitive, Onika was wary of him, and Rurekans tended to think they were better than everyone else. But he couldn't very well turn him away.

Kal stepped close, chest to nose, and glared down. "Cause trouble and you deal with me. We have no extra bedroll, so you'll have to make do with dirt."

"Making do is my specialty," Burk said, stepping around Kal to crouch by the fire.

Grayson returned and glared across the flames at the thief, but Burk either didn't see the boy or pretended not to.

Continuing northwest the next day, they met several travelers who claimed Hebron and the Cross Canyon Bridges had fallen in an earthquake. The news silenced all but Grayson.

"Think Novan made it?" he asked.

"Should have," Kal said, uneasy that Onika's prophecy continued to become reality. Novan was smart. If the bridges were gone, he would have gone south. "We head for the Ebro Tip."

They camped that night in an empty cistern. By now Jhorn had carved two canes from cat's claw branches and used them to vault himself around, sticks and stumps acting like horse hooves in a slow-motion canter. His speed and balance were amazing.

"How do you do that?" Kal asked.

"Years of practice," Jhorn said, inspecting the canes. "These aren't as comfortable as my old ones. I'll likely get some blisters."

"You should see him with his pegs," Grayson said. "He can kick a man in the face."

"*Grayson*," Jhorn admonished.

But Kal didn't doubt it.

They sat around the campfire and ate roasted wattlelop, which Burk had caught. Grayson and Burk told tales of their heroic exploits, each trying to one-up the other. Burk put his arm around Onika's shoulder and whispered in her ear. Whether by his words, touch, or both, she somehow looked even paler. Kal was about to intervene when Grayson knocked into Burk, separating him from Onika. Grayson took her hand and pulled her up and away to her bedroll. Rustian stayed behind and hissed at Burk.

Kal was glad to see Onika had plenty of protectors, but the words she had said still haunted him. *The one comes who will seek to end my calling . . .* What mischief was Burk going to try, and how might Kal prevent it?

"Onika is a beautiful woman," Burk said, still watching her and Grayson.

"I'll thank you to keep your hands off her," Jhorn said. "I don't need legs to kill a man."

Kal liked Jhorn more and more each day.

Burk forced a laugh. "Like I'd bother with a blind girl. I want a woman who can cook and clean and keep house."

"What house?" Kal asked.

"I'll have one someday," Burk said. "A mansion."

"Best wait till you have that mansion to be looking for a wife, eh?" Kal walked to the entrance of the cistern to stand watch, eager to cease communications with the pompous child. Burk went to bed, and eventually Jhorn did too. Kal walked above ground to scan the landscape. The moon had waned but still shone bright. He wondered where Novan was, if Wilek was home, what Mielle might be doing, if Amala was in bed yet.

A yelp brought him to attention. A grunt. The dull thuds of punches.

Kal ran around the cistern and found Burk pummeling Grayson in the dirt outside. The lad was getting a terrible beating, but he had clamped his teeth onto Burk's leg like a rabid dog.

"Enough!" Kal grabbed Burk's shoulder, Grayson's arm, and wrenched them apart. Shook them hard. "What are you doing out here?"

"He threw a stone at me," Burk said. "Then ran away."

"He was bothering Onika," Grayson said. "Jhorn said it's my job to protect her."

"You couldn't protect her from a spider," Burk said. "Besides, I'm not going to hurt her. I like her."

"Exactly why she needs protecting," Grayson said. "And Onika loves me. She told me so."

"Like a brother, maybe," Burk said. "An annoying brother."

"Shut up, both of you." Kal shook them again. "Neither of you has a thing to offer Onika. No sense fighting over a woman who'd never have you."

"She'd have me, given time," Burk said. "I'm good with women."

Kal pulled him close; the boy reeked of body odor. "Just you push that thought out of your mind, Burk, you hear? If I catch you anywhere near her, I'll bury you alive in a box of drice."

The boy shrank a little, and Kal felt they finally understood one another. "To bed, the both of you." He shoved them away.

Burk stomped back into the cistern.

But Grayson lingered. "Don't make me sleep near him, please. He'll beat me again when you're not looking."

Why had Jhorn, a former soldier, not taught this boy a thing about fighting? At Grayson's size, Kal had been fearless. Then he remembered the boy's true age and sobered. "You must learn to fight your own battles."

"Jhorn won't teach me," Grayson said, his voice forlorn. "Says violence begets violence. But I don't know what *begets* means."

Kal fought back a smile. "It means to create. He means that violence only creates more violence. And he's right." It wasn't Kal's place to usurp Jhorn's authority over the boy. "I'll give you some advice."

"Oh, thank you, Sir Kalenek! You won't regret it. I'm a fast learner."

Oh, this boy . . . "Keep your enemies close," Kal said. "Get to know Burk, and you'll learn his weaknesses. He may even confide in you. Then you'll know how to thwart his plans."

Grayson nodded. "Keep him close to thwart his plans. Yes, sir. I will."

"Good. Now get some sleep."

The next morning they continued south toward Ebro and saw at least two dozen mule deer moving in a herd.

"Haven't seen so many travel together before," Jhorn said. "And never this far north."

The deer were not the first animals to cross their path. There were squirrels, jackrabbits, prairie dogs, ossabey, lizards, snakes, dune cats, quail, rats, a torterus . . . even a fang cat that picked a fight with Rustian and lost.

A dusty cloud bloomed on the horizon. First Kal wondered if there might be a fire, but as they came closer he realized it was dust, not smoke. Foreboding kindled in his gut.

That afternoon they met a group of travelers who claimed Ebro was blocked off.

"A quake two nights ago," the man said. "The ground caved in from the Ebro Tip to the Great Ice Canyon."

It couldn't be. "How wide is the gap?" Kal asked.

"A league or two, and fifty paces deep. There's no way to cross."

"I'd like to see it," Kal told Jhorn. He could never believe it otherwise. "We're nearly there."

They continued on, and Kal discovered the travelers had been in earnest. The new canyon looked like any other, except that it was fresh. He recognized the signs of a fall-in from what he had seen in Farway, the way the soil was smooth along the walls but for the river holes that dotted the side. Water gushed from several, making muddy waterfalls.

"River holes," Burk said.

"Not all of them." Grayson pointed at smaller holes that were either dry or partially caved in. "Those are root holes."

"Then where are the roots?" Burk asked.

"Gone," Grayson said. "Evenroot tunnels often collapse after being harvested. That's partly why smugglers pay so much for children to harvest root."

"So we turn back?" Jhorn asked.

Kal pictured a map of the Five Realms in his mind. "If Hebron and the bridges are gone, and Ebro and all of Sarikar are cut off, we have no choice but to head north. We can stop in Lâhaten for supplies. Empress Inolah is a friend of mine. She'll help us, I'm certain. Then we go on to Jeruka and catch a ship for Everton."

"Friends with the empress?" Burk snorted. "Sure you are."

"Don't be stupid," Grayson said to Burk. "Sir Kalenek Veroth is shield to Prince Wilek Hadar, the empress's brother."

"If he's a shield, what's he doing in Magonia?" Burk asked.

"My business is my own," Kal said. "Our journey has just lengthened, friends. We're nearly one hundred fifty leagues from Lâhaten. Three weeks, I'd guess."

"It might as well be forever!" Burk said. "I didn't leave Kaptar to die in the desert."

"You're free to go your own way," Kal said, wishing the boy would.

"I only hope we have enough time," Jhorn said.

"I'm open to other ideas," Kal said, but he knew there were none.

"Could we climb down the canyon and cross on the bottom?" Grayson asked.

Leave it to Grayson to find an actual alternative. "I suppose we *could*."

"I'm not going into the canyons!" Burk yelled. "Barthos will eat us."

"I'm not aware of a low enough place to enter the canyon," Kal said, ignoring the thief. "We could keep watch for one. I'm not opposed to trying to cut across."

"We'd still have to find a place to climb up on the other side," Jhorn said. "And, god or not, something lives in The Grays. I'd rather not be trapped down there when whatever it is feels hungry. Lâhaten would be safest, if we hurry."

Kal nodded. "We head for Lâhaten. May the wind be at our backs."

QOATCH

By twilight on the twenty-second day, Priestess Jazlyn's delegation reached the city of Lâhaten in Rurekau. Its stone buildings stood like soldiers surrounding the fortress. The setting sun caught on the glass windows of Castle Lâhaten and glimmered like orange jewels. In the distance, Mount Lâhat smoked. It had been years since it last blew ash into the sky. The Great Ladies of Tenma all agreed it would soon pour forth again.

A Kushaw assassin knew ninety-six different ways to kill, and Qoatch had gone over them all on the journey. He had focused on passive ways to fulfill his oath: poison, accidents, or deadly insect bites. It mattered not. He could not kill Jazlyn. He did not want to.

He hated himself.

He should have told Duvlid the truth, asked for reassignment. To say nothing . . . He selfishly risked everything so many men had struggled for, for so long.

As he berated himself, the delegation rode under the city gate. Bald Igote soldiers dressed in brown leather armor with gold accents stood on the wall above, longpole spears in hand. The city was shutting down for the night, but those who were out stopped to stare at the stately procession. Tennish Protectors wore white. Even covered in dust, they looked like demigods compared to the Rurekan commoners.

They stopped before the gates to the Imperial Quarter. Moaba, Jazlyn's head Protector, got off his camel to speak with the gatekeeper. The Veil was void of shadir at the moment. Gozan had gone ahead to search the castle, taking his slight and common shadir minions with him.

It wasn't long before Jazlyn lost patience. "What's taking so long? Qoatch, go find out."

Qoatch commanded his camel to sit, dismounted, and approached Moaba at the gate. They were speaking Kinsman, which Qoatch knew well.

"We will not be put off," Moaba was saying. "This is an insult to the Great Lady."

"I have my orders," the gatekeeper said. "No foreigners allowed in the Imperial Quarter without Emperor Nazer's approval."

"Then send for it," Moaba said.

The gatekeeper's gaze fell on Qoatch. His eyes popped wide as he took in Qoatch's attire. "Sands! Who are you supposed to be?"

"This is Qoatch," Moaba said, "eunuch slav to our Sixth Great Lady."

The gatekeeper and the two guards behind him snickered.

Qoatch had received such reactions from foreign men before. Many found eunuchs pitifully amusing. Others merely laughed at his uniform, which was a long white kasah skirt, a bare chest, and the pelt of a fang cat tied over one shoulder. At least he wasn't forced to shave his head like these common soldiers.

"A messenger rode ahead to announce our arrival," Qoatch said. "Did he come here?"

"His scroll was taken to the emperor's attendants, but he wasn't admitted."

"Where is he now?"

"How should I know where the man took hisself? Now get! You won't change my mind."

Qoatch walked back to Jazlyn. Gozan and his followers had returned, clouding the Veil as they swarmed around the Great Lady.

"Well?" she demanded. "Speak, eunuch."

"The gatekeeper has orders to let no one inside the Imperial Quarter," Qoatch said. "I do not understand the emperor's reason for snubbing you. He is either extremely rude or hiding something."

"He insults you," Gozan said. "You will need to use magic to get inside, perhaps kill several guards."

"I am tired," Jazlyn said. "Have my girls do it, Qoatch."

Qoatch said nothing. Simply remained in place, head bowed.

"I gather you disagree, eunuch. Answer, then."

"These people see magic rarely, Great Lady. Seize this opportunity to show your strength. Let them fear you, not your servants."

Jazlyn stared at the gate, passive. Qoatch hoped she wouldn't punish him for offering advice. She waved to her guards. "Get these people out of my way!"

Qoatch cleared a path for the priestess, whose camel pranced behind him, head held high. Gozan flew at her side, invisible to all but the mantics and Qoatch.

Jazlyn shouted down in Kinsman from her great height, voice magically magnified by Gozan. "Open the gates!"

The gatekeeper trembled but still denied her. "I cannot, lady."

"Then I shall do so myself." Jazlyn thrust her palm forward. Gozan flew toward the guard, picked him up, and carried him through the air. The guard screamed, oblivious that he was being carried. Gozan slammed the man's back against the gates and held him there. The great shadir had the power to make the man fly without touching him, but Gozan liked to play with humans. To the common eye the guard's body hung suspended in the middle of the iron doors.

"Put me down!" he yelled.

Jazlyn nudged her camel forward a step. "If you wish it."

Gozan pushed the man into the gates. Hinges creaked. The doors parted slightly. Light from the sunset spilled through, slowly growing as the breach widened. The guard's back sank into the gap, causing his arms to extend out in front like he was trying and failing to touch his toes. His leather armor scraped against the iron until, in one great rush, Gozan pushed him through and out of sight. The doors yawned open. Jazlyn waved her guards forward.

Two by two the delegation from Tenma passed into the Imperial Quarter. Qoatch ran back to his camel and mounted, quickly taking his place behind Jazlyn.

Inside the gates a wide stone path ran under a looming archway to Castle Lâhaten. The path soon was the scene of a battle between the white-clad Tennish Protectors and the Imperial Guard of the Emperor.

"Imbeciles." Jazlyn murmured a command to Gozan. The shadir blew into the melee, appearing to humans as a sudden gust of wind surging forward. It picked up the Rurekan Igote. The Protectors fell back, staring at their enemies, who were now suspended in air by the force of Gozan's power and Jazlyn's desire.

"Your hospitality is abominable," Jazlyn shouted. "I could crush each of your skulls with the snap of my fingers. I ask nothing more but for you to announce my arrival to your disobliging emperor. Do so now."

Gozan released the Igote, who dropped to the ground with thuds of leather-clad bodies against stone.

Jazlyn urged her camel under the arch. It stopped in front of the castle entrance and she ordered it to sit. Several attendants scurried from the vestibule and stood in a line.

Qoatch stopped his camel beside Jazlyn's, hoping this was the end of the disrespect toward his Great Lady. Her eyes were ringed gray, her skin had begun to wrinkle, and her hair, once black, was now streaked with gray. She had drained herself and must purge soon to find rejuvenation. Qoatch felt responsible. He should not have suggested she use magic when fatigued.

A short man stepped forward. "Welcome, weary travelers. I have sent word of your arrival to the emperor. I hope to hear his instructions soon."

"Must I destroy you all?" Jazlyn yelled.

"We have traveled a long way," Qoatch told the man, knowing Jazlyn had no more magic in her. "The Great Lady would like to rest before meeting with the emperor."

"Any moment and I'm sure we will have our answer," the man said.

"Set up my umbrella and altar mat," Jazlyn demanded.

Qoatch did as asked. He instructed the slavs to erect the umbrella shade just outside the front doors, where it would be most inconvenient. He bade them hang a curtain around the umbrella to give Jazlyn privacy to conduct her sacred ritual. Once her cushions had been arranged, Qoatch led her inside and helped her sit. Her face was lined and pallid. Her girls began fanning her with palm leaves. The altar mat lay at her feet, ignored. She had done too much too quickly. Curse Gozan, anyway, for riling her so.

Qoatch unrolled her mat. "I would be pleased to prepare my Great Lady a drink or something to eat," he said aloud, technically to no one.

"Chalabba," Jazlyn whispered, "with two doses of root. And some peres."

She should wait before taking more root, but she would never heed his cautions. Qoatch prepared the chalabba himself, pouring the frothy drink made from camel's milk, spices, and rock sugar into the jar and carefully adding two doses of evenroot.

He could kill her now. Ten doses should be enough.

The thought came unbidden, deep from his years of training. He pushed it away and fixed the drink properly. She devoured it and the fruit, then knelt on her altar mat to purge the evenroot poison to Gozan. Jazlyn was resting when word arrived from Emperor Nazer.

"The emperor has offered your priestess a place in his castle," the short man told Qoatch. "The rest of you must take rooms outside the Imperial Quarter."

"The Great Lady's Protectors will not abandon her," Qoatch said.

"Her quarters have two adjoining rooms," the man said. "She may bring as many guards as she can stuff inside. Emperor Nazer has also invited her to dinner in the great hall tonight, where she will have the opportunity to state her business."

"The Great Lady would prefer a private meeting with the emperor," Qoatch said.

Jazlyn stepped out from her makeshift tent, looking herself again, though tired. "Never mind that. Qoatch, have Moaba choose five Protectors for each room. You and my girls will sleep in my chambers. Send everyone else to wait in the city until I send word. And you . . ." She approached the short man, whose eyes widened as he took in her beauty. "Lead me to my chambers immediately."

"Of course, Great Lady." The man bowed and scrambled into the vestibule, Jazlyn behind him. A green-and-brown cloud that was Gozan materialized suddenly and drifted in her wake. Jazlyn would mend fully.

Qoatch gave the necessary orders to the rest of the contingent, then followed his Great Lady inside.

İΠΘLᴧH

Inolah was lying in bed, praying to the God, when a parade of servants entered her chambers. Two men carrying a tub, another three with buckets of steamy water, and two maids—one carrying a gown, the other a tray of jewels and Inolah's crown.

"What's this?" Inolah asked, sitting up.

"An emissary from Tenma has arrived," one of the maids said. "The emperor has asked that you bathe and dress. He'd like you to eat dinner with the emissary in the great hall."

An emissary? "Why has she come?"

"I know not, lady."

Always the servants were so polite. *"The emperor has asked . . . The emperor would like . . ."* Inolah knew better. Her husband had *demanded*. He had *ordered*. And he expected to be obeyed.

Perhaps if Inolah could befriend this Tennish woman, she and her children could ride with the emissary when she left. From one of the Tennish ports, Inolah might book passage on a ship to Armania and be home in a month. She could have her baby at home with her mother.

The prospect so thrilled her that she climbed from her bed and started to undress.

The dining hall was shaped like a quarter circle that reminded Inolah of the shells she had collected from Seacrest as a girl. The entrance came in on the

321

lowest level, in the center of the widest arc. Ten levels had been built along the arc, each a step higher than the last and growing narrower as they ascended. All were filled with tables. The top level belonged to the emperor and his heirs.

Nazer had not yet arrived, but Ulrik stood behind his chair, arguing with a Tennish priestess. Oh dear. Inolah needed to get the woman down a level before the emperor arrived. She hurried up the aisle and found that her son was applying himself to that very task.

"In Rurekau, women sit below the men, Priestess," Ulrik said firmly.

"I will *not* sit below men," the priestess replied in accented Kinsman. She was a stunning woman who couldn't be much more than twenty years old. Dressed in a shimmering white gown embroidered with gemstones of every color, her red-tinted skin and gold-and-pearl diadem marked her a mantic priestess. Her eyes were large, her lips full, and they showed immense displeasure.

"I have told you, lady, there is no seat for you here," Ulrik said. "Must I call the guards to remove you?"

"You dare threaten me?" the priestess said. "If this were Tenma, I'd make you a eunuch."

Ulrik smirked. "My talents would be wasted as a eunuch, Great Lady."

The priestess's nostrils flared. "Impudent, hairless child!"

"*Ulrik*," Inolah said, before the woman could cast a spell to destroy her son where he stood. She would berate him later for his terrible manners.

Ulrik flushed when he saw Inolah. "Mother! Good. Deal with this woman." He took his seat, dismissing them both.

Inolah smiled wide. "I am Empress Inolah. You are the emissary from Tenma?"

The woman looked her over, eyes narrowing at Inolah's pregnant belly. "Priestess Jazlyn, the Sixth Great Lady," she said.

"I would be honored, Priestess, if you would dine at my table. Only the emperor's table sits above mine. Surely that is understandable?" She motioned to the second-highest level. It was twice as long as the emperor's and, along with Inolah and her daughter, sat the emperor's harem and his illegitimate daughters. It also sat above the rest of the hall.

Priestess Jazlyn studied the room. "This is acceptable." She stepped down to Inolah's platform.

Good. Inolah walked to her seat in the center and offered the priestess Vallah's chair, wondering again where Nazer had sent their little girl. A beautiful man came to stand behind the priestess. He was tall and muscular with silky brown skin, thick black brows, and a flat nose. His hair was cropped short, as was the case with all men in the mother realms, and he had a Tennish slav tattoo around his neck.

"Have you a request of my eunuch, Empress Inolah?" the priestess asked.

A eunuch? Inolah nearly gasped to see his slit earlobes. What a shame. "No. Um, what brings you to us, Great Lady?" she asked.

"I demand restitution on the issue of human trade. Rurekans have been buying women and girls from Tenma, some even kidnapped from our schools. The sale of females is forbidden in our realm. These crimes also violate the Ten Year Truce."

Nazer and his wretched noblemen were obsessed with Tennish mantics. Now they were stealing little girls? "I am grieved to hear this, Priestess. I hope my husband will help."

"I am no longer certain he intends to speak with me. I was forced to use magic just to enter the castle."

Inolah would have liked to have seen that. The conch sounded, and everyone stood. Everyone but Priestess Jazlyn, which earned her a dirty glare from several of Nazer's concubines.

Nazer swaggered up the steps in the center aisle, stopping when a new serving woman caught his eye. Inolah averted her gaze while he whispered in the woman's ear but kept her head pointed in his direction so he couldn't claim she had publicly disrespected him.

The moment he fell into his chair at the high table, Inolah sat and attempted to make small talk with the emissary. "How was your journey, Priestess? Was the weather fine?"

"Do not feel obligated to entertain me, Empress. I have come for one reason. I was told the emperor would address me at dinner. When will this happen?"

"I know not," Inolah said. "He has never conducted business during meals before."

"I see." Priestess Jazlyn stood, muttering something foreign under her breath. A spell.

Inolah steeled herself, praying that the woman's rage would spare Ulrik.

The priestess spoke, and her voice magnified as if there were a thousand of her, all speaking at once. "Emperor Nazer of Rurekau, my people are eager to raise the sword against yours for the abduction of our women and girls. I journeyed here in hopes of finding a peaceful solution. Will you hear my petition, or do you prefer war?"

The room felt quiet. Inolah had never before heard anyone speak so boldly to the emperor, let alone in public.

"Empress," Nazer said, without looking Inolah's way, "you will control your guest."

Inolah gritted her teeth. Typical that he would blame her. She bowed her head in submission and reached for the priestess's hand, took hold, and squeezed. "Have mercy, Priestess," she whispered. "I'll do what I can to help your cause, but I beg you not to speak publicly again to the emperor."

Priestess Jazlyn's large eyes met Inolah's with frightening intensity. "What is that man's hold on you?"

"Our children. He keeps the boys from me and traded my girl in marriage, at only six years old."

A grunt. "You care for your offspring?"

"They are everything to me."

The priestess took a deep breath and sat, studying Inolah's pregnant belly. "In Tenma we do not raise children in family units."

Inolah knew all about Tennish culture. "Birthing and rearing my children has been the best experience of my life." The mere words brought tears and made her voice crack.

"What is so fulfilling about pain?"

"Many of the most rewarding life experiences cause some pain," Inolah said.

Priestess Jazlyn hummed her understanding. "I find that true of taking evenroot. How can you help me?"

"I can find out who is selling the girls once they enter Rurekau. You could send an assassin to end it."

"But if the problem comes from the throne?"

Inolah did not care. "Send your assassins to kill whom they must."

The priestess chuckled. "You claim familial love yet wish your husband dead. Empress Inolah, the assurance of your investigation is not enough to satisfy me or my queen. With the emperor's refusal to negotiate, the option to reconcile has passed. Tenma is ready to wage war."

Which was unsurprising. There was nothing for Inolah to do now but make sure that she and her boys were gone before the fighting began. "In that case, perhaps it is you who can help me. I and my children must leave Rurekau. Nazer keeps me confined to my chambers. This is the first time I have left in weeks."

The priestess raised one eyebrow. "I all but declare war on the emperor, and you want me to steal his wife and heirs too?"

"I have lived twenty years in Rurekau," Inolah said. "When I first saw how badly the women were treated, I tried to help. But these people do not want change. They are comfortable in their oppression. I must take my children away before their father ruins them or kills one in a fit of rage."

"How many of this brood do you claim?"

Inolah looked up to the high level. "Just those two boys sitting with the emperor. Prince Ulrik and Prince Ferro."

Fire kindled in the priestess's eyes. "That hairless puppy is your son?"

"I thought that clear. Did you not hear him address me as Mother?"

"In Tenma, all carriers are called Mother."

"Oh, well, Ulrik is my eldest and heir to the throne of Rurekau. Ferro is our second son."

The priestess laughed, delighted. "Once your husband falls, we will crush this realm easily."

Such words prickled Inolah. "Prince Ulrik might be young, lady, but he would not hand over the empire so easily." She lowered her voice. "Which doesn't matter if you will help us escape." Let these mad realms have their gender war.

"Prince Ulrik will not travel with me," the priestess said. "He cannot be trusted. You must choose whether you will remain here with that wolf pup or leave with me and your other son. I shall come to your chambers tonight when I leave to see what you have decided."

The priestess stood and walked to the end of the platform. Her handsome eunuch followed.

Inolah looked down at her plate of untouched food, eyes swimming with tears. Choose? How could a mother choose between her sons?

Hinck

Hinck was riding to Seacrest when Oli rode up beside him on his silver stallion.

"May I accompany you?" Oli asked.

"Of course, Your Grace."

Oli chuckled. "I broke your nose, Hinck. That earned you the right to call me Oli."

Hinck nodded, and they rode in silence for a long stretch.

"What's your ambition in life?" Oli asked.

Hinck had no idea how to answer such a question. "I'm not sure."

"That's fair," Oli said. "I'm not yet two and twenty and I'm still unsure myself."

"Don't you mean to be a general?" Everyone knew that.

"That's what my father, my mother, Janek, even the rosâr wish for me. So I suppose that will be my fate."

"What would you rather do, if you had your own way?" Hinck asked.

"A warden, perhaps. I don't like to see young people corrupted—to become slaves to one way of thinking. The young must be taught to think for themselves. To test everything. To seek the truth of life. They must gather information and weigh it carefully."

Hinck had never heard Oli say so much in one breath. "How does one become a slave to thought?"

"Take me, for example," Oli said. "I've always done what my father and Janek asked of me. I obey them. But if I do nothing but blindly obey my whole life, at what point do I become a man capable of making my own choices? Do you ever struggle with this?"

"Trevn orders me around to test my loyalty. He wants me to agree, but I am free to choose. I could leave his service anytime and—while he might be upset—he would still be my friend."

"Friend. See, that is key. I don't believe Janek has a real friend in the world besides his garden. We are his to command, to play with. If we die or become difficult, he will replace us. Sâr Trevn is different?"

Hinck thought about how Trevn had commanded him to infiltrate Janek's group. It wasn't the same, though. "He bosses me all the time, but he would never intentionally humiliate me."

Oli studied Hinck. "You truly wanted to befriend Janek?"

Not ever. "I simply wondered about him."

"He collects people," Oli said. "People he can use to his benefit."

"You are tired of being used?" Hinck asked.

"Indeed, but I am his. I cannot escape. You can. That is why I tried to scare you away. Janek ruins lives, Hinck. Take care."

"I will," Hinck said. "Thanks for the warning."

Oli nodded. "Race you!" He kicked his horse into a gallop and Hinck gave chase.

They arrived at Seacrest and left their horses with the stable boy. Inside the house Timmons greeted them.

"His Highness is still in bed this morning," he said. "You may wait in the garden."

"It's past the midday bells!" Oli said.

"His Highness was up very late," Timmons said.

"With who?" Oli asked.

"Forgive me, Your Grace, but I cannot recall all of their names."

"*Who*, Timmons?" Oli asked. "If you don't tell me, I'll go back and see for myself. Don't make me tell the sâr you let me in."

The onesent sighed. "Lady Eudora remained behind, Your Grace."

Hinck's arms pimpled.

"Gods!" Oli yelled. "Must he bed every woman in Armania?"

"Only the ones he wants, Your Grace," Timmons said.

"Well, I shall skip my visit with the sâr today," Oli said, clearly annoyed. "Are you leaving, Hinck, or staying?"

"Leaving," Hinck said, feeling sick. Eudora and Janek? Five Woes!

The pair returned to the stables and waited for the grooms to resaddle their horses.

"Sorry this happened," Oli said. "I know you admired her, but it's best you know she's a drick."

The word made Hinck's cheeks burn. "There have been others?"

"Loads. Sir Jayron, Marek Ortropp . . . half the King's Guard, I swear. She favors men in uniform. Especially older men."

Hinck shuddered. "Fonu?"

"Never Fonu, much to his indignation. She despises him." Oli chuckled and rubbed his face. "We are not a pious family, Hinck. Are you shocked?"

"No."

"You're a terrible liar. The devastation is plain on your face. Do not fret. We will find you a nice woman. Maybe from Sarikar."

"I don't want a nice woman." Hinck had only ever wanted Eudora.

"Be patient, then. Janek will be finished with her by the end of the week. And Eudora *hates* being cast off. She will be looking for someone to claim just so it appears that she was the one who moved on."

"You think I stand a chance?" The words sounded so pathetic, Hinck instantly wished them back.

"Sure—well . . ." Oli looked Hinck up and down, frowned. "You're a trifle thin. You might spend more time on the practice field. Eudora loves nothing more than a muscular arm to hang from. I'll instruct you in technique, if you'd like."

"Thank you," Hinck said. "I'd like that very much."

"I still think you should forget my wayward sister. You're too good for her. But if you do manage to catch her, know it won't last. No one holds Lady Eudora Agoros for long."

When Hinck returned to Castle Everton, he went directly to Queen Thallah's apartment and Trevn's bedchamber within. It was empty, so he had to wait until Queen Thallah went to dinner so he could sneak through her bedchamber to the secret room.

Cadoc met him at the inner door, sword bared. Once recognition in the dim light set in, the shield nodded and let Hinck enter. Trevn sat at the desk, writing with a quill pen. Above his head and down the walls hung lines with sheets of drying parchment. Trevn didn't look up, even when Hinck sat on the corner of the desk.

"I rode with Oli to Seacrest this morning," Hinck said. "Janek was still in bed. With Eudora."

Trevn's head jerked up and his eyes met Hinck's. "But she's his cousin."

"Since when does that matter?" Hinck said. "People marry their cousins all the time."

"It matters to me," Trevn mumbled.

"Well, I can rest in the knowledge that you, at least, won't chase after her," Hinck snapped.

Trevn frowned. "Why are you yelling?"

"Because, as always, Your Selfishness, you miss the point. The very man who placed this ridiculous task on my shoulders has taken Lady Eudora for himself. I'll be flogged on the pole."

Trevn set down his quill. "Did Oli and Janek fight?"

"No. Apparently Lady Eudora has no honor to protect. Apparently I'm more naïve than a newborn babe to have ever found her virtuous."

"I heard rumors about Eudora, but I never believe rumors."

"Believe them where she is concerned." Hinck took a moment to wallow in his pain. "In spite of this, Oli seems to think I can win her. He says Janek will cast her off by the end of the week."

"That sounds like Janek. So why the glum face?"

"Besides the fact that Oli also says his sister prefers muscled, uniformed, older men?"

Trevn snorted at that.

"I thought she was honorable, Trev. She was to me like the goddess Thalassa. But she is no different than a temple prostitute or a common street whore. At least they get paid. Eudora gives herself away for nothing."

"I'm sorry, Hinck, I truly am. Do you want to quit? You can if you must."

That comment made Hinck smile. Trevn was different from Janek. "No. You didn't send me there to make a bride of your cousin. I need to find out about the rune."

"Thank you, Hinck. Eudora could be the key to everything. In fact, I've been thinking that Lady Lebetta and Father Tomek's deaths might be related."

"What makes you say that?"

"Father Tomek was poisoned by magic. Drice don't kill intentionally. Someone must have ordered them. And since drice cannot be trained, magic is the logical explanation. I think there might be a sect of the Lahavôtesh here in Everton, and that Eudora and Lilou Caridod might be adherents."

Magic. Secret sects. This was the making of a great tale. "Trev, I am blundering here."

"You'll figure it out."

Hinck sighed. "Between Eudora and Janek, I'll be lucky to live long enough to complete your quest."

"You must, Hinck. You are the best chance we have at figuring out any of this."

İꟼOLAH

A noise outside in the hallway. The priestess must have arrived. Inolah grabbed a candlestick—in case she need to join in the fight to subdue the guards—and dropped the unlit taper on the floor. She slipped up beside the door, clutching the iron holder like a club.

But the door opened to nothing. No, wait. A guard, sliding forward on his back, feet first. Behind him a second guard floated through the doorway, his body folded in half.

"Who is there?" she asked.

"I am eager to leave this place." Priestess Jazlyn's voice.

Inolah could see nothing of the priestess or her men. Remarkable! "Praise Arman."

"This is not Arman's doing, but mine," the priestess said. "There is nothing my shadir cannot do. Your husband plots against me. I want to be gone before he tries anything. Have you made your choice?"

The only choice she could. Inolah crouched beside her bed and heaved her bundle over her shoulder. "I am coming with you."

"On one condition," the priestess said.

Inolah's heart dipped. "What do you want?"

"When I returned to my chambers after dinner, the emperor had taken my belongings. I require more evenroot if we are to make it to Tenma."

"I cannot say where he would have stored your things," Inolah said. "But there is an evenroot mill in the Open Quarter. Perhaps you could find some there?"

"I hope you are right," the priestess said. "If I lose the aid of my shadir, we will not make it far. *Pasas.*"

The reality of the situation dampened Inolah's joy at the coming escape. They might not make it! She forced herself to think positively. "Can you make me vanish as well?"

But Inolah's body was already fading. *How strange.*

"Do you see this stone?" the priestess asked. A gray stone the size of a biscuit hung in the air, waving from side to side. "It is how you can find me."

"Yes," Inolah said. "But how will you see me?"

"It is my spell. I can see you all. Now, lead the way to your son, Empress Inolah. And go silently. We are invisible but can still be heard."

Inolah crept from her room and down the hallway. All was deserted until they climbed the stairs to the high level. Then she had to move carefully, slipping into the alcoves to avoid knocking into patrolling guards.

The night bells rang just as they reached Ulrik's new quarters. Two Igote were stationed outside. Inolah hoped the maid had been truthful when she said both boys were here. She motioned to the door, hoping the priestess could see. In seconds the Igote crumpled as invisible Protectors attacked.

"Wait," the priestess warned. "*Both* your sons are inside?"

"Please let Ulrik come, Priestess," Inolah said to the air, wishing she could plead directly into the woman's eyes. "He has made mistakes, but he is a much better man than his father."

Silence fell in the hallway.

"You deceived me," the priestess said.

"Not entirely," Inolah said. "The boys are together. We cannot reach one without the other knowing."

The stone hung in place. Inolah could imagine the priestess scowling as she weighed the situation.

"Fine," the priestess said. "Let us enter and see what Prince Ulrik will do."

Praise to the God. Inolah made the sign of The Hand.

The gold-leaf door opened and the stone entered. There was a small commotion as much of the group collided in the doorway, unable to see each other. Eventually they were all inside and someone closed the door.

Ferro was jumping on a canopied bed, oblivious that the door had opened. Ulrik, on the other hand, stood against the wall, sword in hand, staring warily around the room.

"You told your father not to underestimate me," the priestess said, making only herself visible. "In that you showed the first hint of wisdom."

Inolah's arms prickled. Something had happened that the priestess had neglected to share. Had Inolah put Ulrik in danger by bringing the mantic here?

Ulrik twitched and his gaze fixed on the priestess. "Priestess Jazlyn, good midnight. You look . . . tired."

Inolah walked around the bed to get a better view of Jazlyn. The woman's cheeks were pale, and heavy circles ringed her eyes. Her magic was waning. They needed to go. Now. "Ulrik," Inolah said, "we've come to help—"

The priestess lifted her hand and silenced Inolah's voice.

"Mother?" Brow furrowed, Ulrik's gaze darted around the room.

Inolah touched her throat and yelled for Ulrik, but no sound came forth.

"What have you done with my mother?" Ulrik asked.

"What does your father want from me?" the priestess countered.

Ulrik shook his head. "I cannot say."

"*Hey*," Ferro's small voice said. "Father said no women in here." He jumped to the floor and ran toward Ulrik. Jazlyn moved to intersect, but before she could reach Ferro, Ulrik tucked the boy behind his back. Good.

"Priestess Jazlyn is a powerful mantic, Ferro," Ulrik said, "so we must be careful to show her our respect."

He was catching on. Appealing to the priestess's pride might induce mercy. Inolah moved to stand near her sons. She did not touch them, however, did not want to frighten them.

"Can you make me fly?" Ferro asked the priestess.

"Certainly." Her voice was sweet, but Inolah knew better. The woman wanted Ulrik to answer her question and would not rest until she succeeded.

Priestess Jazlyn lifted one hand above her head. "*Ra'am*."

Ferro shot into the air, whooping and giggling. Inolah cried out silently, reached for him, and missed. Ulrik caught hold of his foot, but Ferro's small boot slipped off in his hand. Ferro continued to rise until he lay against the ceiling.

Ferro laughed and flapped his arms. "Look, Rik! I'm a bird!"

Ulrik moved beneath his brother, looking up. "Please don't hurt him."

"Tell me," the priestess said, "and I won't."

"Father has been learning magic," Ulrik said. "He hopes to trick you into teaching him."

That fool! How could Nazer meddle with black spirits?

"His shadir swears to be stronger than any other," Ulrik added.

"They all claim that," the priestess said.

"This one hates women," Ulrik said. "Father calls it Dendarholn."

Priestess Jazlyn's eyes narrowed. "Dendron?"

"The god?" Ulrik asked. "Surely not."

Inolah had the same thought. If Nazer could petition the god of nature, he would need no instructor.

"If Dendron is here, my shadir would sense him," the priestess said. She waved her hand, and Ferro floated down into Ulrik's arms. Another wave, the word "*pasas*," and both boys vanished.

"Thank the God." Inolah's voice had returned. "You witch!" she yelled. "How dare you silence me?"

"It was necessary to discover the emperor's intentions," the priestess said.

"Mother?" Ferro cried out. "I can't see you. I can't see my feet! Rik, are you—"

When he didn't finish, Inolah called out. "Ferro? Where are—" Her voice muted again.

"I have silenced you all!" Tension rang heavy in Priestess Jazlyn's voice, more like pain than frustration. "Empress, lead on. The rest of you, follow the stone. We must hurry."

Inolah pushed aside her own impatience and led everyone down a back stairwell into the bowels of the castle. From there they went to the laundry room and out a chamber off the back end to a hidden door that led to a tunnel. This they traveled for quite some time before exiting through an abandoned tailor's shop in the middle of the city.

Moonlight covered everything in a bluish glow. They passed through a labyrinth of stinking, muddy alleyways and out onto a wide street. There Inolah stopped, trying to discern which way to the evenroot mill. She tapped her throat, wishing to speak, and fixed her eyes on the floating stone.

"Why have . . . you stopped?" the priestess asked, speaking slowly. "Answer."

"We have left the Imperial Quarter," Inolah said. "Where are your Protectors?"

"Camped in the . . ." The priestess panted. "In the Open Quart—No!" She faded into view, pale, like a ghost.

"What is happening?" Ulrik asked. His voice came from behind Inolah.

"She is fading," Qoatch said. "She must purge, but she sent her shadir to watch the emperor."

"It's too late, anyway," Ulrik said. "If she hadn't silenced me, I could have warned you."

"What . . . you mean?" the priestess rasped.

"My father's shadir will know we have escaped," Ulrik said. "And even if he doesn't, the guard changes at a quarter past night bells, which rang just before you arrived in my chambers. They will have found the guards you attacked and—"

"Enough!" the priestess hissed. "Gozan is here. What have you learned?" The priestess and her eunuch were focused in the same place, but whatever they saw was invisible to Inolah. "Empress!" Jazlyn yelled suddenly. "To the Open Quarter. Hurry!"

Inolah became visible then, only partly. They all did. Like specters on the Night of Ships. She took three steps toward the Open Quarter, but her son's voice stopped her.

"The first thing my father will have done is close the city gates," Ulrik said. "We are trapped. We should return before he . . ." Ulrik coughed. "Wha . . . ? Stop thaaa . . ." He trailed off in a wheezing breath.

Priestess Jazlyn had raised her hand toward Ulrik. "What are you doing?" Inolah asked. "Don't hurt my son!"

Ulrik fell to his knees in the mud, clutching his throat. Inolah ran to him, knelt in the mud beside him. Ulrik's face darkened a shade.

"Stop it!" Inolah wailed.

Ferro ran to Ulrik, grabbed his arm. "What's wrong, Rik?"

Metal clanked. Dozens of footsteps squished over the muddy ground. Igote guards flooded the street, some on foot, some on horseback. In the middle of the back row, Nazer sat his war-horse.

"One would think that when trying to escape, silence would be key," the emperor said.

Holy God, have mercy! Save us from our enemy, my husband.

Everyone who had once been unseen was now fully visible. The priestess looked to be using all her efforts to punish Ulrik.

"Let us go or . . . I will kill . . . your heir," Jazlyn warned, a trembling hand still raised against Ulrik.

The emperor shrugged. "I can make more sons. This one betrayed me."

"No!" Inolah lunged at the priestess, grappled for her hand. When she failed to catch it, she gave up and punched her.

Priestess Jazlyn flew back a full two paces and landed on the muddy ground. Qoatch knelt beside her. Inolah rushed to Ulrik, who was gasping. She helped him stand.

Fighting broke out behind them. Nazer's Igote attacked Priestess Jazlyn's

Protectors, who were hopelessly outnumbered. Five to one, the Igote cut them down, all but the eunuch and Jazlyn, who seemed too ill to perform any magic.

"Arrest the Tennish witch!" Nazer said.

The guards advanced. Qoatch stood between his Great Lady and two dozen Igote. He kicked the nearest guard in the chin and, as the man stumbled back, drew the sword from the Igote's scabbard. He spun to face a second guard, slicing the sword across the man's neck and partially severing his head. He faced the third and fourth with ease. As he fought, his sand-cat pelt slid from his torso and into the mud. He had killed eight guards when the emperor called out.

"Stop!"

The fighting ceased. Qoatch backed up, bestride over the legs of his priestess, who lay on her back, muttering at the dark sky. The eunuch lifted the bloodied sword to the emperor. "Get back," he said, his voice a low growl.

Inolah stared at Qoatch. My, but he was a glorious warrior.

The emperor applauded. "How long might you last in one of my arenas, I wonder? Look around you, slav. You could kill more of my men, but in the end you would die, and I would take your priestess. Wouldn't you rather live and continue to serve her?"

On the ground, Jazlyn shifted, whispered, "Stand down, Qoatch."

The eunuch dropped the sword. The guards quickly bound his hands and feet and tossed him into the back of a wagon.

"Bind them all," the emperor yelled.

Priestess Jazlyn was trussed and thrown in beside her eunuch. Inolah and Ulrik were also bound and loaded into the wagon. They huddled together.

Qoatch squirmed until he was beside the priestess. "Great Lady," he whispered to her, "you must purge."

Her eyes moved as if they were the only part of her that could. She looked ghastly, on the cusp of death.

The guards lifted Ferro up onto Nazer's lap. His massive war-horse tossed its head as Nazer steered him to the wagon.

"You will learn what it means to betray me," he told Inolah.

"Mamma!" Ferro reached for her.

"I made the boys come," Inolah said. "It was all my fault."

"I am not a fool!" the emperor screamed. "You will remain in the dungeon until you give birth. Then you will die. And after I publicly disinherit my ungrateful son, I will execute him as well."

"No!" Inolah screamed.

"Ferro shall replace him. You are young enough to forget your mother, Ferro, aren't you?"

Ferro continued to reach for her. "I want Mamma."

Nazer chuckled. "You won't for long, boy." He steered his war-horse away.

The wagon tugged forward in a jerky fashion, squishing over the muddy ground. Inolah leaned against Ulrik and wept. How could everything have gone so very wrong?

"Can you purge without your altar mat, Great Lady?" Qoatch asked the priestess. "I fear the poison is taking you from me."

Her face was chalky gray and had started to wrinkle. "I cannot . . . sit up."

The guards had bound Qoatch's hands in front, which enabled him to help the priestess to her knees.

"What are you doing?" Ulrik asked.

"She must pray," Qoatch said.

The priestess slouched sideways, completely limp. Qoatch settled beside, propping her up with his own body.

"Purge now, Great Lady, please."

Priestess Jazlyn wheezed in two shallow breaths and tried to speak, but all that came out was a raspy bray. Purging the poison to a shadir was the only way to heal when one had taken too much evenroot. Wait too long, and death would come. The eunuch stayed close and began to pray for her.

Inolah had never seen a more devoted servant. Sadly, it did not look as if Priestess Jazlyn would survive the night.

TREVN

Trevn clutched the dry pages of the Book of Rôb to his chest as he ran through the halls of Castle Everton, head pounding with each jolt. He had worked until his hand cramped, managing to transcribe all of chapter five. Those pages he had hung to dry in the secret room. Chapters one through four he carried with him.

He ran all the way to Hinck's chambers, where he found his friend still in bed. He set the pages on the side table and pulled the covers off. "Hinck, wake up." He shook his shoulder, then pinched his nose. "Hinck."

"Get off!" Hinck slapped Trevn's hand away.

The volume of Hinck's voice rattled Trevn's headache. "I completed four chapters of the book. You must take them to Rogedoth."

"What time is it?"

"Morning. I've been up since dawn." Trevn sat on the edge of the bed and sighed heavily, hoping to guilt Hinck into action. "If they kill me, it will be your fault."

Hinck's eyes squinted open. "Why can't Beal deliver your precious papers?"

"Because Beal is already delivering a message."

"To Miss Mielle, I suppose?"

"See how clever you are?" Trevn walked to the door. "I must return to my work. You will take the chapters to Rogedoth?"

"Yes, yes."

"Remember, you misunderstood that he wanted everything and figured four chapters would be enough. Come to Mother's apartment and tell me what he says."

"Yes, yes, yes!"

"You are terribly grumpy in the mornings, Hinck, you know that?"

Before Hinck could throw something, Trevn departed and returned to his mother's apartment. There he found that Beal had returned with company. His mother sat in the front room with Lady Zeroah and Miss Mielle.

Trevn paused on the threshold, both thrilled and terrified by the scene. Mother and Mielle in the same room? Dangerous, indeed. Though perhaps Lady Zeroah's presence would diffuse the situation somewhat.

"Trevn, my son!" Mother cried, rising. She curtsied deeper than she had in ages—survived it—and waved for him to sit. "I hoped you had not gone far."

Lady Zeroah and Miss Mielle stood and curtsied as well.

The furniture was arranged in a rectangle. Two long couches faced each other with a chair on each end. Mother sat alone on one of the couches; Miss Mielle and Lady Zeroah occupied the other. Trevn glanced at Beal, hoping for a hint as to the current mood, but his ashen-faced onesent gave nothing away.

"Lady Zeroah, Miss Mielle, good morning." Trevn bowed his head politely and sat on one of the chairs.

"We felt it best to bring our reply in person," Mielle said.

Mother scowled at Mielle. "They will not say what you wrote to them."

"There was no secret in my message, Mother," Trevn said. "I simply expressed my condolences to Princess Nabelle after the loss of Father Tomek."

"Oh," Mother said. "I had forgotten Father Tomek was related to your father, Lady Zeroah. My deepest sympathy to you and your mother."

"Thank you, Rosârah Thallah. You are most kind." Lady Zeroah smiled wanly and turned back to Trevn. "His Grace, the Duke of Odarka, is still coming to terms with the loss of his father. He asked me to convey that you are welcome to visit him anytime. In fact, he said he was eager to speak with you about your future."

"Future?" Mother turned her scowl on Trevn. "Have you reconsidered marriage to Lady Brisa?"

"No, Mother. I simply wanted to pay my respects after the death of the duke's father."

Mother humphed, clearly annoyed by something. Everything, likely.

"Your Highness," Lady Zeroah addressed Trevn, "has there been word from Sâr Wilek or his abductors?"

"I'm afraid not, lady," Trevn said. "But do not lose hope. I know of no man more persistent than my brother Wilek. He has taught me much."

Mother sniffed. "And I suppose I taught you nothing."

"On the contrary, Mother. You taught me how to dress for a ball. I daresay that is a skill I will need throughout my life."

Mother narrowed her eyes as if she knew Trevn had somehow insulted her but could find no criticism with his comment.

"I have always been impressed by Sâr Trevn's courtly manners," Lady Zeroah said. "He is a very good dancer too. Do you agree, Miss Mielle?"

"I've never danced with his equal," Mielle said.

"Nor will you," Mother snapped. "An honor maiden is fortunate to have ever danced with a sâr."

For sand's sake, Mother!

Mielle smiled warmly. "Then I am fortunate, indeed, Your Majesty. Rosârah Brelenah has declared us her favorite pair and insists we dance exclusively in her presence, hasn't she, Trevn?"

"You will address the sâr by his proper title!" Mother yelled, stomping one foot.

The room fell silent. Mother glared as if hoping the anger might shoot from her eyes and burn Mielle to ashes.

Mielle frowned apologetically. "Forgive me, Your Majesty. I misspoke. It is only in private that your son asked me to call him by his given name."

Trevn closed his eyes.

A knock on the door kept Mother from exploding. Hinck entered, wide-eyed, as the scene presented itself. He looked from lady to lady until his gaze fell on Trevn. He tipped his head slightly. When Trevn didn't move or speak, he jerked his head to the side.

"Uh . . ." Trevn stood. "Excuse me, I . . . must speak with my backman."

"We should go as well," Lady Zeroah said, standing. "Rosârah Thallah, thank you for your gracious company." She curtsied to Mother. Mielle mirrored her movements. They again thanked Trevn and bid him contact them should he hear anything about Wilek, then swept from the room.

The moment the door shut, Mother started railing. "Of all the rude, obnoxious . . . That chit is forbidden from entering my apartment again, you hear? And what is this talk of dancing for Rosârah Brelenah?"

"Excuse me, Mother," Trevn said. "It seems Hinck has urgent news."

"If Hinckdan barges into my private apartment bearing urgent news, he can speak it in front of me."

"In that case, Mother, I too shall go." Trevn left. Cadoc and Hinck followed him out the door.

"Impertinence!" she yelled. "That honor maiden has corrupted you! I will not—"

Blessedly, the door fell closed. The threesome headed toward Trevn's chambers.

"Well . . . what news, Hinck?"

"Rogedoth wants all your pages. I told him I misunderstood and would ask you about it. Once you came back from your outing with Miss Mielle, of course."

"Good man."

But when they entered Trevn's chambers, the tumbled mess made it clear someone did not want to wait. Tapestries had been ripped from the walls. The mattress hung off his bed, a gutted mass of feathers and straw. His pile of maps, which he had left in a tidy stack on his table, lay in a crushed heap on the floor, trampled and sullied by dirty bootprints. Everything in his wardrobe had been pulled from its shelf, carpeting the floor in tangled clothing.

"What in sand's sake happened?" Hinck said. "I just left Rogedoth."

Trevn picked up a map that displayed a smudge of a bootprint with the even-spaced holes of hobnails. "These were soldiers, not priests." He handed the map to Cadoc. "Hobnails in the print."

"Someone besides Rogedoth is looking for the book," Cadoc said.

"But who would send soldiers?" Trevn asked.

"King Jorger is visiting," Cadoc said. "The Book of Arman might be important to him."

No . . . "If King Jorger wanted something, he would simply demand it," Trevn said. "But I like your thinking, Cadoc. We need to cast a broader net of suspicion. Hinck, have my things moved to Mother's apartment. As much as I hate spending time with her, I am safer in her company. I must return to work." He had half a manuscript to finish. And now, another mystery to solve.

CHARLO⊙N

C ome." Mreegan waved Charlon closer.

Charlon could not. She remained on her knees. Looking up. Up at the throne. "You'll find no child in me," she whispered. "I've not tempted the prince a second time." *Or a first.*

Mreegan's brows sank. She was angry. Disappointed. "Explain."

Searching for courage, Charlon reached across the distance. Found the prince. Pulled from his strength. "The bond," she said. "His emotions weigh heavily. I cannot—"

"You've been given a great honor," Mreegan said, stroking her newt, which sat on her knee. "Do you think my other maidens would fail me?"

"No, Chieftess." She knew they would not. Already a child would be growing.

"Perhaps you're not Mother after all."

"I am!" Charlon pleaded. "I want to be." Had to be.

"You have until the next full moon. If you're not with child by then, I'll choose another. Now go. Do not fail me."

Charlon lowered her gaze. Left the tent into the darkness of the night. Needed to run. Run far away.

Farther from the red tent, the fear faded. Each step lighter.

Betrayal, her heart said. And her mind understood.

The Chieftess had used magic. To inspire fear, contrition, obedience. Charlon bit back anger. Fool woman had no idea. Magon supported Charlon now. Yet if Charlon failed, Magon might leave. She must not fail. Must not!

342

She ran back to her tent. Stepped inside.

She felt the prince. Determination. Scheming. Her eyes adjusted to the low light from the smoldering fire. Saw him in his corner. Hating her. She lurched, his rejection too much to bear. *Hide*, her heart said.

No! She could not hide. She must conquer him. But how? How could she? Too heavy, the burden. Too great for Charlon to master.

She threw herself on her bed of furs. Sobbing. Again a broken child. So unfair. If only she were stronger. Could use magic to manipulate. The way Mreegan did. But she was too weak. Too small. Too broken. She would never be Mother. Never be Chieftess.

A hand touched her shoulder.

"Don't!" She rolled over. Pulled the knife from her leg sheaf. Held it up in the darkness.

The prince drew back, eyes wide. "Sorry," he said. "I thought you were hurt."

"Why do you care?"

He shook his head, and his bewilderment pulsed through her. He didn't care. Didn't *want* to care. "I only wondered." He started back to his corner.

"Wait. Come here."

Compelled, he strode toward her, frowning. Hated being forced. Hated her.

"Take my hand." She thrust hers toward him, hoping action would inspire confidence.

His revulsion choked her. But he crouched. Reached out. Grabbed hold. His skin was icy. Distracted her from the terror. She was touching a man! *Stop!* her heart said. *Get away!*

She wouldn't. She would stay. She must. "You are cold."

He shrugged. "The one nice thing about your magic. Makes the summer heat almost pleasant."

Kind words. Friendly. Yet fear kept her tense. She stared at their hands. Touching hands. So strange. "Kiss me."

The order brought disgust. Anger. In the Veil, the slights pushed him forward, crowing as they did. He fought them. Teeth gritted. "No." He groaned. Agony sliced. Stabbed within. Through their bond.

Charlon screamed. Released the order but held tight. "Kiss my hand!" she yelled. But that also brought rebellion. Released the order again and asked, "Will you kiss my hand?"

The pain fled. Confusion pressed down. His dark eyes met hers. "What?"

"Men kiss the hands of maidens," Charlon said. "It means nothing."

His familiar loathing returned. "Kissing a woman's hand is a sign of respect and honor."

"You don't respect me."

"Right you are, witch. Why don't you just force me? Why did you stop forcing me?"

Shook her head. Silence. Her hand in his. Flesh against flesh. *No*, her heart said. *Flee!*

She tugged her hand back. It slipped a little. But he squeezed tighter, brow knitted in thought. He leaned down slowly, watching her. She flinched. He pressed his lips against the back of her hand.

A ragged scream from within. Charlon yanked free. Scrambled across the bed. Tears blurred him from sight and helped her hide. It was the eyes. Eyes that changed everything. Eyes that saw within. "Don't look at me!"

His gaze instantly lowered. "You're afraid of me?"

She wiped away tears. Felt his curious thoughts. He crawled toward her. She yelped, flipped to her feet. Backed toward the tent wall. "Stay!"

He froze on his knees. "I don't understand."

Hands trembling. Too much too fast. No more tonight. "Back to your corner!"

The prince moved to obey, but the slights in the Veil massed around him. Still on his knees, they pushed him off the bed of furs and across the dirt floor, mats bunching behind him. He glided toward the fire. Caught hold of the center tent pole. Held on. His legs stretched out behind him. He fell to his stomach. The slights continued to pull him, cackling.

"Stop!" he yelled. "I'll go!"

Charlon released her order. The shadir dropped his body.

Thankful. Glad it was over. He pushed to his feet. Hurried to his bed. But as he lay still, his mind spun. Puzzled. "You won't force me," he said from his corner. "Someone hurt you. But if you're so afraid, then how did you manage to . . . ?"

Comprehension dawned. He knew.

"We never . . ." he said. "You lied." First joy, then overwhelming relief. "I remember now. You had me convinced you were Lebetta. Then you got scared and put a spell on me."

"Silence!"

But it was too late. His heart soared. Triumphant. He knew she could not. Not do what the Chieftess wanted.

"Please don't tell." Her voice, soft and pathetic. She hated her weakness. Her fear. "Mreegan will kill me. Will choose someone else. Someone stronger. Kateen . . . Roya. They will not fail."

The prince shuddered. Understood perfectly. Those maidens would enjoy being Mother. They would hurt him. And because of the soul-binding, hurt her in the process.

The prince turned on his side. Facing away. His back a wall between them. The sight brought more tears. How she wanted to be near him. To make peace.

Foolish! Men could not be trusted. These feelings were a lie from the binding. She must control them.

Control.

That was the answer. Magic could force Charlon to do what she could not by herself.

She got up. Fetched her altar mat and a bottle of ahvenrood juice. The goddess would help. Help defeat this man. Defeat fear. Help her become Mother. Become Chieftess.

She only need ask.

KALENEK

The first week passed quickly, but once they met the endless ripples of the Painted Dune Sea, the days crawled. This, surrounded by dust with no break in the horizon, was how it would be for the next few weeks. Sand in Kal's boots and beard and nose. He did not welcome it.

Now that they were far enough from the red lakes, Kal went back to traveling at the coolest times of day: in the early mornings and from late afternoon until dark. They stopped during the day when they found sand dunes that offered the least bit of shade. At night they slept out under a shelter of stars. The second week passed slowly.

"A shame that Novan is not here to describe the sky," Onika said one night as they sat around the campfire.

Kal, who sat beside her, smarted, knowing that the prophetess had been growing friendly with Novan before Kal had sent him away. He wanted to ask her if Novan was alive but held his tongue.

"The sky is black as tar and sprinkled with diamonds," Grayson said.

"Ever held a diamond?" Burk asked. "I have. Don't look like nothing but a shard of glass."

"How about you, Sir Kalenek?" Onika said. "How would you describe the sky this night?"

Kal glanced at the vastness overhead, and his heart pinched to think of Livy, looking down. "I see a million tears. The gods weep for mankind, weary of watching their creation destroy itself. We hate each other to the point of hopelessness."

"Is he always so joyful?" Burk whispered to Grayson.

"Not tears, Sir Kalenek," Onika said, "but glimpses of hope. Hope is seeing light in the darkness. No matter how dark life seems, hope is never far away." Her words sobered Kal, and he looked again to the night sky.

"May I feel your face, Sir Kalenek?" Onika asked.

So strange was her request, Kal turned toward her, intending to ask her to repeat herself, but her hand was already reaching out. It slid over his bearded cheek, making him jump.

"I don't mean to frighten you," she said.

Not frightened. Stunned.

She palmed his cheek, pulled her hand forward, fingertips trailing through his beard, up over his lips and nose, between his eyes and along one eyebrow. He should stop her. Her blindness had kept his scars hidden from her all this time, but now she would see everything. She would know. Yet no one had touched him so tenderly in so long that he couldn't move. Her fingers found the scar on his forehead and traced the line down over his other eye and across his cheek.

"There are two types of pain, Sir Kalenek," Onika said, fingers lingering on the pinched scar just above the line of his beard, "that of lifeless existence and that of growth. Let go of the pain, embrace growth, and only beauty will remain."

Her words destroyed the thrill of her touch. Kal grabbed her wrist and pushed her hand away. "Nothing beautiful about me, Miss Onika. If you'll excuse me." He pushed to his feet and left the campfire, desperately needing time alone.

As Kal walked into the darkness, he heard Burk ask, "Will you feel my face, Miss Onika?"

"Not tonight," she said, "but perhaps in another time and place."

"How long should we wait for you?" Jhorn asked.

They had finally reached the outskirts of Lâhaten. Jhorn was given coin to purchase supplies while Kal attempted a meeting with Empress Inolah.

"If you don't hear from me before tomorrow at dawn, set off without me. Take the east road toward Jeruka." It was Kal's hope to send a messenger to escort Jhorn and the others to the palace, but Emperor Nazer had never been a sane man. Kal didn't dare put the group in danger by bringing them along until he was certain they would be safe.

"Arman will cover your path in blessings," Onika said.

Her warming words made Kal want to embrace her. Instead he said, "Thank you, Miss Onika," fixed her in his mind, and set off on foot toward the smoking mountain. The camel brayed as if to protest his leaving, but Kal didn't look back. Jhorn needed the animal more than he did.

By the time Kal reached the city gates, it was after morning prayers. The gates were open, and no one questioned him as he entered the city. The streets in the Open Quarter were filled with vendors setting up market stalls. A few urged him to come inspect their wares. He ignored them, though the Kinsman language they spoke gave him a measure of peace.

The mother realms were behind him now.

Unlike the filth of Hebron, the city of Lâhaten was pristine. Emperor Nazer and his fathers before him were obsessed with immortality and built cities to last, made of stone. The streets were hard-packed gravel. Both kept the city safe on those rare occasions when the mountain rained ash and fire. The houses were tapered, slightly smaller on the top than the bottom, which helped prevent collapse in earthquakes. The castle itself was built of stepped pyramids, four small around one so tall it tweaked Kal's neck to tilt and see the top.

He reached the gates to the Imperial Quarter and found them closed. "Good morning," he told the guard, whose head was shaved like all Imperial Guards of the Emperor.

The Igote stared at Kal's scars. "Five Woes! Who took a knife to you?"

Where Kal's scars were concerned, he preferred blunt rudeness to silent stares. "I am Sir Kalenek Veroth, High Shield to Sâr Wilek Hadar of Armania." Kal showed his shield ring. "I come on urgent business on behalf of House Hadar."

"The Imperial Quarter is closed by order of the emperor," the guard said. "No one enters."

A typical response. "I don't wish to bother the emperor. My message is for Empress Inolah, my sâr's sister."

The guard shook his head. "The empress is unwell. Emperor Nazer has ordered her seclusion."

Inolah sick? The news stunned Kal. "What are the symptoms?"

"What do you think I am? The emperor's favorite friend? How should I know?"

Kal had half a mind to slit this man's throat, but he reined his temper. "If I cannot see the empress, would you announce me to Prince Ulrik?"

"He's sick too," the guard said. "I'll send word to Emperor Nazer that you're here with a message for the empress. Can't do more than that. I have my orders."

Kal fumed inside but nodded. "Emperor Nazer should be proud to have such a man guarding his gates."

"I thank you, sir."

Thanks wouldn't help Kal speak with Inolah. He walked away, uncertain what to do.

A boy approached and offered to lead him to an inn. For a price, of course. Kal gave him a copper for directions to the city barracks.

It had been seven years since Kal last stepped foot in the Rurekan barracks. Then it had been on the Imperial Quarter's side. Guards had been able to pass into the IQ through an inner gate—one hidden from common folk. Before Kal could see whether that route still existed, he needed a uniform. Should he look for the laundry or take one off a guard?

The barracks were across from the guards' stables. Men came and went freely from the entrance in singles and pairs. Most headed deeper into the city; some walked into the market, some to the stables, and, every so often, one went up a platform and into a small shack. It wasn't until a man drove a mule and wagon—carrying a noxious load—from the back of the little building that Kal realized it was an outhouse.

Perfect. But the mere thought of killing a man made his arm tingle. Panic shot through him that he might again lose the use of it. He would kill no one, then. Simply detain a man and steal his clothes.

He entered the outhouse. Inside was a bench with four holes, two of them occupied. Kal sat between the two guards and waited. One finally got up and left. The moment the door shut, Kal attacked the other.

The guard attempted to fight back, but with trousers tangled around his ankles, he fared poorly. Two blows to the head knocked him senseless. Kal quickly stripped off his uniform. He tied the man's ankles with the tunic, his wrists with one leg of the woolen stockings. The other stocking leg he stretched and shoved in the man's mouth to gag him.

Kal pulled the uniform over his own clothes, noting the stripes on the sleeve. Some kind of officer. He tucked his thick warrior's locks up under the man's helmet and left.

On his way down the ramp he passed a guard coming up. The man saluted. Kal nodded and hurried into the barracks. It wouldn't be long until his victim was discovered. He followed a long hallway, walking past a dining hall, armory, laundry, bathhouse, then room after room filled with sets of stacked beds. He rather liked wearing a helmet. It was nice not to have everyone staring at his scars.

Up ahead, at the end of the hall, a door opened and an officer stepped out. "Ho, up! Squad! Every man in the palace! Some prisoners have gone missing. Step it up!"

Men poured from the bunks and ran toward the officer. Kal joined the rush.

"Who are we looking for?" someone asked.

"The empress and Prince Ulrik have escaped the dungeons. The emperor wants them found."

Kal stared dumbly at the officer as guards passed him by. "The royal family was in the dungeon?"

"None of that now," the officer said. "You just help find them before the emperor blames the guard for their escape."

"What of Prince Ferro and the princess?" Kal could never remember the girl's name.

"Prince Ferro is safe with the emperor. And everyone knows the princess was married off. Where have you been?" The guard shoved Kal through the door.

Kal stumbled along with the horde of guards. Married off at six years of age? Who was so desperate for a royal marriage to marry a child? No wonder Inolah had revolted.

Kal followed the guards through a tunnel that ran under the inner wall and into the barracks of the Imperial Quarter, then through to the inner bailey of Castle Lâhaten. The guards entered the palace through a side door, then down a stone spiral staircase until they reached the dungeons. They wove from one cell bank to the next, bumping into other guards doing the same. There was no organization here. And why would Inolah still be in the dungeon if she had escaped? She would be trying to leave the castle.

Except that Nazer had Ferro. Mothers always went after their children.

Kal pushed back through the men. Find the boy, and Inolah would not be far away.

QΘATCH

Qoatch shifted on the stone floor and shivered. The cell was terribly cold, and he had lost his pelt in the fight. For three days in this cell, he thought he might not have to worry about whether or not to complete his mission of killing Jazlyn. Her shadir had shown mercy in healing her, but her overuse of evenroot had left her in a haze. Just this morning she had finally begun to speak clearly, a sign that she would be herself again soon.

In the darkness of the cell, Qoatch's thoughts drifted to home. Had the Kushaw killed the other Great Ladies? It could be that Jazlyn was the last of her kind. He glanced at her and his heart seemed to swell into his throat. Fool! Why did he let her kindness to him count for so much? He should have told Duvlid about his affection. The Kushaw would have replaced him.

"Gozan tells me he released the empress from her cell," Jazlyn said.

Why didn't the creature release them as well? Where had he been?

"Someone comes," Jazlyn said. "Help me with this. Quickly!"

Uncertain what she wanted, Qoatch scrambled on hands and knees across the sticky floor to his lady's side. She was struggling with the coil of hair atop her head.

"What do you need, Great Lady?" he asked.

"There's a vial of evenroot inside the twist."

She hadn't fully healed from her last purge. It would be too much, especially if Dendron served the emperor as shadir. Qoatch pulled her hairpin and the coil of hair loosened. He unwound it. Something slid off the back of her head

351

and clattered to the floor. He felt for it, hands closed on the vial. "Great Lady, please. You must take care with . . ."

Footsteps clacked outside the cell door.

"Give it to me now!" she hissed.

Qoatch handed it over and stood to meet the visitor. A shadow blocked the crack of light under the door. A key scraped in the lock. The door opened.

Light spilled inside, illuminating a spider that scurried back into the dark shadows. A guard entered, squinted. His gaze found Qoatch.

"Get the woman up," he said. "His Eminence wants to see her."

Qoatch crouched beside Jazlyn. "Great Lady, you must wake. It's time to leave this place." He studied her face and hoped she hadn't taken any root.

Jazlyn extended her hand. "Help me stand."

Qoatch did as she bade. Once she was on her feet, she stepped up to the guard.

"Take us to the emperor," she said.

"Oh no," the guard said. "Just you. Your fighting man stays here where he'll cause no trouble."

"I think not." Jazlyn waved her hand at the guard and whispered, "*Nahshaw.*" She passed her left hand over Qoatch, said "*pasas,*" and his body vanished, invisible again.

Qoatch's heart sank. She had taken the root.

He stepped into the corridor and jumped, startled to see Gozan when the shadir had abandoned them for so many days. The shadir glowered at him, which made Qoatch look away.

"Well?" the priestess said to the guard.

"What was I about?" The guard frowned and scratched his head. "Oh, right." He bustled out of the cell. "Follow me."

Jazlyn did, and Qoatch stayed right beside her. Gozan followed behind. The guard had forgotten Qoatch ever existed. As they traveled out of the dungeons, they passed a cluster of Igote, standing outside a cell.

"No sign of forced entry," one guard told another. "Someone must have freed them."

"Impossible!" another guard said. "No one came in or went out."

Jazlyn smiled and glided past the puzzled Igote, her head held high. Behind Qoatch, Gozan chuckled.

Their guard led them up several flights of stairs and on such a twisting journey that Qoatch had no idea where they were. More of Gozan's flock had joined them along the way. The Veil was clouded with colors and eyes that only Qoatch and Jazlyn could see.

The guard finally led them through a set of gold-leaf doors and into a dining room. A long table, which Qoatch guessed could seat some thirty guests, was set for two. At the end of the room, floor-to-ceiling bay windows protruded in a half circle.

The emperor stood in the bay, his back to them, looking out on the view of the Upper Smoke Canyon, Dendron's Tail, and Mount Lâhat, which oozed charcoal smoke from its missing peak. Gozan and his flock floated farther into the room. The great shadir put himself between Jazlyn and the emperor. Qoatch stayed at his lady's side.

"I hope you have good reason for keeping me in your dungeons, Emperor Nazer," Jazlyn said. "I should think you would have been happy to see me leave."

"Not when you took my wife and sons with you."

"They wanted to go. They know the Tennish army will rake this city to dust."

The emperor smiled. "Still set on war, are you? Woman, you have no concept of who I am. I'll speak plainly so your feeble mind can comprehend. I am Emperor Nazer of Rurekau. There is none higher than me in all the realms. I have at my disposal the favor of the gods and shadir, which you yourself worship. They fall at my feet and tremble."

This made Gozan and his companions laugh.

"You dare rank yourself so high?" Jazlyn asked. "You are a greater fool than I imagined."

"You will help me," Nazer said, "or you will die."

"Oh? Why does one as great as you require assistance? Let alone help from someone as low and feeble as I?"

"I have secured the assistance of a powerful shadir but have not yet learned how to craft spells."

Gozan shook his head at Jazlyn. *His shadir is nothing.*

"Yes, I can smell the magic on you," Jazlyn said to Nazer. "But a measly persuasion spell will not subdue a Tennish priestess. Nor will it stop me from killing you. Do you have any idea how much power I wield?"

"Your words do not scare me, Priestess," Nazer said.

"They should." She glared at the emperor. Qoatch knew that look. She was trying to rein her temper. He almost wished she would strike this arrogant man in a way he would never forget. "Is this why you abduct our women?" she asked. "To learn magic?"

"Your mantics have proved too ignorant for the spells I wish to cast."

"What is it you want me to teach you?"

"First, put a spell on Ferro." He snapped his fingers and a guard entered, pulling the frightened boy by the arm. "Ferro will replace his traitorous brother as my Heir. But I need him to forget his mother. She is dead to us."

"She's not dead!" Ferro yelled.

"She will be," the emperor spat. "And once this *great* lady assists me, you will believe it."

The boy began to cry.

"You have abducted my people and insulted me in every way," Jazlyn said. "Why would I ever help you?"

"Because I have taken your evenroot supply. And if I send you back to the dungeon, your shadir will leave you in search of one who can feed it."

Humans are such fools, Gozan muttered.

Fools, fools! a slight sang.

"You may have seized my belongings," Jazlyn said, "but I had a vial hidden on my person. I have taken it."

The emperor's confidence wavered. "You bluff."

"Show me your shadir," she said.

"My shadir wishes to remain hidden."

"Mine does not," Jazlyn said. "*Herah aht etsemek, Gozan.*"

Gozan faded from the Veil and into the human realm. He appeared more vivid here: coal-black skin blacker, hair thicker, smell stronger, muscles bigger.

The emperor gaped. Ferro yelped.

"*Letpev avet!*" Jazlyn yelled.

Gozan lumbered toward the emperor, who took one step and froze at a command from Jazlyn. The creature picked up the emperor in his hairy fist.

The emperor screamed. "Don't eat me!"

"This is Gozan, Your Highness," Jazlyn said. "Call forth *your* shadir. Now!"

The emperor grunted and tried to pry open Gozan's hand. The shadir turned him upside down, and the emperor yelled, "Fine! *Herat at-tat, Dendar-holn.*"

With a tiny *pop*, a second shadir appeared between Jazlyn and where Gozan held the emperor. A slight! It stood no taller than Prince Ferro. It had yellowish-green skin and three bulging, toad-like eyes. A slender tongue darted in and out between fat lips as it glanced around the room. When it saw Gozan and the emperor, it squeaked and stumbled back into a dining chair.

"Your mantic has summoned you, slight," Jazlyn said. "It seems he requires your assistance."

The tiny shadir bowed before Gozan. "Has my wielder caused you trouble, mighty one?"

Jazlyn answered, "He told us your name was Dendarholn."

"What? That's incorrect. Fool wielder! Are you deaf?"

"What is your name?" Gozan asked, his voice a rumbling growl.

"Of little importance. We must learn why this human lied. I'm of a mind to part from him for such a blunder. I think I will. Emperor Nazer, I absolve our bond as of—"

"Not so fast," Jazlyn said. "I have declared war upon this emperor and therefore you."

The slight whimpered. "Great Lady, have mercy on a shadir of the lowest level."

He vanished. Ferro screamed. The slight had somehow crossed the room and grabbed the boy.

"*Lesherr avet!*" Jazlyn yelled.

Gozan's swarm of minions flew at Prince Ferro, snatched him from the slight's arms, and threw the boy toward Qoatch, who caught him, despite still being invisible.

Ferro screamed and kicked. "Put me down!"

"Take the boy to the empress," Jazlyn commanded Qoatch. "She will be worried for him."

This quieted the boy. A wave of Jazlyn's hand sent the swarm of shadir into the wall. The stone shattered, leaving a dusty doorway into the adjoining room.

"I will return for you, Great Lady," Qoatch said, ducking through the opening with the boy.

"Only when you have seen the empress and her family to safety," Jazlyn said. "This city will not see dawn. Make sure she understands that."

"Yes, Great Lady." Yet Qoatch lingered, watching his lady turn her attention back to the trembling slight.

With the thrust of her hand, the emperor's shadir shot out of the room like a pitched stone. He smashed through the wall of windows and soared higher and higher, arching toward the distant, smoking mountain.

"*Radaph!*" she yelled to Gozan's minions, who soared out the broken window in pursuit of the slight.

Jazlyn walked to the broken window. The wind snaked inside, blew her dress against her and her loose hair back. In the distance the shadir, now no bigger than a swarm of flies, sank into the smoking hole. The ground shook once—hard and violent—then Mount Lâhat exploded.

KALEИEK

Kal was halfway up the dungeon stairs when a rumble shook the walls. "Earthquake!" someone yelled.

Not again! Kal flowed with the crowd as they pushed up the spiral staircase as one. On the ground floor the guards scattered across the foyer. Kal headed up the grand staircase, trying to recall where the emperor's chambers were. On the second floor a large group of guards joined him, all talking at once about a witch and her magic.

"What's happening?" Kal asked.

A guard beside him answered. "The Tennish witch destroyed the emperor's dining room—blew out all the windows. She's got him trapped there."

"She shook the earth," said another.

"Called forth her shadir," said a third. "It took form."

Kal shivered. He hadn't seen a shadir take form since the war.

As they rounded the landing halfway between the second and third floors, a woman's scream snaked down to them.

Inolah. Kal spilled off the landing with the guards and ran toward a set of towering gold-leaf doors, one of which was open. The guards stood ten deep before the doors; there must have been five dozen, all looking in. Over the helmets and bald heads, Kal saw a massive dark shape pass by the doorway.

Not merely a shadir, but a great. Gods help them all.

"My child is in there! My Ferro!"

Kal's gaze found Inolah a good twenty paces down the hall. Two guards

357

were holding her arms. She fought to pull away, straining toward the dining room, her stomach great with child. Behind her, pressed against the wall, Kal recognized a much older Prince Ulrik, bald head covered in black henna tracings. A barrier of guards boxed them in.

A general approached the pack of guards, who all began talking at once. "Report!"

"A shadir has the emperor!"

"Prince Ferro floated away!"

"A witch is killing the emperor!"

"She set the mountain on fire!"

"The emperor is a mantic!"

"Silence!" the general yelled. "One at a time. Where is the emperor?"

"In the dining room. The shadir has him."

"Prince Ferro?"

"Floated away, General. Through a hole the witch blasted in the wall."

"Which wall?"

"The east wall, sir."

The general's scowl landed on Kal's stolen uniform. "Commander! Take ten men and find Prince Ferro. Captain!" He faced another guard. "Get those men back and open that second door."

Kal took the opportunity his uniform provided and walked toward what he thought must be the east hallway. If he could get Ferro, Inolah might leave with him. "Ho, up!" he yelled. "Who is with me?"

A gaggle of men surged around him.

"Too many!" he yelled. "Castle men, step forward!"

Nine men did so. "Good enough," Kal said. "I'm a city man. What's on the east side of the dining room?"

"The drawing room, which leads to the royal ballroom, then the guard's chamber," a guard said.

"Does each have its own entrance?"

"No, sir. The rooms open into one another."

"Lead the way," Kal said. "Hopefully we'll come upon the prince from the opposite end."

The man took off, Kal right behind. They passed through the Igote guard's chamber to the royal ballroom, and there they met Prince Ferro.

The boy was indeed floating. Not in a menacing way. His arms and legs were wrapped around . . . something, as if he was being carried by an invisible

358

man. A shadir, no doubt. Like his older brother, henna tracings covered Prince Ferro's shaved head. Rurekan royalty and their bizarre customs.

"Witchcraft!" a guard on Kal's right shouted.

The guard on Kal's left pulled his sword.

"Hold!" Kal raised his hands and took two steps forward. "Prince Ferro, I come on behalf of your mother."

The prince wriggled, his arms stretched toward Kal. "I want my mother."

"Stay with me," a voice whispered.

Kal went down on one knee, held out his arms. "I will take you to her."

The boy floated back a step. The carpet wrinkled on the floor beneath.

"Who holds you, boy?" Kal asked.

"Ko-ach. He's taking me to Mother."

"Qoatch is the witch's eunuch," a guard said.

Not a shadir, then. Good. "Leave the room, all of you!" Kal yelled, standing. "Wait for me outside the doors."

"But, sir—"

Kal waved them back. "Out! Now! Keep the doors shut so he can't escape. Open them only when I say."

The men scrambled out of the room. The door shut.

Kal turned back to Prince Ferro and spoke softly. "I speak to the man holding the prince. My name is Sir Kalenek Veroth. I am shield to Sâr Wilek Hadar of Armania, brother to the empress and this boy's uncle. When they refused to let me see the empress, I stole a guard's uniform." Kal pulled off his helmet to reveal his hair. "If escape is the empress's goal, I will assist her."

"There is little time," a man's voice said. "The mountain has ruptured. My Great Lady and her shadir will see that it destroys the city."

Such foreboding words sent a thrill of fear through Kal. A mantic conjuring spells of that scale would fall into a haze soon enough, but she could do immense damage before then, especially with no one to fight her. "Give the boy to me and return to your lady. I'll get the empress and her children to safety."

Silence stretched between them. Ferro wiggled in those invisible arms.

Distant breaking glass made Ferro float several steps back toward the drawing room.

"Your lady needs you," Kal said.

Ferro slowly sank to the ground until he was standing on his own feet. He ran into Kal's arms.

"Tell the empress to go quickly," the eunuch said. "We will follow, but do not wait for us."

Not a problem. "I'll tell her."

Footsteps scuffed the floor, fading. Kal reached out and felt the place where he thought the man had been standing. "I guess he's gone."

"He went back to the mantic witch," Ferro said. "She made me fly."

Kal shivered and replaced his helmet, tucking his hair out of sight. "Did she?"

"All the way to the ceiling. Are you really from Armania?"

Kal took hold of the boy's shoulders. "Listen to me, Prince Ferro. Your mother and brother are being held outside the emperor's dining room. What I said is true. I'm from Armania. I'm an old friend of your mother's, and I want to help. What is the quickest way out of the castle without being seen?"

"Through the wall tunnels. We can get to them from the library. It's not far from Father's dining room."

"Excellent, Your Highness," Kal said. "Say nothing of our plan. I will suggest the guards move you and your mother to the library to keep you safe from the mantic. Once we are there, I'll attack the guards. When we're fighting, you must lead everyone to the secret door. Can you do this?"

"Sure I can. I know just how to—"

"We must hurry, Your Highness. Shall I carry you or would you rather walk?"

"I can walk. I'm almost a man, so my father says."

"He is right to say so. You've been very brave."

Ferro beamed and tugged Kal by the hand toward the door. "I want to see my mother now."

"I live to serve." Kal approached the doors and banged with his fist. "It's the commander. Open up."

The doors opened to a wall of wide-eyed guards.

Kal shoved through, pulling Ferro along. "I'm taking the boy to his mother."

"But the emperor said—"

"The emperor would want him far from the mantic witch." Kal walked on. Bootsteps pattered after him. No one argued.

Back in the main hall the number of guards seemed to have doubled. Kal made it through half the men before anyone noticed who he was walking with.

"He's got Prince Ferro!" said one.

Surprisingly, no one tried to take the boy. The crowd parted, and he and Prince Ferro walked easily up to the guards surrounding Inolah and Ulrik.

"Ferro!" Inolah pushed through the guards and embraced her son.

Glad of the helmet, Kal hoped she would not recognize his voice when he said, "The emperor wants his family away from the mantic. We're to move them to the library, where they'll be safe until the witch is captured."

The guards seized Inolah, Ulrik, and Ferro by the arms and dragged them down the hallway and through another set of gold-leaf doors.

Kal passed into the library and raised his hands to stop any other Igote from entering. "The emperor said there were rebels in the castle who were trying to help the empress escape," he said. "They'll say anything to get into this room. Guard this door from the outside, and keep the rebels away at all costs."

"Yes, Commander," a guard said, and he pulled the doors shut.

Hopefully that would buy them some time. Kal examined the doors. No way to lock them. He would have to move quickly.

QOATCH

Qoatch ran back to the shattered stone wall and stepped into the dining room. Jazlyn stood beside Gozan, who still held the emperor in his fist. The other shadir were gone. The end of the dining room no longer had a roof. Guards stood clustered in the doorway, several dead bodies piled up before them. Out the window, smoke hung above the city like a thunderstorm. Jazlyn had been busy. Her face was gray and wrinkled, her hair white. She had little strength left.

The emperor was blathering, his face covered in tears and snot. "I'll take no more women from your realm. I'll give back those I've taken. I'll send men to you. You can—"

"It is too late for you, mighty emperor," she said. "Life is more blessing than you deserve."

"Don't kill me! My people will be lost without me. I am this city."

"Then you can join it." Priestess Jazlyn chanted a long string of mantic words. Gozan carried the emperor out to the shattered bay windows and set him down.

Hunched and trembling, the emperor asked, "What are you going to do?" But Jazlyn was still speaking her spell.

"What are you saying?" the emperor yelled.

Gozan thrust his hands at Nazer's feet. The balcony, which was made of stone, began to soften.

The emperor's feet sank slowly. He yelped, tried to lift one leg, then the other, failing both times.

The soft mixture grew over his feet, turning his ankles to gray stone that crept slowly up his legs and hardened at mid-thigh.

"No!" Nazer squatted, tried to scrape away the stone. "Stop this at once!"

"You claim to be part of this city," Jazlyn said. "I have made it so. Watch your city burn until you burn with it."

Emperor Nazer reached for her, cursing her name, but she stood just outside his grasp. She shouted spell after spell in the ancient language. Qoatch understood none of it. Out the broken bay windows he saw the other shadir had returned. At their touch, buildings fell and gardens withered. In the distance, a new smoke cloud shot from the mountain like steam from a kettle.

Qoatch came to stand on his lady's left, where he could see the ground below. People ran from the crumbling structures, screaming. One man staggered from the garden shed, covered in blood. A dog stood over a fallen child, barking, a shadir pulling on its ears. Out in the open spaces the people of Lâhaten stood staring in wonder at the smoking mountain.

Jazlyn's eyes were ringed with withered gray skin. Her cheeks were sallow. She was dying, and in her anger could not even feel it. "Great Lady," Qoatch said softly. "Take care of your strength. I fear the haze will take you."

"I have strength enough with Gozan beside me. Did you see how his swarm brought fire from the mountain? He is truly the most powerful shadir in all the Five Realms." She swiped her hand through the air, and the slights sent a group of servants flying into the stable wall. Another motion brought liquid fire up from the mouth of the mountain. It slid slowly, menacingly toward the city.

"The emperor has wronged you," Qoatch said, "but must his people die too?"

Jazlyn turned to him, eyes ablaze. A muttered "*Athah*" turned him visible. "Contradict me again and you will join them."

So Qoatch remained silent and watched his Great Lady and her shadir destroy Lâhaten.

KALENEK

Only three guards had remained inside the library. Kal would need help to defeat them. He glanced at Prince Ulrik, wondering if the young man could fight. He hated to put Inolah and her unborn child in the path of a sword, but the guards had been ordered not to harm the royal family. She should be safe.

"You men, check the windows," Kal said. "Make sure they're secured."

Two of the guards crossed the room. Kal approached the third, knowing he might have to kill this time. The thought made his fingers tingle.

Voices rose outside the door.

"Let me into the library at once," a man said.

"No one enters," said another. "My orders are from the emperor."

"There is an impostor in there!"

Kal needed to hurry. When the two guards reached the windows, Kal asked the third, "Is there any other way out of this room?"

"I don't believe so, sir."

"Good." Kal struck a hard punch to the guard's face while he disarmed him. The guard stumbled. "Nola!" Kal tossed the guard's sword to Inolah and drew his own. The moment he raised it to the guard, who was pushing back to his feet, Kal's hand went numb and he dropped the weapon. "Five Woes!" He growled and kicked his sword toward the prince. "Prince Ulrik!"

The guards at the window rushed Inolah, who faced them, sword in hand, gods help her. Prince Ulrik scooped up Kal's blade and went to join his mother.

Kal tackled his guard. They hit the floor and squirmed over the wood, stopping partly under a table. The violence took Kal back in time. His enemy rolled on top and punched him. Kal bashed his head against the man's temple while he used his left hand to pull his knife. He rammed the blade between the side laces that held the man's leather armor in place. The man croaked, his glassy eyes pinched, and he slid off Kal to the floor.

Kal's mind went blank. He lay on his back under a table, paralyzed, metal clanking somewhere above. A helmet on his head . . . He pulled it off. One thought emerged. The helmet was Rurekan.

"Surrender your sword if you refuse to fight," a woman said.

"I cannot do that, Empress," a man answered.

Inolah. Kal came to his senses. He scrambled out from under the table and took stock of the room. Prince Ulrik had wounded his man. Inolah's guard had his back to Kal. Inolah looked furious, jabbing and stabbing while the guard merely defended himself and dodged her blows.

Something banged outside the doors. Kal looked for Ferro and found the prince in the corner of the room, watching and waiting, a narrow door open behind him.

Good boy. A moment more and they could escape. Kal reached for his sword. Gone. His knife was stuck inside the man he had killed. He had to use his left hand to pull it out since his right was still limp and useless. Arman, why? Onika had said this was the God's doing. Would the God let Inolah and her children die?

A heavy grunt drew Kal's attention. Inolah's guard crumpled, fingers grasping a line of blood blossoming across his throat. Seconds later the prince finished his man with a stab to his chest.

"Well done, Ulrik," Inolah said.

The elder prince picked up his opponent's sword and tucked it and Kal's blade under his arm. "We must hurry." He pulled his mother toward the secret door, slowing when he passed Kal. Narrowed eyes took in Kal's hair and scars.

"Kalenek." Inolah was staring too. "This is my brother Wilek's shield," she told Ulrik.

"Hello, Princess," Kal said. "We did not know you were expecting another child."

"Nazer will not send my letters," Inolah said, palming her belly. "He is keeping me prisoner in my own—"

"There will be time to catch up later," Prince Ulrik said, slipping through the doorway. He kept hold of his mother's wrist, pulling her after him.

She paused in the doorway and said to Kal, "I'm Empress here, you know." She grinned and ducked in after her son.

Kal went back and grabbed the sword from the guard Inolah had killed. At least his fingers were working again. Behind him the doors slammed open. A dead guard fell inside the room, followed by the real city commander from the outhouse, still in his underclothes.

"Stop them!" he yelled.

Kal ran to the secret door, squeezed inside, and looked for a latch. "How do you close this?" He peered into the darkness on each side of the corridor and saw no one.

"Above your head!" Inolah yelled.

Kal dropped the sword and fumbled overhead. The guards were coming. His fingers found a dangling string, which he pulled so hard it snapped.

But the door fell shut.

Outside someone slammed against it. Pounded. The movement shook the entire wall.

The door remained closed.

Someone grabbed Kal's arm. "Come, Kalenek!" Inolah.

He crouched, found the sword at his feet. "How can you see?"

"I cannot, but I have taken this route before."

A distant boom shook the castle.

Inolah gasped. "That woman. We must hurry."

Kal had no argument there. "I live to serve, Princess—sorry, *Empress*."

"I prefer Princess."

Kal grinned as he crept along behind her. "As do I, Your Highness."

They emerged in the Open Quarter beneath a billowing cloud of gray smoke that made it dark as night, though it couldn't yet be midday. An orange glow reflected off the bottom of the clouds near the mountain. The air crackled with heat and ash. People were dashing everywhere at once—merchants, guards, and commoners, howling at one another, at no one—all running toward the North Gates.

"Something burns!" Prince Ulrik yelled.

"She has awakened the mountain," Inolah said. "We must hurry!"

"She who?" asked Kal.

"Priestess Jazlyn of Tenma," Prince Ulrik said. "My father insulted her."

She must be dry by now, though. No mantic could last this long.

Inolah led the way down one filthy alley after another to avoid the frenzied horde scrambling for the North Gate. Ash continued to rain down, and Kal pulled his tunic up over his mouth and nose.

They reached an inn. The attached stables had been abandoned—most of the horses taken—but they found three cow-hocked workhorses and saddled them. Inolah mounted and Kal handed Prince Ferro up to her. Ulrik returned Kal's sword and climbed on the second horse.

"Which way from here?" Inolah asked.

"To the East Gate." Kal sheathed his own blade and kept the extra guard's sword in hand. "The North is closer but likely overrun. We will reach the Nindera road faster if we head east now. I have companions waiting there."

"Lead on," Inolah said.

Kal mounted the third horse and set off against a tide of chaos. The horse could do no more than walk around people hauling carts filled with all they owned, pushing, shoving, and trampling each other. Behind Kal, fire climbed from the mountain into the sky on ropes of smoke.

Inolah screamed. A man was pulling her off the horse. Kal rode alongside and bashed the pommel of the guard's sword against the man's head. The man fell into the flow of people. So did Kal's sword, his hand limp. Kal roared, weaving his horse hard left and right through the crowd to make a path. He wanted out of this city. Now.

"This way!" Ulrik called, turning down another alley. He'd found yet another twist of near-empty backstreets and soon exited just south of the East Gate, where a much smaller group of people was flowing from the city.

Once they passed through the gates, Kal kicked his horse into a gallop. They rode hard, due east. Overhead, the darkness spread above and blocked the daylight.

A league or so later the ground rocked with the roar of a thousand sand cats. A pulse of wind shoved them from behind. Kal slowed to a stop and looked back.

The mountaintop had exploded yet again. Tendrils of fiery smoke spiraled out like curling ribbons. Rivers of fire swelled down the sides of Mount Lâhat, surging toward the city in a flood of liquid fire. Kal stared in horrified wonder. Sour fear pooled in his throat.

It couldn't be possible.

"We should keep moving!" Ulrik yelled.

Right. Kal pulled away from the devastation—from prophecy fulfilled. There had been earthquakes, sinksand, floods, and now this: fire from the mountains. The fourth of the Five Woes.

TREVN

Barek Hadar, Duke of Odarka, kept a stone mansion on High Street for when he visited Everton. Trevn had spent little time in this area of the city. The houses were so grand and the estates so vast, he couldn't jump from one roof to the next. Besides, most of the people who lived here spent more time at court than in their own homes. If Trevn wanted to see one of them, he could usually find them at the castle.

A manservant ushered Trevn and Cadoc to a cozy sitting room on the first level, where the duke was already waiting. He was average height with squashed features and Father Tomek's eyes. He stood and bowed.

"Thank you for seeing me, Duke," Trevn said.

"Your Highness, you honor me, the island of Odarka, House Barek, and all of High Street with your presence. Do sit down. Can I offer you anything?"

Trevn sat on the proffered chair. It was soft and oddly resembled a throne. "Nothing but privacy." He glanced at the servants.

The duke waved them away, all but Cadoc, who remained by the door. He sat across from Trevn on a noticeably smaller chair. Was the man trying to flatter him? Or was Trevn reading meaning where there was none?

"The official report from the palace physician is that your father died from natural causes," Trevn said.

"Yes, I saw the report," the duke said.

"The report was false. Your father was poisoned. I was with him when he died."

"I figured as much," the duke said. "He had powerful enemies."

As Trevn well knew. "He told me to come to you, and so I have."

"I admit, we did not expect you to," the duke said. "Father was never certain where your loyalties lay."

"Did he think me a traitor?"

"Nothing like that. He wasn't certain about your faith. Which gods you served, if any. It's common knowledge that you openly disdain adherence to any standard of belief or tradition for the sake of it. But what a man does and professes with his mouth is sometimes different from what he believes in his heart."

Trevn had never served any of the gods, had always made a point of ignoring them. "And Father Tomek hoped I followed Arman?"

"He did. He also wasn't certain where you stood on the Heir War."

"I thought that obvious. Everyone knows Janek and I don't get along."

"People believe it an act. Rumors say your backman is well established in Sâr Janek's retinue. And Sâr Janek's concubines claim that you may summon them at will. With Sâr Wilek missing, Sâr Janek is raising a great deal of support. It's suspected your father might declare him Heir."

"Before knowing whether or not Wilek is dead?"

"Wars are anything but fair, Your Highness."

Trevn supposed that was true. "Father Tomek wanted me to choose a side. Publicly?"

"He hoped you would. He left a letter for you, should you come to call." The duke stood and walked to the hearth, removing a scroll from the mantel. He crossed the room and handed it to Trevn. Trevn unrolled it and read.

Sâr Trevn,

If you have come to my son, the situation is dire. Years ago Rosârah Laviel conspired with Rôb priests to murder all the Armanite priests in our realm. I am speaking of the Great Priest Scourge of 865 that we studied together. My mentor was one of those killed. There was so much more I hoped to teach you about Arman. Now I must leave that to the God himself.

Because I was a sâr, privately tutoring you in Sarikar, my faith escaped the notice of Rosârah Laviel and the Rôb priests. I had hoped that yours would as well. But if you are reading this, the priests have discovered me and grown suspicious of you. They will find a way to test you. Be wary! They will do all they can to ascertain which god you serve.

You are well aware of the factions fighting over whether Sâr Wilek or Sâr Janek will inherit the throne upon your father's death. It was always my hope that you would advise Sâr Wilek in the days to come, that you might present Arman as the Only God. I know I ask a lot, that you are uncertain in matters of faith. I charge you to study this matter until you determine the truth for yourself.

I have included along with this letter the words of a prophecy we discussed together. This third version comes from an Armanite prophet. My son has the original clay tablet in his possession. If you would like to see it, simply ask him.

I believe this prophecy is about to be fulfilled—that both the Root of Arman and the Five Woes are upon us. If our people are to survive, we must find The Prophet. We will also need a king with a strong vision and a strong god.

No god is stronger than He Who Made the World.

You are a clever young man, but faith is not based on knowledge or even logic. You cannot simply follow the rules of the Holy Book and call yourself a follower of Arman. Put your trust in the God—the one who wrote the Book—for Only He is above reproach.

Blessings on your life until we meet in Shamayim,

Father Tomek Hadar

The second page was the prophecy transcribed in Father Tomek's hand.

Behold, I say to you, that in those days the root of Arman will be destroyed and usher in the end of all things. There will be mourning and great weeping heard throughout the land. Realm will rise against realm, brother against brother. There will be earthquakes, floods, and fire from the mountains. Rocks will crumble, and the ground will sink into the depths. Not one stone will be left atop another—each and every one will be thrown down. And then the end will come. And Armania, the glory of the Five Realms, the beauty of Arman's eye, will no longer be the head of all things.

Therefore Arman will raise up for you a prophet, who is not of your people. The prophet's words will save all who listen and obey, and will bring peace between mother and father.

—Armanite prophecy from the prophet Ottee, House Hadar 168

Trevn let the scrolls fall to his lap. "My father might live many more years—might live longer than Wilek."

"He might," the duke said, "but no one lives forever."

Trevn glanced over the prophecy again. "Do you think the Five Woes have come?"

"I do. And I am not alone. There is a group of believers who are preparing for this."

"Athosians?"

The duke grinned. "Oh, no. Do not lump us in with their ilk. We are Armanites who have formed a council of sorts. We call ourselves the Nahtan. We each oversee or contribute to a task."

A secret council. The idea piqued the Renegade in Trevn. "What kind of tasks?"

"Storing food, animals, water, supplies, weapons, coal. Building or buying boats."

"Boats? Why?"

"If the Five Woes come, this land will end. We will need to take to the waters. Sail into the unknown and find new land."

Trevn's arms prickled. "What is your task, Your Grace?"

"I am in charge of navigation."

Trevn scooted to the edge of his seat. "Have you sailed beyond the bowl?"

"Not I," the duke said. "But I have funded the exploration."

"Who have you sent?"

"Aldair Livina."

"But he is mad!"

The duke leveled a reprimanding stare at Trevn. "King Echad declared him mad. What does that tell you?"

That the man had likely gotten in Father's way. "Where has he gone? Has he found something?"

"He can tell you that himself. I would like you to join us, Sâr Trevn. I would like you to consider taking up a task of your own."

"Which is . . . ?"

"Convincing Sâr Wilek to join us, then making evacuation preparations in Everton."

Trevn pushed aside the excitement of exploring and tried to think through the consequences of joining such a group. How could he be certain the duke and his associates weren't as mad as the Athosian doomsayers? "Where is this Prophet? Father Tomek said there were no true prophets left in Armania." He shook the scroll. "This says The Prophet will not be of our people. A Sarikarian prophet?"

"My father believed The Prophet would not be from any of the Five Realms. There are verses to corroborate his theory in the Book of Arman. I can list them for you."

Trevn vaguely recalled transcribing something about a prophet. "I would appreciate that. But if this Prophet is from outside the Five Realms, how will we know him when he comes?"

"Father said we would know when we heard The Prophet speak."

As Trevn pondered the vagueness of such a statement, the house shook. An earthquake. A small one.

"Well, I hope he speaks soon," Trevn said, "because we are running out of time."

He bid the duke farewell and made his way with Cadoc through the house to the exit. As they walked down the hallway, Trevn's gaze caught on a portrait on the wall. He stopped.

Portraits hung side by side all the way down both sides of the hallway. There was one of the duke, one of Lady Brisa, one of her sister Trista, and on and on, but these held no interest for him.

"Fetch His Grace at once," Trevn told Cadoc.

Cadoc and the duke appeared moments later, the duke slightly out of breath. "What is it, Your Highness?"

Trevn pointed to the portrait on the wall. "Who is that man?"

The duke glanced at the portrait, then Trevn, and squinted in confusion. "That is Prince Mergest III of Sarikar. It was painted when he was about your age, I believe. King Ormarr sent away all the paintings of his eldest son where he would not have to see them. King Jorger did not ask for them back."

"Prince Mergest . . ." Trevn stared at the portrait, chilled as the revelation came over him. The young man in the painting looked very much like Janek. They had the same ridged brow and piercing stare, the same cheekbones and condescending smirk. "That," Trevn said, his voice wavering slightly, "is the Pontiff Barthel Rogedoth."

KALEΠEK

Kal's party reached Jhorn's camp by what he guessed was sometime after midday, though the sky was charcoal gray with no horizon in sight. While Kal had been in the city, Jhorn had purchased two tents, a poured-stone wagon with two mules, and a great deal of food. He had also refilled their water jugs. What would they have done without him?

While Jhorn saw them all fed, Kal tried to study Lâhaten through his grow lens, but the curve of the land blocked his view of the mountain and what was left of the once indestructible city.

Ulrik came to stand beside him. "May I?" Kal handed over the lens, and the young prince held it to his eye. "Unbelievable. Oh, there's a bird."

"Indeed, carrion birds will eat well this night."

"The flesh of my people," Ulrik said. "Of my father."

The words nipped at Kal's conscience. "The emperor might have escaped."

"No. She killed him. And I'm glad." Ulrik scowled, as if anger might erase any love he once held for his father. He looked through the grow lens again and shouted, "It's her! Priestess Jazlyn comes!"

What? Kal snatched back the lens and looked through it. "The road is empty."

Ulrik laughed, beaming into the sky. "Because she flies."

Kal looked up and located a bird—not a bird. Two people. Riding what looked like a massive bat. It was easily bigger than the camel and mules combined.

Inolah came to stand beside him. "The priestess?"

"She rides her shadir," Ulrik said.

The words sent a tremor of heat through Kal. Only great shadir were powerful enough to fly, to carry passengers, to appear so long in this realm.

"How can she ride it?" Inolah asked.

"Shadir can take any form they wish," Ulrik said. "But only the magic of their wielder can make them visible."

Ulrik had that last part backward, but Kal saw no point in correcting someone so smitten. "You seem fond of the mantic."

"She's a most impressive woman," Ulrik said. "And gloriously beautiful."

"Tennish women are dangerous, Your Highness," Kal warned.

The young prince winked. "All women are dangerous."

"*Ulrik*," Inolah said. "She tried to kill you."

"She wouldn't have done it," Ulrik said, squinting at the approaching creature. "She is coming to join us as she said. She'll be tired, like before. We should prepare a bed. In your tent, Mother?" Inolah nodded, and Ulrik hurried back to the camp.

"What is he, seventeen?" Kal asked.

"Nearly. Stubborn like me and fearless like his father. But I believe in him."

"Good," Kal said. "Because he's about to gain a thousand burdens. An obsession with a mantic witch should not be one of them."

"Never fear, Kal. She hates him," Inolah said.

"That will not keep her from making use of his affection." Kal and Inolah stood side by side and watched the approaching beast. Perhaps the woman would die from her haze and Kal would be free of the burden and danger she and her shadir would bring upon them.

"Your scars," Inolah said. "That happened in the war?"

"A few weeks after I left here. I was captured in Magonia."

"I am sorry. When you came to Lâhaten that day," Inolah said, "I thought it was to save me. But you were only here to negotiate with my monster of a husband. You left me here. A letter from my mother years later told me you were married and expecting a child. Later another letter informed me you lost them."

Kal glanced at Inolah's pregnant belly. "The last time I saw Livy, she was as far along as you are now."

"Oh, Kal. Do you still mourn them?"

He nodded. He would always mourn them.

The creature circled the camp and landed in the sand, sending a great dust cloud over them. Kal pulled his tunic up over his nose and walked slowly toward the shadir. Inolah followed.

A Tennish man slid off the side and reached back for the priestess. He carried her limp body toward Kal. The massive, bat-like shadir stood on its hind legs and began to shift and change. It vanished slowly, fading, its dark eyes fixed on Kal until they disappeared last.

Good riddance.

"We are here, Great Lady," the Tennish man told the unaware mantic. This was the voice of the invisible man who had given Prince Ferro to Kal. His cropped hair and slit earlobes marked him a eunuch. He wore a long white kasah skirt. His chest was bare.

The mantic looked dead. She was rail thin with sunken cheeks and skin like a moldy prune. She wore a dirty white gown and the diadem of a Tennish priestess. Only her eyes, shifting and gazing around the camp, let Kal know she still lived.

This Prince Ulrik had called gloriously beautiful? But then, she was a mantic. Who knew what she truly looked like.

"Can we help, Qoatch?" Inolah asked.

"She is in a haze," the eunuch said. "She must purge the poison."

"She may use my tent." Inolah led him to it and held open the drape.

"Do not disturb us," the eunuch ordered, carrying the priestess inside.

Kal drew Inolah away from the tent. "Why would you help someone so dangerous?"

"She concerns me too," Inolah said, "but she helped us escape. I owe her."

Prince Ulrik pushed out of the tent, scowling. "The eunuch demanded I leave. I wanted to see her return to normal."

"She likely prefers no one see her that way," Inolah said, embracing her son.

Kal seized that moment to escape. He walked to the campfire, where Jhorn was sitting alone. "Where is everyone?" he asked.

"In the other tent, where they'll be safe."

Safe from what? "The mantic is near death. She couldn't harm us even if she wished to."

"Her shadir will not be far away," Jhorn said. "It's unwise to let either of them near Onika or Grayson. They can't come with us, Sir Kalenek."

"I don't want them with us either, but it's not my decision," Kal said. "I'm taking the empress and her children to Nindera. If Inolah invites her Tennish friends, I won't and can't deny them. Keep Onika and Grayson away when the mantic is near. For their own safety."

When Grayson and Burk ignored Kal's orders to rise the next morning, Kal collapsed the tent on their heads. The fallen fabric bubbled as the boys sought out the exit. Kal left them to it and carried his pack to the wagon, where Onika stood waiting.

"Good dawning, Onika," he said.

"The air smells of death," she said. "We must hurry if we are to escape Gâzar's reach."

Kal's chest throbbed from her words, but it no longer gave him the scare it once had. "We'll go as quickly as possible," he promised, moving toward the horses. He saddled all three and the camel, feeling all the while like Onika was watching him.

Ulrik approached one of the horses. "Remarkable, isn't it?"

Kal wouldn't call the horse that. "We would've died without the animals, that is certain."

"Not the horse, Sir Kalenek. The way the priestess changes. She amazes me."

Kal followed the prince's gaze. The eunuch was carrying the mantic in his arms, and though she was awake and looking around, Kal guessed she was far from herself. He could see the potential for great beauty in her features. Some of the wrinkles and cracks had faded from her burnished red skin.

"She looks younger already," Ulrik said.

"Overdoses of evenroot don't age a person so much as suck out all the bodily fluids."

"Oh, I know," Ulrik said. "I'm just pleased she'll be herself again soon."

"With a mantic, how can you ever be certain what her true self looks like?" Kal asked. "She could be two hundred years old wearing a mask of youth."

Ulrik shrugged. "I care not, so long as she takes on the form I am familiar with."

Foolish prince. Kal would again caution Inolah about her son's obsession with the priestess. It would not do to have the new Rurekan emperor a puppet of Tenma.

Jhorn vaulted through the sand to Kal's side. "A storm is coming."

Kal regarded the thick, gray clouds overhead. "It's only smoke from the volcano."

"No," Jhorn said, pointing behind Kal. "The wind has carried that to the north. This is coming toward us."

Kal considered this as he studied the sky. Indeed, there were two very different groups of clouds. "Rain in the desert?"

"Desert torrents fall hard and long," Jhorn said. "A hand's depth of water can rush along the sand and sweep everything away."

Twice more Jhorn remarked on the clouds, and sure enough, some five leagues into their journey, it started to rain. The patter of water into sand soothed Kal's nerves. He couldn't imagine it would become a hazard.

"Should we make camp?" Burk asked.

"No," both Jhorn and Kal said at once.

"We must find high ground," Qoatch said.

"There is none," Kal said. "Not in these parts."

"Can you help us, Priestess?" Prince Ulrik asked, but the woman was asleep.

"How far is Nindera, Empress?" Kal asked.

"Some ten leagues more," Inolah said.

The storm would surely catch them before then, but Nindera was the only plan they had. The rain grew heavier. Water rushed along the ground. The camel moaned as her feet began to slip in the mud. Kal's clothing hung heavy, and he shivered. It was against his instincts and training to travel through a rainstorm with women and children, but he kept up a soldier's pace.

"It's getting worse," Jhorn said.

Kal wished Novan was with them. He could use one of the boy's brilliant observations right now. He glanced at his bedraggled entourage and tried to think of what Novan might say. They had horses, tents, mules, a poured-stone wagon. The wooden wheels spun, searching for traction. It would not roll much longer.

"Jhorn? Does a poured-stone wagon float like a poured-stone boat?" Kal asked.

"They're made to," Jhorn said. "Most traders in these parts pull their loads on land, then take off the wheels and sail north on the ream."

Then Kal's plan should work perfectly. "Let's remove the wheels to protect them from collision, and we can hole up inside the wagon. If the water gets high, we'd be safe enough, wouldn't we?"

"Yes," Jhorn said, grinning. "I believe we would."

Removing wheels in a rainstorm was no easy task for any man, but with Qoatch and Ulrik's help, Kal and Jhorn managed. By the time they were helping everyone back into the wagon, a thin layer of moving water had covered the ground.

"It's wet in here," Burk said.

"It's wet everywhere," Jhorn said.

"Let me see." Grayson jumped over the side, making a huge splash. Inside, the water was already two hands deep.

"Start bailing," Kal told the boys.

Kal and Ulrik gathered the saddlebags, the harnesses off the mules, and all the tack, and loaded it in the makeshift boat. The road had become a muddy river, carrying along the occasional tumbleweed. The animals lifted their feet over and over, searching for dry ground. Kal and Ulrik finally got inside and hunkered down under the length of folded tent everyone was holding over their heads. A few fingers of water still covered the bottom, soaking Kal's backside and legs.

The rain came down hard, drumming on the top of the canvas. Kal peeked out and could no longer see the animals or where the road had—

The wagon shifted.

"It's happening," Jhorn said.

The wagon lurched again, sliding several paces. On the ground outside, brown water surged around them as if the desert had suddenly become a dirty, turbulent sea. The water reacted to the terrain beneath, rushing here and pooling there. The wagon jerked along until it was picked up by a gush of water and carried a distance of several paces before dropping again.

Ferro began to cry. Kal didn't like feeling helpless. He held tight and waited for the rain to stop, but it did not. Endless apprehension brought fatigue, and Kal's fingers, cold and stiff, ached from gripping the tent edge for so long. Beside him, Grayson's teeth began to chatter. A violent gush sent them shooting over the ground. Water cracked against the outside of the wagon. They slammed against something, twisted around. The gods continued to drop water on their heads, so there was nothing to do but hold on.

Hinck

Hinck still couldn't face Janek. Not after what he had learned about the prince and Lady Eudora. After days of training with Oli and, well, *hiding* in the castle, his only plan to avoid the pole was to beg Lady Eudora for mercy. It was a risky move. She could very well laugh in his face—likely would—but he was running out of time. He had to try.

The Agoros family kept a house on High Street, and Lady Eudora also had a private apartment on the east wing of the castle. Hinck went there first. To his delight, the maid greeted him warmly and led him into the sitting room to wait.

Hinck wandered the room, seeking any sign of runes, hopeless he would ever fulfill either of his quests. Eudora clearly liked rocks. They were displayed on shelves, tables, and pedestals. A rock mosaic of the people tree hung on the wall. No sign of the runestone, however, so he sat down on a footstool to wait. His nerves were so frazzled that he soon stood up and circled the room again. He picked up a crystalized chunk of rock.

"Lady Eudora to see you, lord," the maid said.

Hinck spun around so fast he dropped the rock. He crouched to pick it up, and when he rose, he found Lady Eudora standing before him in all her glorious beauty. He stared into her amber eyes, and words evaded him.

"I do believe you're blushing, Lord Dacre," she said, taking the rock from him. "Oli told me what happened. I'm sorry if the situation caused you any discomfort."

"I'm not your mother, lady," Hinck forced himself to say. "You owe me no explanation."

But Eudora went on as if she did. "It's odd. I can never manage to say no to him. He is most persuasive."

That Lady Eudora's interlude with Janek had not been the first was yet another blow, though now that Hinck thought about it, how else would Janek have known about Eudora's bodymark? Oh, Hinck was the biggest of fools.

"He will be king someday," she whispered. "One does not refuse a king."

"Sâr Janek isn't likely to rule," Hinck said before thinking it through. "The king's health hasn't worsened. And Sâr Wilek is strong, or are you afraid he won't return?"

Eudora sighed, as if she had better things to do than listen to the ramblings of a fool. "Everyone who matters knows that Sâr Wilek will be a terrible king." She narrowed her eyes and set the rock back on the shelf. "You'd be wise to change your allegiance to a stronger candidate, Lord Dacre. I'll say no more."

Hinck found himself momentarily speechless. In light of present company, he'd completely forgotten to play his role. Yet this might be good. He might be stumbling onto something important. He grasped for words that might open up the conversation further. "I've sworn my allegiance to no one but my king and my master, Sâr Trevn. To either of his brothers, I've made no pledge."

"And what of Sâr Trevn?" she asked, eyes blazing eagerly. "Would he ever support Sâr Janek?"

Not in the five levels of the Lowerworld or beyond. "I cannot say, lady. Sâr Trevn and Sâr Wilek have become close."

Eudora groaned, disappointed. "That's what Janek says."

Janek, this time. Such familiarity spoke volumes about Lady Eudora's relationship with the Second Arm of Armania.

"Janek is hoping you can persuade Sâr Trevn to, well, broaden his mind a little."

Oh really? Apparently Hinck's time with Janek had not been spent in vain. "I can certainly try."

Eudora beamed, touched his arm. "Oh, I knew you would, Lord Dacre. You're so obliging."

Hinck's cheeks burned at her praise, despite how manipulative it had been.

"How rude of me," she said. "You must sit. I'll ring for refreshments. What do you prefer? It is early for wine, but if you would like it . . ."

Hinck sat on a silk-covered longchair. "Nothing for me, thank you."

"Nothing?" Eudora sat across from him. "Then why have you come?"

Gods help him. "To confess, lady." He studied the floor and cursed his cowardice. "First that I have always loved you. I only came to Seacrest to see you."

"Lord Dacre, please."

He glanced up, and upon seeing her horror-struck expression, he instantly focused back on the floor. "I know you care nothing for me. I will, in time—should Yobatha have mercy—get over my infatuation with you. But Sâr Janek has challenged me to a task he knows I'll fail."

She huffed. "That sounds very much like him."

Her tone gave him the courage to look up again. "I've come to beg your mercy, lady." He took a deep breath. "If you'll tell me a small secret, it will save me from the pole."

"Janek has threated to have you whipped?"

Hinck swallowed his fear. "Unless I can tell him what mark adorns your body."

She gasped and stood. "That pig!" She stomped across the room with the finesse of a soldier, arms crossed, muttering indiscernible words under her breath. She spun toward him, then away again, speaking this time to the hearth.

"I'll tell no one," Hinck said, thinking it might help to remind Eudora that he was still in the room.

She glared at him. "Why should I believe you?"

He stood and tried to look noble. "I can give you my word as an earl. I'm young, but as far as I know, my reputation is excellent."

Eudora stopped pacing and stared at him before falling into a fit of giggles. "Oh, Lord Dacre. You're so incredibly droll."

"Thank you. I think."

"Oh, but we must punish him." She walked past, spun back. "That is his test, you know." Her gaze met his. "To see how well you play his game."

Hinck shook his head. "I confess I know not how to play this game."

"You came to me, did you not? That shows a certain shrewdness *and* humility. Janek has plenty of shrewdness, but no humility. That, my dear earl, is your strength over him."

She had called him dear. "But how can humility stand against shrewdness?" Hinck pictured a dune cat eating a beetle.

"Because you asked nicely, where he is trying to manipulate us both."

"Ah." Hinck still didn't follow her logic.

"I could simply give you the answer," she said. "You would be safe from the pole, and Janek would wonder how you came by the information."

"I'd be most grateful, lady," Hinck said, feeling hopeful for the first time in weeks.

"But wouldn't it vex him so much more if it were true?" She grinned wickedly.

If what were true? "The location of your bodymark?"

She sauntered toward him, chuckling softly. "No, dearest Hinckdan. Sâr Janek's darkest imaginings as to how you discovered that mark."

Hinck's eyes widened. She had called him by his first name and was standing ever so close. The moment her lips touched his, he thought for the briefest moment that his heart had stopped. When it began to thunder in his ears, he realized that Yobatha and Mikreh had accepted his offerings, and he applied himself fully to the cadence.

"I knew there was something!" Hinck stood beside the desk in Trevn's secret room. Trevn was transcribing, as always, but had stopped to tell Hinck about the painting of young Prince Mergest III he had seen at the Duke of Odarka's home. The news lightened Hinck's sorrow for the moment. "So the banished prince came to Everton to live in secret, created a new identity, rose within the ranks of the Rôb church, and eventually carried on an affair with Queen Laviel."

"I am not convinced, as you are, that he is Janek's father," Trevn said. "But it sure did look like him. And it does explain the runes and his contempt for the Armanite faith."

"What are you going to do?" Hinck asked.

"Nothing as yet. Hopefully Wilek will return soon. If he does not, I will have to think of something." He stood to hang a completed page on one of the lines. "How did your visit with my cousin go?"

Hinck sighed, eager to shock his friend, though the end result of his day had left him bitter and depressed. "She gave herself to me."

He watched Trevn for a reaction but, of course, none came. The prince merely sat down again, set a clean sheet of parchment before him, and picked up his quill.

"Afterward"—Hinck swallowed—"she insisted we travel immediately to Seacrest, which we did. We entered the garden together. Timmons even announced us together." Another glorious moment. "She hung on my arm and didn't let go the entire afternoon. Janek could tell something was different, and he toyed with us until I tired of his games and announced that I had accomplished the task he had set before me. He looked rather shocked, which was, I confess, delightful for me. Then he demanded I give the answer aloud, in front of everyone."

Trevn had yet to look up from his writing, so Hinck forged on. "I had to choose between obeying the sâr or humiliating a lady publicly. I simply couldn't shame Eudora and told the sâr as much. This made him laugh, and he bid me whisper the answer in his ear. With Eudora's permission, I did so. Then he announced my words to the entire assembly! Lady Eudora flew into a rage, had the audacity to slap Janek, then stormed out. Since I had arrived with her, I made my apologies and left. Her driver had just shut her into her carriage when I caught up. Then I did something stupid. I offered to challenge Janek to a duel, to avenge her honor. Trev, are you listening?"

"I am."

"Don't you want to know what she said?"

"If you wish to tell me."

His indifference angered Hinck. "No, I don't think I will."

Trevn looked up and pursed his lips. "I am being hunted by corrupt priests, Hinck. I've given you a task. If you have information about that task, report. If not, say what you like, but don't expect me to pause my transcribing to laud the fact that you slept with a woman who has bedded half of Everton."

"I knew you'd say that." Insufferable royalty cared only for themselves. "Well, she laughed at me, Trev. When I offered to defend her honor, she laughed a very long time."

"Because she *has* no honor," Trevn said. "It's really quite funny."

"Let me finish! She thanked me for my courage but said she didn't want me to die, and if I dueled Janek, he would kill me. Then she said the most insulting thing of all."

Trevn looked at him, and Hinck knew that his friend truly did want to know what had happened, even if his pride wouldn't let him admit it.

"She said I was a sweet boy, and that I'd make a charming man someday."

"Oh," Trevn had the decency to say. "So that's why you're not dancing around my table."

"She doesn't love me, Trev. I'm not even sure she's capable. She used me to punish Janek. She lifted me to the height of all I ever wanted, made me feel as though I was the only man alive who could ever please her, and then she squashed me under her heel like a beetle. I *am* a beetle."

"You're a beetle?"

"I'm brokenhearted. Spent. The abuse is too great. I cannot face them and pretend she hasn't eviscerated me like the cruelest soldier on a bloody field of battle."

"*Enough*," Trevn said. "I know you're upset, but you've played their game well. They're livid with each other, but your reputation to both remains unscathed." He sighed and went back to transcribing that infernal book.

"How did you throw off the humiliation when Shessy betrayed you?" Hinck asked.

"I knew everyone was watching me, so I pretended I didn't care."

"So must I, then." Hinck couldn't let Eudora know how she had devastated him. "There's more." He told Trevn all Eudora had said about supporting Janek for king.

This news was grave enough that Trevn set down his quill. "If Eudora is talking openly about this to you, she must believe you are one of them. That is excellent. But I cannot let anyone believe I support Janek. With Wilek gone, that might embolden Janek to make his move. He has been campaigning hard in Wilek's absence. What can I do? The people will support Janek."

"Surely not," Hinck said. "Everyone knows Janek's reputation."

"So? My father's reputation is incorrigible. Maybe that is what people expect in a king."

"Isn't this beyond us?" Hinck asked. "It is your father's decision to choose his Heir."

"My father hasn't made a decision on his own in years. The men and women who whisper in his ear rule Armania. At this juncture, I'd set the crowns on the heads of Rosârah Laviel, Janek, and Pontiff Rogedoth."

"Get closer to your father, then, so you can whisper too."

"There's no time. They've been at this for months. Years, likely."

Hinck did *not* want Janek to be declared Heir. "What can be done?"

Trevn's eyes went glassy as he stared into nothing. "I will make a public statement of support for Wilek. It's what Father Tomek wanted."

"Won't that be dangerous?"

Trevn met Hinck's eyes. "It will give the people something to gossip about that involves Wilek—to remember that he is still a viable choice for Heir. And by drawing attention to myself in such a public way, the villains who seek to threaten me will be forced to lie low for a while and bide their time. Hopefully until Wilek finds his way home."

"Unless those very villains are keeping him away."

"We must pray to Arman they are not."

Trevn, pray? "You're not the praying sort."

"It was Father Tomek's dying wish that I weigh Arman for truth. Cannot hurt to try."

As long as Hinck didn't have to. The father god had too many rules for his tastes. "What about me? What should I do?"

"Ride to Seacrest first thing tomorrow. Tell Janek I was in a foul mood and cast you out. That way you won't be here to know what I've done. You'll learn about it with Janek and the others. Better yet, tell them my mother forbade me to see Miss Mielle because we don't match in fives. Tell them you're afraid I'll do something rash because I'm madly in love with her."

"Are you?"

Trevn shrugged. "How should I know? You tell me."

"Can't help you, Your Cluelessness, for I'm equally clueless. My experiences with women have taught me less about them, not more."

"Well, it has been far too long since I saw Mielle. Perhaps I will have to visit Fairsight Manor and face the princess."

"That should get someone talking," Hinck said.

He left Trevn to his scribblings and wandered toward his chambers on the fourth floor, overwhelmed with the mere act of breathing. He still ached over Eudora's words. How long would it take for the wound to fade?

As he passed the servants' stairwell, a man in a cloak stepped out and grabbed his arm. Hinck yelped and reached for his sword, but the man had already disarmed him. He pushed Hinck against the wall and held Hinck's own blade to his throat.

"The gods have taken notice of your worthiness, Hinckdan Faluk." The voice was a scratch of cat's claws on leather. "A hundred souls have their eyes on you. You're being measured. Will you listen carefully for the call?"

Hinck stammered and managed to utter, "I-I will, sir."

The man grunted. "Your answer is noted and will please the tribe. Discuss this with no one." He dropped Hinck's sword on the floor and fled.

Hinck remained against the wall for quite some time, dizzy with fear. Finally he crouched to retrieve his sword. As he sheathed it, it occurred to him that he might have accomplished what Trevn had asked him to do. This was an invitation. He replayed the cloaked man's words again. Yes, he was sure of it. He was being measured. He would, indeed, listen for their call.

WILEK

Wilek mashed his pole into the urn. This batch was broken down enough. Good. The sun was already low on the horizon, and he was starved. He carried his urn toward the dry screens and the wagon. No sign of Four. Odd.

Behind him, flesh smacked flesh. A man grunted.

Wilek tensed and kept walking, hoping Roya wouldn't bother him today. He dumped out his mashed root onto an empty screen beside a wagon and caught sight of a man's feet on the ground. He stepped around the wagon to see who it was.

Four. Bleeding from the chest. Eyes closed. Dead?

Wilek spun around. Three Magonian slavs lay motionless on the ground. Over by the laundry lines, two men shrouded in black were attacking two acolytes.

Who were they? Should he run? Join them?

"Wilek Hadar!"

A middle-aged man with twisted locks of hair ran toward him from the rocky cliffs.

"You Sâr Wilek Hadar?" the man asked, slamming to a stop beside him.

Hope rose like a wave in Wilek's chest. "That's right."

The man grabbed Wilek's arm and pulled him away from the harvest yard. "Ready to go home?"

"Yes!"

They sprinted away, but as they neared the rocky ledge, Wilek's legs began to slow. He was getting too far from Charlon.

"I cannot leave."

"By that hair I assume they compelled you." The man glanced at the back of Wilek's neck. "Sick witches. A shame, that. Gonna have to fight it. And it's gonna hurt. I'd knock you out, but I kill too many people that way. If you're dead, I don't get paid."

"Thank you for taking the precaution. Who are you?"

"Call me Rand."

Wilek stopped entirely. "Randmuir Khal of the Omatta?"

The man beamed. "You've heard of me! A learned man, you are, Wil. I like that."

Wilek wasn't sure he wanted to leave with the famous assassin. "Who are you working for?"

Rand laughed. "Let's save the niceties for later, eh? If I wanted to kill you, you'd be dead. Keep moving!"

Wilek ran beside Rand, who kept a tight hold on his arm. His leg muscles ached. He had abandoned his work without permission. Now he was straying too far from camp.

Charlon's fear stabbed through him. She could feel him leaving. He saw her then, in his mind. She was kneeling on her mat, casting a spell on herself. One that would remove her fear.

Sands, she was beautiful. The idea of leaving her seized his heart. "Wait!" He stopped running of his own accord. "There is a woman."

"It's a Magonian camp, man. There are a lot of women."

"But only one that did this." Wilek held up his palm bearing the rune. "She is wearing a necklace with this same mark. I need it to be free."

"Someone soul-bound you? Where's this crow?"

"In her tent. The maidens usually rest before the evening repast."

"'Course they do, precious lambs." Rand turned back to the rock face. The two black-clad men were a few dozen paces behind. "Hey!" he yelled. "Fetch us a woman called . . . ?" He glanced at Wilek.

"Charlon," Wilek said.

"Charlon! Bring her to camp. Don't get killed."

The men started back up the rocks. Rand and Wilek continued on. Ten more steps and Wilek's knees locked. He had to start dragging his legs one at a time. Rand hefted Wilek over his shoulder and carried him. Wilek writhed, trying to get down. Pain stabbed through his neck, cold and deep. He gritted his teeth and fought the urge to scream.

"It would be easier if you stopped thrashing about," Rand said.

Wilek made a sound like a dying buck.

"Woe-bound crows," Rand muttered. "Nothing I hate worse than compulsions."

Wilek continued to fight the magic while the magic fought Rand. Fear from Charlon suddenly gripped him. The black-clad men had found her. Struck her. Wilek kicked Rand so hard in the back that the man dropped him. Desperate to keep Charlon safe, Wilek scrambled away, sprinting toward the Magonian camp. Until something bashed against his head.

He tripped, fell to his hands and knees, dazed.

"All right, Wil? Tried to go easy." Rand heaved him over his shoulder again. "Got to be some trick to head-bashing I never learned."

Wilek floated away on a flurry of icy wind. He smelled a horse. They were galloping over a darkening prairie. The compulsion snatched at him with icy fingers but found no purchase on his addled mind.

Sometime later voices pulled him back to focus.

"Where are the others?" a man asked.

"Right behind, should be." Rand slung Wilek off the horse and into the arms of another. "Get Teaka over here. The rest of you, bind him to that tree. Cursed crows compelled *and* soul-bound the poor slig. See if you can find him some real clothes too."

A bit later, intense pain cleared Wilek's vision. It felt like someone was carving out his brain. He had gone too far from the Magonian camp. Did the pain increase the farther he went? Would it kill him?

The sky was charcoal gray, just light enough to display the shapes of several tents in the distance. A bonfire glowed fiercely and cast light over the occasional nomad who wandered past. They had tied Wilek to a squat whitethorn tree on the outskirts of their camp. Rand and a man closer to Wilek's age paced around the tree.

"You said I was going home," Wilek said, breathing through his teeth.

"Welcome back, Wil." Rand crouched before him. "It's these woe-bound crows. Hate them. Always have. Never liked anyone who thinks they're better than the rest of us."

Sands, Wilek's head hurt. "Then you cannot much care for a sâr."

"Don't," Rand said, waggling his eyebrows. "Care for my coffers, though, and they've been light of late. Earthquakes have people scared. Not much need for mercenaries when you're too frightened to get out of bed."

Wilek could understand that. "But the Omatta hates the monarchies. You cannot be *that* desperate."

The younger man chuckled. "Got you there, Father."

"My son, Meelo," Rand said, nodding at the younger man. "But you're right, Wil. The one who's paying your ransom is an old friend. So, despite your being royal spawn, his wish is good enough for me."

"Who is this person?" Wilek asked.

"Rayim Veralla," Rand said. "We were boys together before he went into training."

Rayim! "Captain Veralla friends with Randmuir Khal of the Omatta? I never would have guessed that," Wilek said.

"Shows how clever a sâr is, doesn't it?" Rand said. "Ah, here they come."

Two more men ushered an old woman over to Wilek. She was so slight she might have been mistaken for an adolescent girl if not for her white hair and lined skin. She walked with her arms out to the side as if trying to keep her balance.

One of the men dropped a pile of clothing and pair of boots beside Wilek.

"Thank you," Wilek said, though he couldn't very well dress while tied to a tree.

The other man spread a leather mat on the ground before Wilek and set a bowl on the end. A pale lizard was curled inside it.

"Who is this?" Wilek said, suddenly nervous, thinking of Mreegan's lizard.

"My mother, Teaka. Grew up in Magonia," Rand said. "She's going to undo the spells they put on you."

Thank the gods. Maybe she could stop the pain. "Why the lizard?"

"That's Errp," Rand said. "Mother's pet. He's a letaha newt, not a lizard."

Newt? Strange that both Teaka and Chieftess Mreegan had a pet newt.

Teaka leaned close to Wilek and sniffed. She ran her finger over a scratch on his cheek, examined the spot of blood that came away, smelled it. She hobbled back to her bowl and wiped the blood inside the basin, knelt on the altar mat. The newt slithered out of the basin and onto her knee.

A ragged scream rent Wilek's heart. Charlon! He twisted to look beyond the tree. The black-clad duo approached on horseback, one holding a struggling woman over his lap.

Wilek tried to stand, pulling against the ropes that bound him. "Don't hurt her!"

"Calm, Wil," Rand said. "It's only her magic making you worry."

It was. But that knowledge didn't take away his fear.

The man pushed Charlon off his saddle into Meelo's arms, which made her scream louder. Meelo set her on her feet but kept hold of her wrist.

"Don't!" She elbowed him and spat in his face. "Let go of me!"

Meelo simply grinned, leaving her spit glistening on his cheek. "When you're through with her, Father, I want her."

"No!" Wilek and Charlon yelled together.

Rand snapped his fingers and pointed at Wilek. "Put her over here."

Meelo pushed Charlon down on Wilek's lap. She slid to the ground and stood, rocking from one foot to the other. "Let us go."

"So you can order the sâr to attack us?" Rand said. "Why don't you sit down."

The black-clad men dismounted and drew their swords. Charlon knelt beside Wilek, leaving a hand's breadth between them. Her nearness lessened the pain in his head.

"Get free," she whispered. "Help us escape."

Her command swelled inside, and Wilek strained against his bonds.

Rand growled. "Fight it, Wil. You know this is her magic."

Fight. Wilek whimpered and curled his head to his knees but was unable to stop tugging at his bindings.

"How you coming along, Ma?" Rand asked.

"Almost," the old woman said.

"What is she doing?" Charlon asked, seeming to notice Teaka for the first time.

"*Undoing*, crow," Rand said. "She's undoing your spells."

"No!" Charlon yelled. "Don't take him from me. I mustn't fail." Charlon scrambled toward Teaka, pleading with her to leave the magic in place. Meelo stepped in her way, and Charlon drew back.

Teaka continued muttering without even a glance toward Charlon. In a sudden rush of warmth, the compulsion broke and the pain vanished.

Wilek gasped, shocked at how light he felt. "It's gone. The compulsion is gone!"

"Untie him," Rand said.

The men removed Wilek's ropes. He stood and massaged his hands. The warmth was already coming back, but he was still cold within.

"What of the soul-binding?" he asked.

Teaka shook her head. "Not without knowing which spirit powered it. I must question the mantic who cast the spell."

"She did." Wilek gestured to Charlon. "She wrapped our hands with the twine of that pendant." Wilek pointed at the charm that hung around Charlon's neck.

Teaka's beady eyes locked onto Charlon. "You have your own shadir, girl? What's its name?"

Charlon lifted her chin. "Magon."

The woman cackled. "Magon serve *you*?" She shook her head and told Wilek, "She won't tell us the truth."

"But she did," Wilek said. "That's the shadir's name. I've heard her say it."

"A great shadir would not bond with one so small," Teaka said. "Take the pendant, at least. You'll be safer in possession of it until you can find out the real name of her shadir."

Wilek spun around and grabbed for the necklace, but Charlon ran. Meelo and his companions gave chase. Moments later her shrieks pierced the night and her irrational terror stabbed Wilek. He shook it away, reassured himself that she was fine. No one would hurt her. While he waited, he pulled on the trousers and boots, which were both a little large, then untied his kasah skirt and dropped it in a heap. *Good riddance.* He was just pulling on the tunic when they dragged Charlon back. Her eyes rolled with terror as she thrashed against the men's hold. *Gods, what had happened to make her so afraid to be touched?*

Wilek braced himself against the tree, fighting her fear. This needed to end. The moment she was near enough, he lurched toward her and ripped the pendant from her throat.

She went limp in the men's arms; they nearly dropped her. Had Wilek killed her by taking the pendant?

But no. She suddenly squirmed out of their hold, crawled between Meelo's legs, and sprinted away. She had been faking. Again the men gave chase, and a few minutes later they dragged her back, crippling Wilek anew with her terror.

"Let her stand on her own," Wilek said. "She hates being touched."

"She hasn't given me much chance," Meelo said. "I think she'd like—"

"Hands off!" Rand yelled.

The men backed away from Charlon, which lightened the fear in Wilek's chest. He lifted the pendant between them. "If I break this, will it end the spell?"

"Don't!" Charlon said.

"Breaking it will bind you forever," Teaka said. "You must have the token to attempt a soul-loosing. And no mantic will perform it without knowing what type of shadir powered the spell."

Figured. Wilek put on the necklace and tucked the pendant into his new tunic. He would keep it safe until he could undo the magic. "Tie her up. She comes back to Everton with me. And remember, whatever happens to her happens to me. I'll know if you so much as look at her too much."

"Royalty . . ." Meelo took hold of Charlon's arm and dragged her away. Charlon shrieked. Wilek gritted his teeth, waiting for it to be over.

"Feel better?" Rand asked.

"I will once they stop touching—" A shard of terror stabbed his throat, and he yelled.

In the darkness something exploded in a tiny cloud of orange flames. Rand and his men sprinted toward it. Wilek followed, peaceful now that he knew Charlon had escaped.

Five Woes! She escaped?

Rand and Wilek pushed through a huddle of men to where Meelo sat on his knees, holding his face in his hands and keening.

"What happened?" Rand asked. "Where's the girl?"

"Meelo kissed her," one of the black-clad men said. "She said some magic word, and his face melted."

"What's that crow done to you?" Rand wrenched Meelo's hands away from his face. A gasp rose around them. The man's lips were gone, shriveled into two lines of raisin-like skin that bared his teeth in a perpetual snarl. His teeth were coated in blood, which dripped down his chin in a streak, as if he'd taken a bite of a living creature.

"She dares disfigure my son?" Rand stared into the dark toward the Magonian camp, his face pinched with a venomous look. "I'll kill the witches. All of them!"

Meelo covered his mouth and ran off into the night.

No one spoke or moved. Wilek kept his gaze averted from Rand, uncertain what he might do in his anger. But the man suddenly rubbed his face and sighed. "I'm starving. Let's get some food."

Wilek followed Rand into camp, his thoughts fixed on Charlon. He could feel her intent to return to the Magonian camp. She was frightened. Worried how Mreegan would react to her losing him.

Wilek sat with Rand beside the bonfire and ate dry bread and meat in silence. Throughout his meal, Wilek struggled to rationalize his way out of making plans to rescue Charlon from the Magonians.

Teaka came and sat beside her son. "I cannot help Meelo if he hides from me," she said.

"He's sulking," Rand said. "Knows he's a daft fool for not listening. He was warned to leave that witch be."

The woman turned her gaze on Wilek. "It was powerful magic for one so young. Could be I was wrong. Could be she *is* bound to Magon."

Errp the newt crawled out from the woman's apron pocket and sat on her shoulder.

Wilek's mind flashed to Mreegan, then to Charlon. He pined over Charlon a moment, then forced his thoughts to Lebetta and how horribly she had died. This brought the rune to mind.

"Teaka," he said. "If I drew a rune for you in the dirt, could you translate it?"

She shrugged one tiny shoulder.

Wilek drew the rune in the sand in front of Rand, hoping he'd done so correctly.

The old woman squinted at his drawing. Her thin lips twitched and curved into a smile. She chuckled, a raspy sound that reminded Wilek of a wheezing goose. "This one here"—she traced it with her forefinger—"means five. But when drawn inside the rune for fire, they become one rune that means five fires or five flames. Then there's the rune for shadir." She traced it as well.

"Five flaming black spirits?" Wilek asked.

"Five flames of the shadir," she said.

"What does that mean?"

She leaned forward and traced two of the lines, then drew them apart from the rest and added five short lines of a sunburst atop them. "This one isn't a rune."

A shiver ran up Wilek's arms as he took in the mark of the Knife—the king's assassins. "It's upside down," Wilek said.

"Because they work from inside," Teaka said. "The king thinks he rules, which is what they want him to think. But a man can't rule a city that's already being ruled in secret."

Wilek could hardly believe what she was implying. "Who is *they*?"

"The men who rule Armania. The priests of Havôt."

Wilek had never heard of them. All this time, mantics were in Everton, manipulating his father? "How do you stop a mantic?"

"Take away their power." Teaka drew a glass vial from her apron pocket and held it up. Evenroot dust.

"If I find where they keep their root dust . . ."

"You can destroy it. Or give the root to me." Another chuckle.

"But how can I find it? Where would I look if I know not who the mantics are?"

Her smile wrinkled her face. She uncapped her vial and said, "Errp, *matsa ahvenrood*."

The newt lifted its head, eyes alert. Its nostrils twitched, then it scurried down Teaka's arm to her wrist and sniffed at the open vial. "The letaha live off root. They can find it anywhere."

No wonder Mreegan had one. "Teaka," Wilek said, an idea forming in his mind. "Would you and Errp help me save Armania?"

PART THREE

THE END OF ALL THINGS

CHARLON

"Explain yourself!"

Charlon cowered before Mreegan in the red tent. Face covered in dirt. Gaze on the floor. "They came for the prince. Had a mantic with them. She broke the compulsion. Refused to meddle with the soul-binding. The prince took our token and wears it now." Sobs came forth, deep and heavy. Such longing. Wilek gone. Gone before she could test her new plan.

"You failed and must be punished." Mreegan lifted her hand.

A spell was coming. Charlon braced herself for pain.

Nothing happened.

Mreegan frowned, thrust her hand forward again. Stood and circled Charlon.

Show yourself, Favored One, Magon said within. *It's time to stand as Mreegan's equal.*

Charlon rose slowly, mustering courage. She lifted her own hand. Whispered a spell.

Mreegan stopped moving, frozen just by Charlon's words. Only the Chieftess was supposed to have the power to perform magic without runes.

Mreegan's gaze met Charlon's. "The slight Eemahlah is no match for my shadir. Who powers your spell? Tell me the truth!"

"Magon gives me strength," Charlon said.

A gasp. "You dared petition *my* shadir?"

"I was desperate. I prayed to the goddess and she answered."

"But she hasn't cast me down from my position as Chieftess. Why would she serve us both?"

The two women looked at one another warily.

"What does it mean?" Charlon asked.

"She must want us to work together."

Why? The goddess had promised. Promised Charlon would be Chieftess someday. Perhaps this was a necessary step. She released her hold on Mreegan, determined to try things Magon's way. "Magon told me I am Mother. But I despise men. Cannot touch one. Hate being touched by anyone."

"Ridiculous," Mreegan said.

"You saw within. When you healed me. You know why I fail. But I have a plan. I must place a compulsion on myself. I have been practicing."

Mreegan scoffed. "That's impossible."

"You doubt Magon's power?"

"No, but—"

"You said only the Chieftess could petition Magon. I proved you wrong. Anything is possible with Magon. I can do this. But I need your help."

Chieftess Mreegan stared within, saw that Charlon spoke the truth. "Very well. But I will not risk our camp by abducting the prince again. This time you must cast a mold of his betrothed and go to him masked in her form. Ask Magon to help you find the woman's location."

"Yes, Chieftess," Charlon said.

"We leave for Everton tomorrow."

As the Magonians journeyed toward Everton, Mreegan taught Charlon all she knew of compulsion spells. Charlon practiced. Forced Kateen to crawl on all fours like a dune cat. Made Five believe he was One and pick a fight with Rone for wearing the lure. Once compulsions on others were mastered, Charlon practiced on herself. Cast a spell that she hated furs and could not sleep that night from the chill. Made herself loathe water until she could barely speak for her dry throat.

Charlon became proficient at placing spells on herself. Finally capable, she retreated to her tent and cast the spell she needed. To banish her fear of men. Her fear of human touch.

But had it worked? Could she even know?

She must test it. But not on any man. Torol had always been kind. Torol she trusted.

She petitioned Magon for cleansing, then walked out of her tent. Three passed by with a tray of food. "Fetch Torol," she ordered, and he scurried away.

She went back inside to wait. Soon Torol entered her tent.

"Are you well, Mother?" he asked.

"I must test my spell." She reached for him. "Take my hand."

He walked to stand before her. His fingers slid over hers, up her palm, and bent around the side of her hand.

She shivered. Not from fear. She found his touch pleasant. Only in the back of her mind did the soul-binding cause her to hesitate.

"Will you kiss me?" she asked. Not a compulsion this time. Torol's choice.

He looked hesitant. Stepped closer. Ran his fingers up the back of her arm.

Her mind did not scream. She did not flinch. Had she done it? *Please, Magon!* Say that she had.

Torol's eyes searched hers, afraid. Likely wondering if this was a test. If she would punish him later. Roya played too hard with the men.

"You're safe," she whispered. Her stomach fluttered within.

Torol pressed his lips to hers. Soft lips. Prickly beard. Solid arms. An intense sorrow seized her. This was not the prince—not her soul-bound.

She pulled Torol closer, fighting the soul-binding magic. Shocked and delighted. No fear of being touched. Only the nagging horror that she was betraying her prince.

She shoved aside that guilt. Drew Torol to her bed. They knelt, fell together. Arms clutching each other. While she felt no fear, she wept for Prince Wilek. She was betraying him in the worst way and sensed that he knew it. These emotions would be too strong for him to ignore.

So she let herself cry while at the same time celebrating. With Magon's help, she had mastered men. She had mastered fear. Now nothing could stop her from mastering Prince Wilek.

She only had to beat him back to Everton and his betrothed.

WILEK

Wilek had been a boy the last time he had ridden through this part of Sarikar. He found it vastly altered and suspected the changes were recent. A half dozen fall-ins had claimed large sections of the road, forcing their party to take alternate routes that added at least two days to their week-long journey. They came upon Cheyvah's Maw ten leagues too soon. Somehow the crack had lengthened, likely from the recent earthquakes. This would delay their return even more.

As they followed the crack north, Wilek thought about Charlon constantly. Not since adolescence had he felt such random longings for a woman.

The soul-binding was to blame, no doubt.

Panic seized him suddenly, and he found he couldn't breathe. Waves of conflicting emotions surged through the soul-binding link. Confusion, affection, remorse, pleasure, desperation, but strongest of all, joy.

Charlon was free! She had overcome her fear.

With someone else.

Wilek found his own unworthiness suffocating. He had failed to save her and she'd chosen another. Torol! She'd chosen Torol. Wilek would kill him.

Madness! He forced himself away from such deep thoughts, studied his surroundings, and started counting shrubs in a desperate attempt to distract his mind. He'd reached seventy-six shrubs before his emotions tapered off.

Illogical or not, Charlon's rejection remained heavy on his heart. Wilek would ask Teaka again to reconsider breaking the soul-binding. The old woman feared Charlon had been truthful about Magon being her shadir.

"Magon is too powerful," Teaka had said. *"To tamper with the spell of a great shadir is foolishness, indeed."*

And so Wilek was left to suffer.

The sun was high in the sky when the city of Pixford came into view on the horizon. Wilek's heart quickened, knowing he would soon cross the border and into his own realm. The road descended into a canyon that would wind and twist before letting out a mere league before the Pixford gates. Halfway through the canyon they came upon a contingent of Armanian soldiers blocking the road.

"You Armanians forget that Sarikar isn't your realm?" Rand called out.

"You have our sâr," one of the Armanians said. "We want him back."

Dressed for battle with helmets hiding their faces, Wilek couldn't be certain these were Armanians at all. He nudged his horse to the front. "Your sâr is here. Who leads you?"

"It is I, Your Highness." A man in the center of the line removed his helmet. Agmado Harton.

"Hart! What have you been doing these past weeks?" Wilek asked, wondering where his men had gone after he had been taken.

"Looking for you, Your Highness. You're my responsibility."

"He's my backman," Wilek told Rand.

"Seems your backman failed you," Rand said, a little louder than necessary. The Omatta laughed.

Harton's face clouded. "Hand over our sâr or die."

"I'll turn him over to the man who hired me," Rand shot back. "That wasn't you."

Harton drew his sword and nudged his horse forward. "I will fight for my sâr."

"Wait!" Wilek rode his horse in front of Rand's. "I am safe, Harton. Take word to the king and my mother that I am coming home."

"You're not yourself, Your Highness," Harton said. "They've bewitched you."

What madness compelled Harton to openly defy a direct order? "Have I not suffered enough? Do as I command, Hart, or you shall face the pole!"

Harton seemed to consider Wilek's threat a real one, which it was. He signaled to his men, who turned in retreat. "I'll send a man to Everton with word of your coming, Your Highness," Harton said. "But as your shield I'll remain nearby."

Sands! Wilek had forgotten he had assigned Harton as acting shield when he sent Kal into Magonia. The king had likely threatened Wilek's men with sacrifice if they returned without him. "You set my mind at ease, Hart. I thank you."

The Omatta group followed the Armanians through the remainder of the canyon and along the outskirts of Pixford. Wilek was shocked to see the city decorated for the Feast of Rain, which celebrated the arrival of the stormmer season. Every house had some kind of blue bow or ribbon mounted on the door with a bucket underneath.

If stormmer had already arrived, that meant Wilek was twenty-five now. His ageday had come and gone. Had his trip to Farway gone as planned, he would have married Lady Zeroah sometime last week.

He felt sick at the idea of marrying anyone but Charlon—obnoxious, unfaithful, soul-binding witch—and sicker still when he realized he had been gone ten weeks longer than planned. Ten weeks. Had his mother given him up for dead? Harton hadn't, so that was some comfort. He hoped Father had not yet named Janek as Heir.

The Omatta made camp that night before the first link in the Cobweb Bridge. Wilek didn't trust Harton not to get antsy and attack, so he asked one of the Omatta to invite his temporary shield to join them.

Harton rode into camp, three men on either side, all with swords drawn.

Wilek stormed out to greet them. "What is the matter with you? I am safe with these men. Why do you continually ignore my commands?"

"They might have you under a compulsion," Harton said. "They cut your hair, and you have a rune on the back of your neck."

Wilek shivered at the word *compulsion*. "Well, I'm no longer with the mantics, am I?"

"No, but—"

"A compulsion would have forced me to go back. Put away your swords, all of you." Wilek waved at the guards. "The Omatta mean us no harm. They will escort me home."

"We can do that without their help," Harton said.

"I'm aware of your skills, Harton. But the Omatta freed me from the Magonian camp, and that is the report I will give my father. These men deserve our respect. I'll have no more of this rudeness from you, is that clear?"

Harton glowered. "Very, Your Highness."

They remained locked in a stare until Wilek said, "Well? Dismount, Harton. Come, enjoy the food."

Harton obeyed, though it seemed to pain him greatly. Did the man have some bad history with the Omatta?

They all ate around the bonfire, and Wilek lost track of Harton for a while.

He next saw him dancing around the fire with a pretty woman. Back to his old ways, apparently. At least he had put down his sword. Wilek hoped the man didn't do anything foolish to upset Rand.

A rush of cold desire flooded Wilek suddenly. Too embarrassed to move, he sat uncomfortably and stared into the fire, unwilling to risk eye contact with anyone for fear the smile of a pretty woman would undo him. Curse that witch. What was she doing now? He rubbed his forehead with his icy hand, and the coolness brought a tingle of relief.

"Your man Harton has the temperament of a nomad."

Wilek looked up into Rand's weathered face. "Which is . . . ?"

"Eager, hungry, and savage, with greater mood swings than a woman in her courses. Meelo would like him." The man spat. "Wish the fool boy would quit hiding and let his grandmother heal his face. How do you fare this night?"

Wilek sighed. "As well as a man can be when his every thought and feeling is twined with another."

"Can I do something to help? Get you anything? Food, drink, a woman?"

Sleep was all he needed. "Thank you, no. I shall retire soon, I think."

Rand sat down beside him. "You should know, a few hours after I accepted the assignment to bring you home, another man from Armania petitioned me to capture and kill you."

That was always happy news. "Strange that two sought to hire you on the same day."

"Not when you consider that it was the same day the messenger from your contingent informed the king of your abduction."

"Who was this second patron?"

Rand shook his head. "Only a messenger. And the request wasn't signed."

"What did he look like?"

"A priest, I think. He wore blue robes under his cloak. And an anklet of the five gods."

A Rôb priest, then. "Someone in the Rôb faith wants me dead." Teaka's words came back to him. He needed to find out what she meant about the priests of Havôt who secretly ruled Armania. It brought to mind the priest scourge during the war and Janek's mother, who had championed it. "Rosârah Laviel has given more to Temple Rôb in petition for my death than the entire realm gives in guilt offerings. But would she risk treason?"

"I cannot say." Rand tossed a twig in the fire. "Rosârah Laviel hates me as well. Because of her, I'm not permitted inside the Everton city gates."

Janek's mother was as hideous a monster as Barthos. "How did you offend her?"

"Not me. Sâr Janek became enamored with my daughter. But rather than give in to him, Zahara put a knife to his throat. Said the only way he could have her was if he married her first."

Wilek chuckled. "I like that."

"Yes, well, Sâr Janek didn't. He kept after her, but my girl was always armed with an array of daggers that left the sâr with several scars." He touched the tip of his nose.

Wilek snorted. "That liar! He told me he cut his nose replanting a thornberry bush."

"Yes, well, Rosârah Laviel was outraged that the daughter of a nomad had refused her son. She summoned me, ordered me to give my daughter to Sâr Janek as a mistress. I refused. The rosâr banished us that very day."

Typical. "Was your daughter upset?"

"She had no interest in the sâr. She'd been spying for me and had already learned what I needed to know. So we left and haven't returned."

"Is your daughter here?" Wilek asked. "I'd like to congratulate the woman who got the best of Janek."

"Zahara captains a ship out of Tal. Bit of a pirate, I'm proud to say."

"Well, I insist you accompany me back to Castle Everton," Wilek said. "I will speak to my father about lifting your banishment."

"That's good of you, Wil." Rand picked up another twig and pitched it into the fire. "Also, I'm not one to fret, but my mother senses something with the land. She's got the women all stirred up. This is the first time in decades I don't know what to do. Would you alert me if you learn anything?"

Wilek wished he had an answer about these strange disasters. "The moment I learn anything, you shall know it."

Wilek finally went to his tent and bedded down for the night, but he tossed and turned, plagued with dreams about Charlon, her voice and smell, her deep eyes and soft skin. And wanting to kill Torol. Long after the distant night bells rang in Pixford, he was still wide awake.

The moment he was back at Castle Everton, he would send a squadron of King's Guards to scour the Five Realms until they found a mantic willing to reverse the soul-binding spell. There had to be someone willing to *"tamper with the spell of a great shadir."*

Trevn

Trevn woke to Beal, who brought news of Wilek. Word had come that very morning that he had been found! The First Arm, the Dutiful, was on his way back to Everton. It would be another day or two before the full contingent arrived, but Wilek was alive.

Trevn pulled the covers over his head and fought back tears of relief.

Once he had dressed and broken his fast, he went to Wilek's onesent, Dendrick, to express his joy over the news of his brother's return. Dendrick had come back shortly after they'd received word of Wilek's abduction, and while the rest of Wilek's men had continued searching for him, Dendrick had remained at Castle Everton, carrying out Wilek's orders to send aid to Farway.

"It's nearly morning bells, Your Highness," Cadoc said. "You must prepare for court."

"Spending time with your father this morning?" Dendrick asked.

"I am visiting the court of Rosârah Brelenah today," Trevn said, unwilling to let even Dendrick know of his plans until he had followed through.

"I must visit the armory," Dendrick said. "I'll walk you partway."

The three exited Dendrick's apartment and made their way down the hall. As they passed by the crossbar, Trevn glimpsed a soldier exiting one of the chambers: Father Tomek's old room, it looked like. Trevn backed up and took a closer look. Indeed. A soldier stood there, nervously looking at the floor as if that might keep him from being seen.

"You there!" Trevn yelled. "What are you doing?"

The soldier jumped to attention. Trevn jogged toward him. Cadoc and Dendrick's footsteps pattered behind. Filthy with ragged clothing, the soldier looked to have survived a harrowing journey.

"Novan Heln," Cadoc said. "You were with Sâr Wilek's party to Farway."

A thrill of hope blossomed in Trevn's chest. "Has Wilek returned?"

"No, Your Highness," Novan said. "Sâr Wilek sent Sir Kalenek and me on an errand while we were in Farway. I arrived alone this morning with a message for the sâr, only to hear from the stableman about his misfortune."

Trevn tried not to let his disappointment show. "My brother will be home soon. Who is this message from? And why were you in Father Tomek's chambers?"

"I . . ." Novan took a deep breath. "The message is from Sir Kalenek Veroth. He bid me show it to no one but Sâr Wilek, Father Tomek, or Dendrick." Novan met the onesent's gaze.

Dendrick blinked, glanced at Sâr Trevn. "With your permission, Your Highness?"

"I insist you read the message this instant," Trevn told Novan.

The soldier seemed to shrink. "Perhaps we could go somewhere private?" he asked Dendrick.

Of all the insolent things the man could have said. Trevn's eyes widened, and he glared so harshly that the soldier looked away. "Pretend Cadoc and I aren't here, Guardsman Heln, if that helps you," Trevn said with as much authority as he could muster. "We will not intrude, nor will we depart until Dendrick assures me all is well with my brother."

Novan opened his mouth . . . closed it. He removed a battered scroll from his pocket, glanced at Trevn again, then held it out to Dendrick.

Trevn wanted to strangle the man.

Dendrick took the scroll between thumb and forefinger. "The seal is broken," he said.

"Yes." Novan swallowed. "I was waylaid by thieves outside Batira. Sir Kalenek wrote the message in code, however, and my captors were unable to read it. The cipher is *pilaster*."

Cipher? "You were taken captive?" Trevn asked, forgetting his promise not to intrude. "Who held you?"

"A Sarikarian ranchman."

"By himself?" Cadoc asked, smiling.

"Oh, no. He had a wife and three unmarried daughters to help. He wanted me to stay and work his farm."

Cadoc snorted a small laugh. "And marry a daughter, no doubt. Lucky you got away when you did."

"I was, indeed," Novan said.

Trevn watched Dendrick, who was frowning. "Well?" he prodded.

"It will take time to decode this." Dendrick glanced at Novan. "You know what this says?"

"I have a general idea, sir. I'm to act as a witness to the events described within."

"You can trust Cadoc," Dendrick said. "Sâr Trevn as well."

"As well?" Trevn was tempted to snatch the scroll and decode it himself. "Why am I an afterthought?"

"I meant no disrespect, Your Highness," Dendrick said. "Clearly this guardsman has been through an incredible ordeal. I only wish to reassure him he has not failed his orders."

Chastised, Trevn shrugged one shoulder. "Do continue."

"I shall decode this." Dendrick lifted the scroll. "But there is no reason Master Heln cannot tell us his tale first. Let us hear it in Father Tomek's chambers." He pushed in the door, and they all went inside.

Trevn was afraid.

He didn't like being afraid.

That Janek might be conspiring against Wilek . . . That his father might send a Knife to kill whomever he pleased . . . How Sir Kalenek's warning so eerily echoed Father Tomek and Barek Hadar's talk of the end of the world . . . And the pale prophetess Sir Kalenek had not only discovered, but believed had prophesied the coming of the Five Woes . . .

Could she be the one from the prophecy? The Prophet that Barek and his companions were preparing for? And what was Trevn going to do with all he had learned?

For now, he could only proceed with *his* plan. He crossed the castle foyer, keeping out of the way of the builders who were repairing the broken pilasters. Dendrick and Cadoc walked on either side of him. Trevn missed Hinck's company. He needed a laugh, but unfortunately there was little to laugh about these days. At least Wilek was well and on his way home. Trevn had asked Dendrick to inform the gate guards that he was to be awakened the moment Wilek returned, no matter the hour.

Queen Brelenah's guards saw him coming. They were used to him now and opened the doors, likely assuming he had come to dance with Mielle.

He wished that were true.

Trevn passed into the courtyard and climbed the steps to the colonnade.

Some three dozen courtiers were present today, well over half of them women. Several honor maidens and matrons sat on pillows, talking to one another. A lutist played a rengia, and three couples were dancing before the queen. Mielle was one of them, dancing with Sir Kamran DanSâr, the youngest son of Father's first concubine.

Trevn hated him. He hated anyone who danced with Mielle.

None of that, now. He focused his attention on the queen and the task at hand.

He had trained every herald in the castle to stop announcing his arrival with the trumpet. Today he had to ask the man to play the hateful tune.

The herald looked confused but quickly obeyed. The sound of the horn halted the music and dancing and drew the gaze of everyone present. The silence was so complete, Trevn could hear a bee buzzing in the garden.

He disliked so many staring at him when he had an important task to accomplish. But this had to be done in public. That was the whole point.

Do your duty, Renegade.

"His Royal Highness, Trevn-Sâr Hadar, the Third Arm, the Curious," the herald said.

Trevn approached the wicker throne. People bowed in deference to his rank. Two of the queen's dogs charged, jumping and yipping at his legs. He stopped before the throne and tried to look brave despite how his insides felt like liquid leaking out the bottom of his boots.

His mother was going to be furious.

Mielle stood so close he had to force himself not to look her way. Since he outranked the queen, he did not bow but smiled, hoping to ease her confusion. "Your Highness," he said in a voice loud enough that all could hear. "I'm elated at the news that my brother Sâr Wilek is well and will soon be with us again."

The queen's concerned expression brightened. "As am I, Sâr Trevn."

Before she could set him dancing, he went on. "There are few men who have mentored me in such a way as my brother, your son," Trevn said. "He has given me much, and I wish to return the favor."

The queen's brows furrowed, and she tipped her head to the side. "How so?"

A deep breath. It seemed as though the silence was even greater than before. "In this time of uncertainty, I felt it would be opportune to voice my loyalty aloud." He knelt then, on one knee, as men did before being knightened. "Your Majesty, I pledge my loyalty and service to Wilek-Sâr Hadar, the First Arm, the Dutiful, and in doing so, I pledge my loyalty and service to you, should your ambitions remain constant with that of your son."

The queen's eyes glittered with moisture. She extended her hand. "Sâr Trevn, I accept your pledge gladly on behalf of my son and welcome you."

Relief filled Trevn at a task well done. She had accepted him. Let the people talk.

He rose and kissed her hand. The crowd murmured their approval. Some applauded.

"You have been gone from us for too long, Sâr Trevn," the queen said. "Miss Mielle has been without a satisfactory dancing partner." She glanced toward the dance floor. "Oh, do not mistake me, Sir Kamran, you are very charming. But I've always felt that your beard aged you too much to stand with Miss Mielle. You'll dance instead with Lady Duvelle." She waved Sir Kamran toward one of her older maids, and he obeyed. "Much better. Now, Sâr Trevn with Miss Mielle. Lutist? Something merry."

The lutist began a nevett. Trevn offered Mielle his hand. She quickly curtsied and placed her hand in his. Her touch sent tingles up his arm.

Trevn led her in the dance. The moves were constant. Not slow, but not terribly fast either, which enabled them to speak softly to one another.

"Why did you say those things to the queen?" Mielle asked.

"By announcing my loyalty to Wilek, I publicly stand against Janek."

Her intense gaze made him tremble. "I think you are incredibly brave."

Well, that was kind. "I certainly don't feel brave."

"Have you missed me?" she asked.

Desperately. Every moment. They held hands, and he turned her in a circle. "I would much rather climb into caves with you than stand in the way of a plot to murder my brother."

"What if they come after you?"

"I have Rosârah Brelenah's protection now. Her guards will watch over me, as will my own."

The dance required a twirl, which ended with Mielle briefly in his arms.

"I'm still afraid," she whispered.

Afraid for Trevn's life. How would she feel if she knew the world might be ending? He hoped he would never have to ask her.

Trevn crawled into his bed, exhausted from the day. He didn't like being responsible. All in all, though, his plans seemed to have gone well. Queen Brelenah had been delighted with his oath, and he had greatly enjoyed the unexpected pleasure of spending time with Mielle again. It would likely be a few more days until Wilek returned. Trevn hoped he had startled the enemy long enough for Wilek to fix any harm Janek had caused.

Raised voices in the hall caught his attention. He pushed to one elbow and strained to hear. The guards were arguing with someone. His chamber door swung open.

"Please wait until morning, Rosârah," a guard said.

Mother. Of course. He had expected her sooner.

She charged to Trevn's bedside, a sheepish King's Guard in her wake. "How *dare* you!" she screamed.

"Dismissed," Trevn told the guard, who quickly exited the room and closed the door behind him.

"By my own son, my *only* son. Betrayed."

Trevn took a deep breath and sat up. "I did not betray you."

"How is pledging your service to the rosâr's first wife not a betrayal to his third wife?" She waved her hands. "He who brings trouble on his family will inherit the wind."

"I did it for Wilek."

She paced to the end of his bed and back. "Why? If he is crowned rosâr someday, then yes, pledge your service to him and his mother. But until then she is not Mother Rosârah and deserves no extra respect."

"My life is in danger. By voicing my support for Wilek as Heir, I garnered extra protection until his return."

Mother stopped her pacing. "What do you mean? How is your life in danger?"

Trevn swung his legs off the side of the bed. "A war is brewing. I had to choose a side."

"I have guards too. I can protect you."

She would never understand. "I am being watched. In pledging my service to Wilek, I showed them that I am not a child to be bribed or frightened. I am a sâr of Armania. And I will choose my own path."

She shook her meaty fist. "You will go to the king and take it back. Tell him you pledge allegiance to him alone. That you want no part of this war between your brothers. I am your mother. You *will* obey me."

He met her gaze. "Not in this."

Her eyes bulged with fury. "You are a man now, is that it? Well, there is a way that seems right to a man, but in the end it leads to death." She stomped to the door, wrenched it open, spun back. "Do you want to die?"

"My mind is set."

"I always knew you would betray me." She left, slamming the door behind her.

The walls shook. *Sands!* Was that her, raging down the hallway?

Glass shattered in the distance. Someone yelled. The candlestick on Trevn's bedside table rattled to the edge. He caught it just before it fell.

No, this was an earthquake.

He sat still, feeling the motion, wondering how it worked. Was the ground caving in far below the surface? Was it the river holes? Coal mines? Harvested evenroot tunnels? A combination of all?

He noted that this shaker moved differently from the last. It rattled rather than rocked. And still going! He had never felt such a long one.

A crash. Stone rumbled, loud and long, worse than thunder. The floor rattled with the impact. In the distance Mother screamed.

Trevn jumped out of bed and ran into the hallway. Dust filled the air. He pulled his tunic over his nose and squinted, trying to understand what he was looking at. The shaking had stopped. He crept along, reached the hallcross, and turned right, toward the crossbar of the castle's A shape.

The crossbar had been ripped away entirely. Ahead on the left, he could see down into the queen's garden. On the right, the front steps to the castle and the fountain of the Rôb Five were visible. Where had all the bedchambers gone? The walls?

He edged toward the broken floor. Three guards were crouched by the jagged edge that had once been part of the hallway. His mother was hanging over the side, gripping the ledge with both hands, sobbing and screaming. The guards were trying to pull her up. Fear spiked through Trevn, and he lunged toward her, wanting to help. Beyond her—below—nothing but dust and darkness.

Cadoc caught hold of him. "Let's keep you back, Your Highness. They'll get her."

Trevn's mind raced, trying to figure out if he knew anyone who resided in the crossbar of the castle. Hinck was on the fourth floor of the west wing. Princess Nabelle's apartment was on the fourth floor of the east wing. Of those he knew, only Father Tomek had lived in the cross.

"Get me up!" Mother screamed. "Get me up right now, you fools!"

"Be calm, Mother," Trevn said. "All will be well." Though how could it be? Their world was dying.

"Trevn! Tell these pathetic guards to pull me up this instant!"

"Make haste, men," Trevn said, wincing as the three struggled to drag his overweight mother up onto the floor.

When they finally got her on her feet, she smothered Trevn in a hug. "Oh, my son! Praise Mikreh you are alive!"

"You as well, Mother." Trevn hugged her back, truly thankful she was well. He pulled her aside and tried to make peace. "I am not afraid of Janek."

"You should be."

"No, Mother. I must do what I feel is right."

"You're too young to know what you're doing."

Trevn lowered his voice. "Listen to me, and listen well. I am no fool. I have thought this through. Mother, I want you to be part of my life. But it is my life, and you must let me rule it. If you take that from me again, if you continue to berate my every choice, I will renounce you. Do you understand?"

Her eyes went wide and her bottom lip trembled. "Why are you doing this?"

"Because I must. Do you want Janek as rosâr?"

Her watery eyes went hard. "You know perfectly well I do not!" A moment of silence passed, and she began to weep. "But he is too strong to stand against."

Fear again. Always afraid. "I disagree. So trust me, Mother. I am asking you to trust me."

A sniffle. "Very well, my son. I will trust you."

Though she looked unhappy, Trevn realized that she truly cared for him. Perhaps, in time, his mother would become an ally instead of an adversary.

The dust had settled some, though it was difficult to see the extent of the damage in the darkness. From the chasm came a commotion of voices and screams. Trevn felt helpless, but he could do nothing until he saw his mother to safety.

But was there any place safe in all Armania?

"Sâr Janek said you have sided against him," Hinck said. "Said it's his fault he lost your loyalty. That he neglected you for too long. Should have put in more effort."

"More?" Trevn asked. "What does the man consider effort, I wonder? I cannot see that he ever put in any."

"Mocking you takes great effort, of course," Hinck said.

"I suppose." They were sitting by the fire in Trevn's tent. The King's Guard had set up a small village of military tents in the Rosâr's Garden behind the castle. No one was permitted inside until the master builders could conduct an examination in daylight. So far it seemed that the earthquake had felled the entire east wing of the castle, the crossbar, and part of the inner west wing connected to it.

"Janek told me to watch you close, to tell him all you say and do," Hinck said. "This is my second test, and I'm not to fail him."

Wonderful. "This earthquake has overshadowed my fealty to Wilek," Trevn said. "Father has commanded we all go to Canden, where he can sacrifice the wounded to Barthos. He thinks Barthos meant to kill all who are injured—that they were disloyal to the god of the soil. Since Janek and Laviel's rooms were also destroyed, I suggested that perhaps Barthos meant to kill them. Father did not find that amusing, nor did Rogedoth, who jumped in to tell my father that Barthos had made sure Janek and his mother were at Seacrest before he took out his vengeance on those in the castle."

"Wasn't Princess Nabelle staying on the east wing?"

"Yes, but Cadoc learned from some guards that she left after the queen's court this midday, angry, it seems, that Miss Mielle danced so long with me. My appearance in Brelenah's court today likely saved all their lives."

They sat in silence. Trevn couldn't stop thinking about how Mielle might have died tonight. One doomsday theory, he could easily ignore. But all of them together, matching the ancient tablets, affirmed by men he respected . . . It left him with but one choice.

"So, to Canden," Hinck said.

"You, yes. But not me."

"What does *that* mean?"

"Father has commanded I go to Canden, but I must wait for Wilek. So I will defy the king."

"You're insane," Hinck said.

He was. He would likely face the pole for ignoring his father's command. Unless the Five Woes culminated before then. "I plan to ask my mother's help. Send her to me."

Hinck stared at him. "Beyond insane."

Trevn simply waited for Hinck to obey. His friend eventually got up and walked toward the exit.

"Hinck," Trevn said. "Be careful."

"Yeah," Hinck said. "You too."

KALENEK

A rotten breeze wafted over Kal. Something wet and rough brushed his face. He opened his eyes to rank and matted white fur. A camel's neck. The animal nipped at his hipsack.

Kal patted the camel and laughed. "Caught up with us, did you, girl?" He dug half a carrot from his hipsack and fed it to her. "That's all I have, so don't ask for—"

The wagon trembled. The camel brayed and spun in a circle.

"Take it easy," Kal called after her. "This barely counts as an earthquake." He sat still until the shaking stopped. Everyone else was still sleeping. Kal stood, stretched, and carefully climbed over the side of the wagon. His boots squished into goopy mud. A quick inspection showed that a mud drift had buried the back bottom half of the wagon. They would have to dig it out before they could replace the wheels.

Grayson stood, hair frizzing out like a sticky snare. "What's to eat?"

"Mud." Kal turned and took stock of their surroundings. Mud and more mud. No sign of the other animals. The camel nibbled on some limp desert plant. Kal searched through his grow lens but saw no sign of civilization. He had no idea where they were.

"Are you the mantic?" Grayson asked.

"I am Priestess Jazlyn, Sixth Great Lady of Tenma," a woman answered.

Kal spun back to the wagon and regarded Grayson and the woman, who looked no more than eighteen. She was all eyes and mouth and curves and coils of the blackest hair. Still wearing her filthy white gown and diadem.

Kal shivered. The mantic had successfully purged, which meant her shadir was nearby, whether Kal could see it or not. He didn't want the creature here, yet he'd like to ask the woman about Wilek's rune. First and foremost, however, he needed to keep Onika and Grayson out of the woman's sight.

"Grayson," he said. "Get down here and help me with this mud."

"Sure thing, Sir Kalenek." The boy scrambled over the side.

Kal was pleased to see the priestess lie back down. He set about digging the mud drift away from the wheel. He had no shovel and had to stab the mud with his sword to loosen it, then Grayson dug it aside with his hands.

Eventually, Ulrik joined in. Jhorn climbed out and tried to help, but the soft mud made it difficult for him to move on his canes.

Inolah awoke and started work on the other side of the wagon. "Why not harness the camel and see if she can pull us out?" she asked.

"The pulling points on the harness are in the wrong places," Jhorn said. "Mules pull from their chests. Camels pull from their shoulders and hump. I suppose I could try to rebuild it."

"Can you help us, Priestess Jazlyn?" Ulrik asked the mantic.

"I have no evenroot," she said. "My magic is gone until I locate more. The empress promised to take me to the evenroot mill in the Open Quarter in payment for my rescue. I have kept my side of the bargain."

"I am sorry, Priestess," Inolah said. "I suspect we could find some root in Nindera."

"How far is that?" the mantic asked.

"A seven-day journey from Lâhaten," Inolah said. "Though I cannot say how far we traveled already, or if we even went in the right direction."

Kal suspected the torrent had carried them north and that they were closer to Jeruka than Nindera, but he kept his theory to himself. He would tell Inolah later but had no desire to help the mantic regain her power.

"If the boy mantic would share, my shadir could fly me and my eunuch home to Yobatha."

"Me?" Grayson's eyebrows shot up into his hairline. "I'm no mantic."

"Your skin shows signs of needing to purge."

"It's a birth rash," Jhorn said. "The boy takes no evenroot."

Her eyes narrowed. "That is impossible."

"Give me a sip from your water bag, Jhorn," Kal said. "It's already starting to get hot."

Jhorn vaulted in front of the priestess, blocking her view of Grayson. He handed Kal the water bag.

Kal took his time drinking and glanced at the place Onika rested, relieved the blind woman had kept herself under the blankets so far.

"Burk isn't helping," Grayson said, glaring into the wagon.

Sure enough, the young thief was still asleep, curled into a ball near Priestess Jazlyn's feet. Kal reached in and poked Burk's backside with the point of his sword. "Get up, Burk! And, Nolah, you get back in the wagon and rest."

"I know what I can handle and what I cannot," she said, taking a stab with her sword.

"You speak too informally to the empress, Sir Kalenek," Prince Ulrik said and went around to join his mother.

Kal supposed he had. He was about to apologize when Burk leapt to the wet sand beside him. The ground shifted. The wagon lurched.

"Nobody move!" Kal held his breath. He scanned the ground, looking for moving earth, but all was still.

Until the camel jogged up to them and the dirt beneath Kal's feet crumbled.

Arms flailing, feet pedaling, he searched for anything solid. The remains of Farway flashed in his memory. They'd be buried alive!

Voices cried out as they sank. Grayson tumbled over the side of the wagon, which was now beneath Kal's feet. They weren't falling fast—at the speed of a walk. All around him, dirt poured, silently, deadly. The light faded as they fell deeper. He couldn't see the others now. Nothing but dirt. It churned around him, cool and moist and heavy.

Then he stopped.

His head was uncovered; he could still see sky above. He heard the camel braying, heard Grayson yelling for help, heard someone screaming. A man.

Kal's body was packed in strangely, arms lifted out to his sides, knees bent—one leg forward, one back, as if frozen midleap. He tried to move. Couldn't. Panic seized him, and he strained to thrash his arms and legs. His right arm shifted. More dirt fell around it.

He paused, waited, tried to relax. A deep breath brought granules of sand into his nose and mouth. He took shorter breaths. Listened for the others.

"My legs! My legs hurt!" This from Ferro.

"I'm coming, Ferro. I see you." Inolah.

"We must lift the wagon." Ulrik.

"I can't breathe!" Burk, somewhere behind Kal.

"If you can talk, you can breathe." Jhorn.

"Qoatch?" Jazlyn yelled. "We must push the dirt away from the sides of the wagon so we can see where we are."

"We're in a hole, Priestess," Jhorn said.

"Qoatch?" Jazlyn called again.

"I am here, Great Lady," Qoatch said weakly. "I am injured."

"There's a tunnel," Grayson said. "I'm going to see where it goes. Come on, camel."

The camel brayed.

"I can't move!" Burk yelled.

Ferro continued to scream about his legs. Inolah and Ulrik worked to free him. Jazlyn questioned Qoatch, who couldn't feel his body at all. Kal did not hear Onika, though Rustian was growling nearby.

Kal put all his effort into his right arm. He wiggled it until more dirt fell. The dune cat hissed, and Kal felt sharp claws against his wrist. More sand fell away, freeing his right shoulder. Kal saw the wagon below and Rustian sliding toward it on his side, hind end flailing. Kal was trapped above the wagon, legs buried in dirt that sloped sharply up to the fall-in's edge. The wagon was mostly uncovered. Jhorn and Onika were inside, as were their supplies. Kal watched Rustian glide down the drift and flop over the wagon's side. He righted himself and stretched. In the distance, far past the fall-in, Kal could see Grayson holding a lantern, leading the camel into a tunnel. Fool boy had better take care.

A flash of dark hair on the other side of the wagon and Ulrik lifted Ferro into his arms. The boy was screaming. Inolah popped up beside them. She pulled the crumpled tent from the wagon, and they moved down the tunnel, the way Grayson had gone. Kal still could not see Jazlyn, Qoatch, or Burk.

He dug with his right arm until his right leg was free; then he dug out his left shoulder, which enabled him to free his left arm. The sand around him shifted suddenly, and he slid fast toward the wagon with a pile of sand, everything crashing in a wave over the wagon's edge.

Jhorn cried out in dismay and brushed the dirt off Onika's face.

"Sorry," Kal said, recovering. "Are you both well?"

"We are fine," Jhorn said. "Prince Ferro broke his leg."

"Help me!" Burk yelled.

Kal looked up. Just behind where he had been, Burk was sticking out of the sand from the waist up.

"Hold still, Burk." Kal had brought down a lot of sand with him. He didn't want Burk to bury Onika and Jhorn completely. He did not see the mantic. "Priestess?"

"Here." She stood near the front end. "My eunuch is pinned under the wagon. I must find evenroot to free him."

Mantics were useless without their root. "Go look if you like," Kal said. "But I say we pull him out now before the landslide buries him forever."

The woman stared, as if weighing Kal's worth. He didn't wait for her judgment. He rooted around for the mule harnesses and the tangle of tack and dragged it away from the landslide. He needed the camel.

"Grayson!" Kal yelled into the tunnel. "Come on back!" He set about hauling supplies from the wagon in case it got buried. He found all four wheels and moved them. He lifted Onika from the wagon and helped her sit beside Inolah and her boys. He backsacked Jhorn there as well.

"See if you can make these harnesses fit the camel," Kal told Jhorn.

A scream brought Burk down in a gust of dirt that filled the wagon. Kal waited for the dust to settle. He found Burk's foot sticking out of the sand and yanked. The boy slid out from the mound of dirt and onto the ground.

"Argh!" Burk cried. "You hurt my ankle!"

"I'll hurt more than that if you don't start listening," Kal said. "I told you to wait."

"I couldn't help it."

"Get up and help me with the eunuch." Kal glanced back to the others. "Prince Ulrik? I could use your assistance as well."

Burk whined about his ankle and did little to help, but Kal and Ulrik managed to lift the exposed side of the wagon enough for Jazlyn to pull out her servant. His breathing was labored and shallow. When they lowered the wagon again, more dirt slid down upon them. Kal and Ulrik carried Qoatch to the others. Grayson had returned with the camel and Jhorn's lantern in hand.

"The tunnel just keeps going," Grayson said. "I saw a bunch of dead newts. At least twenty."

"Letaha," Jazlyn said. "Did you see any living?"

Grayson shook his head. "Only dead ones. Why?"

"Letaha live on evenroot. Was there any?"

"No, ma'am. Plenty of root holes, but all the tubers had been harvested." Kal sought Onika's gaze. Her face was turned toward his, covered in so much dirt she looked like one of them. He walked to her and whispered, "Onika, are we to take the tunnel?"

"It is the quickest way to the sea," she replied, her words warming him.

Good enough for Kal. He turned back toward the others. "If we can harness the camel, she can pull the wagon out of there. Then we can see where this tunnel leads."

"The tunnel?" Ulrik cried. "We should climb back up. It's far safer to travel on land where it might fall beneath our feet than underground where it might fall down upon our heads."

"The wall is too soft to climb," Kal said. "It will bury us." He examined the ground. The tunnel was old, its walls packed and dry, yet there were fresh footsteps on the ground that were not their own. "Someone else has used this tunnel recently. There is likely a way out."

"It leads to Jeruka," Ulrik said. "This is one of my father's evenroot shafts."

"The emperor was harvesting evenroot?" Jazlyn asked.

"He wanted to keep it from Tenma," Ulrik said.

"Give me the lantern," Jazlyn said. "I must find some root to heal my eunuch and the boy prince. I don't need much. Some broken tails will do."

Ulrik took the lantern from Grayson and carried it to her side. "I'll go with you."

Kal watched them leave. When they were out of earshot, he said to Inolah, "He sure changes his mind quickly when that woman speaks."

"He admires her," Inolah said.

"One should not engage with a worshiper of demons," Jhorn said. "If she finds her poison, do not let her use her dark magic on your son."

"But he is in pain," Inolah said.

"Pain will fade in time," Jhorn said. "A soul is not so easily won back from Gâzar."

"He cannot lose his soul when magic is forced upon him," Onika said. "Only when he gives his soul freely can it be lost."

"Being healed will open his mind to favor the demon magic," Jhorn said. "It's too risky."

"So is death," Onika said, "when a soul has not found the God."

Time to change the subject. "How is that harness coming along?" Kal asked.

"See if this will fit around the camel." Jhorn held up the two harnesses, which he had lashed together into one.

Kal used his knife to cut up the tent for padding. He tore a spare kasah into strips and lashed the harness to the folded tent to keep it from slipping. He and Ulrik removed the camel's saddlebag and set the padding and harness over her shoulders.

"Ready to help pull, girl?" Kal asked.

The camel brayed and nipped at the harness. Kal hooked her to the wagon, but she wouldn't pull. Kal tried getting excited, he tried begging, he tried yelling. It wasn't until Grayson dangled a carrot before the camel's nose that it moved.

"I thought those were gone," Kal said.

"In her saddlebag," the boy said.

It was hard work for the camel. Kal and Ulrik had to dig out most of the dirt before the wagon even budged. Finally it broke free from its dirt prison and scraped along the tunnel ground.

A cheer rose up even as more dirt crumbled down, but they were now able to clean out the wagon and replace the wheels. Two were on by the time Jazlyn and Ulrik returned triumphant. The priestess held what looked like a tangle of hair in her fist. These turned out to be evenroot tails that had broken off from harvested root.

She set to work grinding them while Kal and Jhorn replaced the last two wheels. They had just finished when an argument began. Inolah stood above Ferro, in front of Ulrik, Jazlyn, and Qoatch, who now stood perfectly healthy at his Great Lady's side.

"Mother, don't be foolish," Ulrik said.

"Ferro is my son. I decide."

"But she can stop the pain," Ulrik said.

Kal shivered, his memory flashing back to the war, to the torture. They would heal his scars if he confessed all he knew. They would stop the pain.

"I am emperor now," Ulrik told his mother. "Let the priestess help."

"You are *not* emperor," Inolah said. "Not until you have been crowned. The empress rules Rurekau until then. And I will not have my son healed with the black magic that killed his father. My decision is final."

"I thought you to be an intelligent woman, Empress," Jazlyn said.

"I will hear no more on this matter." Inolah turned her back on them and crouched at Ferro's side.

"I'll take some healing on my ankle," Burk said, limping toward the priestess, who murmured one word and declared him well.

Kal splinted Prince Ferro's leg with a spare trace from the remains of the second mule harness, then he helped Jhorn, Onika, Inolah, and Ferro into the wagon. The others would go on foot to ease the burden on the camel.

"But my ankle," Burk said.

"He can walk," the mantic told Kal, and his resolve to hate her crumbled a bit.

Kal led the camel forward. Ulrik still held the lantern. Jhorn kept a second, smaller lantern in the wagon. The low light was just enough to see by.

Grayson walked on Kal's left. The boy remained silent, casting fearful looks toward the mantic. Kal would have to ask the boy why he suddenly feared her.

Every few steps they passed holes or side tunnels that branched off the main route. Dead newts lay in the empty root holes. Some shafts were tall enough for Kal to stand in.

"Does evenroot truly get this big?" he asked the mantic.

"Even bigger," she said. "Under Tenma, some root grow as high as three men and hundreds of leagues long."

No wonder there were so many Tennish mantics.

"Yet the tunnels under my home are much like this," Jazlyn said. "Empty. We have harvested root for centuries, and there is little left. We grow it fresh each season, but it takes much longer to grow than it does to harvest. As a result we train fewer mantics each year."

Kal thanked the gods for that.

"Have you thought of harvesting elsewhere?" Ulrik asked.

"The other realms are unwilling to help," the mantic said. "They fear our magic and refuse to aid us in our quest to continue the art. We once had a trade agreement with Sarikar to harvest in the scablands, but they sold their harvesting rights to Magonia. Our sisters in the south will not share root with us and waste it on unnecessary rituals. Emperor Nazer refused to discuss our harvesting Rurekan root. Now I know why."

Kal had no response to this. He tried to mentally calculate how many days it might take them to walk to Jeruka. If they were traveling in a straight line, it might be fifty leagues, more or less. If they were going to make better time, they needed to get to the surface. There had to be a way.

WILEK

Wilek traveled with the Omatta and the Armanian guard along the rocky coast of the Four Fingers and over the Cobweb Bridges. Two more days to reach Everton. To the west the Eversea looked still, yet far below the bridge, raucous waves crashed against the cliffs. Wilek admired the beauty of his homeland, the way the river holes expelled water from the cliff walls like fountains from the deep.

Throughout the day he counted nine ships sailing south. It seemed a lot for this time of year, too early for harvest. He would have to ask his father about it when he reached the castle.

Sometime after they stopped for a midday repast, they met a group of pilgrims from Armania. Wilek sent Harton to question them. The news he brought back was dire.

"They flee Everton," Harton said. "An earthquake destroyed the castle. The rosâr has gone to Canden."

Dread clogged Wilek's throat. He felt Charlon's distant concern rise up in response to his emotions. "The king evacuated the city?"

"Not officially," Harton said. "Left it up to the people whether to stay or go. Apparently your mother remained behind with the Mother Rosârah to await your return."

Unsurprising. "Deaths?"

"One said hundreds died in the castle fall-in. Another said Mikreh spared the rosâr's family. Who can say for certain until we see for ourselves?"

"Indeed." But the report that Mother and Gran had stayed behind gave Wilek hope that they, at least, were well.

As they continued north, they passed many more refugees from Everton. All carried different versions of the same story. The only facts that matched were that some portion of Castle Everton had suffered damage in the earthquake and that the rosâr had fled to Canden.

Every bridge their party crossed put Wilek's senses on high alert. The Cobweb Bridges had always been rickety. Now he felt certain one could break any moment, dropping him and his men into the ravine where the Eversea would swallow them whole.

By the time they met solid ground again, twilight had fallen. There, on the south side of the final bridge, they came to an Armanian encampment.

"Ah," Rand said. "Here is the man who will fill my coffers."

Wilek instantly recognized the tall Queen's Guard standing by the road.

Rayim Veralla was staring at their party, searching, Wilek supposed, for him. It was no surprise the man could not root out Wilek when he looked like a Magonian slav. He spurred his mount toward the captain.

Rayim's gaze shifted to Wilek. He frowned, cocked his head to the side. "That you, my boy?"

Wilek forced a confident smile. "Yes, Rayim. I've come home at last."

"By the gods, the sight of you brings me joy. What's happened to your hair?"

"A long story. Mother is well?"

"She and all her dogs. She asked me to find you, so I hired Rand."

"What of Sir Kalenek?" Wilek asked. "I sent him on an errand in Farway. Has he returned?"

Rayim frowned. "He has not. Where did you send him?"

Wilek's heart sank, and when he didn't answer, Rayim waved to him. "Come rest in my tent. We will camp here and cross Echo Crack in the morning."

Wilek dismounted and spotted Rand atop his horse a few paces behind. "Randmuir Khal of the Omatta has been banished from Everton. I wish to vouch for him and allow him and his tribe to enter the city without hindrance."

Rayim lit up in a smile. "Excellent, Your Highness." He nodded to Rand. "I knew you'd find him, old friend."

"Magonian witches done a number on him," Rand said, "but he's still breathing."

"Indeed he is. And he welcomed you back. I suspect you'll have no trouble as long as the rosâr, Sâr Janek, and Rosârah Laviel are away. They likely won't return soon."

"Is the castle destroyed?" Wilek asked.

"Not fully. The east wing and the crossbar collapsed along with a section of the inner west wing. The rest stands. There was a lot of damage in the city too. Hundreds of buildings down."

"Death toll?"

"Just under six hundred, last I heard."

Wilek's heart sank. "Trevn? The sârahs? The other rosârahs?"

"They are all well and have gone with the rosâr to Canden, except your mother, grandmother, and Sâr Trevn."

Trevn stayed behind? "Something happened to Trevn?"

"He is perfectly healthy, but there are some matters to discuss in private."

Wilek looked to Harton, who was still on his horse. "We'll camp here for the night. Have the men ready to leave at dawn."

"Yes, Your Highness," Harton said.

Wilek handed his reins to a young soldier and followed Rayim into a familiar blue military tent. It almost felt like home. Rayim had even brought some furniture.

Wilek settled onto a wicker longchair cushioned in blue velvet and released a deep breath, feeling truly safe for the first time in weeks. "Tell me of my brother."

"The very day we received word of your safety, Sâr Trevn visited your mother's court and swore fealty to you through her. He has attended the court of Rosârah Brelenah every day since, much to his mother's vexation."

"Did he give any reason for this sudden pledge of devotion?"

"Just that he was thankful you were alive and wanted to show his loyalty in these uncertain times."

A purposeful slight to Janek, perhaps? "Has Janek vexed him?"

"Not that I'm aware of, Your Highness, though the Earl of Dacre has been spending nearly every moment at Seacrest with Sâr Janek. For the past month, I'd guess."

"Hinckdan and Janek?" A ludicrous pairing.

"I thought the same, but it's true. I've investigated. And there's more. A message from Rosârah Thallah gave word to the others traveling to Canden that Sâr Trevn is ill and confined to her tent. The truth, of course, is he remained in Everton secretly. Your father might still be unaware that he is not among the Canden contingent."

"If Rosârah Thallah went to Canden, why did Trevn stay behind?"

"I know not, Your Highness. Such a deception is routine for Sâr Trevn, but I cannot guess why Rosârah Thallah would play along."

Trevn wanted everyone to believe he was headed to Canden. "What's he up to?"

"That, Your Highness, I would very much like to know. But his young lady friend left for Sarikar with your betrothed, so I cannot blame her for his actions."

"What young lady friend? Do you mean Miss Mielle?"

"The very girl. I caught them kissing in the garden once. And he danced his first with her at his ageday ball. Rosârah Thallah forbade their friendship, which likely only encouraged it to bloom. I am glad Princess Nabelle took the girl to Sarikar, for I feared he might soon fulfill his mother's dream of his siring the rosâr's first grandchild."

Janek had already done that several times over, illegitimately, of course. But Wilek wouldn't put it past his idealistic youngest brother to marry in secret. He sighed, but it felt good to be part of the drama of court life again. "I'll speak with him."

"Thank you, Your Highness. Sâr Trevn is a clever young man. He doesn't act without reason, even when he seeks to shock."

Wilek could attest to that.

"I fear someone has threatened him. Father Tomek died while you were away. Most mysteriously, I might add."

"No! What happened?"

"The physician declared it a natural death, though rumors of poison abound. His room had been ransacked—and a few days later Cadoc told me Sâr Trevn's chambers suffered the same fate."

"It does seem like a lot of trouble, even for Trevn. Though it could simply be more of his games."

"Perhaps," Rayim said. "But I sense it's something more."

Wilek couldn't help but agree.

The next day passed slowly. The procession set out before dawn, yet it was long after the night prayer bells when they finally reached the gates of Castle Everton.

It was too dark to see the damage. They entered through the west wing. While Wilek was eager to see his mother, grandmother, and brother, he didn't want to wake anyone, so he ordered a servant to have him roused at the dawn bells and went straight to bed.

The abduction almost seemed unreal now that he was home. He lay awake, wondering who might be numbered among the priests of Havôt and if they were the ones who wanted him dead. Were they here in Everton or with his father in Canden? And when they discovered Wilek had returned, would they attempt to kill him?

Kal had always slept with a dagger under his pillow, which, tonight, inspired Wilek to do the same.

Tomorrow. Wilek would find answers then.

Trevn

Sometime after night bells, Cadoc woke Trevn with word from the watch that Wilek had returned. Trevn sprinted to his brother's chambers, but the guards refused him entry. Trevn didn't care. He had waited long enough.

He returned to his bedchamber, climbed out his balcony, and scaled the wall. It occurred to him that he should have told Cadoc his plans. He should also tell Captain Veralla and Captain Alpress how easily he could sneak into the royal bedchambers. He was loath to give up his secret, but if he could do it, so could an assassin.

Trevn slipped over Wilek's balcony and heard groaning. He froze, hoping he wasn't interrupting his brother with some woman. But then he heard a snore, a body shift on the bed.

He crept inside and opened the fireplace to light a candle, then used the candle to light a lantern. A pale yellow glow lit the room.

Trevn stepped up to the bed. Wilek thrashed back and forth and moaned. The way the bedsheets had twisted around his body made him look like a corpse wrapped for shipping.

"Wilek?"

"No!" Wilek yelled. "Leave me be."

But Trevn could not. He had waited so long. "I must talk with you."

"Release me from this spell, witch. Release me!"

Oh, he was dreaming. "Wilek," Trevn said louder. He hung the lantern on the hook above the bed, reached out, and shook Wilek's shoulder.

Wilek grabbed his arm just above the elbow and pulled him close, eyes open. His free hand drew a dagger from under his pillow and held it to Trevn's throat. The blade scraped over his skin.

"Stop!" Trevn tried to pull away. "It's Trevn. Your brother."

"Liar!" Wilek's eyes were wild. He was bone thin, had cropped his hair short, and wore a scruffy beard covering his cheeks and chin. "I told the guards to let no one pass, yet here you are, wearing Trevn's skin. Have you captured him? Cut his locks?"

Trevn had never been so terrified, not even when Father Tomek had died in his presence. Had Wilek gone mad? "I scaled the wall and came through your balcony."

Wilek's brow pinched. "All the way to the fifth floor?"

"It's not terribly difficult. The stone bricks are filled with cracks that make great handholds."

Wilek lowered the knife but kept his grip on Trevn's arm. "Trevn?"

"Yes! It's me, I swear it!"

"Tell me something only you would know. What was served at dinner the night Lebetta died? When we ate with Lady Zeroah and her honor maiden."

Dinner? "I-I don't remember."

Wilek shook him. "You *are* Charlon!"

Who? Trevn forced his thoughts back to that night. "Um . . . I, uh, don't recall what we ate. Mielle wore an orange dress with black beads and a white sash. She had little orange flowers in her hair." It came to him suddenly. "We had carrot soup. I remember thinking it matched her dress. And whitefish."

Wilek let go.

Trevn backed up a safe distance, touched his stinging throat; a dab of blood came away. *Five Woes.* "Wh-who is Charlon?"

Wilek grunted. "It's no matter. Someone in Everton wants me dead, but who?"

Trevn had several guesses. "Janek's supporters. They want him on the throne. He's been helping Father in your absence."

Wilek climbed from the bed and walked onto the balcony, skin tight on his bones. He looked over the edge, then turned and peered up to the roof. "No rope. Did you come from above or below?"

"From the side. I free-climb. Wilek, are you listening? It's urgent I speak with you."

Wilek came back inside. "I gather it must be urgent if you are sneaking into my chambers like some kind of Knife."

430

"It couldn't wait, not even until dawn. Besides, I thought you wanted to know who killed Lady Lebetta."

Wilek frowned. "Her murder was solved?"

"Not solved," Trevn said, "but I have a theory."

Wilek sat on the edge of his bed. "Forgive me, brother. I am not myself. Being held prisoner . . . it has made me overly cautious. Please, sit and say what you must."

Trevn claimed a footstool and the words spilled forth. "Eudora had a stone etched with the same rune Lady Lebetta had drawn in blood. So I sent Hinck to befriend Janek and try to find out why. Hinck thinks it's a secret circle. He has received visits from hooded men, telling him an invitation is coming."

"That's . . . bizarre."

"Yes, well, Father Tomek said the runes Lady Lebetta drew come from a cult started by Prince Mergest III—the very cult that lost him the throne of Sarikar to his brother, Jorger. Hinck also learned that Eudora supports Janek for Heir. My guess is their group will make a move now that they have Father cloistered in Canden. Then there's the information in Sir Kalenek's message."

Wilek perked up. "Kal sent word?"

"Through his backman. He found no translation for the rune except that one of the symbols was the mark of a Knife. Sir Kalenek thinks Father had Lady Lebetta killed, but I think this secret circle is involved. Eudora's stone had no Knife symbol upon it."

"The priests of Havôt," Wilek said.

The familiar word stopped Trevn. "Who?"

"The men who rule Armania in secret. An old mantic woman told me the rune is their mark. The upside-down Knife symbol is their way of making a command outside the king's authority."

"*Havôt* means great shadir in ancient Armanian. Prince Mergest's cult is called *Lahavôtesh*, which means followers of the great shadir. I read about it in a scroll Father Tomek left me. I bet they are one and the same."

"A mantic cult in Armania," Wilek said. "Who would be part of it?"

"Rogedoth," Trevn said. "He is really Prince Mergest III."

"What?" Wilek roared. "Father Tomek discovered this?"

Relief washed over Trevn to finally be getting this all out. "No. Father Tomek is a whole different problem. I saw a painting of the young Prince Mergest III at the Duke of Odarka's home. I recognized Rogedoth right away.

Hinck believes Rogedoth is Janek's father—*that* I'm not convinced of. But Rogedoth—or Prince Mergest—has been killing Armanite priests for years. I think he killed Father Tomek to destroy what they believed was the last copy of the Book of Arman, but I copied it in my lessons, and now they're watching me. Father Tomek said to show you the Book of Arman when it was safe. He hoped you'd read it."

"Slow down, brother. What does the book say that is so offensive?"

"I confess, I never paid attention. Just copied the words. But I've begun to read it again. So far it says that Arman is the Only God. Any other deity is false—black spirits that want to consume us. They feed off our souls when we make offerings. To pledge our lives to them gives them control over us. Any time a spirit creates a false god, it creates trouble for Arman."

"To fully worship a shadir, one needs evenroot," Wilek said.

"Really?" That made so much sense. "Miss Mielle and I uncovered an evenroot harvesting yard in the city. They were using orphans to process the root. I bet Rogedoth is behind it."

Wilek stood, eyes raging. "I will not let mantics rule this realm."

"There's one more thing," Trevn said, nearly breathless with the excitement of finally confessing all to Wilek. "Sir Kalenek found a woman in Magonia. A true prophet, he says. He is bringing her here. She foretells that only by sea will anyone survive what's to come. Her words match a prophecy Father Tomek left for me. The Five Woes."

"The doomsday prophecy the Athosians preach?"

"Every faith has a version of the Five Woes prophecy. I think it's upon us, Wil, and I'm not the only one. I know that sounds crazy. I didn't want to believe it at first. Still don't. But our land is dying. I think we destroyed it—the priests, the mantics, the smugglers. Our greed took too much. We must leave if we are to survive."

"Where is this message from Kal?"

"Dendrick has it. You should hear Novan Heln's report as well. It's most convincing. He saw the destruction of Kaptar and says Hebron and Ebro are gone as well."

Wilek seemed to shrink under that news. "Let us go to Dendrick now. I'll find no sleep tonight." He started for the door.

Trevn jumped up and followed. "I haven't found sleep for weeks."

Wilek gripped Trevn's shoulder. "I'm glad you woke me, brother. You've done well."

Wilek's words were a balm on Trevn's overwhelmed soul. He had to look away to maintain his composure.

The First Arm had returned. All would be well now.

Trevn assisted Wilek all day. After Wilek read Sir Kalenek's message and Father Tomek's research on the Lahavôtesh, he had three separate interviews with Novan Heln. Trevn brought all the versions of the Five Woes and Root prophecies from his secret room so that Wilek could compare them with Heln's story and Dendrick's translation of Sir Kalenek's scroll.

Trevn wanted to send soldiers to Canden to arrest Pontiff Rogedoth, Yohthehreth, and Lau for the murder of Father Tomek, and he told Wilek as much.

"I cannot arrest them without proof of some crime," Wilek said, then explained his plan to travel to Canden with Teaka and her newt and let the creature seek out evenroot. "If I find root in their chambers, I can arrest them for that, to start."

"Clever," Trevn said, happy to know that the men would be arrested soon.

"I need to confirm or deny this theory of Rogedoth being Janek's father. Perhaps Teaka could ask her shadir to find out?"

The idea left Trevn queasy. "You would solicit the service of a mantic?"

"Worry not. Teaka is a good mantic."

"Black spirits are never good—so said Father Tomek."

"Teaka will speak with them, not me. I know of no other way to discover the truth."

Before Trevn could argue further, Rosârah Brelenah and Gran came to visit Wilek for first sleep, a half dozen dogs with them. That was the only time Trevn was apart from Wilek all day and one of the first times he had ever slept during first sleep.

Cadoc woke him with a summons from Wilek. Trevn ran to his brother's chambers, ready to tell Wilek about Barek's Nahtan group that was working on the evacuation, but this time it wasn't the Five Woes that Wilek wanted to discuss.

"I heard you have been spending much time with Miss Mielle Allard."

Trevn's cheeks burned, but he grinned. "I like her. She went to Sarikar with Princess Nabelle and Lady Zeroah. They believe the Woes are upon us and intend to convince King Jorger."

"My betrothed." Wilek frowned. "Lebetta and I were your age when we discovered each other, though that was different since she was given to me, and Miss Mielle has not been given to you. What is her age?"

Trevn slumped in his chair. "The years are wrong. But superstitions are asinine. Father forced me to sign a betrothal to Lady Zeroah while you were gone so that there would be peace with Sarikar in case you died. Only because I matched her in fives."

Wilek shrugged as if Trevn's confession meant nothing. "That's politics, Trevn. Politics tells me I must marry Lady Zeroah as soon as possible, despite the possibility that the end of the world might be upon us."

"Hinck says his parents aren't the same age and they do fine—most of the time. And Mielle said Sir Kalenek loved his wife very much and they weren't the same age."

"Yet she died. Horribly. Father would see that as Mikreh's doing."

"I want no one but Mielle." Trevn felt foolish. He sounded like a prince throwing a tantrum.

Wilek studied him, nodded. "I'll do what I can to help you, but first we must help our people."

Yes, that was far more important. "To Canden, then?"

"I will go to Canden. You will take a message to King Jorger in Sarikar."

Alone? "But I want to stay with you."

"There is too much at stake. You must accomplish three things. First, tell King Jorger that his son has become our Pontiff and is Janek's father."

Trevn's arm hair stood on end. "The witch told you that?"

"She did. And I believe her."

Trevn did not. "Why should we trust a black spirit? Father Tomek would never."

"I trust Teaka's judgement. And her answer matched Hinckdan's theory."

"Two theories do not equal proof."

"I am decided on this, Trevn. Second, bring Lady Zeroah back here. She and I must marry right away. And the third thing you must do is help Princess Nabelle and Lady Zeroah convince King Jorger to join the Nahtan."

Trevn frowned, confused. "You know about them? How?"

"Gran is their ringleader." Wilek smiled wryly. "Has been for years. I never paid much attention to it before. Thought it was her Armanite nonsense. My mother has joined them as well. She has your orphaned root harvesters filling crates with food and loading reamskiffs. Joining them seems the best option.

My men, my mother, you . . . all the evidence supports a seaward evacuation. We must continue to prepare. So do your best to convince King Jorger to join us. I should be back by the time you return. If not, you must begin the evacuation. And if I never return, set sail without me."

"What? I wouldn't leave you behind."

"It's your duty, brother. Besides, you've always wanted to go to sea. If I don't return, save whom you can. Find new land, and become rosâr over our people."

Trevn felt sick. He did not want to be king.

"Say you'll do it," Wilek said.

"I will," Trevn said meekly. "I promise."

"And I will do all I can to return so that you do not have to. Go prepare. Send for me when you are ready to depart, and I'll see you off."

Trevn left Wilek's chambers and met Cadoc outside. "We are going to Brixmead."

"Shall we sail or ride, Your Highness?" Cadoc asked. "The sea would be faster."

Trevn smiled wide. "The sea it is, then."

KALEⴖEK

Days passed as Kal led the camel from one tunnel to the next through what felt like a never-ending labyrinth. They had only three candles left for the lantern. They rationed their food and water and were still running low. Dead newts littered every path, but Kal didn't dare eat them.

Every crossroads was an argument over which way to go. Priestess Jazlyn seemed to think she should lead. There were times when they reached a dead end or the tunnels got too narrow or low that they had to backtrack and find another route. When any of this happened on one of Kal's chosen routes, the priestess lectured him. When it happened on one of hers, Kal said nothing. This was his caravan to lead, his camel, and his supplies purchased with Armanian coin. But the woman outranked him, as did Prince Ulrik, who always took her side. So Kal practiced silence.

Burk did not. "I should have stayed in Kaptar."

Kal wished he would have. The boy complained more than Jazlyn lectured.

"See that?" Grayson yelled. "See the blue?"

Kal followed Grayson's pointed finger down a tunnel. "What did you see?"

"A glowing blue light. In the tunnel."

Kal saw no such thing. They continued through the musty darkness. The tangy smell of soil overpowered his senses. No matter how much care anyone took, the taste of dirt invaded every breath, every meal.

Kal helped the camel maneuver the wagon around a sharp bend, and the tunnel opened to the shores of an underground lake that glimmered in the lantern light before stretching into darkness. There was no way to tell how big it was. Kal stared, listening. No rivers.

"It's stagnant," he said. "Not part of the ream."

"Maybe not from this side," Jazlyn said.

Before Kal could respond, an earthquake shook the ground. Dirt sprinkled on their heads. Clumps followed. Inolah screamed.

"Under the wagon!" Jazlyn commanded. "The tunnel is caving in!"

Kal stepped toward the wagon, but his boot sank into spongy soil. He held his lantern to the ground, where it met water and hissed out. *Water?* "Stay in the wagon!" he yelled. "We're sinking!"

There was no time. The ground turned to sinksand and the lake advanced, a formidable opponent Kal could not fight. It swelled around him, surprisingly warm, and sucked him into the darkness. *Poison!* Terror gripped him, but there was nothing he could do but swim. His clothing stuck to his body, making him heavy, but no tingle of poison affected his skin.

The rumbling stopped. All was silent but for splashing. He could see nothing. "Ho, up? Who's out there?"

"It's hot!" Grayson yelled. "Like a bath."

"It stinks," Burk said.

The camel brayed, clearly unhappy.

"Us four are still in the wagon!" Jhorn called. "My lantern went out. I'm searching for the flint."

"Rustian is here as well," Onika said.

"Qoatch?" Priestess Jazlyn called.

"Here."

A green ball of light flamed to Kal's left. Priestess Jazlyn floated out of the water, holding the light in one palm.

Kal treaded water, speechless. The light shone over the heads of Ulrik, Burk, and Grayson, who was already shimmying up the side of the wagon. The camel, still harnessed to the front, was struggling. Her stamina amazed Kal. He swam toward her, trying to keep clear of her kicking legs. The knots attaching the harness to the wagon were too tight, so Kal drew the knife from his belt and severed them. The camel swam away. Kal wanted to call her back, but he feared she might capsize the wagon.

Kal moved down the side of the wagon. Inolah and Grayson were pulling Ulrik in. Qoatch and Burk were already inside. The witch was still floating above the water, holding her light orb.

Qoatch and Ulrik lifted Kal in next. "Is this wagon going to hold us all?" he asked Jhorn.

"It should," Jhorn said. "Most poured-stone skiffs this size hold twenty grown men."

"If we have trouble, I will help." Jazlyn floated into the wagon, rocking it when she landed. Kal had to turn away from the brightness of her orb.

"We don't need your magic here, witch," Jhorn said.

"Very well." The light went out. The instant blackness made Kal's arms prickle. He blinked and found he could see.

"Look what you've done," Ulrik said. "Priestess, please bring back the light."

"She already has," Burk said.

"That is not me," Jazlyn said.

The lake gleamed with colored lights. Beneath the ripples drifted swaths of blue, pink, and yellow. Kal found a close one. Green. It was some kind of worm, flat and ruffled.

"The blue ones are bugs!" Grayson yelled, which brought Kal's focus to the nearest speck of blue. Indeed, the blue lights were round and flitted about in the water.

"We are drifting," Jhorn said.

Kal could feel it—could see it by the way the glowing bugs and worms seemed to shift past each other. "Wish we had some longpoles."

A debate ensued over what to do next. Ulrik wanted Jazlyn to use her orb to illuminate the cavern so they could look for exits. Qoatch said his lady needed to purge and rest. Jazlyn said she had enough strength to maintain a light orb. Jhorn wanted someone to get out and swim, to tow the wagon until they found the wall, which they could then follow to an exit. Onika said the answer would come if they were patient.

Patience, it seemed, was not something Priestess Jazlyn was used to practicing. She conjured her green orb, which showed that they were nearing the opening of a tunnel. The wagon picked up speed as it swept toward the river hole.

Kal spotted the camel swimming off on their right. He whistled, but the camel ignored him.

"Kal, watch your head!" Inolah shouted.

Kal looked up. At the mouth of the tunnel, dripstones hung low from the ceiling. He ducked into a crouch.

They sailed silently and swiftly into the tunnel. A sharp turn made the wagon smack a rock wall. Kal winced, hoping poured stone could take a beating. Priestess Jazlyn's light dimmed. Her face had started to thin. She should listen to her eunuch.

The light went out completely, and the eunuch attended to the woman like a devoted son.

"Is she well?" Ulrik's voice. Worried. A second devotee.

"She has been pushing herself too fast, too often," Qoatch said. "She must rest."

She had plenty of time to. Their wagon boat continued to sail along in the darkness, occasionally knocking against the sides of the tunnel. Jhorn managed to work his flint and light his small lantern. Soon they had a small glow of light with them again.

After a while, the tunnel spat them out into a larger river. Kal grabbed the side of the wagon to keep himself from falling on Onika. Again he worried whether there might be poison in the water. The glow of Jhorn's lantern was enough that Kal could see they had entered a massive underground river. It must have been fifty paces across, three times as wide as any river he'd ever seen. The cavern stretched above some three or four levels high. The walls on either side were jagged, like canyon cracks. River holes emptied more water into the main.

"What happened to the camel?" Ferro asked.

Kal didn't have time to worry about the camel. He tried to figure where they might be. This river had to run into the Eversea. Three days—five at the most—he guessed, and they would reach the end. He only hoped the river did not let out at the top of a cliff.

Hinck

The caravan reached Canden House without discovering that Trevn had stayed behind. Rosârah Thallah ordered Hinck to sleep in Trevn's chambers to continue the façade.

There Hinck received a summons to join Sâr Janek and his friends in the rosâr's Throne Room and to dress his best.

Odd. Why would Janek revel in Rosâr Echad's Throne Room?

Intrigued, Hinck changed into the ensemble he'd worn to Trevn's ageday ball and set off.

The guards admitted him without question. A small group of people had already arrived, Rosâr Echad, Pontiff Rogedoth, and the prophet Yohthehreth among them. The king sat in his rollchair looking ill—worse than Hinck had ever seen him. Janek stood with his mother, Timmons, and several other attendants. Also present were Avron Jervaid, Oli, Fonu, several King's Guards, and Sir Jayron standing with a chubby woman and a little girl, who was dressed better than Queen Laviel.

The prisoners he'd seen at Seacrest. Why were they here?

Oli crossed to Hinck. "Good evening," he said in a low voice. "Welcome to the wedding."

Hinck fought to contain his shock. "The what?"

"Janek is marrying the Rurekan princess. The marriage won't be legal until it's consummated when the princess turns fifteen," Oli said, "but it will give Janek the advantage he needs."

To be declared Heir. "So he invited guests?" Hinck asked.

"As witnesses," Oli said. "Twenty-five witnesses must sign to make a wedding legal."

"I didn't know that."

"Stuff it away," Oli said. "You never know when you might want to marry in a hurry."

So Hinck stood beside Oli and witnessed Pontiff Rogedoth join Sâr Janek and Princess Vallah of Rurekau in marriage. The girl sobbed the whole time. To Hinck's horror, only Sir Jayron's knife at the girl's throat could encourage her to speak her lines of agreement. It took three King's Guards to hold back the nurse, who screamed constant curses upon them all.

She drew much attention, but sadly no one stepped in to help.

When the ceremony ended, a contract was signed, and Hinck wrote his name as one of the witnesses. Janek patted his bride on the head, wished her a good evening, and ordered her taken to her chambers. Then he left, dragging Oli and Fonu with him.

Hinck was not invited. Not that he cared.

He wished he could tell Trevn what had happened.

He couldn't believe what had just happened.

His growling stomach led him to the kitchen. Hara was there, arguing with the Canden cook. In Everton, Hinck would have sat at one of the kitchen tables and flirted with the maids when they passed through, but the argument between Hara and the Canden cook seemed to have scared the maids away. Hinck grabbed a bowl of stew and some berry tarts and headed back to Trevn's chambers.

Canden House was nowhere near as large as Castle Everton. Hinck reached Trevn's chambers quickly. He pushed in the door and nearly ran into a man, soup sloshing onto his hand when he startled.

"Beal!" He quickly set the bowl on the floor, then wiped the stew off his hand onto his trousers. "Gods! Are you mad?"

Hinck looked up, glaring, and realized the man was not Beal. The stranger was dressed all in black, hooded, and was holding out his hand, something small and round in the center of his palm. Hinck stepped closer.

A stone marker with a red rune inked onto the surface.

Hinck's stomach twisted. "What's this? Who are you?"

The man placed the marker in Hinck's hand. "You have been weighed and accepted," he said, his voice unfamiliar. "Bring this token to the dungeon immediately after night bells tomorrow. Wear black. At the end of the cells you will find a door. Give this token to the doorman or you will not enter."

"Enter what?" Hinck asked.

"Wear black," the man said. "Tomorrow." And he left.

Hinck stood staring out the open door, heart pounding. He glanced at the stone in his hand, then rushed forward and closed the door.

He had done it. Gotten his own runestone. Wait till he told Trevn! He was going to find out how all this was connected to the plot against Trevn and Wilek, and to Lady Lebetta's murder.

A jolt of fear sizzled through him.

He picked up his stew and sat on Trevn's bed, but he was no longer hungry. Tomorrow night he might come face-to-face with a murderer.

WILEK

The long journey to Canden gave time for Wilek's anger to grow.

Rogedoth had taken over Armania in secret. He'd gained so much influence over Father, and Janek had conspired with him to take Wilek's place as Heir. Somehow Lebetta had gotten caught up in it all—her life cut short. And now Trevn was involved too.

Charlon came to mind then. How Wilek missed her, wished she were near. *Fool thoughts!* He had no time for this bonded nonsense. His people's lives were in danger. He forced his thoughts onto the present crisis. Before he had left this morning, Gran had sent messengers to the Nahtan contact in every city in Armania, telling them of the prophet Kal had found. Wilek worried it might be too soon—that they should wait until Kal returned with the woman. Confirm who she was. Gran wouldn't hear of it. *"Time is short,"* she'd said.

Her seriousness had inspired Wilek to make a contingency plan with Rayim. If things went poorly when Wilek spoke with Father, Rayim knew to ride immediately back to Everton and assist Gran, Mother, and Trevn in the evacuation.

No matter what happened to Rosâr Echad, Sâr Wilek, or Sâr Janek, a remnant of Armanians would survive the Woes.

It was just after first sleep on the third day when Wilek arrived. He sent Rayim and his men along with Teaka and Errp to search Canden House for evenroot, and then he and Harton went to the Throne Room.

Captain Alpress was standing watch outside. When he saw Wilek, his eyes bulged. "Sâr Wilek!" He bowed quickly, as if barely remembering to, then proceeded to stare at Wilek's short hair. "We did not expect to see you in Canden."

"I have come to see my father."

"Yes, of course. Uh . . . he'll be surprised to see you."

Surprised. Not happy or relieved. "What has happened in my absence, Captain? What did my father do?"

"Nothing as yet, Your Highness. Sâr Janek was married last night to Princess Vallah of Rurekau. And the rosâr is planning to—"

"Inolah's girl? She cannot be more than—"

"Six," the captain said.

"That's insane!" Harton said.

Not insane, ruthless. Marriage to a royal ally was one of Father's stipulations for Heir. Janek had blundered his first pairing. And now he had married a child—his own niece—in order to win the eventual crown.

"I'm sorry, Captain," Wilek said. "I interrupted you before. What is the rosâr planning?"

"To induct Sâr Janek as Heir at week's end. He has already given him the ring."

Though Wilek had expected it, the confirmation stung. "Then it seems I arrived just in time. Wait outside, Hart." Wilek pushed past Captain Alpress and entered the Throne Room.

Father sat in his rollchair, clutching a goblet of wine. Three women knelt on the floor around his chair, one massaging his bare feet. Schwyl sat at a table by the window, scribbling on parchment. Two King's Guards stood inside the door.

Everyone stared at Wilek. Father choked on his wine.

Normally Wilek would have demanded privacy, but he needed the gossip and scandal to be wild and swift. He needed anarchy. At the same time, he must tread carefully. To attack his father outright would only make the man defensive.

"My boy!" Father said, his voice weak. He handed his goblet to one of the women. "I'm delighted to see you."

"Surprised to see me yet living, I'm sure."

"What did you do to your hair? Warrior locks are a matter of honor."

"The Pontiff was unsuccessful at having me killed."

"Rogedoth?" Father frowned and waved the women away. "Out," he told them.

The women exited swiftly.

Father licked his lips and squinted at Wilek. "Why accuse Rogedoth of such treason?"

"The day I went missing, the Pontiff attempted to hire Randmuir Khal of the Omatta to track me down and kill me," Wilek said. "Fortunately for me, my mother had already arranged for Rand to bring me safely home."

Father leaned forward in his chair. "Why would the Pontiff do that?"

"To put Janek on the throne—once you die, of course. He likely has plans to kill you once Janek is declared Heir."

"Ridiculous! What of your kidnappers? They are my real concern. What did they do to your hair?"

Would Father hear no evil against Rogedoth? "The Chieftess of Magonia took me captive, hoping I would marry her Heir and join our realms. She now knows that is impossible. My hair will grow back."

"Good, that," Father said.

"Did you know the Pontiff has been harvesting evenroot in Armania since before the war ended?"

"Absurd. Whatever for?"

"At first I thought it was to smuggle it out to Magonia or Tenma and make a fortune, as they have all but depleted the resource in their realms. Then I discovered that Rogedoth is a mantic. He has been using his magic to influence you."

Father waved one hand. "He does no such thing. Why this attack against the Pontiff?"

"Because he seeks to rule, Father. Ever since he lost the throne of Sarikar." He paused, wishing he had a bigger audience. "Pontiff Rogedoth is Prince Mergest III. When his father discovered his preoccupation with mantics, his titles were stripped away and he was banished from the realm. He came to Everton and used his mantic ties to create a new identity. But the Pontiff quickly grew tired of ruling Armania in secret. Since he cannot sit on the throne of Armania himself, he used his magic to seduce one of your wives so that he might sire a son who could rule where he could not."

Father sputtered. "Which wife?"

"Rosârah Laviel."

"Preposterous! I am Janek's father." Yet the king waved his fist at Schwyl. "Fetch me Rogedoth, now!"

Schwyl scurried from the chamber.

"Who told you this, son?"

"Does it matter?" Wilek asked. "Investigate if you must, but there is little time. The Five Realms are dying, Father. The underground rivers of the ream have never made a stable foundation. Mining coal and harvesting evenroot have weakened it further. There's little left keeping the soil in place. Had Rogedoth kept your decree against the use of evenroot and not harvested Armania, our realm might have survived. But he did not. Greed is to blame. Farway, Hebron, Kaptar, Ebro, and now Everton are suffering pangs of what will soon become utter destruction. The Five Woes are upon us."

"The Five Woes are to be heralded by a prophet," Father said. "Where is he?"

"She," Wilek said. "Sir Kalenek found her in Magonia. She said those who will survive will be on ships. We must return to Everton immediately and evacuate the city. We must get on ships before it's too late."

"And go where?" Father asked.

"To a new land, the prophet said."

"New land, Mikreh's teeth! Where is this prophet? I want to speak with her."

"Kal is bringing her back from Magonia."

"Lies." Rogedoth's voice. "Sâr Wilek is stalling, Your Highness."

Wilek turned to find the man standing in the doorway, Schwyl behind him.

"If there was such a prophet," Rogedoth said, "I would know of her."

"If she is true, she would have stayed far away from you," Wilek said.

"Why was your shield in Magonia, Sâr Wilek?" Rogedoth asked. "Perhaps you are the mantic."

"I sent Sir Kalenek to Magonia to translate the rune Lady Lebetta drew as she died. I have recently learned that you control my father with magic. You wanted my concubine dead."

"Holy Rosâr," Rogedoth said, "Sâr Wilek is obviously unwell. He bears the rune of a mantic slav on his neck. I fear he is here under their compulsion."

No! How dare he turn this around? "The compulsion has been broken, Pontiff," Wilek said. "I am here to cast you out of my father's court."

The Pontiff seized the poles of Father's rollchair and swung him around behind Wilek. "See the mark for yourself, sire."

"It's true!" Father cried. "My son is one of them!"

Wilek shook his head and turned to meet his father's gaze. "Their magic no longer works on me, Father. But Rogedoth's magic is controlling you right now."

"Look at me, my king," Rogedoth said, kneeling beside the rollchair. "I do not bear the eyes of a mantic."

That was true. Rogedoth's eyes were brown. Could magic change eye color? "Father, he lies. Can you not feel it? Or are you too blind to know he forces your hand?"

"Watch your words with me, boy," Father warned.

The windows and chandeliers began to rattle. Father cried out and gripped the arms of his rollchair as an earthquake shook the room.

"Another warning that the Five Woes are coming," Wilek yelled over the noise. "We must act swiftly, Father. Arrest Pontiff Rogedoth for treason, then return to Everton and evacuate. Now!"

"The sâr's accusations bring a curse upon us!" Rogedoth said, making the sign of The Hand.

The moment the Pontiff kissed his fingers, the earthquake stopped.

Silence fell complete. Wilek watched his father's expression twitch and fuss. Was Rogedoth controlling him, even now?

"The Pontiff is right," Father said finally. "All was well until you returned."

"You were lost in lies!" Wilek motioned to Rogedoth. "You still are! I bring you truth."

"He has always been difficult," Rogedoth said. "Questions everything."

"Janek favors me more than you ever did," Father said. "Janek does my will. He has even married before you."

"Married a child!" Wilek said.

"Janek will be Heir," Father mumbled. "I can trust Janek."

Arman, forgive him. Wilek had failed. He hoped, at least, that Rayim had found the evenroot. "Trusting Janek is a mistake, Father."

Father's face purpled. "Again you contradict me! I am rosâr. I know best."

"Rogedoth is a mantic!" Wilek affirmed one more time. "He is using magic to sway you. And Janek, Rogedoth's son, plots with him. Once Janek is Heir, they will kill you!"

"He threatens your life," Rogedoth said. "This is treason."

"I will hear no more," Father snapped. "Guards! Arrest Sâr Wilek. Barthos is clearly displeased with his presence here. We must offer worthy sacrifices to ease his anger. I have decided that Sâr Wilek will go first."

CHARLON

Magon brought word. Lady Zeroah had left Everton. Gone to Brixmead. So the Magonians changed their course and their plans. While Charlon and Mreegan entered Castle Brixmead, their acolytes set off to commandeer a great ship. A ship they could sail to Everton. Once Charlon had captured Lady Zeroah.

Then Chieftess Mreegan set her sights even higher.

She wanted to take King Jorger. Wear the man's mask. This, she felt, would give them the freedom to do what they must. Charlon argued against it at first. The risk was too great. If they were caught, all would be lost. But Magon assured her. Magon's sovereignty and powers would be sufficient.

Magon made their company invisible. The rest was easy.

Charlon had been learning to do magic without her altar mat and runes. The Chieftess reminded her that to wear a mask was different. It required a token from the donor. One could not create a mold spell with word alone.

Charlon and three of the men assisted the Chieftess. Once she appeared in the form of King Jorger and the real king was locked away, they moved easily throughout the castle. Invisibility was no longer necessary.

They asked for Lady Zeroah, and servants directed them to a sitting room on the second floor. Chieftess Mreegan let herself in. The small room was sweltering. A fire raged in the hearth. Lady Zeroah was sitting on a longchair. Embroidering. She saw the king, stood, and curtsied, frowning slightly. Her embroidery slid down her dress to the floor.

448

The girl was a twig. Skinnier than Charlon. Taller. Small eyes. Pointed chin. Too much hair piled high.

"Grandfather, hello. What brings you to . . ." Her words faltered as she caught sight of Charlon.

Charlon wore only a blue-and-white kasah. Shoulders, arms, legs, and feet bare. The men entered next, wearing kasahs as skirts. Chests bare. Torol carried the stone basin and rolled-up altar mat. Nuel and Morten carried nothing.

"Who are your companions, Grandfather?" the girl asked.

Mreegan said nothing as she circled the room, inspecting everything with a sour expression. "I suppose this will have to do."

"Do not worry," Charlon said. "I can manage."

Mreegan's gaze fell on Lady Zeroah, combed her up and down. "But I *do* worry," she said, scowling at Zeroah. "Look how she stands. You are not capable of such dignity. No one will believe your mask."

"Magon can do all things, Chieftess," Charlon said. "Do not forget. She chose me."

"As if you would let me." The Chieftess grinned at herself in a mirror on the wall. "I rather like having the body of a man. I now understand why they are such forceful creatures. He is old and sore in spots, but still . . . to have such strength . . ." She flexed her upper arm and smiled. "I would change his title, though. I prefer *Godking* to *the God's king*."

"Who . . . ? Who are you?" Lady Zeroah asked.

Charlon approached the girl. Reached up. Twined her fingers through one dangling curl. Zeroah flinched and pulled back. Charlon saw her fear, fed off it. Grabbed a fistful of hair and yanked. Zeroah's head jerked to the side. She cried out.

"Odd . . ." Charlon said. "The slights told me it wasn't attached." She released Lady Zeroah's hair, reached for the bun on top.

The girl ducked under her arm and hurried toward the door. Upon seeing the men standing there, she changed directions and fled across the room to the fireplace, spun around, and pressed her back to the corner, where the wall met the bricks of the hearth. She grabbed the fire poker. "What do you want?"

Charlon stalked toward her. Stopped just out of reach. Put her hand on her stomach as if cradling it. "To be the Mother. Of Sâr Wilek's child."

Lady Zeroah flushed. Fear strong within. She glanced across the room. To the king. The Chieftess picked up the girl's embroidery. Inspected it.

"Grandfather," Lady Zeroah said. "Why do you allow this woman to insult me? Why do you say nothing?"

"What?" Chieftess Mreegan looked up. "Oh, do as Charlon says, Granddaughter."

Lady Zeroah shifted her gaze back to Charlon. She shook the poker. "I command you to leave this room at once."

Charlon laughed and glanced at Mreegan. "She and the prince have fire in common."

"Stop playing with her and get on with it," the Chieftess said.

"But I need to study her if Wilek is to believe."

Jealousy burned in the girl's eyes. "Do you know the sâr to speak so informally of him?"

"I do," Charlon said. "He and I are soul-bound." She lifted her palm. Showed the rune marking.

Lady Zeroah lifted her chin. "Sâr Wilek is promised to me by his father, the Rosâr of Armania. Just last week Sâr Wilek sent a letter renewing his pledge. We are to be married within the month."

"And you shall be," Charlon said. "Or so Wilek will think." She waved at the men. "Bind her."

Nuel and Morten rushed toward Lady Zeroah. She struck Nuel with the poker, but he snatched it away and grabbed her wrist. She screamed and elbowed him, kicked, pushed at his hands, trying to get him to let go. Morten seized her other arm and pulled it out to the side.

"Release me!" she yelled. "Grandfather, tell them to stop!"

Chieftess Mreegan said nothing. Sat on the longchair, watching. The newt crept out of the king's breast pocket and perched on one shoulder.

The men pushed Lady Zeroah to her knees and bound her wrists behind her. Bound her ankles next. "What have you done to the king?" she asked, tears welling in her small eyes.

Nuel wrapped a cloth over her mouth. Yanked it tight until it forced her lips open.

"See if her hair coil comes off," Charlon said.

Nuel scratched at the girl's hair until the bun lifted away. Tossed it to Charlon. Morten picked up the girl. Carried her to the longchair. Seated her beside the Chieftess.

Charlon took a sip of root juice from her hip flask, then unrolled the altar mat. Knelt on one end. Placed the stone basin on the other end. She unwound the lock of hair. Cut a fringe into her bowl. Poked the tip of a knife into her own finger. Mumbled the proper words as blood joined hair.

Lady Zeroah began to pray. Mumbling to Arman. Such words slowed Charlon's progress. Bothered her. Magonians did not believe in the gods of the father countries. But Charlon had been raised in Rurekau. There, some thought Arman to be a powerful mantic. Others believed him the Father God. The Creator of the world.

She asked Magon for strength. Chanted louder. Waved her hands. Finally felt her face begin to narrow.

Her hair grew longer, coiled, and darkened. Her frame thinned and stretched taller. Breasts shrank. Bronze skin blackened. Eyes shifted. Lips narrowed.

It was done. "Get me her dress."

The men moved toward Lady Zeroah, but the girl was staring, horrified, at Charlon. Staring upon her own face.

Then the girl slumped over and fainted.

TREVN

Trevn arrived in Brixmead four days after leaving Everton. By his figuring, Wilek should have reached Canden yesterday. He hoped Father would see reason and return to Everton at once.

He hoped the same for King Jorger.

The first thing Trevn noticed on his carriage ride from the docks to Castle Brixmead was the large number of foreigners in the city. By their colorful kasahs and bare feet, he guessed them to be Magonians. Why would Magonians walk freely in Sarikar?

When Trevn arrived at the castle, Prince Loran and his daughter, Saria, were awaiting him in the foyer with a handful of other minor royals and nobles he recognized. The prince and his daughter looked very alike. Both were slender, had small ears and narrow noses, coal-black skin, and eyes the color of curry powder. Saria, only two months older than Trevn, had been an entertaining target for Trevn and Hinck's teasing over the years. She had never cared for their sense of humor.

"Welcome, Sâr Trevn," Prince Loran said. "I'm sure you did not expect to see us so far from Pixford. We are visiting my father. I was delighted when your messenger announced you."

"I come bearing urgent news," Trevn said. "I must see the king right away."

"Of course," Prince Loran said. "Ywan, inform the king that Sâr Trevn wishes to see him."

The onesent scurried away.

452

"My father has not been himself of late," Prince Loran said. "I fear he might be too ill to receive you. Can you share this urgent news with me instead?"

"I have orders to tell the king. But if you would join me when I speak with your father, I would be glad to tell you both, for it affects the Five Realms."

"Foreboding, indeed," Prince Loran said. "Ah, here is my sister. Look who has come to call, Nabelle."

Princess Nabelle entered the room like a queen. Her cold stare fell on Trevn, and he fought the urge to shiver, determined not to let her intimidate him.

"Good midday, Princess Nabelle," he said.

"If you have come to see the honor maiden, you will be disappointed," she said.

"I came at the request of my brother Sâr Wilek," Trevn stated. "He has returned safely to Everton only to discover there is nowhere safe in the Five Realms."

"Sâr Trevn is full of ominous warnings, sister," Prince Loran said. "We must wait for Ywan to—ah, here he comes now."

Ywan bowed. "The Godking wishes to see Sâr Trevn."

"Let us go now," Prince Loran said, leading the way.

"Godking?" Trevn whispered to Prince Loran.

"Yes." Prince Loran sighed, his expression pinched. "Father recently announced his new title. If you do address him, please humor us by using it. Until we understand his illness, we hesitate to upset him."

"Why do we tell Sâr Trevn such personal matters?" Princess Nabelle asked. "It is none of his concern."

"Sâr Trevn is like family," Prince Loran said.

"*Like* family is not family."

"It is not your decision, Nabelle, and it is done," Prince Loran said. "Say no more of it."

They arrived in the Throne Room and entered without knocking. King Jorger sat primly on his evergold throne, eating figs. The room felt unnaturally cold, though a fire raged in the hearth.

Trevn approached the king and gave a short bow of respect.

"This is Prince Trevn?" the king asked.

"Sâr Trevn, the Third Arm of Armania," Prince Loran said.

"*Third* Arm?" King Jorger narrowed his eyes and considered Trevn as if he had never heard of him despite the hundreds of times they'd spoken over the years. "Prince Wilek's blood?"

"Sâr Wilek is my half brother," Trevn said, confused why this man no longer knew him.

"Where is your brother Wilek now?" King Jorger asked.

Such informal language. "He went to my father in Canden."

"Wilek has passed his twenty-fifth ageday," the king said. "I demand he marry Lady Zeroah, as promised."

My my. This man was ill indeed. "He fully intends to do so, um, Godking Jorger, but he is preoccupied at present with the destruction of Castle Everton."

The king shifted uncomfortably. "What is it you want?"

Trevn first shared that Prince Mergest and Pontiff Rogedoth were one and the same.

"This confirms our own suspicions," Prince Loran said. "Nabelle has been convinced for years, but Father did not agree."

They all looked to the king, but the man showed no signs of interest in the matter.

"You did not wish conflict between Sarikar and Armania," Princess Nabelle said.

"That's right," the king said. "Very true. Now, if that is all, I am tired and would like to rest."

"I'm afraid that is not all, Your Highness." Trevn then gave the prophetess's warning, telling them about the over-harvesting of evenroot and how he believed it to be the source of the disasters in the Five Realms. "Only those on ships will survive the Woes. We ask Sarikar to join Armania in evacuating the Five Realms before it is too late."

"This again," Prince Loran said. "I did not expect you to be allied with my sister, Sâr Trevn."

"Nor did I," Princess Nabelle said. "But you cannot deny that too many have ignored Arman's ways for too long."

"Tell me about this prophetess," Jorger said. "What does she look like?"

"I have not met her," Trevn said. "The message described her as pale-skinned. 'A winter palomino with eyes like diamond gemstones' were the exact words."

"How poetic," Jorger said. "I've never seen such a person. How can you be certain the man was not drunk when he wrote this message?"

"The guardsman who carried the message met the prophetess as well. His story is the same. She said many things that came true on their journey."

"Give me her words again," Jorger demanded.

"I have a copy of it here." Trevn handed a scroll to the king.

The king unrolled the scroll and squinted. "'Wail, for the day of destruction is . . .'" He went still as he continued reading. "'. . . foundations of the earth . . . violently shaken . . . Mountains will tremble . . . only a remnant will endure . . . remnant will set sail and begin anew . . . In the lands beyond the sea . . .'" Jorger looked up from the scroll. "I have heard many versions of this prophecy in my life. Why are you so certain the time is now?"

"Because it is happening," Trevn said. "Walk with me to the beach and I will show you my theory."

"How academic." The king stood. "Lead on, boy prince. Let us see your theory."

"Very well." Trevn quitted the room.

"Sâr Trevn," Prince Loran said behind him. "Is this really necessary?"

"It is the only way I can think to convince you."

"It cannot hurt, brother," Princess Nabelle said.

The beach in Brixmead came right up to the castle walls on the northeastern side. Trevn slogged through the dry sand and onto the hard-packed grit near the surf. He dropped to his knees and began to dig. By the time the king and his two adult children caught up, he had a good-sized hole.

"Wait and watch," Trevn said.

They all stared. From below, brown water filled the hole, rising slowly. *Perfect.*

"See how the water fills my hole to the same level as the sea?" Trevn said. "That's the problem with our land. The underground of the Five Realms is made up of caverns and canyons and canals that are deeper than the sea's surface. Too many collapses and the sea will rush in and fill all the holes. And with the illegal evenroot harvesting in Armania, there is little solid ground beneath us anymore. It won't be long until, as the prophetess warned, the sea swallows the land."

"Your experiment proves that the sea would flood underground passageways," Prince Loran said, "but it does not prove that the Five Woes are upon us so soon."

"Farway, Hebron, Kaptar, Ebro," Trevn said. "That's four cities gone, that we're aware of, and Sâr Wilek witnessed the growth of many cracks on his journey along the King's Canyon. Sâr Wilek and I are not willing to risk our people. Are you willing to risk yours?"

Prince Loran sighed. "I cannot deny that these disasters have weighed heavily on my mind. How much time do you think we have?"

"The Prophetess said perhaps a few months, but that was weeks ago."

"We will move onto boats at once," the Godking said, walking away.

Trevn chased after him. "Your Highness, Sâr Wilek has requested I meet him back in Everton as soon as possible. I had hoped you would send Princess Nabelle and her daughter back with me so that his betrothed could be there when he returns."

"Excellent suggestion, boy prince," the king said. "They must marry immediately."

"But, Father," Princess Nabelle called out. "If the world as we know it is coming to an end, we cannot dally with a wedding. The prophecies have always said that Armania would fall. If Zeroah and I are there when it does—"

The king turned back to his daughter. "Nothing matters more than this wedding!" he snapped. "It will show our people that all is well."

"But all is not well!" Princess Nabelle said.

"Which is why we will move to the boats." Jorger continued walking.

Trevn did not understand why the man was so intent on the wedding. But if it meant that Mielle would return with Trevn to Everton, he was thrilled.

Prince Loran caught up with Trevn and the king. "How will we decide which people can board the ships?"

"I will decide," the king said.

"That's hardly a fair way to go about it," Prince Loran said.

"I am tired," the king said, entering the castle and turning toward his chambers. "I must rest. Do not disturb me."

Trevn stood with Prince Loran and Princess Nabelle in the northeastern vestibule.

"Do you see it now?" Prince Loran said to his sister. "He is mad, I tell you. Something is wrong."

"Then call the physician," Princess Nabelle said.

"I did. Father refused him."

Princess Nabelle glanced at Trevn. "Ywan will show you to your chambers, Sâr Trevn, where you can rest until dinner is served."

"Thank you, Princess." Trevn was happy to have completed his task and eager to get far away from the discussions of mad King Jorger. Besides, once Trevn was away from the princess, he could look for Mielle.

Mielle

Mielle hurried down the hallway to Trevn's chambers. She glanced over her shoulder, knowing Zeroah was not far behind. She only wanted a minute alone with him.

Cadoc saw her coming. "Miss Mielle, good midday. Come to see the sâr?"

Mielle beamed. "Yes, sir."

He knocked once, pushed open the door, and poked his head inside. "Miss Mielle, Your Highness. Shall I tell her to come back later?"

"No!" Trevn's voice. Her heart leapt. "Send her in, please. Beal, you may go check on . . . um . . . something."

Mielle bit back a smile.

"I shall inquire as to how quickly your clothing can be laundered, sir," Beal said in his breathy voice.

"Excellent, thank you," Trevn said.

The door opened wider. Beal stepped aside to let Mielle in, avoided her gaze as she entered, then slipped into the hall and closed the door behind him.

Well, good midday to you too, Beal.

Trevn stood gazing at her; his eyes seemed bigger somehow, glossier, deeper. His feet were bare, and sand was caked to the knees of his trousers. He'd already found the beach!

She curtsied, clasped her hands, fidgeted, and leaned against the door to try to keep still. Trevn kept staring. She hoped he would speak soon.

Blessedly he did. "Good midday, Mielle."

"And you," she said.

"I've been thinking about you much lately. I can hardly believe you are standing here."

Oh . . . She suddenly felt very hot and . . . exposed. She wished she could sit or hide somehow, which was silly. Why would she want to hide?

Trevn walked to her, took her hands in his, which sent tingles up her arms and down into her belly. His fingers slid over the scab from the Renegade *R* she'd cut on her hand. He closed her fingers and lifted her hand, inspecting it. His eyes lit up and he smiled.

"Is it wrong that I want so badly to kiss you?" he whispered.

She shook her head. "I don't think so."

He kissed her gently, and she breathed in his sandy, salty beach smell. She grabbed his face, pulling him closer, trying to put all her sentiments into her kiss, wanting him to know how he made her feel.

His hands slid around her waist. He was always so timid—no, careful, like he might scare her away. It was the opposite of how she expected him to be, but she liked it. It made her feel in control. Safe.

Trevn broke the kiss and buried his face in her hair. "Mielle, I've missed you."

She loved when he said her name. She reached behind his neck and tangled her fingers in his coarse minibraids. "I missed you too."

Trevn stumbled back a step, tripped on something. One of his boots. He sat down suddenly on a longchair, pulling Mielle awkwardly onto his lap. One of her feet was tangled in her skirt. She felt off-balance and held tight to his tunic.

A knock on the door made Mielle jump. Her sharp movement caused her to slip off Trevn's knees. He held tight, trying to keep her from falling, but it was too late, and she pulled him with her. They hit the floor with a thud.

Trevn started to laugh.

"I'm sorry!" She tried to get up, but he was lying on her skirt and she fell back down.

Another knock.

Trevn twisted out from under Mielle. He stood and helped her to her feet, then went to the door and opened it a crack. "Yes?"

"Lady Zeroah to see you, sir," Cadoc said.

Trevn glanced back to Mielle. He looked her over and his eyes widened. Well, he didn't look any better! His hair frizzed out behind his round ears, and her red ochre lip powder was smudged all over his mouth.

The door swung in. Trevn tried to push it closed, but a dainty shoe blocked the opening.

"Let me in, Your Highness," Lady Zeroah said. "I know Mielle is with you."

Mielle. So unlike Zeroah! She'd wanted to talk to Trevn about how strangely her lady had been acting, the loss of her manners and propriety, but seeing him had sidetracked her. And now they'd run out of time.

Lady Zeroah shoved her way inside and closed the door with a swift kick. She glanced at Mielle, raised one slender eyebrow, then turned her penetrating gaze to Trevn. "Really, Your Highness. Not more than an hour has passed since your arrival in Brixmead. Does Everton have no women?"

Oh! How could she speak so rudely? Trevn choked a laugh, clearly shocked by Zeroah's ribaldry. Surely he must see there was something very wrong with the lady.

"And you," she said to Mielle. "Give everything so soon, and he'll tire of you."

Mielle's cheeks burned. She folded her arms, wanting Zeroah to leave and never return.

"I beg your pardon, lady," Trevn said. "Can I help you?"

"How soon do we leave for Everton?" Zeroah asked.

Trevn smoothed back his frizzy hair. "Um, that depends on King Jorger. You are his to command, not mine."

Zeroah rolled her eyes. "I am no one's to command. I want to go to Everton. Right away. And it is *Godking* Jorger. Don't forget."

Mielle cringed. This was wrong. All wrong! What had happened to her dear friend? Had Zeroah and the king caught some kind of mania?

"I will not go against *Godking* Jorger or your mother," Trevn said. "If they say you may leave, we can set out first thing tomorrow."

"Good. Be ready. I shall have my way." Zeroah opened the door. "Come, Mielle."

Mielle glanced at Trevn, and a moment of boldness seized her. "I will join you momentarily, lady. Allow me to say farewell."

Zeroah sighed heavily. "If you must. Remember, though . . . Princess Nabelle, my mother, said that should anything happen to Wilek, Prince Trevn is contracted to marry me." She left, closing the door behind her.

Mielle stared, dumbfounded, at Trevn. "Is that true?"

Trevn looked everywhere, it seemed, but at Mielle. "What is wrong with Lady Zeroah? I have never seen her behave so strangely."

Mielle crossed to his side and whispered, "She's been acting like this for several days. It's like she woke up with a different personality."

"Just like the, uh, *Godking*?"

"Exactly like that," Mielle said. "I'm sorry she was so rude."

He offered her a kind smile. "I could never tire of you, Mielle."

His words melted her anger, but she could not return his smile. "You're contracted to marry Zeroah?"

He sighed, shrugged. "Only if Wilek died. And he returned in perfect health, so there is nothing to fear."

Mielle's heart seemed to shatter. "You lied to me!"

He shook his head, eyes pleading. "Not a lie, exactly. I did not wish to upset you. Mielle, I am sorry. Let's not fight. We will sail for Everton tomorrow, and Lady Zeroah will plan her wedding to my brother. All has worked out perfectly." He wiped his thumb over her cheek and it came away dusted with red ochre. "I will see you at dinner?"

She frowned. "They will seat you beside Zeroah, won't they?"

He grinned. "Probably, but I'll be able to see you better that way."

Such words! She kissed him softly and breathed him in, happy to have made peace and to have confided her fears about Zeroah. Trevn would help make everything all right again.

Hinck

Hinck considered not going. He thought about playing sick or riding alone back to Everton and begging Trevn's forgiveness for his cowardice.

He could do none of those things, of course. His sovereign had given him an order. More than that, his friend had asked this favor. He could not let Trevn down—especially if he was about to gain insight into the mysterious Lahavôtesh and the plots against Trevn and Wilek. Rumors around Canden said that the king had arrested Wilek for treason. Hinck found this inconceivable. Perhaps he might learn something tonight that could help.

So into the dungeon he went, twisting his way through a grid of cells until he saw a masked man standing before a door at the end of the final corridor.

Oh gods, oh gods. A deep breath and he walked the final stretch on legs of pudding. He stopped just out of reach of the guard, feeling as if he had arrived for his own execution.

The man stood a head taller than Hinck. He wore a white mask shaped like a bird's face. The breast of his black tabard was embroidered with silver spirals.

Hinck held out the runestone. The man grabbed Hinck's arm and yanked him close.

"Why have you come here?" His voice was unmistakably familiar.

"Oli?" Hinck held up the marker again, relieved to speak with someone he knew. "They said to give this to the man at the door."

"Leave. Quickly!" Oli hissed. "Before anyone else sees you. I cannot explain now. Just trust me."

Oli's words made everything worse. Hinck had to know what was beyond the door. He could not fail. "Is this about Eudora?"

Oli shook him. "Fool! This . . ." He tapped the marker. "Once you enter, they'll own you. Forever. They'll consume your soul, use you to hurt those you love, use you against Sâr Trevn. Once they have you . . . death is your only freedom."

Five Woes, the man was foreboding. "What *is* this place? Who are they? I must know."

Footsteps behind Hinck sent him spinning around. A second man approached, this one wearing a bronze fish mask.

"Too late," Oli whispered, snatching the stone from Hinck's hand.

The man stopped before them. "Is there a problem?" His voice was deep and oddly familiar, yet Hinck couldn't place it. Curse his foggy brain!

Oli held up Hinck's stone. "The gods have set you before us, Hinckdan Faluk." His voice was now cold and formal. "You have been weighed and found worthy to enter the Sanctum of Mysteries. First you must take an oath. Will you answer the call with a vow of loyalty?"

Hinck spoke before he lost his nerve. "I will."

A small sigh. "Inside the sanctum you must never use your name. Inside, our identities are hidden. You enter a Spark. Next time you are summoned, hood and mask yourself. Do you understand?"

"Yes."

"Then enter the Sanctum of Mysteries." Oli pushed open the door. Nothing but a dimly lit corridor lay beyond.

As Hinck hesitated on the threshold, the fish man slipped past him and entered. Hinck followed. The corridor was lit with torches, the air clouded with incense.

The fish man walked briskly, and Hinck hurried to keep up. At the end of the corridor, a stone door hung ajar. The man ducked through. Hinck glanced behind him, saw no one. Oli must still be guarding the entrance.

Hinck slipped through the open door and froze in the darkness, blinded. He waited for his eyes to focus. A pale yellow glow on the left beckoned him. He stumbled his first few steps, but once he turned a corner, a rectangle of fiery orange light straight ahead silhouetted the fish man's figure.

Hinck walked forward, praying that the father god—Arman, if Father Tomek had been right—would protect him from whatever went on here tonight.

He reached the doorway and peeked inside, breathless. The room was the size of the great hall above. On the far end, opposite where Hinck stood, a dais stretched the width of the room. In its center, a smaller stone platform stood as high as a man's waist, like a table.

The room was filled with black-clad, masked people—some men, some women—standing in groups, talking. Men wore black ensembles. Women, black gowns. All but Hinck wore masks. He saw every kind of mask: animals, solid colors, multiple colors, one that depicted a huge eyeball, another a yellow sun.

Hinck suddenly wished he had heeded Oli's warning and fled. Everyone here would recognize him, yet he knew only Oli. How was that fair? How could he tell Trevn who was involved in this cult when he could not see their faces?

The smell of lavender gusted over him. "Are you coming in?" a soft voice asked.

A woman was standing behind him. A silver mask covered the top half of her face, leaving her lips and chin exposed.

"Eudora."

"Shh! No names tonight."

"I don't have a mask." A stupidly obvious statement but all Hinck could manage.

"You are being initiated. You aren't supposed to have one."

Initiated? "What will happen?"

Those lips twisted into a smirk. "You'll see." She kissed his jaw and slid past, her body tight against his in the doorway.

He followed her, not wanting to lose the one person he knew in the room. She stopped in a group of men, who greeted her, each kissing her hand.

Hinck felt exposed, standing in the center of the room, the only one without a mask. Eudora and her admirers seemed in no hurry to end their discourse, so Hinck backed into the corner opposite the dais and waited.

More people entered, all masked. The chatter grew until a gong silenced it. Hinck located the bronze disk on the back corner of the dais. A masked man gripping a mallet stood beside it.

"Hinckdan Faluk," a man's voice called out, "come forward."

Five Woes. The voice had come from the other side of the crowd. Hinck couldn't see the speaker. He swallowed his fear and entered the mob. It parted for him, dozens of masked people stepping back, staring.

Trevn owed him for this. He owed him forever.

Hinck reached the front, where a low altar ran along the floor in front of the dais. In the center a fire pit burned. A shallow, silver pan hung above the flames, suspended from an iron chain. A man in black robes stood between it and the platform. He wore a silver mask with fangs around the mouth. His eyes, looking out from two holes in the mask, were gray.

A mantic!

"I am Moon Fang, Inferno and Supreme Master of the Flames. The gods have found you worthy, Hinckdan Faluk. A hundred souls agree. You have been given the call. Do you accept it?"

The room was silent.

Hinck swallowed. "I do."

"The Veil that hides the Sanctum of Mysteries is drawing aside. Will you enter?"

What kind of a game were these people playing? "Uh, I will?"

"Place your right hand over your heart and raise your other to the gods. Repeat after me to make your vow under the name Shadow Claw."

A vow? He would break any vow the moment he saw Trevn. But he couldn't very well back out now. Hinck set his hand over his heart and lifted his other. Moon Fang spoke, and Hinck repeated his words.

"I, Shadow Claw, in the presence of the gods, the shadir, the chosen demigods, and the heroic human worshipers, most solemnly pledge and swear to faithfully obey the commands of my elder Flames, to give my steadfast respect and support, and to heed all mandates, decrees, edicts, and charges set before me. I will divulge to no one the happenings beyond the Veil, upon punishment of death. This oath I seal with my blood."

Oh gods, blood?

Moon Fang reached out, those eyes seeming to look through him. "Give me your right hand."

Hinck held out his hand. It was shaking.

The man pulled a knife from his robes. Hinck drew back and bumped into someone.

A snicker from the crowd.

Moon Fang flipped the knife around, hilt out. "Take the sacred blade."

It looked like a regular blade to Hinck, though as he took it in his hands, he saw that the pommel was made of bone, carved in runes—some he recognized from the stone marker.

"Add the blood of your right hand to the pan," Moon Fang said.

They wanted a blood oath. It was no different from the Renegade *R*s he and Trevn had cut into their hands years before. An oath that superseded this one.

Hinck made a careful cut across the fat edge of his hand and pinched the skin until a drop of blood fell into the pan.

It sizzled.

Trembling, Hinck returned the knife to Moon Fang, who set it on the platform behind him. "The gods accept your offering, Shadow Claw. All initiates must also undergo a physical trial in order to receive mystic wisdom. Do you accept?"

There was more? "I do," Hinck said, and hoped he would not regret it.

"Remove your tabard and tunic and kneel at the altar."

Hinck stared at the man, then glanced over his shoulder at the wall of masked faces, at the eyes glinting from the holes.

Should he make it out alive, he was going to kill Trevn. Cut Trevn's hand and fry his blood. Make him strip down in front of a hundred people. He pulled off his cloak, dropped it at his feet and loosened his belt. He pulled off his tabard, his tunic, and dropped both on top of his cloak. The chillness of the dungeon kissed his skin. He dropped to his knees at the altar.

Moon Fang reached down to the coals, then came to stand before Hinck on the opposite side of the altar. Hinck's gaze clapped onto the branding iron in the man's hand, on the fiery orange glow of its head.

They were going to burn him? Fear pulsed through his veins. He edged back from the altar.

"Hold him," Moon Fang said.

"No!" People lunged up from behind, grabbed his arms, pushed him down on the altar. The stone was cold against his chest and arms. He struggled against those holding him, terror making him desperate. "Stop! I changed my mind. I don't want it."

"You have given your pledge and will honor it," Moon Fang said.

Fire seared the center of Hinck's back, between his shoulder blades. He screamed, shocking himself with the volume and pitch of his voice. It sounded foreign. He hadn't known he could make such a sound.

The hands let go, but the burning continued. Hinck sat back on his heels, trembling, and gasped in air where there wasn't enough. His back throbbed.

"Be discreet," Moon Fang said. "Discuss this matter with no one. Now take your place at the back of the line."

Hands again grabbed Hinck, pulled him to his feet. Someone shoved his clothes into his shaking arms. He hugged them to his chest and wandered through the crowd to the back of the room, glad to put distance between him and the branding iron.

"White Raven. Come forward!" Moon Fang yelled.

Hinck found a place against the far wall and stood wobbling—back, throat, and heart pulsing. The crowd parted as a man wearing a white bird mask made his way forward. It was Oli.

"White Raven, you disobeyed a direct order," Moon Fang said. "Do you deny it?"

"No," Oli said.

"You will be fed tonight, but you will not be cleansed. Do you understand?"

"I do."

"Then take your place at the back of the line."

Oli wove his way back through the crowd, heading for Hinck. He stopped before him. "You should get dressed."

Hinck looked down at the forgotten bundle in his arms. His back ached. He imagined raw skin, cooked skin, peeling . . .

Oli grabbed his arm. "Hey."

Hinck stared at the dark eyes looking at him from behind the mask.

"I tried to warn you," Oli whispered. "Now snap out of it and put on your clothes."

Oli grabbed the wad from Hinck, shook out his tunic, and dropped everything else. He held it up as a onesent might. "Arms in, let's go."

Hinck threaded his arms through the holes, and Oli pulled it over his head. The fabric scraped against the burn like a razor. Hinck arched his back and whimpered, trying to get it off.

Oli did not coddle him. "Now the tabard. Come on."

Hinck gave in and allowed Oli to dress him.

"There will be a moment where you can spit it out," Oli said, cinching Hinck's belt around his tabard. "See how they take their portion, then circle back? You can get rid of it then."

What was he talking about? Hinck glanced back to the dais. A line had formed before the altar. Moon Fang was feeding each person a spoonful of something.

"What's on the spoon?" His raspy voice startled him and he cleared his throat. He needed to snap out of this daze, gather what little wits he had left, and pay attention.

"Evenroot," Oli said. "It allows us to see the black spirits in the Veil."

Hinck moaned. "But that's poison."

"Yes. We take the poison, then pray to the spirits to cure us. The prayer is an oath of allegiance. Tonight the spirits won't accept my oath. That is my punishment."

Hinck met the dark eyes in the bird mask. "But you'll die!"

The bird mask shook from side to side. "Not from one spoonful. They water it down. But I will be painfully sick."

"Then you should spit it out too," Hinck said.

"The spirits will know. They always know." Oli grabbed Hinck's shoulder and squeezed, looked directly into his eyes. "But you must not swallow. Spit out the poison and ignore the spirits. The brand means nothing. As long as you don't swallow, don't pray to them ever, they cannot claim your soul. Don't give them power over your soul, Hinck," Oli whispered. "Death is better."

Hinck shuddered.

Oli led Hinck to the line. As each person approached the front, Moon Fang whispered something, then fed them a spoonful of evenroot. When Hinck reached the front, the man said, "This is the milk of Gâzar, the King of Magic. Taste and become one of his children."

Gâzar of the Lowerworld?

Moon Fang lifted the spoon to Hinck's lips. Hinck opened his mouth and took it. It was sweet and gritty and icy cold and made the inside of his mouth tingle. He turned and followed the line of people toward the back of the room, holding the substance in his mouth. He tripped on his own feet, and a single drop of milky pulp slid down his throat like a shard of ice. He spit out the rest immediately, but it was too late. What had he done?

He grew frigid inside, as if ice had melted into his veins. Every nerve tingled, burned with cold. Hinck gasped, wanting the sensation to stop. Someone grabbed his shoulder.

"What did you do?" Oli. Angry.

The cold intensified. Hinck fell to his knees, shivering, gasping for breath.

A creature dressed in shadow reached out to him. Hinck stretched his arm toward it, then pulled back. No. He must not give himself to the spirit. "Go away," he said. "I don't want you."

The spirit vanished in a wisp of smoke.

Hinck blinked, panted in tiny hitches of air. The room warped and twisted in bands of colored smoke. The candlelight stretched. Drums came from somewhere. People started dancing. Someone screamed. A woman lay on the stone platform on the dais, writhing, shrieking in horror. Chains held her captive. Drums beat louder. Creatures appeared from the smoky air, leathery with wrinkled skin in various colors, some with three eyes. They fell upon the woman. Her wails intensified, then quickly silenced.

People continued to dance. Some fell to the ground and thrashed about. Others got up and went on dancing. The creatures continued to reach out, and Hinck denied them each time.

In the midst of it all, Hinck saw Oli fall to the floor, screaming. He did not rise.

KALENEK

The days passed slowly in the underground river. They ran out of food, so Jazlyn used magic to catch and cook fish. Jhorn, Inolah—and without a say, Ferro—refused to eat for two days, but Inolah finally gave in to Ferro's begging and fed the boy. At that point even Jhorn ate.

But Jazlyn's root tails eventually ran out. Now they were all hungry, and the mantic witch looked haggard and ill.

She wasn't the only one. A crowded, jostling boat made sleep difficult for everyone. Such erratic rest kept the worst of Kal's nightmares at bay, but his growing fatigue was making him irritable.

Jhorn kept the lantern off most of the time, wanting to preserve it. He lit it for short intervals. During one such time, Kal showed Jazlyn the piece of leather with the runes Lady Lebetta had drawn and asked if she could translate them.

"Rune magic is Magonian," she rasped. "Tennish mantics do not use such primitive methods."

This confused Kal. "I thought all mantics were the same."

"An insult to my kind," she said. "Evenroot gives a mantic spiritual eyes to see shadir. Each mother realm has its own ways of communicating with the shadir. Magonian mantics prefer rune magic and potions. Tennish priestesses rely on the language of the gods. We speak to the shadir as equals, which makes us infinitely more powerful."

"Infinitely more indebted," Jhorn mumbled.

This left Kal no closer to having completed his mission than when he had left Wilek in Farway. He hoped his prince would not be too disappointed.

After what felt like a month of darkness, the daylight came like lightning that flashed and remained in the sky.

The river had exited the ream and now flowed along the bottom of a deep, narrow canyon. Kal squinted up at the cliffs, heart swelling with recognition. "The cracks of Jeruka!" he yelled, relieved to know they would not sail off the end of a cliff. "We must be nearing the bay."

Sand sprinkled down the cliff walls here and there like tiny waterfalls. The canyon ran straight ahead, but in the distance it narrowed and turned.

"Everyone get down and cover your heads!" Kal yelled.

The coming bend was not a turn but a section of rock that had fallen from above, leaving only a narrow gap in the canyon for the river to pass through. Kal hoped the wagon would fit. He glanced at Jazlyn, but she was asleep—in a haze, Qoatch had claimed. Kal tucked his head between his knees.

The port side hit the fallen boulder and knocked the wagon in a half circle. The motion threw Kal against the side, sending an ache up his arm. The impact slowed the wagon's movement around the fallen rock. On the other side of the boulder, the swift current sucked them in and quickly increased their speed again. Kal kept low as the wagon banged between the cliffs and more fallen rocks.

"The wagon cracked!" Grayson cried.

Kal glanced at the leak, grabbed a leather bedroll. "Put this against it." He tossed it to the boy just as movement above captured his attention. "Avalanche!" he yelled. "Heads down!"

They swept into a shower of sand and rocks. The wagon bashed against another fallen boulder in the rapids. A stone hit Kal's shoulder, another his knee. Water was filling the wagon quickly. Kal tried to help Grayson plug the crack, but it was too big. They were going to sink.

The wagon rattled through another narrow opening. Up ahead, the canyon yawned into the Eversea.

Almost there. May Onika's god help them.

Chunks of rock rained down and struck the sides of the wagon, chipping at the poured stone. One fell onto a pack behind Burk. The boy yelped and pitched the rock overboard.

"Boulder!" Jhorn yelled.

Kal looked ahead. *Where?* Nothing but clear sea as they shot out into the mouth of the river.

Then they hit. The boulder had been hiding just beneath the water's surface. The impact catapulted the wagon up out of the water, above the submerged rock. Kal's body fell back over the side, and he plunged headfirst into the sea.

Underwater, Kal could still hear the low rumble of the avalanche, but more than that, he felt it. Deep, powerful vibrations surged through the water around him. He opened his eyes, and the saltiness stung. White bubbles spiraled around him as tiny rocks shot through the water. He glimpsed a colorful reef on his right and a wall of white light on his left. He kicked toward the light. He could see nothing overhead. No wagon. No people.

His head burst through the surface, and he thrashed around, looking for the others. The tattered tent they'd been using for a blanket floated before him. On his right, a pack. On his left, Jhorn gripping a water jug, eyes wide with confusion. Beyond Jhorn were several others: Prince Ulrik, Burk, and the dune cat, fur pasted to its skinny body. No sign of the wagon. Kal swam toward them slowly, searching for Inolah and Onika and Grayson. Could they not swim?

Continuous splashes pulled his focus to the cliffs behind him. An avalanche of rocks tumbled down into the water. This was more than an avalanche. It was an earthquake as well.

The vibration became so intense, the water tickled Kal's skin. Clouds of white sand swelled up beneath him, hiding the reef from view. Waterfalls of gravel, dust, and stones poured down the precipice.

As rocks fell from above, he suddenly realized—the Five Woes were upon them. He had seen all five now.

Down the coast, a deafening crack felled a section of cliff as large as Castle Everton. Just before it crashed into the sea, Kal caught sight of houses atop it and heard the distant screams.

Five Woes!

"Sir Kalenek, my mother!" Prince Ulrik yelled. He had a hold of Ferro and Jazlyn. "Help her!"

Kal saw Inolah and Onika at the same time. Inolah was floating facedown in the sea. Just past her, Onika splashed and flailed. Kal swam to Inolah, flipped her over. "Nolah!" He gripped the back neck of her dress and paddled toward Onika, dragging the empress along.

"Onika, I'm here!" Kal reached out. Her hand slapped his face. "Calm down." He grabbed her arm, and she climbed on him, submerging his head beneath the waves. Kal pushed away from her and kicked himself back to the surface. He spat out a mouthful of salty water. "Onika!" He grabbed her wrist. "Relax!"

Qoatch swam up to them. "Pass the empress to me."

Kal handed Inolah to the eunuch and pulled Onika close. "You must calm down," he said. "We ride the waves. We don't fight them."

"I can't . . ." She panted, choking him with her arms. "Can't swim." Her cheeks had flushed bright pink. He marveled at how her pale skin bared every emotion.

"Well, I can. We'll simply float here until help arrives."

The roaring subsided—the earthquake and avalanche over—but the swish of sand still rained down the cliffs and into the water. Then came a rolling wave that must have lifted them three levels—a result of the fallen cliff, no doubt. Onika screamed, but this far from shore, the wave did not curl or swamp them. It merely carried them farther out to sea.

Kal swam in place, supporting Onika's weight. The blind woman clung to him, pressing the side of her head against his tunic. There they waited, riding the waves of the Eversea and the countering swells from shore, which decreased with each passing. In the growing silence, soft sounds became easily noticeable: Onika's breathing, murmured talk from the others, the lap of the water against their bodies, the dripping of water from their hair, the purr of the breeze, the distant hiss of waves hitting the cliffs.

"I can hear your heart, Sir Kalenek," Onika said, pulling Kal from his reverie. "It has been broken but will someday heal and be filled with joy."

The words stunned him. The way she saw into people . . . So strange. But could she be right? Would he ever find joy?

Kal and Onika had drifted apart from the others, who were now clustered in a circle. Kal was relieved to see Inolah awake and swimming on her own. And Grayson, holding tight to Qoatch. A high-pitched growl brought up a chorus of laughter.

"Rustian?" Onika whispered.

Kal chuckled. "Your cat does not sound happy."

"Rustian dislikes water, but he is an excellent swimmer."

"He is an unyielding protector," Kal said. "You are lucky to have him."

"Not luck," Onika said. "Providence. And now I have a second protector. Though I might lose you for a time, Sir Kalenek, you will return to me some-day. Never forget that."

Kal pondered her words as he swam slowly toward the others. Everyone had survived. Grayson was bleeding from his temple, having been hit in the head with a rock, but there were no other injuries reported.

They swam east along the coast, where they could get a better look at the remains of Jeruka and the port. The sight of so many boats, still intact, comforted Kal. Surely one could carry them back to Everton.

It wasn't long before they were picked up by a fishing vessel. The captain was awestruck to learn he had rescued the Imperial family, and they were instantly taken to port. From there, wagons carried them toward the palace. As they moved through the city, Kal observed the destruction. Roads were cracked and uneven, houses collapsed. In the rubble, people held their dead and wailed.

They found the seaside palace eerily silent. When word spread of the Imperial family's arrival, servants came running. Their group was divided and swept in different directions. Priestess Jazlyn insisted Qoatch bathe, and the eunuch was forced to join Kal and Burk in the steams.

Kal bathed, dressed in a fresh Rurekan guard uniform, and was led to a private room, where he lay down, tucked his dagger under his pillow, and dozed off, wondering how long it would take before they could set sail for Everton.

QⵙATCH

After bathing, Qoatch set off for his chamber, which was across the hall from Jazlyn's. As long as he framed his requests as being for his Great Lady, the servants of Jeruka were eager to comply. A maid brought him a length of white linen that could be tied into a fresh kasah skirt. There were no sand cat pelts to be found, so he would have to go without.

Once he was dressed, he set off in search of appropriate clothing for his lady. The only white gowns he could find were plain servant dresses. In high quality he found only ivory. He tried to commission a white gown, but the dressmaker first wanted approval from the empress.

"I'm certain there is a Tennish gown in the palace," the dressmaker's maid said. "A gift from High Queen Tahmina for the empress." But she could not recall what had become of it.

So Qoatch carried his dismal clothing options to his lady's chambers and knocked.

"Enter."

Hearing Jazlyn's voice brought great relief. He hated being apart from her. She was the only person he cared for in the world. They must protect one another. He entered and found Jazlyn wearing a saffron-colored robe, standing at an open window, looking out at the city. Gozan he did not see.

Jazlyn turned her round eyes on him and frowned. "What are you wearing? Answer."

"A kasah I made from a length of fabric."

She grunted. "I suppose you've brought me something equally disappointing."

He laid the two options on her bed. She came to stand beside him, looking down her nose at both.

"These are unacceptable. Did you speak with the tailor? Answer."

"He is waiting on approval from the empress to begin your dress, Great Lady."

473

Jazlyn growled and strode back to the window. "I want to go home. I am tired of living like a vagrant. I have begun to shake from the lack of consistent evenroot. Those measly tails did little for my appetite."

Qoatch nodded. He would have to find his lady some root, but he would take his time. A fast would do her body good.

A knock at the door preceded the dressmaker's maid, holding a white gown and an earthenware crock.

The girl swept inside without being invited. "I found it!" She strode to the bed and laid the Tennish gown beside the other two. "It's going to be a bit big, but I've come prepared." She set the crock on the bed, lifted the lid, and withdrew a shard of yellow chalk.

Jazlyn came to look over her shoulder. "This is acceptable." She shrugged off her robe and handed it to Qoatch.

The maid jumped and looked away, embarrassed it seemed by Jazlyn's nakedness. Qoatch took charge and grabbed the gown, shook it out.

"Reverse it," the girl said. "So I can mark the seams."

Qoatch turned the gown inside out and helped Jazlyn into it. The dress hung off her shoulders and pooled on the floor at her feet. Jazlyn lifted her arms to the side and the girl set to work.

"I'm sorry for your loss, Your Highness," the girl said. "It must be awful to experience such a betrayal."

The words shook Qoatch, prickling his conscience.

"I am not a *Highness*," Jazlyn snapped. "I am a Great Lady. And what do you mean, *my loss*? Answer, girl."

The maid's eyes widened. "You don't know about the rebellion in Tenma?"

Qoatch felt dizzy. The Kushaw. He'd almost forgotten. Had they gone through with it? Had they killed the priestesses?

"I have been in Rurekau these past few weeks on a diplomatic mission," Jazlyn said. "Explain this rebellion at once."

"Yes, Your . . . Great Lady," the girl said. "Four days ago we received a group of Tennish refugees coming from Larsa who told us of an uprising of men in Yobatha. Rebels murdered all the high mantic priestesses and the child priestesses-in-training."

Jazlyn sank to the edge of the bed. "What men could kill a priestess?"

"They were eunuchs," the girl said, glancing at Qoatch. "They're calling it the Eunuch Rebellion."

Jazlyn stared at Qoatch. "Did you know of this? Answer me truthfully."

Qoatch tried to remain composed, but his eyes watered and he looked away.

"Leave us," Jazlyn commanded the maid.

The girl practically ran from the room.

"Wait!" Jazlyn yelled. "Where are these Tennish refugees now?"

"They've set up a camp on the outskirts of the city, Great Lady."

Jazlyn waved her hand at the girl, who fled. The clump of the door brought a heavy silence over the room.

"You knew of this," Jazlyn said. "Speak your answer now."

Qoatch must be careful. He needed to twist the truth just enough so that she would believe. "They are called the Kushaw. They came to me the night before we left Yobatha and told me their plan. They wanted me to take your life."

Jazlyn's stare burned his courage and he looked at the floor. "You've had plenty of opportunities," she said. "Why did you let me live?"

His hands shook. No answer but the truth would possibly convince her. "Because you saved me, Great Lady."

"When?"

"The Kushaw were harsh, but as a boy, I believed in their cause—I still do." He risked a glance and swallowed. "But when I came to the palace in Yobatha, where the High Queen makes us, compels us . . . Her cruelty . . ." He broke off, trembling at the memories of Queen Tahmina's torture. "You claimed me—saved me from her wrath."

"It wasn't compassion. I needed a eunuch."

Qoatch knew better. Jazlyn disdained Queen Tahmina's unnecessary cruelty. And in taking Qoatch as her own, she had spared him further pain—had never used pain against him.

He shook his head. "You saved me, Great Lady." And he bowed low.

Her burst of laughter made Qoatch tense. He straightened and found her in a fit of hysterics. She laughed hard and long and deep.

Qoatch's cheeks burned. He wanted to leave, to flee from this humiliation.

Before he could, she took hold of his hand, squeezed it. "Oh, Qoatch, sweet slav of mine. Do not fear. You have given me rule of Tenma. I will not cast you aside, not ever. Now, fetch that maid to finish this dress. I must visit the Tennish refugees to establish myself as High Queen."

Immense relief washed away shame. Qoatch stood before her—a trained assassin meant to take her life—and again she had granted him mercy. Humbled, his heart swelled. He bowed and departed, eager to please his Great Lady.

He would be devoted to her for life.

İnOLAH

Ulrik son of Nazer, at sixteen years of age, was now Emperor of Rurekau.

The officials in Jeruka had rallied to crown him immediately. They did not like taking orders from a woman. So, just like that, Inolah's power was gone. She still had authority as the emperor's mother, and would continue to have it until he married, but it was not the same.

That was fine. She did not want power. But she wasn't certain her son was ready to handle so much of it all at once.

She sat on a chair in the corner of the council room, watching *Emperor* Ulrik in his first council meeting. So far he was exercising wisdom by remaining silent and listening. He was bare-chested, with henna tracings all over his torso, and wore the medallion of his office on a single gold chain. They had also given him fresh tracings on his head and around his eyes that set off the thick golden crown he wore.

"The city is in chaos, Emperor," the Igote general said. "We cannot offer aid fast enough, and just when we manage to restore some level of calm, another earthquake turns everything upside down again."

"The Tennish refugees keep coming," the sheriff said.

"We have Rurekan refugees coming in as well," the general added. "From Nindera and Lâhaten."

Ulrik lifted his hand. "We will deal with these problems. But first I want to talk of Sir Kalenek's recommendation for relocation."

Inolah was pleased that her son had included Kal in the meeting. The High Shield had yet to speak, but Ulrik had already informed his council of Kal's recommendation.

"It's hogsfeed," the general said. "The earth cannot be destroyed. Perhaps Barthos is merely ridding the land of transgressors."

"My brother was killed in yesterday's quake!" the sheriff yelled. "You know full well that he was a better man than any of us." He turned to Ulrik and spoke calmly. "I think we should go, Your Eminence. These quakes are growing more powerful and frequent."

"It would be madness," the general said. "The fleet isn't large enough to take everyone, and the Igote numbers are too small to stop thieves from stealing smaller crafts."

"What do you think, Mother?" Ulrik asked.

"I trust Sir Kalenek with my life," Inolah said, looking at Kal. "He is honorable and would never deceive us. If he says that Farway, Hebron, and Kaptar are no more, I believe him. I cannot say whether every word the prophetess speaks is truth, but seven major cities destroyed so close together is highly suspect."

"I agree," Ulrik said. "But I cannot desert my people or my land."

"Forgive me, Your Eminence," Kal said, speaking for the first time. "Your land won't be here much longer, and if you insist on staying, your empire will end. I recommend you gather as many of your people as you can and put them on ships."

"All because of the words of an aberration," the general said. "Why should we believe her?"

"Bring her here and ask her yourself," Kal said. "She knows things that are impossible for her to know. She warned of Kaptar's demise before it happened, predicted it to the very hour. Do not make light of her words."

The prophetess had clearly won Kal's support. Inolah wondered if he had feelings for the pale woman. She was at least ten years his junior, but Inolah couldn't deny that Onika was alluring in an alien sort of way.

"Whether you stay or go," Kal said. "I must obey her wish to meet my sâr."

Which meant he would set sail for Everton as soon as possible. Inolah wanted to go too.

"I have spoken to her," Ulrik said. "And I agree with Sir Kalenek. But without land I have no empire. I must do what is best for Rurekau and my—"

An earthquake shook the room. Several of the councilmen cried out. The Igote general dove under the table. The shaker did not last long.

Inolah spoke before anyone else could. "The empire is in the hearts of the people, my son. Rurekau can find new land and build new cities. But only if we survive."

Ulrik took a deep breath. "It is decided. We will sail to Everton and join the Armanian fleet. My next concern is the Tennish people. I cannot trust them. Priestess Jazlyn, whom I greatly admire, threatened war against Rurekau before Lâhaten fell. She is a cunning woman. While she has been a friend to my mother and me during this ordeal, in the end she will do what is best—what is most prosperous—for her people."

Inolah relaxed, glad to hear Ulrik speak some sense regarding the priestess. She still was uncertain they had done right in keeping secret Jazlyn's involvement in destroying Lâhaten and killing Nazer. But to confess Ulrik's knowledge now would risk his crown.

"There are too many Tennish refugees," the general said. "They could overpower us."

"Not without their evenroot," Kal said. "Do they have some?"

"Probably," the sheriff said.

"We must divide the Tennish people between the ships," Ulrik said.

"Won't that give them more power?" the general asked.

"Quite the opposite," Ulrik said. "If we give them, say, five of their own ships, they might, in time, plot against us. But if we separate them, allow no more than twenty per ship, they will be unable to rise up. They will be nothing more than passengers. And we must make sure they bring aboard no evenroot."

"I like it," the general said. "But I won't like telling the priestess."

Ulrik flashed a wide smile. "Leave the priestess to me, General."

Ulrik made Inolah wait outside the council room with Qoatch while he spoke to the priestess alone. It was incredibly foolish. The woman could have found a new supply of evenroot by now. She could kill Ulrik for his attempt to force her hand.

The door was not closed for long. Priestess Jazlyn shot out like a hawk, the door banging in her wake. Nostrils flaring, she stopped before them. Qoatch stood to greet her, but her eyes were focused on Inolah.

"He is starting down a path just like his father," she said.

Arman, help them. What had Ulrik done?

"On the contrary," Ulrik said, strolling out of the council chambers, hands tucked innocently behind his back. "My father would have left your people to die. Compared to him, I am a hero—the savior of your people."

"You are an arrogant man pup who will someday soon be taught a valuable lesson in humility. I will not be sorry to hear you failed to survive it."

A chuckle from Ulrik. "Would you like to divide your people into groups of twenty, or shall I?"

"I will do it." Jazlyn stalked away with Qoatch in tow.

"I'll have a schedule of departures sent to your chambers so you can arrange matters," Ulrik called after her. "Good midday, Priestess!"

She did not reply.

"Ulrik, was that wise?" Inolah asked.

Ulrik turned his delighted expression on Inolah. "I cannot be certain, Mother, but I am beginning to think the priestess likes me more than she lets on."

The next morning, the fleet began to set out. The council had decreed to send five ships immediately, filled with the most important citizens of Rurekau and enough provisions to reach Armania. The rest of the fleet would follow once each ship could be filled with food and supplies. The ships would anchor outside the Everton harbor until they decided on which direction to sail.

There were thirty-three great vessels—both merchant and military—at port in Jeruka, and hundreds of smaller, personal craft. Already there had been riots among the private sector from people fighting over places in boats. The sheriff had his hands full dealing with it all, which pleased Ulrik. Inolah knew her son disliked how the council hovered and gave him advice, as if he were a fool who knew nothing.

Ulrik was no fool. But he was vastly untrained and overconfident, the latter of which Inolah feared might be his undoing.

The day passed in a blur. Ulrik assigned Sir Kalenek and his band to the *Baretam*, the emperor's warship. He asked the High Shield to help him keep an eye on Priestess Jazlyn, whom Ulrik had assigned to the same ship.

Inolah stood on the bow of the *Baretam* and watched the priestess board, her white gown fluttering in the wind. Qoatch, stunning as always, shadowed her. Then came eighteen Tennish refugees.

Inolah's baby kicked, and she pressed her hand to the place she had felt the movement. She had never been so uncertain about the future. Her husband was dead. Her son was emperor. Her daughter was missing. And the place she had lived these seventeen years was no more. She was leaving. Starting over. Yet she had never felt so lost in all her life.

WILEK

Wilek sat with Harton in a metal cage on a cart headed for The Gray, the mist wetting his face. All his life he had feared this moment, yet he found himself oddly calm. He had prepared Trevn and Rayim for the possibility that he would not return. Armania would survive the Five Woes. His only regret was that Father had ordered Harton to be sacrificed too.

"I'm sorry, Hart," Wilek said. "You shouldn't be here."

Harton shrugged, jaw set. "No one really knows what's down there, Your Highness. It's not my destiny to die tonight."

Such confidence amazed Wilek. He didn't want to give up either, but in his over two hundred visits to The Gray, no one had ever survived. Not once.

The caravan arrived at the shrine, and Wilek and Harton were brought before the stone ring. The moon was barely a sliver tonight, so it was harder to see the bronze platform, the circle of stones, and the Barthos pole.

What to do, Arman? Should he fight to get away? Stand with dignified pride? Scream truth to the witnesses?

No option seemed right.

Wilek eyed the chute box warily, knowing he would be sent down first. Right into Barthos's open maw.

He studied the crowd. Janek had stopped his horse in the center position of the arc, where the First Arm belonged, the very place Wilek had sat some two hundred times before. He wore the Heir's ring on his right hand. The blue diamond above Father's Barthos insignia gleamed in the torchlight.

Wilek had earned that ring. It should have been his. None of this should be happening. He glared at his father, who sat in his rollchair beside the Pontiff, just outside the stone barrier. The man looked more bloated than ever. Thick coils of herbs hung heavy around his neck. They would do nothing against Rogedoth's magic.

Wilek turned his glare on the Pontiff next—Prince Mergest, the banished. What had become of Rayim and Teaka and their search for evenroot? Had they found it? Or had they already started back to Everton to help Trevn flee the coming Woes?

"Tonight we sacrifice two worthy men to Barthos," Father yelled, drawing Wilek's attention. "The value of a sacrifice is gauged by how much value it has to the offerer. As my eldest living son, Sâr Wilek's value to me is beyond measure. He is the most I can give to Barthos. And Barthos will honor my sacrifice."

No, he won't. They'd both die, and Rogedoth and Janek would rule until the Five Woes sucked them into the ground, straight to the Lowerworld.

"Are there any others who would give their lives to the god of the soil?" Father asked. "His anger against us burns. He continues to shake the earth, so we must honor him, that he might let us live. Good men of Armania, who among you who would sacrifice to save our worthy realm?"

Father gave this talk every so often, especially when ruled by fear. No one had ever taken him up on it—not since the day Chadek had died.

The men on horseback shifted uncomfortably as they waited for the king to move on.

"If there are none," Father said after another moment, "we shall begin the—"

"I will sacrifice!" a man yelled. "I will go into The Gray."

What was this? The crowd murmured and parted, revealing Oli Agoros, Duke of Canden, dismounting his horse. He approached the king, his expression somber, and dropped to his knees before the rollchair.

"Mighty rosâr, may you live a thousand years," Oli said, his voice choked. "I give my life for this noble cause."

Why would the duke do such a thing? Was this some trick of Janek's?

"No!" a voice yelled from the crowd.

"I'm the prized heir of my family," Oli said, louder. "My life should delight Barthos."

"Don't be daft!" Oli's father, Zeteo Agoros, ran out of the crowd. He gripped the neck of Oli's tunic and dragged him back from the king. "Get on your horse, fool!"

Oli fell to his rear. He pulled free of his father's hold and knelt again before the king.

Janek dismounted and came to stand beside the king's rollchair. "We have enough offerings tonight, Oli. Obey your father."

"I have given my life to the rosâr, may he reign forever," Oli said, glaring at Janek. "The decision is his."

"The offer has been made," Father said. "To rescind is to insult Barthos."

"No!" Janek glared at Father. "This is *my* servant. He belongs to me."

"Don't you kill my boy, Echad!" Zeteo yelled.

The king raised his hands above his head, making his tunic stretch taught against his bulbous stomach. "My word is law! Any who disagree may feed Barthos as well." He lowered his arms. "Zeteo? Janek? Will you die for Armania?"

The silence was absolute. Everyone stared at the four men. Finally Zeteo spat on the ground by Oli and charged back into the crowd. Janek slunk back to his horse and mounted.

This was madness!

The guards stripped Oli of his belt and sword and checked his boots for knives. Pontiff Rogedoth stepped over the rock barrier and approached the pole. He knelt before it alone and muttered a prayer, while two guards pulled Father's rollchair up the steps of the shrine. Rogedoth circled the pole five times before ascending the shrine to stand with the king.

"Bring the offerings," Father yelled.

Wilek let out a short breath, fighting to keep his fear locked away where Charlon might not feel it and make everything worse. Two pikemen nudged Wilek forward. He knew them. A King's Guard named Marret Gells and Trevn's friend Hinckdan.

"Since when is an earl a pikeman?" Wilek asked.

"I volunteered," Hinckdan said.

Strange. "Trevn said he told you that Pontiff Rogedoth is a mantic. I informed my father, but the Pontiff controls him."

Hinckdan glanced at the king but did not answer.

Wilek tried the first pikeman. "Gells? If we do not stand against the Pontiff, he will see to it that my father kills more innocents. Is that what you want?"

"I'm sorry, Your Highness," Gells said. "I have a wife and five children."

Wilek nodded. "I understand. But if you let me die today, there will be no one left to stand against my father when he decides to feed you all to Barthos."

Gells looked away.

Hinckdan narrowed his eyes, then squeezed one shut.

Was that a wink?

"Assume the formation," Father yelled.

The audience took their places. Wilek, Harton, and Oli stepped inside the barrier and knelt before the Barthos pole. Wilek bowed his head and spoke to Arman.

Father Tomek believed you real. After Rogedoth's behavior, I'm inclined to agree. So I pray to you, Arman, not to this Barthos pole. I pledge my life to serve you and all of your decrees. If you are merciful, as Trevn thinks you might be and as Kal's prophetess claims, have mercy on me. Save my life so I can save my people. I must get them on boats, to obey your prophetess. Help me help you, mighty god.

Wilek looked up to see Janek on his horse, looking down on him, expressionless.

"You will go to the utter depths of the Lowerworld for this, Janek," Wilek said. "Gâzar has set aside a special place of torture for Rogedoth and his son."

Janek smirked. "I am not his son, you fool."

"Silence!" Father waved to Gells. "Circle the pole!"

"Will you stand, Your Highness?" Gells asked Wilek.

Wilek and Harton leaned together, used each other's weight to stand. They started around the pole, Hinckdan behind them. A third pikeman steered Oli along.

Wilek considered running, but that would only make him look cowardly. He must continue his show of fearless bravado, even if it was a lie.

Pontiff Rogedoth began his diatribe. "We, the children of man, sit in the shadow of Barthos's glory. Our sins bind us in misery and we deserve his wrath. Barthos shakes the foundations of the—"

"Arman is god over all!" Wilek yelled, suddenly inspired. "Barthos is false! Arman is god over all! Barthos is a fabrication!"

"Silence the prisoner!" Father yelled as Rogedoth continued his speech.

"What are you doing?" Oli asked Wilek.

"Challenging my father one last time." He yelled all the louder, until Hinckdan whacked his pike over Wilek's head so hard that he fell to his knees.

"Get him up," Father said. "Finish the last lap."

"I've got him," Hinckdan told Gells. "You stay with the others."

Gells and the third pikeman walked on with Harton and Oli. Hinckdan crouched beside Wilek. The earl grabbed his arm and helped him stand, slipping something cold and hard up Wilek's right sleeve.

"Sorry I can do no more, Your Highness," Hinckdan whispered.

A blade! Wilek ripped away from the earl and walked with his head held high, hoping to drive off all suspicion. The dagger was cold against his skin. He held his wrist carefully, desperate to keep the dagger in place. He finished the circle just as Rogedoth reached the end of his speech.

"We thank Barthos for his kindness," Rogedoth said, "and proclaim his wonders to all who have ears."

"Bring forth the offerings," Father said.

The three men came to stand at the bottom of the steps. They would go one at a time. Wilek first. He climbed the steps on his own, looked down on his father, and considered using the knife to kill him, but that would put Janek on the throne. Instead he said, "As we stand here my men are working to end this tyranny. You might kill me, but your reign is near the end. Not even your mantic puppeteer can save you."

Father's eyes flashed. "You have been sentenced to die as an offering to Barthos, god of the soil. Tonight you atone for yourself and all Armania."

"I atone for no one," Wilek snarled. "You murder me, just as you murdered Chadek and hundreds of others."

"Put him in the box!" Father yelled.

Hinckdan opened the half door of the chute box, and Wilek stepped inside. Hinckdan closed the door, gave Wilek one last desperate look, then walked to his position at the outer edge of the platform.

The box reached above Wilek's waist, hiding his hands from the crowd. He could cut his bonds now. Try to escape. But there were too many guards. One dagger against two dozen pikes and swords would swiftly fail.

He lifted his bound hands and gently ran his finger over the shards of broken glass that ringed the top edge of the chute box. No place to hold on. Not for Chadek. Not for him.

Arman, help him. He would face Barthos and fight.

Rogedoth looked to the top of the Barthos pole. "This man dies so that we might earn your favor and proceed to peace and long life." Rogedoth smirked at Wilek. "Tell your concubine Moon Fang says good evening." He yanked down the lever that opened the trapdoor.

The floor under Wilek's feet vanished and he fell.

He felt Charlon then, for the first time all day. His terror reached across the distance and pulled her to him as he slid down the chute, one hand pressing the dagger against his stomach to keep from losing it. The journey seemed endless and he held his breath, waiting for the bottom, wanting to somehow brace himself for impact.

But there was none. He slid over a tiny bump, which made a bell clang overhead, then the smoothness of the chute changed to dirt, and he came to a stop over packed sand.

He sat up and shook the dagger from his sleeve. It fell between his legs. He felt for it, wishing he had a torch. His fingers found the hilt, and he carefully began sawing the rope around his wrists. The sharp blade quickly severed the hemp.

Many thanks, Hinckdan.

Hands free, he gripped the dagger and stood. He found himself in a narrow wedge of canyon. The walls rose high on either side, leaving the land before him open for Barthos's approach. The sliver of moon hung above, seeming to smile upon his misfortune. Wilek gripped the dagger tighter and stepped forward, kicked something. Sticks covered the ground. He reached for one and stopped. Not sticks. Bones. Human bones.

He shivered, thinking of Chadek here, just a boy, crying, afraid, then eaten by a god.

Not a god, Trevn had said. A falsehood. A fabrication.

God or not, something had eaten all these people.

Rôb priests claimed that Barthos inhabited The Gray, despite there being dozens of Grays throughout the Five Realms. Father believed Barthos was omnipresent. Others maintained that the creatures in The Grays were servants of Barthos.

Wilek didn't know what to believe anymore.

A snap above sent him spinning around. Something whirred in the chute. Harton was coming. Wilek waited, but before Harton arrived, the chute door above snapped again, and the whirring increased. Oli was coming too. Wilek's words had affected Father. The guilt-ridden man wanted to leave The Gray.

A bell clanged above, sounding much louder outside the chute. Harton exited face-first, coughing and spitting dirt from his mouth. Wilek ran over and helped him stand. The moment he cut through Harton's binds, the bell clanged once more. Seconds later Oli arrived, sitting upright as if he took this adventure every week.

Wilek held up the dagger. "Give me your hands, Oli."

"Where did you get that?" Oli asked. "They took mine."

"Hinckdan gave it to me by the Barthos pole," Wilek said, slicing through the ropes.

"Good man, Hinck!" Oli said, laughing. "I hope he survives Janek without me."

Something rattled in the distance.

"I doubt that's a snake," Hart said.

"I think the bells called him," Wilek said. "Why would a god need a dinner bell?"

"Curse that splintered moon," Oli said. "It would help to see better." He crouched and picked up a long bone.

"I think that's someone's leg," Wilek said.

Oli gave it a swing. "You have a knife. I need a weapon too."

The rattling grew louder.

Harton sat down and pulled off his boot.

"Have you a knife too, Hart?" Wilek asked.

"No." Harton fiddled with something, put it in his mouth. "Gods, my throat is dry. I need water."

"What are you doing?" Wilek asked.

The rattling swelled into an ear-piercing cackle. How Wilek hated that sound! He backed against the chute bottom, holding out the dagger.

Oli came to stand beside him. "I have a feeling your dagger and my bone are only going to make Barthos angry."

"You have a better plan?" Wilek asked.

Oli snorted. "I came down here to escape my father and Janek. My plan ended there."

To their left, Harton slumped to the ground.

"Hart!" Wilek ran to his side and leaned over him.

"Did he faint?" Oli asked.

"I think not. His eyes are open." Wilek kicked Hart's leg, but the man simply stared into the black sky, breathing heavily, almost panting. "Harton, get up!"

Out in the darkness, sand crunched as if someone had thrown a boulder into it. Another crunch. Another.

"If those are footsteps . . ." Oli said.

A shriek pierced the night, bringing with it a rancid smell on the wind. *Barthos.*

"I say we feed him Harton and make a run for the chute," Oli whispered.

Harton groaned. "I heard that."

"Hart, get up!" Wilek whispered. "He comes."

An immense shadow rippled before them, blocking the sliver of moon. Three eyes the size of coconuts flashed in a body the color of sand. The creature screeched. Wilek trembled, squeezing the dagger as if that alone might save him.

The three eyes flashed again, and somewhere high above came the rattle of countless hollow sticks clacking together. Another wail sent a gust of rotten breath over Wilek, who caught sight of a mouth bigger than he was tall. Gods, he must be huge!

Harton was still on the ground, on his knees now. The fool would be killed if he stayed there.

Barthos took another ground-shaking step . . . another . . . then three at once. The air rippled before Wilek, and he squatted.

He could see Barthos clearly now, looming over him. His head looked similar to a rabid dog. Scaly ridges covered his body. He walked on his hind legs like a man and stood as high as a two-level house.

Barthos lowered his head, so Wilek darted between the legs, keeping low. The creature moved his nose over the ground, sniffing, and Wilek slipped out the back between his legs and tail, raking his dagger over the hock of the beast's left foot.

Barthos howled.

Wilek ran to the right. The creature twisted to look for him. Wouldn't Barthos speak? Was this a god or an animal?

Oli clubbed the side of Barthos's head with the leg bone, which splintered, leaving the top half of the bone hanging limp from the bottom.

The beast growled, wrenched around to get at Oli. Wilek slashed at the creature's hip.

This time Barthos turned back to Wilek so fast his snout batted him to the ground. Wilek hit the sand crawling and quickly rose to a run.

"Hey!" Oli yelled, holding the two halves of his leg bone, splinters out. He whistled, as if calling a hunting dog.

The creature spun back to Oli, who plunged his two bone halves into one yellow eye, giving Wilek the chance he needed. He stabbed his dagger high on the creature's other leg. Barthos screamed and sent a kick to Wilek's chest. Wilek landed in the sand and skidded all the way to the rock wall. He gasped, trying to find his breath, saw the creature whirl toward him, stomp closer.

Oli ran up behind Barthos and swung another bone at the back of his leg. The beast swiveled his head around and roared. Wilek seized the moment and ran.

God or not, they could never kill the beast, not like this. They were like two mice fighting a desert cat that could swallow them whole.

Oli screamed in agony. Wilek glanced back and saw him on the ground, cradling his arm. The creature's head looked up at the moon as he choked down something.

Oli's arm? Gods, he would truly eat them alive. "Oli!" Wilek yelled.

In a snap Barthos lowered his head to the ground, nose pointed toward Wilek, nostrils flaring. Behind the creature, Oli tried to stand but fell, moaning, his arms curled against his chest.

Wilek backed away from the beast and held out his knife.

The rattling increased—where *was* that coming from?

Wilek's feet tangled in a pile of bones. He struggled for balance, keeping his eyes on Barthos. He crouched, grabbed a bone, and threw it. The bone bounced off the creature's face and earned Wilek a snarl. He switched the dagger to his left hand and tried again, this time getting some heft into his throw. The bone smacked Barthos's snout.

The beast merely growled.

Wilek edged backward through the bone pile until his heels hit the rock wall of the canyon. Barthos crept upon him and roared, blowing hot, rancid breath into Wilek's face. Wilek gagged, gripped the knife tightly, and prepared to fight for his life.

Behind Barthos, a green light brightened the night. Wilek wanted to look to see what it was but didn't dare take his eyes off the creature.

Barthos, however, tucked his head between his legs and moaned like a frightened pup.

The beast didn't like the light.

The brilliance shifted, spilling across the sand, growing brighter until a green ball of fire struck Barthos's right shoulder. The creature howled and spun around.

What in the Five Realms was that? Wilek looked back.

A second ball of fire blazed into light, centered on Harton's palm.

Wilek lost his breath. Harton was a mantic?

Harton hurled the second fireball, which struck Barthos in the ear. The beast shrieked and ran into the cliff wall. Hit hard. Fell. Another ball of fire bloomed and sailed, this time hitting Barthos in the stomach.

Barthos howled. He struggled to rise onto his legs but slumped back to the sand.

Harton had injured him.

It. Barthos was no god. That much Wilek now knew for certain. This creature was all animal. Looking for an easy meal.

A third ball of fire sparked, grew slowly on Harton's hand. He hurled the fire against the creature's head. It wailed and thrashed in the sand.

Then Harton collapsed.

Wilek started toward his backman, but a snort from the creature changed his mind. He ran toward it. He needed to finish this.

The beast lay on its back, chin pointed to the sky, neck exposed. Wilek gripped the dagger and dragged it hard across half of its throat.

The beast flailed, head jerking up and spraying blood across Wilek's chest. Wilek stumbled back, waited. The creature rattled and moaned, tossed and turned. When it fell silent again, Wilek came around its head and sliced the other side of its neck.

This time the creature merely twitched. The growl in its throat was more of a death rattle. Encouraged, Wilek set to work, hacking his dagger across its neck. The blade scratched over tendons and bone. Hot blood drenched his arms and steamed the pores on his face, sending up a sour smell. He kept at it, pouring his fury at all this creature had done into every stroke until he managed to sever the head completely.

The creature was dead. Had never been a god. Wilek crouched over it, noticing for the first time that it had two horns on its head—rather than the long ears Barthos was always drawn with. Each horn was as long as Wilek's leg and curved slightly forward.

He walked around to its tail and found it had a rattle, like a rattler snake, though this rattle was as long as Wilek's arm. He realized with a jolt that the beast had all the likeness of the cheyvahs of myth.

A moan reminded him of Oli and Harton. Wilek grabbed one of the horns and dragged the head back toward the chute. Once he was a good arrow's shot from the carcass, he let go and ran to Oli, who was lying on the ground, moaning.

In the darkness Wilek couldn't tell what he was looking at. Oli's tunic was drenched in blood. His left hand gripped the right . . . No. It gripped the stump of his right arm just above the elbow. The rest was gone.

Wilek peeled off his tabard and wrapped the stump. The duke screamed, and Wilek went as quickly as he could, twisting the tabard tight until Oli's arm ended in a fat roll of fabric.

"You going to live?" Wilek asked, laying Oli's arm at his side.

Oli panted, grunted, and gasped out, "It feels like a god bit off my arm."

"I'm sorry," Wilek said, which sounded completely hollow.

"Am I hallucinating?" Oli asked. "Or did your backman do magic?"

"He did magic." Time to see about that. Wilek pushed up and walked to where Harton was kneeling and muttering.

"You're a mantic, Harton?"

"A moment, please," he said. "I have to purge."

The poison. Charlon had called it cleansing. Wilek waited, furious and thankful at the same time. He never could have killed the cheyvah without Harton's fireballs, but his own backman a mantic? The revelation stung.

Harton looked up suddenly, eyes clear. "I'm sorry I didn't tell you, Your Highness. I knew you wouldn't employ a mantic."

"Because mantics are illegal in Armania," Wilek said.

"I don't use it much, I swear. A little love spell here and there. Extra strength on the practice yard."

Love spells. "Why doesn't it change the color of your eyes?"

"It's an easy enough spell to mask eye color," Harton said.

Which explained how Rogedoth hid his gray eyes. "Where did you learn?"

"From my father, who learned from a Tennish whore. After he died, I pretended to be Armanian to get out of Rurekau."

"How old are you, really?"

"Twenty-nine."

Unbelievable. "You're older than me!"

"Please don't discharge me. I'm a good soldier. I'll try again to quit. It's just . . . root is addicting."

Wilek knew—had felt Charlon's cravings for the stuff. His sympathy angered him. "The need for evenroot has destroyed the Five Realms! You have seen the results firsthand."

"I know. I'm sorry. But I never grew my own. I always bought it."

In Everton, even, he had known where to purchase it. "That does not make it right, Hart. I must think on what to do." Wilek turned back to check on Oli, then stopped, an idea forming. He twisted back to Harton. "Can you heal Oli's arm?"

Harton glanced over to where Oli's body lay. "Perhaps. How bad is it?"

"Come and see." He offered Harton his hand, pulled him to standing, and they jogged to where Oli lay.

Harton knelt at Oli's side, staring at the blood. Wilek unwrapped his tabard from Oli's arm. The fabric was now soaked through. Oli groaned, tried to move away, then passed out.

Wilek pulled the rest of the tabard free and regarded the oozing stump. If Harton could heal Oli, perhaps he would be willing to attempt a soul-loosing spell. Wilek didn't want to hope too strongly, and praying to Arman that a mantic would free him seemed wrong somehow, so he pushed the thought aside for the moment.

Harton grimaced at the wound. "I don't . . ." He shuddered. "I don't know how to replace his arm without having it here. I'll just, um, stop the bleeding. Put a confusion in his mind so he doesn't feel pain." He laid his hand on Oli's bleeding arm and spoke in ancient Armanian, just as Charlon had. Unlike Charlon, or even Teaka, he did not use a bowl or blood.

"*Izog âthâh. Âtsar dâm. Râphâ zōt chêts.*"

Wilek watched the bloody mass, waiting for it to dry up. Instead, blood seeped between Harton's fingers, dripped down the side of his hand.

"You're making it worse," Wilek said.

Harton scowled. "Shh!"

The cold crept upon Wilek like a shadow, pimpling his arms. Icy air snaked down his throat. The oozing blood frosted. Oli screamed.

"What's happening?" Wilek asked, shivering.

"A moment more," Harton said, breath misting from his mouth.

"I won't!" Oli yelled. "You cannot force me. Get away!"

Harton slumped over, unconscious. Wilek shook him, found him breathing. The air around them warmed. Oli's arm now ended in a smooth stump, just above where his elbow had once been.

Wilek looked down on the duke. "Oli? Are you well?"

Oli simply stared into the night sky, breathing steadily.

Wilek sat on the ground between the two men, wondering if there were more cheyvah in this Gray. The silence chilled his arms as he waited anxiously for Harton to wake. Oli groaned and shifted several times before Harton sat up.

Wilek wasted no time. "Can you cast a soul-loosing spell?"

The backman simply stared.

Frustration filled Wilek's chest. "Answer me!"

"I-I don't know," Harton stammered. "I've never tried."

"You will try. Now." Wilek drew the pendant from inside his tunic and pulled the cord over his head. "She wrapped our hands in this. It burned a rune onto my palm."

Harton took the pendant, pressed the amulet to Wilek's palm, and wrapped the cord around his hand. Wilek could still see the burn scars where the cord had seared him.

Harton tucked the end of the twine under itself, then pulled off his other boot. A packet fell out onto the sand.

"More evenroot?" Wilek asked.

"It only lasts so long."

Wilek waited while Harton ingested the drug and fell under its stupor. It surprised him how differently Harton and Charlon reacted to evenroot. Wilek had never once seen Charlon behave like this. Perhaps one reacted to root juice differently than powder? Or maybe Charlon was more gifted or learned as a mantic. She did ask for cleansing, though not after every spell.

When Harton became himself again, he spoke the words of his spell without asking which mantic had cast the soul-binding. Would Harton's ignorance of spells keep him from success?

"*Izog âthâh.*" Izog, come.

"*Bâqa ze ecâr.*" Break the bond.

"*Nêzer illek nephesh.*" Separate the souls.

"*Bara châphash netsach.*" Make free forever.

Wilek felt Charlon briefly, as if she were being ripped away. Tears flooded his eyes and he screamed as the incredible loss consumed him. He collapsed in the sand and wept.

Then came a sudden warmth.

Wilek was lying on the dirt, Harton looming over him. His backman pulled the cord off Wilek's hand. The lines from the twine were still there, but the rune mark on his palm was gone, as was the cold within. Wilek sat up. "You did it."

Harton winced. "You don't feel the bond?"

"Nor the cold."

"Good." Harton shifted onto his knees. "I must purge again."

Wilek sat in silence, thankful to be free from Charlon. He watched Harton, curious. The spell hadn't seemed like it had cost much effort. Harton was still lucid this time, while healing Oli had rendered him unconscious. Why had Teaka been afraid to try?

"The shadir are coming for me," Oli said.

Wilek crawled to Oli's side. "No one is here but us. Harton healed you."

"Healed my arm?" Oli lifted his stump and uttered a small cry.

"I'm sorry," Wilek said. "I mean he stopped the bleeding."

Oli's gaze shifted to Harton, who lay on his face in the dirt, mumbling a prayer. "He's asking his shadir to cure him of the poison. It's the same with Lahavôtesh."

Prince Mergest's cult that Trevn had talked about. "Which is . . . ?" Wilek asked.

"A secret order of those who worship black spirits. I figured if I died, they would lose their power over me. I should have died."

"That's why you volunteered for sacrifice?" Wilek asked.

"I wanted my life to have meaning." Oli's eyes glossed with moisture. "But they owned my life, so . . ." He shrugged.

"Are the priests of Havôt part of them?"

Oli flinched at the words but said nothing.

Wilek pressed on. "Did they kill Lebetta?"

"Likely. She was inducted shortly after me. They give us tasks. People who refuse . . . Things happen. Sometimes people die."

"Tell me about them. What is the draw?"

"I knew Janek and Fonu were part of something secret. They would talk, make me feel left out. So when the Feelers came asking if I was interested, I said yes. But I should have stayed away. When I found out they wanted Hinck, I tried to warn him, but he refused to listen. I know not whether he . . ." Oli shook his head and stared at his missing arm. "I shouldn't talk of this while I still live."

Wilek needed to know more. "I command you to talk about it."

Oli chuckled. "See now, that matters not, Your Highness. Kill me if you must, but a shadir can torture my soul for eternity. Forgive me, but I will obey the shadir over you."

"What does that mean, 'Obey the shadir'?"

"Evenroot is poison," Oli said. "But mantics make a deal with a shadir, who will heal them of the poison. Some shadir have stipulations for that healing."

"Why deal with shadir at all?" Wilek asked.

"If you take evenroot in any large measure, you need a shadir to heal you or you will die."

Wilek looked down on Harton. "That's what he is doing now? Asking to be healed?"

Oli nodded, turned his head, and stared across the canyon. "You cut off Barthos's head?"

Wilek followed his gaze and shivered. "Harton did most the work. I just wanted to make sure it stayed dead."

"Wait until the minstrels hear about this," Oli said, smiling wryly. "You'll be the Godslayer for all time."

"Harton killed it."

"You killed it together," Oli said. "But since you cannot let anyone know your backman is a mantic, we will say you killed it alone."

Wilek shook his head. "I won't take the credit."

"You must, Your Highness," Oli said. "Carry that head into Canden House and throw it at your father's feet. There must be witnesses to see you do it too. It's the only thing that will win back the ring from Janek."

This coming from Oli? "You want me to reign? You're Janek's friend."

Oli snorted. "Janek has no friends. He is self-absorbed and dishonest. I have never condoned his actions, but I could not escape his control either. I wanted to make my own life, even if it meant death. Now that I still breathe, he will likely demand I return to his service."

"You are welcome at my table anytime, Your Grace," Wilek said.

Oli stared at Wilek, eyes watery and bloodshot. "Thank you, Your Highness. I might have to take you up on that. Though I should warn you, I seem to have injured my sword arm."

The next morning Wilek, Harton, and Oli began the day climbing out of the canyon. It went slowly, especially with Oli's missing arm and the struggle to drag the cheyvah head between them. By the time they reached the city, the sun had started to set.

They made quite a stir as they took the long way through town. Three men, two covered in blood. Wilek, who dragged Barthos's head behind him, followed by Harton, and finally Oli, who had no way to hide his missing limb. People drew back from both the sight and smell.

By the time they entered Canden House, Rayim was waiting in the foyer with a squadron of Queen's Guards. When he saw Wilek, he rushed forward and embraced him. "Gods be praised! We were just about to leave for Everton when word reached us that Sâr Wilek was marching toward Canden House carrying Barthos's head. I dared hope it was true. How did you survive?"

"It was not easy," Wilek said. "Did you find any evenroot?"

"In five chambers, belonging to Rogedoth, Yohthehreth, Lau, the Honored Lady Zenobia, and Rosârah Laviel. The newt spent a very long time in Sâr Janek's apartment but found nothing. I wonder if he somehow moved it before we arrived and the newt sensed that it had been present."

Wilek was disappointed that Janek had managed to evade his trap, but catching the other five with evenroot should be enough to stop their plans. "Arrest those five individuals immediately and send a messenger to my father. Tell him that Barthos and I await him and his Wisean Council in the Throne Room."

Rayim chuckled. "With pleasure, Your Highness."

The undead prince carrying Barthos's head startled at least a dozen servants on the short walk to the Throne Room. Word must have spread, because by the time Wilek, Oli, and Harton reached the fifth floor, several nobles had gathered outside the gilded doors, including Kamran DanSâr, Lady Durvah, Lilou Caridod, and Hinckdan Faluk, who gave a whoop when he saw them.

"You're alive!" Hinckdan shouted, ogling the severed head. "Is that Barthos?"

"What's left of him after the sâr attacked," Oli said.

Harton opened the doors, and Wilek entered the chamber first. Father was sitting in his rollchair, surrounded by Janek and three of the Wisean Five: Danek and Canbek Faluk and Avron Jervaid. Wilek had eyes only for the king.

Sweat had beaded on Father's pale face; his bottom lip quivered. "Are you a ghost that stands before me, my son?"

Wilek swung Barthos's head toward the men and let go. It rolled twice before stopping at Father's feet, leaving a sticky trail of red goo on the marble behind it.

"Back!" Father ordered, and his attendant pulled his chair away from the head.

Wilek bowed deeply. "I am very much alive, Father. But your god is not." Harton stood holding open the doors for the crowd gathered there. Perfect. Wilek wanted all to hear. "Barthos is dead. He will never feast on Armanians again, be they criminals or innocents." He looked his father in the eye. "I faced Barthos and defeated him. I demand Justness."

"Of course, my son," Father said, a tremble in his voice. "Ask me for anything you want and I shall give it to you."

"Three things," Wilek said. "First, that all mantics found in Armania be arrested and put on trial."

"What mantics?" Jervaid asked. "There are no mantics in Armania."

"Second," Wilek said, with a glare at Jervaid for interrupting. "I be declared Heir of Armania."

"But I am Heir!" Janek yelled, glancing wide-eyed from Father to the severed head.

"You are not even a prince of Armania," Wilek said. "You are the son of Pontiff Rogedoth and Rosârah Laviel."

The crowd gasped and began to murmur.

Janek lifted his chin. "That is a lie!"

The king reached out to Janek. "Give me the ring."

Janek held his fist against his heart. "But it's mine!"

"Your parents," Wilek said, "Pontiff Rogedoth and Rosârah Laviel are, as we speak, being arrested as mantics. Captain Veralla and his men found evenroot in their chambers. The abstaining fast forced upon them as they sit in the dungeon will be proof enough, Janek, that they have an affinity for the poison."

The crowd exclaimed over this announcement. Janek glared at Wilek. He pulled the Heir's ring from his finger and handed it over. He knew his parents were guilty. He knew he had lost.

Wilek shoved the ring onto his finger, confidence filling him at the feel of the warm metal against his skin. "Harton," he said, "escort this false prince to his chambers and put five guards on his rooms until the king can decide what to do with him."

Harton drew his sword. "After you, Your Highness."

"Father, this is insulting!" Janek said. "I demand a private word."

"Go with the guard, Janek," Father said. "I must investigate this matter before I can speak on it."

"When you find the truth, I will demand Justness from you both." Janek strode between the men. The crowd parted for him at the door. Harton followed like a shadow.

"What is your third demand, my son?" Father asked.

"That we evacuate Armania before the Five Woes destroy us all."

"Evacuate?" Canbek exclaimed. "And go where?"

"To sea," Wilek said.

This set the men to talking. Even those outside the doors began discussing the impossibility of Wilek's demand.

"Barthos was never responsible for the earthquakes and destruction of our land," he told the crowd. "Mantics are to blame, along with those who have profited from the sale of evenroot. Greed and selfish ambition have brought the Five Woes upon us. We must evacuate our cities before it is too late."

"Not to sea," Jervaid said. "There is nothing beyond the bowl."

"We don't know that," Danek said.

"We do!" Jervaid shot back. "Explorers have searched for centuries and have found nothing. Sailing into the unknown will be the death of us all!"

"So will staying here," Hinckdan said.

"We can go south," Jervaid said, "to the Polar Desert. Or at least to Faynor or Verdun."

"Verdun is too close to the ice canyons," Canbek said. "The canyons collapse first when the earthquakes come. Why not live on ships to see what happens? My houseboat is very comfortable. We can anchor in the harbor."

"Ships and boats are not safe from the Woes," Danek said. "Ask the admiral how many boats have been lost in the swells."

"Besides," Wilek said to Canbek. "There are close to forty thousand people living in Everton. Do you plan to take them all on your houseboat?"

"Surely you don't mean to evacuate commoners," Canbek said.

"We must do something!" Wilek shouted. "A plan is being devised. Mother Rosârah and Rosârah Brelenah have formed a council to prepare for the coming Woes. They know how many can be saved. They will have charted a course. Let us return to Everton right away to aid them in their cause."

Father nodded, eager, penitent. "As you say, my Heir. We will leave for Everton at dawn."

"Good," Wilek said. "And you will investigate Lady Lebetta and Father Tomek's murders. I believe the Pontiff is responsible."

CHARLON

The first night Charlon spent back in Everton, she had a nightmare. Prince Wilek was being attacked. By a great beast. When she awoke the next morning, she could no longer feel their soul-binding.

He was gone.

She climbed from bed. Barred the door to Lady Zeroah's bedchamber. Drank root juice. Dropped to her knees on her altar mat. Called to Magon.

The goddess did not make her wait long. The room grew frigid and foggy, and Magon stepped out of the veil, fiery eyes locked on Charlon.

What is it? Magon asked.

"The prince," Charlon said, voice shaky. "I can no longer feel him. Our bond is severed."

That cannot be.

Charlon swallowed her fear and dared to contradict. "Unless he is dead."

Did you feel his death?

"No. I felt fear. But now I don't feel our connection at all."

Magon's smoldering eyes narrowed. *If someone has meddled with my spell, I will find out.* She faded away.

The room warmed. Charlon remained on her knees, terrified. If Prince Wilek were dead, how would she birth the Deliverer? She would have to marry Prince Trevn instead, which meant she would have to get rid of Mielle.

Such a mess.

Someone knocked at her door.

"Who is there?" she asked.

"Flara, miss. A message has just arrived for you. From Prince Wilek."

The prince!

Charlon hurried to the door and unlocked it. The Chieftess swept inside, holding a scroll. She looked identical to the housemaid Flara. She pushed the door closed and thrust the scroll at Charlon.

"Hurry," the Chieftess said. "That doorman will inform the mother any moment."

Since King Jorger did not reside at Fairsight Manor, Mreegan's mask of him was useless there. So she had taken captive the maid Flara as well, wearing whichever persona she found most useful. The real King Jorger, Flara, and Lady Zeroah were hidden in trunks in the undercroft—all three close enough to maintain the spells.

Charlon broke the seal and read the letter. He was alive. Tears overcame all emotion. Filled her eyes. *Fool*, her heart said. "He is coming back!"

"King Echad returns as well?" the Chieftess asked.

"Yes, yes, everyone is coming. They mean to evacuate the city. Onto ships, just as Prince Trevn said."

"When will he arrive?" Mreegan asked.

"He does not say. Just that he has set out. How many days does it take to travel from Canden to Everton?"

"Perhaps three or four?" Mreegan guessed. "More with a large group."

Fear settled within. This letter must have been sent before the bond had been severed. Prince Wilek could very well have died.

"He had better come quickly," Mreegan said. "I only have enough root juice for another week or so. We need this wedding to happen soon."

"Why not go to the *Vespara* and get more?" Charlon asked. The entire Magonian encampment was now living on the ship, which they had stolen from King Jorger and anchored down the coast.

"It is too far away at present," the Chieftess said.

A knock on the door and it opened. Mielle entered. "You have word of Prince Wilek?"

"He is on his way back," Charlon said, hoping it was true.

"Oh!" Mielle clapped her hands and laughed. "What glorious news. Trevn will be so relieved."

Awkward silence descended.

"Is there anything else?" Charlon asked.

Mielle pursed her lips. "I wanted to talk with you about something."

So annoying, this girl. "About what?"

"We are best friends," Mielle said, nearly crying. "You said so."

Such a weakling. "And . . . ?"

"You are not yourself. Everyone has noticed. Even Flara."

This again. Charlon caught Chieftess Mreegan's smug expression. "Perhaps I am tired. Of being myself. Tired of acting like a child. I want to be a woman. Is that so wrong?"

Mielle sniffled. "Of course not. I just . . . I want to know what changed you."

"No one thing," Charlon said, scrambling for a lie. "A woman has only one life. She must make the most of it. She cannot wait around for men or mothers to tell her what to do."

"I know your mother vexes you, but you have always respected and admired Sâr Wilek. He is a cautious, reserved man. Your new boldness might shock him. What if he decides not to marry you? I do not wish to see you hurt, my lady."

Panic burned within. "You think he might reject me?" This was terrible! The Chieftess was practically smiling. She had always criticized Charlon's portrayal of Lady Zeroah.

"I know not," Mielle said. "He will notice how much you have changed. I only wanted to . . . I felt like I should . . . I am worried, that's all."

Charlon smiled, tried to look like she meant it. "I will think about what you said, Miss Mielle. You could be right."

"Oh, thank you for listening!" Mielle smothered her in a hug that lasted far too long.

When Mielle left, Charlon knew the Chieftess was about to lecture her once again, but Magon appeared between them.

Your prince lives, Magon said. *A male mantic broke the soul-binding. His shadir was a slight. I punished it. It will never serve that careless human again.* Magon faded away.

Prince Wilek lived! What a relief. And a blessing. Before, the prince would have felt the soul-binding through the mask. It would have given Charlon away. Not so now. But if the Mielle girl was right and Charlon could not behave like the real Lady Zeroah, she might fail still.

Later that evening, Mreegan returned as Flara, a lidded wicker basket tucked in the crook of her elbow. "I was right, wasn't I?" she asked. "You have been careless. You cannot behave like Lady Zeroah."

It was too difficult! "What can I do?"

"Go see her. Talk with her. Study her."

"I have. She is only ever angry." Which reminded Charlon of the brothel. Seeing the girl bound and gagged brought back nightmares. Charlon wanted to kill Zeroah and be done with her. The Chieftess said it was too dangerous to wear the mask of a dead person for so long. Said they needed the spiteful child alive for now.

Chieftess Mreegan was watching her, grinning.

"Why do you smile?" Charlon asked.

"Because I have done you a favor. I made myself invisible and searched Prince Wilek's chambers. Found a collection of journal scrolls. There were dozens. Several have passages where the prince writes about Lady Zeroah."

A spark of hope. "Give them to me!"

The Chieftess opened the lid to the basket and withdrew a roll of scrolls.

Charlon snatched it away. Sat in the longchair and searched through the scrolls. Spied Zeroah's name. Her heart quickened. So honest, these words. She scanned the rest of the page. Found Zeroah's name again. Then again, farther down.

She flipped through two more scrolls. So many clues. The girl was timid. Smelled of rosemary. Served the poor. Cried easily. Trembled in his presence. Seemed almost afraid of him, though had attempted boldness in conversation. A gift of a dagger. A single kiss.

"Will it help you?" Flara's nasal voice pulled Charlon away from the scroll.

So much. "Yes, Chieftess. This is exactly what I needed. I must find a bottle of rosemary water right away."

TREVN

Trevn set out for his mother's apartment to check on the Book of Arman. He was pleased to see that no more damage had come to the castle, though repairs had not yet started. The cross section was still damaged, so he and Cadoc took the servants' stairs.

Queen Brelenah had invited Trevn to a meeting of the Nahtan tomorrow, and he looked forward to discovering who in Everton counted themselves Armanite and helping in any way he could.

When he and Cadoc arrived at his mother's apartment, they stepped into a shambles. Furniture had been overturned, cushions ripped open, and his mother's clothing was strewn over every section of the floor.

"Someone is still looking for the book," Trevn said. "I would have expected the villains to have followed us to Canden."

"Unless they knew you did not actually go," Cadoc said.

Who besides Hinck, Cadoc, and Mother could know that?

Cadoc searched the apartment and found it empty. Trevn trod over the carpet of clothing and checked the secret room, pleased to see it had not been disturbed. He touched the Book of Arman and wondered if he should move it. To Barek's houseboat, perhaps?

Not yet. It was safest here.

"We must discover who is doing this," he said. "Can we lure him out somehow?"

"Perhaps you could visit the Temple Arman each morning," Cadoc suggested.

It took Trevn a moment to understand what Cadoc meant. "With a manuscript pouch over my shoulder, you mean?"

Cadoc grinned.

"I will make a scene as I come and go each day," Trevn said, "quoting the Book of Arman and inviting others to join me. Could you muster a contingent of guards you trust?"

"Certainly."

Trevn nodded, eager to do something proactive. "Post your men near the Temple Arman just before morning bells. Instruct them to watch everyone but me. I want a full report of who is present."

"It will be done," Cadoc said.

Trevn made a grand scene in the Temple Arman the next morning. It was located on the ground floor of the castle, near the great hall, and was by far the most dazzling temple in the building. Trevn recalled his father wanting to change it to a Temple Barthos, but something always distracted him from following through.

Despite the noise Trevn made, no one paid him any mind. Perhaps he had come too early. He would have to try again tomorrow.

Trevn and Cadoc arrived in Queen Brelenah's apartment for the Nahtan meeting moments before the midday bells rang. He counted twenty-three people present, a mixture of royalty, nobility, military, servants, and commoners, who were already discussing the population. Trevn recognized over half, including Gran, Princess Nabelle, Dendrick, Hawley, the guardsman Novan Heln, Sârah Hrettah, Barek Hadar and his manservant, Crossett from the stables, and the former admiral Captain Aldair Livina.

"Impossible," the captain was saying. "Even if we combined all five fleets, we would only have some twelve hundred vessels. There are over nine million people in the Five Realms. We would need fifteen thousand boats to save everyone."

"Many have houseboats," Queen Valena said. "Some have several."

"Houseboats might be the fashion," Barek said, "but they won't hold many people."

"Nor will the nobility want to share their precious houseboats with commoners," Dendrick said.

"They would if the people agreed to work," Queen Valena said.

"Indentured slaves, you mean?" a soldier asked.

"I included houseboats in my numbers," the captain said. "Even if we commandeered every vessel in the Five Realms, we could save no more than a quarter of a million people. Yet there is no point in discussing Rurekau, Tenma, or Magonia. Between Armania and Sarikar, we have enough boats for a hundred thousand. But that leaves no room for livestock."

"Can we build more ships?" Trevn asked.

"Not if these Woes are coming as quickly as this Prophetess let on," the captain said.

"We need to speak with her," Queen Brelenah said. "Perhaps I will send a squadron of guards to find Sir Kalenek."

"How would they even know where to look?" Gran asked. "Trust the Prophetess to Arman. We must do our part, and that is to prepare for the Woes."

Trevn listened raptly as the discussion continued. Queen Brelenah gave a report on how the food was being divided among the galleys and merchant cogs at the Port of Everton. The same was being done at the other Armanian port cities. She assigned Novan Heln to assist Crossett in preparing horses for the boats but cautioned them to be careful about how many animals to take, as the beasts ate and drank a vast amount.

Princess Nabelle gave a report on supplies, and when she finished, a soldier presented in Captain Veralla's absence, sharing about the number of weapons his team had gathered.

Barek gave the best news of all. "Captain Livina has discovered land."

A hush gripped every soul in the chamber.

"Where?" Trevn asked.

"It is an island," the captain said, "some four hundred fifty leagues north-northwest from here. No bigger than Odarka. I lost my ship and crew when Cape Waldemar collapsed. I also lost all my charts, but I am confident I can find the island again."

"This brings up a concern of mine," Barek said. "I feel as though Captain Livina should be reinstated as Admiral of the Fleet."

This statement brought a stunned silence over the assembly.

Barek went on. "Only he knows the way to this new island. We dare not sail into the bowl with no plan." He cast his gaze from face to face as if looking to find someone to agree with him.

"I can only speak for myself," Queen Brelenah said, "but I agree with you. The problem is the rosâr and his preference for Admiral Vendal."

"We must commit our plans to Arman," Gran said. "If he agrees with our need, he will deliver success."

Most everyone responded to Gran's comment with nods or hums of agreement. Trevn didn't know what to think of such faith, and the existence of this new island was too much to brush aside. "Do you think there are more islands?" he asked the captain.

"Perhaps," Livina said. "I thought we might set up temporary homes on the island I found, then set out north from that point in search of more."

They discussed the new island at length, and Queen Brelenah closed the meeting. Trevn left, his mind lost in a reverie as to what they might find outside the bowl.

Everywhere Trevn went, he carried a fake manuscript with him. He met with Captain Livina to compare charts of the Eversea. The newly discovered island thrilled him and gave him immense hope during this dark time. Queen Brelenah called on Trevn often, giving him tasks in his new role on the Nahtan. Frequently Trevn asked servants to assist him on an errand, only to find them preoccupied with some task from Lady Zeroah for her upcoming wedding.

Trevn continued his temple visits for the next three days, but there had been no reports of anyone suspicious watching. He ate while working or in meetings, constantly busy with some part of the evacuation plan. At night he poured over his maps and explorer diaries, replaying his meetings with Captain Livina in his mind.

Days passed without Trevn once seeing Mielle. He longed to spend time with her, so he sent a letter, apologizing for his neglect. She replied, assuring him that she understood. No word came from Wilek, so Trevn could only forge ahead and pray his brother would return soon.

WILEK

Wilek arrived in Everton as the sun was setting. He had taken a small group of men and ridden in advance of his father's procession of ships, which were making their way down the Echo Crack. They had gone to Canden on horseback, but now that they needed every possible ship, the king had decided to sail back to Everton. Janek and the other prisoners were being kept in one of the ship's brigs.

Wilek had made sure Harton understood that while he had forgiven his use of magic in The Gray, Harton must never be tempted again if he wanted to remain in his service. Harton had promised to give it up for good.

Harton rode ahead to give word of their arrival, so when Wilek stepped inside the castle, he was unsurprised to find a reception waiting. Harton stood with Trevn, Lady Zeroah with Princess Nabelle. Also present were Wilek's mother and Gran, a gaggle of little dogs, and a large group of staff.

His mother kissed him. "It went well?"

"It did not. Pontiff Rogedoth used his magic on the rosâr, who sentenced me to be sacrificed to Barthos."

Gasps and murmurs flitted through the crowd.

"How did you escape?" Trevn asked.

"I was sacrificed," Wilek said. "I faced Barthos and won." He nodded to Rayim, who motioned Oli and Hinckdan toward Wilek. The men came forward, dragging the smelly Barthos head between them. They dropped it before Wilek and his grandmother. Wilek bowed low and held his breath—the head was starting to rot. "I honored your god, Mother Rosârah, when I killed my

506

father's god. Arman blessed me with victory, and my father declared me Heir."
He raised his fist for all to see the ring.

"Sâr Wilek killed Barthos!" Harton yelled.

"The Godslayer!" Oli added.

And from Hinckdan, "All hail the Heir!"

A cheer rose up from the crowd. Wilek had them. Word would spread.
As long as he continued to starve Rogedoth and his mantics of evenroot, he
might see the other side of this conspiracy of mantic priests.

"Search the castle for evenroot," Wilek commanded Rayim. "Mantics will
not be tolerated in Armania."

Rayim bowed. "It will be done."

"Take that head to the tanner," Wilek told Oli and Hinckdan. "See if he
can preserve it."

The men, thankfully, removed the head at once.

Wilek said nothing of Rogedoth and Laviel's arrest or Janek not being a
prince of Armania. He would leave that to Father. For now, he greeted Trevn
with a nod and approached Lady Zeroah, who curtsied to him. She looked
every bit the skinny girl she had been when last he had seen her.

"Thank you for fetching my bride," Wilek told Trevn.

"Your hair," Lady Zeroah said, her gaze flitting over his head. "You cut it?"

"My captors did." He had refused to wear a wig like his father and resisted
the urge to feel the shortness as she and several others stared. Thankfully he
had found a high-necked tunic in Canden to hide the rune on the back of his
neck. He needed to have the mark removed.

"Were you frightened?" Lady Zeroah asked.

"Let us talk of that another time, lady."

"I'm sorry, Your Highness," she said, eyes downcast. "I didn't mean to offend."

Wilek was too tired to play the courting game. "Do not think on it."

"Lady Zeroah has been preparing for your wedding," Mother said.

He met Zeroah's golden eyes. "Have you?"

"King Jorger was upset that we missed your ageday," she said. "If it pleases
you, we can be married tomorrow morning."

"How thoughtful." Wilek fought to keep his expression plain, but his stomach clenched at the idea of marrying anyone just now. Not knowing what
else to say, he took her hand and kissed it, breathed in the smell of rosemary
on her skin. It took him back to the day she had given him the dagger. He

remembered feeling hopeful for their marriage back then. Now he was not so certain. What had changed?

"Unless you would rather wait," his mother said. "As long as you marry before Lady Zeroah's next ageday, all will be well with the kings."

"I see no reason to wait," he said, pained. Marrying would only strengthen his role as Heir. "But I would like to first appraise the evacuation plans. I might find it necessary to delay a day or two."

Lady Zeroah curtsied deeply. "As you wish, Your Highness."

Wilek sat in his chambers with Trevn, numb from the endless drama in the Five Realms, the fact that he was to be married tomorrow, and now this news of Rosârah Thallah's ransacked apartment. "Rogedoth, Yohthehreth, and Lau were all with us in Canden," Wilek said. "Someone else must be working with them who wants your book. Or they left a loyal man behind."

"I've been home from Brixmead a week," Trevn said. "Any loyal man would have come after me by now if he was going to."

"Might he know you seek to trap him?"

Trevn frowned. "Perhaps."

Wilek's mind drifted to the evacuation and Avron Jervaid's betrayal of the rosâr. The day the procession had started back to Everton, Jervaid had left for Faynor with a host of nobles and the pregnant Queen Ojeda. When the king discovered that his fifth wife had run off with a member of his council, he sent a contingent of soldiers to bring her back and placed charges of treason against Jervaid.

Despite all this, thousands had fled south to Faynor in Sarikar, drawn in by the tale. A bard had already written a song of Jervaid and Ojeda's secret love affair that had begun long before the king had ever met the young actress. Many believed the child she carried belonged to the Elderman.

Even with the small migration south, there was still nowhere near enough boats to save the people of Everton, let alone the rural population or those from other cities in Armania.

"Have the lots been passed out to the commoners?" Wilek asked.

"Yes, but your mother and Miss Mielle have procured another boat to fill with orphans."

That was three boats now that his mother and Miss Mielle had claimed for the poor. "Let them have their boat. There is no way to make this fair. I arrested a merchant for selling places on his ship. Another was hung today for having murdered three families for their lots, which he was selling for a gold a piece." And Father was still ill, despite the mantics being imprisoned.

"Have you and Father decided what to do about the Admiral of the Fleet?" Trevn asked.

"It will be Hanray Vendal. But I persuaded him to make Aldair Livina captain of the *Seffynaw*."

"That's a fair compromise."

"The Admiral plans to sail the fleet first to Odarka, where we can meet up with the ships from the northern cities, then allow Captain Livina to lead the way to his island."

"I confess, I am excited to see it. What about your wedding?"

"There's no reason to wait," Wilek said. "Are you still concerned?"

"I know not. Miss Mielle said Lady Zeroah has been more herself lately. Perhaps it was fear for her grandfather's health that made her act so strangely." He paused. "Are you happy?" he asked. "To marry Lady Zeroah?"

"Happy?" Wilek chuckled dryly. "We are sârs, Trevn, you and I. We have a higher calling. We are responsible for ruling a nation. Our people's happiness matters more than our own. If I become king, know that I will make you Heir immediately if only to keep Janek or any other from trying to claim that role. Now, I hope to live to be an ancient king in my rollchair with my sons crowded around me. If I succeed, you will be free to find every happiness you crave. But should something happen that prevents such a future . . ."

Trevn shrugged off the warning. "Who would dare challenge the Godslayer?"

Wilek smirked at the title, which was already being spread throughout the city. "There is always someone, brother. Will you promise to put our realm first? Before even your own happiness?"

"I pledged my service to you. Is that not enough?"

Unfortunately no. "This is the only wedding gift I ask of you, Trevn."

Trevn sighed heavily. "Fine, I promise. But that makes my goal keeping you alive until you become that ancient king with all the sons, putting me twentieth in line behind your brood."

Wilek chucked at the image. "Good enough, brother. I welcome the help."

Wilek's wedding day began early. First to the bathhouse for the symbolic washing away of his bachelor status and to purify his body for the ceremony.

His father and Trevn were there. Also present were Rayim, Harton, Oli, and Hinckdan.

It was tradition for family and friends to offer advice to the groom. Father lectured on the fickleness of women and how Wilek only needed to get Zeroah pregnant and he could return to his harem. Rayim said that women were sometimes temperamental but simply needed to hear kind words each day. Harton remained silent, and Oli, extra moody since the loss of his arm, gave his condolences on the whole affair. Trevn and Hinckdan surprised Wilek by agreeing that women liked nothing more than a man who was a good listener.

After Wilek's bath, Dendrick dressed him in royal-blue silk and velvet with a sand cat cape as long as his father's. On his belt he wore his great-grandfather's sword and the dagger Zeroah had given him.

Once he was dressed, Wilek's men escorted him to the King's Garden in back of the castle. Zeroah was waiting, dressed in a gown of green and gold, the colors of Sarikar. Miss Mielle stood beside her, holding a sheathed sword—the traditional wedding gift a bride gave her husband.

The king sat in his rollchair throne, which had been parked before the statue of King Halak II. Mother and Gran sat on his left, Trevn on his right. Behind the king stood Janek's new bride—Wilek's niece—six-year-old Princess Vallah. Wilek had met the girl three years ago but doubted she remembered. Ree stood with her. Wilek smiled at his old nurse, wishing he had known she was here so he could have made time to visit. He hoped Father would have a priest annul his niece's marriage to Janek as soon as possible.

With all the castle priests in the dungeon, Wilek sought out a medial priest named Burl Mathal to perform the ceremony. Father Mathal came forward and called the attention of the gods. His assistant carried in a goat that would be sacrificed to Tenma, the mother goddess of fertility. Wilek handed Lady Zeroah's dagger to Father Mathal, who used it to slit the goat's throat. The blood was drained into a consecrated bowl, which Mathal placed on the altar.

Wilek and Zeroah came forward and knelt. Mathal dipped an ironthorn branch into the blood and sprinkled it over Wilek's and Zeroah's heads as he chanted a prayer to Tenma, asking for blessings upon the couple. Then he butchered the goat, cut off a piece, and threw it into the flames. He prayed again for blessings on the couple, then cut off two bites from the roasted portion and fed them to Wilek and Zeroah.

They stood then, and Wilek removed his great-grandfather's sword from his belt and held it out to Zeroah. "This sword belonged to my great-grandfather

King Nathek Hadar. It's the sword of my ancestor for you to hold until the day you gift it to our first son."

Zeroah took the blade and handed it to Miss Mielle, who in turn passed her the other sword. Zeroah held it out. "This sword of my father I give to you, husband. A symbol of the transfer of guardianship and . . . protection from him to you."

Wilek took the sword and marveled at it a moment before clipping it to his belt. It was a hand-and-a-half creese sword with cast fittings of solid brass over an onyx grip. Beautiful, but not terribly functional.

"Kneel again at the altar," Father Mathal said, "and clasp hands."

Wilek dropped to his knees and reached for Zeroah. Her hands were trembling, or maybe that was his hands.

"In the sight of these witnesses," Father Mathal said, "we ask the gods to bless—"

The consecrated bowl began shaking on the altar, stone against stone, rattling and scraping slowly forward, twisting.

"Earthquake," someone whispered.

Wilek held his breath, trying to discern the intensity.

Father Mathal continued, "We ask the gods to bless this couple and—"

The bowl slipped off the side of the altar and smashed at Wilek's and Zeroah's knees. Blood spattered the gray stone and Wilek's left side. He flinched and released Zeroah's hands.

"Remain calm," Father Mathal said. "It will end momentarily."

But the trembling increased. The ground bucked beneath Wilek's knees. A cracking sound pulled his head around. The statue of King Halak II split diagonally across the face. Father's attendants pushed his rollchair forward just as the statue's eyes and nose slipped from the head and shattered on the stone path.

Screams rang out. The audience scattered.

"Stay out of the castle!" Wilek jumped up. "Remain outside!"

The words had barely left his mouth when the earth splintered and yawned open from the castle doors to the broken statue. A man leaped over the crack to a lady on the other side.

His mother screamed. What was left of the statue of King Halak II tipped toward her and Gran.

Wilek sprinted toward them, picking up Gran and carrying her out of the path of the statue, which crashed behind them, splintering to pieces. Wilek's fur cape choked him; a chunk of marble had pinned it to the ground. He set Gran down and yanked off the cape, letting it fall. The ground was still shaking. An earthquake had never lasted this long. Could this be the end?

"To the boats!" he yelled, not willing to risk being wrong. He spun around, found Dendrick and Harton behind him. "Dendrick, prepare a carriage for the queens and princesses. Meet us at the fountain in front. Harton, with me."

Dendrick sprinted away. Where was the king? Wilek searched the crowd. Saw no sign.

"Prince Wilek, don't leave me!" Lady Zeroah appeared beside him, clutching his great-grandfather's sword, Miss Mielle with her. Zeroah looked at Harton and gasped, eyes wider than a whitefish.

Wilek glanced between Harton and Zeroah, wondering over her reaction to his backman. "Find your mother and get to the king's ship. I'll meet you there. Or, if you prefer, you can ride with my mother."

Zeroah tore her horrified gaze from Harton and looked pleadingly at Wilek. "I must go to Fairsight Manor first. My trunks are there."

Trunks? Wilek had no time to think of anything but getting as many people as possible on the ships. He put his arm around Gran and led her to the circle path. Mother, her maids, the dogs, and a half dozen other royal females followed.

Zeroah did not.

Wilek glanced back to see her standing by the fallen statue, crying, holding the sword he'd given her, Miss Mielle tugging on her sleeve.

Five Woes. "Get to the boat, lady!" he yelled, then turned the corner of the building.

The sound of breaking stone induced a cacophony of screams. Wilek looked up at the castle. A crack crawled down the wall, slowly making its way from the roof to the western entrance.

Wilek and Harton hurried the women on. Guilt made Wilek look back for Zeroah, but he could no longer see the King's Garden. He thought of Trevn then, and Oli, Hinck, Rayim, and Kal. The thoughts overwhelmed. If only he could wish everyone on board a ship in an instant.

The earth stilled as they came around the front, but there was no sign of Dendrick or the carriage near the fountain. Wilek spotted Rayim on the porch steps with Queen Thallah. "Take the women to the fountain, Hart, and get them into the carriage when it comes. I'll be right back." He ran toward the castle and sprinted up the steps. "Rayim!"

The captain, clutching the third queen by the arm, looked as if he had been caught stealing. "I am terribly sorry, Your Highness, but I cannot find the other queens."

"There." Wilek pointed toward the fountain of the Rôb Five. "Waiting for the carriage."

Rayim looked past Wilek to the huddle of women, and the panic in his eyes faded. "Thank the gods. Those women have given me the slip far too often."

"The king?" Wilek asked.

"His attendants put him in a wagon and left for the boat."

"Sâr Wilek," Queen Thallah said, "please ask Captain Veralla to release me at once."

"She intends to go looking for Sâr Trevn," Rayim said, "but I must take her to the ship."

"Leave your son to his capable guards, Rosârah," Wilek said.

The ground jolted and again began to shake. Chunks of stone rained down from the castle wall and splintered against the marble steps. A piece struck Wilek's arm. Rayim pulled Wilek and Queen Thallah against the castle wall until the stones stopped falling.

A child's cry drew Wilek's attention to the bottom of the steps. Princess Vallah stood alone, Ree on the ground beside her. *Gods, no!* Wilek ran to Ree and saw her eyes were wide and glassy. Blood matted her hair. No breath. She was dead.

He moaned, shocked with a heavy dose of sorrow. His eyes glazed at the loss of this woman who had raised him and Inolah. He picked up his niece and hugged her close just as the shaking stilled again. "Will you stay with my mother, Vallah?"

She looked down on the nurse. "We must not leave Ree!"

"Ree is gone, Vallah. I am sorry."

A curse from Rayim drew their attention. The man, still dragging Queen Thallah, stared toward the front gates. "I look away for a moment and they disappear!"

Wilek glanced at the fountain. The carriage rolled to a stop, Dendrick inside. Queen Valena and her daughters and their maids were waiting, but Mother, Gran, their maids, and the gaggle of dogs were gone.

Five Woes! Wilek carried his niece to the carriage and lifted the girl inside.

"Stay with Hrettah," he told Vallah, then asked his half sister, "Where did my mother go?"

"Back for her chair," Hrettah said, then screamed as yet another earthquake began.

That blasted wicker throne! "Rayim, stay here and make sure the carriage waits for my mother and Gran. Harton and I will fetch them."

Wilek sprinted back around the castle, Harton trailing behind. His footsteps landed awkwardly on the moving ground, rattling his bones. When they reached the Rosâr's Garden, sure enough, his mother had found two guards and was directing them in carrying her wicker chair.

"Mother!" Wilek yelled. "You would risk the princesses for a chair?"

"The trembling has stopped."

Wilek stilled a moment. So it had. "That is not the point. You endanger the others." He looked around, not seeing his grandmother. "Where is Gran?"

Mother's eyes widened. "She was right here. I thought . . . Oh, no. Wilek, she wants to stay. I did not think she really meant to."

Stay? Was everyone going mad? "Harton, take the chair. You men, find the Mother Rosârah and bring her to the fountain of the Rôb Five."

The guards obeyed. Wilek took hold of his mother's arm and ran, dragging her behind him. They reached the carriage and found that several servants had climbed in with the women. A man stood on the front seat, strangling the driver. Another man fought Dendrick. Rayim lay on the ground, holding his head.

"Stop this at once!" Wilek demanded.

Harton dropped the wicker throne and went to help Rayim. The driver punched his strangler, who stumbled back. His heel stepped over the edge of the driver's bench and he fell. Harton pounced upon him.

Wilek lunged back from his mother and drew his sword. "Get out of that carriage. Now. All of you who do not belong!"

A half dozen servants scrambled out.

"In, Mother. Quickly. The dogs too."

Harton and the driver had run off their attackers. They gathered the mutts and handed them up to the women. Rayim stood slowly, picked up a dog.

"Make room for the girls," Mother said, waving her maidservants forward. Wilek helped all six honor maidens into the carriage, which now looked past capacity.

"May I come too?" Miss Mielle stood at Wilek's elbow, face streaked with tears.

He glanced behind her. "Where is Lady Zeroah?"

Miss Mielle choked back a sob. "They left me!"

What? Wilek had no time to ponder what this meant. "Make room for my betrothed's honor maiden." He took hold of Miss Mielle's elbow and helped her up.

"Wilek, my chair!" Mother said.

Curse that chair! "I will have a new one made for you."

"No! I love my wicker throne."

"It is very light," Queen Valena said. "If you hand it up, we can hold it."

Wilek stifled a retort, and he and Rayim passed the chair up to the women.

"Ride with them," he told Rayim. "See that they all get on the *Seffynaw*. Harton and I will find Gran and bring her on horseback."

"Make sure you reach the docks in time," Rayim said, gripping Wilek's arm. "I shall not let them leave without you."

Wilek nodded, and Rayim climbed up beside the driver just as another earthquake began.

"To the docks," Wilek told the driver. "Hurry."

Mielle

Mielle sat wedged between Princess Hrettah and one of Queen Valena's maids. She held one of Queen Brelenah's puppies in her arms and stroked it repeatedly, trying to calm the trembling animal and herself. The earthquakes couldn't seem to decide whether or not to stop. And while they were frightening, Mielle couldn't stop replaying the scene in her mind when Princess Nabelle had ordered Mielle out of their carriage and Lady Zeroah had allowed it.

She had truly lost her friend. But how? Why? Something had changed drastically after they'd traveled to Brixmead. If only she could understand.

The carriage slammed to a halt. Most of the women inside screamed, pulling Mielle's attention to the street. They were parked at the harbor, a mob of commoners blocking the way to the ships. The driver cracked his whip at the crowd. Captain Veralla was standing on the driver's seat, sword raised, yelling at the people to get back. The mob looked ready to kill them all. Over their heads, Mielle could see a wall of King's Guards blocking the paths to the gangways of the ships, fighting to keep the crowd back.

This was dreadful! For everyone. Why couldn't they make room for all the people?

Captain Veralla climbed down to the street and began dueling a man who looked to be a mercenary.

From the ship, several guardsmen pushed through the crowd toward the carriage. She recognized Novan Heln, one of Trevn's new acquaintances, as the first to arrive. He drew his sword and waved it in an arc. "Everyone move back!" he yelled.

Some obeyed. Others pressed forward. Novan jabbed the point of his sword toward a fat butcher with a bloody apron, who was standing right in front of the horses.

"Get out of the way, man," Novan said.

The butcher pulled a knife. "I've a blade of my own, boy. You poke me, I aim to poke back."

"Don't make me kill you," Novan said. "If you don't have a lottery coin, you cannot board."

"All the lots went to royals and nobles," a woman said from behind the butcher.

"Or soldiers," said another woman.

"It ain't fair," someone shouted behind Novan.

Of course it wasn't. How could it be? Mielle hated this. Where was the Justness in it?

"They are not my rules," Novan said. "But I have vowed to enforce them."

"I've killed enough pigs in my day," the butcher said. "You won't be all that different."

He jabbed the knife at Novan, who dodged and drove his blade into the butcher's gut. The man screamed so loudly Mielle shuddered and looked away. More screams followed as the other guards engaged the crowd. When next Mielle looked, Novan had raised his bloody weapon to the circle of onlookers. "I don't want to hurt anyone," he shouted. "You let this carriage pass, or I'll kill you all. Now get back!"

The people shifted, staring with wide, accusing eyes. Two men grabbed the butcher's arms and pulled him out of the road, leaving a dark line of blood on the dirt.

The driver cracked his whip, and the carriage jerked forward.

"Well done, Heln," Captain Veralla said as he joined Novan in front of the horses. Together they led the way, swords waving before them like deadly flags. People jeered, some threw rotten food, but no one else challenged with force. They reached the *Seffynaw*, and the guards opened up a path for the ladies and the dogs to board the ship.

Mielle climbed down, then turned to help Princess Hrettah. The girl kept hold of Mielle's arm and walked with her.

"That was so frightening!" Princess Hrettah said.

"It was," Mielle agreed. "You will be safe soon."

"But the people . . ."

"I know," Mielle said, hating this.

The ground was still for the moment, and the guardsmen ushered them toward the gangway.

Princess Hrettah stopped before Novan and pulled a blue ribbon from her hair. "Thank you, brave guardsman." She reached up and tied the ribbon around the top of one of his braids. The girl was only twelve, but since such a gesture was meant to honor a brave knighten, Novan bowed low.

"It was my honor, Your Highness."

Such sweetness in the midst of chaos brought a smile to Mielle's face.

"Hrettah!" Queen Valena yelled from the gangway.

Mielle pulled the princess away and hurried the girl onto the ship.

Mielle stood on the deck of the *Seffynaw* watching a group of men load horses onto the ship. The animals were increasingly skittish. Many protested and kicked as they were strapped into canvas slings, then pulleyed over the side of the ship and lowered into the hold. The same was happening on other ships all along the docks. On the *Rafayah*—the ship docked to the south of the *Seffynaw*—a lifted horse nearly bucked himself out of the sling. He hung thrashing, with the canvas caught around his neck and front legs. The men lowered him and tried to put on a new sling, but the horse wanted none of it. He kicked two guards overboard and trampled a third before they managed to subdue him.

As this went on, Mielle glanced between the animals and the angry crowd of commoners in the harbor. Mielle loved animals, but it did not seem right to allow horses to take up space while people died. She wondered if Queen Brelenah would agree.

A sailor looking through a grow lens shouted, "Admiral! There are ships out there. An entire fleet!"

A man in an impressive blue tunic trimmed in gold strode to the sailor's side and looked though his own lens. "Rurekan flags. Send a dinghy out to meet them. Make sure they keep back. We've no room for docking. And if they get too close, the people might try to board them."

"Yes, sir."

The sailor ran off to obey the orders. Mielle left as well, setting off to find Queen Brelenah and do what she could to bring more of the people on board the ship.

TREVN

Trevn started up the servants' stairs, Cadoc, Hinck, and Oli right behind him. Cadoc and Oli's swords clanked, as both had dressed in formal King's Guards attire for the wedding.

"Why are we inside the crumbling castle?" Oli asked.

"There is something I must fetch," Trevn said.

"Wonderful," Oli said. "Send a servant to fetch it and let's get ourselves to the docks."

"I must get it myself," Trevn said.

"Why didn't you load your belongings ahead of time like everyone else?" Oli asked. "You even had a head start on those of us who were in Canden."

"I could not preload this," Trevn said. Perhaps he should have taken the book to the *Seffynaw* already, but he still didn't know who, beyond the priests, wanted it destroyed.

"You could not," Oli parroted. "Princes. I swear you are all so full of yourselves you will kill us all in the end."

"Watch your words, Your Grace." This from Cadoc.

"Yes, yes, I've insulted a sâr of Armania. Send me to the pole, if you must. I survived the god Barthos, I shall survive the pole too."

Trevn grinned. He could see why Hinck had grown to like Oli Agoros and couldn't resist baiting him again. "Wilek killed Barthos, not you."

"Half my arm assisted the sâr, in case you failed to notice," Oli said. "I'd like to see how you would have fared."

"I would have died," Hinck said, panting as they rounded the fourth landing.

"Oh, but we all would have died if you hadn't slipped Sâr Wilek that dagger, Hinck," Oli said.

They reached the fifth floor, and Trevn flung himself around the corner and into the hall. He skidded to a stop at a hole in the floor. The gap was only a few paces, but it surprised him.

"The castle is falling apart." Cadoc grabbed Trevn's arm and pulled him back.

"Which is why we should be outside," Oli said.

Trevn yanked free of Cadoc and jumped the gap. He ran to his mother's apartment, inside her bedroom, and into the privy. He didn't bother being discreet and opened the secret door in plain sight.

"Now see?" Oli said behind him. "I told my father we were not true royalty until our home was filled with secret passageways. I tell you, the man refuses to listen."

Trevn went inside and looped the Book of Arman—which was still stuffed inside a map tube—over his head and left arm. Then he rolled up the maps on his table and shoved them into an empty tube. He handed it to Cadoc, grabbed his other tubes filled with the rest of his collection of maps, and held them out to Hinck and Oli.

"Help me carry these?" he asked as the floor shook anew.

He froze, waiting to see what this shaker would do, but it lasted no more than ten seconds. The men each took three map tubes, leaving no extras for Trevn. He carried only the Book of Arman. He gave the room one last glance, then ran back through his mother's bedchamber and into the sitting room. There he found Beal waiting with five Queen's Guards.

"Sands, I'm coming!" Trevn said, sensing his mother was behind this.

"I care not what you do, Your Highness," Beal rasped. "Give me the Book of Arman or I shall be forced to take it."

CHARLON

Charlon had fought with Nabelle. She hadn't known what else to do! She could not leave. Not without Zeroah. Could not keep up the spell without the girl alive and nearby. Only Chieftess Mreegan's ongoing magic had maintained Charlon's disguise today. The distance from Fairsight Manor to Castle Everton was too great without help. Charlon needed her on board or all would be lost.

Charlon reached the house. Ran down to the basement. Banged on the door to Flara's chambers. "Chieftess, let me in!"

The door opened to Flara in her maid's dress. "Thank the goddess! I almost came looking for you. All the servants left when the neighbor's house collapsed. I considered going to the boat. What's happening?"

"They're evacuating the city. Nabelle tried to take me to the ship, but I jumped out of the carriage. Help me get the trunks upstairs. We must hurry."

"We cannot carry the trunks!" the Chieftess said. "Nor can I use magic on them in public."

"I told Nabelle I needed them," Charlon said. "She'll come for her daughter."

"You'd better be right." Chieftess Mreegan muttered words that lifted all three trunks into the air. Charlon ran ahead and opened the doors. The trunks floated behind her. She ran to the front porch. Saw the carriage approaching. Slipped back inside.

"She's coming! Set them down."

Mreegan lowered the trunks just inside the door, then they worked together, tugging one over the threshold with strength alone.

The carriage stopped out front with Princess Nabelle, Hoyt, and the driver inside. It was the open carriage, intended to have carried the prince and princess through the city to greet the people after they were married.

Still not married.

"Help her!" Nabelle screamed to the men.

The driver and Hoyt ran up the steps.

"Zeroah, get in this carriage now!" Nabelle yelled.

Charlon obeyed, Chieftess Mreegan as Flara beside her.

"How could you forget three full-sized trunks?" Nabelle asked. "They should have gone to the ship days ago."

"The wedding . . ." Charlon lowered her face to her hands. "He left me!"

"He has more responsibilities than any regular man," Nabelle said. "And you are not yet his wife. If we don't get to the docks soon, you never will be."

The trunks were loaded. The carriage circled around. High Street was deserted, but Procession Way was thick with people. None of them willing to part for a carriage of their betters.

Charlon couldn't blame them.

"Make way for the Princess of Sarikar!" the driver yelled.

"She can die like the rest of us!" someone yelled back.

"Insolence," Nabelle muttered.

The ground trembled. Up ahead some two dozen people sank through the cobblestone. Screams ripped through the air. The crowd scattered but for two, pulling up a man from the edge of a crevasse that had formed in the street.

"Drive, drive," Nabelle shouted. "Go around it!"

The driver cracked his whip, and the carriage rolled toward the hole.

KALENEK

The *Baretam* had reached Armania and dropped anchor just outside the Port of Everton. The harbor was filled with so many boats that Kal couldn't see the shore from the main deck. He went up to the quarterdeck, where Emperor Ulrik stood with Captain Durinn.

"Sir Kalenek," Ulrik said, motioning to starboard. "Someone comes to visit us."

Kal walked to the railing, saw the approaching dinghy, and withdrew his grow lens from his pocket. A quick look and he instantly recognized the King's Guard uniforms. What relief! Perhaps Kal would finally get back to Wilek.

"Sailors from the *Seffynaw*," he told Ulrik. "I'll talk to them."

"Excellent," Ulrik said. "I will receive them in the great cabin."

Kal nodded and walked away, uncertain whether or not he would obey the young emperor. The boy had taken an instant liking to his new crown, but Kal's allegiance was to Wilek. If he had a chance to get off this boat, he would take it. And he could not allow Ulrik to claim Onika for himself.

He went all the way to the foredeck, where the dinghy was being hoisted up the side of the *Baretam*. He grabbed a nearby sailor. "Fetch Empress Inolah, the man named Jhorn, the boy Grayson, the prophetess Onika, and her cat," he told the man. "I must have them all. Tell them we are leaving."

"Master Burk as well, sir?"

"No," Kal said. "If he is with them, it cannot be helped. But do not seek him out."

"Yes, sir." The sailor ran off.

Kal felt a twinge of guilt at leaving Burk behind, but the boy did not belong with them anymore. He would need to find his own way.

Kal studied the destruction of Everton. Throughout the city, clouds of dust puffed up like chimney smoke, and actual fires were spreading. Over a dozen ships had already set sail and were headed out of the harbor.

The dinghy reached the top, and the King's Guards boarded. They instantly recognized Kal, though he did not recall their names.

"Sir Kalenek," the first said, "a terrible earthquake has spurred an evacuation of the city."

"The quakes keep coming," said the other. "On and off for the past hour."

"The people have gone mad," said the first. "Admiral Vendal says it's best you keep these ships back, where they'll be safe from the mob."

That message must be given to the captain, but Kal did not want to risk lingering where the emperor might insist he stay. He grabbed another sailor and bid him take the message of keeping the ship back to Captain Durinn.

Inolah approached then. Jhorn vaulted along behind her with Onika, Grayson, and Rustian following a few steps back. No Burk. *Good.* Kal sighed, relieved. They just might escape without trouble.

He watched Grayson. The boy's aging had finally slowed during the long sea voyage from Jeruka to Everton. Had Burk been walking with him, they would have looked the same age, despite Grayson being only eight years old.

So strange.

Inolah reached Kal first. "I must take the prophetess to Sâr Wilek," he told her.

She stepped close and whispered, "Ulrik will not allow it."

"Onika is not his," Kal said. "She must go to Wilek."

Inolah glanced at the pale prophetess. "You must leave quickly then."

Kal set his hand on Jhorn's shoulder and addressed the King's Guards. "Board this man and his companions."

"The youngsters first," Jhorn said.

The guards grabbed Onika and lifted her over the side and into the dinghy. Grayson went next. Rustian leapt up onto the railing, ran along it, and hopped down beside Onika.

Inolah took Kal's hand, tears in her eyes. "I could not bear it if so many years passed before I saw you again, my friend."

Her words pricked his heart. "I hope you will visit the *Seffynaw* soon."

She kissed his cheek. "Tell Wilek I will come. I promise." She released his hand and started up the steps to the stern deck.

Kal hefted himself over the side and sat between Grayson and Onika. He noticed Jhorn then, still on the ship, peeking over the railing, eyes bloodshot.

"What are you doing?" Kal asked.

"I'm staying on the *Baretam*."

"And abandoning your charges?"

"I can't be seen on the *Seffynaw*. If anyone wondered over Grayson's skin, word of a legless man would confirm their suspicions. I'll stay with the empress for now. Keep them safe for me?"

Grayson and Onika were both crying, yet neither protested. Jhorn must have prepared them for this.

"I will guard them with my life," Kal said.

Jhorn nodded, took one last glance at Onika and Grayson, then vaulted away.

Dazed, Kal signaled to the sailors on the *Baretam*. The dinghy jerked and began to lower toward the sea.

WILEK

Wilek's and Harton's inquiries about Gran led them to the Temple Arman. Inside they found the great statue of Nesher the sunbird in a pile of rubble. At the edge of the crumbled stone, the Mother Rosârah was kneeling, hands clasped in prayer. Blood ran down the side of her face and dripped onto her lap.

"Gran!" Wilek ran toward her. He knelt at her side, gripped her shoulder. "Gran, what happened?"

She did not look up from her prayers.

He examined her. Something had gashed open her head. "Gran, please." His voice shook. "We must go."

She opened her eyes, looked upon him, and smiled. "No, Wilek. I will die here in my home, with my God."

"The gods are mere fables. I killed one!"

"No." She gripped his wrist with her gnarled fingers. "You know better than that. Arman is alive. He is angry, and rightly so. We have mocked him for far too long."

"Gran, please."

"Listen to me, Wilek Hadar, the Dutiful, Heir to the throne of Armania. Obedience to your father the king is no longer necessary. His folly has destroyed this great land. If our people are to survive, you must obey Arman from now on." She shook his arm. "He is a jealous God, prone to fits of anger and rage. But in his great mercy he always leaves a remnant." She squeezed his wrist. "Lead that remnant back to his holy throne."

Yes, yes. Whatever you say, Gran. "I will. Now let us go."

"I told you, I will remain here. It is too late for me."

"The physician will be the judge of that." Wilek scooped her into his arms and moved one foot to the floor to stand.

"Wilek Hadar! Put me down at once." Gran took hold of his chin. "You will *not* take my choice from me. That is something your father would do, and you are better than that."

He wavered, wanting to ignore her.

"This wound is too grievous. I would not survive a sea journey. Let me die here, in the place where I first met the God."

Wilek remembered Harton then. "My backman is a mantic. He can heal you, Gran."

"How dare you threaten me with magic! Put me down at once."

Wilek stopped. He squeezed her to his chest and kissed her wrinkled cheek.

"I love you too," she said.

Wilek set her down. She moved back to her knees at the altar, bare feet sticking out behind her. Wilek adjusted her dress to cover her feet and wondered briefly where her shoes had gone.

"Pia belongs to me," she said.

The statement was so odd, Wilek thought he must have misheard her. "I'm sorry?"

"Janek's concubine Pia. The girl is my spy. A good one too. She will help you keep an eye on your brother. Tell her I gave you the word *weed*, and she will serve you the same." Gran chuckled. "All this time there was a weed in his garden that he never thought to pull."

Pia Gran's spy? It was too much too fast. "I cannot do this without you, Gran."

She patted his cheek. "Of course you can. You are a good boy."

He wasn't good. Not really. "I cannot leave you."

"Arman will not let me suffer long," she said. "You must go."

Wilek nodded once and stood.

"Seek him out and you will find him," she said.

Seek him. Wilek nodded again.

"Take care of our people." She bowed her head in prayer.

Wilek backed slowly away, tears clogging his breath and choking his throat. A crash outside in the hall jolted him.

Harton stepped inside the room, looking pale and faint. "We should go, Your Highness."

Wilek nodded and walked from the room.

CHARLON

The driver skirted the fall-in, but the crowd on the other side forced him to stop. The horses tossed their heads and whinnied.

"Get out of the road!" the driver yelled.

No one listened. The mob pushed in. Swarmed the carriage. Grabbed the sides. Rocked it. *Hide!* her heart said. Charlon slid off the seat and onto the floor. Terror surrounded her.

"Do something!" she yelled to the Chieftess.

"I am spent and must cleanse," the Chieftess said, her face a mass of gray wrinkles. "My root juice is gone."

Not all. Charlon had her flask. She must act. To get them to the boats before the masks wore off. She pulled up the layers of her wedding dress. Removed the flask from its leg sheath.

Princess Nabelle was standing now, facing the mob. "Sâr Wilek is waiting for his bride-to-be," she yelled to the crowd. "Will you let Lady Zeroah pass? Lady Zeroah, who has always served you?"

Two men reached inside the carriage. They grabbed the princess's arms. Yanked her over the side. The woman screamed as she fell into the mob. Hoyt reached for her. Seconds later he too was taken. Gone.

The driver hadn't noticed. He continued to crack the whip at the horses. Gained a few paces. Not enough.

Charlon could not be taken. Could not miss the boat. "Magon, help!" She whispered a spell and stood, thrust her hands out. Trusted that Magon would save her.

She saw into the Veil then. Magon stood beside her in the wagon, but only Charlon could see her. The goddess flew into the crowd, shoving people aside. They screamed. From their perspective, people moved without walking. Heels scraped across the dirt. Bodies piled up on one another. Fell into porches and alleyways. Charlon caught sight of Princess Nabelle among them, yelling for the driver to wait. Charlon's heart quickened. Better for the woman to die with Mielle.

The carriage jerked forward. "Many thanks!" the driver called to the people, as if they had moved on their own. The fool. He still hadn't realized Nabelle and Hoyt were gone.

The carriage quickly increased speed. Fatigue growing, Charlon sat down but kept her spell active, watching in amazement as Magon carried out her wishes. The faster the carriage went, the more unnatural the moving crowd looked. Flying aside as if blown by the wind.

Charlon eyed the masts of the ships in the distance. *Almost there.* She held fast, and Magon cleared the way. Without even a prayer mat or runes. With Magon at her side she could not fail.

They rolled into the harbor, and the driver stopped beside the *Seffynaw*, where a wall of guards stood before the gangplank. Charlon and Chieftess Mreegan scrambled out of the carriage. The driver, shocked to discover he had lost Nabelle and her manservant, turned into a blubbering mess. Enough of him. Charlon summoned three King's Guards from the crowd. Ordered them to carry her trunks on board. She and the Chieftess followed the guards. Up to Lady Zeroah's fancy cabin. There she ordered the trunks placed under the bed. Under the bed, where they would be safe and unseen.

Only when she and Mreegan were alone did Charlon fall to the bed and call to Magon for cleansing.

TREVN

Beal wanted the book? Trevn's own onesent? Why?

"Seize them!" Beal yelled.

The five guards advanced. Cadoc drew his sword and stepped toward the guards. Oli fumbled with his, which—now that his right arm was useless—was belted on the wrong side. Even so, he managed to get it out of its scabbard and into his left hand in time to meet the attack.

Hinck had no sword. Nor did Trevn. And Trevn still didn't understand what was happening. Something was different about the onesent. His confidence, for one. But his eyes were odd. They looked gray. "Explain yourself, Beal."

Beal chuckled softly. "You, sir, are no longer my master."

Cadoc attacked one of the guards. Their blades met with a clash. Oli leapt forward to engage a second.

"Hinck! With me!" Trevn ran to the wall and yanked the Rurekan longsword out of its display.

Hinck grabbed the handle of a combat sword that hung framed beside it, but as he pulled the weapon, the whole frame came with it and thudded to the floor. Hinck set his boot on the frame and pulled.

Trevn lifted the longsword, finding it lighter than expected. A quick glance showed Cadoc fighting two of the guards at once, blocking their way to Trevn. A third lay motionless on the floor. Oli stood against the wall, not moving. Beal, hand raised, stood before him. Then Oli's sword flew from his hand and landed across the room.

Oli met Trevn's stare. "Your onesent is a mantic."

A shiver ran down Trevn's back.

"Kill them all!" Beal rasped.

The other two guards edged around the far side of the couches, approaching Trevn.

Beal wanted him dead? Beal? "Hurry up, Hinck!"

With a slow splintering sound Hinck wrenched the blade free of the frame. He came to stand beside Trevn and held out the sword, mounting screws dangling from the top of the tang.

One of the guards stabbed at Trevn. He parried and wheeled to the side, dodging the second guard's blade. The first guard swung at Hinck, who yelped and ducked. Trevn countered the second guard, who came at him with tireless fury.

"This is treason, you know," Trevn told him.

The man answered with a series of cuts and stabs that Trevn wasn't ready for. He parried blow after blow, arms already tiring. *Should have spent more time on the practice yard and less on the roofs.*

The guard struck hard, knocking back Trevn's parry far enough that his blade cut into Trevn's shoulder.

Trevn gasped, shocked at the strangeness of such smooth pain. Hot and pulsing. Not so bad. Until he tried to lift his sword and his arm barely moved. The guard advanced, so Trevn lunged behind the couch to give himself a barrier.

He glanced at Hinck, who was pulling the combat sword from the chest of the first guard. The man lay on his back, clutching the wound, a low keening sound coming from his lips.

"You killed one?" Trevn asked, sidestepping around the sofa as his attacker tried to decide which way to go around. "Get over here and help me!"

Trevn's guard gave up and stepped on the sofa seat. Trevn ran around the end of the couch and stood beside Hinck. Together they raised their swords. Cadoc had killed another guard. Only two remained.

The floor shook beneath them. Another earthquake rattling the weakened castle.

"Sands! It's not going to let up, is it?" Hinck said.

"Not this time," Trevn said.

The map tube's strap snapped, freeing the weight from Trevn's shoulder. He spun around in time to see Beal picking up the tube from the floor, a dagger clutched in his other hand.

"No!" Trevn dropped his sword and tackled Beal before the man had a chance to raise the knife. They crumpled to the rug, struggled. Trevn managed to get on top. Hot pain seared his thigh. He tried not to think about the wound and straddled his former onesent, squeezed both hands around his throat. To his right, Oli picked up Trevn's discarded sword and joined Hinck and Cadoc.

Blades clashed like irregular timpani. Three against two now. *Good*. It would be over soon. Trevn kept his hold on Beal's throat and tried to stall, to wait for help.

The man whispered, "*Redu lee!*" and someone pulled Trevn off Beal and threw him.

He rolled three times before coming to a stop against the wall. A glance back showed no one but Beal.

Thrown by magic?

Beal stood up, knife in hand, its tang bloody. "It's over, spoiled little sâr. You cannot win."

Those sinister gray eyes made Trevn shiver, but he gritted his teeth and pushed down his fear. "Traitor! I thought you served my mother."

"Who do you think sent me?" Beal asked as another Queen's Guard fell to the floor behind him. "She'll be angry you died, but glad to have fulfilled her orders."

"Liar!" Trevn picked up the closest chair and charged, using the chair as a battering ram. He knocked Beal to the floor. The knife went flying. Trevn dropped the chair and pounced. He clapped his hand over Beal's mouth, hoping that silence might keep him from using magic. This left Trevn with only one free hand, and Beal easily rolled him to his back.

Movement overhead. Behind Beal's back.

Beal grinned down on Trevn. "*Hareshet nisge—*"

A sword emerged from Beal's chest as someone stabbed him from behind. A death groan eased Trevn's fear. Beal's face pinched, gray eyes lost focus, and he collapsed on Trevn just as something sharp pierced Trevn's stomach.

"Too far!" Trevn yelled. "Pull back, you fool!"

The sword withdrew, and Trevn shoved Beal's dead body off. Hinck stood over him, wincing.

"I got you?" Hinck asked.

"*Yes.*"

Beside Hinck, Oli held his sword ready. Over by the couches, Cadoc pulled his blade from another guard. The map tube lay on the floor beside Beal. Trevn grabbed it and cradled it in one arm. His shoulder stung, his thigh stung, and Hinck had stabbed him.

Trevn pulled up his tunic and noted the puddle of blood that had filled his navel. The cut was just above, a few fingers wide.

Hinck grimaced. "I'm sorry!"

"Get something to wrap it!" Trevn yelled. "We must go!"

GRAYSON

Grayson wiggled on the boat's bench. They had left the *Baretam* with Sir Kalenek and were approaching the *Seffynaw*. He was going to meet a king! He stared at the Armanian flagship. It was slightly bigger than the Rurekan stoneclad vessel and made of wood painted blue and white. Gold letters spelled out the ship's name across the side. "Sir Kalenek, will we get to see the king?"

"The rosâr, he is called," Kal said. "And I cannot say."

"But we will see Prince Wilek for sure." Onika had spoken much of the prince who would be king.

"Onika and I will see *Sâr* Wilek," Kal said. "I do not know about you."

"But at some point, though, right?" The ship was big but not *that* big.

"Perhaps," was all Sir Kalenek would say.

It grew silent then but for the glub of the oars. Onika held Rustian on her lap and cried. It always made Grayson uncomfortable when Onika cried. She had told Grayson that she would see Jhorn again soon, so he didn't understand why she was so sad. He wished he had something important to say, something to make her smile or to impress Sir Kalenek.

The Veil was filled with shadir today. The smoky creatures were everywhere, swirling and laughing and causing mischief. They loved the destruction the earthquakes had brought to the land. They loved death.

Jhorn had made Grayson swear never to tell a soul he could see into the Veil. At least not until Onika told him differently.

None of the creatures Grayson saw today were as big or as scary as the one that lived with Priestess Jazlyn. On their long journey through the ream in Rurekau, it had been hard work for Grayson to pretend he couldn't see the monster called Gozan. He was thankful to have left it behind on the *Baretam*.

Grayson didn't fully understand what was happening on shore. Sir Kalenek, Onika, and Jhorn had been talking about it all morning. The closer the dinghy came to the docks, the louder everything became. People were screaming or crying or running or fighting. Some carried bundles. Some carried nothing. And some jumped right into the ocean and started swimming toward the boats in the harbor.

Grayson watched a man on a small fishing boat lift a sack of grain and hand it down into the hold. This reminded him of something. "Sir Kalenek, I was wandering around the *Baretam* this morning and found a room in the hold that was filled with evenroot. Sacks full of it. Powder, fresh tubers, even some plants. Heard one sailor tell another that it was what they confiscated from Priestess Jazlyn and her people. Do you think she knows it's on the ship?"

Sir Kalenek's eyes filled with interest. *Ha!* Grayson knew the High Shield would want to know that. He smiled, happy to have finally impressed the man.

"My guess is no. And the young emperor had better hope she doesn't find out. You'd make a fair spy, Grayson."

A spy! Grayson liked the sound of that. "Is it bad that he kept it, do you think?"

"It's a risk," Sir Kalenek said. "If the mantics get ahold of it, they could take the ship."

"Would they attack us?"

"Not right away," Sir Kalenek said. "Survival is all that matters at the moment. But once we find land, the mantics could take power."

"Do not fear the magic of our enemies," Onika said. "Arman has a plan."

Arman did. And Grayson couldn't wait to play his part, though he still didn't know exactly what that meant. Jhorn and Onika had been talking about it for years, and Grayson had a feeling he was close to finally finding out.

The dinghy scraped against the side of the king's ship. They were here! Someone above lowered two ropes.

Sir Kalenek and one of the oarsmen stood up, and each caught a rope. Sir Kalenek hooked his to the front of the boat, while the oarsman hooked his to the back. When they were done, Sir Kalenek called up to the men on the ship, he and the oarsman sat down again, and a few moments later the boat lifted right out of the water as the sailors above began to pull it up.

JILL WILLIAMSON

Grayson grinned at the way the boat suddenly felt weightless. He looked up to the pulleys and watched the ropes move through the wheels. On the deck, he could just see the men there, working the cranks that lifted them. Above, the ship's masts stretched high into the clear sky. The sails were tied up, making the yards look like the rungs of a giant's ladder.

The boat lifted past a small, round window, but Grayson had been too slow to see inside. They were already halfway up!

Grayson smiled and looked over the side, watching the water drizzle into the sea below. Something moved under the dinghy. It looked like a foot. Grayson frowned, turned around to get a better look, and saw two hands holding tight to the end of the boat. He leaned over the side and met a man's dark gaze. The man was holding on to the back of the dinghy.

Grayson gasped and leaned back, out of the man's sight. "Sir Kalenek," he said softly.

One of the oarsmen said something to Sir Kalenek, who laughed.

"Sir Kalenek," Grayson said a little louder.

The man still did not hear.

They were over halfway up the side of the ship. Grayson stood up and took a step, but the wiggling of the boat made him lose his balance and he fell onto the middle bench, where Onika was sitting.

"Stay seated, Grayson," Sir Kalenek said. "We're almost to the top."

As Sir Kalenek looked his way, Grayson pointed to the back of the boat, but the man went back to his conversation with the oarsmen.

"Stay close to us on this ship, Grayson," Onika said. "I am not yet ready to be parted from you."

"Onika, there is a man who—"

The boat stopped, and Sir Kalenek and an oarsman climbed over the side.

"Sir Kalenek!" Grayson yelled.

"Patience, Grayson," he said.

"But . . ." He glanced back to the hands. Still there.

The men helped Onika climb over the railing. Rustian crouched and jumped up.

The second oarsman glanced at Grayson. "Come on, boy."

Grayson motioned to the side of the boat and mouthed the words "*Man down there*" just as the man crawled up and over. Grayson stumbled back from the stranger and tripped on an inner rib of the boat. He fell hard on his backside and cried out.

Another man climbed over the front end. He shoved the oarsman out of the boat. Grayson heard the man scream, then a splash. The two men inside the dinghy held knives to the ropes on each end.

"Cut!" the first yelled.

They sawed against the ropes, and the boat jerked and twisted.

"Sir Kalenek!" Grayson called.

The first oarsman looked over the ship's railing and down into the dinghy. "Hey!"

Sir Kalenek appeared next, reached for Grayson. "Stand up! Grab my hand. Hurry!"

Grayson stretched his hand toward Sir Kalenek, but the boat fell. His stomach twisted and he screamed.

Sir Kalenek, still reaching out, yelled, "No!"

The boat crashed into the water, knocking the back of Grayson's head against one of the ribs.

The thieves grabbed the oars and began rowing.

"Get out of the boat, Grayson!" Sir Kalenek's voice, from somewhere above.

Grayson wanted to obey, but he couldn't swim. Sir Kalenek had saved him when he fell in the floodwaters. Would he do it again? Grayson looked over the side and into the dark and cloudy water. *Too scary*. He glanced up at the king's ship. A group of soldiers were tussling with Sir Kalenek, trying to hold him back, as if he wanted to jump in to rescue Grayson. That made Grayson feel good.

Onika stood to the right of the fighting men. It looked like she was watching Grayson, which was silly—she was blind. Still, he lifted his hand and waved just as the dinghy floated under the pier.

The darkness frightened him. He wanted to ask the men where they were going, but he remained silent, afraid that if they remembered he was there, they would throw him over.

They rowed under the pier for a very long time. When they came out again, the sun made Grayson wince. People started jumping into the boat. Someone stepped on him. He squeezed under the center bench and hugged his knees to his chest, trying to be smaller, but he'd grown so much in the past few months that it was much harder to do than it used to be.

People kept coming. Squished against Grayson. Men, women, children. How many could this dinghy hold? Grayson peeked out from under the bench and tried to count them but lost his way when he came to fifteen on a girl he had counted already.

"Everyone sit still or you'll sink us!" a man yelled.

But people kept shifting, trying to make more room. Finally the dinghy moved away from the shore, out into the open sea. The people were all talking at once. Grayson clapped his hands over his ears. He was shaking. He was scared. How would he get to the king's boat now? How would he ever see Jhorn again? Or Onika? He gasped. How would he protect Onika if he wasn't there? Burk would find her. Even though Sir Kalenek had left Burk on the Rurekan boat, he would find Onika, just like she said would happen. And Grayson wouldn't be there to stop him.

Why had this happened? Why hadn't Grayson been smart enough to get out of the boat? Who cared if men were trying to steal it? No wonder Grayson annoyed everyone so much. Right now he annoyed himself.

WILEK

Wilek was surprised how clear the road was. People stood clustered in the ditches, yelling and shoving each other, but not one entered the street. He and Harton rode easily, skirting several fall-ins, cracks, and crumbled buildings. By the time they reached the harbor, however, the crowd converged upon them as if suddenly remembering they wanted to leave too.

Wilek and Harton had to draw their swords to keep people out of their way. Eventually they reached the wall of guards keeping the commoners from the gangplank to the king's ship.

"Make way for the Heir," Harton yelled. "Sâr Wilek is here."

When the guards saw that Harton's words were true, they moved aside and let them both ride their horses right over the gangplank and onto the deck.

Wilek left Foxaro there and made his way to the quarterdeck, where he found Admiral Vendal. "How does the register look, Admiral? Are we all on board?"

"It's been a nightmare to count the commoners, Your Highness," the admiral said. "Rosârah Brelenah insisted we let another five dozen people board. I'm sure we're past maximum capacity. Also, I'm sorry to say that the prisoners never arrived."

Wilek stiffened in alarm. "Pontiff Rogedoth?"

"He and the other four." The admiral shook his head. "No one knows what became of their carriage."

Sands! What did it mean to have Rogedoth out there, free? "Anything else?"

"As to the royal family, the Mother Rosârah has not yet arrived, and—"

"The Mother Rosârah is dead," Wilek said, fighting the rush of emotion that came over him at speaking those words.

"Oh," the admiral said. "I'm sorry to hear that, Your Highness. I always admired her."

"I interrupted you," Wilek said. "Who else is still missing?"

"Sâr Trevn has not yet boarded."

Wilek groaned. *Where are you, Trevn?* "Did anyone see him?"

"A guard saw him enter the castle with the Earl of Dacre and the Duke of Canden."

Wilek nodded, dismayed at the thought of leaving Trevn behind, Oli and Hinckdan too. "We'll wait a bit longer." On the pier, the mob fought the guards. Some tried to climb the dock lines, but the guards pushed them off into the sea. "Is there room for commoners aboard the other ships?"

"I cannot say," Admiral Vendal said. "If I send a runner to another ship, he'll likely never make it, let alone return with an answer. Perhaps once we put out to sea, we could send skiffs back and forth to determine whether there is any more space. To the Rurekan ships as well."

"What Rurekan ships?" Wilek asked.

"A fleet came in this midday from Rurekau. Sir Kalenek Veroth boarded with some passengers just moments ago."

Kal! "Take me to him."

The admiral ordered a sailor to do so. Wilek, eager to see his High Shield, followed along with Harton. They found Kal's cabin guarded by two armed men.

"What's this?" Wilek asked. "Is my High Shield a prisoner?"

"He attacked several sailors," a guard said.

"Why would he do that?"

"Some commoners hijacked his dinghy with a boy inside."

A boy? "Let me in."

The guards opened the door. Wilek entered, only to be tackled to the floor. A short struggle followed. Guards pulled off Wilek's attacker. It was Kal.

Kal's eyes gained recognition. Anger melted into heavy sorrow. He fell to his knees and hung his head. "I have failed you, Your Highness."

"On the contrary. I received your message from Master Heln. We are evacuating the city, as you suggested."

"I lost the boy. He was important. They have kept me here, where I could not give chase."

"Who is lost? What boy?"

"His name is Grayson. Thieves stole the dinghy we came over in with the boy still inside. If anyone finds out what he is . . . our enemies could use him against us."

What enemies? It was unlike Kal to behave with such defeat. "Let us go to the quarterdeck. If commoners stole a dinghy, they will fill it with people and try to board a ship. We will watch for it."

Kal stood, expression eager. "You'll let me out?"

"Of course. Let's see if we can find this boy."

Kal nodded. "Thank you, Your Highness. We must hurry."

TREVN

Trevn stood with Hinck, Cadoc, and Oli on the corner where Procession Way met the Sink road. The path to the docks was crammed with debris and people.

Oli lifted his sword. "We'll have to fight our way through."

Trevn pressed his hand to his abdomen. "We would never make it. I have a better way." He walked toward the bakery. Its windows had been smashed; it looked to be abandoned. He opened the door and went inside. Empty. Even the food shelves had been cleared out.

"You know a shortcut?" Oli asked.

"Indeed I do," Trevn said.

Hinck groaned. "Not the roofs."

"It's the fastest way. By far."

"Last time, at least," Hinck said. "It will take years to build enough roofs for you to run wherever we land."

"What do you mean *run*?" Oli asked.

Cadoc chuckled. "You'll see."

"Put away that sword, Your Grace," Trevn said. "You will need that hand."

Trevn led the way out the back of the bakery and up the ladder. His wounds hurt with each rung. The rooftops were delightedly vacant. He instantly started running, which hurt his gut. He pressed one hand tight against the cut and ran anyway, clutching the map tube tightly to his side with his other hand.

They ran. It was the same path Trevn had taken dozens of times before, but this time he didn't much enjoy it. His mind dwelled on Beal's words about his mother, and he wondered where Mielle might be. He almost didn't see the missing chandler's shop and barely stopped in time, his feet skidding over crumbled masonry. A peek at the street showed that the building had collapsed into rubble.

Five Woes! Trevn took in the destruction and backtracked to the butcher's shop behind the Lazy Man's Inn. He had to stop before reaching the leatherworks to catch his breath. He doubted he could make the jump with his wounds. Below, the streets were chaos, people packed together like wheat in a sheaf.

Cadoc reached him. "Are you well?"

"I'll live," Trevn said. "We could have jumped here if someone hadn't *stabbed* me."

"I said I was sorry, Your Ungratefulness," Hinck said. "Guess we go my way today." Hinck led them to the rear of the leatherworks, down the half ladder to the roof of the weaver's, and on from there.

Another tremor came, and they stopped to wait it out. Across the street a tenement crumbled. People on the ground screamed and scattered, but with the street so packed, they only trampled each other. Trevn looked away as the chunks of stone from the building crushed the crowd. On the other side of the temple, an angry throng of people swarmed the pier. Leagues inland much of the city was burning.

They climbed down to one of the lower roofs that edged the harbor, approaching from the south. Trevn's feet had barely touched ground when a familiar voice yelled his name.

"Sâr Trevn!"

A filthy, blood-spattered man staggered toward them. Who *was* that? He was wearing part of a guard's uniform—no tabard, belt, or sword. Boots were gone too. Yet he wore a woman's ribbon tied in his hair like he'd just won a match at tournament.

Cadoc drew his sword and moved to engage.

The man lifted his hands above his head. "Cadoc, no! It's me, Novan Heln."

Cadoc lowered his sword. "Five Woes, man, what happened to you?"

Novan shook his head, eyes hollow and distant as he studied the mob. "We're all going to die, aren't we?" His voice cracked.

"Not on my watch," Cadoc said.

Trevn took a deep breath and considered the mob. "We're going to have to fight our way through."

"You mean *we* are," Oli said. "Not you."

"Exactly." Trevn grinned. "I seem to have forgotten a sword."

"Mine was taken," Novan said. "But I will stand behind you, Your Highness."

"Very well," Trevn said. "Let us board the ship."

Oli, Cadoc, and Hinck waved their bloodied swords to clear a path. Novan shoved aside anyone who came near, and they slowly made their way across the harbor toward the gangplank of the *Seffynaw*.

"It's the sâr!" someone yelled.

The crowd surged around them. Someone grabbed Trevn's hair, another his arm. His feet left the ground. Sands, they were going to kill him! He hugged the map tube tightly.

Novan charged Trevn's attackers like a bull, knocking them away. Hinck grabbed Trevn, and the crowd went for Novan instead. Novan punched one man in the face, kicked another. Trevn snagged the guard's arm and dragged him through the press of bodies. Cadoc lunged into their wake, sword darting out and scaring back the mob.

When the guards at the gangplank saw Trevn, a small cheer went up.

"We've been waiting for you," one of them said.

Trevn's men ushered him onto the ship, where Mielle embraced him.

Trevn gave the Book of Arman to Mielle and asked her to hide it in her cabin for the time being, knowing that he would need to find a better place. At some point he would also need to convince Wilek to read it.

Cadoc dragged Trevn to the physician, and once he'd had his wounds dressed, he evaded his mother by sneaking up to the stern deck. He wasn't ready to deal with the woman yet. Wasn't sure how or what to say. Still didn't understand Beal's words. He would ask Wilek's advice later. For now, Wilek was busy.

Trevn sat cross-legged at the center of the stern rail, squished between the bodies of commoners who had drawn lot numbers. People covered the deck, sitting side by side, some with children on their laps. No part of the stern deck was visible.

The *Seffynaw* had set sail moments ago. Trevn stared at the carnage that was Everton, both horrific and majestic. The maps he had pored over for so many years, drawn and redrawn—they were relics now. The cataclysmic earthquakes had riven the city into shards. The southern coastline had crumbled all the way to Echo Crack, which now looked more like a gorge. Debris filled the water. Animals and people too, the latter holding on to anything: doors, barrels, the occasional straw roof. People capsized smaller crafts, fighting each other to get inside. Behind them on shore, houses crumbled or sank beneath the ground. Despite it being so early, the tide had risen. Trevn thought back to his demonstration on the beach. It was happening. As the ground collapsed, the water rolled in to fill the holes.

Trevn saw a man push another from a skiff. The first man struggled in the water, clearly panicked and unable to swim. Up he came, then down again. Up and down, until he no longer came up.

Trevn closed his eyes. *Let them go quickly, Arman, with little or no pain. Forgive us for not making room for more.*

He couldn't bear to watch more death but felt that his people—those left behind—deserved to be remembered. So he forced himself to watch until the ship carried them out of sight. He didn't have his grow lens with him, so he said one last prayer for the people of Everton, Armania, and the Five Realms. *May Arman have mercy on their souls.*

Trevn got up and walked carefully through the seated crowd. Cadoc, who'd positioned himself near the stairs, walked with him down to the quarterdeck. There they found Wilek and Kal at the port rail, each peering through grow lenses at the other ships.

"There!" Kal yelled. "That's the dinghy, headed for that merchant ship." He pointed to a ship ahead on their right.

"Looks Sarikarian," Trevn said.

"Can we mark it somehow?" Kal asked. "I need to go over there and find him."

"Patience," Wilek said, peering again through his lens. "*The Wanderer*. We only need remember that name, Kal."

Kal nodded. "*The Wanderer*."

Trevn left them and headed toward the main deck, Cadoc following in silence. They wove between people, climbed up to the foredeck, and walked all the way to the bowsprit. Down the steps and into the nose of the ship. Some younger boys were already there, looking over the rail at the figurehead of Thalassa, goddess of the sea. Trevn stood behind them and gazed into the distance ahead. He had always wanted to know what was out there.

Now he would get his chance.

Not the End.

A Note From the Author

Thanks for reading *King's Folly*, the first book in THE KINSMAN CHRONICLES. Continue the adventures of Wilek and Trevn in *King's Blood*.

This book was a challenge for two reasons: its scope and the darkness of its storyworld. I spent a lot of time researching the kings of the Old Testament and the world in which they lived. And while THE KINSMAN CHRONICLES does not directly parallel any story in the Bible, I wanted to capture the darkness and superstitions of that ancient world and show how those things continually led God's chosen people astray.

I'm excited to lead the Armanians back to He Who Made the World during the course of this series.

I'd love to hear from you. You can email me through my website and sign up for my newsletter to get updates on upcoming books and events. If you'd like to help make this book a success, tell people about it, loan your copy to a friend, or ask your library or bookstore to order it. Also, writing a book review for online stores is very helpful.

Discussion questions for THE KINSMAN CHRONICLES series can be found online at www.jillwilliamson.com/discuss.

If you'd like to see a larger version of the map of the Five Realms, pore over the book's Pinterest page, or look at family trees, flags, sigils, and runes, visit my website at www.jillwilliamson.com/books/kinsman-chronicles.

Acknowledgments

This book was a huge undertaking, and many people helped me at various points along the way. Thanks to John Otte, Jason Joyner, Cathyln Dyck, and Kathryn Freeman, who helped with an initial brainstorming session at ACFW 2013. To Larry Nielsen and Michael Vernor for helping me work out the magic and for reading the very first draft. And to Crystal Nielsen for listening patiently while all this went on. To Amanda Luedeke, Stephanie Morrill, Shannon Dittemore, Nadine Brandes, Melanie Dickerson, and Chris Kolmorgen for letting me vent about the story, helping with brainstorming, and critiquing. To Kerry Nietz for talking science with me. To Tom Luque for his help with sailing. And big hugs to Luke Williamson for listening to the whole spiel, and to Corinne Stennett for your consistent prayers. Thanks as well to the talented and organized team at Bethany House Publishers, including Dave Long, Elisa Tally, Noelle Buss, and Amy Green. You guys are awesome.

About the Author

Jill Williamson writes fantasy and science fiction for teens and adults. She grew up in Alaska, staying up and reading by the summer daylight that wouldn't go away. This led to a love of books and writing, and her debut novel, *By Darkness Hid*, won several awards and was named a Best Science Fiction, Fantasy, and Horror novel of 2009 by *VOYA* magazine. She loves giving writing workshops and blogs for teen writers at www.GoTeenWriters.com. She now lives in the Pacific Northwest with her husband, two children, and a whole lot of deer. Visit her online at www.jillwilliamson.com.

More Fantasy From Bethany House

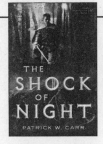

When one man is brutally murdered and the priest he works for mortally wounded, Willet Dura is called to investigate. As he begins to question the priest, the man pulls him close, cries out in a foreign tongue—and dies. This strange encounter draws Willet into an epic conflict that threatens not only his city, but his entire world.

The Shock of Night by Patrick W. Carr
THE DARKWATER SAGA #1
patrickwcarr.com

As a dynasty nears its end, an unlikely hero embarks upon a perilous quest to save his kingdom. Thrust into a world of dangerous political intrigue and church machinations, Errol Stone must leave behind his idle life, learn to fight, come to know his God—and discover his destiny.

THE STAFF AND THE SWORD: *A Cast of Stones, The Hero's Lot, A Draw of Kings*
by Patrick W. Carr
patrickwcarr.com

◊BETHANYHOUSE

 Stay up-to-date on your favorite books and authors with our free e-newsletters. Sign up today at bethanyhouse.com.

 Find us on Facebook. facebook.com/bethanyhousepublishers

 Free exclusive resources for your book group! bethanyhouse.com/anopenbook
an open book